GREEN AS GRASS.

A JOLLY SCHOOL STORY.

"PITY THE POOR BLIND!" MOANED SHARP SENIOR.—"OH! MY NEW HAT!" GROANED GREENE JUNIOR.

No. 1.

GREEN AS GRASS.

By the Author of "FOLLOW-MY-LEADER."

CHAPTER I.

THE GREENELY GREENE FAMILY.

WHEN an elderly gentleman of respectable appearance is observed to cast his spectacles at his wife, empty a jug of boiling water over the pet cat, pound the cups and saucers into fragments with the teapot, kick his chair over, box the ears of the page for no other fault than that of being within smacking range, and finally conclude by shaking his fist insanely at his own reflection in the looking-glass—and doing all this without apparent cause—two inferences naturally suggest themselves to the mind of the observer —namely, that the aforesaid elderly gentleman is either mad or is visited by a severe and sudden spasm of the toothache.

But Greenely Greene, Esquire, who had just completed each and every of the above-named eccentricities at his breakfast-table, did not appear to be afflicted with either of the aforesaid maladies. Moreover, his proceedings seemed to be taken as a matter of course, as Mrs. Greenely Greene extracted the spectacles from her hair with perfect composure, and the page, holding the knob of the poker to his eye, picked up the chair, and removed the damaged crockery with his disengaged hand.

"Feel better, my love?" said Mrs. Greene.

"A little," responded her husband, with a sigh so deep that he seemed to fetch it out of his right boot.

"Bad noos in them letters you just opened, Mr. G.?"

"Horful!" replied Mr. G., with an emphasis which set the rules of pronunciation at defiance. "We was a deal 'appier afore we came into this property, Jemimar."

Mrs. G. looked down complacently at her green satin morning robe, trimmed with yellow velvet, and sniffed as if she thought that *some* things, at least, were improved; but she only said—

"What's the letters about, G.?"

"The fust," replied Mr. Greene, putting his spectacles on his nose, and handling the letter as if it had been a particularly repulsive specimen of toad— "the fust is from Diddler Hook about the Fish-catching Company ——"

"Flat-fish, wasn't it?"

"You're right, my dear. And a beautiful plan I thought it was, too. You reklect it? The sea was to be baited with winkles, with needles stuck through 'em, and when the fish had swallered the needles all you'd got to do was to get in a boat, and throw a powerful magnet overboard, tied to a rope, which would attract the needles inside of the fish, and so you could catch as many as you wanted. It seemed to me a good idea."

"So simple!" said Mrs. Greene.

"And yet Diddler Hook writes to say that he can't get the public to take the shares, and so he encloses two and ninepence-ha'penny in stamps as the balance, and says the affair 's wound up."

"Is that all that's left out of your thousand pounds?"

"That's all, Mrs. G., except 'alf a ton of needles as he says he's sent on by Parcel Delivery."

"My good gracious!" gasped Mrs. Greene. "Why, where's the money gone to?"

"I don't know. Mostly to the promoter, I think, and the director and manager and seckitary."

"Who's the promoter?"

"Diddler Hook."

"And who's the director?"

"Diddler Hook."

"And the manager?"

"Diddler Hook likewise."

"And I s'pose the seckitary's him, too?"

Mr. Greene nodded.

"He must have worked very 'ard, G., to get through all that money in a fortnight."

"Very."

"I think, Mr. G., that you'd better give up these speckilations. We aint had a minit's peace since you took up with 'em; and the money you've lost ——"

"Sunk, Jemimar ——"

"Sunk, then—it's all the same, for it'll never come up again. I say the money you've lo—sunk— is something fearful. When we kep' our little chandler's shop, afore Uncle Jolliffe left us his fortune so unexpected, you never threw things at me, nor yet b'iled the cat; and, as for hearing a bad word out of your mouth, I never did. Give 'em up, G."

"I will, my dear."

"And we'll be 'appy again, and dewote ourselves to the eddication of our dear boy, Jolliffe."

"Ah! there it is again," said Mr. G., taking up another letter. "It's this wot upset me, and not Diddler's affair."

"There's nothin' the matter with him, G.?" exclaimed Mrs. G., turning pallid with maternal anxiety.

"Oh! no—there's nothin' the matter, only he seems to have been makin' a hass of himself, as usual."

"Poor boy!" said Mrs. Greene. "He's always being decomposed upon. But why don't his tootor look arter him? I'm sure his wages is high enough."

"That's the party, my dear. We're took in again."

"What! and him a clergyman?"

"Ah! but you see, my dear, he wasn't a clergyman, arter all," replied Mr. Greene, consulting the letter with a very rueful expression. "It's old Biggs as writes. He happened to be passing through Jellyborough, when what should he see but our boy and his tootor being dragged along the street by 'arf a dozen perlicemen, drunk, and swearing fit to make a weathercock's hair turn grey!"

"What!" squeaked Mrs. Greene; "our Jolliffe drunk and swearing?"

"Biggs ses so in his letter, my love. He gives the werry expressions. I'll read 'em to you if ——"

"I don't want to hear the nasty lyin' rubbish. But if that Biggs has got a single hair left on that bald head of his, I'll have it out the fust time he comes here. Now, you mark my words!"

"Don't be onreasonable, Mrs. G. Biggs took a deal of trouble. He went to the station, and got Jolliffe off; but they wouldn't let him bail the tootor, because the perlice suspected him to be a chap there was warrants out again for pretty nigh every crime there is, from manslaughter to mooching."

"To think of our poor boy being in such company as that! Oh! G., once let me get him 'ome again, and he shall never go out of my sight no more!"

"Nonsense, Mrs. G.! The boy's sixteen, and you can't have him tied to your apern-strings now. He must see life."

"He aint a-goin' to see life through the keyhole of a jail, G."

"Well—no, since you put it that way, Jemimar; he might have a better prospeck. But wait till Biggs comes—he'll bring Jolliffe home to-day—and then we'll take his advice."

"Advice! And about your own son, too. Why, G., you ought to be ashamed to ask anybody how to manage him. Who's to know how, if his father don't?"

To this important query Mr. Greene found it difficult to discover a fitting reply, and he was about to get out of the difficulty in his usual manner—by breaking some crockery, and punching the page's head—when there was a noise in the street as of some vehicle being stopped in a hurry in front of Mr. Greene's door, then the unmistakeable sound of the breaking of glass, followed by the breaking of that divine law which prohibits swearing.

"That's Biggs' voice!" exclaimed Mr. Greene, starting up, and hurrying to the window.

"And that's Jolliffe's!" was the remark of Mrs. G., as she followed her husband's example.

She was right—it was Jolliffe; and Master Greene was uplifting his voice for a very excellent reason—two excellent reasons. In the first place, his head was jammed through one of the windows of the cab which had brought them to the door, and the broken glass was sticking into his neck; and, in the second, a stout, wrathful-looking, middle-aged gentleman was boxing his ears with a vigour and regularity which proved that he was no novice in the art.

"Hi, Biggs!" roared Mr. Greene; "what are you up to with the boy?"

"Oh, the brute!" exclaimed Mrs. G. "I'll give it him!"

And, being a lady of prompt action, she tucked up her sleeves, flattened the page behind the door—where he had been listening—sallied out into the street, took Mr. Biggs by the ears (he had no hair available as a handle), banged his head against the hind wheel of the cab, lugged Master Greene out of the window—scraping him frightfully in the process—and re-entered the house in triumph, having accomplished all these feats in exactly one minute and a quarter.

As soon as Mr. Biggs had got rid of the complicated fireworks which the contact of his head with the cab-wheel had set going he made for the house, red-hot with bumps and fury; but the cabman barred the way.

"I'll take my fare afore you go, guv'nor."

"Dash you and your fare!" growled Mr. Biggs. "Get it from that—that woman who's just gone in. It's her dashed cub that's been the cause of all the row. I'm not going to pay. Knock at the door, and ask for Mrs. Greene."

"No, thanky!" said the cabman. "She aint the party for me. I've drove Mrs. Prodgers, and I knows the breed. I'll trouble you for three and six, and the broken winder two bob—that's five and a tanner. Come, pay up. You hired my cab."

"I—I'll hire a blunderbuss, and have somebody's life!" gasped Mr. Biggs, whose bumps were getting more and more prominent every moment. "Get out of the way."

And, charging straight at the cabman, Mr. Biggs butted him down the area steps, and rushed into the drawing-room of the Greene mansion in a state of mind which defies the power of words to express.

Master Greene was a stretched-out youth, with a general appearance of having more than the average number of joints in his limbs, and all of them weak. He had a large head, two-thirds of which was nose; and as his neck was long and limp, like that of a very young bird, this arbitrary nose was perpetually overbalancing the head to which it was attached, to the intense discomfort of nervous people, who were in momentary dread of seeing it snap short off the parent stem.

When Mr. Biggs made his entry Master Greene was in the hands of his mamma, who was picking out the pieces of broken glass, while Greene senior hovered around with bits of sticking-plaister, which he dabbed on to the wounds whenever he got an opportunity; and so absorbed were they in this interesting occupation that the intrusion of Mr. Biggs passed unnoticed, until he emphatically announced his arrival by giving the page—who was holding a basin of hot water, and crying into it out of sympathy—a smack on the side of the head.

Of course the unlucky page dropped the basin, and, equally as a matter of course, the hot water filled Mr. Greene's slippers, scalded his feet, and made him use language and dance in a manner most unbefitting his years and station.

"Edgardo," roared Mr. Greene—Edgardo was the page's fancy name; he was christened Peter—"Edgardo, fetch a policeman!"

"If he moves a step," said Mr. Biggs, "I'll skin him, and pickle him with vinegar and salt."

The page's sense of duty was not strong enough to induce him to dare this more than Bulgarian atrocity—he retreated to a corner, and fenced himself in with the coal-scuttle.

"Biggs," said Mr. Greene, in a voice trembling with emotion, "I respect you as a man who was once a friend of mine, and always paid reg'lar for his two hounces of tea and butter and his 'apenny dips when I was in the chandlery line; but, Biggs, I ham a father, and you 'ave houtraged my feelings as sich. Look at my boy, with his neck scored like a line of pork ready for the baker's, and tell me wot you mean by it?"

"Mr. Greene, sir," replied Mr. Biggs, in a manner that would have been full of imperious majesty if he had had a little less mud about him, and his bumps had not been quite so prominent, "bis'ness fust, and pleasure arterwards, has always been a motter of mine. Therefore, afore I has the felicity of punching your 'ed, I'll trouble you to send down five and six to the cabman—money doo for his fare and a broken winder."

"And may I ask you, sir," said Mrs. Greene, with a calmness that was perfectly awful, considering the angry storm which raged in her maternal bosom—"may I ask you who's going to pay for my broken boy? Look at his poor dear neck!"

"Look at his poor dear ——" repeated Mr. Biggs, in a tone of deep disgust. "Look at my poor dear head, ma'am! If that idiot of a boy of yours is fool enough to ram his thick skull through a cab window it's not my fault."

"Idjot yourself!" retorted Mrs. Greene, indignantly. "As if my poor dear Jolly could do such a thing! Speak up, Jolly, my love, and tell us all about it."

But Master Jolliffe—or Jolly Greene, as he was called by the more rude of his acquaintances—was in far too bewildered a state of mind to do anything but howl in a minor key.

"Now, Mr. Greene, sir," repeated Biggs, upon whom the howling of Green junior was evidently producing a most distressing effect, "I have only to say this—your wife's sex prevents my asking her for satisfaction; but, if you're ready to take her part, I know you've a back garden, and I'll wait your convenience there."

And, nodding his head significantly, Mr. Biggs moved towards the door.

Greene senior had plenty of pluck, and did not want a hint of that nature twice. He laid down his sticking-plaister, said, "Take care of the boy, Jemimar—I shan't be long," and began to pull off his coat to show that he was ready.

But though, as we have seen, Mrs. G. had no objection personally to giving Mr. Biggs one or two for himself, marital affection would not allow her to stand by and see her husband endangered.

"Greene," she said, and in such a voice that the partner of her joys and sorrows shook visibly, "if you move another step I'll claw your hair off; and if some of the skin comes with it, don't blame me. And as for you, Biggs," she added, turning to that gentleman, "if you aint out of this house in two minits of your own accord, I'll try what I can do."

Mr. Biggs was not a coward. He would have tackled two male Greenes, and have given a very good account of three even; but one Mrs. G. was too much. He was near the door, his hand upon the handle. He hesitated; Mrs. Greene raised her right hand suddenly—it was only to brush a fly away, but it decided Mr. Biggs, and within the stipulated two minutes he was in the street, where he was instantly pounced upon by the cabman, who had been waiting for him.

"Open the door," growled Mr. Biggs.

"Did you get the fare, sir?" inquired the cabman, with a grin.

"Yes, and something over," was the reply; "and so will you if you don't drive off sharp."

"Vere to, sir?"

"The d——!"

"Better go back and ax the lady for the party's address," thought the cabman. "It strikes me as she must be hintimate with him."

But, wisely judging that, if he wanted his money, he had better keep his reflections to himself, the cabman got on his box, and drove off, with Mr. Biggs inside, audibly invoking ruin and desolation upon the heads of the Greenely Greene family, but especially upon Mrs. Greenely Greene.

CHAPTER II.

THE SHARP FAMILY.

ON either side of that classic thoroughfare of filth and frowsiness known as Drury-lane are a number of tributary courts and alleys, the very existence of which, to nine thousand nine hundred and ninety-nine out of every ten thousand of the inhabitants of London, is unknown.

The principal reason for this ignorance of these courts and alleys is, that nobody ever wants to visit them except the people who live there, and they are of such a retiring and modest character that they seldom come out except very late at night, and if any one should by chance stray into their precincts they cannot be persuaded to let him go again. There is a legend current that an enthusiastic young Bible-reader did venture into Angel-alley; but he was never heard of any more. For some week or so afterwards an Irish family, consisting of a father, mother, and ten children, were noticed to be looking uncommonly plump, while the father sported on the following Sunday a rusty black coat so much too small for him that in less than ten minutes he had split it up the back; and his youngest son, Dennis, might have been seen entombing a cat in a shoe of canoe-like build (much resembling those usually worn by the Bible-reader), and subsequently holding a wake over the remains with all the rites and ceremonies (barring the whiskey) generally observed by the "finest pisantry in the wurreld."

Angel-alley itself was not much larger than the area of a Belgravian mansion, but it held a wonderful amount of smell. Tradition said that in this very Angel-alley the Great Plague of London first broke out. If that be true, what could it have smelt like then? We shudder at the bare idea, and pass from Angel-alley to those of its angelic inhabitants with whom our story has to do.

Number One in Angel-alley was exactly like all the other numbers in dirt, dilapidation, and smell, and would therefore have been undistinguishable from them but for one circumstance, which was truly phenomenal in such a locality; and that was, the presence on the battered door of a large brass plate—and a bright one, too—which bore the inscription, in fat Roman capitals, "S. Sharp, Solicitor."

Amidst the filth and squalor of Angel-alley that brass plate looked like burnished gold. It may seem a wonderful thing that any member of one of the learned professions should have taken up his abode in such a place; but it was yet more wonderful that a piece of metal which would fetch at least a shilling at the marine-store dealer's should have remained for only ten minutes in such an exposed position. The secret of its immunity from annexation will be told by-and-bye.

In the back parlour of Number One sat the owner of the brass plate, and of the name thereon inscribed, busily writing with the stump of an ancient quill-pen upon a large sheet of blue foolscap paper, and opposite to him was his son—a boy of about fourteen years of age, watching the movements of the pen with a most discontented expression.

Sharp senior was a little withered old man, aged about fifty by years, and a hundred and fifty by dissipation. He had originally been built on a very small scale, and had shrunk so much since that it was wonderful how his skin continued to hold the framework of his bones together. He was quite bald, and the keenest observer could not have traced any vestige of beard or moustache. In that barren soil there was not nourishment enough for a single hair to grow with comfort to itself.

Sharp junior presented in some respects a perfect contrast to his parent. True, he also was as yet beardless; but he had a plentiful crop of light curly hair. He was plump to an exasperating degree in such a place as Angel-alley, where a good solid hunger-subduing meal was a thing unknown; and his features, instead of exhibiting the preternatural sharpness and cunning distinguishing his parent, had a sweet, infantile, innocent expression, which could not have been surpassed in imbecility by the fattest cherub ever carved upon a tombstone.

At length Mr. Sharp senior laid down his pen, and fetched up a sigh of relief.

"That's done," he said. "Now, Billy, what have we got for dinner?"

"Same as we had yes'rday," was Billy's short reply.

"And what's that?"

"Sim'lar to wot we dined off the day afore," said Billy, with a mournful sniff.

"What was that?"

"Nothin'."

"That's filling, Billy."

"At the price," replied Sharp junior, more shortly and mournfully than ever.

Mr. Sharp rested his chin upon his two withered claw-like hands, and looked at his son in a meditative way.

"What astonishes me, Billy," he said, "is the way you keep your fat up. Dinner or no dinner, you look just the same—you never lose an ounce."

"I should if it was genuine muscle I had on me," growled Billy; "but it aint. I'm blowed out—that's all; and if any one was to prick me with a pin anywheres, I should double up like one o' them air b'loons."

"Don't talk like that, Billy. You're solid enough. Why, only yesterday, when the perlice was after me, and you dropped down in front of him to save your poor old dad, he fell on you with a whack that would have bust anything less solid than a rock. Don't tell me, Billy."

"I'm going to give up all them games, though," said Sharp junior, doggedly.

"What games?" demanded Sharp senior.

"Why, thievin'."

"I say, Billy," exclaimed Sharp senior, in sudden alarm, "have any of them School Board fellows been after you? I should like to catch one trying to corrupt the principles of a son of mine, after all the pains I've taken with his education."

"No," replied Billy; "it ain't the School Board—it's somethink inside of me. I wants to be able to walk about the streets without feelin' my 'art jump into my mouth at the sight of a slop. I wants to be able to look at a well-dressed old cove without reckonin' up how much he's got in his pocket, and how I can get it without bein' copped. I wants to airn a honest livin', and I'm goin' to do it."

Sharp senior's cunning little eyes twinkled, and the corners of his mouth curled up with a grin.

"Billy," he said, "there's nothing I would like better myself; but it can't be done."

"Why not?"

"In the first place, Bill, my boy, what do you think of doing for an 'honest living,' as you call it? Do you know a trade to work at?"

"You know I don't."

"What would you do, then?"

"Anythink—run of arrands."

"And what do you think would be the first question put to you?"

"About wages, I s'pose."

"No, Bill, my boy; the first question would be about your character. Who'd give you work when that was known?"

Poor Billy looked hopelessly mournful. He knew at once that his father was right, and that his hopes of getting an honest living were small indeed.

"It's no use, for I've tried it. If a man's once down in the mud he's got to stop there, Billy. Come, cheer up, my boy. I've finished the petition, and a beauty it is. If we don't make five pounds out of it to-day call me—an honest man. Ha, ha, ha, Billy!"

"Them petitions ——" began Sharp junior, when his parent interrupted him.

"*Those* petitions, Billy. 'Those,' not 'them,' my boy. We are going amongst some particular people to-day, and, if you slip in your grammar after that fashion, you will spoil the game."

"The less I has to say the better I likes it," was Billy's reply.

"Very good, my boy. Your looks are invaluable, but your tongue is a most unruly member. Go and wash yourself, Billy; and put the soap in your pocket when you've done with it."

"What's that for?"

"To smell of it, of course. It's a fine thing among these charitable people to smell strongly of yellow soap. They hold that 'cleanliness is next to godliness,' and believe in your Christian principles according to the number of times a day that you wash yourself."

Billy grinned. His honest principles were not so strongly rooted yet but that he could smile at those who were the dupes of his parent's sharpness.

The necessary operations of the toilet were soon completed. Billy came forth radiant, and so strongly flavoured with soap that he smelt like a washing day. Sharp senior had attired himself in a wonderful costume of seedy black, consisting almost wholly of coat, and that such a large one that at times Mr. Sharp disappeared altogether. Indeed, once, while he was looking in at an old clothes shop, the proprietor thought that he had dropped off a peg, and hung him up again for more than an hour, much to his discomfort.

Father and son were soon clear of Drury-lane, making for the West-end by way of Covent-garden, Sharp senior casting many a thirsty glance at the public-houses en route, and licking his lips as he saw their swinging doors open and shut as the customers passed in or out.

"Quite sure you haven't got twopence about you, Billy?"

"You know I aint. If I'd had so much as a farden you'd have screwed it out long ago."

"I *must* have a drink somehow, Billy. It's frightfully hot, and when we get to the first house on my list I shan't be able to patter a word."

"It's no use askin' me to nick anythink, dad," said Billy firmly, "becos' I won't."

"Very well, my boy. Then you'll see your unhappy parent drop a corpse on the pavement. Stop a bit, though. We'll try the blind dodge."

"Wot's the little game now?" demanded Billy, as his parent hauled him up a court.

"I can't stand it any more," replied Sharp senior. "There was a swell in that pub having a shilling's-worth of brandy and soda. Catch hold of my hat. That's it."

And, with a rapidity worthy of Maccabe, Mr. Sharp had drawn a card from his pocket with "BLIND" printed on it in staring capitals, had tied it round his neck, and then, rolling his eyes up in an awful manner till only the whites were visible, he caught hold of Billy's sleeve with his left hand, and, tapping the ground with the stick he held in his right, he whispered to Billy to "cut away."

"Look out, Billy, and when you see a soft kind of old gentleman or lady shove me up against them. They can't help noticing me then, and it's always good for a penny, at least."

Sharp junior was too used to the many "dodges" of his father to express any wonder at this one, and he obeyed his directions as a matter of course, and in a few minutes they had turned out of Bow-street into Coventry-street, where, amidst the full tide of humanity thronging that thoroughfare, there was an excellent chance of finding that "soft kind" of old lady or gentleman whom Mr. Sharp designed to prey upon.

Opposite the great drapery establishment of Stabb and Mangle, Billy thought he had a chance. A gorgeous chariot, painted a pale gingerbread colour, picked out with blue, was drawn up at the kerb, and a stout lady of benevolent aspect was preparing to get in, when Billy, dutifully following his directions, shoved his parent gently against her, and at the same time knocked a vacant-looking young gentleman into the gutter.

"Pity the poor blind!" moaned Sharp senior, in a tone so doleful that it produced the effect of a complicated stomach-ache upon the listeners.

"Poor man!" said the lady, instantly feeling for her purse. "Greene, here is a poor blind man. Have you got any change? I've only got notes in my ridicule."

Mr. Greene—for it was none other than our friends whom we introduced in the first chapter—picked a sovereign out of his waistcoat pocket, and dropped it into the hat which Billy held extended.

"Bless you, my noble duke!" said Sharp senior,

fervently; then he added in a whisper to his son, "Out away, Billy. I'm gasping for a drink."

"He seems uncommon fond of you—that boy of yourn," said Mr. Greene. "It seems to me that you don't divide the wittles reg'larly."

"He's my only delight, my noble duke," replied Sharp. "It's my pride and pleasure to have him weighed every day after supper, and feel how fat he gets, while his poor old father dwindles and dwindles away into an early grave."

"Poor man!" murmured Mrs. Greene, who was in tears already at this instance of paternal devotion. "There's my card. Come there any hevening after seven, and we'll see what can be done for you. Jolliffe, did you hear? Why, where is he? Jolliffe!"

All that was visible of Master Greene just then was the soles of his boots sticking out between the wheels of the chariot; but a mother's eye is keen, and Mrs. G. had him out in a twinkling, very dirty, and considerably damaged.

"Oh, my dear Jolly!" exclaimed his mother. "Whatever made you get under there?"

"I didn't get under there," replied Master Greene, sulkily. "I was shoved. Somebody's always shoving me."

"John," demanded Mrs. Greene severely of the footman, who had been carrying on an ogling flirtation with one of the young ladies in Messrs. Stabb and Mangle's establishment, "who pushed your young master under the carriage?"

"Sure I don't know, mem."

"Then you ought to know. You're an idjot, John, and I've a good mind to discharge you. Help Master Jolliffe into the carriage, and tell William to drive home."

In her maternal anxiety Mrs. Greene had forgotten all about the existence of the "poor blind man," who was already in a quiet little public-house with the faithful Billy, devoting the proceeds of his dodge to the purchase of brandy and water.

"Billy," he said, when he had disposed of his second sixpenn'orth, and while a third was mixing, "our fortune's made. If ever I saw a green lot, it's those who gave you that sovereign. We'll call on them, Billy, this very evening. Our luck's going to take a turn."

And thus it was that came to pass the first meeting between the families of the Greenes and the Sharps—a meeting that was destined to have such important results for both.

CHAPTER III.

THE AREA SNEAK "SHOCKED."

MR. SHARP senior drank brandy and water with a neatness and dexterity, and, above all, to an extent which fairly roused the admiration of the landlord of the public-house, and he insisted upon "standing" glasses round at his own expense.

"I've got customers," he said, "who take their lotion as Britons ought to do, but gents who liquor up as free as you is scarce indeed. Three sips to a 'go' of brandy, and a 'go' every ten minutes! You're a man, sir, as his country ought to be proud of. If I had a dozen customers like you I'd retire in two years."

Mr. Sharp was touched by the landlord's appreciation of his drinking powers, and took a glass with him. Then he would insist upon returning the compliment, and so they went on for an hour or two, until the landlord was crying drunk, and Mr. Sharp had only three and ninepence left out of his sovereign; but, beyond the fact that his eyes twinkled a trifle more, and that he was a trifle swelled about the region where the bottom button of his coat ought to have been, he seemed neither the better nor the worse for the brandy he had taken.

Arrived at this point, Mr. Sharp senior deter-

mined to return home, and prepare for the important interview of the coming evening, which, he had already decided in his own mind, was to make the fortunes of himself and his son.

"They're rich, Billy," he said—"the turn-out spoke that as plainly as if I'd seen their banking account—and they're vulgar. The first words they spoke were enough to decide that point. Now, there's nobody in this world so easy to come over as a rich snob, if, Billy—if you only know how to set about it."

"You might let 'em alone," said Billy, who could not forget his inward yearnings for an honest life. "They tipped you a quid."

"A quid!" exclaimed Sharp senior contemptuously—"a paltry sovereign—a poor piece of twenty shillings! Bah! Billy, you're not worthy of your father. I tell you, my boy, those Greenes will be worth a fortune to us, and honestly, too, Billy."

Billy looked at his father doubtfully. There was nothing implied in the doubt, for he was so well acquainted with that gentleman's principles that the idea of any honest notion proceeding from his father was more than doubtful—it seemed impossible.

"You'll see, my boy—you'll see," continued Sharp senior. "You trust your old father, and before a week's over you'll be as big a swell as that noodle you shoved into the mud—ah, and riding in the carriage, too!"

"Don't cut it quite so fat, dad," said Billy, as he looked down upon his tattered clothes. "Why, we should be lucky if I could only get a page's place alongside such swells."

"Page! Nonsense, Billy—you shall be master, I tell you. But let us get home, and I'll have a nap, my boy. I always think better after a little sleep. Hal-lo! Hush, Billy; there's somebody after our plate."

They had reached the top of the alley by this time, and, looking down, they could see a lad of about seventeen or eighteen making a cautious survey of as much of the interior of Number One as he could see through the dingy window panes of the parlour.

Satisfied, apparently, that there was nobody inside, he took a short thick "jemmy," or crowbar, from under his coat, and approached the door.

"Who is he, Billy?" whispered Sharp senior.

"A stranger, dad," replied that young gentleman, with a grin. "Hark! there he goes."

The area sneak, after hovering about the plate like a fish round a tempting yet doubtful bit of bait, made a dash at it, and, inserting his crowbar between the metal and the door, was about to give a vigorous wrench, when suddenly he uttered a yell of dismay, dropped the crowbar, and staggered back into the centre of the alley as if he had been shot.

It was worse than being shot, for then at least he would know what was the matter with him; but now he stood glaring at the brass plate as if it had been a ghost, his knees knocking together, his arms dangling limply from the shoulders, like Punch's, when the showman's hand no longer animates that lively puppet.

"Oh, murder!" he was heard to mutter hoarsely.

"Wot is it?"

The voice of Mr. Sharp, bland and polite, answered—

"What is it, my dear young friend? I can tell you. It is a very fine piece of metal, warranted to weigh four pounds. It did scale four and a half, but polishing has reduced it. Will you make a bid? Come, what do you say for that noble brass plate, with a tin of polishing powder and a leather thrown in?"

The young man glared at him with a savage eye. "Is it yours?" he said.

"It is, my dear young friend. I venture to say that nobody will dispute the ownership with me."

"DON'T TOUCH HIM, MADAME," INTERRUPTED SHARP SENIOR—"THE RASCALS STRIPPED HIM, AND HE HAS NOTHING BUT THE BOARDS ON!"

"Then *wot's* the matter with it?" growled the young man wrathfully.

"Matter! Matter with it? There is absolutely nothing the matter with it. As a brass plate it is simply perfect."

"Then," demanded the young man, in a high and quarrelsome tone, "why did it go nigh to knock my bloomin' arms orf when I went to—to—look at it in a cashwill kind of vay? Come now, tell me that."

"Knock your arms off! Did it, now? *Your* arms, too! Such a nice gentlemanly young man as you! I *am* astonished!"

"Oh, yes, I dessay y'ar. But who's a goin' to pay me for 'avvin my harms knocked orf?"

"I should advise you—but stop a moment. Have you got six and eightpence about you?"

"No, I aint; an' if I had, wot then?"

"Only that I'm a lawyer, my good young man, and six and eight's my fee."

"You don't git no fees out o' me for your adwice. Who wants it?"

"Then I'll give you some gratis. That brass plate has injured you, you say? Well, take the brass plate for the damages. I can't make you a fairer offer. There it is—go and take it."

But, instead of expressing gratitude for this munificent offer, this strange young man flew into a violent passion, and, with a variety of extraordinary oaths, declared his readiness to extract Mr. Sharp's liver for the extremely moderate charge of half a pint of cold fourpenny.

"My good young man," said Mr. Sharp, calm and polite as ever, "I would willingly oblige you, even to the sacrifice of a portion of my vitals; but you can't have my liver. And why? Because I haven't any. But I'll tell you what you *may* have."

"Wot's that?"

"*The brass plate if you can get it off!*"

At this the young man's patience, sorely tried, gave way, and he blasphemed in a way that was vigorous even for Angel-alley, and which elicited open-mouthed admiration from several juvenile candidates for Newgate who were looking on.

"Crimey! Carn't he slam!" exclaimed an accomplished pickpocket, ten years old. "He'd cuss Jewey Samuels blind in ten minnits."

"Why don't he go and cuss down his own court, then?" remarked an eminent burglar of fourteen, made jealous by the praises bestowed on the stranger. "He aint one of our lot. Let's give 'im the frog's march."

The proposal at once aroused that patriotic feeling which leads an Englishman to regard an intruder as a mortal enemy.

There was plenty of mud in Angel-court, and the angels were good marksmen, of which fact the slim young man at once received convincing proof.

One dab fitted into his right eye, a second filled up his mouth, two others accommodated themselves to his "yere'oles"—as the facetious young pickpocket termed them—and a dozen others did their best to make themselves at home.

The young man, naturally disgusted, made a blind rush at his tormentors, but only succeeded in tumbling over Sharp junior, who, with kindly forethought, had laid himself down on purpose.

"Oh! swelp me, if I could only kitch 'old o' one of yer!" he gasped, as he scooped the mud out of his eyes; but just then he received his own crowbar in the pit of his stomach, and doubled up as neatly as if he had a well-oiled hinge in that portion of his anatomy.

That fall was fatal to his hopes of vengeance. In an instant two had hitched themselves on to his legs, and dragged him down the alley, while the balance of the jovial crew heaped mud, oystershells, and foul abuse upon him all the way to the gutter, where they rolled him, and then scattered.

Five minutes after a policeman who wanted a job found him, and ran him in for being drunk and disorderly. Such is life!

CHAPTER IV.

MR. SHARP DREAMS.

MR. SHARP the elder had the sleep he so ardently desired. He also had the nightmare—a supplementary blessing which he would have modestly declined had the choice been offered to him; but it wasn't, so he groaned, and choked, and snored, and suffered, until Sharp junior—who had been suffering, too—could stand it no longer, and threw a bundle of firewood at his parent.

Sharp senior woke with a terrific yell, and, jumping up with a suddenness that scattered the dingy counterpane, glared in a wild manner about him.

"Wot's the matter now?" demanded Sharp junior wrathfully. "Wot are you makin' all that row about? Aint you made enough in the night? I aint had a blessed wink."

"Then I *am* awake?" queried Sharp senior.

"Time, too!" growled Billy. "If it 'ad bin anybody but me they'd ha' woke you up long ago. Wot's the matter? Wot are you looking about like that for—somethin' to eat?"

"Oh, no, Billy!" said his father, with a shudder. "I've had enough of that in my sleep. Oh, Lord! such awful dreams! I dreamt that I was a cannibal."

"A cannon-ball!" repeated Billy. "Ah! I should think so, and somebody kep' a lettin' of you orf all night. That was the noise I heerd."

"No, a cannibal, Billy—a devourer of human flesh—and I thought I had you for supper; and very nice you tasted."

"Was I biled?"

"No, Billy—roasted. Done to a turn, with the gravy in, and the crackling nice and crisp. Well, I polished you off ——"

"Wot, all of me?"

"Every morsel, Billy."

"Why, you couldn't hold me. I weigh more'n you do."

"Never mind, Billy; I got you down, and then I began to feel ill ——"

"No wonder, arter swallerin' and gorgin' yer own kid."

"I began to feel ill, and then I was sick ——"

"And you brought me up ag'in, I s'pose?"

"No, I didn't, Billy; and don't interrupt so often. It's extremely rude. Well, I was sick, and I began to throw up the most extraordinary things. First there was King Charles's statue, then the Duke of York's monument, steps and all."

"Draw it mild, now!" expostulated Sharp junior.

"And then, Billy, came St. Paul's. That was awful. The cross tickled my throat dreadfully; but when it came to the dome, Billy, I thought I should have burst. It was just coming up when I woke."

"I wonder wot you would a brought up nex'. It's lucky you had sich a good supper, though, father, as there aint nothink for brekfuss."

"Never mind, my boy; it will not be for long. We shall soon revel in the fat of the land."

"You means that lot you gammoned yes'day in the swell turn-out?"

"Yes, my boy. They're green as grass, and we'll make hay of 'em, Billy."

"Better make bread an' cheese an' beer of 'em," said Billy. "Wot's the good of 'ay to us? We don't keep no moke."

"I was speaking metaphorically, Billy. The hay I mentioned means, not vulgar bread and cheese and beer, but venison, partridges, pheasants, turtle, champagne, horses to ride, carriages, servants to order about—everything, in fact, you can think of."

"That's a rayther rich kind of 'ay," said William. "I should call it clover."

"Never mind what it is called, my boy. We'll have it—that's the main point."

"It sounds good," said Sharp junior doubtfully. "But there, wot's the use of talkin'? You're always a hatchin' of some new kind of hegg, and it's always haddled."

"You're a dutiful boy, you are, William, to compare your own father to a hen who doesn't know her business. But, never mind; you cut away down to old Samuels with this note, and take care you bring an answer."

"If it's the sort o' answer I generally gets to your notes, I'm sure to bring it back, and behind me, too," grumbled Sharp junior.

"Then thank Providence and your father, who have provided you with a natural buffer for 'em, you ungrateful rascal," retorted Sharp senior.

Sharp junior took the note, and, muttering something concerning the "blowing" of buffers, departed.

The residence of Mr. Samuels was not very far distant, for in less than a quarter of an hour William reappeared, in company with a very plump and very dirty little Hebrew gentleman, smelling strongly of fried fish and old clothes.

"Aha! ma tear vrend," began Mr. Samuels, directly he caught sight of Sharp senior, "you're going to pay dat little loan you porrow of me—eh? I got him all town here, ready reckon up. Five bob de loan, and fifteen weeks' interesht at fifteen per shent per week; dat makes ——"

"Oh! never mind what it makes, my dear Samuels," said Sharp senior blandly. "We won't talk about paltry shillings now. I've got a scheme in hand which will bring us gold by the hundred-weight, and bank-notes by the quire."

Mr. Samuels' nose appeared to let out an extra joint like a telescope, and his beady black eyes fairly watered with avarice.

"On de cross, Mishter Sharp?"

"No, no; I've done with that. This is as square as a paving stone."

"All de petter, mishter—all de petter. If monish can be made without rishk it's de shafest way."

"So it is. Now, I've got a regular soft-roed one in tow, Samuels, and, if we work him together, we can lay our hands on a nice little lump without putting a finger in danger."

And thereupon Mr. Sharp gave Samuels a sketch of the Greene family, only judiciously altering name and residence, as a precaution lest the amiable Hebrew should go poaching.

"Vell, you are a goot judge o' character, Mishter Sharp—I vill shay dat much; and so I shpose I must chance it. But it's an awful rishk. Two shoots o' closhe, a umberreller, two pairsh spectacles, and a quid. Holy Moshes! I shall be ruined!"

But, after many similar expressions, and inquiring whether "five shillings wouldn't do? Shay sheven and shix—ten bob? Holy Apraham! fifteen bob? Oh, blessed Aaron! sheventeen and shix, then?" Mr. Samuels produced from his inexhaustible bag the two suits of clothes, the spectacles, and the umbrella.

"That's the style," said Sharp senior gleefully. "Now for the quid."

"Holy Jacob! can't you do without the monish? It's awful scarshe."

"If I could I would; but I can't. So out with it."

At last it did come out, and Mr. Samuels, having received an acknowledgment from Sharp, promising to pay something like three hundred per cent. for the loan, departed, mumbling that he was ruined, and that he was so soft-hearted that he never could refuse a friend anything.

"Now, William, my boy, prepare for action," said Sharp senior briskly, as soon as they were alone. "Is there a bit of soap?"

"Yes."

"It's fortunate that soap isn't good to eat, William, or we should have had to change that sovereign, and buy some. Go and borrow some hot water somewhere, my boy."

"You aint going to wash yourself, father, are you?" said Sharp junior, with a dawning look a alarm on his plump features.

"Never you mind, William. Go and fetch the water."

"Think of the shock to your system! You aint used to it, you know," remonstrated Sharp junior.

"You bring the hot water, William, and in a hurry, too, or I'll shock your system with something stronger than soap and water."

Sharp junior departed, wondering, and when he returned with the hot water in a battered beer-can he found his revered parent busily engaged in putting a fine edge on a very old razor.

"Oh," murmured William, "it's only for a shave."

"That's all, my boy," replied his father. "Sit down."

"Why, who are you goin' to shave?"

"You, William," replied Sharp senior, fixing a steadfast eye upon his offspring the while he made a plentiful lather with the soap and hot water.

William was young and plump, and no egg was ever more destitute of hair than were his cheeks. He was sure of this; and yet so grave were his parent's tone and expression that he passed his hand hastily over his face, as if expecting to find that a luxuriant crop of whiskers had sprouted without warning.

"But there aint nothin' to shave," remonstrated William.

"I'm not going to shave your face, my boy. I'm going to shave your head."

"Here, I say now! Come, none o' that! My 'ed don't want shavin'; I aint a wiolent loonatic."

"On the contrary, my boy, you are a professor of every known science, of all languages—ancient and modern; and a head that holds so much knowledge must be bald, you understand, William."

A light dawned upon Sharp junior, and he grinned as he said—

"Wot! is that the dodge to play on them Greenes up yonder?"

"That's it, William. You are about to apply for the post of tutor to Greenely Greene esquire, junior; but at present you are too young. When I've done with you, you'll look about sixty, and wise enough for a Lord Justice of Appeal."

"And ugly enough, too."

"Just so. Now, hold steady, William, in case the razor slips, and I take off some of the hide as well as the wool."

William obeyed, and, with a stolid grin of enjoyment, sat perfectly still while his father soaped and shaved him until his head was as bald as his chin.

Then his eyebrows were carefully whitened, a huge pair of blue-glass "goggles" mounted on his nose, and his plump body and limbs encased in a rusty black swallow-tailed coat, a clerical waistcoat, and a pair of pantaloons to match.

At last the transformation was complete, and Sharp senior looked at his handiwork in wonder and delight.

"It's beautiful, William—beautiful! Although I've done the job myself, I can hardly believe it's you."

"You don't think the green 'uns will twig me, then?"

"Impossible, my boy."

"All right, guv'ner. So far so good. You've done up my outside; but how about my hinside? If I'm a perfessor I orter know summat, and I knows nothin'."

"That's a drawback, certainly, my boy; but it's to be overcome."

"As 'ow?"

"Shake your head and frown when you're asked anything."

"That might do for once or twice."

"Well, if they get you into a corner, and I'm not there to help you, say something like this—'It would depend upon the pacific or prehensile periphery of the perihelion.'"

"Oh, my eye!" gasped Sharp junior. "'Ow the blazes am I goin' to patter all that? Wot do it mean?"

"Never mind what it means. You can pick up thieves' Latin fast enough. Now learn what I tell you."

"Say it again, then. Wot was it? Sumthin' about a queer old file and paregoric."

"Bah! 'the pacific prehensile periphery of the perihelion,'" repeated Sharp senior, with alarming distinctness, and an angry flourish of the razor.

William contrived to master the difficult phrase after a dozen attempts which nearly drove his father to the verge of insanity; but, having a good memory, he managed to retain the pronunciation of the words, only changing their places, which, as Sharp senior observed, didn't matter in the least.

Then, having carefully dressed himself into the likeness of a very shabby street preacher, Sharp senior sallied forth with the transmuted William, to, as he humorously remarked to an acquaintance, "cook them Greenes for dinner."

CHAPTER V.

THE "CONFIDENCE" DODGE.

NOW it chanced that at the very time that the Sharps were on their way to the Greenes, full of such benevolent intentions, the parental Greenes were once again in trouble on account of their beloved son.

The fact of their being troubled concerning Greene junior was nothing new—he was always in some mess or another; but this was an alarming case—he had been missing all day, and no trace of him could be found.

The servants had been despatched in every direction, with a promise of a whole year's wages as reward to the one who should bring him back. Scotland Yard had furnished its most able and intelligent inspector, who, with a couple of sovereigns on account, instantly put himself in communication with the nearest public-house, where he received so much information from a whiskey-bottle that he was obliged to retire to the tap-room and give his overburdened brain a little rest.

Meanwhile the Sharps, father and son, with that charming modesty which ever leads the truly great to shrink from public notice, proceeded by the dingiest of back ways towards the palatial residence of the Greenes.

They had nearly reached Regent-street—the western boundary of that once fashionable but now frowzy region known as Soho—when Sharp junior caught his father by the arm, and pointed across the road.

Sharp senior looked, and saw a Roman-nosed youth, with a pallid and vacant countenance—mud-bespattered—a chimney-pot hat of the most fashionable style on his head—a couple of full-sized advertising boards slung over his shoulders after the manner of sandwich men, and just below which peeped out a couple of slim naked legs and feet, quite blue with cold.

"Why it's—no, is it? Yes, by jingo, it's young Greene!"

And so it was. Without stopping to speculate as to how he had got into that condition, Sharp senior hopped across the road with the agility of a sparrow, and embraced as much of Master Greene as the boards would allow him to lay hold of.

"Oh! my dear young friend," he exclaimed, pathetically, "what awful catastrophe has reduced you to this shocking condition?"

Young Greene looked vaguely and tearfully over the top of the front board, and then said—

"Where's my mar?"

"Come along with me, my dear young friend," said Sharp senior, trembling with excitement as he thought of the chance in his hands. "We'll go to her directly. William, run ahead, and get a cab. This is indeed a fortunate day!"

"Where's the other men?" demanded Greene junior at this point, and after a careful survey of Sharp senior. "You weren't one of them, you know. Where's my watch and chain, and my rings, and my purse, and my clothes? They said they'd come back in ten minutes, and give me fifty pounds for trusting them, and I've been waiting here—oh! ever so long—and I'm so cold!"

"The 'confidence' dodge," thought Sharp senior. "Well, they've cleaned him out, anyhow. Why, by George, he hasn't got anything on but the boards!"

It was true. Beyond a short under-shirt the unhappy young Greene had parted with all his clothing to the confidence men. Verily they had a rich and easy haul that day!

Cabmen have curious "fares" sometimes, but surely never did a more curious "party" than Greene junior get into a "growler." The cabman thought so, too; but, before he could object, Sharp had hustled his prize into the cab, and shouted out the address to the driver, bidding him "go" as if he had Mrs. Giacometti Prodgers after him.

The swell address mollified the cabman a bit and he started off with a jerk, which sent young Greene—who couldn't sit down on account of the boards—flying against Sharp senior.

"Prop him up on your side, William. Keep him steady, or he'll spoil the look of our new clothes; and that won't do."

It was an awkward journey, and Greene junior suffered fearfully, for every time that he was "propped" up the shock drove all the breath out of his body, and by the time the cab stopped he was as short of breath as if he had been pearl-diving for a wager.

It was very evident that something unusual had happened. A page—pallid and ill-tempered, through deprivation of his meals—stood at the wide-open front door; at the area-gate was the cook, in unconcealed and defiant converse with her favourite, Sergeant Onety-one, of the X reserve—but a careful listener would soon have discovered that their speech had more reference to rabbit-pie than to lost heir; while at the front window were Mr. and Mrs. Greene, receiving messages and messengers, and despatching miraculous telegrams, which must have driven the telegraph clerks to the verge of insanity before they found out the meaning thereof.

In the midst of this confusion the cab drove up with that compound rattle and bang only to be achieved by a "growler" in the last stage of dilapidation, while Sharp the elder waved his hat out of one window, and Sharp junior "hurraed" out of the other.

The fond and anxious mother caught one glimpse of her darling's "beak" as it rested on the advertising board, and then she flew to meet him.

The page was half-way upstairs, eager to be the first to carry the joyful news, when Mrs. Greene came in contact with him.

It was a very one-sided collision. Mrs. Greene weighed fourteen stone—the page scaled six; she was coming down—he was going up; consequently he made a Zazel-like flight into the hall, where his head wedged itself into the umbrella-stand, and where, in the general joy, he was left to enjoy himself upside down for about two hours and a half.

Meanwhile Sharp senior had to get his prize out of the cab, and into the house, where his fond mother instantly embraced and scolded him after the manner peculiar to fond mothers in general.

"Oh! you naughty, naughty boy! How could you run away and break your mother's heart?"

Then she bestowed another hug, and, finding the boards in the way, gave a tug at the string which held them together.

"Don't, madam! Pardon me," interrupted Sharp senior. "Dreadful thing to relate; but—rascals stripped him. Nothing else on!"

That was enough for Mrs. Greene. She gave one look of horror at her bare-legged child, and then hurried him out of the drawing-room upstairs, whence she set the bedroom bells ringing furiously.

With the aid of a bath, and of a footman as valet, Greene junior soon appeared in more befitting costume; but he had a sense of injury upon him which soap and water could not remove, and he appeared dissatisfied.

"Ah! now my boy looks like himself again—don't he, Mr. G.? Come here, Jolly darling, and thank these gentlemen for their kindness. Really, Mr. Shark, I don't know how ——"

"Sharp, if you please, madam."

"Sharp—certainly. Excuse me; but I am naturally a little confused just now. Jolly, express your gratitude to Mr. Sharp and his friend, the Professor, and then tell us all how you contrived to get into this trouble."

"Oh—ah—yes!" began Greene junior, who had taken such an interest in the personal appearance of Sharp junior that he could not keep his eyes off. "Very much 'bliged, 'm sure. Er—don't you find it rather cool?"

This latter observation was addressed to Sharp junior, who, as my readers will remember, had had his head shaved.

"Jolly, my dear, how can you?" remonstrated Mrs. Greene.

Thus checked, Greene junior stared harder and breathed louder, but said nothing until he felt for his watch-chain, to finger which was an immense resource in time of mental disturbance.

It was gone, of course, and Greene junior broke out into lamentation.

"I say, mar, where's my watch and chain? Why don't you send somebody out to see whether those men have come back? I ought to have stopped—they were going to give me fifty pounds."

"You shouldn't have had anything to say to the wretches, Jolly," replied his mamma. "If you wanted money, why didn't you come to me? You know I never deny you anything."

"Those rascals, my dear ma'am," interposed Sharp senior, "would take in the seven sages of Greece, they are so artful. Not long ago, as I know for a fact, two of 'em swindled one of the chief inspectors of detectives at Scotland Yard."

"Lor' bless my soul!" exclaimed Greene senior, aghast with wonder.

"They did, sir, upon my professional word of honour; and now they go about London openly, and never a policeman dares touch them."

"Not touch 'em!" cried Mr. Greene. "Why, I should almost have thought that they could have hanged 'em for it!"

"Not a bit, my dear sir! Don't you see, said Sharp, counsel for the prisoners examines 'em—gets the whole story out. Fine thing for the newspapers—letters from indignant ratepayers—incompetency of the police—dreadful show-up. No—no go at all; and now the police are naturally afraid of these chaps, and they do as they like."

"Perhaps it's the very two rascals who robbed my poor dear boy," said Mrs. Greene.

"Very likely, madam. They've got almost a monopoly of that 'lay' now; and it's almost as profitable a 'lay' as that of the goose who used to turn out golden eggs for its master. Ha, ha!"

This humble little joke—specially adapted by the artful Mr. Sharp to the capacities of the Greene family—took effect, and in about two minutes Mrs. Greene began to smile. Mr. Greene followed suit

with a loud "Haw, haw, haw!" but Greene junior—who seldom laughed, except at a pantomime, when somebody was burnt with the clown's hot poker—remained quite serious, and inquired, in a doleful voice, "what there was to laugh at?"

"Your amiable son is quite right," said Mr. Sharp, at once resuming his gravity. "There is indeed nothing to laugh at. A scandalous outrage has been perpetrated, and the offenders are yet at liberty. We must leave their punishment to time, my dear madam; but it is quite in your power to prevent the repetition of such a thing."

"I'm sure," replied Mrs. Greene, "that I don't see how it's to be done, unless I tie poor dear Jolly to my apron-strings, or lock him up perpetually in his pa's big iron safe."

"A nice thing that 'ud be," growled Greene senior. "Why, we should have some o' the Sassieties for the Perwention of Everythink down upon us in no time, and I should get three months for cruelty to my own boy."

"Very possible, my dear sir," replied Sharp senior. "This is a strange country for justice. One magistrate will fine a man ten shillings for beating his wife nearly to death, while another will sentence a schoolmaster to imprisonment, and consequently to ruin, for giving a few strokes of the cane to an incurably vicious scholar. Your sound sense has again led you right, sir."

This was very agreeable flattery to Mr. Greene. His "sound sense" was invariably leading him into scrapes and losses, but he liked to be "soaped;" and where is the man who does not like the operation, if skilfully conducted?

"I wish Jolliffe had a little of it," said Mr. Greene, mournfully; "but he'll never be a credit to his parents. There's Mrs. G. now—why, when we kep' the chandler's shop, she used to make a couple of pound a week hextra by short weight, and——"

But at this point Mrs. Greene gave her husband a look, compared with which the head of Medusa was bland and child-like, and he wound up with a feeble laugh, and said he was "only joking."

"You joke again like that," said Mrs. Greene, in a whisper, which seemed to curdle his blood, "and I'll give you something worth joking about! Lowerin' on us before these strangers. Think of your persition in society."

Sharp, senior, of course, pretended not to have heard Mr. Greene's injudicious remarks, and took up the conversation at the preceding point.

"As I was saying, my dear sir, it is quite in your power to prevent such a misfortune occurring to your amiable son again."

"As how? Blest if I haven't tried all I know!" growled Greene, senior.

"Easily enough. Provide him with a man of the world, who is also a man of learning—one who will be a guide, philosopher, and friend, one who——"

"I say," interrupted Mr. Greene, "you don't mean a tooter?"

"A tutor is the very thing I do mean," replied Sharp, senior, with one of his most amiable smiles.

"Then we've had enough o' that game a'ready," retorted Mr. Greene, groping in his pocket for Mr. Biggs' letter, and then handing the missive to his new friend. "Jest cast your heye over that."

Mr. Sharp did "cast his heye" over it, and, not in the least dismayed by this check, handed it back with a smile—

"Ah, I see, your good nature was imposed upon, Mr. Greene, no doubt, and you took this person upon his own recommendation?"

"Blessed if I did. I warn't in b'isness for nigh on forty year to do such a trick as that. He had a crackter from the Dook of Bagnigge Wells, a yard and a half long, and another from the Bishop of Banbury Cross, in his lordship's own handwritin', and blessed bad the writing were too for a bishop."

"False characters, my dear sir, no doubt."

"I went and sor the dook myself," continued Mr. Greene, heated with the idea that he should be thought what is vulgarly called a "mug," "at his lodgin' in Lambeth-fields, where he was stoppin' while the place was bein' done up, and nice haffable gent he was—not a bit o' pride. There he was, smokin' a yard of clay, and drinking mild arf-an'arf, just like a hordinary man."

Mr. Sharp grinned inwardly, but he saw that the Greene one's self-conceit was wounded, and sighed a sigh of commiseration.

"His grace the duke confirmed the written character, no doubt, sir."

"Hevery hinch of hit," said Mr. Greene, with slow and aspirational emphasis, "and so would the bishop, only I didn't see him. He was away wisitin' some of his flock at Pentonville."

"Well, my dear sir, since you have resolutely made up your mind against the employment of another tutor for your amiable son, I will not attempt to dissuade you."

"It wouldn't be a bit of good. I've made up my mind, and so has Mrs. G."

"My Jolly never goes out of my sight again if I knows it," added that amiable lady.

"That's all stuff and nonsense, Mrs. G.; the boy must be heddicated, and he must go to school."

"Again you show your admirable good sense, my dear sir," said Sharp, "and if you have not yet made your selection, my friend, the Professor here, is the very man to aid you in your choice."

"We thought of Hoxford," said Mrs. Greene. "I mean my Jolly to mix with the hairystocrats."

"Very good, my dear madam," replied Mr. Sharp, blandly. "Master Greene is admirably formed both by nature and position to mingle with the bright and beautiful of society, but he is as yet too young for college. What do you say, Professor?"

The Professor was ready, and repeated with much gravity the cabalistic phrase his father had taught him.

Naturally it produced a profound impression upon Mr. and Mrs. Greene. The former sighed, and shook his head at Master Greene, who was sucking his thumb, and apparently deriving much satisfaction from the process.

"Ah! my boy, when will you be able to talk like that? Why don't you come here, and listen to these here gentlemen's improvin' conwersation?"

"I am listening," replied Greene junior in an injured tone.

"Then what did the Professor say just now?—come!" said Mr. Greene, confident that he had posed his son.

"I don't know."

"I'll give you such a oner over the year directly, my boy," said Mr. Greene, in a warning tone.

"Give him time, my dear sir—give him time. The greatest geniuses are always longest in ripening. You will be proud of him one day yet. My friend, the Professor, has noticed that his phrenological development is something marvellous."

Mr. and Mrs. Greene were rather uncertain whether this was an allusion to the shape of their son's nose or a remark upon the way his hair was cut, but they looked wise, and nodded their heads, which did just as well.

"I'm sure," said Mrs. Greene, after a pause, "we shall be only too 'appy to take Mr. Shark's advice."

"Ever—ever," said Mr. Greene; "and I've got somethin' on my mind, Mr. Shark, which if you'll be so good as to allow me, I'll let out."

"Only too happy to listen to you, sir," replied Sharp senior, with a bow, while his mouth fairly watered with anticipation.

"You see," Mr. Greene went on, leaning confidentially forward—"you see, I've a pretty good deal o' property of one kind and another, and I aint so young as I used to be, and letters, and figgers, and things bother me horful. Now, if you wouldn't mind coming as a sort of sekittary——"

"Say no more, my dear sir," exclaimed Sharp, jumping up, and wringing his new friend heartily by the hand. "Consider it done, and on your own terms. I had almost promised myself to the Chancellor of the Exchequer, to help him with his new budget, but I felt from the first moment we met that we were made for one another."

"You're a good feller, Shark. I know of the way you behaved to my son, and it won't be my fault if we don't get on well together. But talking is dry work, what do you say to a toothful?"

"Really I seldom take anything so early," replied Mr. Sharp, modestly, "but upon this joyful occasion, I—er—"

"Come along then," said Mr. Greene, heartily; "your friend, the Professor, will join, of course. Come along."

And arm-in-arm the new-made friends marched out of the room, the Professor following, very grave outwardly, but boiling internally with suppressed mirth.

CHAPTER VI.

IN WHICH THE BOND UNITING THE GREENES AND SHARPS IS DRAWN MORE CLOSELY THAN EVER.

WHEN the Sharps left the mansion of their new patrons, about three hours after the interview faithfully recorded in the foregoing chapter, Mr. Greene was peacefully reclining with his head in the grate, and his feet on the ornamental coal-box, softly murmuring that somebody was a "jol-goo-fler," while Mrs. Greene, and Greene junior were vainly endeavouring to drag him to a more comfortable place of repose.

It was evident that the new friends had been having a very jolly time, for even the seasoned Mr. Sharp betrayed a slight unsteadiness in his walk, and there was a twinkle in his eyes which betrayed something more than satisfaction.

"Billy, my boy," he said, "this is indeed a great day for us. I knew something good was going to happen, but nothing half so rich as this. Why, we shall make our fortunes in a year."

"No game, mind," said Sharp junior.

"What game, Billy?"

"Why, nothink on the cross."

"Why, you ungrateful young rascal!" exclaimed Mr. Sharp. "Here am I making your fortune, and the first thing you do is to insult your poor old dada."

"Oh, insult be blowed!" said Sharp junior, who was a matter-of-fact and practical kind of youth. "You'll do it if you gits the chance—you know you will."

"Ah, Billy, necessity is a stern task master, but there'll be no need for anything of this kind now. We shall get all we want by asking for it. Lord! what lovely dry sherry that was!"

"Ah! there's another go," grumbled Billy. "What did you want to go and make the hold gent tight for? You'll have the missus down on you for that, and p'raps get the game spiled."

"Well, that wasn't quite prudent, I own; but that sherry was enough to make a man forget everything. How many bottles did we have, Billy?"

"You had five, and the hold gent had three; and where you puts it all to I don't know."

And Billy eyed his parent sideways, with a look of intense disfavour.

"Never you mind, my son. You'll see me put away more by-and-bye. That was a good idea of mine, wasn't it, after the 'Professor' dodge failed, to recommend your son as my amanuensis? Your son! Ha, ha, ha! Oh, my!"

And Sharp senior was compelled to pause while he laughed so heartily that his new hat rolled into the road.

"There you go ag'in!" grumbled Billy. "There's the tile spiled now!"

"Never mind, my boy; we'll have a dozen a-piece to-morrow. Oh, my! what a game it is!"

GREEN AS GRASS.

A JOLLY SCHOOL STORY.

"THE NEW BOYS!" EXCLAIMED THE MASTER.—"WHOEVER SAW BOYS EIGHT FEET LONG."

And well might he call it a game. A well-played and profitable game it was, too. Mr. Greene had formally engaged him as manager and secretary, at a salary of five hundred a year and commission, while Sharp junior—otherwise the son of Professor Popper—was also liberally provided for.

"No more banyan-days, my boy!" continued little Mr. Sharp, rubbing his hands rapturously together. "No more starving, or scheming, or sneaking round back ways to avoid the police! Lots of money, and the fat of the land to live on; and when young Greene goes to school you shall go too—I'll manage it!"

"I aint so heager about that," said Sharp junior. "I'd rayther have a crib somewhere in the kitching. School's a place where they gives yer too much cane, and too little grub."

"Always thinking of that precious inside of yours, Billy!"

"Ah! and why shouldn't I? It's always a worryin' of me—aint it?"

"Think of the nobler and better part of your nature, my boy—the moral and intellectual—never mind your grosser appetites!"

"Well, why don't you set a hexample, then? How about all that sherry this arternoon?"

"That's got nothing to do with it, Billy. That's only a matter of business."

"So's mine. How am I goin' to live if I don't peck?"

By the time this unanswerable argument was concluded Angel-alley was reached, and Sharp senior hastened to make his final preparations for quitting that scurvy abode for ever.

"There's nothing here, Billy, that we need take away with us; so the packing up won't last long. All the family pictures and the plate are at the Bank, and the furniture we'll make a present of to the next tenant."

"There's the door-plate," suggested Billy.

"So there is! What a pity that young man who took such a fancy to it didn't leave his card! He should have had it cheap."

"And there's old Samuels to pay," added Billy.

"Ah, yes! we must square him, or he'll blow upon our little game—he's sure to find us out if he suspects anything—and when we've done that, Billy, we'll buy our outfit, and bid adieu to Angel-court for many a long day."

"Hooray for that! But, somehow, it don't seem real," said Billy, doubtfully.

"You'll find your first good dinner real enough, my boy. But, there, cut away to Samuel's; there's no time to spare. Don't forget the wig."

Billy ambled off on his errand, and soon returned with the wig.

"Well, Billy, what did he say? I was afraid that he'd come back with you."

"And so he would; but he's laid up with roomattics, and the langwidge he used is awful."

"That's lucky, Billy; otherwise he would have been round here asking questions, and I should have been obliged to burden my conscience with a few lies. Where's the wig?"

Billy handed it out—a most artificial production, looking more like a choice selection from a haystack than an imitation of human hair.

However, Sharp senior regarded it with admiration when he had well gummed it on to Billy's bald head.

"There you are, my boy! Nobody 'd know you now. And mind this—when you're in company, run your fingers through the wig now and then, and scratch it a little—it looks natural."

"Blowed if it feels natural," grumbled Billy. "It's most horful uncomfortable; and what'll it be like when the glue dries?"

"Never you mind, Billy; think of the object we've got in view. That's worth a little discomfort, I should think."

"But I gets the lot on it," remonstrated Billy.

"Even now we've got a fortin' in the distance I can't stay—I'm goin' to be packed orf to school alonger young Greene."

"My dear boy, you'll enjoy yourself just as much there; and more—when you come to my age you'll say that school-time was the happiest of your life."

"Oh—ah—yes, I dessay!" grumbled Sharp junior, not at all convinced by his parent's argument. "I've heard about schools afore to-day, and I prefers a place as a page, with the run of the kitching."

"You're a nice low-minded boy for a professional man's son—a man who is a gentleman by Act of Parliament. You'll never rise in the world with those low tastes, Billy."

Billy looked very discontented, and "blowed" everything in general in an under-tone until all his parent's preparations were complete, and once more they sallied forth to the abode of the Greenes.

Sharp senior presented much the same appearance as on his first visit; but the younger Sharp had thrown off the professorial attire, and was once again the chubby innocent with whom the reader is already acquainted.

With the exception of his wig—and therein lay the source of a frightful amount of torture to Billy.

It was not alone that it was heavy and made his head ache. Either the wrong sort of glue had been used or else too much of it; but there the fact was, that by the time the Greene mansion was reached Billy itched so dreadfully that he could hardly refrain from pulling his wig off, and scratching his scalp until it would have looked as if a Comanche Indian had had an interview with it.

"What are you wriggling about like that for?" said Sharp senior, in a fierce whisper.

"Oh!" groaned Sharp junior, "I can't stand it much longer. My 'ed do hitch to that degrees."

"Nonsense, it'll go off directly, and you keep still, here's the Greenes coming."

A moment after Mr. Greene, looking rather bilious, and Mrs. Greene, who appeared to have taken a rather strong dose of vinegar, entered the room. Mr. Greene left the door open. Mrs. Greene muttered something sarcastic about "manners," and banged it to, whereupon a howl of agony arose from the passage.

"My poor Jolly!" exclaimed Mrs. Greene. "You brute, you're always knocking the boy about, you brute you."

"Me, why I never touched the boy. It was you who banged the door, Mariar!"

"And who left it open?" retorted Mrs. Greene, as she tucked the injured Jolly under one arm, and gently caressed his nose. "If you'd had manners, and 'ad shut the door as a gentleman, then I couldn't have banged it—could I?"

"Oh! shut up, Mariar, you're enough to drive a feller wild. Excuse the missus, Mr. Sharp, she's a little out o' sorts. And now to bisness. Is that the young gentleman you were speaking of?"

"It is, sir, at your service."

"Most 'stounding likeness," muttered Mr. Greene. "Why, if he was only bald, and had specs on, blow me if you could tell him from his father."

"The likeness is very strong, indeed, my dear sir," replied Sharp, "and I am happy to say that the resemblance is mental as well as physical. Master Sharp Popper inherits the intellect of his distinguished parent."

"Ah, he must be a 'appy man. Now, Jolly, you go and show Master Popper over the house while we talks bisness."

Popper, otherwise Sharp junior, desired nothing better than to scratch himself, and in less then ten seconds he had opened the door, and banged young Greene into the passage.

"What did you do that for? said Greene, plaintively. "I've taken all the skin off my elbows. Somebody's always a-shoving me."

"Look here," whispered Sharp junior, "you've

got to show me the house. Now, where's your bedroom?"

"Up stairs. What for?"

"Never mind, you cut along, and show it to me."

"I don't see why I'm always to be ordered and shoved about," remonstrated Greene junior, but at this moment Sharp inflicted a neat little pinch on his calf which gave him a fair start, nor did he stop until he reached the door of his own bedroom on the third floor.

"Now you stop outside there till I call you," said Sharp junior, "and don't you move, or I'll wring your blessed neck."

"Oh—ah, I dessay now. Come, I'll tell my mar."

But young Sharp was already in the room, making frantic efforts to get the wig off.

That was by no means an easy job. The glue was strong, and held tight. Billy tugged until tears of agony ran down his cheeks, but the wig held fast.

"Blow it, I can't stand it!" he muttered, as he glanced wildly round the room. "Hallo, there's a bath! That's a good idea. If we can get some warm water I'll soon have it off. Here, young Greene, come in."

Master Jolly obeyed, staring at his new companion in a wonder-stricken manner. In truth he had been looking through the keyhole, and fully expected Billy was a conjuror capable of pulling his own head off.

"I say, can we get any warm water?" said Billy.

"Lots."

"Enough for a bath?"

"Yes; it's always laid on in the bath-room."

"Come on, then, I want a bath. It's so precious hot. Don't you?"

"I don't mind. But, I say, will it really come off?"

"Wot?"

"Why, your head."

"Wot d'ye mean?"

"I looked through the keyhole just now, and I saw you trying to unscrew your head. Wasn't you?"

"Look here, young Jolly, that peeping through keyholes is a bad 'abit, and you'd better get rid on it. I knowed a boy once who looked through a keyhole, and the man on the other side went to unlock the door and the key stuck in the boy's eye, and fixed him there. They couldn't get it out for more'n a week, and he was starved to death."

"Did you see that?"

"I heerd him. I used to parse the 'ouse every day, and his 'owls were frightful."

Greene junior paled and shuddered. He inwardly resolved never to peep through a keyhole again unless he was certain that the key was lost. Such is always the result of a nice little tale with a moral to it.

CHAPTER VII.

IN WHICH YOUNG GREENE DYES—AND A GOOD MANY COLOURS, TOO.

THE bath-room, like every other room in the Greenly Greene mansion, was very handsomely and completely fitted up. A man could have there any kind of fancy wash known to modern refinement.

"That's the chap for me," said Sharp junior, pointing to one similar in size and shape to a marble sarcophagus. "But, somehow, I don't quite like the idea of being washed all over all at once. 'Ow orfen do you get a scrubbin', young 'un?"

"Every day."

"Lor', no wonder you're so precious thin! Wot a fool you must be to scrub yourself away like that! I think I'll try this here happyratus over the basin. Do the water come down this injyrubber pipe, Jolly?"

"Yes, that's the shampooing basin. Hold your head under, and turn the tap."

Billy did. The water spirted forth in a warm and genial shower, and in a very few minutes he had the satisfaction of feeling the gum melt, and the insupportable tickling cease to trouble him.

"That's prime," he thought, "but if I takes this blessed wig orf afore the young 'un he'll be sure to split. Blow him! and he's undressin' for a bath now. I'll chance it. He's such a hass, perhaps he won't notice nothink."

Billy "chanced it," and gently lifting off the wig, rubbed his itching scalp with the softest of Turkish towels, and having carefully removed every trace of the aggravating gum, replaced his wig, and felt happy.

By that time Greene junior had disrobed, and climbed over the edge of the bath, when, with his usual good fortune, he slipped, and fell into it all of a heap.

"Hurt yourself?" asked Billy.

"I'm always hurting myself," groaned Jolly, "or if I aint some one else is. Turn the water on, please—the cold first. You'll see it marked on the tap."

Now Billy's literary acquirements were of the very slightest description. He looked gravely at the words carved on the handles, and taking hold of one by chance turned it on full.

For a moment Greene junior sat there smiling in anticipation of a luxurious warm bath, then a look of doubt and suspicion shaded his features, and then, with an awful yell, he sprang upright in the midst of a cloud of steam, and rolled into the middle of the room, kicking with terrific energy.

"Poor chap!" murmured Billy, gently. "I s'pose I turned on the wrong tap. Lor! wot a row he's makin'. We shall have the old 'uns up here d'reckly."

Billy was a boy of infinite resource. He argued instinctively that cold water was likely to be the best antidote for hot. There was a shower-bath close by, with the curtains drawn, and a card pinned to them, on which was written, "NOT TO BE USED."

Billy did not stop to spell that out. A bath was a bath, and had but one use to his mind.

He dragged open the curtains, plunged Jolly into the middle, and pulled the string with a jerk.

The water came down like a thunder shower. Billy heard sundry gasps and snorts and feeble kicks, but never left go of the string until the water ceased to flow.

"That's done him good, I lay," thought Billy, as he opened the curtains to let young Greene out. "Why—oh! here's a go! Blest if I haven't dyed him."

It was awful, but it was true. There in the bottom of the bath sat the unfortunate Greene, gasping for breath, and dyed a brilliant gamboge yellow from head to foot.

An enthusiastic inventor had induced Greene senior to invest some money in a new system of dyeing, and Greene junior, with his usual luck, was the first article submitted to the test.

"I've done it now," thought Billy, as he gazed upon his gamboge handiwork. "This'll spile the whole blessed game. They'll think I did it a-purpus. I'll try if it'll rub orf while it's wet. Come here, Jolly."

And with very scant ceremony, Billy, in a perspiration of fear, hurled Greene junior out of the bath, laid him out on the floor, and scrubbed away at him with a flesh-brush, as if he had been polishing boots for a wager.

Unfortunately he selected the very place where Greene had been most severely scalded. It was more than human nature could endure, and with a yell, equal in shrillness to the whistle of a locomotive, Jolly Greene bounded up, overturning Sharp junior, and, without a thought of his utter want of anything in the shape of clothing, fled down the stairs, loudly calling for his "mar!"

CHAPTER VIII.

GREENE JUNIOR EXPLAINS.

THE ears of maternal affection are sharp, and at the sound of Jolly's first yell Mrs. Greene hastened to the rescue.

"Where are you, Jolly, my poor dear? Oh, my good gracious!"

The poor lady no sooner caught sight of her beloved offspring in his frightful condition than she uttered a scream, and fell back fainting upon Mr. Greene, who had come out to see what was the matter.

Mrs. Greene, as my readers already know, was not distinguished for a sylph-like elegance of form, and the collision floored her husband with alarming suddenness. Mr. Sharp would have suffered too, but he had just time to dodge behind a chair.

"Wotever's the row, Mrs. G.?"

"Oh! my poor dear Jolly!"

"Blow that boy! He's always up to something," growled Mr. Greene. "Where is he Mariar? Wot's he bin a-doin' of?"

"Oh! go and look at him, Mr. G.! He's got the yaller fever or the janders. Send somebody for a doctor."

Mr. G. was just expressing his opinion that a good bamboo cane would be the best kind of physic for the boy, when that victim himself limped into view.

"Oh, Lord!" ejaculated Mr. Greene, and sat down with a jerk upon the carpet. "What is it?"

"Don't be frightened, guv'nor, it's nothink," said the voice of Sharp junior, and that amiable young gentleman ambled leisurely towards Greene junior, nodding in a friendly manner at Mr. Greene.

"Nothink!—isn't it?" exclaimed Mr. Greene. "Look at his colour. Wot has he been doin' of?"

"I haven't been doing nothing," moaned Master Greene; "it was done to me. He turned the hot water on, and all the skin's off, and I am so sore, and then he put me in the shower-bath, and I come out all yellow, and then—Oh!"

Sharpe junior, thinking it quite time to put an end to these indiscreet revelations, administered a stinging pinch, which made the unfortunate Jolly dance with agony.

The cry of her beloved in agony roused Mrs. Greene to action. She arose with wonderful rapidity—considering her weight—sent for a doctor, took an overcoat from a peg in the hall, flung it over Jolly, and bore him to a sofa.

The process extracted fresh howls from the injured one, for he was dreadfully sore where he had been scalded.

The doctor soon arrived—for the Greenes were wealthy and influential, and less important patients could wait.

"Well, my dear madam," he said, with his blandest professional smile, "how is our young friend? A little bilious—eh? Why, good gracious!"

Just then he caught sight of Jolly, and jumped back as if he had been called in to prescribe for a lion in a fit of delirium tremens.

"Ah! you may well be startled, doctor," said Mrs. Greene, tearfully. "It's awful, isn't it? Hevery care's took of him, and yet such a boy for getting into trouble there never was."

"I don't get into trouble," protested Greene junior, tearfully; "I'm shoved into it."

"We're going to send him to school," said Mr. Greene, resolutely. "I won't have my peace of mind broke like this. There's always some game on, and me and Mrs. G. is reg'lar miserable."

"An excellent plan!" observed the doctor, as he put the finishing touches to Jolly's scalds. "How do you feel now, my young friend?"

"All right, thankee."

"And now for this unfortunate dyeing business," said the doctor. "You have told me how it happened? Have you any of the dye left?"

"Plenty; and I wish the chap was here as persuaded me to buy it. I'd dye his inside yaller for him."

A cupful of the dye was brought, and the doctor, after carefully eyeing it, and smelling it, and even tasting a little, shook his head gravely.

"I'm afraid I can't do anything here, Mr. Greene."

"What?" ejaculated Mr. and Mrs. Greene together.

"You see this is a very mordent dye, the base of which is, I think, peroxide of chromium; and in that case——"

The doctor paused.

"Well?" said Mrs. Greene, breathlessly.

"In that case nothing can remove it."

"Oh, Lord!" exclaimed Mr. Greene.

"Oh, my poor dear Jolly!" and Mrs. Greene flung herself upon the recumbent form of her son—much to his discomfort—and wept aloud.

"Except one thing, of course," added the doctor. "It will wear off—in time."

"How long?" groaned Mr. Greene.

"Say seven or eight years."

"Seven or eight years! My boy to walk about all that time sich a colour! I'd rather have him scraped."

"Come now, pa!" moaned Greene junior. "I'm not going to be skinned—so now then!"

"Can't nothink be done, doctor?"

"I'm afraid not; but you have one chance—consult the man who made the dye. He knows its composition better than I do, of course. Good morning!"

And away the doctor went, leaving the unfortunate Greene family in a state of great consternation.

The Sharps, too—both father and son—were not without their misgivings lest this mishap should damage them in the estimation of their new patrons; but, fortunately, they looked upon Master Jolly as being the author of his own trouble, and were, besides, too occupied in devising a remedy.

"Wot a pity you kicked that chap downstairs the last time he called, Mr. G.!"

"Who? The man who sold me the dye?"

"Yes."

"Well, it was unfortunate; but who'd a thought of sich a thing as this?"

"G.?"

"Well, my dear?"

"I dessay the chap would take a 'pology of you, backed up with a tenpunnut."

"We'll try him, my dear. I'll go round there at once."

Here Mr. Sharp saw an opportunity to cut in, and he did so accordingly.

"Allow me to act for you in this matter, my dear sir," he said, persuasively. "My profession has accustomed me to deal with delicate and difficult cases, and I will pledge my reputation that I succeed in this."

"Thanks!" said Mr. Green, cordially, as he took out his pocket-book. "That's the man's address, and there's a twenty-pun' note. If you can do it cheaper, though, do."

"You may rely upon me, sir. But persons of his class are very avaricious—dreadfully so."

"That's true," sighed Mr. Greene. "The money that chap had out of me for his precious dye no one would credit if I told 'em, and now all it's done is to turn poor Jolly as yaller as a guinea."

"Not an inappropriate colour, my dear sir, considering that your amiable son is as good as gold."

And Mr. Sharp gave a little laugh to call attention to his little joke. But joking on the subject was dangerous. The Greenes didn't even smile and Mr. Sharp wisely took his departure.

CHAPTER IX.

OUT OF THE FRYING-PAN INTO THE FIRE.

NOW it is a remarkable instance of the force of habit that, although Mr. Sharp had within his reach, at the mansion of the Greenes, any quantity of wine and beer and spirituous liquors, yet he could not resist the temptation of entering a public-house the instant he thought himself safe from the observation of his new friends.

He passed the first—urged by the importance of his errand; he paused opposite the second for a moment, and then passed that also—but only because he remembered a better one in the next street.

"Lord," he murmured, "of course, there's old Foxey's house! I wonder if he'll remember me defending him when he was charged with receiving stolen goods. How we made the liquor fly when he was discharged for want of evidence! Ha, ha! the jury never knew that I'd bounced three of the witnesses, and made a fourth so blessed tight that the judge gave him seven days for contempt of court the minute he showed his nose in the witness-box."

By the time these humorous reminiscences were over Mr. Sharp had reached the public-house, where he found the eminent Mr. Foxey in the private bar, tossing for champagne with some very flashy-looking customers, composed apparently of equal parts of betting men and swell mob.

Foxey was hardly what the world would have called a respectable citizen; but, among his many faults, that—to use his own words—of "cutting an old pal who was down on his luck" was certainly not to be reckoned.

The moment he caught sight of Mr. Sharp he saluted him cordially, and asked him what he'd take to drink.

"Me and my friends here are just going Tommy for some fiz. You shall stand in."

"I'll have a go, too," said Sharp, in an offhand tone. "A pound or two won't make much difference to me."

"What! up in the stirrups again, Sharp? That's the sort! Flimsies, too, by the Lord Harry! What mug have you got hold on now?"

Sharp winked a wink full of meaning as he spun a battered halfpenny, and the tossing began.

The champagne went round merrily, and, as the landlord and his friends had been moistening their clay pretty frequently already, they began to feel rather sleepy after the fourth dozen—two of which, at a hundred and twenty shillings a dozen, had fallen to Mr. Sharp's share.

"That's twelve pound out of twenty," he thought, as he quitted the public-house, leaving the landlord and his friends reclining in various postures of unstudied elegance upon the floor and the sofa. "It's no use going round to that chap with only eight pounds left; and time's up, too. I've been in that crib nearly three hours."

It was a fix; but a man of Mr. Sharp's infinite resource was not likely to be daunted—especially when his wits were sharpened by half a dozen bottles of Moet's best.

He sauntered along, thinking deeply, until he reached the street corner, where a little crowd was collected round a hawker, who was bawling forth the many virtues of his most miraculous cleansing paste.

"There aint no deception about it," he was saying. "Blood-stain, pitch-stain, grease-stain, mud-stain—even the stain off of a guilty conscience—a cake of this will remove 'em all, and the price is only a penny; and all you've got to do is to wet the paste, and rub a little on. If wot I say aint true I'll return the money and eat the cake. Who says next? Here you are, sir. Sold again!"

A brilliant idea struck Mr. Sharp as he listened to the man's voluble patter.

Here was the very thing. It would be easy to say that the dyer was dead or had retired from business, and that this was his successor. Nothing came easier to Mr. Sharp than lying.

He waited until a policeman had dispersed the crowd and ordered the hawker to move on; then, while he was shutting up his tray, and condemning the whole police force to the infernal regions, Mr. Sharp accosted him.

"Trade don't seem very lively."

"Lively! No, it aint," replied the man, with an emphatic oath, which I decline to reproduce. "How the blank is it goin' to be, when the blank slops moves a man blank well on just when his blank patter's beginning to fetch 'em?"

"How would you like to earn a couple of pounds?"

"Wot's the use of arsking such a question? Kin you show us how?"

"I can, and easy, too—no trouble. Come and have a liquor, and I'll tell you."

Mr. Sharp had already taken enough to make four men with the ordinary kind of heads, drunk and incapable; but my readers are already aware of his genius—for it was nothing less—for drinking.

"Now, wot's the little game?" said the hawker.

"First, what's your liquor?"

"Ah, you knows how to treat a man, I see! A 'go' of rum hot, then. That patter's horful dry work this weather."

Mr. Sharp, in order to seem sociable, ordered two, and, after a few preliminary sips, proceeded to unfold his scheme.

"Now," said Mr. Sharp, "about that stuff of yours. What's it made of?"

"I don't know. I buys it 'olesale of a cove in the Minories, who swears that he'd make a fortun' out on it if he 'ad only chips enough to advertise it, and give it a six-j'inted name like a tallerscope."

"Will it take dye out of anything?"

"Dye! Ah, that's just wot it will do! Why, when I first took to the line my missus had a noo yaller shawl as she was werry proud on, and one day the kid upsets 'arf a pound of dripping on to it. She wollops the kid, and I give him a oner, but that wouldn't take the grease out, so I thinks of the stuff I'd bought, and we melts a cake up in some bilin' water and shoves the shawl in."

"And it took the grease out?"

"Ah, more than that—it took all the colour out, too. My missus was furus, shied the tub at me, and laid me up for a week."

Mr. Sharp's face brightened.

"The shawl was yellow—eh?"

"As yaller as a blank quid; blank me if it wasn't!"

"That'll do!" exclaimed Mr. Sharp, in an ecstasy. "If it'll take the dye out of a shawl it'll take it out of a boy. Have another 'go' of rum, and come along."

"Out of a boy?" said the hawker. "Wot kind of a boy?"

"The ordinary kind, only he's rather a bigger fool than usual."

"And he's dyed?"

"All over, as yellow as that shawl you were speaking about."

"That's a rum go; but, then, it don't matter to me. If there's two quid to be made out on it, I'm the cove for yer."

"You're a trifle shabby, certainly," said Mr. Sharp; "but it don't matter. Professional men are always careless in dress, and the cleverer they are the dirtier they are, as a rule. When they begin to wash themselves every week, and put on a clean shirt every month, it's a pretty sure sign that their intellect is failing. Come on, we'll have a cab."

In a quarter of an hour they had reached the Greenly Greene mansion, the drawing-room window of which was occupied by Mr. and Mrs. G., who had been flattening their noses against the plate-glass without intermission ever since Mr. Sharp's departure.

"Here he is, Mariar," said Mr. G., in a state of intense agitation, "and he's brought the dyer feller with him."

"That aint the party, G.," replied the lady. "The man you kicked downstairs was twice as big, and he had red air."

"Never mind, it's somebody; and that Sharp knows what he's about. I'll lay it's all right."

The next moment our little friend entered the room, heaving with exultation.

"All right, Sharp, my boy?"

"All right, Mr. G., sir—all right. The party you sent for has retired from business, and this gentleman, an old friend of mine, bought the concern. I found him engaged in some most important chemical experiments for the Government laboratory, and he wouldn't have left them for another soul but me —would you?"

"I'm blanked if I would."

This was rather strong language for an eminent chemist, but the Greenes were too much excited at the prospect of restoring their dear Jolly to his natural colour to heed a little bad language.

"The doctor's been again since you went out, Sharp, and he says as Jolly's body, where he was scalded, mustn't be touched yet awhile, but if you can get the dye off of his face and 'ands, you'll find me hact liberal."

"I've settled all that, my dear sir," interposed Sharp, hastily, for, as may be supposed, he was by no means anxious to let Mr. Greene know the real terms on which the "eminent chemist" had been engaged.

"Come along up stairs, then. We've put Jolly to bed. Will it be necessary to take him hout?"

"Oh, no, you can perform the operation in bed I think, professor," said Mr. Sharp.

"Anyweres," was the great man's reply.

"You'll have a little refreshment, gentlemen, before you proceed to business?"

"Sence you are so kind, a little drop o' rum wouldn't be bad," said the eminent chemist.

"I'll send some up, and remember, gentlemen, that two anxious parients is awaiting down below."

"Ah! my dear young friend," said Mr. Sharp, amiably, as they entered the bedroom of the luckless Jolly, "and how are we by this time?"

"Better, thankee," replied Master Greene, eyeing the new comer with much disdain. "Who's that chap with you? What's he come for?"

"To cure you, my dear young friend. To restore to you your natural lovely complexion, and bring joy to the hearts of your fond parents."

"Look here, I'm not going to have anything done to me. Somebody's always doing something, and it's sure to hurt."

"I'll pledge you my candid word of honour, my young friend, that it won't hurt a bit. It's only just like washing your face."

"Well, if that's all I don't mind, but I know something's going to happen. I feel a kind of pricking all over me."

A can of hot water had been brought up, in addition to that necessary for the grog. The eminent chemist poured it into the basin, and he said in a hasty whisper—

"How much stuff shall I put in?"

"Better make it strong," replied Sharp, also in a whisper.

"Arf a dozen 'll be enough. If that don't do we can try some more."

And half a dozen of the mysterious cakes were thrust vigorously into the basin, while Mr. Sharp stirred with equal vigour at the grog in the punch bowl.

"It's all ready," said Sharp, tasting a ladle-full. "Come on, before the stuff cools."

It was the perfection of grog—hot, strong, sweet, and aromatic.

Glass after glass was swallowed, and the eminent chemist began to get a little hazy and struck up the chorus of that specially stirring ode to Saint Jingo, which is stated by well-informed persons to have caused the illness of Prince Gortschakoff, and the Emperor of Russia, to make an attempt at suicide.

"*We don't want to fight, but by Jingo——*"

"Dry up, you noodle," exclaimed Mr. Sharp angrily, "do you want to spoil the whole game? Here, the stuff's cool enough now; come on and help me with the boy."

The eminent chemist arose, and reeled unsteadily to the bed-side, where he instantly fell upon the suffering youth.

Jolly howled, of course, and Mr. Sharp hurled the eminent chemist off the bed, and propped him up in a corner.

"What a head you've got," said Sharp, contemptuously. "Why, I've got a boy fourteen years old who could chuck you under the table."

"I'm aw ri'."

"Then how is this stuff to be used?" demanded Sharp in a ferocious whisper. "Do you lay it on with a rag?"

"Yesh."

Young Greene watched all the preparations with anything but happiness expressed upon his features.

Something was going to be done to him, and, as he knew by sad experience, whenever anything was done to him it was sure to hurt.

If he had his hair cut the barber was certain to snip a little bit out of his neck or his ear; if he had a tooth drawn it was always the wrong one. Nothing ever went right; it was fate.

"Now, Master Greene, we are quite ready," said Sharp, cheerfully, as he placed a protective layer of towels round Jolly's neck. "Keep still, it'll soon be over."

Jolly resigned himself to his fate with a groan, and Mr. Sharp proceeded to dab a flannel saturated with the mixture all over the patient's interesting features.

The first application produced apparently no effect. Mr. Sharp wetted the flannel, and tried afresh.

This time there was a slight change in the aspect of Master Jolly's face and neck, but so slight that it was impossible to define.

Nevertheless it encouraged Mr. Sharp. He laid on a third coat, and then sat down a little way off with his head on one side, like a connoisseur regarding some work of art.

"Isht aw ri'?" murmured the eminent chemist, who was yet capable of taking a maudlin interest in the proceedings.

"It's doing *something*," said Mr. Sharp, whose hopeful look was now changing to one of doubt.

"Knew wash all right," murmured the chemist, with a bland smile of contentment.

"I'm not so sure about that," muttered Mr. Sharp. "There's a change entirely. Why, oh lor'! I'm blanked if he isn't turning green!"

It was too true. Some unexpected chemical combination had taken place, and the unfortunate Jolly was ornamented with a pea-green face and neck, and a body and limbs of a brilliant yellow.

Nothing but emigration was possible for him now. The natives of the Sandwich Islands, with a taste for colour, would have made a king of him, but civilisation would laugh him to scorn.

CHAPTER X.

MORE TROUBLE.

MR. SHARP'S exclamation and the sight of poor Jolly's pea-green visage sobered the eminent chemist, and he gazed horror-stricken at the result of his handiwork.

"Who'd a thought it?" he muttered, hoarsely. "It never did such a think afore."

"Because it never had the chance," growled

SHARPE JUNIOR QUIETLY ENJOYS THE DISCOMFITURE OF THE "SWELL" AND THE CONSTERNATION OF THE COMPANY IN GENERAL.

Sharp senior. "Here's a mess. I'm blanked if I can see my way out of this. It's worse than before—blank it! He's double-dyed now. You'd better cut and run before the old people come up."

"Wot about the two quid?"

"Blank the two quid! Think yourself lucky if you get off without being collared and locked up."

The fears of the eminent chemist for his personal safety overcame his covetousness, and he made for the door with a tolerably steady step, and gained the street in safety.

"I say," exclaimed the voice of Greene junior, "what has that man gone away for, and what makes you look so white, and why don't you take this stuff off my face, it tickles so, and where's my mar?"

Mr. Sharp looked at him with a thoughtful eye. Where was his mar, indeed, and what would she say when she came?

Another brilliant idea came with the inspiration of despair.

"It's all right, Master Greene," he said, "your mamma will be here directly, and wont she be pleased? But now I must cover up your face, for if the light gets to it, when it's dry the consequences would be awful."

"I knew something was going to happen," moaned the unlucky Jolly. "Why didn't you cover me up then?"

"Plenty of time, Master Greene. I've rung for a needle and thread, and we'll put you to rights in no time at all."

The needle and cotton were brought, and Mr. Sharp desired the servant to inform her mistress that everything was going on beautifully, and that Master Jolly would be ready to embrace his beloved parents in a quarter of an hour.

That quarter of an hour Mr. Sharp diligently employed in sewing up poor Jolly's head and neck in a couple of handkerchiefs, leaving only two little holes for his eyes, and a larger one for his mouth.

"There now, isn't that nice and comfortable?"

"No, it aint," grumbled Master Greene, "it tickles dreadfully, and it makes me hot too."

"Never mind, my dear young friend, "it won't be for long, and then, if you only knew how nice you'll look."

"Oh, ah, yes, I dare say," growled Greene junior, who, in reality, looked rather like a Roman-nosed corpse, floured to keep it fresh in warm weather. "I want my mar. I won't stop here any longer."

"No, more you shall, my dear Jolly," said Mrs. Greene, who with Mr. G. at that juncture entered the room. "Oh, my, how pale he is!"

"Pale as a corpse," said Mr. Greene. "Why it's worse than being yaller."

"Excuse me, my dear sir, that is only the handkerchief sewn over his features, to preserve them from the air, while the bleaching operation is going on."

"It's all right then?"

"Quite right, dear sir. Your beloved son will be restored to you as beautiful as ever."

"Where's the other gentleman?" asked Mrs. G. "You ought to do something handsome for him, G."

"He's gone, madam. He is a modest man, and cannot bear to be thanked; besides, he was amply content with the liberal douceur you commissioned me to give him."

"That's right. I'm glad the fellow's not greedy. Twenty pounds is no joke in these hard times."

"Can't we just have a peep at Jolly?" said Mrs. Greene.

"Not so much as the thousandth part of a wink, my dear madam, unless you wish him to be green—I mean yellow—for life."

"No—no, of course not. We leave it to you, Mr. Sharp; but where is your young sekittary? I declare I've been so decomposed all the morning that I haven't missed him."

"Studying, my dear madam, no doubt. That boy will be a great man some day. He never loses an opportunity of acquiring some kind of information."

Just then a shrill voice, upraised in tones of anger unmistakeable, was heard proceeding from the regions below, and in a moment the cook appeared, flushed with rage and trembling, till she shook like a blanc-mange.

"Which I'm not used to it, mum, and I'm not a-going to put up with it nayther," she began, rather incoherently, but with a great amount of decision.

"Whatever is it, Jane?"

"A great lazy boy, as is fat enough for a paupers (porpoise?), not content with eatin' enough at his meals to satisfy three ordinary Christians, must go a-poking his nose into my larder d'rekly he thinks my back's turned, and he calls hisself a sekittary too! I'd have sekittaried him with the rollin'-pin, but he was too artful, the willin, and it went through the clock instead, which you can see for yourself, mum, and a month's warnin' if you please from this moment, as is things I'm not used to, and am not a-goin' to put up with."

"Blank that boy!" thought Mr. Sharpe. "He's always after something to eat." Then he added aloud—

"My dear good girl, you are mistaken, I assure you. He was only analysing."

"There's no Anns ner yet no Elizas in my kitchen," retorted the cook; "and, if there was, what business would a boy like that have down there?"

"She is mistaken again, my dear ma'am," said Mr. Sharp. "I meant to explain that my secretary was merely taking samples of food, for the purpose of ascertaining their purity. Adulteration is carried on to such a fearful extent nowadays."

"That's true," said Mr. Greene. "Things aint as they ought to be. Why, when Mariar and me was in the chandlery line——"

"Hold your tongue, G., for goodness sake!" said his better half, with a suddenness that caused Mr. Greene to bite the offending member sharply.

"And you, Jane—you hear what this gentleman says. What was being done was for the good of us all, to prevent these nasty grocers from choking us with their rubbish."

"Good, indeed!" exclaimed the cook, with a toss of her head. "As if I didn't know what was good better than a saucy hupstart of a boy, as is far too fat ever to have got a honest livin'!"

Mr. Sharp, with the keen scent of a sharp attorney for a libel, had his note-book out in an instant.

"These words are actionable, my good woman—mind that. I shall advise Master Popper Sharp to bring an action against you for defamation of character."

"Deformation of crackter!" snorted the cook. "His crackter is deformed enough a'ready, I'll lay a wager. But I can't stop idlin' here no longer. Now, mum, is this fat lazy feller to come hangin' about my kitchen or not?"

"Your languidge is oderous, Jane. If I hadn't sich a good c'rackter with you I should say that you had been drinking."

"You'd better not, missus," retorted Jane, her face flushing scarlet, while she trembled with wrath. "You say such a thing as that and I'd see whether your 'air was real or false in the twinkling of a hi."

Matters were now assuming a serious aspect, and a battle royal seemed imminent, when a diversion was effected by the appearance of Sharp junior, who ambled placidly up as though nothing was the matter, nor ever had been, nor ever could be.

The cook waited till he was well within range, and then let out a round-handed spank, which would have made Billy see stars manifold if it had hit him, but he ducked just as nimbly as the clown in Punch's show, and the cook went down the back stairs with far greater speed than she had ascended.

"Oh, dear me, there's nothing but worrit in this world!" sighed Mrs. Greene. "Only let me get you safe away to school, Jolly, and I shall get a little peace, perhaps."

"Oh—ah, come now!" said the injured Master Greene. "I get a lot of peace, don't I? Do you ever get scalded to death nearly, and dyed all manner of colours that won't come off? Yes, of course you do. Ah, I shall be glad to get away to school! I can't be worse off than I am here, and it'll be a change. Only I hope that they won't send the fat chap; he means well, but I'm never in his company for ten minutes without getting shoved. Somebody's always shoving me."

CHAPTER XI.

IN WHICH MASTER JOLLIFFE IS MADE "BEAUTIFUL FOR EVER."

IT was many a long year since Mr. Sharp had been so puzzled. He might have confessed that the experiment had failed, and thrown the blame upon the "eminent chemist;" but he had committed himself by stating that it had succeeded.

Then, again, he knew that his influence with the Greenes would be considerably diminished if he acknowledged the truth; and a good all-round lie that would fit the circumstances he could not think of for the life of him.

In this dilemma he sought out the ever cool and collected Billy.

Mr. Greene had given him about half a hundredweight of letters and accounts to sort, examine, and answer; but, in his then state of mind, he could think of nothing but Master Jolliffe's green and yellow complexion.

Billy thought for a moment, with his hands plunged deep into his trousers' pockets, and then said—

"Why don't you come the Rachel fake?"

"Billy, my boy," exclaimed the enraptured Mr. Sharp, "you're a genius—a trifle too fat, perhaps, and not quite hair enough for the character; but you've inherited your father's intellect. Rachel him! Of course—the very thing!"

They never thought of consulting Master Greene as to whether he would like the operation. No one ever did. If any one coveted some of Jolly's property they took it, without going through the ceremony of asking; or, if one was out of temper, or had the toothache, Jolly was sought out, and his unoffending head smacked.

So Billy was speedily despatched to a chemist's with a liberal order for glycerine, pearl powder, rouge, small sponges, and other such articles, well-known to devotees of the Rachel persuasion.

"And how is our dear boy a gettin' on, Mr. Sharp?" asked the plaintive voice of Mrs. Greene, who was perpetually hovering about the bedroom, and was only restrained from pulling the covering from off her darling's face by the warning of Mr. Sharp that he would be dyed for life.

"Better ma'am—better; getting on favourably. You shall see him to-morrow, or perhaps to-day, looking more beautiful than ever."

"Bless you, you have saved my darling boy!" said Mrs. G., beginning to evince alarming symptoms of a desire to embrace her benefactor. "Me and G. will never forget you, Mr. Sharp."

"Don't mention it, ma'am—don't mention it. And now, if you'll excuse me, we'll go in and attend to Master Jolliffe."

They found the gentle youth on his back, fast asleep, but evidently suffering from a severe attack of nightmare, to judge by his gasps and groans, and the convulsive movements of his limbs.

"He's a nice beauty to make all this fuss about," said Mr Sharp, eyeing the hapless Jolly with a look of much disfavour. "I wonder now if he got smothered—by accident of course—whether these Greenes would adopt you instead?"

"Come, now, none o' that! You said you t be up to any games."

"You're a nice boy to round on your poor old father. Why, I can't leave you alone five minutes, but you must go sneaking into the pantry, gorging that precious inside of yours."

"I can't help it. I was born with a happetit, warn't I?"

"That'll do, you ungrateful young ruffian. Cut along, and get those handkerchiefs off young Greene's face while I mix the complexion in the basin."

Billy obeyed, and as the coverings were removed he stared in astonishment, for his parent had not informed him of the change in Master Jolly's colour.

"Why he's worse than he was afore."

"Never you mind whether he's worse or better. Just wake him up, will you?"

Billy woke him up by the short and simple expedient of punching him in the wind. It was very effectual, and Jolliffe awoke immediately with a howl which would have echoed through the house, had not Billy promptly checked it back with the pillow.

"You let me alone. You're always shoving me about."

"It's all right, my dear young friend," said Mr. Sharp. "We have come to restore to you your primitive beauty of complexion."

"Oh, ah! all right. Go on, I don't care what you do," said young Greene, abandoning himself to despair. He was the toy of fate, and to struggle against his destiny was beyond his power.

Mr. Sharp laid on the paste with a liberal hand, and indeed more than one coat was necessary to hide the brilliant green beneath; but at last it was done, and Master Jolliffe looked uncommonly like one of those lay figures which decorate the tailoring establishments of Moses and Sons.

"It's beautiful," said Mr. Sharp, admiringly, "only I hope his mother won't want to kiss him. It won't stand too much of that," he added, in a whisper.

"Tell her that he aint quite cured yet, and that the complaint's ketching," suggested Sharp junior.

"Right again, my boy, and now get the looking-glass, and let him have a look at himself."

Billy obeyed, and held the mirror up before Master Jolliffe.

He had been rather a pasty and bilious boy with regard to his complexion, and as Mr. Sharp had been very liberal with the pearl powder and rouge the change was great indeed.

Greene junior gave a sniff of satisfaction, and eyed himself with exceeding glee.

"Thankee," he said, "that's very kind of you. 'Pon my word I'm sorry if I said anything rude just now, but you've no idea how I get shoved about. I'll go down to my mar."

Mrs. G., having been duly warned of the danger in store for both herself and her darling if they got too close, was permitted to see Jolly, and, suspecting nothing in the innocence of her heart, called down blessings on the head of Mr. Sharp, while Mr. G., in the first burst of his gratitude, wrote out a cheque for such an amount that Sharp calculated it would take a month to spend it in champagne at a guinea a bottle.

"But," she said, firmly, in conclusion, "both G. and me have made up our minds that Jolly goes to school this week."

And for once at least their wishes were fulfilled without a check, for on one memorable Thursday morning, amidst tears and wailings, Masters Jolliffe Greene and William Sharp Popper drove away to Warmington grammar school.

The last words of Sharp senior to his son were—"Whatever you do, Billy, *don't let young Greene wash himself.*"

CHAPTER XII.

SCHOOL.

ON a bright clear morning in early summer, the Rev. Copley Cobbem, M.A., head-master of the Warmington Grammar School, sat in his study with a bewildered expression of countenance, remarkable in a gentleman who (as his scholars believed) was acquainted with every language, living or dead, and who had all the sciences and "ologies" securely stowed away in handy corners of his cranium.

Morning prayers and breakfast had been duly discussed, the young gentlemen were letting off steam in the playground, previous to the summons to the class-rooms, and the Rev. Copley Cobbem, according to custom, was reading his morning's correspondence.

There was only one letter; but that one might have been written in the hieroglyphics of "Cleopatra's Needle," judging from the way in which it puzzled him.

He rested his elbows on the table, and his cheeks on his fists, and glared at the epistle, while his nose was within an inch of the paper. He held it out at arm's length, looked at the back and front, the address, the superscription, and the signature, and seemed to derive no comfort whatever from any of these processes. Let us introduce our readers to the letter, and let them share the head-master's bewilderment.

"REV. AND DEAR SIR,—Mr. John Brown, of London, whose son was at one time under your charge, has so strongly recommended your great ability as a teacher of youth, that I am induced to confide my two boys to your care. They are extremely good boys—docile and affectionate—only possessing a natural peculiarity which renders them sometimes the butt of the unfeeling. In a word, they are very tall and slim for their respective ages (12 and 13); but this I know will not influence your benevolent heart against them. As it is highly probable that the bedsteads in your dormitories would be unsuited to my sons' requirements, I take the liberty of forwarding by rail—carriage paid—two substantial iron cots, twelve feet long, which can be lengthened, if necessary, by means of a screw at the foot. "I am, Sir,

"Yours obediently,

"WILLIAM SMITH."

"Now, what in the name of goodness does this mean?" muttered the Rev. Mr. Cobbem. "Bedsteads twelve feet long! It must be a mistake, and yet the letter is written very clearly. And who on earth is Mr. Brown? Who recommended him here? I have five Browns in the school now, and I've had fifty in my time. And who's Mr. Smith? There's no address beyond London. It must be a slip of the pen. At any rate the boys will be here to-day, so the letter says, and I must wait till then."

And, dismissing the subject of the "twelve foot" boys from his mind, the Rev. Copley Cobbem gathered up his books and papers, and strode away to the class-rooms just as the bell ceased ringing.

As he pushed open the green baize-covered door a sharp "crack" sounded, followed by the jingle of falling glass; then a hurried shuffling of feet, as the boys scudded into their places as quick as rabbits to their holes in a warren. Only young Greene remained standing in the middle of the room, jerking his elbows convulsively up and down, and making the most hideous grimaces.

The Rev. Copley Cobbem took no apparent notice of young Greene, and young Greene was equally oblivious of the master's presence until a terrific bang of a cane on the desk made the culprit jump three feet into the air, and let off a tremendous sneeze before his feet touched the ground again.

"Greene, come here," said the head-master, with another emphatic bang of the cane on the desk.

"Oh if you please, sir, it wasn't me," murmured young Greene, anticipating that the cane would next descend upon a more sensitive organism than the deal desk.

"It wasn't me," repeated the head-master, with scornful deliberation. "Perhaps you will have the kindness to explain what you mean by that sentence? Do you learn grammar in this school, sir?"

"Ye-es, sir."

"And a pretty use you put your learning to, sir. Repeat the rule concerning verbs and their nominative cases at once."

Greene couldn't of course. He had not nearly recovered from the combined shocks of the sneeze and the unexpected coming of the head-master.

"Very well, Greene, you are obstinate, but I will ask you one more question. Who broke that window as I came into the class-room?"

"I—I don't know, sir—indeed I don't. I—I was busy, sir."

"Yes, busy quivering like a mountebank; I saw you."

"I—I was trying to sneeze, sir; I'd been trying for five minutes, sir, and I couldn't do it till you come in, sir."

"I'll teach you to try and pass off lying excuses, Greene," said the Rev. Copley, grasping his cane, and marching towards Greene junior, whose complexion matched his name by reason of sheer terror.

But before the first juicy cut was made there came another sharp "crack," and the glass of a second window fell jingling to the floor.

This was awful. To break a window in his very presence, and while yet a culprit was undergoing punishment for a similar offence! Who was the audacious offender?

He glared around again. There were dozens capable of the act, but not one upon whom he could fix the guilt with certainty.

He marched to his desk, and prepared for the business of the day with an energy that made every boy with an imperfect exercise tremble in his shoes.

Suddenly the hush of fear that had fallen on the schoolroom was broken by a rustle and a movement as every boy turned towards the door.

The Rev. Copley turned too. His eyes almost came out of his head—the very tassel of his skull-cap stood on end.

"Who—are—you?" he demanded, in a faltering voice.

"The new boys, sir."

"The new boys!" exclaimed the master. "Who ever saw boys eight feet long?"

CHAPTER XIII.

THE FURTHER HISTORY OF THE TALL BOYS.

THE task which Sharp senior had intrusted to Billy was no joke, and before twenty-four hours had passed, his life was a burden to him.

Young Greene had a strong propensity for washing himself, and Billy's orders were strictly to prevent anything of the kind.

"If ever you touches that mug o' yourn with soap and water you'll be yaller for life—now mind."

"But I must wash myself sometimes," remonstrated Greene; "you have no idea how it tickles."

"Never mind that; you've got to put up with it."

"I never knew anything like it," moaned Jolly, dismally. "I can't even wash my hands, because I've got to keep these gloves on. It's all your fault. If you hadn't shoved me into the shower bath I shouldn't have been dyed. Somebody's always shoving me."

"You wait till we get to the school, Jolly, and I'll put you all right with some of the stuff Mr. Sharpe give me; only think how you'd get shoved about by the other boys if you washed your face and turned all yaller and green agin."

At the first interview with the Rev. Copley Cobbem, Billy was in an agony of terror when he saw that gentleman gaze rather curiously at Jolly's complexion through his double eyeglasses; but nothing was said on that point just then, and Billy breathed more freely.

With the boys it was tolerably easy. Billy hinted in a general way that his chum was suffering from a sort of scurvy, and found it necessary to powder hi face a little. They thought it was catching, and left him alone for a time.

For a similar reason the housekeeper allotted a separate room to young Greene and Sharp. The latter might have had one to himself, but he dared not leave Jolly for a moment, lest he should be seized with a sudden temptation and wash himself.

But the life was becoming dreadfully monotonous to Billy. He was chained to Jolly's side as effectually as if tangible fetters of iron bound them.

"I can't stand much more of it," he thought. "Blow it! I'll let him wash hisself and git it over, if I can't hit on some better dodge in a day or two."

The climax came at last with the event which closed my last chapter.

*   *   *   *   *   *

Perhaps no man on earth was ever more staggered by visions unearthly than the Reverend Copley Cobbem, M.A., was by the spectacle before him. If King Neptune, accompanied by his favourite mermaid, had suddenly shot up through the floor of the room, and made tender inquiries after his mother, he could not have been more overcome.

"Who are you?" he asked again, as the strange figures with rather uncertain movements, advanced two steps into the room. The foremost had a narrow escape of falling upon his nose.

"Hold up, Dick," said the hindermost.

"All right, Nick," replied the other, "but I fancy some of the straps are wrong."

Both were perfectly cool, and seemed to regard the spectators as so many automatons. The Rev. Copley who had taken an ink-bottle in his hand in a mechanical way, took young Greene's head for an inkstand, and poured about half a pint over that luckless youth, as he asked the question, "Who are you?" for the third time.

"The Reverend Copley Cobbem, I believe?" said the foremost.

"Yes."

"You received a letter this morning advising you of our coming?"

"I received a letter, but—when—really——"

"You did not believe in it?"

"I did not."

"But now that the letter is authenticated, and we are here, kindly inform us where we can sit down to begin."

"I say, Dick," expostulated the other, in an undertone, "you can't do it."

"You mind your own business, Nick," replied the other; "leave me to work it."

"Before—beginning—studies," said the bewildered Mr. Cobbem, "I—I—should like to have a few words with—you—young—gentlemen."

"We are entirely at your service," said the foremost, bowing, and in so doing he lost his balance, and put a hand on young Greene's head. Young Greene promptly gave way, and the two came down with a crash.

"I'm jiggered," said young Sharp, rising in his seat, "if that chap aint got dummy legs—fust-rate padded stilts."

These words fell on the ears of the Rev. Copley Cobbem, and the light of intelligence beamed in his eyes. He let the fallen one lay, and went for him who was yet perpendicular. Up came one of the long legs, and caught him in the pit of the stomach. The blow was painful, but he bore it, and the long youth, having shot his bolt, went and joined his brother on the floor, the pair having young Greene under them.

The nature of their limbs was revealed in the fall. A variety of straps came down as their toes turned up. The Rev. Copley Cobbem seized the legs, and began lugging the wearers about the room in a sort of frenzy, and they, clinging to young Greene, took him with them.

"Hooroar!" cried Billy Sharp, "go it. Let 'em have it. They've got no friends."

"You let us alone—will you," said one of the fallen youths. "Look here, we've done nothing to you. Kick him, Dick."

"Can't, Nick."

"I'll not have—the—the—peace of this—peaceful house—disturbed," gasped the Rev. Copley. "I will—not—have my domestic hearth—as I may say—shattered—by intrusive pantomimic ruffians—the scum of the lower—orders. No—I won't——"

"You let us take our legs off, and then we can talk to you," said Dick.

"I'll have you leave the room at once."

"Then let us alone."

"Take off those false limbs," said the rev. gentleman, letting go of their legs, but continuing to dance around them in a wild fashion, that would have gained for him the position of dancing master to the cannibal islands, if such a post had been vacant, and he had applied for it.

"We are doing so—are we not?" asked the one who had been called Dick, regarding the Rev. Copley with lofty scorn.

They were still remarkably cool, and took off their false limbs like innocent youths who had been going in for a little legitimate pastime in the playground. This done, they stood up, and revealed the form of two lads, about twelve and fourteen, fairly grown, with the bright "sprack" look, as they say in Wiltshire, of intelligent young Britons, with something of the Tartar, and a good deal of the devil in them.

"Now, gentlemen," said the Rev. Copley Cobbem, sarcastically, "will you have the goodness to follow me?"

They bowed, and taking their legs (I mean the dummy legs) under their arms, followed him downstairs to the hall. On the way down the rev. gentleman palpably gave off heat like so much red-hot pig-iron.

In the hall he paused, and looked about him for some weapon suitable for the chastisement. A number of boxes met his eye. They were six in number, all carefully labelled.

Three bore this inscription—

"Master Richard Stager."

Three had this—

"Master Nicodemus Stager."

"Our boxes," explained Dick Stager, coolly. "Better have 'em taken upstairs at once."

"Before doing that," said the Rev. Copley Cobbem, white as snow with anger, "I shall want to know all about you."

"You received a letter from us signed Smith," said Nick.

"From you!—from your father—your guardian, or somebody of that sort."

"From us," said Dick. "That letter was gammon. I have the real article in my pocket."

He produced a good fat envelope, with a good fat seal upon it.

There was a solid look about it that pleased the experienced eye of the reverend gentleman, and he became a shade cooler.

"Come in here," he said, leading the way into his own breakfast-room. "Put your caps down on that chair."

Their caps and dresses, by the way, were of a very antique order—out of fashion at least fifty years.

Mr. Copley Cobbem now perceived this for the

first time. Hitherto all his powers of observation had been concentrated on their legs.

"You are dressed very oddly," he said.

"We bought this lot for ten-and-six of a travelling showman," said Dick. "Our real togs are in the boxes."

"Indeed! Hand me that letter."

It was passed over.

The Rev. Copley Cobbem examined the seal. He knew something of heraldry, and saw that the writer, at least, was of good family. He broke it, and read—

"DEAR SIR,—Being confined to my couch with an attack of gout, inherited from my father, I am unable to accompany the two boys, Nicodemus and Richard Stager, to your house, so send them with this letter, which makes them the messengers of their own doom. I should like to have sent them to a public execution, but as the times have changed, and a trial is necessary before any one can be thus disposed of, I fall back upon a school. Take them, make them, or break them, as you can, and you will earn my everlasting gratitude. They are no sons of mine, being the offspring of my brother, who married on nothing, and, dying, left his children something less. The mother is dead also, and a good thing for her. But to the point. I have these boys in my care, and I must keep them whether I will or no. They have been the plague of my life—the bane of my friends—the curse of the neighbourhood in which I reside. Being confined with gout (hereditary, and not personally acquired), I have been unable to exercise that supervision over them which erratic natures demand, and, in consequence, they have run a little wild—nay, very wild. At the present moment I do not think they care for any living man under the sun, nor do I think they would hesitate to do anything. Give them the chance, and powder for the deed, and they would blow up Parliament. I am informed that you are a firm man—just the guide and strict mentor these boys want. I frankly admit they will give you trouble—most likely drive you wild for a week or two; but make them or break them, and I shall not grumble at paying double terms. Write to me to the Elms, Southsea, and let me know if you accept my offer. I send the boys so that you may see them. If you like them, keep them—if not, turn them into the street.—Yours truly, "HEAVY STAGER, C.B., Admiral R.N."

"Humph!" murmured the reverend gentleman; "a good, open, frank letter. Double terms—tempting; but Warmington College must not be upset. I wonder whether I could break them in?"

He took a covert glance at them from under his eyebrows, and both of them were in their meekest mood. Ice-cream would have become solid ice in their mouths.

"I'll try it," he said. "I can but turn them out if they are too much for me. Hark you, young gentlemen!"

"Did you speak, sir?" asked Dick, waking out of an apparent day-dream.

"I did," said the Reverend Copley, firmly. "Do you know what is in this letter?"

"No, sir," they both said. "How should we?"

"But you can guess at it?"

"Yes—our uncle wants you to keep a tight hand over us."

"Just so, and I am going to try. You have been a sad trouble to your uncle, it seems."

Both the innocents were overwhelmed with surprise.

"A trouble to dear uncle!" said Dick.

"Somebody has been poisoning his mind," said Nick.

And both showed a strong tendency either to laugh or shed tears—it was difficult to say which.

"You don't seem to believe what I say."

"It comes as painful news to us," said Dick,

producing a pocket handkerchief, with more hol[es] in it than one generally finds in a colander; "w[e] love him, and thought our affection was returned."

"I was certain of it," added Nick, "poor de[luded] uncle!"

All this would have done very well if they ha[d] not come to Warmington College on stilts, but a[s] they had chosen to appear in that eccentric fashio[n] to the scandal of the place, the Rev. Copley Cobbe[m] was not to be taken in.

"You are to remain here," he said, loftily, "a[nd] in the first place, I wish you to understand that [I] will have no nonsense. You comprehend?"

"You wish us to be circumspect in our condu[ct] sir," said Dick.

"And of studious habits," added Nick.

"You have put my wishes almost into the word[s] I would have used myself. What are your names[?]"

"Nicodemus and Richard Stager."

"Oh, yes, that is in the letter."

"What are your respective ages?"

"We are considered by our friends to be O[ld] Stagers," said Dick.

The Rev. Copley Cobbem frowned. Was [it] possible that the grave boy who uttered the[se] words was joking with him? Was it credible th[at] he would venture to trifle with a man of his gra[ve] and reverend demeanour?

"What your friends consider may have no bea[r]ing on fact," he said. "What are your ages?"

"I was born on a Tuesday," said Dick, though[t]fully; "it was a wet day, and there was some co[n]fusion in the house, I have heard nurse say, as t[he] sweep came drunk and knocked the doctor down [as] he was coming upstairs."

"You were not born on a Tuesday. I was," s[aid] Nick.

"Don't fib, Nick. Friday's your day."

"The particular day in the week does n[ot] matter," said the Rev. Copley. "How many yea[rs] have you lived? How old are you?"

"Oh, I understand now, sir," said Nick, with [a] sprightly air. "Dick's fourteen, and I'm thirtee[n]."

"You look older."

"Yes, sir, but we've seen a world of troubl[e]," said Dick.

"And you will see more," said the Rev. Cop[ley] Cobbem, "unless you conform to my wishes, a[nd] endeavour to act in a manner creditable to t[he] establishment. To prevent mistakes, I have a co[py] of the rules in a printed form presented to eve[ry] new boy. Here are two—you will please to stu[dy] them forthwith, as you will not be allowed to pl[ead] ignorance after twenty-four hours have elapse[d]. Ring the bell, there, please."

Dick rang it, and the servant who responded [was] desired to take their boxes up to the Blue Dormito[ry.] The Rev. Copley arose, and walked towards the do[or.]

"In the ordinary course," he said, "I should h[ave] desired your immediate attendance at school; bu[t as] your—shall I say eccentricity, or call it somethi[ng] worse—has upset the ordinary decorum of the scho[ol,] I think it would be better if you waited until af[ter] dinner before you take your places. The pl[ay]ground is open—take a stroll there; a quiet str[oll] if you please, walking arm-in-arm as young gen[tle]men should. I like to see my young gentle[men] arm-in-arm; it gives a tone to the school. But [now] —you must change your clothes. I will s[end] Perkins to show you the Blue Dormitory, and g[ive] him instructions to burn those masquerading leg[s."]

CHAPTER XIV.

BILLY SHARP FINDS HIS MATCH.

PERKINS was not rung for, but called in a [?] peremptory tone, and in a few seconds a sm[all] round boy—with a head like an apple, [?] arms and legs the very image of a roly-p[oly] pudding—came shuffling up the passage in a [pair] of slippers which, in all probability, had once b[e]

GREEN AS GRASS.

A JOLLY SCHOOL STORY.

THE VOICE OF YOUNG GREENE WAS FEEBLY HEARD FROM THE DEPTHS OF THE BASKET, SAYING—"WHERE'S MY MAP?"

worn by his reverend master. His other garments consisted of a pair of time-worn tweed trousers, a soiled linen shirt, and a green baize apron.

"Perkins," said the Rev. Cobbem, "show these young gentlemen to the Blue Dormitory and burn those legs."

Perkins looked at the legs and was no doubt astonished, but he only showed his emotion by a curious snuffling in his nose, which might have proceeded from a cold, or lofty sense of independence, or merely the offspring of habit.

"You hear me?" said the reverend gentleman.

"In coorse I does," replied Perkins; "I aint deaf."

"Don't you give me any of your impudence," returned his master, "or I'll box your ears."

"Box 'em," loudly said Perkins; "you are allus at it, hittin' a norphan over the 'ed. My 'ed's nigh addled by the way I'm pitched into by one and the t'other. Cook give me a buster this morning with the ribs of beef; they're allus at I."

"You are a great burden to me," said the Reverend Copley; "it was an evil hour when I promised your dying mother to take care of you."

"Why don't you do it, then?" asked Perkins. "I aint 'arf wittles enough. It aint a norphan's fault if he's given to layin' on fat. I aint 'arf fed."

"Show the way to the Blue Dormitory."

The Reverend Cobbem, none the better for his encounter with Perkins, retreated upstairs to the school, and the boy and the two Stagers were left together.

"Come on," said the norphan, "pick up your traps and foller me. We'll go and burn 'em in the washus. They are brewin' table beer for us."

"It seems a pity to burn 'em," said Dick.

"So it does; but I've got orders, and I allus obey 'em. I'd rather die than fail in my dooty, although I am a norphan."

"But suppose I gave you sixpence to take care of them," said Dick, "do you think you could stow them away for us?"

"Rather. I've got a cellar as I keeps for myself," said Perkins.

"Then here's the sixpence."

"All right," said Perkins, pocketing it with a satisfied face. "I reckon that you are two liberal coves. Come on. The Blue Dormitory I think you said."

"Yes, that's the place."

"It's the habode of the refractories," said Perkins, "and a sharp eye is kep' on it. I reckon your advice note is bad."

"Not very good, I fancy," said Dick, laughing.

"Then you will get it hot," said Perkins, candidly. "Come along."

He was a nice boy take him all round. No stiffness—so free and easy—so affable, that one was at home with him in a moment.

Dick and Nick winked at each other as they followed him, and appeared to relish his society very much.

The Blue Dormitory took its name from its walls, which were painted a light shade of that colour. This Perkins graciously explained as he ushered them in.

"All on 'em," he said, "is painted some colour or t'other, and they takes their name from it. There's a yaller, a red, and a white and a black besides this. The black used to be papered green, but the paper was p'ison, and all the boys in it was took sick. Old Cobbem thought they had the measles, and treated 'em out of his family medical chest, but he only made 'em worse, so he called in a doctor, who said it was the paper. He stuck out it wasn't till a boy died, then he come round to my opinion. I say, you've got a father?"

"No."

"Nor a mother?"

"No."

"The you are both norphans."

"I am afraid so," said Dick.

"Then mind this, when Cobbem's down on you I'm your friend," said Perkins; and, fearing he might reduce the value of this promise by staying, departed forthwith.

"Nice boy," said Dick.

"Some good fun to be got out of him," added Nick. "Have you the keys?"

"Yes."

"Unlock the boxes, and give me some fresh toggery."

"I say," said Dick, as he was changing his clothes, "what do you think of this crib, Nick? Will it break us in?"

"I don't know," replied Nick, thoughtfully. "There's something in Cobbem's eye which I don't quite like. But we are two to one, and ought not to be licked. Are you ready?"

"Come along to the playground, and let us walk arm-in-arm, as young gentlemen should. Capital idea that, Nick—so eminently genteel!"

"Which is the way?"

"Oh! follow your nose downstairs, and take the first door that comes. It is sure to lead us somewhere."

The first door at the bottom of the stairs led into a cupboard full of dirty boots and uncleaned candlesticks; but the second introduced them to a back yard, where they found the amiable Perkins beating mats, and he directed them to the playground.

"Past the water-butt, round the corner, and through a green gate," he said. "This way is in gineral private; but I don't mind letting you go for once."

"Much obliged, I'm sure," said Dick. "You are about the kindest fellow I've met for a month."

"I don't want to be unkind to nobody," returned Perkins; "but when they're down on me I'm down on them."

They went past the water-butt, round the corner, and through the green gate, and found themselves in the playground—a howling wilderness and waste, as playgrounds usually are.

It was fenced round and about by a high wall—the highest part being on the side where the garden was.

Dick and Nick, dressed in becoming apparel, were two good-looking lads, with a heap of fire in every look and action—the right sort of stuff from head to heel. Tall and symmetrical, each looked the very *beau ideal* of an English boy.

They conducted themselves with great propriety, and the Reverend Cobbem, who made little excursions to the window every half-hour, was nonplussed. The admiral's letter had the ring of truth in it, and their first prank carried conviction with it; but why this orderly conduct now—why this eminently genteel promenading, which would have done credit to the offspring of Beau Brummel—if he every had any?

The time passed, and, the morning duties over, the caged spirits in the schoolroom were set free. Among the first was Master William Sharp Popper, and the last was young Greene, who came downstairs, without any assigned reason, head first.

The new-comers became immediate objects of attention, and William Sharp Popper, with the assurance of ignorance, and the impudence of vice, elected himself as examiner for the school in general.

"You are new coves," he said. "What's your name? Brothers, I can see."

Dick and Nick, leaning against the wall, took no notice of his query. This tried Master William, who, being in society where he had no right to be, was especially anxious to keep up his position.

"You new coveys," he said, sternly, "mustn't come the stiff-backed business with me."

He was very indignant, but he could hardly keep his countenance when Dick Stager turned his quiet eye on him. He covered his confusion by violently blowing his nose.

"On what terms," asked Dick, "do you come here?"

"Me come here?" demanded Billy, "why shouldn't I come?"

"A school at Pentonville," said Dick, "I should fancy, would be more in your line."

"Oh! come—dash it, where's Pentonville?"

"Come aside with me a moment," said Dick.

Billy Sharp Popper hesitated.

"You had better come."

"I don't see why you should drop on to me," he said, uneasily. "I never did you any harm."

"If you don't come you will be sorry for it."

"All right—go ahead."

"Excuse me," said Dick, to the wondering boys, "but a little private conference with this individual is necessary. If you want any information, my brother Nick will give it to you."

He walked off, and Master Popper, with an invisible tail between his visible legs, followed him. When far enough away to be out of hearing, Dick turned round and faced him.

"How came you here?"

"Me, why I was sent by my friends, in course," replied Billy.

"Your friends, who are they?"

"The parients of Jolly Greene, who are my guardians."

Dick never moved a muscle of his face as he rejoined—

"You are a liar."

"Come, now," remonstrated Billy, "that's rather strong language to use to a gentleman in a gentleman's school. You ought to know better—you do."

"It is only about six months ago," said Dick, "when I was in London, walking down Pall Mall—"

"Yes," said Billy, turning pale, "that's a fashionable strolling ground."

"A carriage stood at the door of Epitaa's, the confectioner's."

"There ginerally is a carriage there."

"A rug was in it."

"Wot carriage, as is worth the name, iver goes out without a rug? Come, there's nothing in all this."

"The occupants of the carriage," pursued Dick, coolly, "were inside partaking of refreshments. A fellow, very much like you——"

"There's lots of chaps like me," said the tortured Billy.

"I never saw one," said Dick, "except on that day when the beggar stole the rug from the carriage, and tried to bolt with it. I seized the rug, and kept it, but I lost the thief. He was too nimble for me."

"And you mean to say as that was me?" demanded Billy, on whose noble brow the perspiration lay like drops of rain upon a window pane.

"I mean to say it was no other," replied Dick.

"Oh! yes, go it, ruin a poor chap as have repented of his sin, and been reglar swore in at Hexeter Hall," whined Billy—"don't be down on a chap as aint got no mother, and troubled with a father who aint got no witals, and would as soon swindle me as hanybody. I thought you was a gentleman when I fust see you, and a kind 'arted one too, but now I sees you aint."

"If you tell me I'm not a gentleman I'll knock you down," said Dick.

"I don't say as you aint a gentleman," returned Billy, "I only says that you don't appear to me to be one when you go to crush a repentant cove."

"I don't want to crush you, but I won't have any of your impudence, and that's flat. You sing small here—will you?"

"I won't sing at all unless you tell me to," returned Billy, wriggling. "All I axes is that you

won't sever the friendship atween me and young Greene."

"Who is young Greene?"

"That young party up agin the pump, a-wiping his nose with the back of his hand, and looking as if he was born skeered and meant to die so."

"The fellow seems a little short in the noddle."

"Well, he aint quite right," said Billy, candidly, "and that is why I am sent here to look arter him. His father have got a great opinion of my abilities."

"I have very little of his then," said Dick.

"You won't split on me?" asked Billy.

"No, not unless you deserve it. If your repentance is all humbug look out."

"It's the most genuine harticle as ever was invented," said Billy, fervently. "I was took right aback when I thought of my evil ways—indeed I was."

Dick did not answer him, but rejoined his brother, who meanwhile had satisfied his querists, whose name was legion, as to who he was, where he came from, and which side of the school he intended to take—the wicked and rebellious, or the soft-spoken and hypocritical?

Billy Sharp went over to young Greene, who was not aware of his presence until he received a friendly dig in the ribs that brought him out of a day-dream in a seared condition.

"You let me alone. I wasn't doing anything," he said. "I wish my mar was here."

"You'll never see her again, unless you are precious careful," said Billy Sharp, savagely.

"Oh! don't say that," pleaded Jolly Greene—"it makes me so miserable."

"But I must say it, because your life's in peril. You see them two new chaps as have just come?"

"No, I don't."

"Yes you do, up in the corner; them together. They came on stilts this morning and skeered you."

"Oh, yes, I know; and very bad they made me feel. Oh, I wish I could go home to my mar."

"As you can't, you must make the best of your time here. You see them two chaps?"

"Oh, yes."

"Did you ever see two more murderous villains?"

"Oh! are they—mur—murderous?"

"Yes; one is the son of Greenacre and t'other the nevvy of Rush. They've come here under false names."

"Oh! dear—oh! dear, what shall I do?"

"You stick to me,' said Billy, firmly, "and don't have nothing to do with them. If they speak to you walk away."

"I shall run—I'm sure I shall."

"Run, then, but don't speak to 'em on any account. They've got artful ways, they have, and the first thing they'll do will be to try and pison your mind agin me; then they'll pison your body with double-distilled prussic acid, you'll die in tortures, and there'll be an end of you."

"This is horrible," cried Young Greene; "oh do let us go home."

"You can't leave without a special Hact of Parliament," returned Billy Sharp, "but I'll take care of you."

"Oh, do."

"Whatever they says you tell me, and don't you give them no answer. Believe me they are a bad lot—they're all Greenacres and Rushes."

"Who were they?" asked poor Jolly, trembling all over.

"Greenacre used to kill and cut up chaps about your size, and Rush went out every night to murder, invading of peaceful homes where the family was a sitting round the fire, and he used to let fly at 'em with blunderbusses, and blow 'arf of 'em bang into bits."

"And have these—these—boys—done—anything that way?" asked Jolly Greene, trembling like an aspen leaf.

"Not yet; but I fancy they will begin directly,"

replied Billy. "They are only waiting for a fair chance. I heard one say to the other that you was a likely sort of chap, but you stick to me."

Young Greene promised to do so, and he and Billy were close companions all that day. At night the following letter was sent to Sharp, senior, by his dutiful son :—

"GOVERNOR,—Ere's a preshus gaim afloat. Two cooves cum as kno me, and hif I hadent cum the repenter's dodge would hev blode on me, and got me up a tree. i aint afrade on em haltogethere, but i must run clooze, or get into a trap of their setin. can you run doon? thare's a pub arf wai up the rode, the wite hart, ware you could put hup, and i could snake out to see yer.—Your haffecterate sun,

"BILLY."

CHAPTER XV.

THE WASHING.

THERE was no escape from the necessity of washing this time. It had to be done. The ink had soaked into the enamelling, and Billy thought that scraping alone would not be effectual.

After the exit of those boys of Stager's, the under masters endeavoured to restore discipline by the short and simple method of walking round the desks with a cane apiece, and bestowing a good juicy cut upon every youth not engaged in the legitimate pursuit of learning.

Young Greene suffered, of course. He was stooping and tenderly caressing the bruises of his shins, when a cut from the cane of the second master made him leap forward with a shriek of agony.

"Don't make that noise, sir."

"You made me," moaned the sufferer. "I didn't want to make a noise."

"Don't be impertinent, Greene. Go to your seat at once, and ——. Why what's the matter with your face? How dare you come into the class-room in that condition."

Young Greene looked at him tearfully. He knew nothing about the ink stains on his face, he was only aware that he was a martyr, an innocent being bound always to suffer for some crime he had never committed.

"Did you wash your face this morning, Greene?"

"No, sir, I——"

"Ah! I thought not. And how long is it since you did perform your ablutions?"

"Er-er about three weeks, sir."

"Three weeks!" exclaimed the master. "Why you must be absolutely filthy, Greene. You are enough to breed a fever in the school. Come with me at once—I'll see that you wash yourself."

Billy Sharp gave a groan of despair, as he saw Greene junior hauled from the room by the indignant second in command.

"It's all over," he thought. "T: ïud it all out, and write home to his guv'nor, and then won't there be a jolly row?"

In about a quarter of an hour the second master came down, looking very pale and with a wild glare in his eye.

The Rev. Copley Cobbem had just returned from his interview with the juvenile Stagers. To him the second master marched with unsteady steps, and whispered in his ear.

The Rev. Copley started and turned pale also.

"What!" he said, in a hoarse whisper, "green did you say?"

"As—green—as—grass!" repeated the second master with slow emphasis.

"But he had a beautiful complexion. I remember noticing it when he first came."

"It's the sad and solemn truth, sir, I assure you. I tried soap and water at first to get the ink stains out, and it was just like magic, I assure you. He changed colour all at once."

"Won't it come off?"

"I scrubbed him with a tooth-brush myself, sir, until he screamed with pain and kicked my shins, but it was of no use."

"This is dreadful. It must be the effect of the ink. What is to be done?"

"Better send for the doctor."

"I suppose that will be the best," said the Rev. Copley, "but really it is very unfortunate. What will Greene's parents say if they hear of it? This must be kept a secret."

"You may depend upon my silence, sir."

The doctor came, and was shown up to the dormitory, where young Greene sat, melancholy, but resigned.

"Bless my soul!" he exclaimed. "Why, what is the matter with the boy?"

"That is exactly what we wish you to tell us, doctor," said the Rev. Copley.

The doctor looked, and was, indeed, quite as puzzled as the schoolmaster. He made the luckless Jolly put out his tongue—he felt his pulse—pinched him about the chest and ribs, and, finally, stood looking at him with his head on one side, as men regard some wonderful natural curiosity.

"There is evidently some very serious affliction of the liver, Mr. Cobbem. I never saw such a colour in the whole course of my practice. We must put him to bed at once, and administer a strong dose of calomel——"

"You don't think there is any danger, doctor?"

"I should say not. Not immediate. But we shall see in the course of the next few hours."

Greene junior began to cry, and to feel dreadfully ill.

The grave words and graver looks of the doctor and the Rev. Copley Cobbem alarmed him inexpressibly, but he offered no resistance, only murmuring something feebly concerning his being always "shoved about."

The dose of calomel was given, and Greene junior suffered dreadfully all that night and the next day, but it only had the effect of making him very weak and still queerer if possible.

The doctor ventured on another dose, but only with the result of bringing Jolly to such a state of prostration that he could only feebly gasp at intervals like a newly-caught fish.

Then the doctor tried stimulants and tonics and high feeding.

Jolly grew rapidly strong again, but the colour changed not in the least, and the doctor gave the case up in despair.

"I can do nothing," he said. "It must be constitutional."

"Inherited, possibly," suggested the Rev. Copley Cobbem. "Have any of your family been similarly afflicted, Master Greene?"

"Nobody's afflicted but me," murmured that unhappy youth. "It was the shower-bath that did it."

"The shower-bath?"

"Yes;" and then Greene junior explained the mystery.

"Why didn't you tell me all this before?" said the Reverend Copley, angrily. "Here have I been wasting my sympathy, and the doctor his time and skill. Why—why I've the greatest mind to flog you soundly for this."

"Nobody asked me—did they?" retorted the injured Jolly.

"Don't answer me in that manner, sir!"

"I was all right when I came here, and if that chap hadn't washed——"

"That what, sir? How dare you speak of your tutors in that disrespectful way?"

"Well, so I was!" said Greene junior, desperately. "Ask Sharp—he knows all about it. He said I wasn't to be washed."

There was a mystery in all this which the Rev. Copley Cobbem was unable to solve. Certainly the boy had seemed to be " all right " when he arrived, and the premature washing *might* have changed his colour.

"I don't know what to do," he said to the second master. "The Greenes are wealthy people, and pay very highly. In all probability, if I write to them, and state what has happened, they will take him away. Think over it, will you, Mr. Bailey, and let me know to-morrow if you have hit upon anything?"

"I will, sir."

And thus the conference ended for the time. But other heads had been thinking, too. The busy brains of Nick and Dick were laid together. They had spotted young Greene at once as a " mug," and resolved to make him the instrument of a little joke.

"He's a regular soft 'un," said Nick; "but I don't quite know what to make of that fat chap."

"He *looks* soft," replied Dick.

"Yes, he does. Innocent as a cherub; but I think we shall find him precious deep."

"Let's see if he'll join us in our lark with Greene!"

"They're too chummy—come here together, you know."

"It'll be awkward without him, for they're always together, Nick. Sound him a bit, and see if he'll take a hint."

"I will, my boy, and with him for a chum we'll be able to do pretty well as we like in this school. We'll make it pretty warm for old Cobbem before many days are over."

And they kept their words, as my readers will see in the next chapter.

CHAPTER XVI.

THE COMPACT BETWEEN PERKINS AND SHARP.

THE doctor having so signally failed in restoring young Greene to his normal colour, the housekeeper put in a claim to be heard. "There's nothing like the old-fashioned remedies, sir. You just let me try what soda and water will do."

Young Greene, of course, objected; but nobody took any notice of *him*. The housekeeper tucked him under her arm, and in about an hour brought him back—the colour of a boiled lobster, and hardly a trace of the dye left. At a distance he had an aged look, but when close by he was like one of those boys who think they wash when they rub a damp flannel on the more prominent part of their faces, and leave the rest to time.

An " hurrah!" was on the lips of young Sharp, but he turned it off into a cough, and resumed his labours with an energy quite foreign even to his industrious nature.

The change was, of course, remarked by all, but the able guide and mentor who looked so kindly after his interest came to his rescue again.

"The doctor said the change would come of a sudden," he said, "and as soon as the sun have warmed the holler parts he'll lose the lot."

Jolly Greene was not quite so elated. He was very miserable, and it did n'ot matter much to him what colour he was. He would just as soon have been a deep red as any other colour.

"There must have been something in the ink to take out t'other stuff," said young Sharp. "Oh! what a day of rejoicing this ought to be!"

"I don't care," said Jolly. "All I want is to go home, or to have my mar come here."

"I should like to see your mar here," replied Billy. "Oh! what fun it would be!"

Young Sharp's bliss would have been perfect but for the presence of the Stagers, and, as they knew so much of him, he was terribly uneasy. But he was cunning, and quick at catching the points of character.

"They are well-bred 'uns," he said to himself "and won't lie. I've got a promise that I shan't be split upon, and it will be kept. But I must be careful. As soon as the guv'nor comes I'll lay the case afore him, and p'raps he'll arrange to have me sent to another school."

Billy was not much of a favourite, perhaps; but he was not, on the whole, disliked. The boys saw through him as to the lowness of his origin, although they failed to perceive its viciousness. He made himself agreeable, and was up to so many dodges and tricks that he was looked upon as amusing, if nothing more.

Perkins and he were soon close chums, having much in common, and, after writing the letter referred to in a previous chapter, Billy crept down to the boot-hole to enjoy half an hour's real companionship.

The norphan was hard at work cleaning plate—breathing on a spoon, and rubbing it with a piece of wash-leather as if he meant to shave himself by its aid. When he had finished, Billy, with a professional eye for valuables, began to handle some of the plate, and to appraise it.

"Real stuff, this!" he said. "None of your swindling nickel, which takes in the 'ardworking poor! Worth fifteen bob a fork or more."

"I've heerd the doctor say that his plate is worth two hundred puns," replied Perkins; "and aint he pertickler about it neither, and don't he take it upstairs with him every night!"

"Takes it upstairs, does he?" said Billy, carelessly. "And where does he put it—under the bed?"

"No—in a big iron box let in the wall of his dressin'-room."

"Must be heavy work to take it up every night."

"He don't use it every day," returned Perkins; "only when company comes. He's got a lot of rubbishin' Britannia for common use. There's a dinner party on to-night—a lot of big swells coming."

"Your master mixes with swells—does he?"

"Yes, reg'lar nobs."

"And where does they hang their overcoats?" asked young Billy, with as much indifference as he could assume.

"Jiggles, the butler, puts 'em in the breakfast-room, anigh the front door," replied the innocent Perkins.

"You hates dinner parties, I suppose—gives you a lot of work."

"No, I likes 'em."

"That's odd! Why?"

"Jiggles brings the trays and empty plates to the door—also the dishes. I don't get too much to eat here, and on the way I sweats 'em."

The liveliness of young Sharp was a pleasing sight as Perkins boldly revealed this malpractice. He was like a man just come into some valuable property, or like a traveller who has discovered a well of water after days of drought.

"Perky, old boy," he said, "you and I is friends."

"In course we are," replied Perkins, "or I would have you hout of here in a twinkling."

"Well, then, bein' friends, we ought to share the hups and downs of life together."

"Wot's yer meaning?" asked Perkins.

"A little hextra sweatin' would be a marcy to me," said Billy. "I'm fallin' away to nothin' here."

"Oh, I can't promise nothin' that way," returned Perkins. "Everything is looked so preciously sharp after here that you can't get more than odd bits, and sich as is left on the plates. Jiggles allus studies the anattlemy of every cut fowl, and he could swear to it if you picked a bit."

"But only a leetle," urged Billy, "even gravy and potatoes would be something; then I'll show you how to toss so that it will come a head or a tail just as you like."

"Will you? I'd like to know that."

Perkins was a very willing and apt pupil at the dodging business.

"Yes, and you'll let me have some of the pickings?"

"I'll tell you what I'll do," said Perkins. "You know the cupboard in the hall close to the dining-room door?"

"Where the master keeps his boots, etceterar?"

"How did you know that?"

"I peeped in one day as I was passin'."

"If he had seen you he would have warmed you. It warn't long ago since somebody put cobbler's wax into his boots, and I shall niver forgit the time we had of it to get 'em off."

"Well, but about this cupboard? I gets in there?"

"Yes, and I'll pass in such bits as I can spare. You be ready to lay hold as soon as I puts my hand in."

"Don't you fear! I won't miss a bit. Perky, you are a good feller!"

"I aint bad to them as I takes to. You must have seen a lot of life?"

"Heaps!'" replied Billy.

"Are you a norphan?"

"Not quite," replied the virtuous youth. "Mother dead, and father livin'. But I t have nothin' to do with him. He went a little wild a few years ago, and I cast him off. It went agin my feelin's; but I must keep myself respectable. Once lose your respectability, and you are gone."

"So I should suppose."

"Well, then, to-night. What time?"

"Company comes at seven. Get in there about half-past six."

"I'll not fail, my ancient friend," replied Billy, facetiously. "Now for the trick. Have you got a penny?"

"No."

"Then I'll lend you one. Look here."

And the next ten minutes were occupied in the acquiring of the desirable trick mentioned. By that time Billy declared his pupil to be perfect.

CHAPTER XVII.

ARTFUL DODGING ON THE PART OF YOUNG SHARP.

MASTER William Sharp Popper was not the sort of young gentleman to get himself into trouble if it could possibly be avoided. His education, his instincts, and his experience, all prompted him to proceed through the narrow lanes of life with due caution, and as he left the private apartment of his friend Perkins his mind was busy with plans bearing upon the dinner party, and what was to be got out of it.

That such a mind and, we may say stomach, as he possessed would be satisfied with such crumbs as Perkins chose to give him was ridiculous. A tithe of the black mail levied by a brother marauder never suited him yet, and was not likely to do so on this particular occasion.

"There will be a pile of good things," he mused; "bits of fish, fowl, patties, cutlets, jam tarts, and wines of all sorts, and I'll have some of 'em, but I aint going to get into trouble through it. Young Greene must do the work, and I'll have the profit, which is only in the usual course of natur."

No, he never did pull the chesnuts out of the fire if he could help it, and, keeping up one of the fixed principles of his life, he sought the hapless Jolly, and found him in their private bedroom fathoms deep in the mysteries of Lindly Murray, drowned as it were for a time, and dead to all the world.

Master William Sharp made him leap to the surface of his ordinary life again by the careful application of a severely pointed pin, extracting at the same time a dismal howl from his lips.

"You let me alone," said Jolly. "You are always sticking pins into me."

"Why, you howdacious young himp," said Billy regarding him with pained surprise, "what do you mean by saying that? Did I ever stick a pin into you before?"

"If you didn't you are always doing something," said Jolly.

"And why do I do it?"

"I don't know."

"I do. It's to keep you alive. If you wasn' shook, or punched, or pricked, or done something to you would sink down into the wegetable state in no time. But I'm the saving of you, and I means to go on. One day you will be everlastingly grateful."

"No, I shan't."

"Oh, yes, you will. Sit down."

"What are you going to do now?"

"Nothing but talk to you. Now, Jolly, I am about to open a question which, no doubt, is of great importance to you. It is about the grub in this house. How do you like it?"

"I don't know. I don't remember anything about it. I swallow it," said Jolly, dismally, "but that's all. Look at the life I lead. It's enough to drive me mad! I wish my mar would come and take me away!"

"The grub's bad," said Billy, ignoring everything else; "you know it, and I know it; and unless we gets something a little nourishing both on us will be carried to a hearly grave. I can see 'corpse' written all over you as it is."

"Oh, come!—what now? You are always calling me something nasty," said Jolly, with a shiver.

"No, I aint. Only, as facts are you must have 'em. Now, I've just seen the reverend party as is at the head of this establishment, and laid afore him our miserable condition. He was took aback, and said he was sorry for us, and would begin to feed us up at once."

"It's very kind of him," said Jolly, mournfully, "but I don't want feeding up."

"Do you want to get the man hanged for starving you to death?" asked Billy, sternly. "What's he ever done to you that you should want to get him into trouble?"

"I don't want to get him into trouble," said Jolly.

"Then don't do it. He's a kind-hearted man, and when he shows hisself manly, come for'ard and meet him half way. He says he'll grub us well now and then, but it must be when he's got a dinner party on. There's one to-night, and I've a feed in my mind's eye."

"Have you?"

"Yes, I have; but we must take it as he chooses to give it, or go without. 'There is some things,' says the reverend gent, 'as ought to be done open, and some as must be done in secret. If I feeds you open like, I must give all the boys a blow-out; so you must have your extra grub in secret.'"

"Up here, I suppose?" said Jolly Greene.

"Yes," replied Billy; "but we must get it fust, and bring it here. And these was the further instructions of the reverend gent—'You and young Greene,' he says, 'had better get into the cupboard close to the dining-room door, and as Jiggles brings the dishes out lay your hands on whatever you can, but be sure you don't let Jiggles, Perkins, or nobody see.' Them was his words, and we should be ungrateful monsters if we didn't hact upon 'em."

"It seems a very odd way of feeding us," said Jolly.

"How mean of you," said Master William Sharp Popper, savagely, "to go and look a man's gift horse in the mouth! When a man makes an offer like that, take it free."

"But I don't know that I want it."

"I do. How do you fancy I should think and feel if I went out of this place, say, a week hence, and took your cold corpse home, and laid it at the feet of your mar?"

"I wish you wouldn't talk in that way," moaned Jolly.

"OH, DEAR!" YELLED YOUNG GREENE. "COME AND TAKE IT OFF! YOU'VE NO IDEA HOW IT HURTS!"

" Then take grub when you can get it, and live in 'ealthy wigorous life," said Billy.

" I will, if you wish it."

" I do wish it; and you stop here until I come for you. I shall be ready to take you down to dinner about half-past six, or a little afore. You needn't dress in a choker, as the party is small, hearly, and limited."

With this parting jest Master Sharp went his way, and left Jolly Greene to the awfully bewildering task of getting up his studies for the morning.

What a maze every book was to his woolly brain! The words—such as he got into his head—were ever dancing Scotch reels, turning somersaults, and leaping about like so many imps. All his attempts to arrange them in some definite form were utterly futile.

" I can't do it!" he moaned, as he closed the book, and laid his head wearily upon the pillow. " If my mar don't come soon I shall die!"

When Billy came for Jolly he found him sound asleep, and the temptation to administer a second dose of the pin came upon him. But, his mind being softened down by the prospect of the coming feed, he forbore, and merely gave him a respectable pinch on the calf of his leg.

" Now, don't you holler or make a row," he said, as Jolly sprang up like an indiarubber ball; " but come along quietly. I've tucked all the reverend gent's boots into a corner, and our dining-room is ready. We will go down at once. Take my harm."

Jolly Greene was too far gone in abject misery to dispute on any topic, and, linking his arm in that of his friend, he allowed himself to be led down by that gentleman, who frequently halted in dark corners to see if the course was clear.

The hall was the last place he inspected, and, as nobody was there, he ran young Greene sharply into the cupboard prepared for his reception, and spread-eagled him on a pile of boots of various ages.

" Oh, dear!—oh, dear!" groaned Jolly.

" If you open your mouth again without my telling you I'll strangle the life out of your body!" said Billy. " Sit down, and don't move a hyelash until there's work to be done."

" It's very dark here," moaned Jolly, as the door closed.

" Well, did you want a hall illuminated at the public hexpense?" asked the other. " Can't you take your grub in a humble way for once?"

" It's very hot here, and I'm almost stifled— I am!"

" Will you hold your tongue, or do you want our dining-room hinwaded by all the ushers of the house, who would leave us nothing but bones, and wery few of them?"

" But I don't like eating in a cupboard. I never did such a thing when I lived with my mar."

" You shall never dine with your mar again if you speak another word! Shut up, you persuming, dissatisfied—gourmod!" and Jolly, rather alarmed by the tone of his companion, became silent.

CHAPTER XVIII.

THE DINNER PARTY—A HEAVY SHOWER.

A GOOD half-hour passed, and the two occupants of the cupboard remained undisturbed. The time passed very slowly, and Master William Sharp was beginning to think he had been the victim of a practical joke on the part of Perkins, when a ring and a knock was heard, and the voice of the Rev. Copley Cobbem was distinguished, calling upon Perkins to be prompt and open the door.

" The first nob's come," whispered Billy, getting rather excited. " You sit still while I open the door a quarter of a hinch, and have a look at 'em. There's Perkins letting 'em in."

" Two old 'omen," he said, " and never married I'll bet; been good-lookin' too, but now appears little sour and disappointed."

" What names, mum?" Perkins was heard to say.

" The Misses Trebeltom," replied the foremost lady.

Perkins ushered them upstairs to the drawing-room, and presently his voice was heard from afar announcing them as the " Missus Tremblebones."

Then came another knock and a ring, and the active Perkins came flying down head first.

" Old party, major on half-pay," explained young Billy, to his indifferent companion—" stout, red in the face, well trimmed whiskers, and a leery eye. Nice old party when he's at home, I'll bet. What are you doing now?"

" Some of the boots slipped," pleaded Jolly.

" There's a pair of long Wellingtons close behind you," said Billy, " and if you make that row again I'll shove you into one of them. Here's another—two on 'em—lady and gen'leman, and been quarrelling all the way I can see, because the old gal was so long agettin' ready or somethin' of that sort. How sweet they tries to look, but they are reglar soaked in the winegar of domestic hanimosity.

" More on 'em," he said, a few moments later, " Oh! here's a swell—a honourable at least—perhaps he's a markiss. The Markiss of Dawdleham, and knight of the horder of the garter and chief companion of the washing basin. Aint he got a pair of lavender gloves neither, and don't they fit him serene? I should think so. They beat his skin into fits. What are you doing of now?"

" I've slipped and got on to a pair of cricket shoes, right on the spikes," replied Jolly, with a groan.

" Hold your row—will you?" said Billy, putting a hand on his mouth. " Do you want us to be ruined? Do you want our sanctified santorium to be inwaded? Oh! you precious beauty, if your mother had a dozen more like you what a blessin' it would be! Keep still, here's the company coming down to feed."

" I don't believe Mr. Copley knows we are here," said Jolly between Billy's fingers.

" Oh! you ungrateful young willain. It would serve you right if you was left to starve. Now, you keep as st'll as a mouse while I takes stock of the courses as they go in."

Returning to his old post by the door he reported first—soup, two sorts, then fish—salmon, he thought, by the look of the head which just peeped out from under the cover.

" We can't do nothing with the soup, Jolly," he said, " but when the fish comes out we'll have some of it if 'h re's a chance."

The natural disposition of Perkins favoured them, for if ever there was a boy who laboured to be out of the way when particularly wanted it was he.

When Jiggles brought out the remnant of the fish and put it down on the hall table Perkins was not there.

" Confound that boy," said the butler, " what's he doing? Perkins!"

Perkins did not reply, because he was at that moment engaged in a struggle with the cook—a form of entertainment he partook of about every half-hour in the day. Jiggles in a fury darted towards the kitchen, and Billy, seeing the opportunity he desired had come, took young Greene by the collar, and thrust him forth from the cupboard.

" Take the head," he said, " and shove it into that umbrella in the stand. Quick! We can put everything we gets into it and take it upstairs."

" But we shall spile the umbrella," said Jolly.

" Will you go and do as I tell you?" growled Billy; " who's to know who spiled it? We can chuck it out of the winder into the playground, and when they've found it they can put the job on who they likes."

" But——"

"Will yer go? The head, mind yer—it's the sweetest."

The salmon had been cut in two—the head and tail, with a considerable amount of the toothsome flesh remaining on each. Young Greene, urged on by Billy—of whom he stood in considerable dread—seized the head and thrust it into the umbrella.

"Come back," hissed Billy, "here comes that precious Jiggles."

Jolly never would have got back if Billy had not gone out and dragged him in. Barely had the door closed when Jiggles, holding Perkins by the collar, arrived upon the scene.

"If yer don't keep here to receive the dishes," said Jiggles, "I'll knock your head off, yer little aggravating beast."

"Can I be in two places at once?" asked Perkins a little louder than was necessary to make Jiggles hear. "If the cook collars me in the kitchen and hammers me with the soup ladle, can I be here? Come, now."

"Be quiet—will yer?"

"Then you let me alone."

"Good gracious," cried Jiggles staggering back; "where's the salmon's head?"

"Perhaps yer think I've swallowed it," said Perkins sarcastically; "maybe yer think I've got a arm ninety-two feet long, and grabbed it while I was having a mortial fight in the kitchen."

"It's the cat," groaned Jiggles; "but take the rest away, and bring in the ontrays."

Perkins had his own idea as to where the head of the salmon had gone, and having got the entrées in he opened the cupboard door, and confronted Billy.

"Hand out some o' that," he said.

"Some of what?" asked the innocent one.

"The salmon's 'ed. You hadn't got no right to touch it."

"But you don't think we've got it here?" said Billy; "we can't have swallowed it; to put it under the boots would spile it, and you don't fancy that we could put it in our pockets."

"It's in the——" began Jolly, waking up from a trance. Billy backed against him, and knocked him over.

"Look out!" cried Billy, "Jiggles is coming!"

Perkins darted out, and the door was closed just in time to prevent detection.

"I know you will blow the whole game," said Billy, in a thrilling whisper. "If you do, the reverend gent, who has a heart of milk and butter when people don't go agin him, will never forgive you."

"I don't believe it's right," said Jolly; "it seems to me like stealing."

The amazement and horror of Master William Sharp was apparent even in the darkness. It was quite five seconds before he could reply.

"What!" he said, overflowing with virtuous indignation, "do you mean to say that I would be led into such wile habits by all the reverend gents as ever lived? Do you mean to insinervate that I can suddenly turn agin the careful bringings up as I've gone through, and take to prigging? Master Greene, reflect—will you, afore you proceed?"

"You said it was all a lark, but I don't see anything funny in it," replied Jolly. "Oh! I am so miserable, I wish I was at home."

"Here's the hontrays coming out," said Billy. "I'll do the next bit if you'll only go to sleep, or do something in the way of keeping quiet."

Again Perkins was not there, and Jiggles, indignant, returned to the dining-room to whisper a complaint in his master's ear. Ere his tale was half told, Billy had got two oyster patties, three veal cutlets, a mutton cutlet, and about half a pint of tomato sauce into the umbrella.

Perkins came up a second afterwards, and whisked away what remained. He helped himself to as much as he dare, and brought a small bone, with very little on it, to the cupboard.

"This aint much," said Billy.

"Its all I can spare."

"Perkins!" said Jiggles, "bring in the joint."

"I'm acomin' aint I," replied Perkins. "Do you want me to keep agoin' as if I was in the thick of a trottin' match?"

"You'll get it if you aint quick."

"It's heasy to holler, but hard to run about in this way," said Perkins, as he hastened after the joint, which he presently brought in, leaving a broad trail of gravy behind him on the floorcloth.

Jiggles jerked the dish out of his hand, and Perkins hurried away to consume a couple of cutlets he had stowed away inside the eight day clock. Billy came out to roam for a minute about the hall; he also paid a brief visit to the breakfast-room.

In this way the dinner proceeded, and Billy, by means of great skill and management, got a great variety of articles inside the umbrella—fish, cutlets, the outside cut of the joint, five drumsticks, three jam tarts, part of an ice pudding, and a bottle of champagne.

His labour over, he retired to the cupboard, to await an opportunity to escape with his plunder.

"The company will go upstairs presently," he thought, "Jiggles will retire to the kitchen, and then——"

He could not help smacking his lips. The prospect of such a feed was delicious. But, feeling it was indiscreet, he bade young Greene be quiet—a totally unnecessary command, as that most unfortunate of unfortunates was sound asleep, worn out with fatigue and tribulation.

The ladies went up first as usual, and the gentlemen remained behind.

Jiggles took in half a dozen decanters, and came back to the hall.

"He's a going now," thought Billy, peeping through a slight opening he made with the door.

But Jiggles was not going just yet. He, too, had a certain black mail to levy upon the festive board in the form of such sherry, claret, and champagne as remained from the dinner table. These he partook of seated on the umbrella stand, within two inches of the umbrella.

He was in no hurry. Jiggles was no base wine-bibber who drank hard and fast, but a connoisseur and epicure, who loved to make the best of every drop. He sipped and sipped until Billy thought he must have gone stark staring mad.

"Of all the aggrawating chaps I ever see he is the most," he muttered. "I believe he knows we are here, and does it a purpose."

But Billy knew very little of Jiggles, and did not understand his character. Jiggles was not in his own estimation by any means a common man. He aimed at society, was refined and polite after a way with all living things, until he came into personal contact with Perkins, who, as the steel draws fire from the flint, drew his innate vulgarity from him. He always forgot himself with Perkins—a fact which caused him much irritation and disgust.

Seated on the umbrella stand he was not merely sipping wine, but entertaining an imaginary company, producing in his mind, in fact, a duplicate of the party inside. He was passing the bottle round, conversing and attending to the wants of his guests.

In this way he spent an agreeable half hour, inflicting so much suffering on the leading spirit in the cupboard that it was a wonder every hair of his head was not turned to white, or, at least, to a respectable grey. His sufferings were none the less for having to be borne in silence.

At last there was a move in the dining-room, and Jiggles, rising from the umbrella stand with an inflamed eye, put a question to the empty air.

"Won't yer have any more wine, gentlemen? A glass of sherry? No! Then we will join the ladies."

His intention was to join the ladies in the

kitchen; but, before he could get away, the heavy swell, who had been noticed by Billy, came forth with a good cargo of eatables and drinkables inside him.

He was not drunk. Gentlemen do not get drunk in public nowadays, but he had taken enough to mellow him. The small details of life were of no moment to him just then—broad facts only could he deal with.

"I'll just go and look at my horse," he said, "if you will show me a light. It's a rule of mine to look at my horse and have a cigarette before joining the ladies."

"It's raining a little," said Jiggles.

"Then I'll take an umbrella—any one—this will do."

"Oh, lor!" gasped Billy, "he's got the one with our grub in. Come out, Jolly, we must stop him somehow."

He went out in a fever, and Jolly Greene instinctively followed him. Billy was bent upon getting hold of that umbrella at all hazards, but he was too late.

The swell had a hazy indefinite idea that the umbrella was rather heavy, but he hoisted it up and opened it.

Billy forgot his vexation in what followed. Down came all the good things in a shower—fish, patties, cutlets, limbs of fowl, sauce, and tarts. The champagne bottle dropped and went off like a promising Woolwich Infant, alarming the whole house, and bringing the Rev. Copley Cobbem and all the rest of the guests upon the scene.

"Stand back, Greene," cried Billy, "we are in for it. Behind this door; now then—there's a staircase of some sort ahead of you; go on, and shut yourself in the first room you come to. I'll wait and see if I can save anything from the ruin.'

CHAPTER XIX.

BILLY FIRES A SECRET SHOT AT HIS ENEMY.

THE place in which Billy found himself was a small ante-room, into which the inferior visitors were generally shown. Not being in use that night it was quite dark, and the sweet youth, in hiding there, would command a view of all that transpired in the hall.

Young Greene had gone up the small staircase, just inside the door, thereby leaving Billy without any source of anxiety, and free to concentrate himself upon other things.

The confusion in the hall was terrible. The heavy swell, whoever he was, raged and fumed like a wild beast, and would have been fearful to look upon if dabs of sauce, jam, and bits of meat, stuck all over his head and manly breast, had not made him rather comical.

"It is a gross insult—an infamous outrage!" he gasped.

"Double-dyed villain!" cried the Rev. Copley Cobbem, shaking his fist at the quivering Jiggles, "I see your hand in this."

"Oh, no! I don't know where any of 'em come from," replied Jiggles, looking at the ceiling, "or who chucked 'em over him."

"They came out of the umbrella," said the sufferer.

"And you put them there, you scoundrel!" said his master.

"Why should I go for to do it, sir?" asked Jiggles, with tears in his eyes. "It's more likely to have been Perkins. He's quite wild to-night—more fit for a 'sylum than a 'spectable gentleman's house; or it may be them two boys as was here just now."

"What two boys?"

"Didn't you see 'em, sir?"

"No. I—how should I?—I was too bewildered by the confusion created by this dastardly outrage."

He might also have added that his vision was a little impaired by the arduous task of entertaining his guests, and keeping the bottle going; but he did not.

"Did you recognise the boys?"

"No, sir," replied Jiggles; "I was too much hoccupied in the catastrophy that come about with these fragments of wittles."

A brilliant notion entered the head of young Sharp. He had enemies at school—here was an opportunity to have a dig at them. Of course, it would not do just now, but when the assembly in the hall dispersed he would go and ask to have an interview with the Rev. Copley.

How the things got into the umbrella nobody could explain. Perkins denied it so indignantly as to secure belief for once in a way, and no other person could be fixed upon. The swell—being unpresentable in the drawing-room without a change of clothes—went home in a huff, and the reverend gentleman, with a mournful countenance, accompanied his guests, male and female, upstairs.

Half an hour or thereabouts had elapsed when Jiggles came in, and whispered to the Rev. Copley a request from one of the boys, who wished to speak to him.

"What impudence is this?" he asked. "Who is it?"

"It's Master Popper, sir—him as come with the hidiot chap."

"Who do you mean by that?" asked the Reverend Copley.

"Well, sir, in the kitchen we thought——"

"How dare you think in the kitchen?" asked his master. "That is the place to work in—not to think. If I hear of you thinking again you will have to leave my service. Tell Master Popper that I am engaged."

"He said it was something important about the game that's been going on this evening."

"Jiggles, I never have gambling in my house. What fresh impertinence is this?"

"I mean, sir, the wittles in the rumblerellerer."

The potations of Jiggles had not quite worked off, and it seemed as if he never would have finished the last word.

"Where is Master Popper?"

"In the corridor, sir."

"Say I will come in a minute."

He found the guileless one with a countenance where indignation and sorrow struggled for supremacy. It was quite apparent that the feelings of Master William Sharp Popper had been outraged in some way.

"I'm very sorry to have troubled you, sir," he said; "but I couldn't sleep till I told you what was on my mind."

"You have a rugged countenance, and an unpolished tongue," said the reverend gentleman, kindly; "but I am sure you have a sound heart. What have you to tell me?"

"It isn't much; but I heard an explosion to-night, and, thinking that the kitchen biler had bust, I was comin' down to see if I could do anything for the sufferers. Half-way down I met two of the poopils coming up, larfin' as if they would bust, too."

"Well?"

"I think, sir, they must have something to do with the explosion whatever it may be, although I shouldn't like to say so."

"Two boys coming up laughing—hum!" said the Reverend Copley. "It points to something. Who were they?"

"Afore I gives you the information I have to ask a favour."

"You shall have it if it is anything in moderation."

"It is that you won't say who told you. I am a new boy, and they don't treat me too kindly as it is, and if they knowed I said anything my life would be very miserable indeed."

"I promise not to say anything."

"Thanky, sir. It was the two Stagers, sir—them

as came with the long legs, and disgusted all the respectable boys in the school."

This was coming it very strong, and the Reverend Copley was not quite credulous enough to take it in.

"If I mistake not," he said, "most of my pupils so far forgot themselves as to laugh, you among the number."

"I am sorry if I did, sir, for I didn't mean it. I hates low and unfair tricks. What I want is to get on and take in a regular soaker of learning."

"You express yourself in a tongue somewhat foreign to me, but you are a good boy. Good night, Popper."

"Good night, sir."

"I'll have 'em out before they are a month older," muttered Billy, as he walked away; "I'll make the place too hot for 'em."

He went into the schoolroom, where some were at their books and others at play. Young Greene was not there, nor the Stagers either, and he did not stay.

"They will try to pison his mind," he said, "and I must keep my eye on 'em."

On the landing he met the Stagers by themselves, and his mind was relieved of one fear. He greeted them with a faint smile, and said the evening was "unkimmon fine." They nodded in reply, but said nothing.

"Stuck up like all trumpery people," he said, looking after them ; "but mind you, my lads, I'll bring you down like cocoa-nuts with three shies a penny."

He went everywhere about the house where he dared ; and could find no trace of young Greene. What had become of him he could not possibly think. It was risky to return to the hall, but he could get down into the pantry, where he was likely to find Perkins, and he went.

That youth was then in a gloomy frame of mind, in consequence of having upset his liver with a feast of fragments, in which sauces, foreign to him, were fairly mingled. He received Billy's affectionate greeting with gloomy disdain.

"Aint you well?" asked Billy.

"A norphan, crushed and wolloped, can't expect to be well," replied Perkins. "I've had nothing but fighting all the hevening. The way the cook lays about her aint fair. I'm a mash of bruises."

"Take it out of her in another way," said Billy; "but I want to ask you a question. There's a small room downstairs on the left hand side of the door."

"The ante-room ?"

"Yes, I suppose so, and there is a staircase in it."

"Who said there wasn't," demanded Perkins, with a sudden twitch, as if the feast of the evening had revolted within him.

"Not I, but there is, you know ?"

"Oh! yes, I know. What then ?"

"Where does it lead to ?"

"Across a small passage, and down again into the front garden."

"Oh! that is it. What a capital arrangement ! Good night. I hope you will be better in the morning."

"I shall never be better," said Perkins, shedding tears. "I'm reg'lar broke by the treatment I gets here. I've received a wital injury to-night. If I dies, you can say so at the inquesh. I hope they'll hang the cook."

"I'll stand up for you like a friend," said Billy. "Good night."

"Where can that aggravating beggar be ?" muttered Billy. "If he got outside he'd be lost, for he's downright dazed by being in that cupboard. Perhaps he's come down again and gone upstairs to bed."

But young Greene was not there, and Billy, at a loss to know what else to do, lighted a candle, and sat waiting for him. A couple of hours passed away, and yet he did not come.

"I must have another look," muttered Billy. "I

shall get into trouble if I'm found out, but I can't help it."

All the other boys had retired long before, and after the usual light skirmishing, sank into sweet repose. Not a sound, save their heavy breathing, kept company with Billy's footsteps as he crossed the corridor.

He stole downstairs, but was pulled up by the noise of the departing guests. The Rev. Copley Cobbem was gallantly escorting the ladies to their carriages, and the men were selecting cigars from a box held by Jiggles.

"I can't go down now," thought Billy, and drew back into a dark corner.

When everybody was gone the reverend gentleman went round and locked every door, being especially particular about the ante-room, and went off with Jiggles to count the plate.

"I'm done!" gasped Billy, "if young Greene is there he's in for the night. Perhaps he's fallen asleep on the stairs, and if he wakes up he'll blubber and holler until all the house is up. Then all will come out, and I'm done. What a ass I was to let him leave me for a moment! Oh, Billy, your genius was asleep when you did that!"

He went back to his room heavy at heart and sad within generally. Sitting down on the side of the bed he took his boots off by degrees, and lay down with his clothes on.

For a long time he was kept awake by the peril of his position and the want of food, for he had lost even the ordinary supper usually provided. Grasping at the shadow he had missed the substance, and the loss of a meal was a great trial to one of his rapacious appetite.

At last he fell asleep, and slept soundly until dawn. One glance at the bed usually occupied by young Greene revealed that he was not there, and despair came upon him.

"I'm done, I'll bet a penny!" he groaned. "I'm ruined, and so is my guv'nor! Here's a chance of a lifetime thrown away!"

Billy pulled on his boots in a desperate kind of way, with a groan between every jerk.

"Wot the old 'un will say to me, if the game's spoilt, I don't know. When I do get a hold of young Jolly I'll have him in a corner, all to myself, and give him such a leathering."

Time passed on, prayers were read, breakfast disposed of, but no Jolly appeared.

The Rev. Copley was alarmed, and instituted a close search throughout the house and grounds, but no trace of Jolly could be found, beyond a small puddle or two on the corridor, where it was supposed that he had stopped to weep.

Dinner time came and went, and still no Jolly. The Rev. Copley Cobbem grew desperate, and talked of sending for the police, when his attention was distracted by the arrival of the whole of the servants, headed by the cook and Jiggles, both very pale, and with a wild and excited look about the eyes.

"What ever is the matter?" he faltered. "Jiggles, explain yourself."

"It's the ghost!" replied Jiggles, in a hollow whisper.

"In the store-room," said the cook.

"In a hamper," added Jiggles; "and the way it's going on is horful."

"Jiggles," said the Reverend Copley, "you are drunk."

"I haven't touched a blessed drop, sir."

"A ghost in a hamper! Ridiculous! Bring it up here to me at once."

Nobody stirred.

"I am going into the drawing-room," said the Reverend Copley, "and if that hamper is not brought to me there in ten minutes every one of you shall leave my house this day."

It was a dreadful alternative—the loss of a good place, or the carrying of a groaning ghost in a hamper. The odd man and Jiggles were the only two men of the party. They tossed up for it, and the lot fell upon Jiggles.

He had to carry the ghost; and half of the ten minutes had already expired!

CHAPTER XX.

THE GHOST IN THE HAMPER.

"ROBERT," said Jiggles to the porter, in tones of touching pathos, "we were ever friends. Think of the cold wittles you've had out of my pantry—think of the time when I accidentally lost the key of the beer cellar, and you found it! Be a friend, Bob, and carry it up!"

Robert shook his head with a vigorous emphasis which signified far more than words.

"You've tossed, and you've lost," said the porter. "Carry it hup yerself."

"I'll stand whatever you like to drink," urged Jiggles.

"Not if you was to give me the run of the 'ole blessed cellar!"

"I'm a poor man, as is well known; but you shall have the five shillings I was going to send to my haged mother this afternoon."

The porter visibly relaxed. Skittles was his weak point, and he had been puzzling his brains how to raise the stakes for a match he had made with the potman of the Welsher's Arms.

"Make it 'arf a quid, and I'll do it."

"I should be ruined!" said Jiggles.

"You can't expect a man to carry a blessed ghost about for nothink. Better make up your mind. There goes the guv'nor's bell."

Just then the mysterious sound from the hamper again made itself audible.

Jiggles jumped a little way into the air, and everybody turned pale.

"If you don't say 'yes' at once, I'll make it fifteen bob," said the porter, and, with trembling fingers, Jiggles extracted a half-sovereign from his pocket.

Robert took it, bit it, spat on it for luck, and then, with a pale but resolute visage, marched towards the store-room.

"Mind," he said, "you foller me, and give me a buck up."

"You won't let go on it?"

"In course I won't, onless it—it tries to fly away with me. I couldn't be expected to stand that."

The groaning seemed to have ceased now. The odd man shouldered the hamper, and proceeded as far as the first flight of stairs, where he set it down in a hurry.

"What is it?" said Jiggles, in a hoarse whisper.

"I heerd it," replied Robert, "quite close to my year—a reg'lar holler groan!"

"There goes the bell again," said the cook. "Oh! dear me, we shall all lose our places!"

"Be a man, Robert," said Jiggles, "and get it up to the guv'nor quick. He's a clergyman, you know; and they can do what they like with ghosts."

"You orter stand a hextry five bob," said Robert, "I didn't reckon on it's going on like this here."

"I'll stand half a crown, but I couldn't go no further. Get it over, there's a good feller!"

Robert assumed a look of desperate determination, plunged at the hamper, and started off, two stairs at a time, butting at the drawing-room door without the ceremony of knocking, and landing the hamper upside down at the feet of the Rev. Copley Cobbem.

The head-master was not alone. There were two ladies with him, who gave a small scream a-piece, and stared wonderingly as Jiggles, Perkins, the cook, and a housemaid all crowded in, keeping as far away from the hamper as possible.

"So," said the Rev. Copley, "this is the ghost—is it?"

"That's him, sir," replied the porter.

"You're quite certain of it—eh?"

"If you'd carried him upstairs, sir, and had him 'ollerin' in your ears all the time, you'd be certain, too."

"Well, now, just open that hamper, and let it out."

The porter advanced slowly, much as a man approaches a dog whose intentions as to biting are rather doubtful. His hand was just on the lid, when a hollow blood-curdling moan came from the interior.

Robert jumped back six feet, and knocked Perkins over a console table.

The Reverend Copley had hitherto treated the matter lightly; but there could be no mistake about the groan. He seized the lid, flung it back, and discovered—not a ghost, but the head of young Greene, whose voice was feebly heard saying—

"Where's my mar?"

"Good gracious! What on earth—why, how is this?" exclaimed the Reverend Copley, in broken sentences. "How dare you get into that hamper, Greene, and cause all this trouble and commotion?"

"I didn't get in," murmured young Greene, tearfully. "I was shoved. I'm always being shoved, and I want my mar."

"Come out at once!" said the Reverend Copley, wrathfully. "Why don't you help Master Greene out, Jiggles, instead of standing grinning there? I'll have this put a stop to at once. There is a demon of mischief abroad in the school, and I must lay it at once."

Young Greene was hauled out with no little difficulty, for the straw was pressed in tightly, and then it was found that his ankles were tied, and his arms bound behind him.

The Rev. Copley regarded the victim with an eye of severity. He was certain that Jolly knew who had played him this trick, and he went, in schoolboy phrase, to "get it out of him."

"Now," he said, "have the goodness, Greene, to explain how this occurred?"

"Well, the things came out of the umbrella, and then somebody shoved me, and I came along a passage, and——"

"Stop, one moment. Who pushed you, and what do you know about the articles in the umbrella?"

Jolly was just on the point of giving a clear an abstract of his adventure in the cupboard as his brain would permit, when Sharp junior ambled into the room and gave him such a look.

He curdled Jolly's blood, and he became at once more hopelessly muddled than ever, and he could only stare at the Rev. Copley in a fishy sort of way, and gasp.

The head-master felt a perfect itching to go in at Jolly Greene with a cane, and get something out of him if it was only howls, but he restrained himself, and went on mildly.

"Now, Greene, you must know who treated you in this shameful way. Only tell me their names, and they shall be severely punished."

"I don't know. I was going along, and I heard somebody say 'here's a lark!—there he is,' and then I was shoved about, and the straw got into my mouth, and I hollered, and then somebody pulled me out, and—and I'm here."

"If you fancy, Greene, that I am credulous enough to believe such a lame story as that you are very much mistaken. You are only endeavouring to screen those who have been guilty of this practical joke. You may consider it honourable not to inform, but I consider it rebellious, and I tell you plainly that, unless in five minutes from now you give me a more coherent account of the affair, I shall flog you soundly."

But young Greene only exclaimed feebly, "I was shoved," and gave no other information whatever, until the Rev. Copley had checked off the time on his watch, when he was walked away to the library

GREEN AS GRASS.

A JOLLY SCHOOL STORY.

THE REV. COPLEY COBBEM BEHELD A ROUND OPAQUE BODY WITH A SYLPH-LIKE FORM UPON IT FLYING THROUGH THE AIR.

No. 4.

and had a private interview with the longest and most limber of the head master's special canes.

He was allowed ten minutes to remove the traces of his night's lodging, which had accumulated about him, and which the cane had failed to shake off, and then he was ordered to rejoin his class.

Billy Sharp had already made up his mind as to the real perpetrators of the joke. He was certain that they were Dick and Nick Stager. If he could only supplement his first shot by fixing the guilt of the hamper on their shoulders, expulsion from Warmington was certain. A saint couldn't stand it, Billy was certain, and the Rev. Copley Cobbem was anything but a saint.

CHAPTER XXI.

IN WHICH YOUNG GREENE DISCOVERS THE PIRATE'S TREASURE.

MANY readers may have remarked that young Greene, although amply supplied with everything — except brains — which his doting parents could think of, was yet of a greedy and covetous disposition.

Thus the confidence tricksters found a very easy prey in him, and numberless were the sovereigns he had paid for smuggled cigars, made of brown paper soaked in tobacco juice, and for diamond rings, watches, and other brass and glass jewellery, which cunning men assured him they had just found, and allowed him a peep of under a gas lamp.

To covet is a sin, as we all know, and young Greene was a dreadful sinner in that respect, only he invariably expiated the crime by paying heavily, as he did in this particular instance, which forms the basis of this chapter.

Warmington College was very near the sea. The Rev. Copley having a due regard for the health of his pupils, was in the habit of sending selected parties on alternate days to bathe, under the charge of one of the masters.

The second day after the memorable dinner party it fell to the lot of our friends—amongst others—to make the excursion, in care of Herr Optoshnoff, the professor of German.

Young Greene jumped at the idea with joy. He was fond of washing himself—of washing *himself*, that is, in the most literal sense of the word. As to being washed by others he had a very hearty aversion, and with tolerably good reason, as my readers already know.

During the morning he was actually observed to laugh—a phenomenon which so astonished Master Sharp that he crossed the class-room under the desks, at the imminent risk of being detected and caned.

Arrived within easy pinching distance, Billy felt for the calf of Jolly's leg—there wasn't much of it—and nipped him gently.

"Ow!" yelled the unfortunate one.

"Hush!" said young Sharp, in a thrilling whisper. "It's me. If you say a word I'll skin you."

The Rev. Copley was close by, cane in hand. He heard the exclamation, and naturally wanted to know what was the cause.

Fear of Billy silenced Jolly. The Rev. Copley set his silence down to obstinacy, and gave him three or four juicy cuts with his cane, which made him wriggle dreadfully, and cause the boys next him to blot their copy-books.

"I'll warm you for that, young Greene," said the right-hand one, wrathfully; "you see if I don't."

"I shall have to do mine all over again," said the one on the left, with a ferocious glance at Jolly, which made his blood run cold, despite the warming he had just received. "I'll wait on you, my boy!"

"I couldn't help it," moaned young Greene. "Somebody's always shoving me, or pushing me, or doing something. Oh! *where's* my mar?"

By degrees, however, the pain passed off, and back came the recollection of the afternoon's excursion. The Rev. Copley seldom kept any boys in on that day, out of consideration for their health—he said, but principally because the youngsters spent their money on stale pastry and flat gingerbeer, and spoiled their appetites for their legitimate dinner.

It was a very pleasant coast, with low white cliffs sloping down to the sea, and masses of brown rock cropping up from the sand at low water.

Bathing was safe at all times, the water being very shallow for half a mile out, even at high water, so that the usher in charge had no great responsibility, and usually employed his time, if young, in looking out for a cheap flirtation. But Herr Optoshnoff had brought a pipe with him—one that was put together in joints like a telescope — and a German philosophical work with a twenty-syllabled title.

"Go on mit you, poys," he said, as they reached the shore. "Don't preak nodings, and don't drow stones, und but your heads in de vater ven you shouts."

And with these final instructions Herr Optoshnoff lit his pipe, and forgot all about the dozen of pupils in his charge.

The two Stagers were of the party as well as our friends, Greene and Sharp, and Perkins was in attendance to look after the clothes of the young gentlemen during such time as they disported themselves, *puris naturalibus*, in the briny.

"This is a nicish place," said Nick Stager.

"Jolly," said Dick. "I suppose it's on account of having an admiral in the family, but I always seem to swell and grow taller when I sniff salt water."

"'Taint bad," observed Perkins, cutting into the conversation with that free and easy manner peculiar to him. "But years ago a party durstn't show his nose within forty miles of here."

"How's that?"

"On account of the pirates. Horful coves they were, with long beards and sashes, stuck full of pistols and daggers and swords, and they used to cut parties' eyes out and fry 'em, and make 'em swaller 'em like pills."

Young Greene was looking with his mouth so wide open that Dick Stager couldn't resist the temptation, and pitched a pebble in.

It nearly finished poor Jolly, for the pebble lodged in his gullet, and could not be extracted until he had been held upside down for a couple of minutes, and his back thumped, by as many as could get at it.

"I never see such a chap," said Perkins, indignantly. "You're always cuttin' in and spilin' the conwersation."

"Never mind him," said Nick; "go on about the pirates. Who told you about 'em?"

"An old cove who lives along the beach, a precious old party, nigh two hundred years old. He was one of the pirates hisself. He's put here to watch over the treasure wot the others 'id away, and he can't die until somebody finds it."

"Where is it?" exclaimed the others, simultaneously.

"Over there," replied Perkins, pointing to a mass of rocks which the advancing tide had just reached, "there's a 'ole just hunder that lump to the left, and all you've got to do is to crawl in, turn round three times, say 'Hullaboloo!' and then a lump of rock falls down, and you sees the treasure."

"Have you seen it?"

"Lots of times. There's gold in tons, and jools by the bucketfuls. Lor'! it makes my mouth water when I think of 'em."

"But why don't you go and help yourself? You know the way."

"I wish I did; but all you can do is to git a peep. This hold pirate, he told me that there's only one chap in the world as can get it."

"Who's he, then?"

"Nobody knows—only he must be about fourteen, and his name must begin with a G."

"Why, my name begins with a G!" said Jolly, suddenly waking up to the fact.

"So it do," said Perkins; "and you're about fourteen—aint you?"

"Fourteen last birthday."

"Then I shouldn't wonder," said Perkins, solemnly, "if you aint the very chap as is 'signed by Providence to have all that treasure. You won't forget me when you gets it all—will you?"

"You shall have your pick," replied Jolly, who was struggling frantically with a tight boot.

The others saw now that a "sell" was intended, and Nick said to Perkins, quietly—

"Is there a cave?"

"Yes," replied Perkins.

"Anything in it?"

"Crabs," said the page, with a solemn wink. "Such claws! he'll catch it."

CHAPTER XXII.

SHARP SENIOR ARRIVES AT THE WHITE HART IN AN AFFLICTED CONDITION—A PAINFUL INTERVIEW WITH HIS SON.

SHARP SENIOR was a man of retiring disposition, and never intruded himself upon any one when he thought the intrusion might lead to unpleasant results to himself or others—especially to himself—and therefore it need excite no particular comment when we state that he paid a visit to the White Hart, in accordance with the expressed wish of his son, strictly incog.

With the object of fully concealing his identity, he got himself up in drab shorts, a blue coat, a broad-brimmed hat, a white tie with many folds, and blue spectacles. He also swathed his right leg in a dozen yards of calico, surmounted by a large silk handkerchief, and became an intense sufferer with gout.

On arriving at the railway station nearest to Warmington College he excited some sympathy, and a little comment, by the way he groaned when two active porters—who ought to have had souls above tips, but hadn't—bore him to the one fly in waiting, and deposited him therein.

"There you are, sir!" said one, smiling a smile which expressed a firm belief in getting a shilling. "Quite comfortable, sir? Go easy, Jim; for the gentleman's wery bad."

"All right," replied Jim, looking at his horse, which only fairly woke up once a year, when it was put out to grass. "We shall go easy enough."

"Bless you, my friends!" said Sharp senior, sweetly smiling on the porters. "You have been extremely kind. May you be rewarded for it—by-and-bye! To the White Hart, if you please."

"He's a nice 'un!" growled one of the porters, as the carriage went off with a deal of rattling and clattering. "But let him come back here, and see if he don't have to get into the carriage hisself!"

Sharp senior did come back, and got into the carriage without assistance, much to the surprise of—— But we anticipate. Let us pursue the thread of this most veracious story.

The White Hart was a good inn, and had been a better one in its prime, when the coaches ran along the road, and changed horses there. It was a good, solid, square building, built of stone, with a dozen gables, and a perfect wilderness of stables behind, in three-fourths of which colonies of rats dwelt together in harmony and peace.

Arriving there, Mr. Sharpe asked for a room where he could be private without paying extra for it, and was accommodated at once with the coffee-room, which was seldom occupied in the day. Then he asked for pen, ink and paper, and a glass of stiff brandy-and-water, and wrote the following letter to the Rev. Copley Cobbem:—

"DEAR SIR,—By accident I have just learnt that a nephew of mine—the sole offspring of a dear de-parted sister—is in your well-conducted establishment. I allude to Master William Sharp Popper, with whom I have had, as yet, very little communication. I am afflicted with a chronic gout, which forbids travelling on pain of suffering, and I am thereby compelled to keep at home as much as possible. Just now, however, I am from home on urgent business, and halting here, by the way, at an inn, I regret to say, for I hold such places to be ungodly; but there was no other haven of rest, and a desire to see my nephew came over me. You will understand the desire when I tell you that I was his godfather as well as his uncle, and therefore his welfare, both temporal and spiritual, is of the greatest interest to me. In the few letters I have received from him he speaks of you in the highest terms, and feels sure, if he can only remain long enough, you will lay the foundation of what I desire him to be—a good and wise, and possibly, a grave man. May I ask that he be permitted to see me at once, as my stay here is very short.—Yours, most earnestly and faithfully, "HEZEKIAH BROWN."

Having read it carefully over, to see if the hoof of his real nature peeped out anywhere, Sharp senior rang the bell, and sealed up the letter carefully.

In a few seconds a fairly brisk waiter entered the room.

"Ha, John!" he said—"or, let me see, is your name John?"

"My name is Ralph, but I'm ginerally called William, sir. It comes handy to the customers, and they don't forget it," replied the man.

"William is a good name," said Sharp, senior, thoughtfully. "There was William the Conqueror, William Shakespeare, William the Third, and a score others. The name is impressed upon the nation's mind, and you were honoured when they gave it you. But I have no doubt you deserve it."

"I does my best endeavours, sir," said William.

"You are married, William, I think?"

"Yes, sir."

"Any family?"

"Four gals and three boys—two in arms, twins."

"Twins come heavy, William."

"They does, sir. It takes a lot of calkerlation to make two ends meet."

"No doubt—no doubt, William. But the Lord will provide. Send this letter to my friend, the Rev. Copley Cobbem. Tell the bearer to wait for an answer, and bring me a little more brandy and water and a cigar. Good brandy like this, and an occasional smoke, are the only things which will, as it were, stultify the gout."

"I had a touch on it once, sir," said William, and the doctor told me to take nothing."

"A country doctor, I presume?"

"Yes, sir."

"And you suffered much?"

"My foot was red-hot for three weeks, and you could hear my 'owls three parts down the willage."

"That country doctor was an ignorant man. The next time you are afflicted, William, go to town, see a first-rate man, give him his two guineas, which is the fashionable fee nowadays, and come home, rejoicing in the certainty that the efforts of the clever man will be blessed. Send the letter at once, William, and be as quick as you can with the brandy and water, as I have one of my attacks coming on."

William, much impressed with the visitor, hastened to obey, and Sharp senior smoked and drank until a reply came back from the Reverend Copley. It was all that could be desired. We give it verbatim.

"DEAR SIR,—It affords me much pleasure in releasing Master Popper from his duties for half a day, although I must freely confess the time, from an educational point of view, cannot easily be spared. Master Popper is diligent, but he is a little behind the boys of his age, and the knowledge of this, I fear, acts upon his sensitive nature, and weighs him down. Perhaps you can, in a confidential way, cheer him with the assurance that he has my sympathy and support in all things. He will be with you in half an hour.—Believe me, my dear sir, yours very faithfully,   "COPLEY COBBEM."

William the waiter, who brought the letter in, hovered about the room for a few minutes, and Sharp senior, apparently oblivious of his presence, read the letter aloud. William was much impressed. The very air of the room was impregnated with the odour of sanctity which hovered around the guest.

"Any further orders, sir?" he asked.

"Oh! still here?" said Sharp senior, starting. "Well, being here, you may bring me a little more brandy and water and another cigar, in case I should want it. Smoking as a habit is pernicious, but indulged in as a medical requirement it is decidedly efficacious."

This was a little too much for William, who only indulged in or understood the English language in its simplest form. He hurried out of the room, and returned will all speed with the things required, ushering in at the same time Master Billy Sharp, whose exterior had been swept and garnished by the housekeeper to do honour to the arrival of Uncle Brown.

His face was remarkably clean, and shone with a recent application of yellow soap, his clothes were well brushed, and he had also been fitted up with a clean dicky. Thus renovated and restored, he looked like a decent member of society.

His ready wit had told him who Uncle Brown was, and he was quite prepared for any guise his father might appear in. The shorts, the white tie, and the blue spectacles were thrown away upon him.

As a rule Billy was remarkably discreet, but this time he forgot himself, and while William, the waiter, was still in the room, he hailed his father in this fashion—

"What cheer guv'nor!"

William, the waiter, started, and a shade of wonderment gathered on his brow. Sharp senior dispelled it in a moment.

"I see," he said, "that all my admonitions have been thrown away. You are still the same reckless, thoughtless boy who embittered the prime of my life, and compelled me to send you forth from my roof. But I do not yet give you up. I trust what I have to say to-day may turn you aside from your evil ways."

"It's only now and then I forgets myself," said Billy, hanging down his head. "I'm sorry, sir—indeed I am."

"The soil is good, and with careful cultivation will yet bring forth good fruit," murmured Sharp senior. "William, my friend, leave the room, and, if possible, let no one enter until I have ceased to commune with my so—— ahem! nephew."

"Nobody shan't enter," said William, his uttered determination being, from a grammatical point of view, the very opposite of his amiable intentions. "If anybody comes I'll put 'em into the back parlour."

"Thank you, my friend," said Sharp senior, and William departed, but only to plant his ear against the keyhole outside, and catch few and far between fragments of the following dialogue:—

"What an ass you are, Billy," said Sharp senior, as soon as the door was closed, "to come blundering into the room in that way. I thought you knew better. All your education is thrown away."

"The words were out afore I could stop 'em," replied Billy, sorry for his blunder, but not over penitent. "What do you mean by comin' down in this way? Why not show up openly like a man?"

"How could I," asked his father, "when I've been persuading old Greene that it would be better

for you and that son of his to be here undisturbed for a few months? Mrs. Greene fell in with the notion, as I told her it would make a man of her noble boy."

"I don't think it would be advisable for us to stop," said Billy, gloomily.

"Why not?"

"There's a couple of kids in the school who know too much."

"Too much what?"

"Of me. One of 'em saw me when I tried to fake the rug outside Hepitoe's shop. He bowled me out, and was the one as first guve chace. It was no small run—took at least five pounds off me—as you know; but I did him."

"So you think the young chap knows you?"

"I am sure on it. He said so."

"When?"

"T'other day in the playground, when he got me into a corner."

"And what did you do—knock him down?" asked Sharp senior.

"No—no! I should have got the wust of it. Not such a hass! I put myself in a humble hattitood, and come the repentant dodge."

"Do you mean to say you admitted it?"

"What could I do?"

Sharp senior raised his gouty foot, and brought it down with a bang upon the floor. William, the waiter, who had temporarily shifted his ear, and planted his eye at the keyhole, saw the action with his own optic, and afterwards took a solemn oath—sworn on the tobacco-box in the back parlour—that the old man did not even wince.

"Of all the confounded asses," said Sharp senior, "you, Billy, are the worst! Where's your brains? Where was your intellect when you did such a thing? Why didn't you deny it?"

"I never thought of it. I was struck all of a heap."

"What's the name of the chap?"

"Stager—nevvy to old Hadmiral Stager."

"Here's a fortune thrown away!" exclaimed Sharp senior, rising, and pacing up and down the room with the gait of a man who had never known the gout. William the waiter saw it with his own eye, and took a second oath to that effect. "Here's a pile of money chucked away in the dirt," continued Mr. Sharp, "and all because you can't keep your head. The Stagers are rich, and we could have got a thousand at least for defamation of character. Oh! Billy, what were you thinking of?"

"I was weak," replied Billy, with a penitent air; "but I don't seem quite myself down here. I'm out of my helement. You can't expect me to be otherwise."

"Were you alone when he came out with this?"

"Yes, we were."

"And he said nothing in public?"

"No—not a word."

"Then there's a chance yet, Billy. Let him come out with it before the whole school; take down his words, pick out a few of the most friendly witnesses, and leave the rest to me. I'll get enough out of the Stagers to retire on and take a pub. Once start, there's a lot to be done. I know a couple of detectives who will work in with me, and, if we only keep the melting-pot going, there's a pile to be done out of plate."

"Well, that's all I wanted to see you for at fust," said Billy, "as I was in a fix. But do you think this defamation of character will pay?"

"Of course it will. No man has a right to say a thing of that sort, even if it's true; but when a chap is innocent—as you are, you know, Billy—the jury will give us a fortune. Greene's lawyer shall take the case in hand."

"It might spile all."

"No, Billy, it won't. You go and taunt this chap, and when he's fallen into the trap—as he will—write straight to me."

"How are you going on with the Greenes?"

"Swimmingly. I live in clover. Everything of the best, and not much to do."

"That's all right. Talking of plate as you was just now. There's a nice little lump at the college."

"Is there? But it won't do, Billy."

"We might make a note of it, and get a man to work the business when you start a melting-pot. I've got a reglar plan of the house made out, where everything is kep', and so on."

"Billy, my brave boy, come to my arms," said Sharp senior.

William, the waiter, who had, in his thirst for ocular demonstration of what was taking place in the room, sacrificed his hearing for sight, again beheld a startling yet pleasing sight with his own eye. The boy from Warmington College and his uncle Brown, embracing, danced a light fandango brief but brilliant, and at the conclusion of the performance the boy was allowed to wet his whistle with some of the old man's brandy and water.

"It is a game here, I can tell you," said Billy, as he resumed his seat. "Down here there are all sorts of things going on. There's a boy here in buttons who would be useful if you ever went in for a staff of your own."

"Not I," said Sharp senior, shaking his head. "Let others do the work, and I'll do the fencing. You get ten times the profit, with a hundredth part of the risk."

"As you like," returned Billy, mechanically taking another sip at the brandy and water. "The reverend chap is a merry one. He gave a spiff dinner party t'other night."

"Did he?"

"Yes, and people come and put their things in the breakfast-room."

"What things?" asked Sharp, senior, regarding his son curiously.

"Hovercoats, and so on," said Billy. "Look here. I found this silver snuff-box in one of 'em. What's it worth?"

Sharp senior did not appraise it, but, rising, he seized Billy by the throat, and shook him as a dog would a rat.

Those who doubt this assertion have only to call upon William, the waiter, and he will, if necessary, affirm it on oath. He saw it with his own eye, and ought to know.

"You confounded young fool—you ass!" growled the old man. "What do you mean by running such risks as these?"

"Here, let go, will you? Wot next, I wonder?" demanded Billy, wriggling out of his father's grasp. "Come now, wot have I done?"

"Do you mean to say this hasn't been missed?" asked Sharp.

"Of course it have."

"And inquired about?"

"Yes, but nobody knowed anything, and there was an end of it.

"But why did you do it when you was aware that some people about you knew too much? I can't trust you, Billy—you will ruin all."

"No, I shan't. Who's to know? You take it away, and there's an end of it."

"I'll take it away and chuck it into a pond, the trumpery thing. What's a snuff-box to the game we have in hand? Oh! Billy, why don't you rise in your business instead of grovelling in the dust?"

"I won't do anything in that way any more," said Billy, "but if I remember rightly, your last words was——"

"Never mind my last words. They bore on young Greene, I think?"

"Yes, the downright last, but just afore you told me if I saw a chance of getting anything conwertible I was to do so."

"Then I recalls 'em."

"But you might ha' done that afore you choked me."

"Excitement, Billy, carried me away for the moment, and you weren't hurt much. Touch nothing more, Billy. And now, I suppose our business is over?"

"I haven't got nothing more to say," said Billy, sullenly.

"Then let us go and chuck this bauble into a pond."

"Yes, and I'll see you do it," returned Billy. "I'm short of money, and I thought you'd have given me five bob on it."

"Not while I'm on a respectable lay, Billy—no, never."

"All right," said Billy, bitterly, "you know best."

"Now give me your arm, Billy, and let us walk into the air."

William the waiter, then saw again with his own eye the afflicted gentleman walk lustily across the room, and become suddenly lame as he reached the door. He had barely time to get into a dark recess when the suffering man came out groaning, supported by the noble boy, on whose face were stamped sincere sympathy and affection for his dear relative.

"Waiter!" cried Sharp senior.

"Here, sir," said William, coming briskly forward, but keeping in the shadow to hide the distortions made upon his face by contending emotions.

"I am going forth to breathe the fresh air for awhile," said Sharp senior, "but I shall not be long gone. William, my friend."

"Very good, sir. Shall I order dinner?"

"Not until my return; but you may bring me a little more brandy and water and a couple of cigars. I will drink the spirituous compound here."

William brought it, and the two Sharps slowly and solemnly went forth from the inn, followed by the gaze of William, whose optics, having looked upon so much that was strange and wonderful, were slightly wild.

They turned down the road towards the station, and having passed a corner, the whole demeanour of the lame man changed.

"Billy," he said, "is anybody coming?"

"I don't see any one."

"Then I'll be off. There's a train in half an hour, and I shall just catch it."

"And how about that snuff-box?"

"I'll chuck it into a pond as I go along, Billy."

"No, you won't," said the sweet youth, planting himself before his father. "I know you too well to trust you. Hand out five bob."

"I haven't so much about me."

"Then give me the box."

"Take half a crown on account, Billy."

"No, I won't."

"Three bob. It will leave me penniless; but, as it is for my child's sake, I do not care."

"Three bob, then," said Billy; "but it's wery mean of you."

"I'll throw in these bandages," said Sharp senior, as he hastily unrolled them. "Here they are, and here's the tip. Good-bye, Billy."

Billy bit each shilling separately and carefully before returning the adieu, and then he only favoured his father with a nod. Sharp senior, in great haste, set off towards the station.

On the way he changed his white tie for a black one, and took off the blue spectacles; but there was still enough of the original article left to stagger the two porters who had helped him into the carriage.

Fortunately for him, they had not much time for inspection. The train and Sharp senior arrived at the same time, and as the former took his seat with a face oblivious of having seen the porters before, they only caught a glimpse of him.

"It's wery like," said one, as the train moved on.

"Unkimmon!" said the second.

"But he warn't lame."

"And t'other was."

"He had a black tie."

"And the tother a white 'un."

"T'other wore spectacles."

"And he didn't."

"I don't know whether it be he or not."

"No more do I."

And it is a question which they have never been able to settle to this day.

William, the waiter, waited for the return of his guest, and waited in vain. He—William—had paid for the brandy-and-water and cigars, and it was his duty to look after the repayment thereof. The host of the White Hart would have nothing to do with it.

Two days afterwards, William, having a slack hour or two, went up to Warmington College to lodge a complaint with the Reverend Copley Cobbem. Young Billy was called in, and he declared that his uncle must have forgotten to pay, and, as he was on his road to India, there was nothing else to do but to await his return, when he would, no doubt, act with the honour which had always distinguished him. This would not do for William, who became offensive and pressing; so the Reverend Copley paid the amount, and put it down in young Greene's bill, under the head of "extras."

CHAPTER XXIII.

SUBSEQUENT HISTORY OF THE PIRATES' TREASURE.

EVEN as one nail will drive out another, so will one vice neutralise another—for a time. Young Greene was naturally funky, but he was also naturally greedy; and in this case greed got the upper hand.

He was afraid of the water, but the prospect of that rich hoard of gold and jewels made him brave.

"It isn't deep—is it?" he had the precaution to ask, as he struggled with the final sock.

"It wouldn't drownd a cheese mite," replied Perkins, fervently. "Go in and win, and holler when you comes to the jools. We'll help you fetch 'em."

Then Greene waded out, and his troubles began. Perkins had told the truth. The water was not deep, but the shore was very uneven, the stones sharp, and the sea-weed slippery.

Every step was an irregular wobble, and when he wasn't wobbling he was falling down, much to the detriment of his knees and elbows. Long before he reached the cave he was dreadfully sore; but the thought of the pirates' treasure kept him up, and he struggled gamely on.

The hole in the rock which Perkins had indicated was very narrow, and there was only just room for Greene to crawl in, which process entailed a further loss of "bark;" but his mind was set on the treasure, and he held on until he was fairly through.

It was fearfully dark and slippery, and not a thing could young Greene see.

He had some dim idea that when once he had passed the gloomy portal a bright vision of beauty and magnificence would burst upon him—perhaps a genii would appear somewhere in the neighbourhood, a hundred feet high, demanding, in an awful voice, "What is thy will?"

"I wish I'd brought a light," thought young Greene; "but I s'pose I'd better go on, and get it over. Let's see—I've got to turn round three times, and say 'Hullabaloo!' Here goes!"

He turned hastily round to the left, and brought his head into violent contact with a rock, instantly lighting up a brilliant illumination; but it wasn't of any use to him.

"Oh, dear! How it hurts! I s'pose I turned the wrong way."

He rested for a moment, and then wheeled to the right. He had made a half turn when he slipped, and rolled into a hole.

He was on his back, gasping for breath, when he the sea-weed move beneath him.

He put one hand hurriedly down, and instantly felt something like a powerful vice lay hold of his thumb.

Young Greene forgot all about the treasure—his one thought was of the agony he suffered. Heedless of the rocks, he scrambled towards the entrance; but there a fresh horror awaited him—the tide had come up so rapidly that the narrow entrance was already full of water.

Fortunately for him, he did not stop to reflect, but charged into the water—crab and all—took in one huge mouthful, came up to the top gasping, and climbed the rock, the venomous crab still holding tightly to its prey.

Young Sharp, the two Stagers, and Perkins were at the bathing-place, calmly waiting the result of their joke, and a roar of satisfaction hailed Greene as he made his appearance.

"He's got one of the jools!" shouted Perkins. "Wot is it, Jolly—a dimond or a hemerald?"

"Oh, dear!" yelled young Greene. "Come and take it off! You've no idea how it hurts!"

Unable any longer to bear the pain, he fell off the rock into the sea.

"Look sharp there!" said Nick. "The young beggar will be drowned."

"You help him out," said Billy, coolly. "I can't swim."

"But you will never drown," said Dick. "Another end is in keeping for you."

"You will have your joke," replied Billy. "Perhaps I'll have mine one day."

The last words Dick did not hear. He was busy fishing out young Jolly by the hair of the head, who, having taken in a large stock of water, was gasping for dear life.

They got him out, and carried him up the beach. Then they laid him down and removed the crab by main force, who was game to the end, and took away pieces of flesh for a keepsake.

Then they rubbed him, and, opening his eyes, he asked for his "mar."

"Where's your clothes?" asked Dick.

"I don't know. I left 'em somewhere," replied Jolly.

"But where did you put them?"

"I don't know," said Jolly, with a dazed look. "Perhaps somebody has been shoving them about."

"He's getting off his head," said Billy Sharp. "Let's run him up and down."

"I can't be run up and down without clothes," said Jolly.

"You must."

"But I won't! I shall be taken up."

"Here's Herr Optoshnoff coming," said Dick.

The good-natured German, with his pipe in his hand, came up in a great hurry for him, and looked at the figure of young Greene in dismay.

"Vat is tis?" he said. "Vat is it? Can it be a fight of nakeds? Oh! it is not glean and tecent."

"Nobody knows what he's been up to, sir," said Billy Sharp. "You can't get nothing out of him."

"I was shoved into a hole, and bitten all over," said Jolly, wildly.

"He is a veak boy," said the German professor, "and he gets into de wrong holes at all dimes. But he must be tressed. Go and get him a suit of glothes. Ask of te fishermens vat tey vill take for te loans of a suit."

A disinterested fisherman was soon found, who, for the sum of five shillings, was willing to lend a tarpaulin suit worth about one and threepence, on condition of its being returned within two days, as his boy "would have to lay a-bed till he got 'em back."

The clothes were brought, and young Greene was put into them. As an illustration of the comfort they brought to the wearer, it may be remarked that the trousers had the power of standing alone, and when young Greene got into the jacket the arms stood out like railway signals, but did not rank in

THE TAIL OF THE MONSTER KITE WAS SURREPTITIOUSLY ATTACHED TO YOUNG GREEN'S UNMENTIONABLES—THE RESULT WAS LAMENTABLE.

usefulness with them, as they would neither work up nor down.

Young Greene had three happy hours at the seaside in them; but his companions were not so kind as they might have been. They laid him down and buried him in the sand; they stood him up, and made an Aunt Sally of him, using jelly-fish and other soft missiles; and, no matter what they did, he was perfectly helpless. He had no more control over the clothes he wore than a man in the pillory.

If he was "shoved" he went down stiff, like a clown in the pantomime; and when others laughed he saw no fun in the business. Nor did he see anything humorous in the fact of being unable to sit down or to bend his knees—nor, in the climax to a great effort he made to take a seat, when his nether garment folded up suddenly in the rear, and split across like a sheet of horn.

He was got home at last, and they shot him out of his clothes and put him to bed. Then he laid his head wearily upon the pillow, and said—

"I want my mar!"

CHAPTER XXIV.
THE IMPERIAL CIRCUS—YOUNG GREENE DISTINGUISHES HIMSELF.

EARLY one morning a gentleman of majestic and refined deportment called upon the Reverend Copley Cobbem. He was a man of perhaps forty years of age, with a lot of dark hair rolled up in a lovely manner at the back of his head; his moustache was long and thick, and his clothes gorgeous in colour and ultra-fashionable in their cut.

The buttons alone represented a considerable amount of private property, and his watch-chain, if it had been gold, would have excited the envy of a Rothschild, and brought down in its owner's wake half the enterprising pickpockets of the British Isles.

He rang the bell and he knocked, and, while Perkins was getting his apron off, and his official jacket on, arranged his hair with the easy grace of a man accustomed to society.

When Perkins opened the door and gazed upon him, all the courteous expression he usually wore on such occasions faded out, and, in a short, sharp, peremptory way, worthy of a boy who never did and never would stand any nonsense, he asked—

"Now, then—wot do you want?"

"Is the reverend gentleman at the head of this establishment visible?" asked the stranger. "If so, will you say that Signor Joansmethe desires to see him?"

"I say, mister," said Perkins, suddenly becoming confidential, "are you one of 'em as come down with the circus yesterday?"

"I," said Signor Joansmethe, proudly, "am the proprietor."

"Then," said Perkins, promptly, "you give me a horder, or you shan't come in. I knows what you want wery well; but it can't be done without me."

"Indeed!" said the signor, his dignity ruffled considerably. "But you will find out your error there, my lad."

"No, I shan't," replied Perkins. "I knows what my horders are, and I obeys 'em. Give me a pass, or you shan't come in! When the tother came the chief chap gave me a horder, and I talked over old Cobbem until he took every blessed kid into the best seats."

Signor Joansmethe opened his lips to express his doubt of the truth of this assertion; but ere he could speak he was astonished by hearing a loud smash, and young Perkins went over against the door-post like one smitten.

Then a form came forward, and in it he rightly recognised the Reverend Copley Cobbem.

"How do you do, sir?" said the signor, taking his hat off. "Glad to see you."

"What has this impudent boy been saying to you?" asked the reverend gentleman, with two eyes like stars in his head.

"I aint been saying nothing," said Perkins in a loud tone, "except ax for a horder, and I'm drove to that because you never give me no pocket money. Axing for a horder aint a thing to knock a boy's head off for."

"Go on," said the Reverend Copley. "Now, sir, your business?"

"I think, sir," replied the signor, "that I will leave a few prospectuses, and call at a more convenient hour."

"I think you had better do so," was the reply, and the signor, with another conciliating bow, handed out a dozen circulars and retired.

In acting thus he showed much tact and discretion, for most assuredly if he had pressed the matter then, the Reverend Copley, in his irritated condition, would have declined to have anything to do with him or his. Two hours afterwards he called again and was received most graciously.

"My pupils, signor," he said, "have need of a little relaxation. What is your charge for the best seats?"

"Three shillings."

"I of course am admitted free and the boys come in half-price?"

The signor looked a little glum, and hesitated before answering.

"We shall come sixty strong," said the Reverend Copley.

"Well then, sir, we will say half-price," returned the signor. "Will you come afternoon or evening?"

"Afternoon, I think, and to-day."

The Reverend Copley wrote a cheque at once, and received a pass for all the school. Then he dismissed the signor, and went upstairs to book a seat to each of the boys at full price. Taking them to a circus was very profitable work.

Meanwhile Perkins, with a burning thirst to see the show upon him, and without a penny in his pocket to assuage it, turned the knife machine in a frenzied manner, vowing all manner of vengeance upon the signor and the Reverend Copley Cobbem, who, according to his wild reasoning, had between them ruined the prospect of a pleasant afternoon. In the midst of his sorrow and rage Billy Sharp came in, and heard of his grievance.

"If I was you," said Billy, "I'd take it out of Copley in some way."

"I can't," replied Perkins. "He wouldn't fight, and if he would where should I be?"

"I'd have the money to go somehow," said Billy.

"But how?" asked Perkins.

"I knowed a boy who was served infamously like you," said Billy, looking steadily at him, "and he took something—boots, I think it was—out of the house, and sold 'em to some gipsies in the lane."

"There's some gipsies in the lane now," gasped Perkins, "come down with the circus."

"Is there?" said Billy, innocently. "Well, that's odd—a cove-incidents I call it. Never mind, Perkins, perhaps you'll go to the next circus."

He left Perkins to himself, and for half an hour the knife machine was still. Perkins was in the throes of temptation, and he fell. A pair of short Wellingtons in good condition, and a pair of carpet slippers, were sold to an amiable old gipsey woman for fourteenpence. She asked no questions, and Perkins told no lies about them.

When the thing was done, repentance came upon him, and he went back to the old woman with the money, and asked, with tears in his eyes, for the boots; but she repudiated the purchase, vowed she had never set eyes on Perkins before, and set the dogs at him.

"I suppose they won't be missed," he muttered, as he went mournfully home, "and if they are it won't be for a long time. Who's to say I took 'em?"

A little thought brought him a fallacious feeling of security, and next he turned his mind upon the result of going to the circus without leave. This he decided would, at the worst, be only a thrashing, and he was too used to that sort of thing to trouble his mind about it. Go he would. Having gone so far it would be most cowardly to retrace his steps.

So he went, and when the Rev. Copley Cobbem, with the gravity of a man who only went to a circus for the benefit of the young, headed his school into the upper seats, which had a carpet over them, and were clear of the sawdust, he beheld in the front row, squeezed tight in the midst of a band of youths, Perkins, hot and noisy, yelling and shrieking with the best of them.

"That boy here," he exclaimed, "and without leave! I will dismiss him instantly."

While the school was settling down, he fished for the eye of Perkins, and at last caught it.

"Go home!" were the words the reverend gentleman shaped with his mouth, and waved his arm.

Perkins looked through him, but made no responsive sign.

"The impudent scoundrel!" muttered the Rev. Copley. "What shall I do with him?"

Again he signalled for Perkins to leave, and what was the reply that youth vouchsafed him?

A defiant one.

Most assuredly, and a vulgar one to boot, for like the little vulgar boy of Ingoldsby renown, he put his thumb up to his nose, and spread his fingers out.

What was to be done?

Would it be wise of the rev. gentleman to descend from the lofty attitude of the three shilling seats into the sixpenny ones to have a verbal and perhaps more violent contest with a boy? No, assuredly not. Better let him have his fling, and punish him afterwards.

The Rev. Copley Cobbem sat down, and shut his eyes, as far he could, to the presence of Perkins.

But it was impossible for him to utterly ignore the presence of so prominent a being.

Who took off a boy's cap and shied it into the ring, just as the first prancing steed was led in?

Perkins.

Who closed with the wronged one, and fought most valiantly, to the infinite delight of a crowded audience, rolling into the ring, locked in his opponent's arms, and stopping the first act for just half a minute?

Perkins.

And finally, who defeated the boy he had wronged and returned to his seat, which, having been filled up by sheer pressure from each side, necessitated another struggle, and much bandying of words, ere he could squeeze himself in again?

Perkins.

But who applauded loudest? Who gave encouragement to the author of this disgraceful scene?

The boys of Warmington school.

Yes, to a boy, they applauded most rapturously, and high above the din was heard the cry of "Go it, Perkins!" Even young Greene was seen to smile, and him the Rev. Copley fixed upon.

"Sit down, Greene," he said, giving him a push, "how dare you?"

"Shoved again," growled Jolly, dismally. "I aint done nothing."

"Don't be impudent to me—sit down," said the Rev. Copley; "pray consider you are with gentlemen."

Order being in a measure restored, the performance proceeded, and gave great pleasure to the lookers-on. Ladies in muslin did all sorts of feats on horseback, some of them of a most pathetic nature. Young Greene was quite overcome by the act of the "Lonely girl on the prairie," when she knelt down in terror at the approaching storm, and

prayed for shelter. Dick Stager saw the tears in his eyes, and asked him what he was up to?

"Oh! aint it lonely," said Jolly, "and isn't she nice?"

"Oh! come," said Dick, "we are not going to have that sort of thing. Now, softy, wipe your face and look pleasant."

Jolly wiped his eyes, and did his best to comply with the request; but he never was anything but dismal, and never could be. His laugh was the sort of thing to give one the toothache.

Act after act proceeded with varied applause. A man who ran about on the top of a globe was particularly popular, and Jolly was seen to beat his hands frantically. Billy Sharp, however, turned up his nose in disgust.

"That's easy enough," he said.

"Easy, is it?" replied Jolly, "I don't think you could do it."

"I've done it," returned Billy, "fifty times."

"I'd give anything if I could do it," said Jolly.

"Will you give me ten bob?"

"Yes, I will."

"Then, when we get home," said Billy, "I'll give you a lesson."

"But you haven't got a globe."

"Oh, yes, I know where to get one."

The conduct of Perkins at this time became unbearable. He not only struggled with those upon his right and left, but exchanged words of warfare with boys on the opposite side of the ring. A recklessness had come upon him, and he poured out challenges wholesale.

"Come on," he said, to a bullet-headed boy in a suit of faded green. "Come on. I'm ready for yer!"

The boy in green had done nothing to him, and he had done nothing to that boy. But one of those peculiarly instinctive aversions which make foes of men at first sight was upon them both, and could only be appeased with blood.

The ring was clear for a few moments, and no more.

"Come on!" cried Perkins.

"Half ways!" yelled the boy in green, and they rushed into the ring and closed.

Yells and cat-calls filled the show, and high above all rose the cry of—

"Go it, young Cobbem!"

Now, with reference to that cry it may be here remarked that when the Reverend Copley Cobbem showed an interest in young Perkins, and took him a workhouse orphan, beneath his roof, there were not wanting people to make sarcastic reference thereto, and base calumniators boldly asserted that, although the male parentage of Perkins was a mystery to most people, his mother having died in giving him birth, and no father named, it was none to the reverend gentleman. This report had come round to his ears long before, and hence the cry of "Go it, young Cobbem!" was particularly and peculiarly offensive.

"This must be stopped," said the Reverend Copley. "Words of admonition at least ought to be given. I will step round and see the proprietor of the circus."

"It was indiscreet of him to leave the school alone, for, as soon as he had disappeared, they descended en masse to get a nearer view of the fight, which was being carried on with great vigour. Perkins was approaching a second triumph, and the friends of the boy in green were going to his rescue.

"Come on!" cried Nick Stager. "Now, my lads, all down, and see fair."

All this happened so quickly that the authorities of the place had no time to interfere before the ring was crowded with the various supporters of the combatants, and then they found it no easy task to clear it.

Ring-master, ring-men, tumblers, and clowns, all

came to the mob, and met with resistance on every side. Blows were freely exchanged, but the men, as might be expected, prevailed. The boys retreated, all but young Greene, who, led away by the spirit of the hour, was engaged in a mortal combat with a clown.

It may be that the wrongs of years had told upon him at last, or it may be that for the time a new spirit was in him, but in either case he fought well, and in addition to having lamed Mr. Merryman with a kick in the shins, had got his wig off, and exposed his natural hair to the light of day.

To an ordinary clown this would have been an insult indeed, but when that clown is the proprietor of the establishment it becomes unbearable, and Signor Joansmethe, with his cranium revealed to the public eye, never felt more venomous in his life.

The absurdity of the struggle soon drew all eyes, those of other combatants included, upon the pair, and as young Greene, carried away by the demon within him, fought, and clutched, and kicked, and scratched, the enthusiasm of the lookers-on knew no bounds.

The humble servitors of Signor Joansmethe looked on aghast, and in the midst of the turmoil the Reverend Copley Cobbem returned, after a vain search for the owner of the show, to the arena.

His eagle eye took in all at a glance, and his natural intelligence pointed out to him how derogatory all this was to the gravity and decorum of Warmington College.

With one fierce leap he went through the circle round the ring, and rushed towards young Greene, bent upon inflicting chastisement upon him; but at that moment Jolly got clear of the furious signor, and beat a precipitate retreat.

The signor rushed forward, and fell into the arms of—

The Reverend Copley Cobbem.

Trumpets, pipers, and strings!—how deadly was that closing! The signor had got hold of something or somebody, and that was enough for him. He let out left and right, then right and left, and the reverend gentleman, with his long-lost college training roused within him, let fly back again.

It was a glorious fray.

Caps, hats, and walking-sticks were tossed into the air, voices grew hoarse with shouting, eyes gleamed, friends danced together, old enemies shook hands, and the joy was general. Such a scene as this had not been looked upon in the memory of the oldest inhabitant, who sat in a quiet corner of the booth, with a pint of nuts and two oranges in his right-hand waistcoat pocket.

"Hoop la!" cried the circus men. "Go it, signor."

"Bravo, Cobbem," shouted the boys, and a well-directed blow laid the signor on his back in the saw-dust.

"Call in the police!" he yelled. "Lock this feller up."

"Fellow yourself," replied the Rev. Copley. "You travelling tramp—you gimcrack performer. I'll have you locked up as a rogue and vagabond."

The signor had only one eye to look out of, but that shone like ten. The paint on his face was coming off in flakes from the heat raging within him. He would have got up and gone in again, but his worthy antagonist was dancing round him like a cork, and working his fists in a very scientific manner, calling upon him also to "come on."

This sort of thing could not go on for ever, and in a few seconds the Rev. Copley began to cool down, and getting sensible of his being in a public arena, he resumed his dignity, and addressed a few words to his fallen foe.

"If you or your low show ever come here again," he said, "I'll prosecute. Boys, fall in—we will go home. Perkins, leave this disgraceful scene, and follow me."

Perkins dared not disobey that voice, and a little

crestfallen, as most people are after a scene of excitement in which they have gone further than they intended, he got upon his feet and followed his master.

The school, in various stages of convulsion, got itself in order, and filed out, leaving the signor and his followers to entertain the rest of the public as best they could; but we may add, after what had happened, all their efforts were stale, flat, and unprofitable.

CHAPTER XXV.

A SPHERICAL PERFORMANCE.

ON their return to the college the boys were sent into the schoolroom to study, and Perkins received an invitation to visit the private room of the Rev. Copley. There he was, to use his own expressive words, "warmed up" with a flexible cane, and dismissed to the boot-hole, where he spent an hour in assuaging the agony of his wounds with a pat of butter surreptitiously obtained from the larder.

Study, of course, was out of the question, and in the schoolroom the one great topic was young Green's valiant fight with the clown Signor Joansmethe. For the time the unfortunate one was a perfect hero.

"How he come to do it I can't never think," said Billy Sharp, "for I niver thought it was in him."

"He's got more pluck than all the school together," said Bob Larry, a knowing-looking youngster, with a round face, and twinkling eyes. "It was the most scientific thing I ever saw."

"Unrivalled," said Nick Stager.

"How did you do it?" asked Dick.

"I don't know," replied Jolly; "all I know is that he hit me about, and shoved me frightfully. I'm all bruises, and like a jelly."

"Oh! but come, you mustn't mind your bruises," said Billy. "It was a great performance, and arter that you could do anything."

"Even the globe trick," suggested Dick.

"Oh! don't talk about the globe trick," said Jolly, "I'm so sore."

"Well, doing the globe trick won't make you any worse."

"I can't do the trick without a globe."

"I'll find the globe if you'll try it," said Billy. "Now, Jolly, what do you say? There's a clear run for you in the passage."

"I don't think I can do it," said Jolly.

"But suppose I teach you?"

"Well, I don't mind, but you mustn't let me fall, or I shall hurt myself."

"Fall!" said Billy, "never."

The desire to see some fun took possession of all, or perhaps Billy's little joke would have been spoilt. He was not much of a favourite, as we have said, but in the presence of a joke boys easily sink personal differences.

Billy speedily came back, rolling in front of him a solid globe with the map of the world printed thereon, which he had taken from the library. It was not one of the usual pasteboard things, but a good solid wooden affair, which had been in the family of the Cobbems for at least five generations.

"All outside," said Billy, "and be as quiet as you can."

The passage was speedily filled with two lines of expectant youths, and for once they were all quiet. At the end of the passage was a short straight staircase, at the foot of that the Reverend Cobbem's room, and any noise above the ordinary was likely to attract attention.

"Now, Jolly," said Billy, rolling the globe to the further end, "up and hoff!"

"But how am I to get on?" asked Jolly.

"Somebody help him," said Billy; "one on each side."

GREEN AS GRASS.

Dick and Nick Stager volunteered for this service, and Jolly was hoisted up.

"I can't stand here," he said, as his legs underwent a series of contortions. "I shall be down!"

"Keep him up," said Billy, firmly, "and I'll work the thing behind. "Now, steady it is, and on we go. Stand back, and silence!"

The start resulted in Jolly getting the ball ahead and having his legs at an angle, but Billy kept the ball rolling backwards and forwards, and Dick and Nick held him up, and so they got half down the passage to the great satisfaction of all.

"Can you do it alone yet?" asked Dick Stager.

"Oh! don't think of it!" groaned Jolly. "I shall come down at once."

"You'll never do it alone if you don't try," said Nick.

"This is horrible," moaned Jolly. "Let me come off—will you?"

"Not until you've done it alone. Not so fast, you pushing there. Give him a chance to distinguish himself. I say, Dick."

"Yes, Nick."

"I think he ought to try to perform alone."

"I shall fall and kill myself!" gasped Jolly. "Oh, do hold me! I had no idea it was like this. The man in the circus seemed to do it so easy."

At that very hour the Reverend Copley Cobbem, scarce recovered from his struggle in the arena, was seated in his private room at the foot of the staircase, studying Roman history and a glass of cold brandy and water. The latter was necessary after his recent exertions, and went far towards restoring him to his usual placidity of temper.

The evening was fine, and the window of his room looked out upon the west. There was the glory of the setting sun, and as he looked at the purple and golden clouds he swallowed his brandy and water, and felt at peace with all men.

"The night is fine," he said, and, as if to contradict him, there came a rumbling noise like distant thunder.

"Dear me," he said, rising, "from what direction is the storm coming?"

He went out by a private door into the garden, and looked around. Save in the west, there was not a cloud to be seen, and certainly nothing like an approaching storm.

Returning puzzled to his room, he sat down. "I must have been mistaken," he said, but immediately the rumbling sound came again.

"It's above," he said. "I have it! In the schoolroom. I will send Perkins up and stop it."

He rang the bell, and Perkins came very promptly, with traces of recent tears lingering about his eyes. At least half his usual defiant spirit was in the dust.

"Did you ring, sir?"

"I did. What noise is that in the schoolroom?"

"I don't know, sir. There aint no noise as I knows of."

"Don't be impertinent. I hear it, and that's enough."

"But it aint in the schoolroom, sir. It's in the passage."

"Well, what is it?"

"I don't know, sir. I only heard it as I come along."

"Go and see what is doing then."

Perkins bowed with mingled pride and humility, and went out. The next moment he was heard shrieking.

"Good heavens!" exclaimed the Rev. Copley, "What is it? Thieves, burglars, fire, or what?"

He ran hurriedly out, looked up, and beheld, to his amazement, a round opaque body, with a sylph-like form upon it, flying through the air. Visions of Mercury, as he had seen that god in pictures, came into his mind, but ere they took a definite form the opaque object was on him, and he was sent flying back into the passage, breathless and bewildered.

Perkins, at the foot of the stairs, uttered a wild shriek, and other voices lent their aid to the confusion. The Rev. Copley, feeling he was the victim of some practical joke, thrust forth his arm, grasped something like tow, and held on with a deadly grip.

His mind was chaos for awhile. Sounds like shrieks of despair, and the rushing noises of demons filled his ears, but he could make out nothing definite for awhile. When he came round a little he found himself lying on his back, holding young Greene by the hair of his head, and close by lay the globe which had been familiar to him from his boyhood.

What did it all mean?

He could not say, and, therefore, like a wise man, he asked the only person who was in a position to offer him any information.

"What new foolery is this?" he asked. "Speak, you idiot!"

But all young Greene could answer was "Oh! my poor head" and "Where's mar?"

"I'll get at the roo tof this," said the Reverend Copley, sitting up. "Speak, or I'll strangle you."

"I don't know anything; I don't know anybody," replied Jolly. "Take me home."

"He is not alone in this," said the Reverend Copley, darting into his room, returning with a cane in his hand, and rushing upstairs with the activity of a harlequin.

He was so quick that quite a host of legs were struggling through a door at the end. He charged upon them and smote many, but the passage being in a dark part of the house he could not say who had been smitten.

They got through somehow, and he followed them upstairs.

The boys were half mad with pain, and took refuge wherever they could—some in odd rooms—some in cupboards, and one boy of timid nature ran right up to the top of the house and plunged into the cistern. Fortunately it was nearly empty.

"I'll kill some of them," said the reverend gentleman, dancing about the upper corridor when it was clear. "I can stand no more of it. I wish I could have seen who they were, and taken their names. I believe I saw the two Stagers."

This was true, and they had taken refuge in a room fraught with much peril, of which more in another chapter.

The rest had got into places of comparative safety.

Returning to the hall the Reverend Copley saw Jolly Greene still in the same position upon the ground, and made another effort to extract information out of him, but it was all in vain.

"Go to your room," he said, at last, "and remain there until I send for you."

Jolly, really very much shaken by his recent flight downstairs, crept up to his room, and found Billy Sharp Popper behind the door.

"Well, Jolly," he said, furiously, "did you split, you little beggar?"

"Yes," replied Jolly, vacantly, "I'm split all to pieces."

"That isn't what I mean. Don't gammon me."

But Jolly was not gammoning. He could not give a clear reply, and Billy, after worrying him for awhile, let him alone, and helped him into bed.

Meanwhile Dick and Nick had got into a part of the house quite strange to them, where the furniture was superior to any they had seen there hitherto. In their hurry they forgot to note the door they entered by, and as there were several in the passage they were puzzled which to take.

"Let us try this," said Dick.

"I don't think it was that."

"No—it is fast. Here is another. Hallo! what a jolly bedroom!"

"Somebody's coming," said Nick, hurriedly. "In you go—if only for a moment! I think it is Cobbem with the cane."

Dick, without debating with himself upon the

propriety of the step he was taking, darted into the room. Nick followed him and closed the door.

CHAPTER XXVI.

A NIGHT OF HORROR.

AS Nick and Dick drew back from the bedroom door the footsteps outside drew near, and the voice of the Rev. Copley Cobbem was heard calling for Perkins. For a time he called in vain ; but anon the youth was heard to respond—

"Comin', sir!"

"Coming! Yes, and so is the millennium!" returned the reverend gentleman. "Why don't you keep your ears open?"

"So I does, sir."

"No, you do not."

"I does!" returned Perkins, doggedly.

"If you are impertinent to me I will box your ears."

"Box 'em, then !" replied Perkins. It aint nuffin new if you does."

Judging by the sounds which followed, the Rev. Copley endeavoured to carry out his threat without success. He dodged about the passage after Perkins with great perseverance ; but the boy was too nimble for him.

"I'll give it to you to-morrow!" he gasped, as he gave in. "I'll teach you to serve me in this way!"

"Wot next?" asked Perkins. "Do you want me to stand still and have my head knocked off?"

"Go and get me some hot water—do you hear?" said the Reverend Copley.

"Yes ; and don't you wish you may get it!" said Perkins.

"What new insolence is this?"

"The cook let the fire out hours ago, and she's gone to see her mother, who's took bad."

"Then ask Jiggles to light a fire."

"He's out, too—gone to see a friend of his at the White Hart."

"Was ever man so tormented as I am?" muttered the Reverend Copley ; "and all because Mrs. Cobbem chooses to go away for a month. Never mind, Perkins ; I'll do without the hot water."

Mrs. Cobbem—to whom we hope to shortly introduce our readers—was away, and the housekeeper ought to have looked after the domestics ; but she and her employer had been at loggerheads that morning, and she was out, too.

In no pleasant humour the Reverend Copley entered his bedroom, and banged the door behind him. The noise he made covered the slight scampering sound raised by Nick and Dick as they disappeared under the bed.

"That Perkins must be got rid of," said the reverend gentleman aloud, as he contemplated himself in the glass. "He gets more unbearable every day. What a dreadful mistake it was for me to take him as I did! But I thought a workhouse boy would come cheap, and having him for a term of years would, in a measure, bind him to me. I must have been mad, as it brought on me contumely, and ill-natured suggestions, and domestic sorrow. Bother, confound, d——ahem!—the boy! What's that?"

He paused, and looked round the room, as if he expected to see a ghost or some other awful visitant. There was nothing more than usual visible to the eye.

"I thought I heard a smothered laugh," he muttered ; "but it could only have been fancy."

Slowly, and with much care, he proceeded to undress. Each article, as he took it off, was folded and put into a certain place, and fully half an hour passed before he was ready to get into bed.

Even then he lingered with the extinguisher in his hand, musing as he looked upon the candle.

"Mrs. Cobbem is a self-willed woman," he said. "She comes and goes as she pleases, and she never consults me. She is a gadabout is Mrs. Cobbem—

a vain frivolous woman ; but—she is young! I ought to have married an older woman. Too late to think of that now. Well, I really must— Ha! that laugh again—just outside the door! It's that Perkins. I will stop his nonsense at once. I'll open the door and pounce upon him."

Stealthily as a cat in expectation of surprising a mouse the Reverend Copley crept towards the door, opened it quietly, and made a grasp at a figure dimly defined in the gloom of the corridor.

"How dare you?" he cried, shaking the figure furiously. "This gross impertinence shall end in your dismissal. Take that, and that! Now, then!"

"What's this for? Oh, dear! I'm always being knocked and shoved about!" exclaimed a voice which was not that of Perkins.

"Why, it's young Greene!" exclaimed the Reverend Copley, and, suddenly becoming aware that he was hardly in the sort of apparel in which a teacher of the young ought to appear in public, he darted back into his bedroom, and held conference with Jolly through an opening six inches wide.

"What are you doing here?" he asked.

"I don't know," replied young Jolly. "I'm all wrong—I'm going quite mad! Where's my mar?"

"Go at once to your room!" said the reverend gentleman, and, for the want of knowing something better to do, he thrust forth his arm, and shook his fist at him.

"But I don't know the way to my room," said Jolly, pitifully.

"Find it, you young imp—find it, or—or—I'll be out again in ten minutes, and teach you the way!" was all the reply given him, and the door banged to.

Jolly Greene, in a state of great mental distress, wandered off, whining—

"I've lost everything and everybody! I can't find my room, and I don't know where my mar is!"

The Reverend Copley Cobbem was in a great heat, but he had no intention of dressing himself to have another interview with young Greene. Jumping into bed he rolled the things about him and tried to get a sleep.

But a man of his nature, when excited, could not expect to find the balmy. He turned this way and he turned that, he counted thousands, he thought of sheep going through a gate and tried to count them, and all the time he was occupied in this way two boys—Nick and Dick Stager—were lying under the bed as quiet as mice and scarcely daring to breathe.

At last the cramp set in—Dick got it first. The pain was excruciating, but he tried to get rid of it by quiet rubbing. Cramp is an obstinate thing, and generally will not retire unless the possessor of it walks about.

How was Dick to walk about?

It was out of the question, and manfully did that boy bear the pain until it mastered him, and his right leg went up with a convulsive twitch, the foot striking the old-fashioned sacking which formed the bottom of the bed.

He struck just under the spot where the Rev. Copley lay as that gentleman was settling into sleep. It acted like a galvanic shock, and he was awake instantly.

"What's that?" he asked himself, and the hair of his head began to rise slowly. "The bed was shaken. Is the land visited by an earthquake?"

A low scraping noise under the bed fell upon his ears, and his hair—which had been slowly sinking—went up in a moment, stiff as a wire broom.

"Something under the bed," he said. Then came a happy thought. "It must be the cats."

"Hish! hish!" he said, but made no attempt to get out of bed. Only just the tip of his nose was visible over the counterpane after he had spoken.

The noise he made had some effect, for the scraping sound ceased ; but in a minute or so it began again, and increased in power. Both Nick and Dick were suffering from the cramp, and the

GREEN AS GRASS.

A JOLLY SCHOOL STORY.

YOUNG GREENE FORMS ONE OF A FISHING PARTY AND IS NEARLY TRANSFORMED INTO A MODERN JONAH.

agony upon them was a little more than they could bear.

In addition to the scrapings there were whispers. The Rev. Copley Cobbem heard them, although he could not distinguish the words; but what was said is here written—

"I'm half dead," said Nick. "All my bones seem twisted the wrong way."

"I'm red-hot about the body, and cold as ice in the legs," said Dick. "Oh!"

"Don't make that row."

"I must. Oh! let us get out of this, and run for it."

"You go first, and I'll follow."

"I've forgotten," said Dick; "to the right, I think."

"No, the left. Hush! he's speaking. Keep quiet, will you?"

"If—if there is anybody in—in—the room," said the Reverend Copley Cobbem, in quavering tones, "it—would—be as—well—for them to get out of it as quickly as possible, as I've pistols here—ahem!"

Nick and Dick lay quite still, but both were cold. The notion of pistols was very unpleasant.

"There is not much of value in the room," pursued the Reverend Copley; "but—if—anybody wants it—they can take it—and go. My watch is on the dressing-table—and my purse is on a chair."

No answer, and the cramp having subsided a little, the boys were able to lie quite still.

Silence reigned for five minutes, and the reverend gentleman was beginning to think he had been the victim of fancy. He grew bold, and put his head and an arm out. He also felt about for the pistol, which he really had in a leathern pocket by the side of the bed. It was an old affair, which had been loaded quite five years before. Whether it would go off he could not tell. It was as much as he knew how to fire it.

Pistols were not quite in his line. He fired one once when he was a boy, on the occasion of a public celebration of the battle of Waterloo; since that time he had not touched guns or gunpowder. It was Mrs. Copley who insisted upon keeping that weapon, and with her own fair hands she had loaded it.

As the conviction that he had made a mistake grew stronger the worthy schoolmaster grew bolder. Firmly believing he was addressing the empty air he sat up in the bed and poured out further threats.

"I give you," he said, "ten seconds to get out of the room. I am a splendid marksman, and can hit anything in the dark as well as in the light. I never missed anything I fired at yet—ahem!"

"Do you think he'll fire?" whispered Nick.

"Anyhow," replied Dick, "we had better get out. Take off your boots and carry them in your hand."

Getting off boots is not a very difficult process in ordinary life, unless the boots happen to be uncommonly tight, but tight or loose it is not an easy matter when you are lying on the flat of your back, and have the bottom of a bed within a few inches of your nose.

Nick tilted up his right foot, and Dick tilted up his left, and at it they went.

Both wore elastic sides, which was an unfortunate thing under the circumstances, for a laced boot with the laces undone would have come off without a struggle, but the elastic was another style of thing, and as soon as it was stretched the boots began to creak and groan.

The Reverend Copley heard it, and grew cold. He put his hand out, and laid it upon the pistol.

"In self-defence," he gasped, "I must use it! There are burglars under the bed."

Having got hold of the weapon the next thing to know was what to do with it. The trigger he was aware had something to do with the letting off, and it was a proper thing to take hold of the butt.

Thus far he was all right, and having got it into position he uttered a last trembling threat.

"I'm just—going," he said, "to fire under the bed."

"Come out," said Dick; "he'll do it."

And with as little noise as could be expected they both crept out, side by side, and lay down in the dark by the bedside.

"Which way, now?"

Dick was certain the door was one side of the room, and Nick was positive it was the other; but Dick was the guiding spirit, and Nick, with a pressure of his hand, intimated he was prepared to follow him.

They got half way across the room on their knees, and then Dick ran into a tin pail, and upset it with a crash.

The Reverend Copley, who had been fingering the trigger in the most gingerly manner, gave it a sudden pressure, and off it went, sending the shot with which it was charged into the water jug.

Having achieved this feat the worthy man fell out of bed, and at the top of his voice—and what a voice he had!—began to roar—

"Murder!—fire!—thieves!"

"Come on," said Dick, "we must bolt. Keep up, Nick. Here's the door."

And opening what he fancied was the door to let them out he bolted in, and Nick followed him, but immediately he discovered he had made an error.

"This won't do," said Dick. "This is a cupboard. Get out again."

"Too late," replied Nick. "There's a mob of people coming into the room."

And so there was, a veritable mob of frenzied people, headed by the German professor, who had been smoking in bed, and had been the first to come to the rescue.

"Vat—vat shall be ze matters? Oh, vere shall ze pad tieves be?"

He was armed with a long pipe, smoking, and a poker. Behind him was Jiggles with a carving knife, next to him Perkins with a bootjack, and in the rear a long array of domestic servants and boys—all in a state of dress more suited to a private than a public life.

"Stop them!" gasped the Reverend Copley. "Stop them!"

"Vere shall they be gone?" was the question asked by the German.

"They are in the room now. Search the place. But first," said the Reverend Copley, rising in great haste, "bid the female domestics retire."

These fair maids required very little pressing, as, realising their position, they turned and fled.

The boys, however, remained, with Master William Sharp and his friend, Jolly Greene, in the foreground. Master Sharp was especially interested, as he took a lively interest in burglars in general.

"Shall ve sarch ze room?" asked the professor.

"Yes," said the Reverend Copley. "And, first, let us look under the bed."

They looked, and saw nothing there worth finding, which relieved the Reverend Copley Cobbem, who had put on a dressing gown to carry out the work. They next looked into the fireplace, and then up the chimney—nothing there.

"They are not behind the curtains," he said, shaking them. "I fancy they must have escaped. It only remains for us to look into this cupboard."

He threw open the door, and there was, apparently, nothing in it but a variety of clothing, the property of Mr. Cobbem, hanging upon pegs. As the idea of anybody being behind them was supremely ridiculous the Reverend Copley closed the door with a sigh of relief, and declared the burglarious visitants must have left by the door.

"The house," he said, "must be searched. Jiggles, go and do it, and I will remain here to receive your report. Perhaps, professor, you will remain with me. I have some little affairs to talk over with you, which may as well be talked over, as I am kept for a time from my rest."

"I shall be delighted," said the professor.

"And you boys get to bed at once. There is no occasion for further alarm. You may sleep in peace."

The boys made their bows and retired. Jiggles remained behind, a little exercised in his mind.

"May I ax, sir," he said, "if I am to go round this house alone?"

"Yes, of course," said the Reverend Copley, surprised. "Why not? Are you afraid?"

"I ham," replied Jiggles, with great emphasis, "and so would any man be."

"Pooh—pooh! nonsense!" said the reverend gentleman. "This fear is very childish—unbecoming. Go and do your duty like a man."

Jiggles made no response to this, but went out with a dogged face. He was absent about half an hour, and returned with the intelligence that he had searched all over the house, and found—nothing. His search, however, extended no further than the landing, where he passed the time in fear and trembling. As for going over the house it had never been his intention from the first.

"I'll see old Copley further fust," he said, and he kept his word.

CHAPTER XXVII.

THE AWFUL NIGHT CONTINUED—YOUNG GREENE SEES A GHOST.

"SO far all is well," said the Reverend Copley Cobbem to the professor, when Jiggles had given in his report and retired. "But somebody has been here; the overturned pail proves that, and the question is, where are they?"

"I do not tink dat purglars have been here," said the professor.

"What then could it be?"

"Ze cats."

"Why, of course it might have been. How odd! I thought so at the time, but fired my pistol as—as a precaution."

"Ah! zes so. But see, Mister Cobbem, dis is how it vas. Ze cats shall be under ze beds—scratch—scratch—and zen as you tell me a leetle vile pack, you call on zem to come out. Zey come, run again ze bail—so like ze cats—and in ze creat fight grunch down by ze vasherstand; zen ven ze door shall open zey rush out, and you shall see zem no more."

"You have hit it," said the Reverend Copley. "But in case the—the cats should come again I think I will burn a light."

"Ah! it shall be vise."

"Good night, professor!"

"Coot night, Mistair Cobbem!"

The German waddled out, and went back to his own room to finish his pipe in peace. The Rev Copley Cobbem lit a candle—a very long one, and got into bed again, but not to sleep. Ah, no! cats were all very well as a theory, but they scarcely fitted in with all the facts.

"Dick," said Nick in the cupboard, "I must come out from behind these clothes; I'm nearly stifled."

"So am I," said Dick. "But come out quietly, as all is not safe yet."

"Is he asleep yet?"

"Who?"

"Mr. Cobbem."

"I don't know. There's a light burning; I can see it through the keyhole."

"Shall I have a peep?"

"Yes, do. But mind those hat-boxes we blundered over as we came in."

Dick went cautiously to the keyhole and peeped through. He could just see the interesting countenance, or as much of it as peeped above the bed clothes, of the Reverend Copley Cobbem, and he was apparently sound asleep.

"He's quiet enough," said Dick.

"Do you think we might venture out?"

"Not yet, Nick."

"I can't wait much longer; I'm nearly dead with the heat of this hole."

Meanwhile the boys for the most part had retired to bed, and, after talking over the disturbance, had fallen asleep. In the dormitory where Nick and Dick slept they were missed, and many comments made upon their absence, but it was thought they had slipped out on some wild spree or another. Nobody associated their absence with the alarm about burglary.

Two boys were, however, very wide awake. Master Sharp and his friend Greene had, it is true, retired to their private apartment, but not to sleep. Master Sharp was restless. The very word "burglar" had aroused some half-dormant instinct within him, and the feeling which comes over a man in a strange land when he hears of some of his own countrymen being in the neighbourhood, was upon him.

"I say, Jolly, did you hear that?"

"Hear what?" asked Jolly, who was sitting on the bedside, dozing.

"Burglars been here. I wonder whose lot it is?"

Jolly Greene did not answer him—he was dozing; but Master William aroused him with a pinch.

"Wake up, will you?" he said. "I never did see such a beggar to sleep."

"That's what I came to bed for," replied Jolly.

"Did you? Then you will not go to sleep just yet. I want you to come round the house with me, and see if we can find 'em."

"Find the burglars!" exclaimed Jolly, looking, as well he might, considerably staggered.

"Yes; but only to look at 'em, and see if— But, there, are you ready?"

Jolly Greene, in mortal terror, sank down upon his knees.

"Don't take me near the burglars!" he pleaded. "They'll murder me!"

A scornful laugh escaped the lips of Master William Sharp.

"Murder you!" he said. "They are not such fools. All they want is swag, and if we don't interfere with 'em, they'll be only too glad to get away without touching us."

But Jolly was not prepared to go. He had heard of burglars under the parental roof, and the pictures drawn of them there had been always the same—square-set, beetle-browed, murderous rascals, thirsting more for blood than plunder. In his way he explained this to his friend William, who was much amused thereat.

"That sort of thing," said Billy, "is gone out. Burglary is redooced to a science—a reg'lar perfession, such as only a gentleman of means can hope to get on in. You must be up in the fine harts—have a knowledge of society—be as good as a walking guide to the aristocracy—or you won't make enough to keep you in tooth powder. No, Jolly—the old sort of thing is done with, and a low burglar aint got no more chance of a livin' than a chap who has never learnt his letters have of gettin' the post of hediter of the *Times*."

This learned discourse, delivered with great fluency and rapidity, was thrown away upon Jolly Greene, who was quite limp at the thought of going about a house where burglars were known to be at such an hour; and, as far as even the brave William was concerned, it may be said he was in no hurry to go alone.

But go he would, and as poor companionship was better than none, he was determined Jolly should go with him.

"Wake up, will you?" he said, hauling up Jolly by the collar. "Come along!"

"Oh! don't, please!"

"If you 'owl like that you'll bring the burglars on you. Have you got your boots off? I see you have. Now, keep by me—hold on to my jacket, and don't you open your mouth unless you want to leave this wicked world behind you."

So they crept out of the room. Billy Sharp closed the door, and with careful steps they threaded their way down the passage—Billy turning his footsteps towards the Rev. Copley Cobbem's room.

It is now time to return to the two young gentlemen in the cupboard, who were in what may very reasonably be called "a fix." In the first place, that cupboard was for some reason a little hotter than cupboards usually are, and in addition to its ordinary heat, there was an assemblage of stuffy garments, quite sufficient to make any shut-up place quite tropical. Furthermore, they were heated by the exciting nature of their position, and finally they were awfully tired and horribly sleepy.

"Do you think he is asleep?" asked Nick, after they had taken about a dozen surveys of the reclining figure of the rev. gentleman.

"He may be, and he may not; at all events, he is still," replied Dick.

"Then let us get out of it."

"Steady. If we are bowled out in this business we shall get it very warm indeed. I've got an idea."

"So have I, Dick."

"Listen to mine, and don't shuffle your feet about, unless you want to bring the house down upon us again."

"I beg pardon, old fellow, go on."

"Take down one of those dresses—skirts I think the women call them, and shove it over your head. Leave an opening big enough to see through, and follow me. The right door is on the other side—let us make for it—quietly, if he is asleep—as hard as we can if he is awake."

"But then I don't see how that will help us."

"Oh! Nick, Nick, my brother, can't you see that with these things about us we are disguised from head to foot? Here's one, I can tell by the feel, that is a good stout material. Here, let me help you. Now, is it over?"

"Yes, but I can't breathe."

"There's an opening at the top—put your mouth to it. Now."

"All right," said Nick.

"Can you see?"

"Oh, yes! I've got my eye on the key-hole."

"Then wait a moment, and I'll be ready."

Dick, rapidly and quietly, got inside another dress or skirt, and pushed open the door a few inches.

"Ready, Nick?"

"Yes," was the soft reply, given in a tone rather lacking confidence. But that was excusable. The hour was a very trying one.

The Rev. Copley Cobbem was not asleep, but his eyes were closed. Not that he was at all afraid—oh, dear no, for had he not shown a courage passing that of common men?—but he was thinking of deep and learned subjects, such as wise men love, and mingling them up, as the strongest and bravest are apt to do, with the recent events of the evening.

Burglars, perhaps, were uppermost in his ideas.

He was dwelling upon the accounts of various burglaries he had heard and read of in his lifetime, and, as a matter of course, dished up those in which violence had figured considerably. The bare contemplation of one in which all the household were slain was sufficient to set him shuddering, and, involuntarily, he opened his eyes.

"To look on—what?

Two horrible ghastly headless forms stealing softly across the room. Two awful shadows that would, if they had visited Richard the Third, have settled the business of that royal personage, and spared the mighty Richmond a tough half hour's fighting.

Having got his eyes open the Reverend Copley could not shut them again, but wide and staring they looked upon the midnight visitors, who, stealing along so silently, could not be reckoned to belong to this world.

They advanced towards the door, and could have got out and gone away without let or hindrance but for that blessed tin pail, over which the foremost ghost suddenly went right upon its shadowy nose.

"Get up and run," cried the second ghost, and made straight for the door.

In a moment the Reverend Copley Cobbem was like Richard the Third—when he got over his fright—himself again.

The voice that spoke was youthful, and, although he could not call to mind the name of its owner, he knew it belonged to his establishment.

He leapt from his bed with a great cry. He did not call for a horse, but, stigmatising himself as an ass, he rushed upon the prostrate one struggling in the folds of a skirt.

Ghost number two, who had had just reached the doorway, saw the peril of number one, and, taking up the little mat outside, he aimed it with much dexterity at the head of the Reverend Copley.

It checked him in his wild pursuit, and he, in his turn, went over the piece of tin we have mentioned.

This saved ghost number one, and gave him time to get clear of the skirt and bolt into the passage, but ere he had half traversed it the Reverend Copley Cobbem, burning with a sense of deep and lasting injury, was in full cry behind them.

"Stop thief!" he cried.

"Come on," muttered Dick, as his brother came up with him. "Anywhere out of this! If he collars us you will have aching bones in the morning."

"I'm ready. Lead on," said Nick.

Dick opened the door at the end of the corridor, and his brother closed it so promptly that the Rev. Copley Cobbem, in his eager pursuit, came up against it like a battering ram, and knocked the lock off the door and the skin from his knuckles and knees.

But he laughed all light injuries to scorn, and, springing onward beheld two figures flying before him. One was stout and the other slim, but the stout one was swiftest in its movements, and the slim one barely tottered on. The Reverend Copley Cobbem gained ground, laid his hand upon it. It seemed to crumple up beneath his touch, and captor and captive fell together.

"I've got you," gasped the reverend gentleman, holding on with the grasp of frenzy, "and I mean to keep you."

"Oh, please, Mister Burglar, don't hurt me," said the captured one. "I didn't mean to come—indeed I didn't."

"Is it Greene?" asked the Reverend Copley.

"Yes, Mister Burglar, I——"

"Don't Mr. Burglar me. What do you mean by these tricks? Come back to my room, and explain yourself."

The fact was the heat of the chase was over, and the Reverend Copley was getting cold about the legs, so he went back to his room, and, having planted young Greene in a position suitable for examination, got into bed.

"Now," said he, "perhaps you will have the goodness to explain yourself."

CHAPTER XXVIII.

PERKINS IN THE THROES OF REMORSE.

IF the Reverend Copley Cobbem had asked Jolly to explain the laws that govern comets he might probably have got some sort of answer, but as he wanted an explanation from Jolly concerning himself the subject was a hopeless one. No answer was to be had.

Jolly was, in short, in a state of confusion—his mind was chaos, and giving an explanation—at all times a great tax upon his mental powers—was now an utter impossibility.

"I ask you," said the Reverend Copley, "to explain yourself. How came you here?"

The eyes of Jolly lit up with unwonted intelligence as the last words fell upon his ears. Here was something he could answer.

"Why, you brought me," he said, "by the collar."

"This," said the learned gentleman, ' is mere subterfuge—low prevarication, which a lad of your respectability and—and intelligence ought to be ashamed of."

"I thought you brought me," said Jolly, wearily, "but I don't know—I don't know anything. I'm all upside down. I wish I could go home to mar."

"Your mar be ——" said the Reverend Copley, and paused. "Your mar be—out of the way, this moment! But tell me what you were doing when I—I—met you—akem!"

"I was walking about."

"Why?"

"I don't know—only William Popper said ——"

"Good gracious! where can he be?" broke in a voice outside, which the Reverend Copley recognised as the property of Master Popper. "What a sad thing it is! Where can he be?"

"Is that you, Popper?" cried the rev. gentleman.

"Yes, sir. I'm looking for Master Greene—he's got out of bed, and is a-walking in his sleep, and I'm afraid something wrong will come of it. He'll be getting on to the parripidge, and break his neck, which would break my 'art, for I love him like a brother."

"Come in, Popper. Your friend is all right, as far as his bodily safety is concerned; but he has been playing pranks in my room."

Billy, in his night-shirt, and bearing a candle in his hand, came to the doorway, and bowed.

"Playing pranks, is he?" said he. "Then he's been unkimmon sharp over 'em, sir, as he haven't left the room ten minutes."

"Not left the room?"

"No, sir. We came down when you fired the pistol, and then we went up again. Master Greene was very tired, and lay down in his clothes. I tried to rouse him, and, as he wouldn't be roused, I left him for a little while, hoping as he would awake. Then I went to sleep myself, and, waking up, found he was gone."

"But does he walk in his sleep?"

"Done it at least once a week ever since he was born," replied veracious Billy.

Jolly did not deny it. If he had been accused of walking on his hands from his birth he would have said nothing. It was just possible he had walked in his sleep, or, just as likely, have walked in that way all his life. He never could remember having been perfectly awake.

"It is a strange story," said the Reverend Copley, musing; "but I will look into it in the morning. Take him away, and put him to bed. Close the door also. Good night, Popper!"

"Good night, sir," replied Billy, and, taking Jolly by the arm, he led him unresistingly away.

The Rev. Copley Cobbem, although he had not discovered the real author of the disturbance, was relieved of all ghostly and burglarious fears, and at last slept in peace.

The next morning the topic of conversation was the doings of the previous night. The boys who slept in the dormitory with Nick and Dick were well up in the history of the mystery, but like true lads they held their tongues, and a mystery to most it remained.

To none more so than to Billy Sharp and to Perkins. "For," as the latter remarked, "they've been here and took nothing"—a thing quite incomprehensible to Billy. The doors also were found locked in the morning, and no traces of footsteps were discovered outside—in fact, there was nothing to show that a stranger had been in the place, except the indisputable assertion of the Rev. Copley

Cobbem. He, like a wise man, kept to the burglary theory, as it would never do for him to admit he had been terrified and befooled by a pair of boys.

Perkins was in a very bad way indeed, for in the depths of his sinful mind he arrived at the conclusion that the strange visitors were ghosts, and he went about the house, both day and night, in a state of mind impe——ble to conceive or describe.

And you must understand the reason was Perkins was troubled in his mind, as he ought to have been, about those boots he had purloined, and when a boy or man has a sin of that sort on his mind his nerves are doubly and trebly sensitive. He sees an avenger in every shadow, a voice of admonition in every breath of mind, the creaking of a stair is the footstep of a pursuer, and the opening of every door announces the coming of the minion of the law.

When Perkins saw a policeman standing at the corner of the lane, watching the flight of a pigeon, he was certain he was waiting for him, and went miles round to get to the end of the village, whither he had been sent with a message. He lived in hourly terror of arrest, and, being blessed with a vivid imagination, he tried and committed himself to penal servitude for life a hundred times a day.

What would he have given to recall the fatal act? How far would he have walked to recover those boots? A wild idea of pursuing the old gipsy, and wresting them from her by main force, came upon him, but there was a stumbling block in the way of carrying out the thought. He did not know whither she had gone.

Perkins was wretched and forlorn.

He was sure he would be punished, and here was what he called "a blessed ghost" come to haunt him. He had not seen it yet, but he was sure it would pop in sooner or later, most likely when he was in bed, and he grew pale and thin with fear.

He likewise lost all interest in his business. The knives and forks were never properly cleaned, and the cook and Jiggles waged heavy war with him— a war of triumph, for he had lost all heart and could not retaliate.

They smote him hip and thigh, and he scarce turned upon them.

Perkins was completely bowed down.

The change caused the Reverend Copley to think the boy was ill, and for a moment the hope that he would die warmed within him, but a better feeling prevailing he gave Perkins enough jalap to prostrate a camel, which made him worse.

It was the third day after the midnight alarm when Master Sharp Popper, whose sharp eyes had seen the change in Perkins from the first, asked him what was the matter.

"I can't eat, drink, or sleep, for thinking of them boots," replied Perkins, dismally.

"What boots?" asked innocent William.

"Them boots as I stole and sold."

Immediately there came over William a glaze of horror. He held up his hand, and stood transfixed before Perkins, the image of amazement and grief.

"Stole and sold boots!" he exclaimed. "Who's boots were they?"

"Oh! come, none o' that," said Perkins; "you know all about it."

"I?—me?" exclaimed Billy, turning round. "Come—dash it!—you mustn't say that. I've a character to keep up!"

"You told me to take them," said Perkins.

Amazement and grief gave way to indignation.

William Sharp Popper became sternly remonstrative.

"You mind what you say," he said, "or I'll go to Mr. Cobbem and blow upon you"

"Oh, don't do that!" said Perkins, wearily. "He'd send for a policeman."

"But in a nateral course of dooty I ought to do it," said William, hovering between his sense of right and love for Perkins.

"I don't know as I cares much," said Perkins. "A chap can't die but once, and they may hang me if they like."

"If ever you are hung once," said Billy, "you would never want them to do it again. Now, just you listen to me. This is wery sad, and if I did my dooty I should call in a perliceman at once, but——"

"Oh! don't do that!" pleaded Perkins.

"I won't," said Billy, "but if I stands by you as a friend you must stand by me. I'm kep uncommon short of wittles here, and sometimes I feel as if I could eat a deal door—and that's how you can help me."

"I don't see it," said Perkins.

"Why, aint you got the right of entry to the larder?"

"I *can* get in sometimes."

"Then *do* get in, and get me something to save me from starvation."

"I'm sure to be found out," said Perkins.

"But if you are you won't find it so serus as t'other job. In one case it's a wolloping, and in t'other a prison!"

"Werry well," said Perkins, "I'll try. There's old Cobbem's bell ringing—I must be orf."

Rather glad to get out of the presence of Billy, he hastened into the presence of his master, who was making preparations to go out.

"Perkins," he said, "bring me a pair of boots. Those short Wellingtons I have not worn lately. Be as quick as you can."

But Perkins stood stock still and neither moved nor answered him.

CHAPTER XXIX.

MASTER WILLIAM SHARP POPPER COMES OUT AS A MORALIST.

THE hair of Perkins visibly and painfully stood up, his knees knocked together, and his eyes, usually of a retiring nature, came out and stood boldly in the light of day.

"What is the matter with the boy?" asked the Rev. Copley Cobbem; "get my boots at once."

"The short Wellingtons, sir?" said Perkins, in a hollow tone.

"Yes."

"Oh, sir," cried Perkins, falling down upon his knees, *I can't do it.*"

Now if he, Perkins, had been desired to slay a fellow-creature, or to leap from the top of the house, or to ride two or three times round the wheel of a water-mill, or any other dangerous or terrible thing, the Rev. Copley would not have been astonished at the pitiful declaration which fell upon his ears; but as the boy had only been requested to bring a pair of short Wellington boots, he may well be pardoned for considering his conduct incomprehensible.

"Not do it!" he said; " is the boy mad?"

"No, sir. Not if you was to give me twenty years to do it in."

"Perhaps you cannot find them."

"Oh, sir," returned Perkins, quivering with agony, "*they will never be found no more.*"

The reverend gentleman rose up, then sat down again, and tried to get his bewildered thoughts into something like order. What did all this mean? Had Perkins gone mad, or was it some new devlopment of his mendacious powers. Whatever it was must be known at once, and the Rev. Copley took a slender cane from the table and got upon his feet.

"Perkins," he said, "tell me what you mean. What have you done with my boots?"

Then Perkins told all, putting it rather hard upon Master William Sharp Popper as tempter, and giving a touching description of the remorse he had endured. No doubt the young imp was sorry, but there was the usual fault in his confession—it was not open and full, and he took refuge in the fact of his having been tempted.

To describe the feelings of the listener would require powers beyond the capacity of any living man. He was in that state which comes upon a man when incredibly awful things pass before his eyes, or are poured into his ears. He was the very personification of amazement, and the attitude he took up was particularly striking. It would have served as a model to a sculptor who wished to produce an Ajax who had defied the lightning, and was astonished to find that the electric fluid would stand none of his nonsense.

"Perkins, Perkins," he said, "pause a moment; let me be clear on one point. Do you mean to say that Master Popper instigated you to commit this horrible crime?"

"I'm ready for to swear that he did it," replied Perkins, fervently.

The Rev. Copley Cobbem rang the bell twice for Jiggles.

Jiggles, with a protesting face, appeared. With a boy in the house it was very hard for him to be called from the sweet seclusion of his pantry. But the look of stifled indignation changed to one of joy as he looked upon Perkins in tears.

"Jiggles," said the Rev. Copley, "send Master Popper here."

"Yes, sir," replied Jiggles, with alacrity, and went forth beaming with happiness.

"He's been and done something," he mused, as he sped along the passages, "and Master Popper is wanted for a witness. I wonder what it is, and I wonder if he'll be sent off."

Jiggles wondered all the way until he found Master Popper engaged in a game of knuckle down with young Greene, for coppers, in which he had everything his own way, and won at a rate leading up to the bankrupting of his opponent. Jiggles came up just in time to save Jolly from utter ruin.

"Master Popper, Mister Cobbem wants for to see you in his room."

Master Popper paused in the game and became troubled. There was but one purpose for which the youth of Warmington College were summoned there, and that was to receive a generally well-earned punishment. Billy had his faults, and although his conscience, as a conscience, was none of the keenest, he had something within which prompted him to be ever on the look-out for squalls, and be prepared to meet them.

"In his own room—eh?" said Billy.

"Yes," returned Jiggles. "Perkins have been up to something. He's been shedding pints of tears, and you are wanted for to witness against him."

The unholy and unbrotherly joy of Jiggles was painful to look upon, but Billy had no eye for that. All his thoughts were concentrated on himself. Keen as a razor, he grasped the situation in a moment, saw his peril, and trembled.

But only for a while. Billy speedily became himself again, and declared himself ready to attend. Only pausing to reckon up accounts with young Greene, and swindle him out of fivepence, he put himself under the escort of Jiggles, and was shown into the presence of the Reverend Copley Cobbem.

"Come this side, Popper, with your face to the light. Jiggles, you may go."

Fain would Jiggles have stayed; but it was not to be. He, however, planted himself at the key-hole, but as the key was in the lock, only heard enough to tickle the appetite of his curiosity, and leave him more hungry than ever.

"Now, Perkins, repeat your story," said the Reverend Copley Cobbem.

Billy, whose face was serene in its innocence, looked at the reverend gentleman and smiled. It was plain he did not know what a blow was coming.

But, as the story unfolded, the light of peace left him—amazement and horror distorted his features, and as Perkins finished he burst into tears.

JOLLY GREENE CAME UP FEET FIRST—WELL ELEVATED IN THE AIR—AND HIS BODY HALF FILLED WITH WATER.

"And this comes," he said, "of 'sociating with low boys, and trying to do 'em good. Oh! what will my father say? What will my dear friends say? Oh—oh—oh!"

"Popper, pray compose yourself!" said the Rev. Copley Cobbem, rather alarmed. "Of course I wish to hear your side of the story. Perhaps you can explain."

"I can, indeed, sir!" said Billy, and his eyes grew bright again. "I told him, sir, a story about a wicked boy who stole his master's boots—with a morial to it, showin' how punishment was sure to come of it—and now, after hearing it, Master Perkins——"

"Say Perkins. His name does not need any prefix," said the Reverend Copley.

"I forgot for a moment that he was a low boy," murmured Billy; "but, as I said, sir, how could he go to do sich a thing when all I wanted was to put him in the right way? Oh! it's dreadful!"

"I see—I see!" said the Reverend Copley, gently. "You meant well; but Perkins is a bad boy. Popper, you may go. Perkins, remain awhile."

Billy, with the air of one relieved from an unfounded charge, glided from the room, casting a look of lofty scorn at Perkins as he did so. The eyes of Perkins flashed fury in reply, but lost their lustre when the door closed and he was left alone with his outraged master.

There was music—of the cane—in the room that day, and tears, and supplications, and much capering to and fro, and finally there came forth a boy with a limping gait, and hands employed in rubbing such parts of his anatomy as had been assailed.

To the boot-hole he hied and thither presently came Master William.

Closing the door, he put his back against it, and regarded Perkins with a venomous eye. Perkins tried to look back with defiance; but he lacked the brazen nature which the life in London had given to the other, and his eyes fell.

"You are a beauty—aint you?" said William, scornfully.

"I was took aback by being asked for them Wellingtons," replied Perkins.

"Took aback! Why wasn't I took aback?" said Billy, contemptuously. "But I see I shall never be able to make a pal of you, and I've come to say that I don't want nothin' more to do with you, not here nor nowhere else; so keep yourself to yourself. Do you hear?"

"Yes," said Perkins, meekly; and Billy, with another scornful glance, left him.

"But I don't care," said Perkins to himself when he was alone. "I'm glad I was found out; I'm glad I was whopped; and I don't want nuffin to do with him, and I won't steal never no more."

* * * * * *

There was a boy at Warmington who had gained quite a reputation for kite-making. He seemed to have an instinctive knowledge of the proportions, the weight of the tail, and all things necessary for a successful ascent of the same, as the kites he made never hung fire, or pitched, or performed any of the well-known antics, but went straight up and away in a respectable even manner.

The name of this boy was Christopher Cobble, generally a silent meditative boy—bound to be a philosopher one day, and to astonish the world with chemical sights and sounds and smells—a giver of lectures, an expounder of the past and promoter of new ideas, a star of a period, a guide to the blind, a leader into the ditch of a new and infallible settlement of the working of creation.

In the silence and solitude of his bedroom he made these kites—in the open air, before his fellow-boys he sent them aloft—some fair to look upon, with angel features on their faces, and others with demon-like expression. All shapes and sizes—birds, beasts, and fishes—each in their turn represented in the wonderful productions of Christopher Cobble.

Young Greene took a great interest in the kite-making, and oft, when his heart was sad, stole away, and asked the permission of the kite maker to sit by and watch the building of the same.

"You may come," said Cobble, "if you don't alk to me. I can't stand fellows who jaw—jaw all the time they are with me. They upset my calculations."

Jolly promised to be silent, and kept his word. By the hour together he would watch the putting together of a frame, the pasting in of the paper, the painting, and the general fitting up of these aërial toys; and he and Cobble were often out together in the green fields, sending them up almost to the clouds, and watching their wings fluttering in the wind, with an ecstasy only known to the inborn kite-flyer.

But even in this they could not let Jolly alone. One day Master William and the two Stagers formed members of a flying party, and the former surreptitiously fixed a fish-hook upon the tail of a huge kite, and quietly attached it to Jolly's nether garments.

"Are you ready?" shouted Cobble from afar.

Jolly held up his arms to signify that he was.

"Then let go!" cried Cobble.

Up went the kite with a bound, and Jolly felt himself whirled round, and hoisted a few inches in the air. A mighty lot of cracking and tearing went on behind, and then a huge patch of the most important part of his attire went up to the clouds.

"Oh, dear!—oh, dear!" gasped Jolly, "even a kite can't let me alone. I'm always having my clothes torn. How shall I get home?"

"Sit down until we get the bit back," said Billy, "and then we will patch it on with pins."

Jolly backed to a hedge, and sat down upon some nettles. With a bound he sprang forward, and ran across the field like a dog with a kettle at the end of his tail, and charged blindly at Cobble, whom he upset. The string broke, and the kite, set free, settled down upon a tree-top.

The bearings of that tree were taken, but the trunk was too tall and straight, and its lower branches too high for climbing, so the kite was left to the crows, who pulled it to pieces, and retired to their nests with the softer part of it. As for Jolly, they made him an apron of dock leaves, and took him home by quiet ways. Christopher was very wroth, and vowed he should never go out with him again.

But Christopher was a kindly-disposed boy, and relented towards Jolly, as we shall see anon.

CHAPTER XXX.

MRS. COPLEY COBBEM TURNS UP AND TAKES SEVERAL PEOPLE DOWN.

"DEAR COPLEY,—I return to-morrow by the 6.45 train. Meet me.—Yours affectionately, AGATHA." The above was the simple epistle that put all Warmington College into commotion. In the first place it gave the Reverend Copley a palpitation of the heart, for the end of peace was at hand and trial and tribulation were returning to him; and in the second place the servants—from Jiggles downwards—knew that a new Reign of Terror was coming upon them.

Mrs. Cobbem was, in short, a woman not to be trifled with. If she did not say all she meant, she always meant what she said; and, when bent upon pursuing a certain course, woe to those who barred her way!

In the early stage of matrimony, when the moon was of honey, the Reverend Copley, relying upon his power as a *man*, ventured to thwart her, and he went under—so far under that he had never since returned to the surface. When, at the expiration of the said moon, Mrs. Cobbem came to Warmington College to take possession thereof—a blushing month-old bride—the servants one and all tried to take advantage of her inexperience; they went under too. Even the housekeeper—stout, formidable, and immovable with the world in general—was never fairly on the surface when Mrs. Cobbem was by. What Mrs. Cobbem said was right—what Mrs. Cobbem desired to be done was carried out forthwith.

The housekeeper was a sane woman, and only mad people kick against the pricks. When the hand of real unswerving authority is over us we had better bow before it. Bend the neck, my friends, lest it be broken.

Some of the boys knew Mrs. Cobbem well; others had the pleasure of looking forward to her acquaintance. The general opinion of her qualities may be found in the words of Tommy Whisker—of whom more anon—who, on being asked by William Sharp what sort of personage she was, tersely gave answer, "She's a hot un."

"And you had better keep out of her way," said Tommy, turning to Jolly Greene, "for she don't like your sort."

"I don't care whether she does or not," replied Jolly; "but, whichever way it is, she is sure to shove me about—everybody does it."

Tommy—who was fair, fat, and fourteen—simply repeated his warning.

"You keep out of her way," he said—"that's all."

There were many signs in the house of the coming of a master spirit. The Reverend Copley dressed himself with great care and personally superintended the arrangement of the furniture in the drawing-room. Jiggles, with his own hands, polished the door-bell handle and rubbed up the brass knocker until all creation was reflected in it. The cook prepared toothsome dishes, and Perkins rummaged out from odd corners a dozen pairs of lady's boots—some stout, some thin, some of cloth, and some of leather—and cleaned them up to such a point of perfection that any eye less practised than that of a bootmaker would have bought them for new.

About five o'clock in the afternoon the odd man—who, led away by the feeling of the hour, had put a flower in his button-hole, to cover the fact that he had been drunk overnight, and been taking refreshers all day—brought round the pony carriage, and the Reverend Copley Cobbem, with shawls and rugs, and an umbrella in case of rain, took his seat therein.

Even the pony—a sluggish beast, all rump and head to the passing eye—seemed to know who was coming home, and without waiting to be whipped over the back or under the ribs, or dug in the haunches with the ferrule of an umbrella—forms of stimulation generally bestowed upon him—broke into a shambling trot, and went straight to the station without stopping at the public-house half-way, which he usually did, to the great scandal of his respectable master; but that was the fault of the odd man, who generally drove to the station to meet the friends of his master, and, being a man of weak mind, could not resist a half-way beershop.

All the new boys were in a fever to see their mistress, knowing how much depended upon her love and goodwill. A kind mistress of the house meant good dinners; a stingy, cross-grained one, would pour upon them leather puddings and resurrection pies, without reckoning a thousand minor evils.

Behold them then, at six o'clock, at the head of the stairs looking upon the hall, gathered in a cluster, with Jolly Greene well in front, although he scarcely knew he came there.

In the hall Jiggles and Perkins, in their best, and the housekeeper in the breakfast-room, ready to pop out and give smiling welcome.

A sound of wheels, and Jiggles is at the door. A crush upon the stairs above, and the voice of Jolly.

"Oh, don't crowd so, or I shall be shoved down! Oh, don't!"

The carriage arrives and pulls up. Jiggles throws open the door, and then enters—a woman with dark hair, a slight moustache, and eyes like gleaming spear-heads. These are the three most noticeable things about her. Over all a bonnet, which, like Rome, was never built in a day, or in a week either.

As she enters she turns to Jiggles and spears him up against the wall with a look.

"Have you cleaned that epergne?" she asked.

Jiggles has not cleaned it—he has, in fact, forgotten it, and would gladly now say that he has done so, and sit up all night to redeem the error, but the shade of guilt upon his countenance is seen and read.

"You have not done so, I see. I will talk to you by-and-bye. Is that you, Perkins?"

There is some excitement at the stair head as Perkins, with pallid face, stands forward, and the voice of young Jolly is heard imploring—

"Don't shove so."

"Yes, it's me, mum," says Perkins.

"Have you been quarrelling with the cook? Have you burnt a hole in the new baize apron I gave you, and do you still waste your time playing marbles under the sink?"

Perkins, like Jiggles, cannot lie before the great presence. He attempts a feeble apology, and receives a box on the ears that turns him twice round, and seats him in a giddy state upon the hall chair.

Great excitement on the stair-head, and the voice of Jolly is plainly heard.

"I shall be shoved down. Oh, don't!"

And now the housekeeper, who, with a discretion passing that of womankind, and far beyond her years, had waited until Mrs. Cobbem had expended her heaviest shots upon the lower domestics, comes sidling out of the breakfast-room smiling like a cherub. Her heart is evidently glad, she rejoices in the return of her mistress, but in a moment all her joy is scattered to the winds.

"You bought the last lot of blankets at Smith's," says Mrs. Cobbem; "if you had gone to Brown's you could have had them two shillings cheaper. Such extravagance is enough to ruin any house."

"Indeed, ma'am! I looked at Brown's blankets, and I thought——"

"Thoughts are all very well in their place," says Mrs. Cobbem. "Copley, my dear."

Mr. Cobbem, who has been meekly directing the odd man where to place the luggage, turns smilingly to his wife, who asks him—

"Are all the boys in bed?"

"Well, my dear," he says, "it is a little early—barely six o'clock."

"Are they shut up, then? Are they studying? I have a headache, and don't want to be troubled with any of them to-night."

The Reverend Copley Cobbem fervently assures her that all the young people of the house are deeply engaged in their studies, but while the lie lingers on his lips, Jolly Greene, having been "shoved" a little too far, comes head first down the stairs, and lies like an armadillo on the mat.

Mrs. Cobbem puts down her parasol, takes him by the collar, and jerks him upon his feet.

"Who are you?" she asks.

"I don't know," replies the bewildered Jolly, "I'm always being shoved and thrown about. I wish I was at home and with my mar."

"May I ask, Mr. Cobbem," says Mrs. Cobbem, "how this fool came here?"

The Reverend Copley Cobbem, being only mortal, and having in consequence no power of discovering things beyond his ken, smiles a sickly smile, but answered never a word.

"You know I hate a fool," says Mrs. Cobbem, "and yet you arrange for me to find one on the mat the moment I return home."

"My love, I have not made the arrangement. I assure you, Agatha, I did not know the boy was here."

"That," says Mrs Cobbem, "is mere folly and nonsense. I come home after a fatiguing journey, during which my nerves have been sorely tried by a man singing a low song about winkles for tea, and ——"

"My love," says the Rev. Copley, "you should not travel third-class."

"And who would be the first to reproach me if I squandered money?"

"My love," murmurs the Rev. Copley, "I allowed you first-class fare."

"You allowed me!" says Mrs. Cobbem, with a little laugh; "did you indeed, and very kind it is of you; but I tell you, Mr. Cobbem, that my nerves have been shaken, not only by that low man with his song about winkles, whatever winkles may be——"

"The low person alluded to," murmurs the Rev. Copley, "meant the common periwinkles, found in great abundance upon our coasts, where it clings to the rocks, or grovels on the sandy shores. Its food is——"

Mrs. Cobbem interrupts him with a glare that petrifies him.

"Not only by this man were my nerves upset," she says, "but there were too babies in the carriage, and a woman with a bundle, out of which there was, in the most indecent manner, the foot of a stocking protruding. In addition, there was a man with a red nose, who drank copiously out of a bottle, and kept thrusting his elbow into my side. He asked me if I knew Short's tea gardens, and said there was a hop on to-night, whatever that may be."

"A hop, my love, is, I believe, in the vulgar tongue, a dance."

"You seem to have a perfect knowledge of everything that is vulgar, coarse, common, and repulsive," says Mrs. Cobbem; "and now, after the trials of the day, you must, in your coarse way, add to my suffering by having a fool curled up on the mat to meet me. Take him away."

"Greene," says the Rev. Copley Cobbem, in a dejected tone, "you had better go upstairs."

"Where's my mar?" asks Jolly, staring about him bewildered.

"Does he think I am his mother?" asks Mrs. Cobbem.

"I beg of you, Greene, to retire," implored the Reverend Copley.

"There are others above," says Mrs. Cobbem, suddenly looking up. "Oh! this is more than I can bear," and immediately there is the scampering of many feet, and a general clearing out of the landing above.

"Mr. Cobbem," says Mrs. Cobbem, sitting down on the floor like a collapsed zephyr, "you are a brute. Oh, that I had never left the parental roof!"

"I wish you had died under it," the reverend gentleman says to himself, but in his outward demeanour he shows all anxiety for his suffering spouse.

"Quick, Jiggles, some ammonia—Perkins, water: your mistress is faint. The fatigue of the journey has been too much for her. Greene, will you have the goodness to go to your room?"

"No—no!" cries Mrs. Cobbem, "let him remain here and be a living insult to me."

"You shall not suffer, my love," said the Reverend Copley, and taking her in his arms he bears her into the drawing-room, whither, with cautious tread and bated breath, Jiggles, Perkins, and the housekeeper follow with restoratives.

CHAPTER XXXI.

CROSS-EXAMINATION—A SWIMMING MATCH.

THE arrival of Mrs. Cobbem brought a subdued air upon Warmington College. Hitherto the educational ship had gone along pretty smoothly, but had not kept exactly upon her course.

Fair winds had filled the sails, adverse currents had kept away, and all went well; but now the true guiding hand was at the helm, the master voice was heard upon the deck, and everything was put into its best ship-shape form.

Truly she was a wonderful woman. Not handsome, as men judge women, nor ugly as the rule for beauty goes—a commonplace woman, except for the spirit that was in her.

Aye, that was the thing—the spirit. It was that which subdued her reverend lord, it was that which awed the ushers, crushed the housekeeper, terrified the servants, and scared the boys. Mrs. Cobbem was an Amazon, and her woman-warrior soul broke through all obstacles, refused to recognise barriers, and defied all assaults.

One of the first things she did was to have the new pupils up one by one and cross-examine them. Out of Jolly Greene she got nothing beyond that he was always being "shoved about and wanted his mar." The opinion she had formed of him at first was confirmed.

"He is a born fool," she said, "and I hate a fool."

"My love—my Agatha," replied her lord and master, "the parents of this boy pay well. Let us be gentle with him on the score of his weak intellect."

"I was gentle with you at first," replied Mrs. Cobbem, "and it did you no good. I mean to polish this boy my own way."

"You were gentle with me!" said the Reverend Copley. "When?"

"During the first two days after my desertion of the parental roof," replied Mrs. Cobbem.

"If I remember rightly," said the Reverend Copley, goaded into strong language, "the parental roof was d—— leaky at the time you left it."

Mrs. Copley, who was knitting, rose to her feet, and optically skewered the audacious creature who addressed her.

"Misfortunes," she said, "had at the time descended upon my papa, and others loomed in the distance; but the thing that crushed him was *your* wedding breakfast."

"*My* wedding breakfast!" exclaimed the Reverend Copley. "Is it not the custom for the father of the bride to give it?"

"Custom is one thing, and decency another," replied Mrs. Cobbem, loftily. "You *knew* my dear papa gave a bill to the confectioner, and you were perfectly aware that bill would be his ruin."

"The circumstances of your dear papa," returned the Reverend Copley, "were unknown to me at the time, or perhaps I might have sought matrimonial comfort in another direction."

There are some things a man may say to a woman, and some he may *not*. The Reverend Copley had spoken words which ought never to have been spoken to his Agatha, and she looked about for a missile wherewith to resent them.

There were a variety of articles to select from—

First, the fire-irons—steel and bronze, with many knobby ornaments, and particularly adapted by a skilful ironmonger for the rapid settlement of domestic dissension.

Secondly, a smart travelling clock on the table, with four brass corners, any one of which, properly applied, was sufficient to convince any sane man of the error of quarrelling with his wife.

Thirdly, a fine Japanese vase, with two handles to assist in its projection. It was bombshell-shaped, and splendidly adapted for bringing upon the scene a series of men and women to bear witness to the wrongs of a wife. Well thrown, and well broken, it would make almost as much noise as a Daniel Lambert falling through the roof of a greenhouse.

Finally, there were footstools, books, paper-knives, and a variety of other articles all ready to hand for injured woman to avenge her wrongs with.

Mrs. Cobbem surveyed the weapons ready to

hand, and, with the promptitude of a great mind, decided upon the travelling clock—principally because it was an expensive thing to throw about—and, taking it up, she sent it straight at the reverend gentleman's head.

He meanly ducked, and it went through the French window into the garden, where, with its face knocked in, it ticked convulsively for a few seconds, and, with shattered works, left the clock world behind it for ever. The Rev. Copley, with a perfect knowledge of the fastenings of the window, opened it, cleared the clock and geraniums at a bound, and ran for dear life until he ran up against the odd man wheeling a barrowload of weeds, when he pretended he was trotting about to clear away the cramp, and asked if the vegetable marrows were up yet.

The odd man, who was keen in his way, and had seen his master with the cramp before, replied—

"They beant more than a hinch out, which 'll wex missus, as she hoped you'd look arter 'em."

The Rev. Copley said no more, but retired to an arbour, sat down, and mused o'er the various shades of domestic felicity until the sun went down.

Among others who suffered cross-examination was Master William Sharp Popper, who was grievously harassed by the keen woman who took him in hand. Indeed he suffered sorely, and was in a dejected state for quite two days afterwards."

"What's your name?" was the first question.

"Popper, ma'am—William Sharp Popper," he replied.

"Who's your father?"

"Professor Popper," replied young William, incautiously.

"Professor of what?"

Master Popper was not prepared to reply to this, and had to cast about ere he could say what line his father pursued.

"General science he is professor of," he replied, at last.

"Oh! indeed; and where does he live?" was the next question.

Here was a facer, and had William's education in the art of lying been neglected he would have been utterly floored. But although knocked down he was up again in a moment, and advanced smiling.

"He's a-travelling for a government," he said.

"What government?"

"Haustrian," replied sweet William, boldly.

"Oh! indeed. Mr. Greene pays your expenses here, I believe?"

"Yes, ma'am."

"Why?"

"Oh! he's a friend—at least he's seen—and partly knows my father."

"Indeed. Well, you have a wig on I see; what is that for?"

"I lost my hair in a fever, ma'am. It's coming again."

"Let me see your head."

William took off his wig and exhibited a cranium with a mass of bristles all over it. Mrs. Cobbem inspected it with much curiosity.

"What fever had you?" she asked.

"The halley fever," replied William.

"What fever?"

"The—ahem! the fever which them as lives in halleys has."

"But surely you did not live in an alley?" exclaimed Mrs. Cobbem, horrified.

"Oh, no, mum!" replied William,. "But our best dining-room, which was at the back, looked on a halley, and the fever come up that way. We was all prostrated by it. My mother, two sisters, and three brothers, died of it. My father and me only survived!"

"Poor boy!" said Mrs. Cobbem. "It is a sad story. But you must throw that wig away and let your hair grow. It will soon come on. You may go."

Billy was very glad to get out of this terrible presence, and stole away upstairs to take a little rest after undergoing this fearful ordeal. He threw himself on his bed to rest, and tried to court sleep, but for a long time in vain.

Just as he was dozing Jolly Greene came in and sat down upon the corner of his bed.

Billy just opened his eyes to see who it was and closed them again.

"I say," said Jolly, "I want to speak to you."

"Don't bother," replied William.

"But I want to know if you can swim," said Jolly.

"No, I can't, and don't want to. I hate cold water."

"But most of the boys can swim here, and I want to swim too."

"Then go and learn," returned Billy, shortly. "Don't bother me."

"But how am I to learn?"

"With corks," replied Billy, sleepily.

"What corks?" asked Jolly.

"Oh, bundles of corks! You can buy 'em in the village."

"Yes, I know it. I've seen them. But where am I to put them on?"

"Oh, anywhere!" said Billy, savagely. "On your feet!"

"But——"

"I tell you," said Billy, "to put 'em on your feet, jump in, and you will swim like a fish. Now let me alone. I want to go to sleep."

Jolly, for once in a way, was roused. He had heard the boys talk of swimming, what a glorious thing it was, and he wanted to swim too. He had also heard allusion made to bladders, corks, and other things supposed to assist in the art, and by which means he was assured he was freed from all danger of drowning.

For a good hour or more he sat on his bed, reflecting upon the desirability of acquiring the art, and as Billy slept still he stole out softly, and went down to the village.

There one of the shopkeepers a few days before, had a set of swimming corks for sale. These, however, to Jolly's great disappointment, were gone.

"Sold 'em an hour ago, sir," said the man.

"Where can I get some?" asked Jolly.

"Don't know, I'm sure, sir. There aint much of a sale for 'em here."

"Oh, dear!" said Jolly. "That is just like things I want—always gone."

"Why not try bladders?" suggested the man.

"Bladders?"

"Yes, sir; you get's 'em at the butcher's. Blows 'em up and ties 'em on. Just as good as corks, and better."

Jolly hurried to the butchers, and inquired for bladders. There were at least a dozen for sale, and Jolly selected two of the largest, for which he paid eightpence.

With these in his pocket he returned home rejoicing, and, bent upon astonishing his friends, kept the possession of them a secret.

"I won't say anything," he thought, "but the next time they are going out for a swim I'll steal down first and put on these bladders and jump in. Won't they be astonished to see me swimming about with the best of 'em?"

It was a good idea, and in the end young Greene succeeded in astonishing a good many people.

Billy slept on until the bell for evening studies rang, and this awoke him.

He brushed his hair and went down to the schoolroom. About a dozen boys were there, but young Greene was not amongst them.

"Anybody seen Jolly?" he asked.

Tom Whisker, who was engaged in cutting out a pasteboard man, supposed to be a perfect likeness of the German professor, replied that "he had gone into the village."

"You seem uncommon anxious about him," said Tommy. "Can't he run alone yet?"

"What's that to you?"

"Nothing perhaps," replied Tommy. "But it seems odd the way you two stick together, and he don't seem to be over fond of your company."

"You are mighty cheeky," said Billy. "Stash it—will you?"

"Not for you," replied Tommy, defiantly; "now then!"

As this was equivalent to a defiance Billy asked Tommy Whisker what he meant by it. Tommy replied he meant what he said, and Billy might be bothered.

Nick and Dick Stager were both there, and thereupon they arose.

"I think a ring is necessary," said Dick.

"Certainly," said Nick.

"If one of you had said a cocked hat was wanted the other would have agreed to it," sneered Billy.

"Are you going to fight?"

"Will he fight?" asked Billy, pointing to Tommy Whisker.

"Of course I will," said Tommy, cheerfully.

"Then," said Billy, with professional calmness, "let us have it out at once."

"We must be sharp," said Nick, "or the ushers will be here."

A ring was formed, and Tommy Whisker, with a cheerful face, took off his coat and waistcoat. Billy, relying upon his training—and the training of the courts and alleys is a pretty severe one—removed his upper garments too. He put himself into a perfect attitude, and, to his astonishment and perhaps dismay, Tommy Whisker did so too.

"Who'll see me through?" he asked.

There was some hesitation, but at last one of the boys stood forward. Dick Stager looked after Tommy Whisker.

As the boys stood forward it was plain neither of them would stand much work. Both were too fat—Billy particularly so. It was only a question of one or two well-directed blows as to who should be victor.

Tommy Whisker's eye was a fearless one, and as he moved about there was more agility than might have been expected of him. When Billy led off with the first blow he dodged it neatly, and gave Billy one on the side of the head that made him see squibs.

"Dash it," thought Billy, "this won't do. He knows too much."

Billy struck out blindly, and got another on the other side of his head. This fitted him up with a fine pyrotechnic display, with a full share of singing in his head.

"Confound it!" he muttered; "I won't stand this."

He then tried an old dodge of the home of his youth. He dodged and rushed in, hoping to throw his opponent over his shoulder, but Tommy got him into chancery and so belaboured him that he was glad to get down and feign being knocked out of time.

His second carried him to his corner and moistened his lips with a slate sponge damped with water from the bottle on the Reverend Copley's desk.

Not a sound was made. No encouragement was given by cheering either, for that would indubitably have brought up some of the greater powers to interfere. Indeed, there was one stealing upon them in the form of Mrs. Cobbem, who, hearing a curious trampling of feet, was coming upstairs to learn the meaning of it.

Softly opening the schoolroom door, she peeped in, and looked upon a scene that made her eyes glisten. Billy was still prostrate, in a feigned state of insensibility, and his anxious second was trying to bring him round.

"Prick him with a pin," suggested somebody.

"Here's one," said another remorseless spectator. The first application sufficed. Billy jumped up with an "Oh!" that might have been heard half over the house.

Mrs. Cobbem said nothing, but remained a quiet observer until the two combatants again faced each other—Tommy Whisker confident and Billy a little doubtful of the result.

But the calculations of both were upset by the sudden appearance of Mrs. Cobbem, who, in the midst of a dismayed silence, broke her way into the ring.

Her first act was to take Billy by the arm—her second to secure Tommy in the same way—her third to knock their heads together—and her fourth to lead them towards the door.

"Fighting," she said, "is not allowed here. I always stop it, and take the punishment of it into my own hands."

CHAPTER XXXII.

FISHING—CATCHING AND BEING CAUGHT.

IT was part of the Rev. Copley Cobbem's system of education to encourage all manly, wholesome, and healthful sports—among others, what is very often called an art, the sport dear to the heart of dear old Izaac Walton—viz., fishing.

"The finny tribe," explained the rev. gentleman in a lecture, "are peculiarly adapted to give to man amusement and food combined. They have snouts of a hard, horny substance, splendidly adapted to hold the hook designed by the intelligence of the captor, whereby with a minimum of pain we have a maximum of success."

"But doesn't it hurt the fish?" asked Nick Stager.

The boys had full liberty to ask questions during the lectures, but the Rev. Copley reserved to himself the right of answering them. On this occasion he answered with the promptitude arising out of a perfect knowledge of the subject.

"It does not hurt them in the least," he said.

"Why, then, do the fish wriggle?" asked Dick.

"The natural position of the fish in the water," replied the rev. gentleman, beaming with a ready reply, "is of a horizontal nature. The fish knows this, and devotes its life to preserving it. Hence, when the hook enters the horny substance, which we call snout, and the skilful hand of the fisherman hauls up his prey, the fish finds itself in an unnatural state, and struggles to regain that more familiar with it—that's all."

The boys applauded this explanation, and both Dick and Nick felt themselves put down. But they watched for an opportunity to give the Rev. Copley one in return, and before the lecture was over Dick got it.

"Man," said the Rev. Copley, as his lecture drew to a close, "relies more upon his intelligence. In point of muscular force he is far below the average of creation. The wing of the swallow—the jaw of—of an ass—the limb of the deer, the hound, and the hare are all specimens of superior muscular power—nay, the base and much-despised flea possesses powers which laugh puny man to scorn when comparison is made. It can leap without an effort to forty times its height."

"And yet, sir," said Dick, with a sweet innocent smile, "we crack 'em."

It was wrong of the boys to laugh, and the German professor to choke, and the other ushers to turn aside and apply handkerchiefs to their faces, but the Rev. Copley need not have boxed Dick's ears and sent him to bed. But he did so, and concluded his lecture by abruptly stating that a fishing excursion had been arranged for the morrow, and bade the boys get their tackle ready.

What preparations were made that night! All sorts of tackle—good, bad, and indifferent—came out to the light, and those who possessed the

GREEN AS GRASS.

A JOLLY SCHOOL STORY.

YOUNG GREENE DOES THE ROPE TRICK ALMOST BUT NOT QUITE LIKE THE DAVENPORT BROTHERS.

crudest weapons of the piscatorial art were the most envied of boys. Those, however, who had money could have tackle at cost price (?) of the Rev. Copley Cobbem. Jolly Greene bought a rod, and a host of various sorts of lines and hooks, and before he went to bed he had two of the latter in fleshy parts of his frame, which other boys of surgical tendencies kindly cut out for him with knives that would have found their match in Cork butter.

But all's well that ends well. Jolly got to bed and was up betimes and ready with the rest, and away the school went to Crippleton, where there was shallow fishing, and deep fishing, and all sorts of fishing; and then in various boats, moored for the purpose, they were divided into parties, and set to work.

"And if good luck attend us," said the Rev. Copley, "we will have fish for dinner to-morrow. It will be sweet if it is of your own catching."

Sweet to them, and sweet to him, as he charged for the excursion and filled the dinner table for little or nothing; but he smiled upon them as if the having fish to cut was a sacrifice on his part willingly and cheerfully made.

Jolly was sent out with his constant attendant, Billy, the two Stagers, and others, and with slaughtering thoughts put down his dead lines, and baited that on the end of his rod and began.

He gave his line a twirl, and caught Billy under the arm pit, fortunately only through his clothes. The hook was cut, and the line was cast again. This time he made a bit of net work of it all round the top of his poll.

"I can't make it out," groaned Jolly. "I never saw such an aggravating line."

"You had better give it up, and watch t'others," said Billy, sternly.

"But I gave one pound five for this line and rod," pleaded Jolly, "and I want a little fun out of it."

"You are having some of a sort," cried Dick; "but look to your dead line, you have got something on it."

The line in question was being jerked in the most violent manner, and Jolly, with a bounding heart, hauled it in. There was a fish on it, a big fish with the jaws of a dog, and the eye of a demon. The excited piscator got him into the boat just as he bit the line through, and dropped down with the hook in his mouth.

"What is it?" asked Jolly.

"I think it's a young shark," said Dick Stager, gravely, "but I am not quite certain."

The fish gave a great bound, and would have gone over the side if Billy had not knocked him down with an oar. Then he lay perfectly still, and apparently dead.

"I caught him," said Jolly, in a voice quavering with joy. "Oh! what a beauty he is! What a pity it is we can't keep him alive."

"I don't know so much about that," said Dick, as he cast in his line. "I say, Jolly, do you want your rod?"

"Listen to him," exclaimed Jolly, oblivious of all but his prey, "he's singing."

"Perhaps he's a mermaid," suggested Nick.

"Or a dolphin. Don't they always die singing."

They all gave up their fishing to listen to the noise, which certainly was very curious, and Jolly, desiring to get the full benefit of the sweet music, bent down very low until his nose was within half a dozen inches of it. Then the fish gave up singing, and with a turn of its tail leaped up and laid hold of the most prominent feature of that most unfortunate boy.

"Oh, dear! oh, dear!" he exclaimed, "I'm alldways bein' bidden by someboder. Tag him off."

He spoke as most people would have done under the circumstances, a little imperfectly, but was understood nevertheless. His anxious friends made an effort to get the brute off, but its slippery skin gave them little to hold by.

"Knock him off," suggested Dick.

They smote him until he wagged like a pendulum, but still he held on, and Jolly, in torture unspeakable, yelled "murder!" It seemed as if he and Jolly were thenceforth to be one.

"Perhaps," suggested Billy, "he wants to get back to his native helement. Hang over the side and try him."

It was really getting very serious, for it seemed as if Jolly and his nose were about to part company. They helped him to the side, when he hung the brute over the water, and then, having prolonged its evident enjoyment, it hung on for a few seconds more and dropped.

"I'll never come fishing again," groaned Jolly, sinking down. "Oh! my nose, put me ashore! and let me get out of it before you catch any more."

But this they could not do without permission, and Jolly lay huddled up in terror in the bow of the boat all the live-long day, weary and sick at heart, and unable to appreciate in any way the beauties of the piscatorial art.

The success of the school in general was not very great. There was too much larking about. When a boy gets a bite he does not want anybody to jerk the bottom of his rod, or to throw a crust of bread at his float—or to have people of a light and frivolous turn of mind indulge in a fragment of a hornpipe on one of the seats of the boat; and yet all three things were done almost under the very nose of the Rev. Copley, who fished for awhile on the bank, and remonstrated in vain.

At last he disappeared towards a hotel of respectable dimensions, and was seen no more that day until he returned at evening, to know what good luck had attended his pupils.

A small amount of the smallest fry was shown him, together with four boys who had fallen overboard, and were still wet—Jolly among them, he having been scared over the side by the arrival of an eel, about four inches long, on the end of Dick Stager's line.

"Our success," said the Rev. Copley, who was in a very good humour, "is not very great, but we cannot command the creatures of the deep to come if they are determined to stop away, and let us always be thankful for small mercies. Such fish as we have caught shall take the place of cheese for supper to-morrow."

And smiling sweetly, he led the way to the station and took them home. On arriving there Jolly went to bed, and Billy Sharp made a poultice out of a biscuit and put it on his nose. But many days elapsed ere that organ was itself again.

CHAPTER XXXIII.

YOUNG GREENE HAS AN AWFUL NIGHT.

MRS. COBBEM was a severe disciplinarian and was very fond of mortifying the flesh of other people. Low diet was a favourite prescription of hers, especially when dealing with boys of pugilistic tendencies. Their blood she considered was over-heated and required toning down, and Tommy Whisker and Billy Sharp being of that class of offenders, were toned down accordingly.

They were put into a room especially provided for punishment—a bare apartment, hard and cold enough to give one the toothache to look at it. The furniture consisted of two hard board beds, with just enough bed linen to keep the warmth of life in the occupants.

Here then Billy and Tommy were shut up, with a jug of water and a loaf of bread, which might have done duty as a brick in the erection of a wall, or chopped up would have sold in portions for pumice stone. It was a curious thing, but whenever any of the school were in trouble one of these loaves always came to light. Mrs. Cobbem seemed to have an instinctive knowledge when the boys were going to commit themselves, and to prepare for the occasion.

"There you will remain for the night," said Mrs. Cobbem, "and don't you quarrel, or dance, or sing, or move about, for if you do I shall hear it, as my room is just under you. Ti 's your supper, eat it and be thankful, for you really ought to be made to go without it."

"Yes, ma'am," replied Billy, hoping to soften her by going on the "penitent lay," "I'm glad to have my supper, be it ever so humble; but I dursn't eat that dry bread."

"And why not?" asked Mrs. Cobbem.

"I've got a complaint which dry bread is fatal to," replied Billy. "I can't think the name of it, but I've heerd Doctor Swiggle talk to my dear parpar about it a hundred times."

"I know what your complaint is," said Mrs. Cobbem, calmly.

"I am glad of that, ma'am," replied Billy; "it's an awful thing to bear."

"Your complaint," said Mrs. Cobbem, "is greediness—a thing that gets worse and worse as you encourage it. I am going to cure you with a long course of low diet. There is nothing else of the least service in such cases."

She went out, closed the door, and locked it. Billy sat down upon his hard bed and groaned. Tommy Whisker went to the window, and taking a knife and piece of cardboard out of his pocket, began to cut out a paper model of a wheelbarrow; for Tommy, like Christopher Cobble, was somewhat of an artist.

"Are you going to eat this wittles," asked Billy, after a brief silence.

"I am not at all hungry," replied Tommy; "you may have it all."

"Oh! thank you," returned Billy, sarcastically, as he turned the hard fare over and over. "I'm sure I'm everlastingly and blessedly grateful. Here's stuff for a chap as never had anything less than mock turtles and wermicelly soup for dinner."

Tommy did not answer this, and Billy spent the next two minutes in regarding the loaf in bitter and contemptuous silence.

"If I had my way," he went on, "I'd shy it at that old woman's head. Why, you might shoot this ere lump of tommy out of a cannon straight agin a stone wall and not hurt it."

He tossed it up in the air, with the intention of catching it as it fell, but it slipped through his fingers and came upon the bare boards with a bang, such as the fall of a round shot would have made.

"If you make that row," said Tommy Whisker, "you'll have Mrs. Cobbem up here again."

And barely had he spoken when footsteps were heard outside and a voice came through the keyhole.

"I say, you inside there!"

It was the voice of Perkins, and Billy felt a flash of hope within him. Perhaps Perkins, touched by a knowledge of his sufferings, had brought him something to eat. But the hopes of mortals are too often but a delusion and a snare, and this hope of Billy Sharp's was particularly so.

"Yes, Perky," he said, "we are here—starving. What do you want?"

"Missus says if you go on a-keeping up that jumping about the room she'll come upstairs and warm yer," replied Perkins.

The actual words uttered by Mrs. Cobbem were quite different.

"Go upstairs, Perkins, and tell those wicked boys to keep quiet, or I will most assuredly punish them;" but Perkins always improved and polished a message before delivering it.

"I wish she would," said Billy; "I wants warming."

"If she do come," said Perkins, "you won't be chilly for months arterwards."

"I say, Perky."

"Well?"

"Couldn't you get us a bit o' something to give this flinty old loaf a relish?"

"Dursn't," said Perkins. "But I must be orf. There's stewed meat for us in the kitchen. It's the cook's birthday."

With this parting shot at Billy, for such Perkins, with Mephistophelian cruelty, meant it to be, he went downstairs, and was heard by the prisoners that night no more.

Meanwhile it had got about among the boys that young Greene would be alone that night, and all the active spirits were bent upon making the most of the opportunity thus afforded for the exercise of their jocular powers.

Strings were attached to various movables in his room, and passed under the door, and Nick and Dick Stager got under the bed, with the amiable intention of "lifting it" as soon as Jolly got between the sheets.

This latter joke is a terrible one, but it can only be practised with the old sacking bedsteads. It is easily understood, but to be appreciated must be experienced. Those who practise it get under the bed, and, calculating the time when the occupant is falling into a doze, raise the bed with a jerk, and the result is the said occupant awakes with the idea of an earthquake being about. Finding, however, all is well, he tries to sleep again, to have the performance renewed, until he is terrified into a fainting fit, or in a wild frenzy leaps out of the bed and bolts.

Poor Jolly, content to be alone for one night retired to his room, and, all unsuspecting of deep plots, took off his garments, wrapped his spare form in a night-shirt, and got into bed.

He was tired and weary, and his eyes speedily closed, but lo! he began dreaming at once, and thought he was on a lonely island, which lay flat upon the sea, but presently rose, and assumed the shape of a camel's hump. In terror he awoke, and found his bed had grown up in the centre, and he was rolling over the side.

Suddenly it went down, and he lay in a hollow. The sudden jerk attendant upon the fall fairly took his breath away, and half-petrified with terror he lay still.

Again it rose and again it fell, and Jolly, cold and trembling, peeped over the top of the sheets, meditating a bolt. His eyes fell upon a new source of horror.

The moon was shining through the window, and across the broad band of light it cast upon the floor he beheld his portmanteau travelling like a thing of life, and close attendant upon it were his hat-box and a boot, gliding slowly and easily on their way.

Jolly could stand no more. The room was either accursed or haunted, and, with a bound which an acrobat might have envied, he leaped from the bed, thrust his leg through the front of his night garment, and staggered from the room.

He neither knew nor cared whither he was going, but, with curious leaps and staggers, tumbled downstairs somehow, and got upon the landing below. Barely had he reached the lower ground when the portmanteau and hat-box, bounding like mad things, came after him, and, doubly and trebly terrified, he fled on.

Now, if there is a place handy where a terrified man or boy ought not to get into, into that place the man or boy so terrified is sure to go. The last place Jolly ought to have gone into was the Rev. Copley Cobbem's bedroom; and yet, led on by mocking fate, he opened the door of it and rushed in.

The Reverend Copley was in bed; but Mrs. Cobbem had not yet completed all the retiring arrangements, and was standing by the looking-glass, arranging as much of her hair as she was obliged to sleep in. The rest lay upon the dressing-table, in company with a variety of toilet necessaries.

Hearing the door open she turned and looked upon a boy in a long white night-dress, with a horrified head at the top of it and a long thin leg, that might have served for a pipe-cleaner, thrust through the front of it—a quivering leg, with an enormous foot at the end of it, where five curled-up toes stood out stark and stiff.

Her womanly heart at first shook with fear—for, like most of us, she had a corner in her nature for superstition, and she at first fancied Jolly was the ghost of a schoolboy who a year before had died beneath that roof.

Putting her hands before her face she screamed aloud, and the Reverend Copley—who was just sinking into a doze—awoke.

"My love—my life—what is it?" he asked.

"Oh! Copley—look there! Protect me!" she cried.

The Reverend Copley looked, and saw Jolly, still embarrassed by the position of his right leg, revolving on the left as if it were a pivot. By the light of the candle he recognised the face above.

"It's that fool Greene," he said. "What is he doing here now?"

Womanly fear departed, and the indignation of outraged virtue took its place. Mrs. Cobbem, with one bound, leapt upon Jolly, and smote him on the side of the head. He staggered back, fell over the foot-pan, sat in it, and became lodged there in an almost immovable condition.

"Get out of the room, you bad boy," she said—"get out, this instant!"

"The things all walked about—the bed heaved up!" said Jolly, wildly.

"Get up at once, you infamous boy!"

"I can't get up, and I don't want to," replied Jolly. "Let me die here!"

"Die there, you little villain!" cried Mrs Cobbem, seizing him by the hair of the head. "Who ever heard of a boy dying in a foot-pan? Come along!"

She dragged Jolly along the floor; but where he went the foot-pan also went, and, in addition to this, his legs, sticking up like two broom handles, got in the way, and rather impeded the ejecting movement.

"Mr. Cobbem," said the fair woman, "are you a man to lie in bed and let me be insulted so grossly? Come and turn this boy out."

"I'm coming, my love," murmured the reverend gentleman, "as soon as I find my dressing-gown. I cannot present myself before one of my own pupils in my night attire."

"How I am presented doesn't matter!" said Mrs. Cobbem, hysterically.

"The portmanteau went first, then came the hat-box," said young Greene, talking to the air—"both walking on invisible legs."

"Mr. Cobbem, are you coming; or are we to sleep here with a boy wedged in a foot-pan?"

"My love, I am coming."

And he came. But getting Jolly out of his position was no easy matter, and, after a couple of trials, the Reverend Copley Cobbem was obliged to carry him, foot-pan and all, out upon the landing, there to renew his efforts. As he staggered out of the room with his burden Mrs. Cobbem shut the door sharply upon him, and sent him sprawling in the corridor.

He was very wroth was the Reverend Copley, and he shook poor Jolly about in the most violent manner; but Jolly either could not or would not come out—indeed, he seemed to be unaware of his position, but kept murmuring—

"The portmanteau first; then the hat-box—both on invisible legs."

"Don't give me any of your tricks," said the Reverend Copley, "and don't feign insanity, for I won't stand it. How dare you intrude upon my privacy?"

"Your privacy, indeed!" said Mrs. Cobbem, from the other side of the door. "Mine is no consequence—of course not! Mr. Cobbem, you are a brute!"

"My love, I meant our privacy."

"Don't talk nonsense; but punish that boy, and send him to bed."

"Will you come out?" cried the Reverend Copley, shaking young Greene furiously. "How dare you get there?"

The shaking cleared Jolly's intellect a bit, and he arrived at a partial knowledge of his position.

"I can't get out," replied Jolly. "I'm reg'lar wedged in, sir."

"I'll have you out!" said the reverend gentleman, and, taking Jolly by the shoulders, he put all his strength into a violent tug.

With a noise like the drawing of a tremendous cork, Jolly came out, and the Reverend Copley, not prepared for such a sudden release, fell back against his own door, and burst it open, thereby affording Mrs. Cobbem another sight of Jolly from a different point of view.

She did not scream—her feelings were far too outraged for that—but she pounced upon her better half, and scratched and bit at him in a most furious manner.

"This," she said, "is another of your plots to insult me."

"My love—my life—I never knew of the vicinity of this wretched boy!"

"Don't tell falsehoods, Mr. Cobbem. You brought him here, as you did Perkins, to insult and annoy me."

"I brought Perkins!" exclaimed the astonished gentleman. "Did you not desire me to get a boy from the workhouse, and did you not accompany me, and help to make the selection?"

"I am not blind," Mrs. Cobbem went on, "although I did not see through you at first. It was only when I came to reflect that I saw how that boy was thrust upon me. Mr. Cobbem, you knew Perkins before he came here!"

"I'll swear I did not!" exclaimed the excited schoolmaster.

"You did—you know you did!" returned his wife, who, as reasonable as many of her sex, had formed an opinion on the spur of the moment, and was not likely to change it. "The low craft of a man to have that boy put in front—and well you knew I should choose him—and the low pretence you made of not knowing him, and not liking his looks!"

"It was not pretence. I saw the boy was full of cunning."

"And where did he get it from?" asked Mrs. Cobbem; "not from his mother, but you could not expect him to be otherwise. Cunning is in you, and blood will tell, Mr. Cobbem; yes it will, and you can't stop it."

"This," groaned the unfortunate gentleman, "is more than I can bear."

"And who is to bear your sins if you don't?" asked his wife. "And now one is not enough. You must have another. This young Greene, whom you are always so anxious about, has some features which can't be mistaken."

"Mrs. Cobbem, I'll not endure it."

"You must, and you shall, but I'll have this young Greene out of the house to-night. Let me get hold of him."

But Jolly, with a discretion beyond his years, had fled long before, and as Mrs. Cobbem was not inclined to pursue him, the door was closed, and the Rev. Copley treated to a curtain lecture, which lasted far into the second hour of the morning.

As for Jolly he dared not return to his room, but took refuge in a cupboard, and there upon a heap of general lumber he passed a wretched sleepless night, and would have passed the next day in the same place if Jiggles, coming in search of dusters, had not found him.

CHAPTER XXXIV.

YOUNG GREENE FAIRLY FLOATS AT LAST.

"WHO on earth is this?" asked Jiggles, staggering back.

"It's me—Jolly Greene," replied the wretched youth, as he crept out. Oh! I am so cold. I do wish I could go home and talk to my mar."

"I niver see sich a chap," said Jiggles. "Why didn't you go to bed?"

"So I did," replied Jolly, "but the room is haunted. It's awful."

The idea of a haunted room was pleasing to Jiggles, the more so as it was not its own, and he was anxious to know all about it.

"Come into the spare room," he said; "lie down, and I'll cover you up."

It was a room sometimes devoted to visitors, and Jolly, being put between blankets, was soon warm and comfortable. On being requested by Jiggles, he told as much as he could remember of the events the preceding night.

And how Jiggles did laugh!

"Lor bless yer, sir," he said, "it was only a trick, and a wery old trick of them boys, which their ways of joking is warious. You go to sleep, and I'll see if I can't put you right with Mr. Cobbem."

Jiggles was as good as his word. He sought out the Rev. Copley, told him where he had found Jolly, and all that had occurred. In the passage the portmanteau, with strings attached, was discovered, and all made clear.

"So you see, sir," said Jiggles, "it was all a lark."

"A what?"

"A joke, sir, which is another name for a lark."

"You mean that a lark is a low name for a joke, but pray be more careful of your language, Jiggles. It is very right of you to tell me of this affair, and perhaps, as I am very busy this morning—ahem! you would not mind explaining it to Mrs. Cobbem also."

This Jiggles rashly did, and for his pains, as he afterwards said, "got his head bit clean off"—an assertion scarcely borne out by facts, as he walked about with his head upon his shoulders for many days and years afterwards. With this, however, the matter ended. Jolly was not really to blame, and as the real offenders could not be discovered, there was nothing else to do but to let the business drop.

"But," said Mrs. Cobbem, "if I do find them out woe to them!"

Billy and Tommy were released about now and as it was a half holiday the boys were set free —some to hare and hounds, some to cricket, some to kite-flying, and others to bathe.

Among the latter Jolly Greene, who, armed with his two bladders, walked boldy down with the rest.

"What are you going to do with those things?" asked Billy.

"Swim with them of course," replied Jolly, proudly. "All you have to do is to tie 'em on, plunge in, and there you are—swimming."

"Oh! who told you so?"

"The butcher."

"Ah!" said Billy, drily. "Well, go on, young 'un, swim and prosper."

Arriving at the stream, which was tolerably swift and deep, some half score of the lads took off their clothes, and, being good swimmers, jumped in and rolled and dived about like ducks. Billy took off his clothes, but, having tried the water with his toes, declared it was too cold, and sat upon the bank shivering.

He was too much absorbed with his own feelings to notice Jolly, who, unobserved by any one, tied the bladders round his ankles, and, with the confidence which only the entire absence of brain can give, dived into the stream just where it was deepest.

"Who's that?" said Billy, turning to where Jolly had been sitting. "Good gracious, he'll be drowned! Help!—somebody!—help!"

Up came Jolly, feet first, well elevated in the air, and his body already half-filled with water. The spectacle at once so novel and exciting first sent a thrill through every spectator, then there came forth a roar of laughter.

"Help!—gobble—gobble—help!" shrieked Jolly, floundering about. He found there was a prospect of his swimming upside down, and did not like it. "Help!—gobble—gobble."

And down went his head, but his feet remained on the surface, convulsively kicking about.

"Did you ever see sich an ass?" shrieked Billy Sharp from the bank. "Help him, or I'm ruined and blighted for ever! The governor will half murder me for not looking after him better!"

Larry and the two Stagers having partly recovered from their merriment, went to the rescue of poor Jolly, and by the time they got him out and laid him on the bank he was black in the face.

"He's drowned!" cried Billy, wringing his hands. "Oh, here's a go! I'm broken-hearted!"

"Get out of the way," said Dick. "One would think you were his mother."

"No mother would care half so much for him as I do," said Billy, quite carried away by the fear of Greene being lost to him. "He's father and mother, sister and brother, wittles and drink, to me."

"No doubt," said Dick, meaningly. "But stand by some of you. He's quite full of water—filled up like a bottle."

"Put him on his head, and let it run out," said Billy.

"You must be off your head to suggest it," replied Dick. "Now, then, put him out straight and flat, rub his chest. Nick, take the other arm; I'll have this, and we will work it up and down. Get the lungs into play, and he will soon come round."

Had it been left to Billy the life of Jolly would there and then have been ended, but the great presence of mind displayed by Dick Stager saved him. Little by little his life came back, and, opening his eyes, he said—

"Oh, mar, I've been dreaming that I was at a tee-total meeting!"

"You've been to one," said Dick, "and, against all the principles of the Good Templars, taken a drop too much; but you will be all right in a moment, and you must sign the pledge never to do it again."

"What have I been doing?" asked Jolly, with a

"Swimming," replied Nick.

"With bladders, old boy," added Larry. "And you would have got on famously if your head had been where your feet were."

"I remember now," said Jolly, shuddering, and then the final stage of his recovery came on, and he was very ill indeed.

"I don't know how it is," he said, as he walked home with his friend William, "but nothing seems to go right with me."

"It's because you don't trust people enough," replied Billy.

"I trust you enough," returned Jolly, a little huffed, "and you never pay a farthing back. Only yesterday I——"

"Now don't be mean," said Billy. "Whenever I lend you money I never say anything about it."

"You never do lend me any."

"Well, when I do so you won't hear a word from me—take a hoath of that. You go on trusting me, never mind the t'other fellows. They aint up to much."

"I like the two Stagers."

"Oh! you do?"

"Yes, and Cobble, and Whisker, and Larry, and a lot of 'em."

Young Greene was plucking up a spirit, and Billy felt it was necessary to curb him in.

"I can see how it is," he said; "you are going to ruin."

"Me?" exclaimed Jolly, a little alarmed.

"Yes, to ruin and misery, let alone starvation."

The voice of William was very solemn, almost prophetic in its tone, and Jolly felt a creeping sensation all over him.

"I don't understand you," he said. "Oh, don't go on looking and speaking that way. I've done nothing."

"I shouldn't be a friend to you if I didn't speak out plump and plain," returned William. "You've got among a low lot, and they will be the ruin of you, unless you keep to me, and cut 'em."

"I don't know where to go or what to do," said Jolly, helplessly.

"All you've got to do is to look to me," said his friend. "Don't go a-spending your money in a reckless manner, lavishing it on the idle and dissoloot, but spend it carefully, or, what is better still, let me spend it for you."

"I don't want it spent at all," said Jolly.

"Then let me take care of it. How much have you got?"

"Only one pound five and twopence."

"Then hand over the one pound five and keep the tuppence, in case you should have to go through a toll-gate," said Billy.

"But there isn't a toll-gate about here," said Jolly, helplessly.

"Then you won't want the tuppence," was the calm reply. "Out with it, and let me save you from ruin."

Jolly, after a little hesitation, yielded to the stronger will and brought out the coin; but he sighed most dismally as he passed it over.

"The money's all right," said Billy, after severely testing every coin—not that he mistrusted Jolly, but he thought it just possible somebody might have set him up with a few "duffers"—"and I'll tell you what I'll do, Jolly. I'll come down handsome, and give you a treat to-night. We'll have a grand feed of cold sassingers, faggots, and winkles. I see 'em all in a shop winder. You come and help me to smuggle 'em in."

CHAPTER XXXV.

MR. COBBEM HAS HIS DOUBTS, AND MRS. COBBEM ARRIVES AT A CERTAINTY.

SUCCESS crowned the efforts of Master William Sharp Popper to get in the materials for a feast without observation, and on retiring that night he laid out (upon Jolly's bed, in case of accidents) about a pound and a half of cold sausages, a dozen "faggots," several pints of periwinkles, and a bottle of red currant wine.

"There," he said, "look at that! I'm the chap to look arter you! Is there anybody else in this heducational jug as would give you a treat like that?"

"But who paid for it?" asked Jolly.

The face of Billy was all grieved amazement. Taking up a sausage, he made a couple of bites of it, and swallowed it hurriedly, to hide his emotion.

"There's no gratitood in this world!" he said. "Don't touch none of it if you don't like it."

But Jolly was very spiteful, and, being of a rather grudging disposition, went at the food provided, and ate a lot of it. The toothsome sausage, the fragrant faggot, and the appetising periwinkle had been bought with his money, and he wanted his share—or more, if he could get it.

More he did not get, for Billy was of a class of ship that provisioned rapidly. There was a wide entrance to his hold, and he had studied the art of stowing away with great success. In something under ten minutes the whole of the eatables had disappeared.

"I feels better now," said Billy, as he took out the cork of the wine bottle. "Now, Jolly, where's that mug I bought t'other day?"

"Under the bed."

"Fetch him out, then."

The mug was fetched, and Billy poured out about half a pint of the liquor. It was of village make, with no more sugar in it than was absolutely necessary. As Jolly incautiously gulped down about half the quantity served out to him he gave a start as if he had been stabbed.

"Oh, dear!" he said; "how sour it is!"

"'Taint bad," said Billy, taking a sip of it. "But I don't like to be covetous—you may have my share."

"But I don't want it."

Billy, however, was firm, and Jolly partook of about three-parts of the bottle, and, after clearing away the shells of the periwinkles, went to bed.

He had an awful night—dreamt of demons, lions and tigers, fireworks and thunderstorms—and about five o'clock in the morning his groans aroused Billy from a dead sleep.

"Wot's the matter with you?" he asked.

"I don't know," groaned Jolly. "I think I am dying."

Billy had good cause for alarm. Jolly was doubled up in the most extraordinary way, with his knees against his nose, and his arms clasped round his shins. As for his face it was livid, and only the whites of his eyes could be seen.

"He's done for," thought Billy, as he jumped out of bed. "Don't sit curled up like that. Stritch yourself out."

"Ow—ow!" groaned Jolly. "I'm being twisted and torn. I'm dying!"

"I don't know what to do," muttered Billy. "He ought to be rubbed, and to have hot flannels, and all sorts of things. I wonder whether I could get anything downstairs?"

He put on a few articles of apparel and crept quiety down to the kitchen, where he startled the last of the blackbeetles homeward bound into a sharp run.

He tried the boiler for hot water, but it was empty; he looked about for flannnel, and could find none. The only thing warm which would at all answer the purpose was the round iron top of the kitchener, which still held a considerable amount of heat.

"I must take that," thought Billy, "and carry it up in the warming-pan."

This was not an easy task, for the iron plate rattled most tremendously, but he performed it without arousing anybody.

On his return he found Jolly still in great agony.

"Now, Jolly," he said, "stritch yourself out. I've got something that will put you right."

Jolly, glad of any relief, complied, but he could hardly keep still.

Billy got the lid of the warming-pan open, and, watching his opportunity, suddenly turned it over, and planted it on the spot where most required.

The plate was hotter than Billy was aware of. It was, furthermore, very black—a fact he had overlooked. As soon as it was applied Jolly uttered a frantic cry, that went all over the house, and, acting on the first impulse, held the iron remedy close to him. Then he bounded over, and rolled about the bed until the sheets were in that state dear to the heart of a clown when he is going to put the pantaloon to rest.

Billy looked on aghast, and tried to stop him, but Jolly, under the united pain of inward suffering and outward application, bounded about like a sprite, taking the plate with him wherever he went, until his work was complete, and the bed could not have been improved by a sweep.

"You've done it," said Billy. "Won't there be a bit of wax-ending for this? Here's old Cobbem coming. If you says anything about them sarsinjers and currant wine I'll kill you!"

MR. AND MRS. GREENE VISIT WARMINGTON COLLEGE AND FIND THEIR PROMISING OFFSPRING "PLANTED."

Not only was the Reverend Copley coming, but Mrs. Cobbem was on the way also, both bent upon knowing the origin of the cry of pain which had aroused them from balmy sleep.

"Mr. Cobbem, will you have the goodness to go into that room and see if those boys are dressed."

It was the voice of Mrs. Cobbem that made this request. She was truly delicate, and would not willingly look upon suffering even, unless it was respectably clothed.

The Reverend Copley came into the room just as Billy Sharp drew the counterpane over the agonised Jolly, and the awful work done by the fire-plate. Jolly made an effort to lie still, and Billy respectfully bowed.

"Who is ill here?" asked the reverend gentleman.

"I'm dying," groaned Greene, "oh!—oh!"

"Pray compose yourself, Greene, and tell me your symptoms."

"Pains all over, sir, flying up and down and twistings—oh!—oh!"

"Ha! been eating something abominable, like all boys," said Mrs. Copley from the outside. "I had better give him a dose. Can I come in?"

"You may, my dear," replied the Reverend Copley.

Mrs. Greene, confiding in the word of her husband—as a woman should do—came boldly in, but at that moment poor Jolly got one of the "twistings," and with a great bound he sent all the upper clothes flying. Mrs. Cobbem would have fainted there and then, but her eyes caught sight of the blackened sheet below, and that saved her.

"Good gracious!" she said, "what is all this? Get out, you dirty boy."

She gave Jolly a push, and he went over to the floor, on the other side, where he was left to twist and turn and give vent to stifled howls, while Mrs. Cobbem inspected the couch.

"A fire-plate," she said, "evidently brought to bed with him. What madness is this, Mr. Cobbem? Will you have the goodness to explain?"

"My love, how can I?" he answered. "I am as much astonished and bewildered as you. This is passing the order of common events."

"You are like most men," returned Mrs. Copley, "blind as a bat. This boy—or this lunatic—feeling cold, brought this plate to bed; and yet, Mr. Cobbem, you call yourself the master of the house."

Mr. Cobbem, in her presence, had never but once in his life asserted that he held such a position, and was promptly convinced of there being a mistress who was quite equal, or even superior to, the master. But he dared not even deny that he laid claim to such a position.

"My love," he said, "how can I be accountable for this? Have I the eyes of Argus?"

"Don't bring up your Roman Emperor before me," said Mrs. Cobbem, whose knowledge of heathen mythology was rather defective; "but ask that boy to explain himself, while I stand outside and listen to his answers."

Billy, who had shoved away the warming pan under his own bed, and taken up, for him, a very retiring position, helped the Reverend Copley to get Jolly into bed again, and the cross-examination began, Billy striking in with great effect when the answers were not quite clear.

"Greene, tell me how you came to be so weak and foolish as to bring the plate of the kitchener to bed with you."

"I didn't—I"—began Greene, when Billy put in his oar.

"He didn't know what he was up to. He very often don't" (in a confidential whisper); "a little wrong here, sir" (tapping his forehead), "but getting better every day."

"So you didn't know what you were doing, my poor boy," said the Reverend Copley, tenderly, "but you know what made you so unwell. What have you been eating?"

"Sausages—ow!—faggots—ow!—and winkles—ow!" replied Greene, as he gave another mighty bound, and turned over on his face.

"When?"

"Last night."

"That's it—last night," said Billy, "he dreamt of 'em. He's a most curious dreamer—allers fancying something. If he had been eating sausages, faggots, and winkles, I must have seen him."

"Of course you must," replied the reverend listener. "So it's his fancy?"

"Well, sir, where is he to get 'em from?"

"True, Popper. Where is he to get them from?"

"Where do other boys get their things from?" asked Mrs. Cobbem, scornfully, from the outside. "Oh! you noodle; but go on—I'm listening."

"I don't know that I've anything more to ask," said the Rev. Copley.

"Then come here and take this dose. He'll soon be right."

The Rev. Copley, meekly obedient, went out and took a phial of some size from her fair hand. It contained a black and most unpalatable-looking dose.

"Give him the lot," she said, "and if he won't take it, pour it into his mouth, and hold his nose. Then he must swallow it."

Jolly did not need much forcing. He would have taken poison to relieve himself of his agony. He swallowed the physic, gave two or three violent kicks, and became calmer.

"Are you better, Greene?"

"Yes, sir."

"Then I will leave you to repose. Popper, watch over him."

"I will, sir. I'll sit by him night and day till he's well."

The Rev. Copley joined his wife outside, and together they walked downstairs.

"Copley," said Mrs. Cobbem, suddenly, "what do you think of that Popper?"

"Well, my dear," was the hesitating reply, "I have my doubts of him."

"Your doubts, indeed! I have none. I have arrived at a certainty."

"And what is your certainty, my love?"

"That I am not going to tell you just yet. Only keep an eye on him."

"I will, my love."

"And I will watch young Greene. Do you believe he is mad?"

"I can't say, my dear."

"Or such a fool as he looks?"

"I hope not, my love."

"You can't say, and you hope not. Really, Mr. Cobbem, you are enough to drive a woman mad. But I see I must look after them; and remember this, young Greene is to keep to his own bed and sleep in those sheets till Saturday. As for the plate he took to bed with him, he had better keep it. I will get a new one to-day, and you can charge it in his bill."

CHAPTER XXXVI.

IN WHICH THERE ARE REVELS AND REVELS.

MY country readers will understand what is meant when a village revel is named, but I fear those who live in great towns know very little about the great festival which once a year convulses so many rustic communities, and a little explanation regarding them will not be considered out of place.

A revel in the rustic's mind is the greatest among the few joys that come to lighten his lifetime, and on the day appointed for its keeping those who plough the land and till the earth generally come out of a lethargy of three hundred and sixty four days duration to break the bounds of decorum, to eat, drink, and be merry, to dance, to sing, and perhaps to fight, and finally as a rule to sleep in a ditch, head down, and feet well up in the air, on the borders of a fit.

But the rustic head seldom gives way on these occasions. The healthy inactivity of the brain saves them, and nothing beyond a few days' biliousness seldom if ever follows.

The chief amusements of a revel are knock-'em-downs, three shies a penny, shooting for nuts, tossing the pieman, dancing, drinking, and so on. Occasionally, if the village is a large one, a show or two and roundabouts turn up, as was the case on the day when the revel of the village outside Warmington College took place.

The name of the village is purposely concealed in this story, as many of the events described have transpired so recently: but let us, for convenience sake, call it Smockly, and hasten on to describe the events of the Smockly revel.

At early dawn all the village boys were astir, waiting to receive the various caravans which brought the day's amusements. The proprietors of these caravans belong to a sort of mongrel gipsy tribe, with something of the looks of the old Romany people—all their cunning in poaching matters combined with the cuteness of a town-bred vagabond.

Few of them can read or write, but they have a perfect memory of the days for each revel on their route, and travel round and round in their own circuit, appearing yearly in each place until they die, when the business is taken by their descendants, or, lacking that, their friends.

The first to arrive was the man with the nuts and shooting instruments supposed to be guns—all carefully bent at the muzzle, so as to render straight shooting an impossibility. He fixed up one of his galleries, and, while his wife was arranging a stall with toys, drove a roaring trade at five o'clock in the morning,

The White Hart expected to be lively that day; but the beer-shop lower down—where men could really enjoy themselves with harmony and skittles—made the most money. Before six o'clock the tap-room was chock-full, and the oldest inhabitant—a ditcher and bellringer at the church—was dead drunk in the corner of the skittle ground.

After the nut-dealer came a peep-show, then the roundabouts, then the man with the cocoa-nuts and sticks, and, finally, "Mardle's Entertainment"—a show with a fat woman, a giant, a performing pony, and a great variety of other things which must be seen to be appreciated.

Rapidly and skilfully the proprietors put their booths together, and the real business of the day began. The drums and gongs aroused the oldest inhabitant, who came out comparatively fresh, and had a ride on the roundabouts, which terminated at the end of the first time round by his being pitched off upon his head.

He was a wiry-looking old man this oldest inhabitant, without a tooth in his jaws, and scarce a hair upon his head. He could eat and drink anything, and come out of any little derangement in consequence of excess as bright as a daisy. That fall upon his head did him a lot of good, scattering the fumes of the early-morning bout, and opening to him, as it were, another day.

"Old John" was his name, and—principally on the score of his great age—everybody was supposed to treat him. Friendly hands led him to the White Hart, and by a quarter-past eight he was gloriously drunk again.

It was a fine day, and the sun favoured them—shining out most brilliantly. All the people, old and young, were out and about, and at ten o'clock the boys of Warmington College came down to join the general throng.

The Reverend Copley Cobbem was one of the admirers of the "good old days." He loved and revered old institutions, and, when he could, supported them. Hence the appearance of the boys at the revel—one of the good old festivals left to this steam-benighted land.

It was a day of absolute freedom to his youngsters; but one condition was made—they were to return to the college at an early hour, before darkness developed the more exuberant spirits of the place.

The boys, however, were not popular with the rustics. Their superfine cloth clothes gave offence. It was a "revel," mark you—a revel for fustian and corduroy, and those who wore them, being exactly like other people, wanted their little entertainment to themselves. The boys played pranks, too—boys always will—and although none of them were so cruel and so abominable as the old joke of taking the linch-pins out of the farmers' carts, some of them rather tried the tempers of those practised upon.

As regards the juvenile population it must be admitted they were glad to meet on common ground, and have a little interchange of thought and hard knocks occasionally. It was the elderly portion of the community that resented the coming of the boys of Warmington College.

Not that their resentment ever took an active form. The boys came and went without molestation until this occasion, when the oldest inhabitant, coming out of his second intoxication, elected himself as the champion of the village, and went forth to do battle with the boys—not in blows, but in words.

He had a great opinion of his wit had the oldest inhabitant, and forthwith began to "chaff" them with much pungency and power.

"Ye be a danged nice lot," he said, addressing the Stagers and Tommy Whisker, "a comin' down and swellin' aboot once a year wi' the money that your pars and your mars (the paternal and maternal word given with much emphasis) gi' ye. I dessay ye think ye're better nor most flesh and blood, but I'll ring a bell agin the lot of yer, and I'll clear out a ditch while ye're looking at it."

Getting no answer to this address he swaggered away, just a little inflated with the consciousness of having been "too much for them broad-cloath chaps," and singled out young Greene, who, in company with Billy, was having a go in at the cocoa-nuts.

"Go it, Blathers!" he said. "I'll bet a pint yer don't hit a nut afore Christmas."

This witticism was received with much laughter by a knot of louts, and the oldest inhabitant, strengthened and supported, went over to the row of nuts, and put his hand upon one on the outer side.

"Get out of the way!" roared the proprietor.

"Let be—let be a moment," returned the oldest inhabitant. "I'll bet the soft chap two pints that he don't hit that nut in nine shies. Now, do ye take I?"

Jolly, who held a stick as thick as a rolling-pin, raised his arm to throw, and old John drew back a few paces, and fixing his eye upon the particular cocoa-nut he had pointed out, smiled in derision, as if fully conscious of its being perfectly safe.

But while thinking of that nut he forgot his own, or, to put it more correctly, his head, for Jolly, throwing a little wide of the mark, caught the aged inhabitant on the side of the head, and made him spin again.

He turned round four times and then with a "dang it!" went down in a heap, and lay muttering, "I'll bet a pint he don't hit un," wherein he showed the English spirit of not knowing when he was beaten.

There was a great deal of uproar, and Jolly might have been roughly handled by the louts but for the proprietor, who, having a good customer in hand, stood up for him, and declared it was not his fault. The one policeman also came to the rescue, and the oldest inhabitant was put upon his feet, and led away by some of his admirers to drink.

But drink, generally soothing to him, on this occasion made him cantankerous. It was not that the stick had hurt his head—as nothing less than a cannon-ball could have injured him. The injury lay in his dignity, which had been assailed by what he called one of the "Warminters."

"That chap," he said, "aint such a fool as he pretends to be, and he thought he would give I one for betting him a pint, but no man ever done anything to I and didn't get as good as he sent. Afore the day is out I'll be one with him."

This resolution was much applauded, and the general opinion was old John would be equal to the occasion. He was a great authority in most things —on himself particularly—and was generally looked up to and respected.

Did he not when that teetotal chap came down to the village refute all his arguments in person, by showing how a man could get drunk whenever an opportunity offered, and live on to something near a hundred; and furthermore, did he not by argument show that if he had been a sober man he would have died at an early age, and proved it by his youngest brother, who fell into a water-butt and was drowned at the age of seven; and did he not finally offer to drink more beer than the teetotaller could of water or tea, and "walk a chalk" with him afterwards— an offer never accepted, and the lecturer was laughed out of the place?

John had always been a great man, but this esta-blished his reputation.

Henceforth his authority in any matter was never disputed, and was that the sort of man to be smitten by a "Warminter" on the side of the head with a cocoa-nut stick? Certainly not.

"I'll wait on 'im," said old John, "and I'll gi' it to 'im."

Jolly Greene, sorry for his mishap, but uncon-scious of having provoked such deadly animosity, was hurried from sport to sport by his companions, to banish his regret. He shot for nuts, and shot the man who had the stall in the waistcoat (for which he had to pay damages). He feast d on pickled muscles and prunes, and then indiscreetly rode on the roundabouts, with very painful results. He tried his hand in the lucky bag, and for two shillings got a cracked glass sugar basin and a Jew's harp; then, accompanied by a bevy of his companions, he went to the great show.

It was a canvas booth of considerable dimensions, fitted up with wooden seats, calculated to bear about ten persons, but which, in case of emergency, had to make the best of fifty, ranged round a small cir-cular space, wherein the learned pony and other wondrous creatures exhibited themselves.

The Warmington boys mustered in force, and kept well together. Jolly Greene, Billy, the two Stagers, Larry, Christopher Cobble, and Tommy Whisker were all there, well supported by a little host of their comrades. They had the front seats close to the ring.

Above them was a number of louts, and high above all, on the top seat, with his eye upon Jolly, was the oldest inhabitant.

The booth was well filled, as "Mardle's Entertain-ment" invariably took, and as soon as the audience was in Mr. Mardle put in an appearance.

He was a short pock-marked man, with a fixed right eye, and a left one which was never still. Its restlessness probably arose from its having to do double duty, as the other was quite blind. When Mardle was excited this same eye revolved at a great rate, and sent forth sparks of fire like an electric machine.

The Warmington boys knew him, and he knew them. More than once he had been the victim of their practical jokes, and he felt it necessary to keep his eyes upon them. On this day he had an idea that a little extra vigilance was necessary.

"Ladies *hand* gentlemen," he said, "I have the honour to introduce to you Miss Selina West, haged nineteen, who weighs more than any man or woman alive, is fifty-six hinches round the waist——"

"Let's see her first, and talk about that after-wards," said Dick Stager. "Trot her out. Time, old man, time."

"I takes my own time in all things," said Mardle, his active eyes getting the steam up, "and them as can't wait can go outside, and come in by-and-bye, if they pays another penny."

"What's he saying?" asked the oldest inhabitant, who was inclined to be deaf.

A friend explained Mardle's words as follows:—

"He's telling them Warminton's not to—to come any of their cheek."

"'Ear—'ear," said the old man. "I say, mister, put the soft chap out."

"I'll put you hout if you ain't quiet," said Mardle.

"What does he say?" asked the oldest inhabitant.

Mardle's words were once more explained.

"Put me out—will he?" cried the old man, rising, "let him come and try it. I niver was put out by man or boy yet, and I've been ringer for more than sixty years, and I *can't* be put out."

"Jim!" roared Mardle.

The man who took the money thrust his head through the curtains and asked what was wanted.

"Take that old man out—him with the white fluffy hat."

"All right," said Jim, and the oldest inhabitant, to his great astonishment, was suddenly lifted to his feet.

"Here, come," he said, "you mustn't do that. I've been man and boy for——"

The rest was lost outside, and Mardle resumed his address.

"Miss Selina West can lift sixteen stone over her head, crush a cocoa-nut with her biceps, throw any man, bend a poker on her arm."

Here the aged inhabitant, having found out the private entrance to the booth, appeared behind Mardle, and struck in."

"You can't turn a chap out," he said, "as have been man and boy ringer for over sixty year—so it's no use your trying it."

"What's this?" asked Mardle, turning round. "Here, come hout, will yer?"

"Let him alone!" cried the Warmington boys, suddenly becoming the champion of the old man, and a shower of nuts, pieces of apple, and other suitable missiles, rained upon Mardle.

He was gifted with a temper, this same Mardle, and with a bitter oath he swung round, and looked among them for one on whom to wreak his vengeance. He selected Jolly, principally because he was asleep, and seized him by the collar.

"To the rescue!" cried the boys springing up.

But here the yokels stepped in, and supported Mardle—a number of them tumbling down the seats into the area, and covering his retreat with Jolly, whom he dragged with one hand, bringing up the oldest inhabitant with the other.

"Where's Selina?" he asked, as he got into the private part of the booth.

A woman of enormous dimensions looked out from a screen at the back, and asked what was wanted. She was only partially drsssed, and was evidently diffident about appearing in society in her limited costume.

"There's a row in front," said Mardle, hurriedly. "Take them two and shut 'em up in the wan till I send for 'em."

Selina sank her modesty to meet the exigencies of the occasion, and calmly taking the prisoners up like dumb-bells, bore them away.

Mardle returned to the public part of the place, where he found an active warfare going on. Two of the upper rows of the seats had given way, and about a score of yokels were lying in a heap below. At least a dozen couples were closed in deadly encounter, and black eyes and bleeding noses were getting very nearly as plentiful as blackberries in September.

He and Jim together succeeded in restoring peace. The yokels from below were fished out, the broken seats restored, and the entertainment began. The fat woman exhibited her charms, and was highly commended. The giant stood forth, and fifty Warmington Davids shot at him with peas. The performing pony was asked and answered questions —incorrectly; and, fairly satisfied, the audience cleared out, and went to other revels.

Billy Sharp, thinking Jolly Greene had been simply turned out, thought he would find him wandering about, but he was mistaken. He searched high and low, and at last concluded he had gone home terrified by his expulsion from "Mardle's Entertainment."

It was now about three o'clock, and some of the boys who had spent all their money began to talk of going back to the college to be in time for tea, but Billy was not of the number—he had funds in hand—the remnant of money entrusted to him by Jolly Greene, and he was resolved to enjoy himself.

This he did in his own way, holding aloof from the rest, with whom, as before mentioned, he was not a very great favourite. An inborn rascal, a gambler, and a cheat, it was only natural for him to become the victim of rascals cleverer than himself. Coming across a gentleman engaged in the three-card trick, he invested the money he had, and lost it. Penniless in his turn, he too thought of going home.

CHAPTER XXVII.

WHAT HAS BECOME OF JOLLY?

AS he turned from the village green, Billy Sharp ran up against Christopher Cobble, who was sauntering about with his hands in his pockets, mentally designing a kite, with the fat woman for a model.

"Hallo, Cobble!" he said, "seen Jolly anywhere?"

"You mean Greene?"

"Yes."

"No, not since that affair at Mardle's."

"I don't know where he is," said Billy, uneasily. "I wish he had told me he was going home."

"Are you sure he's gone home?" said Christopher.

"Yes, aint you?"

"No, I'm not. It's my belief he's been stolen."

"By whom?"

"Gipsies," said Christopher. "He's a fine child, and his mother is very fond of him. There will be a handsome reward."

"Gammon!" said Billy, curling up his nose. "Gipsies aint such hasses as to go and steal kids nowadays. It don't pay."

"But you do hear of such things," replied Christopher. "I read a case the other day of an old woman in London who stole a child, stripped it of its clothing, and sent it into the streets in rags."

"In London it's a different thing," said Billy, with a knowing air; "there you can do anything if you've got the genius and the tools to work with. There's lots of slums close upon the big streets, and you can grab a watch, or fake a wipe, or lure a kid, and get out of sight in no time."

"You seem to know all about it," said Christopher, eyeing him keenly.

"I've heard a great deal," replied Billy, rather confused; "but about Greene. I wonder where he is?"

"If he was up in a balloon, I shouldn't wonder," replied Cobble. "I never saw such a fellow for getting into a mess as he is. What was the row last night, when I saw Mrs. Cobbem leading him by the ear to bed?"

"He'd been trying the rope trick."

"Being tied up and getting out? Davenport brothers?"

"Yes, that's it. Greene thought he could do it. And them Stager chaps are a low lot, you know."

"No, I don't know," said Christopher, "but go on."

"Those Stager fellows tied him up in the library and left him—like the Davenport brothers—and gave him half an hour to get out; but he got a bit of the rope with a slip-knot round his neck, and began to choke. Mrs. Cobbem heard him, and come to the rescoo just in time. In another moment it would have been all over. Oh, he's a great hass!"

"I think you ought to speak well of him," said Christopher.

"Why?"

"Because he is fine grazing ground for you. Good bye. I hope you'll find him."

"I can't make these people out," said Billy, gazing after him with a very unpleasant expression of countenance. "Perhaps they think I aint good enough for 'em; but I don't care, so long as I'm all right with the Greenes. That's the party I've got to look to, and I'll see after Jolly at once."

He sauntered back to the college, and was let in by Jiggles, Perkins having slipped away to the revels half an hour before, regardless of the fact that he would have an interview with Mrs. Cobbem on his return.

"Seen Master Greene, Jiggles?" said Billy.

"No," was the reply. "You are the wery fust as have come home."

Billy turned cold.

The ground on which the festivities was going on was circumscribed, and he ought to have found his friend without much trouble.

"You are sure, Jiggles, he hasn't come back?" asked Billy.

"No," returned Jiggles; "and I shouldn't be surprised if he never did."

"Why not?"

"Because he's allers in some mess or another," replied Jiggles. "Only this morning he asked me how much rope it would take to hang a boy!"

"And what did you say, Jiggles?"

"Havin' other things on my mind, I didn't think of him, and I said cashervilly, 'About ten yards,' I ses; and he asks me if I'd got such a thing about the place. I ses, also cashervilly, that I had, and gets it for him. Then he asks me what was the quietest place for a boy to hang hisself in, and I ses, likewise cashervilly—having Perkins's refoosal to clean my boots on my mind—'In a bit of a wood,' I ses; and then he puts the bit of rope in his pocket, and goes away."

"Oh, indeed!" said Billy, with a new horro upon him. "But you don't think he's done it?"

"I'd bet a trifle he's now a dangling copse," replied Jiggles. "By-the-bye, Master Popper, there's a letter for you—come by the mid-day post."

"Let me have it, Jiggles."

Jiggles brought it, and Billy saw it was in the handwriting of his father; but he had no inclination to read it for the present.

"Jiggles," he said, "you can't think he's done it!"

"I hopes not," was the reply; "but apperiences points to sooicide. Had I not been in a cashervill state of mind I could never have given him that rope; but he had it, and took it away."

Billy could bear no more. With a groan he turned aside, and tottered down towards the revels.

"He's done it," he said, "and I'm done for! Let me see what the old man says. Something up in London, I guess."

The letter brought him redoubled grief, for now he knew the immediate finding of Jolly was imperative. Thus the letter ran—

"BILLY,—Don't let that chap Greene out of your sight for a moment. Old Greene has got an anonymous letter from somebody, saying he is in bad hands, and ought to be taken away from school. He and the old woman are coming down. Brace and polish him up for the occasion. Be ready for them, as they may come at any moment—to-day, to-morrow, or at any time.   "DADDY."

"Here's a fix," said Billy, making an effort to tear his short hair ; "they may come this wery arter-noon. Oh, dash it!" Billy when alone was generally very vulgar—"oh, dash it! what shall I do ?"

He hurried back to the village, encountering on the way some of the boys returning. Of these he asked the same question and got the same answer.

"Seen young Greene ?"

"No, not since that row at Mardle's, when he was turned out."

Billy sought the scene of revelry, and made in-quiries of every one he met, and visited the public-houses to see if he could hear of anything concern-ing him.

He watched the audiences going in and out the show, but Jolly was not among the entertained, and as the dusk of evening approached, Billy, among the last to return, again sought the shelter of the college.

Mrs. Cobbem was in the hall, pricking off the boys' names from a list as they came in—an act of super-vision she exercised on these and similar occasions.

"You're late," she said to Billy sharply.

"Yes—ma—am."

"Don't say ma—am to me, as if you were a servant—say, yes, Mrs. Cobbem."

"Yes—ma—Mrs. Cobbem."

"Where's your friend—your companion ?"

"Yer mean Master Green—ma—Mrs. Cobbem," said Billy, as innocently as he could.

"You know very well who I mean—so don't prevaricate or I'll box your ears. Where is he ?"

"I don't know."

"When did you see him last ?"

"At Mardles Entertainment."

"At what time ?"

"About two o'clock."

"What was he doing ?"

"He was a doing nuffin, Mrs. Cobbem," replied Billy, after a short pause, "and he was bein' turned out."

Mrs. Cobbem did not look surprised—but her eyes flashed.

"A boy from Warmington College being turned out of a low show," she said. "Pretty goings on indeed ; but I told Mr. Cobbem what would come of this low business. You may go—and go to bed."

"If so be, ma—am, Mrs. Cobbem, where is my supper?" Billy began.

"There is no supper," replied Mrs. Cobbem, decidedly—"go to bed !"

Billy bowed and retired with a heavy heart. On reaching his room he threw himself down on the bed, thoroughly dispirited.

CHAPTER XXVIII.

JOLLY AND THE OLDEST INHABITANT EXCHANGE COURTESIES.

WHEN Jolly and the oldest inhabitant were left together by Selina West, the strong woman, each had an instinctive feeling that something serious would come out of it.

There was but a very faint light in the caravan, as the only window was a small square opening, such as they have in bathing machines, and this had some perforated zinc over it, presumably to keep the flies out.

The governing passion with the aged inhabitant at that moment was revenge. He had been smitten on the head, which was an insult, to say the least, especially when a "Warminter" dealt the blow, for, although the aged one had spent half his life in insulting and deriding respectability, it was not at all likely he was going to put up without retalia-tion.

The chief emotion in the breast of young Greene was that most awful of awful feelings—mortal funk.

He and the oldest inhabitant regarded each other for awhile in the dim light; at length the latter spoke—

"Ye be the chap," he said, "as hit I on the head."

"I think I did," replied Greene, "but I didn't mean it."

"What did ye mean, then ?" asked the old un. "Come, now, don't go to creep out of it. You hit I wi' a stick when chuckin' at the nut."

A bright idea occurred to Jolly.

"Yes," said Jolly, "I couldn't hit the nut, and you were right, I didn't."

He had a faint hope this would soften the old man down, but the heart of the oldest inhabitant was hardened. He had Jolly in his clutches, and he would not let him go.

"I knowed ye couldn't hit the coker-nut," he said, "but I never told ye to give I a bang on the head. So we'll ha' a fight."

Some sixty years before the oldest inhabitant, then in early manhood, had shone as a pugilist—a country pugilist I mean—but at the best of times his knowledge of the fistic art was confined to keep-ing his elbows well squared, taking hard knocks as they came, and returning them when he got a chance. But for forty years at least he had never stood up as man to man against a foe. If he had he would have, as a matter of course, been knocked out of time in five seconds.

He was not even a match for Jolly now, and Jolly had never done more than kick his nursemaid on the shins—the struggles with Signor Joansmethe ex-cepted—since he was born.

"I don't want to fight," said Jolly.

"But ye must fight," said the old un, putting his hat down carefully in a corner—"man to man—toe to toe—give and take—we'll have it out !"

Never very brisk in his movements the oldest in-habitant in his old days was particularly slow, and Jolly had plenty of time to reflect as he removed his upper garments one by one, folded them, and put them carefully into the corner with his hat.

This done he spat upon his hands, struck an atti-tude that would have served as a model for a statue of Cramp, and invited Jolly to begin.

"Up and down—toe to toe—give and take," he said, "and no kicking wi' boots when down."

Jolly would fain have backed out of it, but the Fates were against him. He and the aged one were alone. No help was nigh—he was bound to fight.

Not having had the advantage of the least pugi-listic training, being ignorant in fact of the very alphabet of the art, Jolly is entitled to forgiveness for the way he began the fight.

Instead of squaring up to the oldest inhabitant in the usual way he ran at him head first, and gave him one on the shins.

Both went down on the old man's hat, which went off like the final bang of a huge cracker, and became transformed into an opera-hat, that would never rise again.

Having got upon the floor the two pugilists re-mained there, and proceeded to have it out.

The aged one had pluck because he had very little feeling, and Jolly might as well have ham-mered at an old aunt Sally as at his foe. He only hurt his knuckles, and did not even raise a bump upon the mahogany features of the old un."

Jolly himself, however, was not quite invulne-rable, and as his assailant raised his arm, and brought down his fist at the rate of a blow and a half to the minute, he soon began to feel like a man who is convinced he ought to have made his will months ago. He also thought of his "mar"—his "par"—his early days, and all the other things which come to a living creature who sees his end suddenly and unexpectedly approaching.

GREEN AS GRASS.

A JOLLY SCHOOL STORY.

JOLLY SHOT DOWN THE BROAD WATER-WHEEL IN A SITTING POSITION AS SOME BOYS LOVE TO COME DOWNSTAIRS.

It may be added, he also saw stars.

The fight, if it may be dignified by such a name, was soon interrupted by the arrival of Miss Selina West, who, hearing the disturbance, came to see how it originated. On seeing the two mortal combatants in the corner, she coolly picked them up, knocked their heads together, and asked them what they meant by it.

Jolly could not reply, for his mind was occupied in studying the revolving of many coloured lights, and the oldest inhabitant would not. He was sulky at being pulled up short at the very moment victory was in his grasp.

"Let me hear you make a noise again," said Miss West, giving them a final shake, "and I'll throw you over the moon. You sit there."

This to Jolly, whom she flopped down in a corner with a sudden ferocity and violence that made him quiver like a jelly for five minutes afterwards.

"And you," she said, to the oldest inhabitant, "keep there," putting him into another corner, "and come out if you dare until I come back. Mind this —I never stand no nonsense."

"No more do I," replied the old un, making a last struggle for independence.

But Miss Selina West, who ruled supreme whithersoever she went, snuffed out the rebellion instantly. She took the old man by the bosom of his shirt, a lovely piece of linen with a bright red ground, and white spots as big as half-crowns, and knocked his head against the wooden side of the caravan.

Impervious as he was to most knocks, this was of startling magnitude, and the aged inhabitant went under.

"I won't move till ye come back," he said, and he kept his word. He sat in his corner, and Jolly sat in his until the sun went down, and the stars came out, and quite two-thirds of the village was roaring drunk.

It was a revel of revels that day, and the stalls and the shows did a big business, and that may account for Miss West forgetting, as she certainly did, the fact of having two prisoners in her particularly private van.

But when a woman is called upon to delight overflowing audiences with her charms time after time, she is apt in her vanity to forget all else. Miss West was but a woman, and she forgot Jolly and the aged one.

The hours rolled on, and midnight drew nigh. All who intended to carry home more liquor than was good for them, had filled their gastronomical cellars, and were wending their tortuous ways towards their places of rest; some to the habitual couch, others to ditches, few to the shelter of friendly ricks. One man, of original turn of mind, tried to go to bed on the top of a milestone, and succeeded fairly well. He was discovered next morning with his nose on one side, and his toes on the other, in the shape of a letter A, on the verge of suffocation.

But to return. The revels were over, and Miss West, having counted over the gains upon the drum with Mr. Mardle, who was indeed her husband, the Miss being a thing of the past, suggested supper, and went to the caravan for certain cooking utensils. There she discovered her prisoners fast asleep.

"Dear me," she said, "I had quite forgotten 'em. Wake up—will you?"

The aged one was first aroused, or rather partially so, and was put outside. His faculties not being fully restored, he came to the conclusion that he had been turned out of the beer-shop at the closing hour, and went staggering home.

With Jolly it was different. He was sober enough when Miss West awoke him, and not a little terrified at finding it so late. Miss West told him it was approaching one o'clock in the morning.

"You get home," she said, "and don't you say you were shut up here, or I'll lock you up one day, and skin you."

Jolly was awfully cold when he got outside, and in addition to other miseries he was not at all certain which way to go. He tried to get his idea of the locality, and failed, and at length was driven to make inquiries of the passers-by.

These were few in number, and principally of a rough character, with more beer than men really need under their waistcoats. All the wisest and best among the people had returned home long before, and were snug in bed.

The first man he spoke to did not answer, but gave a lurch and a hic-cup; the second called him a fool; and the third aimed a blow at him. So Jolly gave up inquiring, and thought he would try to find the way home himself.

He was inclined to think he ought to go to the right, but was almost convinced he ought to go to the left. After debating with himself for awhile he resolved to go to the left.

It led him from the scene of the revels into a lane, which he fancied was strange to him, but as there was a light a little way down which might belong to a house, he kept on.

The light did not come from the abode of an inhabitant of the place. It proceeded from a fire, round which some half-dozen half-caste gipsies were seated, eating their supper.

Greene came upon it suddenly at a bend in the lane, and would fain have retreated, but sharp ears heard his footstep, and sharp eyes perceived him the moment he came in view.

"Jim," cried an old hag.

Jim, a swarthy young gipsy, of twenty or so, was upon his feet and beside Jolly in a moment.

"What news, master?"

"I want to find my way back to the college," replied Jolly.

"What college, master?"

"Warmington College," replied Jolly.

"It's a book-learning cub," cried the old woman. "He's been out on the spree. Bring him to the fire and let him warm himself."

"I must not stop," said Jolly, backing a little. "I ought to have been home long ago."

"Of course you ought, my dear," said the old woman, "but in for a penny, in for a pound, as the old saying goes. Come and sit down and let me talk to you, my pretty dear. Bring him along, Jim. He wants somebody to take care of him, or he'll be robbed of that pretty watch and chain. Perhaps he would like a bit of supper."

CHAPTER XXIX.

JOLLY GREENE'S ADVENTURE WITH THE GIPSIES.

"I WOULD rather go home," said Jolly to the old gipsy woman.

"But you can't till my Jim have supped, and he shall take you home. Sit down, my pretty master, and let the old woman tell you your fortune."

There were five gipsies besides Jim, who escorted Jolly to the fireside—the old hag, whose years might have been something near a hundred, a man of forty, a woman about the same age, a girl of nineteen, and a boy of fourteen. Room was made for Jolly between the two latter.

"Hagar," said the old hag, addressing the girl, "it isn't often you have such a sweetly pleasant gentleman to sit beside you. How proud you ought to be!"

"I am, mother," replied the girl, laughing.

Jolly was immensely flattered. In all the course of his life, except by his mother, he had never been called pretty. Only the most vivid imagination would have been warranted in esteeming him so.

A 'bus driver who nearly ran him down in Baker-street once addressed him with—"out of the way my beauty," but that can scarcely be ranked among the list of compliments bestowed upon young Greene.

The gipsies were uncommonly glad to see him, the old woman wonderfully so; she became quite elated as she looked upon his fine clothes and thick gold watch chain. She even tried to sing.

"Jim," she said, addressing the man, "is it safe, do you think?"

"How should I know?" he asked, surlily. "If you like to risk it—do it."

"It don't matter what I risk, my love," she said. "I've only a few years to live, and it don't matter to me where I spend them. You are fond of the lanes and woods, and might feel the loss of your liberty."

"I've lost it once," he said, with an oath, "and don't want to run any risk."

"But such a soft bit of clay to work on."

"So it is, mother."

"Shall I go on?"

"If you like; it's a good garland that's round the pig's neck."

Young Greene heard nothing of the foregoing dialogue; he was occupied in receiving the attentions of the young gipsy girl—going through a mild form of "canoodling," if the word may be admitted into this story.

The girl had splendid eyes, and knew how to use them; they were regular fixers, gleaming pins, and Jolly was the butterfly. He was impaled.

"You have a father?" she said.

"Yes," replied Jolly, "a par."

"And a mother?"

"A mar," he explained—"common people have mothers."

The young girl grinned, and winked at the gipsy boy behind Jolly's back. That boy went into convulsions. Something amused him.

"I think you very pretty," said the girl, with a frankness which, with a more cunning nature than Jolly possessed, might have laid her open to the suspicion of being a humbug.

"Do you think so?" asked Jolly, feeling his nose as if he mistrusted that feature above all others.

"You are quite beautiful," she said, and taking hold of Jolly's hand she squeezed it.

The position was novel to Jolly, and carried him quite away. His features underwent a series of contortions that would have won him a prize in an agony show; but he meant them to be fascinating.

"Hagar," cried the old woman.

"Yes, mother."

"Ask the pretty gentleman what the time is."

Hagar asked him, and Jolly pulled out his watch.

"Half-past one," he said, "and it ought to be wound up."

"Let me wind it," said the old woman, "pass the watch and the key and I will wind it so well. It shall go beautifully."

"Give me your watch, pretty boy," said Hagar, smiling.

How could Jolly resist her? He handed over his watch and his purse in which he kept the key. The old woman opened the purse, and seeing so little in it (Billy was cash keeper you will remember), asked who had robbed him.

"I got a friend to keep my money," replied Jolly.

"You are in bad hands," said the hag, "you ought to have a friend like me. Now tell Hagar where you came from, and who you are."

In ten minutes they had a brief history of young Greene out of him, and the old hag was keenly interested. She at least understood the position young Sharp held, and was inclined to think she knew him."

"Jim," she said, turning to the man and holding up two fingers, "give him something to drink."

"So strong, mother," he said.

"He wants to sleep—and let him rest until we are far away."

"White or red?"

"White," she said; "he is but a boy—the other,"

dropping her voice, "might kill him. Give him something to drink," again aloud, "and then pretty Hagar shall wait upon him."

Jim, the gipsy, disappeared into a tent close by, and speedily returned with a bottle. This he passed to Hagar with a meaning look, and she, producing a tin cup, half filled it.

"You may drink, pretty gentleman," she said; "it will do you good, and is no stronger than tea."

Jolly drank, for he was thirsty, and the liquid, whatever it was, seemed uncommonly good. It warmed him and made his eyes glisten. He admired Hagar more than ever, and half made up his mind to kiss her.

"You are very pretty," he said, coming out very strong.

"Ah! you say so," she replied, "but you gentlemen like to have fun with the gipsy girl. Have some more wine?"

"I don't mind if I do," returned Jolly, and again he drank.

After the second dose he became hilarious, and did try to kiss Hagar; but somehow the boy got between them, and Jolly nearly kissed him instead. Finding him in the way, young Greene gathered his anger and gave him a push.

"What do you mean by sticking yourself here?" he asked.

"It's likely I'm going to stand by and see you kiss Hagar," said the boy.

"I'll kiss her if I like!" said Jolly.

"No you won't!"

The other gipsies were all silent, and Jolly, ha tasted the blood of pugilism once that day, grew ripe for another encounter.

"I will kiss her," he said; "get out of my way."

The boy laughed and stood his ground. Jolly felt it was necessary to assert himself, or sink for ever in the estimation of that black-eyed little witch. He stooped down and went head first at the gipsy boy.

These tactics answered fairly well with the oldest inhabitant, but with the sprightly young wanderer it was different. He had considerable knowledge of the fistic art, and dealt out to Jolly an "upper cut" that considerably added to the proportions of his already freely-developed nose. Jolly raised his head, staggered back, and sat down staring.

It could not have been the blow alone that so confused him. The whole scene was spinning ound before him. The old hag—a foremost figure —and seemingly stooping over him, was travelling round at the rate of thirty miles an hour.

"Oh! where's mar," asked Jolly.

"Pretty boy is not well," said the old hag—"lie down."

He lay, or rather fell down, and closed his eyes; somebody said, "he's going," but who it was he neither knew nor cared. His agony was now indescribable.

The whirling continued for awhile, and then gave way to an easy gliding motion. He seemed to be going down some stream with a wide, wide sea faintly visible in the distance. The sensation was delicious; he forgot all else, and glided on until a great cloud descended upon him, and he remembered no more.

"Clean gone," said Jim the gipsy.

"Yes," said the old hag, "now out with the change—quick!"

The "change" appeared to be a suit of old boy's clothes, which might have fetched fourpence in Hounsditch. In a twinkling the clothes Jolly wore were whipped off and the others substituted, and a very poor object he looked in his new garments.

"Now the sack," said the old hag, "and stow him away safe."

"What shall we do with him?" asked the man called Jim.

"Anything you like," was the reply. "Perhaps

It will be safer if you put him on the door-step of the college; only beware of the grabs."

"All right," said the man.

A sack was produced, and with the boy's assistance the insensible Jolly was got into it. The man shouldered him like a pig for market, and, followed by the boy, walked away with him.

The college was just across two fields, and the man knew his way well. The path he chose brought him up to the gate of the Reverend Copley Cobbem's private garden.

It was locked, but the gipsy produced a bunch of false keys from his pocket, and speedily opened it, without taking the trouble to put down his burden. Across the garden the pair went until they came to a door.

"Here's the place," said the man, "help me down with him. Gently, or he may wake."

"He would be the first who did so soon," said the boy, with a grin.

They got him down and out of the sack. Jolly was breathing heavily, but quite unconscious of everything around him.

"It's cold for the time of year," said the man, looking up at the stars, "and I don't think he's got much stamina. It's hardly safe to leave him here. I wish we could find a warmer place."

"There's a tub or something over there," said the boy, peering into the darkness.

"I see it," replied the man.

They went over and found it to be a huge flower-pot, such as is sometimes seen in the porch of a gentleman's house. It had no plant in it, but was full of dead leaves and dry earth, the sweepings of the garden.

"We might put him in here," said the man thoughtfully, "and pad him all round with this rubbish. It would at least keep him warm."

The boy seconded the idea. It was pleasant in his eyes, and the man emptied out the rubbish upon the gravel walk. Then they brought over young Jolly, set him upright in it, and filled the vacant space around him with rubbish. When the work was completed he looked like a fine cactus in the dim light.

He appeared to be pretty comfortable, and snored quite musically as the two gipsies stole away, leaving him to be discovered by the first comer in the morning.

CHAPTER XXX.

MR. AND MRS. GREENE HAVE THEIR NERVES UPSET AND SLIGHTLY DISCOMPOSE THE REV. COPLEY.

AMONG other establishments upset by the revels that of the Reverend Copley Cobbem figured conspicuously. The odd man who usually came early to look after the garden did not turn up, owing to his having passed the night in the pound, into which he had been put by some facetious friends, in company with two donkeys, a pig, and a wall-eyed cart-horse.

With these animals he passed the night, and awaking in the morning, found it necessary to have a change of garments before he entered the respectable precints of Warmington College, and having none of his own to hand, set off to borrow a suit of a brother who lived four miles away. Hence it was that when the breakfast hour arrived he was still an absentee.

Perkins was pretty right as his dissipation was for the most part confined to show-seeing (he went five times to Mardle's Entertainment and was the last to leave each time) and shooting for nuts; but Jiggles had the eyes of a dying dolphin, with all sorts of colours in the whites, and had plainly gone in for something stronger than water or cold tea.

When Jiggles did this he was always " bad " in the morning, and his temper was something dreadful. He quarrelled with all his fellow-servants, and was,

when he got the chance, quite brutal to Perkins, who, however, generally kept out of his way.

On this morning he kept so well out of the way that Jiggles had everything to do himself, and in a furious frame of mind he was laying the breakfast table when, to his amazement, the visitors' bell rang.

"Who can this be?" he asked himself. "Is it some howdacious tramp, or is it somebody who's been drunk all night, and come to the wrong 'ouse? Where's Perkins?"

He went to look for Perkins, who at that moment was on the top of the house floating a small paper boat in the cistern, and failed to find him. The bell rang again, and Jiggles felt bound to answer it.

"But who can it be?" he asked himself, as he drew back the bolts and chains.

On opening the door he beheld a stout lady and gentleman, both richly dressed as far as materials went, but without the taste which comes with cultivation. Jiggles put them down as a greengrocer and his wife out for a holiday, and prepared himself to be familiar and condescending.

"Is Mr. Copley hin?" asked the gentleman.

"He aint hup yet," replied Jiggles. "He's had a roughish night. There's a boy lost, and missus have been rampaging at him for letting the poopils go to the revel."

"A boy lost!" exclaimed the lady. "Can it be our Jolliffe?"

It was Mrs. Greene and her husband who had called thus early, having come down late the night before, and put up at the White Hart. Their object in appearing so soon after dawn was to give Jolly the full benefit of the happy day they had designed for him.

And you see how soon the mother's instinct was aroused. A boy was missing, and it must be her own sweet darling—the hapless Jolliffe.

Jiggles was keen in his way, and saw that the parents of young Greene were before him. His plan of action was instantly arranged.

"Mr. Cobbem," he said, "will be down in a few minutes, and as the house aint quite in horder would you mind waiting for a few minutes in the garden? You can get into it through that little green gate."

"But could you not send Master Greene to us?" asked Mrs. Greene.

"I don't think he's quite hup yet," replied Jiggles, hurriedly; "but I'll go and see. The green gate leads into the garden."

"Come along, Mariar," said Mr. Greene. "I'm fond of a garden."

They passed through the little green gate, and entered the land forbidden to all boys, and strolled up the gravel walk, commenting on the plants and flowers as they went along.

"What a lovely what-d'ye-call-'em!" said Mr. Greene, pointing to a myrtle just coming into bloom. "And look at them geraliums! Blessed if it aint like a slice off Covent-garden!"

"I likes the things in pots," returned Mrs. Greene, "'aving growed so many of 'em in our 'ouse. There's something over there which I've never seen afore."

"It looks like a turnip," said Mr. Green, fixing on his spectacles to get a better view of it. "But, Mariar, it's a-moving."

"Being blowed by the wind, love."

"You be blowed!" said Mr. Greene. "It's rewolving like. It's something alive. Come on—let us see what it is."

They advanced, and looked upon—their Jolliffe, just recovering from the gipsy's potation, but hardly able to realise his position.

Of the feelings of Mr. and Mrs. Greene you may judge. Of all the things they had looked upon—of all the scrapes their Jolliffe had got into—and their name was legion—they had never looked on aught like this.

For some moments neither could speak, but stood watching their one little lamb twist and turn his head, rolling his eyes as if he had a nightmare; and probably he had the nearest thing to it you can get in the day.

"Ow—ow!" he said; "let me out! I'm always being tied up or shoved about. Ow—ow! where's my mar?"

"Jolliffe, my love," said Mrs. Greene, awaking, "I am here!"

She threw her arms around his head—it was the only part of his frame she could fairly get at—and sobbed as she nearly smothered him. Mr. Greene walked round the pair with feeble tottering steps, mumbling all sorts of things to himself, and utterly unable to comprehend the scene.

"Jolliffe," cried Mrs. Greene again, "it is me—your mar!"

"Get the boy out of that flower-pot," said Mr. Greene. "Here, I'll do it."

He took Jolly by the collar and drew him out, like a carrot or parsnip, and exposed the garments which he had received from the gipsies in exchange. Mrs. Greene shrieked twice violently.

"How dare they put you here? How dare they dress you so?" cried she. "Jolliffe, my poor, poor boy, don't you know your mother?"

"I don't know nothing nor nobody," he answered, vaguely, "and I don't want to know 'em."

"Jolliffe," cried Mrs. Greene, "them words is harrows to your mar!"

"I don't know, and I don't care," muttered Jolly, glaring wildly about him.

"Mariar," said Mr. Greene, suddenly becoming ferocious, "I want to know if this is really our son?"

"It is the featers and the form," replied Mrs. Greene; "but the intellecks and his clothes are gone."

"I'll know who did it," said Mr. Greene, angrily knocking his hat over his eyes. "I'll have the life of somebody for insulting my son! Here comes somebody. Oh! it's the schoolmaster. He is responsible for this."

The Reverend Copley Cobbem came hurrying up, prepared with a story about Jolly having gone to the revels, and, staying late, had probably gone home with one of his numerous aristocratic friends to sleep; but when he beheld Mr. and Mrs. Greene with a scarecrow between them, and recognised in that scarecrow the missing boy, his astonishment was—as well it might be—boundless.

"Sir," said Mr. Greene, pointing to his son, "look here!"

"Yes," said Mrs. Greene, "how dare you bring him to this?"

Mrs. Greene had got it into her head that Jolly had been subjected to some sort of school discipline, and, as the Reverend Copley seemed unable to speak, she proceeded to express her opinion upon it.

"And this," she said, "is the mild but firm treatment which you promised to use to our darling boy—a-sticking him into filthy clothes, and jamming him into a flower-pot, and packing him up tight with all sorts of rubbage! It's worse than the torturers of the Howly Imposition."

"Mr. Greene—madam!" exclaimed the bewildered schoolmaster, "I give you my word I know nothing about this sad business!"

"Do you mean to say he put hisself there?" asked Mrs. Greene.

"No, I don't, madam——"

"But who is to do it, if you didn't?"

"That's it!" said Mr. Greene. "You did it, or he did it; and I'll tell you what, Mister Copper Cobbing, I'll take it out of you for insulting my boy, who'll have more money than you ever dreamt of!"

"My dear sir, hear me!" cried the reverend gentleman, alarmed at the violence of Mr. Greene, who dashed his hat upon the ground, and entered

upon the preliminaries of a war dance. innocent—I have had no hand in this vil— business!"

"Who had, then?" asked Mr. Greene.

"I don't know.

"Don't listen to him," urged Mrs. Greene; "it him on the 'ed! Oh! Jolliffe, my poor boy, don't you know your mar?"

But Jolliffe did not reply. He only looked about him wildly, and said "Ow—ow!"

"Before you proceed to extremities," continued the Reverend Copley, speaking hurriedly as he dodged away from Mr. Greene, "which may lead to contusions and the shedding of blood, I beseech you to hear me!"

"I won't!"

"But you must," said the Reverend Copley, getting into the thick of a geranium-bed, whither he was followed by Mr. Greene, working his arms in an awe-inspiring style, "as a matter of justice! Hear me—come into the house and hear me—and if I do not prove my innocence I will return with you to an even more sequestered spot than this, and meet you *as a man!*"

"Done with you, then!" said Mr. Greene, slightly pacified.

"Come with me."

"All right. Now, Mariar, bring Jolliffe along. I'll have him afore me until this job is settled."

The Rev. Copley escorted them into the house, and ushered them into the private breakfast-room, where Mrs. Cobbem was calmly arranging the table.

"My love," said Mr. Cobbem, "let me introduce you to my most estimable friends, Mr. and Mrs. Greenly Greene."

"Not forgetting Master Jolliffe Greene," said Mrs. Greene, "who's been tortered out of his born senses by your cruelty here!"

CHAPTER XXXI.

YOUNG JOLLY SPENDS A HAPPY DAY WITH HIS PAR AND HIS MAR.

MRS. COBBEM turned her hard black eyes upon Mrs. Greene, and that amiable lady felt that she was in the presence of a superior power. Mrs. Cobbem calmly asked—

"What cruelty?"

"Sticking boys in flower-pots," said Mrs. Greene.

"Mr. Cobbem, will you have the goodness to explain?" said Mrs. Cobbem, turning upon him.

He did so, as far as he could, and that was as much as anybody but the actual sufferer could explain. Jolly had been found in a flower-pot.

"The question is, how did he get there?" said Mrs. Cobbem.

"That's what I want to know," said Mrs. Greene.

"You shall have all the information that can be given," said Mrs. Cobbem, "if you will allow us to proceed in the regular way. Please be seated. Won't you take a chair Mrs. Greene?"

Mrs. Cobbem was born to rule and she subdued them. They sat down, and Jolliffe was put upon a chair. He was a little better, but still far from being clear of the great confusion the night's adventure had brought upon him.

"Now, Mr. Cobbem, ask that boy where he been all night."

"All night!" exclaimed Mrs. Greene.

"Madam," said Mrs. Cobbem, "that son of your absented himself from the college without leave. Hence his disgraceful position. If you will give us time —"

The cross-examination was long and tedious. It was conducted by Mrs. Cobbem, who never asked a question direct herself, but told her husband to do it. Little by little a dim knowledge of the truth was extracted from Jolly, and Mrs. Cobbem's ready wit made it all clear.

"He got among a low lot of gipsies," she said,

"and they have robbed him, as might have been expected. I hope he will never disgrace himself in that way again, for the sake of the college. If he does we shall not be able to look over it."

This was a bold position to take up, for Mrs. Greene was at first bent upon taking Jolly away at once, and it brought success. Both Mr. and Mrs. Greenly Greene felt Jolly had somehow committed himself, and were rather impressed with Mrs. Cobbem's kindness.

"We are obliged to be strict," continued Mrs. Cobbem, "or we should not be able to keep up the tone of the place. We only take gentlemen, and we expect our pupils to be in every way worthy of the name. We do not have boys of low birth and position here."

"Certainly not, mum," said Mr. Greene, and his wife said so too.

"I should advise your son to change his clothes now," pursued Mrs. Cobbem, "and perhaps you will stay to breakfast."

"Well, I think I can pick a bit," replied Mr. Greene, and Mrs. Greene untied her bonnet strings. The Rev. Copley rang the bell and handed Jolly over to the care of Jiggles, with instructions to let him have a warm bath, and send him down to breakfast as soon as possible."

"And keep him clear of all the other boys," he said, "as I do not wish him to be the victim of unseemly curiosity. We train our boys to be reserved of speech," he said, addressing Mr. Greene. "All gentlemen are so."

"In course," said Mr. Greene.

They did not wait breakfast for Jolly, but before it was half over he came in, looking better than might have been expected. He knew his mar, and kissed her affectionately. He also knew his par, and shook hands with him.

"You must be uncommon hungry," said Mr. Greene; "sit down, Jolliffe, and pick a bit."

Jolly, nothing loth, sat down, and went in for a little all round the table—toast, eggs, ham, marmalade, and tea—to the great dismay of the Rev. Copley and the wrath of Mrs. Cobbem. Both diplomatically strove to check him—things were put out of his reach, and hints given about the evils of over-eating, but Jolly kept on until he really could eat no more, not even if he had stood up.

During breakfast the reverend gentleman and his wife plied the Greenes with stories of the scions of noble houses who had received training at Warmington College. They generally spoke of them as the young Duke of G— and the Honourable M—, as if the full revelation of their names would have brought trouble upon them.

Mrs. Cobbem initiated this mysterious form of conversation, and the Rev. Copley took it up. It answered admirably, and Mr. and Mrs. Greene, so far from entertaining any indignation at the treatment their lambkin had received, were fully convinced that they were highly favoured by his being admitted into the college at all.

The morning event over, the Greenes departed to spend the happy day designed for Jolly. As the door closed upon them the Reverend Copley drew a deep breath and exclaimed

"Thank Heaven I have made it all right with them. I do not want to lose a pupil who pays like young Greene."

"You made it right," said Mrs. Cobbem. "You —why you did your best to spoil all. You would have fawned upon those vulgar people, and they would have sat upon you, and taken their son away. I dealt with them in a different way, and you see the result. You have made it right with them, indeed. What next?"

The Reverend Copley did not reply. Why should he when he knew that a mild defeat might be followed by a complete route? Just then the school-bell rang and he left the room, to vent what little wrath he felt upon the first public offender.

Jolly, with his parents, turned their steps towards the village, as Mr. Greene was going to order a dinner at the White Hart, to be ready by their return from a little ruralising in the woods and fields.

"I aint seen much of the country in my time," said the old gentleman, "but you know'd something about it, Mariar, when you was a gal—didn't you?"

"My mar and par were both of a country family," replied Mrs. Greene.

"What was your par and mar?" asked Mr. Greene, with the dawn of a grin upon his expressive countenance.

"What could they be?" was the reply. "You know, Greene, I've got blood in me."

"Yes, and hot stuff too."

"I don't mean that blood—blue blood—and it's come out in our Jolly, and that is why Mr. Cobbem thinks he's such a gentleman."

"It's my belief," said Mr. Greene, pulling up to meditate, "that Cobbem is a humbug."

"No he ain't; but his wife is a vixen."

"Now, I thought her rather nice," said old Greene, repressing a tendency to smack his lips. "She's got good black eyes and her cheeks was like pippins."

"Oh, indeed!" said Mrs. Greene, all the ornaments in her bonnet quivering like fine grass at eve, "and I suppose she's the only woman that's got dark eyes, and cheeks with a colour in 'em."

Mrs. Greene's eyes were dark enough, and no peony ever boasted a deeper red than her face did then. Mr. Greene noticed these symptoms of a coming flood, and hastened to check it.

"Arter all," he said, "she's a coarsish woman, and got no real manners."

"It's all bounce."

"So it is, my love."

"How our Jolly is enjoying of this day!" said Mrs. Greene, as they resumed their way. "What is married life without one hoffspring?"

"Nuffin," replied Mr. Greene, sentimentally, and the old couple, linking their arms together, went lovingly on.

Jolly was enjoying himself in spite of the rather trying adventures of the preceding night—being, while Mrs. Greene was speaking, occupied in the chase of a butterfly, and caught it he would but for a ditch, which he went into head first just as he was on the point of success.

It was a dry ditch, and his clothes were all right, but nettles grew there, and Jolly, as they took him out, looked as if he had just undergone the first process in tattooing. He howled bitterly, but his "mar" kissed him fondly, and all was peace and happiness again.

The dinner was ordered at the White Hart to be ready at four o'clock, and William the waiter undertook to have on the table the best the house afforded. He also packed them a luncheon basket to take to the wood, and sent a little boy—his own son—with them to carry it.

The son of William was thorough country-bred, sharp as country boys go, and well up in all the histories of birds and beasts and insects to be found in those parts. He was keen enough to see whom he was dealing with, and at once took possession of the party.

"Will ye go to t' big wood," he asked, addressing Jolly.

"Ask my mar," replied young Greene.

Mrs. Greene was asked, and replied she would go anywhere to see the "primroses and wiolets." The boy laughed, and said she could see them in the spring, but he was "afeard there warn't none up just then," as it was autumn.

"Then all I've got to say is, that it's a poor country," said Mrs. Greene. "In the country where I lived with my mar and par we had 'em all the year round."

William, the waiter, convinced that he was dealing with a man of money, and one who might be disposed to be liberal, urged on the cook to prepare a feast worthy of the occasion, and by four o'clock it was ready to be served as soon as the Greenes returned. But the clock struck, and the hands crawled down to the half-hour and they had not come back.

"Where can they be?" said William. "That dinner will be spiled."

He went to the front, and looked up and down the road; he went to the rear, and looked over the fields. No signs of the party could he see.

"It's hodd," he thought. "He said four o'clock; and I told that boy o' mine to get 'em back by that time. He can't have lost 'em!"

Five o'clock struck, and out he went again, but could see nothing. The sun was slowly setting westward, and the mists were just beginning to rise. In another half-hour it would be dangerous for old people to be roaming about the woods or fields.

"I don't know what's come to 'em," said William, despairingly. "Everything is chips and cinders. I'll murder that youngster o' mine, I will—he's always up to some trick or t'other."

Six o'clock, and no Greenes; seven o'clock and darkness, but no Greenes; half-past seven, and a cart drove up to the door.

"Hallo!" roared a voice.

"Who is it?" asked William, rushing to the door.

"Is this the White Hart?"

"It is."

"And is the passage clear, for I've got a gent as can't get out of my cart if there's people about."

"Who and what is it?" asked William.

"I ordered dinner here," said the voice of Mr. Greene, speaking from the bottom of the cart. "You know me."

"It's the gent as brought the young gent from the college," said William, "and alone, sir. Where is the young gent and the lady?"

"I don't know. Aint they come back?"

"No, sir."

"Then the Emperor of Chaney knows more about 'em than I do. But get somebody else to help you, waiter, as I'm inside a sack, and aint got another blessed harticle on all hover me."

"The gent was in a hurry and uncommon cold," said the man with the cart, apologetically, "and so I've done my best."

"But what does it all mean?" asked William, wildly.

"It means this," said Mr. Greene, with a good round oath, "that I came down here to have a happy day, and I'm jiggered if I haven't had it."

CHAPTER XXXII.

MR. GREENE'S NARRATIVE—THE RETURN OF MOTHER AND SON.

WILLIAM, the waiter, took a few seconds to recover his scattered senses before calling upon the ostler to help him in the task of carrying Mr. Greene upstairs, which proved to be no light affair, as that good gentleman ranked among the fleshy men of the world, and being furthermore in an exhausted condition, hung a dead weight upon those who bore him.

But they got him upstairs, and put him into a bed, where he lay full a quarter of an hour before he would explain matters to the landlord, William the waiter, and some half-dozen others who had gathered about the door.

"That chap as brought me home is to have a tuvrin," were the first words he said. "Pay him, and send for the Reverend Copley Cobbem, and ax him to bring a suit of his clothes. They'll about fit me."

"But where's my boy?" asked William, the waiter.

"Is that the himp who took us into the w??]?" asked Mr. Greene, becoming ferocious in a moment.

"No child of mine is a himp," said William.

"Then he aint a child of yourn," replied Mr. Greene, and put his nose under the bed-clothes, as if he had settled the question.

But William was not settled himself. He was not the sort of man to be put down at a moment's notice.

For twenty years or more he had been waiter at the White Hart, where he was much respected. He had married from there, had brought to light a numerous family, which had thriven for the most part on broken "wittles," taken home in hats, umbrellas, red cotton handkerchiefs, and other ways; and he was not going to stand there and be branded as the father of an imp without calling the offender to the bar of explanation.

"Sir," he said, putting his right hand on his hip and bending his right leg in a manner supposed to be easy and graceful—"sir, may I ax what this child—and whether he is mine or not aint no business of yours—have been doing of this day to be stigamartised as a himp?"

"Fust, then," said Mr. Greene, popping his head up like a Jack-in-the-box, "he's been and put my boy up a tree, and he can't get down again."

"Put your boy up a tree!" said William, smiling sarcastically. "No need to do that, I think—he can get up a tree hisself."

"Anyhow," said Mr. Greene, "he helped him up a tree to go and get a bird's nest, which was hempty——"

"Nateral this time o' year," murmured William. "Birds aint chickens, and don't lay all the year round."

"The nest," pursued Mr. Greene, "was hempty, and my son, after convincing himself of the fact, was a-coming down again, when he got hisself wedged in a fork of the tree, and no mortial man will ever get him out of it."

"Wedged in the fork of a tree," said William. "Well, he won't fall off. Where's my boy?"

"He," said Mr. Greene, rising another foot or so, "never went up, and when I told him to go and help my Jolly he said, as he'd see me bothered fust. Now, sir" (this to the landlord, who was a stolid man, and seldom spoke—a sort of human sponge, too, in a way, who absorbed everything, and gave out nothing unless he was squeezed), "I ask if that was the sort of guide to a respectable party?"

"Go on, sir," said the landlord, reserving his opinion. "What did he do next?"

"He said to me, he said, 'Sit down there,' replied Mr. Greene, "a-pointing to a little bit of bank about the size of a cask of butter; 'you sit there, and I'll go and get somebody to help you.' So I sat down, while my missus stood agin the tree offering sich consolation as a mother can give sich times, just to soothe down Jolly's howling, which he gave out strong."

"Being wedged like," said the landlord, feeling called upon to say something as Mr. Greene paused.

William, the waiter, only smiled. His feelings had been grossly outraged, and he could not sympathise with this man.

"I hadn't been a sitting there long," continued Greene, père, "when a sort of creeping sensation, with a dash of tickling, came all up my legs, and began to rub them, thinking I was getting a chill. Then I'm blessed if I wasn't stung and bitten all the way up in the most ferocious manner."

"Hemmets or ants?" suggested William, the waiter, coolly.

"They was little black things," pursued Mr. Greene, "with a lot of 'ed, and some of 'em with bits of straw in their mouths. A lot of 'em came down my legs as I stood up, but there must have been a million at least left behind, and peg away they did, frightful!"

"Some of 'em," said William, the waiter, with icy coldness, "will stick like leeches."

"If that man aint quiet," said Mr. Greene, "I'll up and hout of bed and knock his 'ed orf."

"William, be quiet," said the landlord.

"All right, sir."

"I run up and down," Mr. Greene went on, "and I stamped, and I danced, and maybe I swore a bit, but they kept buzzing away, biting here and biting there, until I thought I was being drilled right through; and I felt it necessary to take everything off. 'Stay here and keep a eye on Jolly,' I says to my wife, 'while I go and have a reglar clear out.' 'I'll stop till the boy comes back,' she says, and away I runs, straight away to a field, where I finds a brook, and there I sits down in a sort of frenzy and tears everything orf. When I comes to look they was all over me, and I looked as if I had the measles."

"Red bumps," explained William, "which bite they will."

Mr. Greene made an impatient movement with his hand, and the landlord shook his head at William, who stepped back a pace, and became a listener again.

"I got into the brook," continued the narrator, "and I begin to wash, for nothing else would move 'em, and I'd got half way through 'em when I heard a roar, and looks up and sees a great brute of a bull, chucking my things right and left, and snorting and banging his feet on the ground, and soon he comes at me, with my shirt on one horn and half my breeches on the other, and away I runs."

Somebody laughed at this point of the painful story, and Mr. Greene said it was William. William, however, denied it, and the story was continued.

"T'other side of the field was the road, and there, as I went through the hedge head fust, I come up agin that chap with his cart, and skeered his horse so that he stood upright, and shot about a dozen loaves into the road. He wanted to fight me, that baker chap did, but while he was picking up the bread he undertook to bring me home in a sack for a pound, but I thought he would come at once and he didn't."

"Where did he go to?" asked the landlord.

"He—what he called it—finished his rounds," replied Mr. Greene; "and whenever he stopped to deliver any bread he made me put my head in the sack, so that I've been nigh smothered a dozen times. He also put up at three public-houses, and at one of 'em he had a fight with another baker. Altogether," said Mr. Greene, with sarcastic bitterness, "I've had a wery happy day."

An impressive silence followed the conclusion of this painful narrative. It was broken by the landlord.

"And where's your boy, sir?" he asked.

"Up in the fork of the tree for all I know," replied Mr. Greene.

"And where's your wife, sir?"

"A sitting at the foot of the tree consoling him."

"And where is that tree?"

"I don't know—somewhere in a big wood."

"There are two, sir," said the landlord, politely; "one is four hundred acres, and t'other six; one is to the east, and t'other to the west—which is it?"

"I don't know, you must go and find out," replied Mr. Greene.

"And may I ax, sir," said William, softly, "where my child is?"

"I only wish I had him here," returned Mr. Greene; "that's all—I'd twist his neck."

"Not while his father was by," replied William, the waiter.

"William," said the landlord, "go downstairs and send James off to Mr. Cobbem's at once."

"And pay that baker," said Mr. Greene.

"How much, sir?"

"A pound. It's all right."

But the baker demanded more. While Mr. Greene had been narrating he had been drinking, and the strong liquor prompted him to charge five shillings for the sack, on the ground that it couldn't be used by a respectable man in business after a porpoise had gone half over the world in it.

Mr. Greene bade them pay him off, and promised the ostler half-a-crown if he would kick him. The ostler took the half-crown, and he and the baker in the tap-room shared the spoil. Such is life—full of craft and villainy. Even those we buy to serve us take an early opportunity to sell us.

CHAPTER XXXIII.

THE FATE OF YOUNG GREENE.

THE complicated events of the night and day were not yet over. When the offspring of William, the waiter, turned up—as he did, alone—his father took him by the collar of his smock-frock, and shook him until his head looked like a dim catherine-wheel, his eyes doing duty for sparks, and his mouth sputtering to perfection.

"You young villain," asked William, "where are they?"

"How should I know?" said the boy, defiantly. "I've been back and looked for 'em—aint I? and do you think you'll know one tree from another in the dark?"

"Why didn't you holler?" said William.

"So we did, and we heard a screeching, but when we moved to the spot it were a howl," replied the boy.

"This," said William, nervously wiping his forehead with his napkin, "will be a case of manslaughter. Didn't you see nothing of the lady?"

"No, and didn't want to," said his son, "for she gave I a clout on the head when the silly chap fixed hisself up, and said it were all my fault. I won't go nigh her no more."

"But they must be found," said William. "I'll go and hear what the old gent says."

He found Mr. Greene and the Reverend Copley Cobbem together, both in a perturbed state of mind.

"Any news, William?" asked the reverend gentleman.

"They can't be found," answered William; "the wood has been searched in wain."

"But they must be found," said Mr. Greene.

"They shall be found," added the Reverend Copley. "We cannot have respectable people perishing in the wood in this way."

"Then all I've got to say is," said William, who was half distracted, "that you had better go and find 'em. I can't do no more—my boy can't do no more; and it was a hevil day that the silly chap cast a shadder on our path."

William was getting metaphorical, he forget he was talking to the father of the missing boy. Mr. Greene quickly reminded him of it.

"May I ask," he said, "if you are deluding to my son?"

"Alluding, my dear sir," murmured the Reverend Copley—"alluding."

"I don't care a rush which," said Mr. Greene; "one or the other suits me, and I don't see that you need grumble at it."

"Oh! certainly not, my dear sir."

"And therefore I ask if that mutton-faced feller there alluded or deluded to my son when he talked about a silly chap?"

"I don't say he's downright silly," William explained, "but to me he have the aperience of not being quite right in his 'ed."

Mr. Greene, who was getting into a suit of the Reverend Copley Cobbem's garments, happened at the moment to have a boot in his hand. This, instead of putting on, he shied at William's head. William, quite an expert at ducking, got down like a sprite, and the boot went through a picture of Joseph's brethren selling Joseph to the Ishmaelites.

It was a lovely picture—all blue and yellow and black, the gift of the proprietors of the "Juvenile Delight" to their subscribers. William, who had always viewed this production as something miraculous in the way of art, looked with dismay upon the wreck, and expressed his opinion that Mr. Greene had done it.

"I'll do for you," said Mr. Greene, looking about for another weapon.

"There was only a limited number issooed," murmured William, "and the plate was destroyed arterwards, and——"

Mr. Greene dived down and took up the other boot. William prudently retreated, and the two gentlemen were left together.

"I see," said the Reverend Copley, "we must manage this affair ourselves. We must organise a regular search. My own servants can be fetched in a few minutes, and I dare say we can get a little volunteer assistance."

The odd man, Jiggles, and Perkins were sent for, and as soon as it was known that assistance was required half a score taproom frequenters, all more or less on the high road to intoxication, turned out and volunteered their services—among them the oldest inhabitant, who generously sank all difference between young Greene and himself, in the prospect of obtaining a little extra beer.

The Reverend Copley undertook to organise the party, and gave directions for the wood to be surrounded, and the party gradually close in, "as they do in jungles, where they hunt the royal Bengal tiger," he explained to Mr. Greene.

"But my son aint a tiger," said old Greene, savagely.

"No," replied the Reverend Copley, with a ready wit that staggered himself, "he is a lion—the lion of my school, I assure you. And, as the Irish would say, 'I *mane* it!' Ha—ha! My dear sir, I mane what I say."

The party having been got together and ready to start, the first difficulty arose. All the volunteers from the taproom wanted beer; so some was brought, and the oldest inhabitant by right of birth was the first to "dip his beak" into it.

He dipped it very deeply, and there were murmurings heard, but he either did not hear, or would not heed them. "When a man gits hold of a pot 'o beer," he said, "it beant right for him to trifle with it. I goes at un—and I drinks un."

They all had beer—Jiggles and the odd man too—and Perkins surreptitiously drained the pots, and immediately fell over the Reverend Copley's feet, doing considerable damage to his corns. Then the party, with a ladder, some ropes, and two lanterns, started.

The oldest inhabitant insisted upon being one of the ladder-bearers, and also in having the leading position. It was no use arguing with him, as he got hold of the end stave and clung to it like an old demon; so they gave in to him.

At the first start he—being now very uncertain on his legs—put the end through the coffee-room window of the White Hart, then he ran into the Reverend Copley, and finally somehow got into the horse-trough.

"Butter gi' it up, John," urged one of the men; "it be too much for ye."

"No it beant," replied John. "I'm as good as any two on ye now, and I'll take this 'ere ladder up to the wood, and I'll get the young chap down, dead or alive—so come on."

And off he went again, staggering from one side of the road to the other, until, in company with two fellow-bearers, he got into a ditch.

"This will never do," said the Reverend Copley. "The object of the expedition will be defeated unless this unfortunate old man is brought to reason."

"Reason be danged!" said the individual alluded to. "I knows what I can do—and I'll do it. That's more than any man about here can say."

"Better carry a lantern," said the reverend gentleman; "you will then become, as it were, a leader of the party."

It was a fatal suggestion, for it pleased the aged one, and having got hold of a lantern he entered upon his duties as a guide. This he performed so well that the ladder was only twice fixed in a stiff fence, and knocked no more than two garden gates to pieces, ere they got clear of the village.

Going up the hill to the wood was exciting sport. The oldest inhabitant fell over every little obstacle, and put out his lantern seven times. One wanted to get along with the other, but he would not hear of it, and all the odd matches of the company were used up in relighting the lantern of that idiotic old sinner.

Just as they reached the wood he went down for the eighth and last time. His lantern went out, of course, and there they left him with an empty match-box, trying to get a light with a headless match.

"I'll be arter ye in a brace of shakes," were his last words, and they saw him no more that night, for the simple reason that, having failed to get a light, he sank into meditation, and finally into a sweet sleep.

The party surrounded the wood, under the direction of the Reverend Copley, who told each man the precise angle he was to take.

"Consider the wood a wheel," he said, "and all of you spokes working to a common centre." That is a simple way of putting it, he explained to Mr. Greene, "which they will readily understand. You and I will go into the wood and make ourselves the centre."

"But how will they find us?" asked Mr. Greene, who did not exactly relish the prospect before him.

"We will keep shouting, and they will hear our voices."

It was all so easy and simple, the men really ought to have carried it out, especially as they all got a shilling on account before starting; but base is the conduct of man. As soon as the Reverend Copley and Mr. Greene left them, they all returned to the village for a little more beer.

Even the odd man, Jiggles, and Perkins betrayed him.

Having got into the centre of the wood, or as near as he could guess at it, the Reverend Copley, who was in his most jocular mood, proposed to adopt a cry he had picked up in his youth, and almost forgotten.

"It's only this, Mr. Greene," he said. "Surilicty—very simple, and easily acquired."

"I'll have a try," said Mr. Greene, and off went the pair shrieking "Surilicty!" at the top of their voices for a quarter of an hour.

"Do you hear them coming?" asked the reverend gentleman, pausing.

"Can't say I do," replied Mr. Greene.

"I thought I heard the bushes cracking. Surilicty!"

"Surilicty, surilicty!" cried Mr. Greene.

"I hear them now," said the Reverend Copley; "here they are."

"At 'em, men!" shouted a stentorian voice, as half-a-dozen brawny fellows dashed upon the pair. "Knock 'em down first, and see who they are arterwards."

"Hold!" cried the Rev. Copley, "there is some error here."

Perhaps there was, but the new comers did not stop to inquire into it. The two gentlemen were tripped up and bound in a twinkling.

"So I've got you at last," said the same voice.

"You shall repent of this," gasped the Rev. Copley; "you are a low lot of burglarious highwaymen ruffians."

"Hold 'ard, Jim," said the same voice; "there's summat wrong in these parties here. Show a light."

Jim showed a light, and by the glare of a lantern the Rev. Copley Cobbem saw half a dozen stalwart men in velveteen around him. A sense of relief came over him—he understood all.

"I see, my friend," he said, "you have mistaken us for poachers."

"Stop a moment," said the man, who appeared to be the leader; "there are some precious rum rigs got up, even the clerical more aint forgotten. Who are you?"

"The Rev. Copley Cobbem."

"Why, so you are, and who is your friend?"

"Mr. Greenely Greene, of London."

"Oh! and what is he doing here?"

"Looking for his son."

"Gammon! You be both poaching," said the head keeper, "and I do wonder at a gentleman of your spectability doing of that—I do."

"I give you my word," said the Rev. Copley, warmly, "that we are innocent of any felonious intent. We came in search of Mr. Greene junior, who had been, as I may observe, lost in the wood."

"Perhaps, Mister Copper," said one of the men, addressing the head keeper, "it's the old lady and boy as we come across."

"Hintelligent lady and boy with haristocratic nose," put in Mr. Greene, speaking for the first time. Hitherto he had been occupied in collecting his scattered faculties.

"The lady screeched," said the man, "and the boy was lying on his back, having seemin'ly come down a buster from the tree."

"He had freed himself most probably," suggested the Rev. Copley.

"And what became of them?" anxiously asked Mr. Greene.

"The boy ran one way, and the old gal t'other," replied the man, and somebody giggled. There had apparently been a little fun going on in connection with that flight.

"Well, I suppose," said the Rev. Copley, "that as we are recognised we may be released and go."

"I can't say that much," replied the head keeper, "for you see I have a dooty to do. Whosoever is found here arter dark aint got no right here, and we has to have 'em up straight."

"But surely you will not haul me—ME, the Rev. Copley Cobbem, of Warmington Hall—up before a magistrate?"

"Dooty is dooty," said the keeper, doggedly.

"So it is, but ——"

"Well, look here," said the keeper, with a burst of generosity, "we will let you off for a couple of quid."

"And what may that be? I am ignorant of the coin you name."

"Two suvrins," replied the keeper, disgusted at his want of knowledge; "and it's dirt cheap."

"So it is," said the men.

"I suppose you had better pay it," said the Rev. Copley, addressing Mr. Greene with an air of resignation.

"But I haven't got it," replied Mr. Greene, gruffly.

"Then I will give it," said the Reverend Copley, "and you can repay me on our return to the public-house."

So they were released, and the two sovereigns paid. Then, in a very melancholy frame of mind, they slowly wended their way back to the White Hart.

There they learnt that Mrs. Greene had indeed returned, but in a speechless condition, and was at that moment in the back parlour consuming gin and peppermint, with the hope of obtaining a little relief and a return of her powers of speech. They went to her at once, and found the gin and peppermint had nobly done its duty. She had not only recovered speech, but plenty of it.

"So, Mr. Greene," she said, "this is how you treat your wife, who have never had an unkind word, or an ill look, or ——"

"Mariar, it aint my fault," pleaded Mr. Greene; "it was all them blessed hants and a ferocious bull."

"I don't want to hear anythink about it," she said. "Where's Jolly?"

"I don't know, Mariar."

"Oh! my precious boy!" cried Mrs. Greene; "he's been and made an inhanimate copses of hisself. Oh—oh!"

"Gin and peppermint!" exclaimed Mr. Greene, readily, and more of the soothing syrup being at hand she underwent a second restoration.

"What is the hour?" asked the Reverend Copley, drawing out his watch. "Past twelve. I think I must return home, or my wife will be anxious about me."

"Your wife, sir, is in safety," said Mr. Greene; "but will you leave my son to his fate?"

"No," replied the Reverend Copley, manfully; "but I must have a little time to think over the organisation of the second search."

CHAPTER XXXIV.

PROFESSOR SHARP POPPER PAYS A VISIT TO WARMINGTON SCHOOL AND SUBDUES THE DRAGON.

NOW it by no means suited the plans of Sharp senior that the Greenes should withdraw themselves from his watchful eye, not only without the ceremony of inviting him, but with some very plain hints that his company was not in the least required.

"They begin to smell a rat somewhere," mused the old schemer. "Who could have written that anonymous letter, saying that young Greene had got into bad company at the school? Those young chaps that Billy wrote about. I must go down and look into this. It won't do to have our little game spoilt just as it's beginning to take."

Old Sharp's mind was soon made up. He was fertile at excuses or lies; there is very little difference between the articles, and he resolved upon accounting for his unexpected appearance at Warmington by saying that his fatherly heart would no longer bear the separation from his son.

"The old girl is so fond herself of that ass, Jolly Greene, that she'll be bound to believe me—so here goes."

Sharp senior had plenty of money, but it was never his plan to spend his own coin while he could borrow—so he had a pound from the cook, ten shillings from the butler, and half a crown from the page. The housemaids would have suffered in proportion, but they had been out with some soldiers to Rosherville, and were, of course, penniless, the gallant warriors having borrowed all that was not spent.

When the dear old gentleman arrived, Warmington College was deserted, save by Mrs. Copley Cobbem and Sharp junior, the rest having been despatched in search of their lord and master, and Mr. Greenely Greene.

Billy was down in the pantry, whither he had gone in search of something to appease his inordinate appetite. It was seldom that such a chance occurred, and he was making the best use of it when the bell rang, and he answered the summons with three parts of a roast chicken inside him, and the balance tucked into the breast of his jacket.

"I never did see such an aggravating chap for a father as you are," he said, in an injured voice. "Jest as I got a chance for a fair tuck-out, you comes in and spiles the game."

"This is a pretty welcome to give your poor old

dad," retorted Mr. Sharp. " What's the game, and how have I spoiled it ?"

" Why every blessed soul is out, 'cept Mrs. Cobbem, who's writing out a notice for the perlice, offering five bob reward for the body of old Copley, and I've got the run of the pantry, and just as I'd spotted a happle pie and a custard you comes a cuttin' in."

" That appetite of yours will be the ruin of you some day, Billy," said Mr. Sharp, regarding his offspring with a steadfast eye. " Why don't you take some medicine and stop it ?"

" Medicine be blowed ! Wot I wants is more grub ; I don't get arf enough. However, since you hare 'ere, come in."

" Stop!" said a very firm and determined voice behind him, and Billy quaked in his shoes, for the voice was the voice of Mrs. Copley Cobbem, and he knew he smelt very powerfully of the cold roast fowl.

" Who is this, Master Popper, and how dare you invite strangers into the house without my permission ?"

" If you please, ma'am," said Billy, backing away, and holding his breath until his voice was almost inaudible, " it's my father, Professor Popper, ma'am."

" Oh!" replied Mrs. Copley, taking a comprehensive view of the old gentleman, and making a complete mental catalogue of him in about three seconds. " And what may your business be, sir ?"

The professor did not reply directly. He had taken off his hat, and now stood gazing, with a look of deeply respectful admiration, at Mrs. Copley.

" Is it possible," he said at length, " that I have the honour of beholding the lovely and accomplished Mrs. Tawdry, whose pictures in the Royal Academy excited such general admiration ?"

Now Mrs. Copley Cobbem was not handsome, neither had her portrait been exhibited in the Academy. She was far too economical to waste her money in any such way, but the compliment " tickled " her vanity, and she almost smiled.

" You are mistaken, professor," she said. " My name is Mrs. Copley Cobbem, and I never had any portrait more expensive than cartes-de-visite at half a crown a dozen."

" Then you must be sisters, madam—twins, most probably. I *never* saw such an astonishing resemblance, and yet it hardly seems possible that there can be *two* such faces in the world."

" Nonsense, Professor Popper," trying very hard to look displeased. " I suppose you wish to see Mr. Cobbem, but of course, like everybody else, he tries to worry the life out of me, and has got himself locked up, or knocked down by highwaymen, or something ridiculous of that sort. Ah! you men— you men, Professor Popper—you have very little consideration for our delicate natures."

" There lives at least one, my dear madam," returned Sharp senior, with an amiable leer, " who will never fail in his duty to your sex. My son William here is too young to remember his sainted mother's opinion of me—I was unworthy of her ; we all are—or he could have told you what Mrs. Popper's last words were."

Mrs. Cobbem softened more and more. It was years since she had a compliment paid her, and compliments are dearer than new bonnets to the female heart, though not nearly so expensive to the masculine giver.

She backed to allow the professor to pass in. She did more—she did a thing unheard of in the annals of Warmington College—she actually asked him to come inside, and take something !

Young Sharp gasped, stared, and nearly let the leg of the chicken tumble out of his jacket.

He felt a warmer respect and admiration for his father grow up within him—admiration for the man who could cast salt (metaphorically) upon the tail of such a crafty bird as Mrs. Copley Cobbem.

Sharp senior accepted the invitation with graceful gratitude.

" Dear madam," he said, almost tenderly this time, for he felt that he was making way, " a crust of bread and a cup of water from those hands !"

" Oh! we'll find something better than that, professor. Master Popper, tell Jiggles to lay a cloth in the parlour."

" Jiggles is hout, mum."

" Oh! I forgot. Then Perkins will do."

" He's hout too, mum. Jiggles sent him, and I heerd him hollerin' ' Fire !' as he went along the back road."

" A nasty, low, vulgar workhouse brat," said Mrs. Cobbem, concentrating all her restrained sharpness into her voice. " Wait till he comes back ; I'll give it to him. Then, as there is no one else, you must go, Master Popper, and bring whatever you think your father will like best."

" Oh, my !" muttered Sharp junior, as he staggered away. " Well, I never ! The old un's reg'lar bewitched her ! Only fancy forgettin' herself, and sendin' me slap amongst the wittles !"

Meanwhile Mrs. Copley and Professor Popper ambled gently on towards the parlour, the professor trotting out a fresh compliment at every yard or so, and Mrs. C. becoming more and more amiable, as she dilated upon the brutal treatment of her husband, and how it was gradually wearing her into her grave.

" Ah! if you only knew what I have to put up with, professor," sighed Mrs. Copley, as she dropped heavily into an arm-chair. " I declare that it makes me quite faint to think of it."

Old Sharp saw his chance, and shot an arrow straight to the mark.

" Then try a little something at once, ma'am. Don't neglect your health. Think how precious your existence must be to all around you. A glass of sherry or a little brandy and water."

Mrs. Copley made a faint show of resistance, but the professor gained the day, and in a minute two glasses of very stiff brandy and water were on the table.

As the potent liquor disappeared Mrs. Copley became more than ever confidential, and the professor more and more tender. So interested indeed were they that neither remarked it as strange that Master William Popper had been away three-quarters of an hour without any signs of supper being forthcoming.

At the end of that time, however, Billy turned up, looking very red and apoplectic, waddling in a painful manner, and breathing in short snorts.

" Which—it's—ready," he gasped, and then vanished round the corner, where he lay down on the mat, and instantly slept a slumber to equal which in intensity the whole Corporation of the City of London would have failed after the most gorgeous of civic banquets.

But neither Mrs. Copley nor the professor took any notice of Billy at all. They had disposed of a second bumper of brandy and water, rather stiffer than the first, and were more amiable than ever.

There was a piano in the room, and the professor asked for a little music. Mrs. Copley was willing, and as she had really a good voice and tolerable execution, the professor's compliments had some foundation in truth.

The music softened them both, and completed what the brandy and water had begun. When they sat down again at the table they were very close together indeed. In fact, I am not sure that Mr. Sharp had not possessed himself of one of the lady's hands, as he murmured—

" Oh! dear Mrs. Copley, what might have been our fate if we had met years ago ?"

Mrs. Copley sighed, looked up tenderly, and gave a short shrill scream as she saw gazing at her from the doorway, with an amazed countenance—

The Rev. Copley Cobbem !

GREEN AS GRASS.

A JOLLY SCHOOL STORY.

THERE WAS A LINE OF SACKS WITH BOYS' HEADS STICKING OUT OF THE TOP—THE HEADS OF JOLLY AND BILLY BEING WELL TO THE FRONT.

CHAPTER XXXV.

YOUNG GREENE HAS ANOTHER NIGHT OF IT.

IT is time we followed upon the track of young Greene, who, after being wedged in the fork of a tree for some hours, came down suddenly, at the very moment when it would have been safest for him to remain there, just as the keepers arrived upon the scene.

As already briefly pointed out, he fled one way and his mother another. Mrs. Greene fortunately found friends to lead her to the White Hart, but poor Jolly, who was perhaps the most friendless fellow on earth when he most needed a friend, had nobody to aid him, and fled in blind terror.

The way he ran up against trees and knocked himself about generally would have killed most people, but he got no harm beyond a few chips and bruises, and with them he got clear of the wood, and reached the open fields.

Still he fled on.

Who the people were who had come shouting after him in the darkness he knew not; nor did he pause to think, but on he ran, until he came to a stream, across which stretched a water-mill.

This was the property of a certain Noddles, who ground corn for himself and neighbours in the day, and spent his nights like an honest man in bed, and so it fell out that the great wheel which earned his daily food was still and silent as Jolly, panting and exhausted, came up.

But the sluice was open, and as the great stream of water rolled thundering down, the noise it made fell with awful portent upon the ears of Jolly Greene, and in his fear he made for one of the back doors of the mill, hoping to find it led him into the habitation of man.

The door was unfastened, for thieves were unknown down there, and Noddles never took the trouble to lock any doors other than those which led into the granary. Panting and weeping, Jolly crept in, and finding a heap of sacks there lay down to rest.

He was quite exhausted, utterly worn out, and could not ward off the sleep that came upon him like a cloud. In a few seconds he was off too soundly for even the thunder of artillery to wake him.

All the night he lay there, and at early dawn came Noddles to open the mill, and see that his men came in time. Noddles was a man of business, and although he could and did get drunk overnight sometimes, no potations were ever deep enough to keep him from his labours in the morning.

He entered by a door on the opposite side to where young Greene lay, and with his own hands closed the sluice and set the great wheel in motion. Then he filled up the corn bin, and let in the half-dozen men who assisted him in the task of grinding.

An hour passed and Jolly still reposed. No sacks were wanted as yet, and no man came in to arouse him, but outside there was an unwonted life and bustle, for a boy came shouting over the fields—

"Jolly Greene—Jolly Greene!"

"What be that, Ned?" asked Noddles, of his foreman.

Ned went to one of the wickets, and looked out.

"It be the Warminters," he said, "broke loose—uncommon early to be sure."

"Close all the doors, Ned," said Noddles, hastily, "or they'll be up to some tricks. Nothing aint safe for them."

Ned put a little extra speed into his movements, and went round closing up the places, leaving that where Jolly lay until the last. As he entered there he saw Jolly sound asleep.

His first impulse was to close the door—that he did; his second to run to his master—that he did also—shouting—

"Measter—measter, I ha' got one on 'em!"

"One of who?" asked Noddles.

"A Warminter!"

"Where?" asked Noddles.

He had suffered from the Warminters in his time, and had never been able to fairly settle with one of them.

"In the sack-room, measter, and the door be locked."

"Get the whip, Ned!" cried Noddles, getting excited.

"Yes, measter."

Ned got the whips, two of them, and he and his master stole softly down to the sack room. There lay Jolly still fast asleep.

"He be asleep, measter," said Ned.

"Foxing," replied Noddles; "there's nothing them boys aint up to. How could he be asleep when he's just come over the fields?"

"That be true, measter."

"Or if he be asleep," said Noddles, with a grin, "I'll wake un."

And he kept his word. He woke young Greene instantly with one touch of the whip. It acted like a summons from a necromancer, and caused him to bound up into the air, and brought him down upon his feet again like a sprite.

Whatever faculties he possessed were then in full play, and with a couple of dodges such as a frightened rabbit might have been guilty of, he dived under Ned's arm and whip, and bolted into the mill.

"Stop un!" cried Noddles, alarmed, "or he'll get among the wheels. Holler to he!"

Ned hallooed, but only scared Jolly more, and he went through the machine-room at the rate of eight miles an hour, and darted up the ladder at the further end.

"He'll be through some of the traps," cried Noddles, "and break his neck. We shall be tried for it, Ned. Stop, my lad, I beän't goin' to harm ye."

They shouted to deaf ears, and to one who was almost blind, too. Jolly went on, regardless of everything, until he came to a room with only a window to escape by, and through this he went, head first, right on to the top of the big wheel, and shot down the broad water boards in a sitting position, as some boys love to come downstairs.

There were friends of his upon the bank—Warminters who had come out in search of him—and when they saw the familiar form upon the wheel they were as much astonished as if they had seen him dropping from the clouds.

Of course he went into the water head first, and equally as a matter of course he disappeared in the eddies and foam. But, though lost to sight for awhile, he was not utterly gone, and they saw him again about thirty yards away, with his fore limbs stuck out like those of a dead pig.

Dick Stager, who had run down with the expectation of seeing him torn up, was one of the first to plunge in to the rescue, and others equally bold went to his aid, and they got Jolly out.

But as they laid him down on the grass he gave no sign of life.

"He's done for this time," said Dick Stager.

CHAPTER XXXVI.

BRINGING HIM ROUND.

IF William, the waiter, lacked one thing it was discretion. Whenever he got a chance of "putting his foot in it" he never missed it, and when there was a thing to say at the wrong moment William opened his mouth and said it.

The Greenely Greenes had passed a dreadful night. The continued absence of their only son, and the utter failure of all efforts to trace his whereabouts, had reduced them to the condition known as "broken-hearted."

" We shall—shall never see him again," said Mrs. Greene, weeping.

" No, he is gone from us, Mariar," replied Mr. Greene, and burst into tears, to keep him company.

They had plenty of help—of a sort—and all the loafers who had shown up so badly in the wood affair, arrayed by the Reverend Copley Cobbem, came to the fore again, repentant and energetic, resolved, like good men and true, to retrieve the past, and make full amends for their former back-sliding.

Mr. Greene had no money, but Mrs. Greene had some. They had also, on the private recommendation of the Reverend Copley, unlimited credit, and the loafers had unlimited beer.

What a thirsty soul a loafer is! The more he orates the more his soul cries out for beer. The loafers of the White Hart were no exception, and the amount of liquor they poured down was sufficient to keep their spirits up for the next two months at least.

They were very energetic. Every half hour they went out and pursued the search in a different direction, but they were soon back again to their malt, bringing with them always the same sad tidings.

" Haint found the young un."

Dawn found them, however, hard at work in the tap-room, except two, who had succumbed to fatigue and refreshment, and gone under—the table.

The rest could still drink, and did so, but their spirits were weary with the search, and they could go out no more.

Mrs. Greene was inconsolable, and Mr. Greene was quietly despairing. The superintendent of the county police was there, and sat down with them to breakfast. The meal, as far as two were concerned, was a mockery. Mrs. Greene only had a round of toast, and Mr. Greene stopped short at two eggs and anchovy paste on half a dozen biscuits.

The superintendent—a quiet, reserved man—however, went steadily to work. He was a father, and could understand a father's feelings—so he told them—but he never allowed his emotions to interfere with his appetite.

" A man has to eat to live," he said; "it's a duty he owes to everybody."

The breakfast was about two-thirds over when William rushed in, bursting with intelligence, which perhaps ought to have been more delicately delivered.

" They've found him, mum, they've found him!" he cried.

" Found him!" Mrs. Greene cried.

" Yes, under the water-wheel—a corpses!"

" Oh—oh!" cried Mrs. Greene, and went down on the hearthrug all of a heap.

Mr. Greene, stunned by the intelligence, staggered over a footstool, and went down on the flat of his back. The superintendent put down his toast, wiped his mouth, and addressed William—

" What a blundering ass you are!" he said. " Go and bring some of the maids, with sal-wolatilly. Go on, man, and look sharp, while I get the poor old creetur on to a sofa."

" But I couldn't help it," said William. " He's dead and gone, and they are bringing him home on an 'urdle."

" Oh—oh! my Jolly!" shrieked Mrs. Greene, and her intense grief took away whatever was ridiculous in her appearance.

The superintendent took William by the shoulder, and calmly turned him out of the room.

" Go and get the sal-wolatilly, and send some of the maids here," he said.

Two servant girls quickly appeared, and helped to get Mrs. Greene upon the sofa. Mr. Greene, left to himself, got upon his feet, and stared about like a man in a dream.

The superintendent took Mr. Greene by the arm. " Come out, sir," he said, " and have a mouthful

of air. The women will look after your good lady. The sex understand each other.

" My boy—my Jolly," murmured Mr. Greene " A happy day—oh, yes!"

" Here's the bar," said his guide, as they reached it, " and I should recommend you to have a wee drop of brandy without spoiling it with water. A little brandy, please. Much obliged, ma'am," this to the landlady, who waited on him. " Now, sir, tilt it off—every drop. That's it. Now, come here. Quick! You ought to sit down."

It was sharply but kindly done. In a moment he had twisted Mr. Greene into a side position, just as the bearers of the unfortunate Jolly appeared in front of the inn. He put him into a chair, and smartly drew down the blind of the window, so that he could see nothing outside.

" You sit here for five minutes or so," he said, " and I'll go and ask that William what he means by coming in with that yarn."

" But my boy is dead!" said Mr. Greene, pitifully.

" So he said," replied the superintendent, " but you can't believe a man unless he's on oath, and not often then. Sit quiet, sir, and I'll soon fathom the story."

Mr. Greene was quite passive, and obeyed him like a child. The superintendent went out, and had not been absent many moments before he was in the room again.

" I told you so," he said, " that man was a liar."

" Aint my Jolly dead?" asked Mr. Greene.

" Not he—only got a little water under his wesket. He'll be all right."

" Hooroar," cried Mr. Greene, and went down on the flat of his back again.

CHAPTER XXXVII.

FARMER JOB.

PROMINENT among the antagonists of the Warmington boys stood Job Grumper, farmer and grazier, a man of forty years of age, and a temper that made the Christian name bestowed upon him by his godfathers and godmothers a misnomer.

Prior to the establishment of the college he had been a man of peace, a rubicund easy-going cultivator of the soil, who went to church on Sunday, looked after his land five days, and devoted the remaining one to the market, where he got regularly drunk, and was brought home by his roan mare at the rate of fifteen miles per hour—he, the said Job Grumper, sitting in the seat, limp and heedless of all that passed by.

In short, Job was a model farmer, a good neighbour, and a man much loved and respected.

But when the Rev. Copley Cobbem came and brought his host of Philistines, Farmer Job became a changed man, and in lieu of the jolly friend and neighbour there speedily came a spiteful hater of his kind, especially of the Warmington kind.

His farm, hitherto standing foremost in the neighbourhood, was, in fact, neglected. He no longer took the prize for mangel or turnips, or for keeping a clean land, and who can marvel at his falling off when it is known that he devoted half his time to thinking over the wrongs he had endured at the hands of the Warmington boys, and studying how to avenge them.

He laid every mishap of his life to their charge— he even blamed them for unfavourable weather, and when he lost a lawsuit with old Joskins, who sold him a horse that died on the way home from the sale, he charged the sharp dealing to the " Warminters." At least, he did so a day or two afterwards, when he got one of the boys into his clutches—a small boy, who was looking round his farm-yard, and, of course, " doing nothing."

That boy went back to the college rather sore— perhaps he was very sore. Two hours afterwards the Reverend Copley, full of dignity, called upon

Job for an explanation. He was shown a double-barrelled gun and a bull-dog, as two forms of inducement to retire. He was induced, and retired rapidly.

The story got about, and the boys, defying gun and dog, visited the farm whenever an opportunity offered itself, and Job was waited upon at his own stable, and twice left in the granary looking on at half a dozen youngsters skedaddling across the fields with the ladder intended to get up and down by.

They rode his ponies and his horses, drove his bull mad, frightened his sheep, and worried Job himself almost as much as Satan of old worried his great namesake; and it came even yet more heavily upon him, as he had not a tithe of his patience.

He was, it may be said, an ingenious man, and came out strong in the way of snares and pitfalls for his tormentors; but as he was continually catching his own men, his friends and relations, and occasional visitors, among whom was the tax-gatherer, who sued for damages, he allowed his inventive talents to rest, and trusted to lying in wait and securing his prey by the chase—in both of which he was occasionally successful.

Of this man neither young Greene nor his guide and friend, Billy Sharpe, knew anything, and, of course, with the good luck that always attended the former, they must needs go over Job's fields for a walk.

It was Saturday, and the Reverend Copley relied upon his boys to conduct themselves properly when out. He always relied upon them, and although occasionally he leant upon a broken reed, and found the good name of the college rolling in the dust through the misbehaviour of some of the ungovernable spirits, yet on the whole the conduct of the lads did him credit.

Neither Billy nor Jolly meant any harm. They were simply taking a quiet walk—talking finance.

"I know I had four pounds, and I gave you three," Jolly said, "for I counted the money—one sovereign for each finger of the right hand."

"No," said Billy, "it was three you had, and you gave me two—one of them I lost and t'other I put into the missionary box instead of a bob, and old Copley wouldn't let me take it out again."

"I don't believe you put anything in," returned Jolly, resentfully; "you put your hand over the hole and gave the box a rattle, but that was all."

"If you go on in that way," said Billy, wrathfully, "I shall git a fine character. What will people think of me? What would them as brought me up to be wirtuous and good have to say to it?"

"All I have to say is," said Jolly, returning to a previous part of the conversation, "that I never seem to have any money and you have lots."

"At the present moment I aint got enough to buy a piping bullfinch," asserted Billy, fervently, "and if a hobject of charity—sich as a father of six kids, who had lost both legs in a corfee mill—I mean in a paper-mill—was to come along this way, I couldn't put a brown into his hat."

Here they got over a stile, and Jolly went forward a few paces alone, Billy remaining seated on the top bar.

Just ahead was a pond surrounded by bushes. In the heart of those bushes lay Job Grumper, rejoicing in spitefulness at the prospect of advancing prey.

"In her last letter," said Jolly, pausing, "mar asked me what I did with all my money."

"And what did you tell her?" asked Billy.

"That you had it."

"Mortial powers!" exclaimed Billy, "what a lie!"

"It aint—it's true," returned Jolly. "And it's no use your asking me for any more, for you won't have it—there!"

This was open rebellion, and as a matter of necessity it had to be put down at once.

Jumping off his seat Billy ran forward and seized Jolly by the collar.

"Look here——" he said, and stopped.

Why did he stop?

Because at that moment something like red-hot wire twisted round the calves of his legs, and immediately his gifted mind went back to a story he had read about a viper that coiled itself round the limbs of a traveller and stung him to death.

Was he stung by a viper?

It was the question of a moment, and it was answered by the voice of Job Grumper and another red-hot application.

"Take that, you Warminter," he said, and again the whip swished through the air.

"Run!" gasped Billy.

He started off himself, and, as ill-luck would have it, towards the farm. Jolly was too much amazed to follow him, until he had a red-hot binding to his legs, and that stimulated him into going upon the track of his friend.

Job went in pursuit, but time had given him fat, and shortened his breath, and the boys got across two fields and into his farm-yard, with him a good hundred yards in the rear. They dodged round a wall, and got well out of sight.

"Dang it," he roared, "I've lost 'em. Smudge, Dick, Jerry, John, some of ye, come out. There's Warminters about!"

The only man who responded to the call was no other than our old friend, the oldest inhabitant. He came out of the stable with two straws on the point of a fork. He tried to look as if he had been hard at work, but a pair of sleepy eyes and uncertain legs made the truth but too apparent.

"John!" said Job, "wake up man, there be Warminters about."

John had been exceedingly drunk overnight, and had not forgotten to refresh himself during the day, but the word "Warminter" scattered the fumes of beer, drove off sleep, removed old age, and made him young and active again.

"Let's be at 'em, master," he said, brandishing his fork. "Where be they?"

"Round here," said Job.

They dashed round the wall together into another yard. There only two pigs met their view. Old John, like an aged bluebottle, buzzed here and there, looking into the stable and outhouses; while Job, his master, darted into the house, and took a view of the country from the various upper windows.

"What luck, John?" he asked, as he came down again.

"Nothing here, master," replied the oldest inhabitant.

"They're about," said Job, "for the country be clear. Bring up Squib, he'll scent 'em out."

"Shall I let him loose?" asked the aged one, grinning.

"No, for if he fastens on, who's to take 'im off? Will you?"

The oldest inhabitant fervently declared he wouldn't take off Squib for all the men that ever was borned. "For," he added, with a knowing leer, "the brute would fasten on to I, and who would take 'im off then?"

"We must keep 'im in leash," said Job, "be quick and bring 'im along."

Squib was the bulldog before referred to, and presently he came round in leash, bringing the oldest inhabitant along with him, leaning back at an angle of forty five.

He was a venomous brute, with murder in his staring eyes, gleaming teeth, and lolling tongue. His ordinary life was passed chained to a big kennel, carefully staked down, and the confinement did not improve a naturally demoniacal temper. Instinct told him what he was wanted for, and he was prepared to bite anybody anywhere at the bidding of his master.

"Hi, Squib, look 'im up, lad!" said Job.

Squib was taken across the farm-yard, and of his own accord took up the trail, so furiously that the aged inhabitant, hanging on behind, followed him more like a tin kettle tied to his tail than a man who had him under his control.

"Ye'll never hold 'im, John," said Job, complacently; "mind, if he fastens on the Warminsters, ye'll be tried for manslaughter."

"Then hold 'im yourself," replied the oldest inhabitant, as he let the brute slip.

Job, well acquainted with the merits of his own animal, uttered a yell of despair, as Squib, with a deep growl of satisfaction, ran towards the yard where he kept his stock.

"Ye old fool, ye've done it," he cried, and smiting the aged one under the jaw, sent him flying into the thick of a manure heap. Then he followed in pursuit of Squib, who had already begun business, and fastened on the throat of a fine fat pig, whose squeals echoed half a mile around.

Job laid hold of Squib by the tail, and dragged him and the pig across the yard, but Squib held on, then he bit the tail and swore, next he kicked him in the ribs, but all his efforts were thrown away, the dog held on, and the squeals of the pig were growing fainter.

"All this comes o' them Warminters," hissed Job, "but I'll ha' damages if she dies."

"She" was the pig, and there seemed every prospect of her yielding up her gentle life, for Squib, with the cunning of his race, had good hold upon a vein from which the red blood was freely flowing.

In a few minutes it would have been all over, and the pig would have become pork, for the London market most likely, for thither come all creatures who meet with an untimely end; but old John, with ocular and aromatic evidence of where he had been upon him, came upon the brute, bringing with him a stout rope. This they put around the throat of Squib. John took one end, and his master the other, and each tugged with all his might.

For a time it seemed doubtful that even this attempt would fail, but Squib could no more do without breath than any other living creature, and his hold relaxed. The pig, released, staggered into a corner, and, curling up in a heap, dug its snout into a heap of filth, and went to sleep."

"Now hold un, John," said Job.

"Hold un yerself," replied John, "or better knock he on the head, for I'll be danged if ever I see so much of the white of his eye afore."

It was sage and seasonable advice, and well for Job had it been taken; but he was a man of obstinate spirit, given to doing things exactly his own way. Besides, the dog was his own; and surely he could do as he liked with it.

"Be quiet, Squib lad!" he said, advancing with the object of loosing the rope from his throat. "Poor old boy!"

"Don't set 'im free, measter," urged the aged inhabitant. "There be too much white, I tell 'ee."

"He's quiet enough," returned Job.

Squib was quiet, and remained so while the cord was being loosened; but the moment he felt freedom at hand he rapidly wriggled his head out, paused an instant undecided which to attack, decided upon his master, and fastened his teeth in the calf of his leg.

"There!" said the aged inhabitant, quite shiny with the triumph of his prophetic spirit, "I told 'ee so!"

"Ho!" was all Job answered, as he staggered back against the wall.

"I said there was too much white," pursued the aged inhabitant; "for I knowed he of old. On the day he fastened on old Fardle's donkey he had a'most as much. I said to Fardle, 'Don't come round the corner wi' he;' but Fardle would come, and Squib did for he."

"Get something!" groaned Job. "Knock his

brains out—kill him—anything! I'll bring an action agin them Warminters for this."

"Let's see," said the aged one, thoughtfully. "What be the best thing to settle him with. A pitchfork wouldn't be bad, only I—— "

"He'll kill me!" groaned Job, sinking into a sitting position.

The oldest inhabitant saw it was time to be up and doing, and trotted off to the house. From the kitchen he obtained a coal hammer, and, thus armed, hurried back.

"Stand steady, measter!" he said.

His first blow was a little out of the mark, and fell upon Job's pet corn; but the second astonished Squib, and the third scattered his senses. His hold relaxed, and he went staggering over the yard like a drunken man, until he suddenly pitched upon his head and lay still.

"That's done for he," said the oldest inhabitant.

His master said nothing, but his eyes filled with tears as he rubbed his mutilated leg, though whether for his own sufferings or for the departed Squib it is difficult to say.

CHAPTER XXXVIII.

THRESHING WHEAT.

IN all his life Job had never been in such a fury before. All that the Warminsters had done previously was as nothing to this. They had killed his pet—his one friend—his best companion—his Squib.

Arguing out events in his usual fashion, he came to the conclusion that he had not been bitten by Squib, but by a Warminster, and nothing less than the life of one of them would ever make amends for his sufferings.

As he sat in his kitchen binding up his wounds he bade John keep an eye on the fields, to see that those he knew were in hiding did not escape.

Old John not only kept an eye upon the fields, but made little excursions to the outhouses; for the feeling in his master's bosom found an echo in his heart. He hated a Warminster more than all else on earth.

Success crowned his efforts. He discovered the Warminsters—Billy and Jolly—in hiding, and rushed to his master, Job, with the glad tidings.

"I've found they," he said—"both on 'em!"

"Where?" asked Job, forgetting his wounds at once, and springing to his feet.

"In the barn—lying under some of the loose shocks o' whate."

It had been an exciting day to Job. Events of a stirring nature had set his blood in motion, and given an impetus to his brain. In an instant an idea of unparalleled brilliancy and power was upon him.

"John!" he said, with a grin, "get a couple o' flails, and if ye see a man aboot get 'im to help of ye to thrash out that whate. Lay on hard, and work well while ye're about it."

The face of the aged one expanded under the influence of laughter, until there were not half the usual wrinkles in it. He saw the idea at once, and beamed.

"Master," he said, "ye be a good un."

But he did not understand half the ability of his master, who had called on others to carry out his vengeance. If either of the boys were killed or maimed it would be no fault of his. He was not supposed to know they were there—he had only bidden his men pursue a usual course of labour—and finally, he himself had not touched a flail.

But there would be no harm in looking in, and he limped out after John, who found a man coming up from the fields, who, after a few whispered words, showed a desire to get to work—quite foreign to his nature.

"Gi' I a flail," he said, "and a thick un."

John got two heavy implements of their class,

and together the two went to the barn. Job lingered by the door with the air of a casual looker-on, but his heart was singing, and he but ill-concealed his joy.

Both Billy and Jolly were under a lot of loose wheat in the centre of the floor. They heard the footsteps, and lay as still as mice. Jolly was horrified nearly out of his wits, and Billy had a return of the palpitation he had often felt when he had been bolting through the streets of London, with a long train of pursuers behind him.

"Mar," said Jolly, feebly.

"Hold your row," hissed Billy, "I never did see such a cove. Perhaps they don't know we are here—OH!"

He got the first blow from the aged one, right across his back, and he gave a great bound that shook half his covering off him, and left a part of his body exposed to view. This the other man saw and laid on with a will. "Oh!" cried Billy again, and lay spread-eagled and helpless.

Jolly had perhaps never been so bright in his intellect before. He appreciated the position, and displayed an alertness which would have delighted, if not astonished, his family.

Springing up he made for the door, with a lot of loose straw clinging about him. Job threw up his arms, and widely extended his legs to bar his way. Jolly came out more strongly than ever; he could not have been surpassed at that moment by a street Arab. Diving down he darted between the farmer's legs, pitched him on his back, and made for the college as straight as a carrier pigeon would have done.

Mrs. Copley Cobbem was in the garden watering her favourite geraniums, and stopping now and then to say a few connubial words of serious import to the Reverend Copley, who was engaged in the exciting pursuit of snails, when a wild figure, like that of a young King Lear, came bounding up the path.

At first they did not recognise the new comer, but as he drew near, and his noble nose stood out in bold relief, they saw it was Jolly Greene.

"What has he been doing now?" asked Mrs. Copley.

Jolly came on, kicked over the watering pot, upset a tin can half-full of snails, and fell sprawling, just in time to trip up the Reverend Copley, who was advancing to greet him. Mrs. Copley saved her geraniums by unexpectedly receiving her husband in her arms.

"What next?" she said, giving him a box on the ears; "you ought to be ashamed of yourself, in front of a house too with fifty windows in it."

"My love—my life," answered the reverend gentleman, "it is really no fault of mine. It was young Greene."

"And you set him on," returned Mrs. Copley. "Bah! I blush when I look at you. Now, young sir, please to tell me what is the matter."

"They are murdering him—beating him to death," said Jolly, staring about him—"knocking his brains out with scaffold poles."

"Whose brains?" asked Mrs. Copley, sharply. "Not yours, I reckon, for you have none."

"Master Popper. They're killing him."

"There is some mystery in the words of this boy," said the Reverend Copley, suddenly coming to the fore—"a mystery that must be investigated."

"Stand back, you fool," said his wife, politely, "and leave this idiot to me. Now, sir, who is murdering this precious friend of yours?"

"Over there," said Jolly, pointing towards the farm. "I am sure he is dead."

"Now, Mr. Copley, don't stand there like a stuck pig, but go and see what all this is about."

"My love, but a moment ago——"

"Are you going or not?"

"My love, I would go if I knew whither."

"Where have you been to?" asked Mrs. Copley, shaking Jolly.

"Farm."

"I have it," said the Reverend Copley. "Popper has been assaulted, perhaps killed by the villain who set his dog at me."

"An insult," sneered Mrs. Copley, "you never avenged."

"My love, I will avenge it now," said the Reverend Copley. "The time has come when the impudence of that man must and shall receive a check."

He put his hat firmly over his eyes, and went forth straight up towards the farm, for when his blood was up the little courage Mrs. Copley had left in him was sufficient to carry him through any ordinary trial.

At the gate he armed himself with a large stone, intended for the departed Squib, and marched boldly in. Job was in front of his house in the attitude of a triumphant warrior, and the two wielders of the flails were seated by the door engaged in the consumption of bread and cheese and beer.

"Here be the reverend gent," said the oldest inhabitant, somewhat unnecessarily, as Job had already seen him, and slightly quailed before the determined air of the schoolmaster.

"Turn him out," said Job.

"Na, na," replied the oldest inhabitant, "he be a harse of another colour. It be dangerous to lay a finger on gentry folk—eh, Dick?"

"It are so," replied Dick.

"Sir," said the Reverend Copley, advancing towards Job.

"Sir to you," replied Job, backing slightly. It was now, indeed, he felt the loss of Squib.

"You are a brute, sir! I come—to—to demand the body of the boy you have—a—murdered!"

"He aint murdered," replied Job; "he's only been well licked."

"And may I ask how you dare lick—as you coarsely express it—one of my gentlemen pupils?"

Job snapped his fingers. It was the least he could do under the circumstances. He felt the white feather coming into his tail, but he dare not show it before his men.

The snapping of fingers is a sign of contempt, and that the Reverend Copley could not endure. All that was Briton-like in his nature was roused, and he made ready for his foe.

"All I ask is," he said, "that those two humble peasants may remain spectators of the coming scene."

"We beant goin' to interfere," said John.

"Before I begin," said the Reverend Copley, as he put his hat upon the ground, "let me ask what has become of the boy who has been so cruelly assaulted?"

"He be a sitting in yon ditch," replied the oldest inhabitant, "a coolin' of hisself arter the lickin' we gave he."

"My blood boils as I think of his injuries," said the Reverend Copley. "Sir, I am ready, if you are."

What followed can be told in a few words—the words which fell from the lips of John in his favourite tap-room that night.

"I never thowt," he said, "that there was half the corky go in the parson. He come up like a dancing chap, and afore measter got his arm up the parson gave he one on the left eye, then another on the right eye, then another on the nose, and another on the mouth. Master's head had no more shape arter that than there is in a football, and he went a tumbling about swearing like a trooper, while parson gave he a punch here, and a punch there, until he got a-nigh the hog tub, when parson took he by the breeches and lifted he into it head fust, and left he with his feet a sticking out like the legs of a duck in a market basket. Then he strikes up a hattitoode like a play chap at the fair, and said, 'He am awenged!' and walked off like an old cock that's just cut the comb off another. Me and

...CAME CRASHING THROUGH THE GREENHOUSE ROOF AND STOPPED THE "SPOONING" OF JIGGLES AND THE COOK.

Dick larfed so that we couldn't get measter out for some time, and then he was very nigh dead."

"Summat will come o' that," said one of the listeners.

"I reckon so," replied the oldest inhabitant. "We shall ha' the Warminters down on us like a swarm o' wopses, and I aint quite certain which side I shall take yet—that I beant."

CHAPTER XXXIX.

IN WHICH THE OLDEST INHABITANT HAS A CHOICE OF SIDES—HE MAKES HIS CHOICE.

WHEN that affair of Job and Billy became known, all the lads at Warmington College were up in arms—not so much on account of Billy, who was, indeed, no great favourite, but simply because one of their order had been grievously insulted and assaulted.

Of the latter there could be no doubt, as Billy for two whole days walked about crab-fashion, and displayed a considerable amount of hesitation about sitting down in school and at meals. Perhaps he made the most of his sufferings, but if he did it was only natural for him to do so, and the whole school rose up to avenge him.

Warmington College was in arms.

The German professor saw it, the other ushers saw it, the Reverend Copley saw it; and Mrs. Copley, with her little eye, beheld it, but never sought to interfere; indeed, the Reverend Copley went so far as to give an extra half holiday, and forgot to mention, as usual, that it was necessary for the boys to keep within bounds.

In a body they went off to the farm of Job, bearing a strong resemblance to a swarm of locusts. The two Stagers played the part of leaders, and were ably backed up by such good knights and true as Christopher Cobble, Tommy Whisker, and Bob Larry. Perkins also joined, as a sort of camp follower, and left his knives uncleaned, to the great wrath and frenzy of Jiggles, on whom the labour of cleaning them devolved.

"Which," as he said to Mr. Copley, "it aint the fust time as he've syrupdeliciously gone out and left his work on me."

"I will speak to him," replied his master slowly, and Jiggles, conscious that Perkins would be served out for his sin, lightly retired to his pantry, and swore roundly.

But to return to the going out of the Warminters. They went swarming across the country towards the farm, and were soon observed by the oldest inhabitant, who was doing a bit of ditching at the bottom of the lane which led to the farm. He saw the boys, and perceiving they were coming as straight as the crow flies, guessed their object, and hastened to his master.

To him—Norval-like—he told his tale, although he had not waited like Norval to have a go in at the enemy single-handed. This is what he said—

"Measter, the Warminters be a comin' on in a bunch, and I think they'll turn the place upside down for ye."

"Get my gun," said Job, roused to action.

"No, measter," replied the aged one. "If it's shooting I'll have no hand in it, as they'll hang ye sure as fate."

"Then get out of my way for a cursed fool!" said Job, and went in to get his gun himself.

He got it, and charged it with a small quantity of powder, and peas on the top of it up to the muzzle.

"I'll make 'em dance at any rate," he muttered, and retreating into his house barred the door, and took up his station at the dairy window.

The aged one got into the hayloft, and having drawn the ladder up, closed the wicket and fixed his eye at the keyhole which commanded a view of the farm-house, his object being to ascertain which was really the strongest side.

"And which that is," he cried, "I'll stand by."

The shouts of the coming foe fell upon his ears, and in a few moments a number of geese and the old barn cock came flying before the advancing party of attack. A few steps behind them were the two Stagers, armed with two sticks.

"Search the place and find the flails," cried Dick.

"And we will give the farmer a taste of his own physic," cried Nick.

The oldest inhabitant shuddered, and began to frame a suitable address of conciliation in case he should be discovered. The boys scattered over the farm-yard, and in two minutes all the flails in the place were in their possession.

They were very noisy and extremely jubilant. Hitherto they had found no foe, for all the men and women of the farm were far away that day down by the marl-field, cutting and binding the last of the golden grain. Most of them thought there was nobody about the place.

But in this they were mistaken, as we know. Job himself undeceived them, for as Dick was giving instructions for the pump handle to be wrenched off and taken home as a trophy, he threw open the small dairy window, and thrusting out the muzzle of the gun, called upon them to desist.

"You touch it, and I'll pepper the lot o' yer," he said.

Dick put his hands to his mouth, and uttered the gathering cry of the Warminters—a very good imitation of the Australian "cooey." The boys came rushing in, and as they saw Job at the window with the gun in his hand more than one pair of cheeks were pale. Billy Sharp most prudently put the pump between himself and the line of fire, and our friend Jolly sat down, quite limp.

"Don't be afraid of him, lads," cried Nick Stager. "He dare not fire it."

"But won't I?—that's all!" roared Job. "Don't you make any mistake, youngsters—I'm on for it."

"Dick!" whispered Nick, hurriedly.

"Yes, old boy."

"Sneak round, and duck under the wall. I'll talk to him until you can get near enough to lay hold of the barrel and turn it up. Comprenez?"

"Yes, so far; but what then?"

"Leave the rest to me."

"All right."

"Tommy!" said Nick, addressing Whisker next.

"Here, general."

"There's a pail of water by the pump. Go over to it, and be ready to throw it into that window when I give the word."

"I'm there!" replied Tommy, cheerfully.

The aged inhabitant, with his eye at the keyhole, watched the scene, and scarce knew what to make of it. He did not believe his master would dare to kill anybody; but he might do it, and, like the selfish old humbug he was, he began to speculate how far he might be implicated.

"Theer's axisserys arter the fact," he muttered; "and they are reckoned as bad as anybody. I think afore he fires I'll go out and 'spostulate;" and he put his hand upon the latch of the door.

"I say, governor," said Nick Stager, addressing Job.

"Well, what now?" asked the impatient man.

"Put that gun down."

"Not likely; and, what's more, I'll let fly among you."

"Nonsense!"

"I'll take an oath of it! Now, then, stand back."

"Whisker, attention! Now, Dick!"

Dick, who, with the cunning of a red Indian, had crept up under the window, sprang up and seized the barrel. Job gave a violent tug, but Dick held on, and the gun was raised to a level with the granary door.

"Now, Whisker, up with that water, and at him."

Tommy raised the pail and ran forward. Job saw what was coming, and in a frenzy pulled the trigger. At that very moment the oldest inhabitant, deeming the proper moment to "'spostulate" at hand, came forth, and received the better part of a half a pint of peas in his aged body.

They peppered him frightfully, and if some five hundred bees had undertaken to sting him all at once, and faithfully carried out their purpose, he could not have suffered more.

The ladder he had taken inside with him, and as he gave a wild leap into the air there was nothing to break his fall except Jolly Greene, who was immediately underneath, and on the top of him the aged one came like a feather bed, and bore him to the earth.

The tumult was tremendous. Job, blinded with water, shouted and swore, and half a dozen noble youths, clinging to the barrel of the gun, shrieked with laughter as they watched his contortions, while the rest capered about like so many imps, unable for awhile to help Jolly, who lay like one dead under the aged one, who wriggled like an eel introduced bodily to the frying pan.

Even Nick, the leader, lost his head for a moment, and laughed and shouted with the rest.

But he was soon himself again, cool and collected. "Order there," he cried, "we must have that gun. Tommy, more water, and there's another bucket handy. Now, boys, in with it. It's all right—Cobbem won't say anything."

"I'll murder you if you throw in any more."

"In with it!" cried Nick.

Job saw it coming in earnest, and let go. The next moment Dick was dancing about with the gun waving above his head.

"Victory!" he shouted, but the cry was premature. Job had suffered, but he was not utterly routed. Nay more, he was only aroused by his disaster, and more like a raging demon than a man, went in search of another weapon.

In the kitchen his eyes fell upon the poker, and when the eyes of angry men or women fall upon that article of domestic utility it has charms few if any are able to resist.

Job at least could not, and taking it from its resting-place in the fender, ran up the passage towards the front door.

With furious haste he pushed back the bolts, raised the latch, and sprang out. He saw a form before him dimly in his mad blindness, and dealt that form a heavy blow. The oldest inhabitant, who happened to be that form, went down for the second time that day.

He was a guileless old man who had lived all his days in the quiet privacy of a country village, but there must have been an evil worm at the root of him, or he never could have so quickly blossomed with the language that came out of him then.

Hard as his head was that poker found a tender place upon it, and made him see bull's-eye lanterns, and more shooting stars than he could have counted without the aid of a ready reckoner.

Job was immediately conscious of his error—he also became aware that the boys were all gone.

"What did ye come in front o' me for, John?" he asked.

"Why did you hit I?" roared the old one, "when I come to tell ye that the boys were all a-chivying the bull, and a-drivin' him wild? Ye must be a blarmed fool!"

"Don't you talk to me in that way. I'm your measter."

"You the measter o' I!" sneered the aged one. "Gi' I another poker, and then we'll see. I ha' had many a man for a measter, but never sich a hass as thou."

This was strong language—unwarrantable language, I may say—and no yeoman of spirit, accustomed to be master on his own farm, could stand it. He gave John his wages on the spot, and told him to go.

"I must have ten bob for plarster for this ere whack," said John, pointing to his head.

"Oh, that's too much!" said Job.

"Ten bob, or I'll have the law on ye!"

Eventually the aged one took five shillings; but the haggling was of considerable length. When it was over the boys of Warmington College were leaving the farm in a body, and Job was gratified with the sight of his gun on the shoulder of Dick Stager, leading the van.

"If I tried to get he back agen by law," he said, "they'd charge me with shooting at they. But I'll ha' 'im back somehow; and as for old John, if he shows his nose here agen I'll —— "

The rest was spoken in his heart, but as he wended his way towards the marl-field, to see how his men were getting on, his brow was black indeed.

The boys of the college had altogether a very joyous afternoon. Having defeated their enemy, they went nutting in his wood, and gathered enough to make them ill for a month.

In joyous procession they were returning home, when, at a narrow part of the road, they were confronted by the oldest inhabitant.

He had a great bandage round his head, a stick in his hand, and several pints of beer in his eye. Altogether there was a good deal of the old savage warrior about him, and Nick, fearing another fray, called a halt.

"It be all right," said he. "I'm your friend. I'm the man to stand by ye. I'm for you, I am. If you want to do for Job I can show you the way."

The announcement was startling but not altogether unpleasant. Having so old and redoubtable a warrior on their side would be an advantage, and great fun might come out of it.

"Shall we close with him?" asked Dick.

"I should think so," said Nick, and so said they all. The aged one was then called up and asked what his terms were.

"I axes for nothing," he said, "but I leaves it to you, gemmen. I've given up a good sitivation to come and help you, but it don't matter. I does it free and 'arty. You do the same, and we shall stand by each other."

"So be it," said Nick, speaking for all.

"Then I'll promise you this," replied the aged one, "that afore the week is out I'll show you how to put Job into a sylum. Meanwhile, if any of you have got the price of a pint about you, I'll not say no to it."

CHAPTER XL.

RIVAL LEECHES.

THE compact was made, and the boys of Warmington College, like Frankenstein, had raised a monster unto themselves. The oldest inhabitant was that monster.

"I'll stand by 'em, and they'll stand by me," he murmured to his boon companions in the tap-room of the White Hart; "and say they only gives me tuppence a week each, which is low reckoning, for that soft chap and sich like is, I should say, good for a bob—say they only gives me that, and as there's sixty of 'em, more will come that way than by being a slave to a farmer."

"That's true," said a man in the corner, "if you only gets the tuppences."

He was a low sarcastic person who spoke thus, an odd jobbing sort of fellow, who could, so he declared, turn his hand to anything. But he was generally so slow in turning his hands that jobs were few and far between, and it was only when the pressure was very great he was employed by anybody. So it arose that he spent much of his valuable existence in the tap-room aforesaid, leaning his head against the chimney, smoking when he had tobacco, drinking when anybody treated him, and cutting in with sage remarks whenever a fair opportunity presented itself.

On this occasion his remark was not received

with the respect it was entitled to. The aged inhabitant took it up in a most resentful manner.

"Look here, Goggles," he said, "you was niver the chap to work, but you could allus cut in and spile the job of another."

"And do you call sponging on little kids a job?" asked Goggles, with a sneer.

Men are always down on their own little weaknesses when they crop up in others. Goggles was perhaps the greatest human sponge in existence, and was therefore very much down upon the oldest inhabitant for showing a similar quality.

"Who's a-sponging?" asked the aged one. "Didn't they come to me in a body and say 'stand by us,' and aint I going to do it? Do you call that sponging?"

"I don't know what took place 'atween you," said Goggles, "but I knows you, and I knows what I thinks."

On this John got upon his feet. Years might have shrunk his muscles, reduced the calves of his legs, and thinned his once luxuriant locks, but his spirit—the spirit of a manly true-born Briton—remained untouched. Carefully rolling up the sleeves of his smock frock, he advanced into the middle of the room, and would have taken up a terror-striking pugilistic attitude if he had not fallen over a spittoon and gone head first under the grate.

He had been drinking heavily that night, and the fall confusing his faculties, he would in all probability have lain there and cooked his head like a potato if friendly hands had not drawn him out of his perilous position.

Goggles, of course, did not help him.

He, with his head leaning against the chimney, made another sarcastic remark.

"What a smell of sheep's head a cooking!" he said.

It was bitterly cruel thus to insult a venerable old man, who had spent all his life in honest labour and simple rustic pastimes. That his head was singed nobody ventured to deny, for the room was filled with the odour of his frizzled locks, but that there was any resemblance between it and the perfume of sheep's head under any circumstances was false. The rustic minds in the room saw this, and more than one said—

"Don't 'ee be hard on the old man, Goggles. He ha' been a good 'un in his time."

"That aint no reason why he should cheek I," said Goggles.

As the aged one failed to show signs of returning life, rum was sent for, and the first few drops had a galvanising effect upon him. He sat up and finished the glass at a gulp.

It was now time for closing, and the potboy came to announce the fact with this brief but indisputable announcement—"Time's hup—all hout"—and at once began to sweep up the place with a long broom.

In a body the company went forth, and the aged one, after one attempt to find Goggles in the dark road, turned his steps homeward, whither instinct must have guided him, as it was impossible to see two feet ahead. He got there, however, and was let in by Jenny Hall, with whom he lived.

She was an old woman, about as old as John, and, like him, she was a living wonder. At fourscore years and more she went into the fields to labour, and did her day's work with the best of them. She also kept her home tidy, and avoided the workhouse as she would a prison.

"You are late to-night, John," she said, "and I'll warrant ye've spent most of thy wages. Turn out thy pockets!"

John meekly complied, and Jenny counted over what was exposed to view.

"You've spent one and fourpence," she said.

"It don't matter, Jenny," replied John, "I've left old Job, and I've come into as good as a fortin'. I'm going to be kep' without work."

"Why, how be that, John?"

"Don't ax me," he said, "ye'll know it soon, Jenny. Give I a light, and let me get un to bed."

"Thee don't have no light to-night, John," replied Jenny, in a most decided tone; "find thy way in the dark. There be the door, and there be only nine stairs. Get up and be gone wi' ye, for the cock's got his throat full o' crowing, and will soon be calling us up again."

The aged one went up to bed, falling over each separate stair, and finally rolled on the floor, with his head just under the bed instead of upon it, and there he slept peacefully throughout the night, unconscious that an evil mind was already working to upset the prospect before him.

This mind lay in the head of Goggles, who in his humble home lay thinking a good two hours or more over certain plans whereby he hoped to supplant the oldest inhabitant in the affections of the Warmington boys.

The home of Goggles was, like that of many loafers, peculiarly humble. The furniture was extremely limited, and might in case of fire have been cleared out in something under a minute. His house, indeed, would have been very bare if it had not been furnished with—a wife and seven children.

What sort of father and husband Goggles made is easily guessed. He married and let his wife keep him, and when children came he considerately left them to look after themselves. But for Mrs. Goggles they would all have grown up thieves and vagabonds, and even her care did not keep them all quite straight, as we may presently see.

Goggles lay a-thinking.

"If there's money or beer about," he thought, "I think I ought to ha' some o' it—and I will, too."

The next day was Sunday, and as he had no clothes fit for that day he kept his bed and smoked. He also abused his wife every half-hour for having nothing better than bread and cheese in the house. He likewise threw his boots at his family whenever they ventured into his august presence.

On Monday morning he was up betime and away to the college, where he, with the aid of a tree, got upon the wall of the playground, and patiently awaited the coming of the boys, who, he knew, had half-an-hour's play before breakfast.

While he is there let me give a brief sketch of his personal appearance, as it is just possible he may be heard of again ere the thread of this story is run off the reel.

He was perhaps forty years of age, but he looked more; he had a broad flat face, small twinkling eyes, a red nose, stubbly beard and thick unkempt hair. For clothes he wore a velveteen coat that must have seen better days but could not possibly see worse—a dingy red waistcoat—knee-breeches, with almost as many patches as there were hairs on his head—dingy stockings—and boots that were but a bitter mockery when viewed as a protection to his feet, as the uppers were full of holes and the soles as good as gone.

Seated on the wall, dangling his legs to and fro, he looked the very perfection of a drunken loafer.

"Here's a kid coming," he said to himself, after an hour's waiting, "and it's the softy chap. Just the right one to begin with. Hist, master, how be you?"

"Oh, dear! Who's that?" asked Jolly Green, the boy whom Goggles had called the "soft chap." "How you frightened me!"

"It wasn't my intentions," replied Goggles; "but look here, master. Don't you trust old John. I'm the man to look arter you. Two bob a week, I'll murder anybody as touches you."

"I'm always being touched and shoved about," said Jolly, dismally.

"In course you are," said Goggles, "and so you will be, until you has I to purtect you."

"But what can you do?" asked Jolly.

"Anything; pint out the party, and I'll finish him off."

"It isn't a him, it's a her," said Jolly.

"I don't care," said Goggles, resolutely; "I'd just as soon lick a her as a he, and sooner."

This was one of the rare occasions in which Goggles spoke the truth. He certainly did prefer a woman to a man to fight with, as he generally got the best of it with the weaker sex, and came off as a rule second best with the stronger.

"Do you think," began Jolly, and paused.

"I never thinks, wot's the good on it?" said Goggles.

Here again was another rare instance of his truthful speaking. The unswerving and everlasting dame had apparently come out of her well to hover over Goggles that morning.

"But she is such—a—a—wonder," said Jolly.

"Who is she?"

"Mrs. Cobbem."

There was a pause. Jolly sucked his thumb, and Goggles for once thought a little, with a leaden eye.

"Oh! that's the party," he said.

"Yes," replied Jolly, "she's always down on me."

"She's down on everybody," returned Goggles. "She couldn't ever let me alone, but come a worrying me about the way I treats my missus, as if a man couldn't do what he liked with his own. I didn't marry her to be bullied by other people."

"I suppose not," said Jolly, scarcely knowing what to say.

"It's a stiff job tackling a woman like that," said Goggles, "and I don't think there's another man in the village as would go in for it, but I'll do it."

"I wish you would," said Jolly, earnestly, "but what are you going to do?"

"I'll try persuasion fust, as I did with my missus," returned Goggles; "but even that's risky, and I hope you will come down handsome."

"Oh! you want to be paid," said Jolly, wearily.

"Yes, I do."

"Everybody wants money of me," groaned Jolly. "Popper gets a lot out of me, and then says he hasn't had it. I am sure I haven't any left for myself."

"But surely you've got five bob," insinuated Goggles.

"No I haven't," replied Jolly, shortly.

"'Arf a crown then?" said Goggles, "that aint much when my time is considered, and a man with a wife and seven children finds his time wallyable. Arf a crown; come, that's cheap as dirt."

"But what will you do?" asked Jolly.

"You say she is 'ard on you."

"Yes, she worries me from morning till night. I'm half silly."

"Nobody would think it to look at you," said Goggles, with his sweetest smile; "for, I said to myself, as I see you coming along, I ses, "Here's a noble young gentleman with the hye of a genus."

"Don't talk such stuff," said Jolly, eyeing him dreamily.

"I won't if you don't wish it," replied Goggles. "But look here; about this Mrs. Cobbem, you want her to let you alone."

"I do."

"Then I'll make her, by persuasion if I can, if not by a way as I brought Mrs. Goggles to see I was right."

"How's that?" inquired Jolly.

"Never you mind. It's my secret. 'Arf a crown. Come, it is cheap."

Jolly meditated over the offer. He had been much harassed by Mrs. Cobbem for some days, and, really, if he could secure a little peace at the price it would not be dear. He decided to close with the offer.

"Here's the money," he said, "and if you get Mrs. Cobbem to let me alone I may give you another, but I won't promise—so don't say I did."

"All right," replied Goggles, pocketing the money; "you may make your mind heasy. In a day or two you'll find I've worked it. All I ax is, that you won't say anything to anybody about my undertaking the job, or it may be sp'iled."

"I won't say a word," promised Jolly.

"Not to your best friend?"

"I haven't got a friend," returned Jolly, "unless it's you."

"And I," said Goggles, "'m your friend for life. Good morning."

He dropped down from the wall almost upon the head of the oldest inhabitant, who was coming to confer with his friends through the iron gates. Had Goggles dropped from the clouds the aged one could not have been more astonished. For a moment, probably, he thought he had, but the truth came quickly upon his intelligent brain.

"I say," he said, "what were you doing up there?"

"Having a look round. They axed me to call," replied Goggles.

"Come, now, I'm not going to have you poaching," said the old un. "That school is mine. If ye want to look arter boys you must find another."

Goggles put his forefinger to his nose, and walked away in the direction of the White Hart. With half a crown in his pocket he had a full day's uninterrupted tap-room bliss before him. The oldest inhabitant looked after him with no pleasant expression upon his face. It was getting apparent to him that he was not going to have things entirely his own way.

"A nice thing," he said, "to have a low loafer cutting in just as my fortune is as good as made; but I'll soon get rid of he. What's that? The boys, in course, coming out for their morning exercise."

CHAPTER XLI.

GETTING THROUGH A GATE.

THE aged John went and fixed his face between two bars of the gate, and took a survey of the playground. All the boys were out, and were enjoying themselves as boys are wont to do. Marbles were in just then, and the square was dotted all over with little knots of earnest gamblers.

"There's a good lot of 'em," thought the oldest inhabitant—"quite sixty, if there's one of 'em; and twopence a-piece will pay handsome. Hist, lads! your friend be here."

Nobody heeded him—if, indeed, they saw him—and in a few moments he cried again—

"Hist, lads! I'm here to stand by you agin old Job Grumper and the lot of 'em."

But again he was unheeded, although Dick Stager looked towards the gate, and must have seen his weazened face thrust through the bars. Old John began to get impatient and peremptory.

"I say, you there," he cried, "don't stand out of your bargain! I'm here—old John's ready, and aint the man to shirk his work if he's set to do it."

Finding he could not get an answer, he took another course. Plucking up a fair-sized tuft of grass he shied it into the playground, and, with the usual luck attendant upon random shots, struck a party he did not intend to. The German professor caught it in his waistcoat, and gave vent to as good an oath as ever found favour in Fatherland.

"Who tid tat?" he asked. "Vat poy was so rude?"

"It was not any of us, sir," replied Billy Sharp. "It was that old man at the gate."

"He shall be an impudent old peggar," said the professor, and, setting all sail, bore down upon the offender.

Old John, whose eyesight was not strong enough to let him see the precise spot where his missile fell, stood his ground, and had not the least idea he had hurt or offended anybody until the professor laid hold of his nose and gave it a wring that

GREEN AS GRASS.

brought water into his eyes and a short and sharp
"Oh!" from his lips.

"Take tat!" said the professor, "and go avays
vith it!"

"What do you mean by a-doin' of that?" cried
John. "That's salt and battery, and I'll have the
law o' ye for that."

"You come and throw rubbish here. I'll have
the laws of you," said the professor. "You are an
impudent peggar, old man."

"I only wanted to speak to one of 'em," said
the aged one. "Them boys and me is friendly."

"Impossibles!" said the German. "They are
gentlemens, and you are an imbudent old peggar.
Go avays, man—go avays!"

How long this would have continued it is impossible to say; but just then the breakfast-bell rang,
and the boys, who had always an inclination to peck,
gave up their games and hurried in. The ushers
followed, and the German professor waddlingly
brought up the rear.

The oldest inhabitant was left alone in his
misery.

"This won't do," he said, "this aint a prosperous
business. That Goggles chap seems to have got up
early and done all the trade."

The playground was empty, but he could not
leave the spot. The prospect of failure held him
like a chain, and there he remained with his face
fixed between the bars, until he suddenly received
a blow behind that sent his head quite through,
and then he was in a sort of snare, hard and fast.

"You are to git out of this," said a youthful
voice, "and be off at once."

It was Perkins, who had come round from the
back way to carry out instructions received from
Mrs. Cobbem. That lady had seen the head of the
oldest inhabitant, and being given to resenting
impertinence in every shape and form, had sent the
young servitor to remove him.

"Tell him," she said, "to go at once, and if he
won't, then fetch the policeman."

Perkins thought it was a case in which he
might take the law into his own hands; but not
being governed by the rules of equity, he had
given the blow first and the remonstrance afterwards.

"Now don't stop staring there," he said, "but
get away at once."

The oldest inhabitant could not see him, and in
the dismay arising from his position, could not even
guess at the voice. It might have been a man's or
a woman's for aught he knew.

"I can't get out," he said, like Yorick's starling
in a plaintive tone.

"Why, you don't mean to say that you've gone
and fixed your head in there?" cried Perkins. "I
say, you've done it now. Them gates is fixtures."

"I didn't do it," said the old un. "You put me
in here."

"If you say that," replied Perkins, "I'll go away
and leave you, and there's a bull coming up the
road—the parson's bull, and you know him."

"Act friendly," moaned the aged one, "and help
me out."

"Keep steady," said Perkins, "and I'll see what
a tug will do."

Taking hold of the old man's smock, he gave it a
pull, but this nearly proved fatal to the unfortunate prisoner, as it brought his gills violently
against the iron bars of the gate, and nearly dis-
located his jaw. He gave an awful howl that reached
Mrs. Cobbem's ears, and brought her again to the
window.

"You are in there for life," said Perkins, calmly.
"I don't see what we can do for you here."

"You did it, whoever you are," moaned the aged
one.

"My name is Perkins," replied the dear boy,
"and as you are inclined to be imperent, I shall
leave you. Here comes Mr. Jiggles, ax him to give
you a hand."

"Missus says that if that old man don't take his
self off at once, she'll have him locked up," said
Jiggles, as he came round the corner.

"But he can't take hisself off," said Perkins,
"for he's been and shoved his head through the
bars, and nothing less than a steam-hengine will
hever get him hout again."

"I didn't do it—you did it," said the oldest inhabitant, driven almost to madness by his position,
and being unable to face that wicked boy.

"Now is it likely I could put him there?" argued
Perkins, "when missus sent me out to tell him to
take hisself off?"

"It don't seem likely," said Jiggles; "but you
have done some rum things in your time. Can't we
get him out?"

"Have a try," said Perkins, "and don't mind his
howling."

"I won't be pulled about in this way," roared the
aged one, clutching the bars of the gate. "You
must have the bar filed through."

"I think," said Perkins, pausing from his labour,
"that you had better go and tell Cobbem to come
out."

"And I thinks," said Jiggles, putting on his
most dignified air, "that you might fust speak of
your master as Mister Cobbem, and then go and
ask him to come yourself."

"I haint a-going to leave this old party!" said
Perkins, firmly. "He's a old un, but he's a strong
un, and he may take it into his head to wrench the
gates up by the roots, and run away with them."

"Oh! you are a beauty," said Jiggles, every hair
of his head bristling.

Seeing there was no help for it, Jiggles went for
Mr. Cobbem, as instructed by Perkins, and in a few
minutes the reverend gentleman, followed by his
wife, came hurrying down.

"Dear—dear me!" he said, "what terrible casualty
is this? How came you here, my man?"

"That's right," said Mrs. Cobbem, "make a
favour of his impudence. You wicked old fellow—
how dare you?"

And then she boxed the ears of the aged one.

"Wot next?" he roared. "That boy of yourn
shoved me through, and now you come and salt and
bully me. I'll have the law on you."

"Me shove him through!" cried the indignant
Perkins. "Come, now, did you see me do it?"

"Don't argue," said the Reverend Copley, "but
let us release him. Let me see—are you at the
precise spot where you came in?"

"I think I've dropped a bit," murmured the old
un.

"Oh! pull him through and have done with it,"
said Mrs. Cobbem, impatiently.

"My love, we may murder him. How then could
we hope ever to rest?"

Mrs. Cobbem said nothing, but turned indignantly
upon her heel, and strolled back into the house. For
the present she left the subject. It could be settled
anon.

The Rev. Copley, aided by Perkins and Jiggles,
set to work to release the prisoner. First he was
hoisted up to get his head higher, then he was requested to kneel, and after that they slid him up
and down, but no position gave success to their
endeavours.

"You have a remarkable protuberance of jaw by
the ears," said the Reverend Copley, "and I dare say
it is elastic in a measure, and you came through
like a spring."

"You've got a lot o' jaw yourself," said the oldest
inhabitant, glaring at him like an evil spirit, "but
you don't do much."

"I fear we must break the gate," said the
Reverend Copley, ignoring the rudeness of the aged
one on account of the painful nature of his position.
"Perkins run for the blacksmith."

"If he ain't quick," groaned the aged one, "it
will be all over with me."

GREEN AS GRASS.

A JOLLY SCHOOL STORY.

THE LITTLE DINNER PARTY IS BROKEN UP, BY THE SUDDEN APPEARANCE OF THE REV. COPLEY COBBEM.

Perkins, for once in a way, performed an errand with unimaginable speed for him, and he and the blacksmith came hurrying back together, the latter carrying files and other implements. There was also a number of other people, whom Perkins had shouted the news to as he ran by, coming up cautiously behind, among them Goggles.

Altogether there was a very nice little gathering outside the gate, but the Reverend Copley was alone within the grounds. He wore an anxious look upon his face, but was calm and stately, as became a man of his position.

"I think, blacksmith," he said, "we had better cut the bar here, so as to save him unnecessary irritation."

"Lor, sir," said the blacksmith, "you don't want to cut no bars. His body is a thin un, and will go arter his head any day."

"Will it, indeed?"

"Of course it will. Now old un, stand steady."

The blacksmith was a strong man, and being aided by those around him, Goggles coming well to the fore, the truth of his statement was speedily verified, and the oldest inhabitant came through the gate like a bolt from an ancient catapult. The Reverend Copley, who had kindly prepared himself to catch, was taken off his balance, and he and the aged one went to the ground together.

But all's well that ends well. The reverend gentleman got up and dusted his clothes with his handkerchief, while the oldest inhabitant carefully tried his head to see if any of his anatomical arrangements were injured. Finding all right, he sulkily demanded to be let out, and went down the road, followed by a long train of admiring friends, who had arrived upon the scene.

As a matter of business the morning's work had been a failure, but it helped to make the oldest inhabitant still more famous, and for many days it was a favourite walk of the rustics up to the gates of Warmington College to see the bars where the aged one had been so firmly fixed.

With these seekers of the sensational Mrs. Copley waged war, and went so far as to allow Perkins to have the garden engine to pump water over them; but some of the roughest began to retaliate with stones, and then she gave in, and in due time the interest of the people died away.

CHAPTER XLII.

A SACK RACE.

THREE days' incessant rain came upon the land around Warmington, and, deprived of their out-door exercises, the boys were put to their wits' end for amusement, especially when their half-holiday came round and the sky was still pouring out its flood of water.

"What shall we do?" said Tommy Whisker. "It's enough to turn a fellow's hair grey."

He was seated in the window of the schoolroom looking out, and put the question generally. Dick Stager answered him.

"Do!" he said, "read like good boys, and get up our lesson for a week ahead."

"Yah!" exclaimed Tommy, "that would be a fine thing—wouldn't it? I wonder you are not ashamed of yourself. No books for me."

"I wonder if the Cobbems are at home," said Dick.

"Mrs. Cobbem generally goes out in wet weather," put in Bob Larry.

"Why?"

"Because her worthy husband is subject to rheumatism."

"I can hear her voice now," said Billy Sharp Popper.

"I'll just go out and hear what she is saying," said Nick Stager.

He was absent a little over a minute, and came

back with a beaming face, such as the fullest of full moons could ill-compare with.

"She is ordering that thing she calls a carriage," he said.

"Hurrah!" cried Dick, "we shall have the house to ourselves."

"Barring the ushers."

"Oh! they don't count. They are in the professor's room, smoking. Now somebody with sharp ears just listen at the door, and let me know when the carriage rolls away, as they say in the story-book."

"What are you going to do?" asked Jolly Greene.

"Well, young un, I don't mind telling you as you appear to be interested," replied Dick. "I am going to have some athletic sports—boxing, wrestling, and foot races."

"Not in the wet, I should think," said Jolly; "we shall all catch cold."

"No, spooney, not in the wet, but in the dry, in the long corridor of this house."

Jolly had a perfect remembrance of that corridor, having had some trifling adventures there. He also knew it was a private part of the house, and said so.

"Private!" said Dick, appealing to the other boys; "hear him. As if this house were not our own. Who keeps it going—eh! spooney?"

"I don't know, replied Jolly.

"Of course you don't know," returned Dick. "Now, lads, who is for the sports, and who is not? All who are for them hold up one hand."

Every hand went up, even Jolly's. Of late his mind had taken a slightly festive turn, and he had once tried a practical joke upon one of the boys, and although he failed the attempt was highly creditable to him. In passing we may as well give a short account of this little affair.

"Bob Larry was always boasting how tough he was, and declared he could take any amount of caning on his hands, "and you may double your fist," he said to Jolly, "and hit the palm of it as hard as you like while I hold it against a brick wall."

"But the wall will hurt you," said Jolly.

"I don't mind that," returned Larry, calmly. "You try it."

"I will," said Jolly.

So Larry put his open hand against the brick wall, and Jolly, who had not dealt a respectable blow many times in his life, prepared to give one now. He struck out, and Larry, faithfully carrying out the old joke, drew his hand away, and Jolly bashed his knuckles.

After due reflection our sage friend arrived at the conclusion that this was a joke, and he resolved to play it upon another, but he chose the wrong party and the wrong place for its performance.

It was Tommy Whisker he tried it upon, and, mentioning the subject in the middle of the playground, merely said—

"I'll give you leave to hit my hand as hard as you like with your fist."

"All right," said Whisker.

Jolly was fixed where to put it, but with his usual keenness decided to hold his hand in front of his face.

"Hit out now," he said.

Whisker let out straight from the shoulder. Jolly drew his hand away, and received the blow upon his nose.

"Oh, dear!—oh, dear!" he said. "I don't think I've got the joke quite right."

And most people will agree with him. There was a defect somewhere.

But, to return to the original subject. As soon the carriage was heard to roll away Dick and Nick proceeded to arrange the sports.

"We will begin with a sack race," said Dick. "There are a lot of sacks in the cupboard by the pantry. The potatoes came in them yesterday. Volunteers are wanted to fetch them."

Plenty were forthcoming, and while they were gone Dick received entries for the race. Jolly and Billy both put in for it, and were drawn for the first heat.

When the sacks were brought the boys, led by the two Stagers, made their way boldly to the corridor, and would no doubt have had a very jolly afternoon but for one thing, and that was the Rev. Copley Cobbem and his wife were at home—he in his room in the corridor, and Mrs. Cobbem in the store-room with the housekeeper.

The carriage had been despatched to the station to meet a relative of Mrs. Cobbem's, who was coming to stay a day or two.

The Reverend Copley was deep in that learned book by Professor Snoozle, entitled "The Origin of Grubs and Slugs, and why they are so fond of Summer Cabbages," and being alone was at peace until he heard a roar, which at first reminded him of the murmur of a distant sea.

"Good heavens!" he exclaimed. "What is it? Not an earthquake."

"Off!" cried a voice in the corridor outside, and then came a frightful yell, as if a thousand demons had invaded his peaceful abode.

"What can this mean?" exclaimed the startled listener. "There is a strange bumping sound in the corridor—very strange sound. Now something falls."

And then there was another yell, and the voice of Dick was heard.

"Rolling home is fair."

"It is the boys!" exclaimed the Reverend Copley. "What fresh audacity is this? But I must disperse them ere Mrs. Cobbem arrives upon the scene."

He opened his door and put his head out, and there he beheld what he very often spoke of afterwards as an unparalleled scene.

There was a line of sacks with boys' heads sticking out of the top—the heads of Jolly Greene and Billy Sharp being well to the front. Jolly, however, was down on his nose, and all the others seemed bent upon going over him.

"Boys!" cried the Reverend Copley, in a voice of thunder.

The firing of a park of artillery in the middle of a rabbit warren could not have had a more startling effect upon the rabbits than that unexpected voice upon the boys. All those who were unencumbered dashed to the door at the far end and melted away like sprites, and those in the sacks struggled to get free.

All but Jolly succeeded, and scuttled off at a great pace. Our friend, however, having been tied in with peculiar care, and not being very nimble in his ways, turned on his back, staring at the Reverend Copley like a boy in a dream.

"What next will you foolish lads do?" said the Reverend Copley. "What are you doing?"

"Sack-racing, sir," replied Jolly; "and I had nearly won."

"But who instigated this outrage? I ask you, Greene, to explain?"

Jolly opened his lips to reply, but the voice of Mrs. Cobbem was heard on the staircase. She, too, had heard the noise, and was coming up for an explanation.

"You foolish lad!" said the Reverend Copley. "If Mrs. Cobbem finds you here she will punish you severely. Get out of that sack, and take yourself off."

"I can't, sir," replied Greene.

"Let me help you."

The reverend gentleman was nervous, and could not unfasten the string. The voice of Mrs. Cobbem was heard several stairs higher.

"Here, come into my room," said the Reverend Copley. "You are a most unfortunate boy, and always in trouble. Can you walk?"

"No, sir."

"Then I must carry you," said the Reverend Copley, taking him under his arm. "But what shall I do with you? Mrs. Cobbem may come into this room. Oh! I must put you into this cupboard; and mind you keep quiet. There! you are upright; and don't lean any way, in case you should fall."

"I won't, sir."

The Reverend Copley closed the door hastily, and resumed his book with affected calmness. Barely had he settled down when Mrs. Cobbem stalked majestically into the room.

CHAPTER XLIII.

MRS. COBBEM APPEARS ON THE SCENE.

"PERHAPS, Mr. Cobbem," said Mrs. Cobbem, "you will kindly inform me what all this rioting means?"

"Rioting!" exclaimed the Rev. Copley, "has there been any?"

His wife cast upon him a look that ought to have withered him, but he was a man callous to the glances of the woman he had sworn to love and obey, and even smiled under it. Yet it was a sickly smile, such as we see on the face of a criminal, who tries to make light of getting penal servitude for life.

"It seems to me," said Mrs. Cobbem, "that you are either deaf or in league with those wretched boys. You conspire with them to make my life a burden."

"I conspire, Agatha?" exclaimed the Rev. Copley. "Oh! my love."

"I would rather be abused by some men," said Mrs. Copley, "than be called 'my love' by a sycophant. Again let me ask you what that disturbance meant?"

The Rev. Copley opened his lips to reply. It was a trying time for him—to be harassed by his wife, and to be in fear of young Greene making some noise and exposing him. In his anxiety, the hearing of the rev. gentleman became unnaturally acute, and he distinctly heard a low grating noise, as if the sack which held Jolly was gradually sliding down.

"Why don't he keep still?" he muttered.

"What do you say?" asked Mrs. Copley.

"I—I said I felt rather ill," replied the Rev. Copley.

"You said something else," returned his wife, "so don't try to deceive me."

"I won't, my love—I never did. I have ever been true to you."

"Oh, bother about that! Now, Mr. Copley, I have something to say to you and I beg you will hearken. There must be better order kept in this house while my uncle is here. Uncle Ruddle is a man of considerable personal property, and although he has a host of nephews and nieces, I do not see why his money should be scattered broadcast. It would be much better if it could be kept together."

"Under one roof you mean," murmured her husband.

"Under *this* roof," said Mrs. Cobbem; "but you are not attending to me. You are listening to something else."

"I!" exclaimed the Rev. Copley, starting as if from a sleep. "Well, yes. No, I am only a little distracted by a mathematical problem——"

"A mathematical grandmother," returned Mrs. Cobbem. "Again let me urge upon you to keep these boys in order. Uncle Ruddle is a bachelor, and likes ease and comfort. He hates babies——"

"We have none," murmured the Rev. Copley.

"You need not remind me of that," returned Mrs. Copley. "One child might have cheered our home, but——"

Here she burst into tears, and the Rev. Copley dropped his book, sprang to his feet, and put his arm round her waist.

"My love, my life, my Agatha, forgive," he

murmured. At the same moment he distinctly heard that sack slide a little further.

"That boy will be down," he muttered half aloud.

"That boy—what boy?" asked Mrs. Copley.

"Oh! no boy in particular," replied her husband. "I was thinking of boys in general."

"Mr. Cobbem, you are a false-hearted monster. You know you were thinking of a boy—of Perkins —who is your chief pride and joy."

"How dare you say that, Mrs. Cobbem?"

"Because I know it, Mr. Cobbem."

"That low child is nothing to me, Mrs. Cobbem."

"He is everything to you, Mr. Cobbem. All the house and the comfort of everybody are sacrificed for that little ruffian."

"Madam," said the Reverend Copley, drawing himself up to his full height, "that boy shall quit this house to-night."

"So like a man that," said Mrs. Copley, with quiet sarcasm; "first pamper a creature, then kick him out on the cold world to starve. You pampered me at first—but now— Mr. Copley, if you look at me in that way I will throw something at you."

"It is not in the power of man always to control his emotions," said the Reverend Copley; "at present I burn under a sense of wrong. Dear me, I am sure he is coming down."

The last words were spoken inwardly, and arose from his again hearing the sound of the sack sliding. Through all he had kept his ears upon the stretch, and his chief fear was that young Greene would cough or sneeze, in which case all would have been at once revealed.

"Mr. Copley—" began Mrs. Copley again, and suddenly pulled up as the threatened fall came at last, and Jolly's head came against the door of the cupboard like a battering ram, and burst it open.

The spectacle that unfortunate boy presented was well calculated to fill the breast of a gentle lady with dismay, for in addition to being tied in a sack, his face was white as a sheet and his eyes fixed. He was, in fact, as far as appearance went, fit for the last sad office of the undertaker.

Mrs. Cobbem looked and believed she was gazing on a dead boy, and in a moment an awful thought came upon her. What could she think but that her husband had murdered young Greene and made an attempt to conceal the body?

"Oh!—oh!" she gasped, and staggered back and sat upon a chair in horrified amazement.

Her awful idea was, however, speedily dispelled by Jolly, who, after rolling his eyes round twice, exclaimed feebly—

"Mar!"

At the same moment the front-door bell rang, but neither Mr. nor Mrs. Combem heard it. Both were engrossed in the scene before them. Silent they stood until young Greene spoke again.

"Please let me out," he said, "I'm choking."

Mrs. Cobbem had recovered—her fear was turned to wrath. Mr. Cobbem, her husband, had deceived her.

"Now, Mr. Cobbem," she said, "perhaps you will explain how came this boy here. Is this a new torture you have devised for this helpless boy? Is this a way of adding to the long list of cruelties you have perpetrated upon those whom their misguided parents place under your charge?"

"My love," said the Reverend Copley, "I found him as he is in the corridor, and while I was attempting to release him you came upstairs, and I, fearing the sight of such a strange object might upset your sensitive nerves, put him temporarily out of the way."

"A fine story—a fine story! but I am not so easily imposed upon."

"Oh! take me out," cried Jolly. "I'm choking —I really am."

"Take him out, Mr. Cobbem."

"Take him out yourself, madam; you drive me distracted.

"Oh, if I—ha! that voice," cried Mrs. Cobbem.

"A pretty thing," roared a voice in the corridor, "to come to this house on a visit and find nobody to receive me."

"They are up here somewhere's," replied the voice of Jiggles; "perhaps they are in master's room."

"He can't come here and see that boy," said Mrs. Cobbem.

But it was too late. Jiggles threw open the door and ushered in a little round man, with a fiery nose and eyes, and a mouth quivering with rage.

"Uncle Ruddle," exclaimed Mrs. Cobbem; "you have come earlier than expected."

"So it seems, Agatha—so it seems," he replied; "and here have I been wandering all over the house at the heels of this stupid fellow, who does not even know where I am to sleep; perhaps you have forgotten all about it."

"Oh! no, my dear uncle," said Mrs. Cobbem, sweetly. "The spare room is ready for you."

All this time she had skilfully shut out the view of Jolly with her dress, but she could not hide his voice, and once again he exclaimed—

"Mar!"

"What is that?" asked Uncle Ruddle.

"Some noise outside, uncle," replied Mr. Cobbem.

"Somebody said 'Mar,'" insisted Uncle Ruddle. "Now, tell me, have you any children in the house? I understood you had none."

"Only the pupils."

"But you assured me they lived in a separate part of the establishment."

"I did, uncle, but come to your room—it is quite ready."

"You must let me out," groaned Jolly, "or I shall be dead in a minute."

"There is somebody behind you," said Uncle Ruddle. "I insist upon knowing who and what it is."

CHAPTER XLIV.

UNCLE RUDDLE HAS A ROUGH TIME OF IT.

THERE are some men who are not to be put upon, and Uncle Ruddle was one of them. He stood upon his rights always with the outer world, and with his relations, who were hunting him for his money, he stood up more.

He did not understand the scene before him, but that had no influence with Uncle Ruddle. He put his own interpretation upon it, and at once went to work.

"This is one of your low practical jokes, Cobbem," he said—"one of your college tricks; but I won't stand it."

"Hear me, sir," exclaimed the Rev. Copley.

"Shut up!" said the amiable old gentleman. "Agatha, show me to my room. I must have at least an hour's rest before I leave this accursed house."

"Uncle, do not talk in that way," said Mrs. Cobbem, tearfully.

"Agatha," he answered, "I always told you not to marry a fool, but you would do it, and the consequences are before you. Will you show me to my room, or will you not? And where is that idiot with my luggage?"

That idiot was Jiggles, who was outside listening, and rebellion entered his heart; but when Uncle Ruddle, like a red hot cannon-ball, bounced out upon him, he caved in, and ran in front with a portmanteau in each hand, and a hat-box under his arm.

The latter Jiggles dropped several times as he walked, or rather shuffled, along. The first time Uncle Ruddle said nothing, the second time he frowned, the third time he swore, and when it fell for the fourth time he tried to kick Jiggles.

"It appears to me, Agatha," he said, "that both the head and tail of this establishment are idiotic."

"With such a master," sighed Agatha, "we cannot expect to have first-rate servants."

Uncle Ruddle was at last got into his room, and being in a passion, which always made him bilious, he went to bed, leaving a command that he was not to be disturbed until he rang.

Meanwhile the Rev. Copley had got Jolly Greene out of the sack, and put him on his feet. For awhile he stood regarding him pathetically.

"You are indeed an unfortunate lad," he said. "You bring misfortunes upon yourself, and on others also."

"I can't help it," replied Jolly. "It aint my fault. I don't mean to do it."

"And yet it is done," said the Rev. Copley Cobbem, sadly. "Now, go to your studies, and—ahem! avoid Mrs. Cobbem, if you can, as she is rather excited with—ahem! the arrival of her uncle; and will you take a message for me to the boys? Say that as there is a stranger in the house, I shall be glad if they will be a little quieter than usual."

Jolly escaped Mrs. Cobbem, and arrived without mishap in the schoolroom. There he delivered his message, which, I regret to say, was hailed with a shout of derision. Then he was questioned, and the story of his late mishap, which he told most dismally, was received with every expression of general joy.

The arrival of Uncle Ruddle excited much curiosity, and Jolly was called upon to describe his personal appearance, and also to point out where he was put to. The former he did to the best of his ability, but with the latter he was unacquainted.

"We must find out where he is to sleep," said Dick Stager, "and prepare his bed and bedroom for him."

"Hear—hear," chorused the delighted listeners.

"Now, how can we get at this place?" said Dick, thoughtfully. "You saw his luggage, Greene?"

"Oh! yes," replied Jolly, "there were two black portmanteaus and a hat-box."

"That's something to swear by," said Dick. "Now, could you go round the house on the quiet, and see where these things are?"

"I won't go round the house again," returned Jolly. "I am sure to meet Mrs. Cobbem."

"But you must."

"I won't," said Jolly, and for once he was very determined. Even Billy Sharp failed to persuade him.

"I think we can manage it," said Dick, after a pause. "What they call the spare room is just over the greenhouse, and there is a strong spout running over the top of that, and a grape-vine to hold by. If you get on this window it isn't far to travel, and if you let go it isn't far to fall, only mind the greenhouse."

Greene looked very dismal, and at first declined to undertake the task; but so many voices were lifted up in its favour, and so many tongues full of praises of his courage, that at last he yielded.

"All you have to do is to peep into the room and see if the boxes are there, and if they are come back, and leave the rest to me. You have nothing to fear. It's raining cats and dogs, and there is nobody in the garden."

"But shan't I get wet?" asked Jolly.

"Not werry," replied Billy Sharp. "You may have a few drops."

"Nothing," said Nick Stager.

The window of the schoolroom was opened, and there, just beneath, was a broad old-fashioned leaden waterspout, full of water just then, but with a good outside edge to walk upon. About twelve yards to the left was the greenhouse, and over that the window of the spare room. A strong old vine covered the building in this part of the house.

"I don't see why I should go any more than any of you," said Jolly.

"You know his boxes and we don't," replied Nick.

"But why can't you leave the man alone?" asked Jolly. "He never did any harm to you."

"Go along, spoony," said Dick, and assisted by many friendly hands Jolly got upon the spout, clutched the vine, and began his perilous passage.

Uncle Ruddle was in the bed, but not asleep. When a man is in a towering passion he finds it hard to arrive at the blissful unconsciousness by which we recruit our health, and in addition to this Uncle Ruddle was not tired. He had gone to bed out of spite, and was naturally very wide awake.

He had the blinds down, but one of them was an ill-fitting article that gave a two-inch slit of the window to gaze at the rain through. This particularly exasperated Uncle Ruddle, who had a very great objection to ill-fitting blinds, and with his eyes fixed on the little bit of murky sky he lay and anathematised the careless housekeeping arrangements of Agatha, his niece.

Just in the middle of a curse of more than ordinary length, he saw a dark shadow slowly crossing the blind, and presently he beheld at the slit aforesaid—

A human face.

A face with a leaden eye, and a nose that at first he was unable to tell the shape of, as it was flattened against the window by its owner, who seemed to be terribly anxious to get a sight at Uncle Ruddle in his little bed.

That he did not succeed in his object at first was apparent, for the individual fixed first one eye, then the other, and finally drew back to get a little rest. Then Uncle Ruddle saw who it was, and recognised in this spy the boy who had been put into a sack and brought into the Rev. Copley's room, especially, as he believed, to insult and annoy him.

The first act of Uncle Ruddle on recognising this second dastardly attempt to destroy his peace was to lay hold of the bell-pull and give it a violent jerk, that brought it down upon him in a serpent-like coil, then he bounced out of bed and laid hold of the blind-cord. It was a spring one, and up went the blind like a rocket.

Jolly, who was about to return to the place from whence he came, staggered back one pace, lost his hold of the vine, and disappeared.

Immediately, Uncle Ruddle heard a crash as if a whole plumber and glazier's shop had been shaken up by an earthquake; and following it came shrieks and yells, as if the plumber and his assistants were shut up in the ruins.

"This house is pandemonium," he said, as the dew of fear moistened his aged brow; "but I'll get out of it at once. I'll have my things packed and be off."

He made a dart at a door which he thought was the one he entered by, and opened it. This, however, was only a cupboard, which he found out as soon as he got inside and mixed himself with a lot of loose ironware, such as fenders, fire-irons, and several shelves of jam pots and pickle jars. Shaking himself free he came forth again, found the right door, opened it, and yelled down the passage for Agatha.

Let us now see what became of Jolly. He had, as may easily be guessed, fallen through the glass roof of the greenhouse. Once through that he got among a pyramid of flower pots, and sweeping each shelf in succession clear, he finally, with a shower of earth, roots, and broken pots, separated Jiggles and the cook, who had been indulging in a little quiet spooning.

It was the duty of Jiggles to water the greenhouse, and sometimes when the cook had time she came and helped him to carry the water. Up to this time Jiggles had not positively declared, but the cook was hopeful, and her hope was on the point of being fulfilled, when Jolly and the ruin he made came down like an avalanche, and spoiled all.

Jiggles was just saying, "How nice it would be if we two was niver to part," as Jolly came and divided them in the most violent and unexpected manner. Jiggles was knocked down by a pot of myrtle, and the cook received in her gentle bosom four fuchsias and their pots, and about a dozen or so of geranium cuttings.

Jiggles was a gifted man, and sometimes formed conclusions in a moment, but now and then he happened to be wrong. On this occasion he shrieked out "cats," but it was Jolly; and, although confused by his fall, and covered with the earth out of the myrtle pot, there was a corner of his fiery intellect in a keenly observant state.

"It's the green un at it again," he said, and got up to help Jolly, who was lying apparently dead.

"Give a hand, cook," he said, I think he's killed hisself.

The cook was not a bad-hearted woman. She had lost a chance that might never come again, and been pretty well scared out of her wits, but she could not bear any animosity against Jolly, who was known to have no very great vices if he had no particular virtues.

"Let's get him out of the way," she said, "afore missus comes."

They got him out into the kitchen, when a little cold water brought him round a bit, and as soon as he could understand Jiggles he was induced to retire with all speed to his room.

"And don't you say nothing," said Jiggles, "and we shan't say nothing."

"I ain't so much in love with my missus as to say anything," said the cook.

Jolly got away to his room, glad to escape, and would have shut himself in, but Billy Sharp was on the watch for him, with power to pour certain threats into his ears on behalf of the school in general.

"You are not to say anything about it," said Sharp; "if you are questioned say it was not you."

"I won't say a word," replied Jolly; "I'll go to bed."

"That's your sort," said Billy; "off with your clothes, get up a sham sleep, and leave the rest to me."

Jolly Greene, with more intelligence than might have been expected from him in his state of mind, hastily pulled off his clothes and got into bed, and Billy Sharp, with one last word of warning, left him to his repose.

The amount of grace received by Jolly was owing to the furious rage Uncle Ruddle was in, for when he at last succeeded in getting Mrs. Cobbem up stairs, he sputtered and foamed for full five minutes before he could utter an intelligent word.

"My dear uncle, I beg of you to compose yourself," said Mrs. Cobbem. "What is the matter now? Oh! do be calm."

"Calm," exclaimed Uncle Ruddle. "Calm, madam, when I've not been an hour in your house without twice being made the victim of a practical joke. Your husband, not content with the tomfoolery on my arrival, must needs send that boy here again to make grimaces at my window."

"To make grimaces at you!" exclaimed Mrs. Cobbem. "Such audacity is incredible."

"Perhaps you disbelieve me," said Uncle Ruddle, every hair on his head bristling like a broom.

"Oh, no, my dear uncle."

"And perhaps you did not hear the subsequent confusion?"

"I heard a breaking of glass."

"That's it, Agatha, just outside my window."

Mrs. Cobbem went to the window and saw the wreck Jolly had made with her greenhouse, and the little sweetness matrimonial life had left in her disposition departed.

"Uncle," she said, "I beseech you not to blame either Cobbem or myself for this. We have a large school, and the boys as a body are very good; but I promise you this, that those who have annoyed you shall be dismissed at once. Come down stairs to the smoking-room, I will send you in a bottle of excellent sherry."

Uncle Ruddle liked few things on earth except himself, but if he had any affection for any two things, they were sherry and cigars. It was raining harder than ever, and he was too fond of his own personal comfort to leave the house that night, so he put the best face he could upon the matter, and went down to the apartment Mrs. Cobbem named.

On the way she said—

"Shall I ask Cobbem to come and keep you company?"

"Yes, do," he replied. "I am not fond of sitting alone."

In a few minutes the Reverend Copley Cobbem, all smiles and gentleness, was seated by his side, offering an explanation of the extraordinary events that had so immediately followed his arrival.

The sherry had a mellowing and the cigars a soothing effect, and in the depths of his crusty old soul Uncle Ruddle had a faint sense of humour. Before the bottle was finished he had laughed heartily a dozen times over the misfortunes of Jolly Greene.

CHAPTER XLV.

MRS. COBBEM IS PUZZLED FIRST, AND THEN CONFOUNDED.

WHILE the two gentlemen were getting into a state of blissful peace in the smoking-room, Mrs. Cobbem was engaged in investigating what was to her the most mysterious affair she had ever known.

On leaving her uncle with sherry and cigars she went straight to the schoolroom, where she expected to find the boys congregated. She was not disappointed—they were all there, with the exception of the one she was seeking.

It was a pretty sight to see how quiet and orderly these young gentlemen were. The catastrophe which had so lately befallen Jolly froze up their spirits, "checked their cheerfulness," and impressed upon them the necessity of orderly demeanour.

As Mrs. Cobbem entered the room they all politely stood up, expecting in their hearts what was coming, but none uttered a word.

"Where is Greene?" she asked sharply.

For a second there was no reply. Then Billy Sharp came to the fore.

"He's in bed, mum," he said.

"I wish," said Mrs. Copley, "that you would get rid of that vulgar habit of saying 'mum' every time you speak. Remember you are in a gentleman's school for young gentlemen. He's in bed, is he? How long has he been there?"

"About two hours," replied Billy.

This astounding lie sent a shiver through the school, and more than one head was bent down. Mrs. Cobbem either did not or would not notice the emotion of the boys.

She asked where Jolly was, and being informed, requested Billy Sharp to accompany her up stairs. There they found Jolly in bed, very pale, with his eyes closed and mouth compressed, and breathing so softly that one could scarcely tell if he were alive.

"Wake him up!" said Mrs. Cobbem.

Billy took him by the shoulders and gave him a shaking sufficient to awaken a dozen ordinary sleepers, but it had no more visible effect upon Jolly than it would have had upon an Egyptian mummy.

"I can't do it," said Billy, pausing from his labours. "I think he must be in a kind of fit mum."

Mrs. Cobbem ignored the "mum," and took the rousing of the sleeper into her own hands. The process she adopted was at once simple and effective

Taking him under the arms she jerked him into a sitting position, and gave him a sound box of the ears on either side of his head.

This form of enlivenment is about the most confusing of all punishments familiar to our early days. But with Jolly it helped him to keep his resolve, for he was really unable to give Mrs. Cobbem anything like a clear account of what had transpired that afternoon.

She put the question first in one form, then in another, threw out suggestions, threats, promises, but all she could get in reply was a series of " I don't knows," and occasional references to his mar.

" This," said Mrs. Cobbem, worn out at last, "is sheer obstinacy. I won't endure it longer. Pack your box, and leave this house at once ; and you too," she added, turning sharply upon Billy, "you low, cunning, good-for-nothing boy !"

Master Sharp was staggered, but he managed to mutter an expostulation.

"Me too, mum," he said. " What have I done ?"

"Everything," she answered. " Pack your boxes and take yourselves to the White Hart. You can write to your friends from there. Perkins shall bring on your things as soon as I can spare him."

Billy looked at the window, through which he could see the pelting rain, and ventured yet again to expostulate.

"We can't go in weather like this," he said.

Mrs. Cobbem answered—

" I cannot have the peace of this house disturbed any longer. A repetition of the doings of this day will deprive me of the dearest friend I have on this earth—one whom I value more than the whole of you troublesome boys.

" You can go at once, and you need not go through any nonsensical leave-taking with your late companions. They are gentlemen, and you are not likely to see much of them in the future."

With this sarcastic reference to the origin of those whom she addressed, Mrs. Cobbem retired, and Billy indulged in a low whistle of amazement and dismay.

"Here's a go, Jolly," he said.

"I don't care," Jolly replied, wearily. " It don't matter much to me where I go. I've always been shoved and pushed about here, and I can't be worse off wherever I go."

"But what will they say at home ?" asked Billy.

" It don't matter," returned Greene.

"Anyhow," said Billy, " it isn't our fault. I think it will be rather jolly at the White Hart. Here, shall I pack your box ?"

"Do," said Jolly. " I don't feel as if I could do anything."

On reflection, Master William Sharp was inclined to think that a few days could be spent at the White Hart in a very agreeable manner.

Of course, Mr. and Mrs. Greene would take their dismissal very ill, but when they came to learn, which they would be sure to do, that it was a misfortune rather than a crime which had led to it, he felt sure that both Billy and Jolly would be sent to another school.

Boxes were packed, Jolly dressed himself, and the two went downstairs together. As they passed the schoolroom door they heard the murmur of voices. Billy paused, undecided whether to go in or not, but remembering Mrs. Cobbem's admonition, he gave up the sad ceremony of leave-taking, and went softly down through the hall. Outside he put up the one umbrella he had, the property of Jolly Greene, and monopolising two-thirds for himself, bade his companion come along.

Jolly, indifferent to the rain, indifferent to the cold, fell in by his side, and in silence they trudged along the muddy road towards the White Hart Inn.

Mrs. Cobbem saw them go, and felt her spirits considerably lightened ; she was even musical, and hummed a few bars of the " Last Rose of Summer,"

a little out of tune, as she went back to make arrangements for the dinner.

As a rule the Cobbems did not dine late, but they could when they liked put a good spread before their friends and acquaintances. On this occasion the spread was to be particulary good.

When baiting your hooks for a fish like Uncle Ruddle, be sure you give him the best of baits.

CHAPTER XLVI.

AT THE WHITE HART INN.

THERE are not many boys of Billy Sharp's age who would have entered the White Hart Inn with the confidence he displayed. But public houses were nothing new to him, and although he had in the old time frequented, in company with his father, places of a low grade, he was not to be daunted by the respectability of any place of public accommodation.

He was tolerably dry when they arrived, but Jolly Greene was little more to look at than a bundle of sodden clothes. A more dejected specimen of humanity William, the waiter, never looked upon.

Having had an acquaintance with both young gentlemen before, he felt less astonishment than he might otherwise have done at their arrival ; but he was speedily put into an agitated frame of mind by Billy Sharp, who had the air of a man of forty at least, and gave his orders with the confidence of an old traveller.

The coffee-room was empty when they entered, but a bright fire was burning in preparation for the usual evening company. It was not, however, bright enough for Billy, who, under the very nose of William, the waiter, took up the poker and stirred it vigorously.

" Waiter," he said, " bring us two glasses of negus hot."

"Yes, sir," replied William, slowly revolving on one leg, but making no attempt to leave the room.

" And I think you had better put a fire in a bed room for my friend," pursued Billy. " He ought to go to bed until he can change. Our luggage will be here presently by—ahem !—special messenger."

"Yes, sir," said the dazed William. " You are going to stop the night ?"

" Siveral nights," replied Billy ; " until we have communicated with our friends. We have left the wretched old school up yonder, and are going to—ahem !—travel a bit. You remember me, when my fa—ahem !—uncle paid me a visit ?"

"Oh ! I remember him," replied William, brightening up. " Uncommon nice gentleman from the Injies, but got a wery bad memory—for bills !"

" Well, get this negus," said Billy ; " and mind it is hot, strong, and sweet—will you ? Jolly, come up to the fire. You seem to have got a cold."

" I've got a gold in my dose," replied Jolly, speaking through the most prominent feature of his face, " and I am shivering all over."

" You should have taken more care of yourself," returned Billy, " and got further under the umbrella. But you are young and thoughtless."

William, the waiter, who had been in search of negus, now returned with it, and with much deference handed it to Billy, who drank his own, and after a little pressing, induced Jolly to swallow his.

"It's bery dice," said Jolly, his eyes glistening a little. " I feel buch berrer dow."

" Of course you do, and until your clothes come take off your jacket, and let it be dried. Perhaps, waiter, you can lend him a coat ?"

" I've one here, sir," replied William ; " but it's a sparrer-tail."

" That will do," said Billy, cheerfully. " On with it !"

The coat was brought, and Jolly was put into it. The sleeves came quite over his hands, and the tails nearly touched the ground.

"It isn't very comferble," said Jolly.

"Roll up the sleeves, and turn the tails on one side when you sit down," said Billy, amiably, "and nothing could be better. That's it! Now that coat might have been made for you."

"Lovely!" murmured William.

"Your opinion," said Billy, with austerity, "wasn't axed. Keep your place, waiter."

William, considerably abashed, retired a few paces, and Billy, with his back to the fire, continued—

"Now, waiter, as to dinner. What have you got?"

"Ducks, sir, killed this arternoon."

"That will do. Any sparrow grass?"

"Out of season, sir—no sparo gross in the hautum."

Billy was not at all confounded by this revelation of his ignorance, but thrusting his thumbs into his waistcoat holes, coolly remarked—

"In town we has it all the year round."

"I am well aweer, sir," said William, the waiter, "that in the great metropolis anything can be had if you've only got the money; but here things is different."

"Just so," said Billy, then let's us say duck, and vegetables ginerally, and a pudding. You would like a pudding, Jolly?"

"I thing that I should like sube bore negus first."

"Waiter," said Billy, "repeat the negus."

Matters were getting a little too much for William, who could not be numbered among the strong-minded men of the world.

He knew Jolly was a boy and Billy was the size of one, but he could scarcely reconcile the great assurance of the latter with anything under middle age and considerable worldly experience.

But he fetched the negus, and Jolly drank the better part of his. Billy put his upon the mantelpiece, and drawing up a chair to the fire, stretched out his legs, and inquired—

"Waiter, can you recommend a cigar? I like a bit of a smoke before dinner."

"Them we 'as," answered William, "are considered by the gents around to be pretty good."

"Then bring me one," said Billy; "full flavour."

William prepared to execute this order, but he was in such a confused state of mind that he turned round three or four times like a slow teetotum before he got out of the room.

Eventually, however, he succeeded in executing this order, and Billy, with a lighted spill in his hand, and rolling his cigar scientifically round in his mouth, gave him a final command, which fairly settled him for the time.

"Hurry up the cook," he said. "We will have claret for dinner, and if you have got any good old tawny port we will have that with dessert."

Whether William hurried up the cook or not is uncertain, but he did not hurry up himself, for after ordering the dinner he spent a good half-hour behind his little screen in the corner of the coffee-room, reflecting upon the phenomenon then present in the inn.

Billy did not smoke his cigar, for after a whiff or two a conviction that it would be too much for him settled on his mind, but he blew a little of the smoke about the room to show he had been smoking, and thrust the weed into the fire.

When William at last came out from his meditative retirement, and began to lay the cloth, Billy made a remark, which would have induced a keener man than his listener to think he had manfully disposed of his tobacco.

"That was not a bad cigar, waiter," he said, "but wants hage."

"I suppose so, sir," said William, feebly, "but master has had 'em for some time."

"How long?" asked Billy.

"Nigh upon ten years."

"Ah!" said Billy, shaking his head sagely, "no cigar's worth much under eleven years; that's about the time I keeps mine."

"He must be a hold 'un," muttered William as he wildly scattered a lot of knives and forks all over the table. "But if so why is he at school?" Then a tremendous idea came unto William—"Maybe he's got into his second childhood."

It was a great thought to emanate from one who pursued such a humble calling, and William was quite pleased with it, and in the end accepted it as a solution of the mystery of Billy's wondrous ease.

The bar bell used to summon William now rang, and he hurried out, glad of something to relieve him of the overpowering greatness of his guest.

Jolly did not count for all this time. He had been sound asleep before the fire, worn out and exhausted by the troubles of the day.

In the bar he found Perkins, who had brought the luggage of the two boys in a barrow with him. William, the waiter, was supposed to be austere, but Perkins soon took that nonsense out of him.

"Don't stand staring there," he said, "but come and help me in with the luggage. I should think them portmanteaus are chock full of water by this time. Now, look alive!"

"My man, you be more civil," said William. "There aint no boys nowadays, they are all men."

Perkins regarded him with lofty disdain, and threatened to report him if he did not bear a hand with the luggage at once.

The boots being out he had no resource but to give the help required, and Perkins discreetly gave him the lion's share of the work to do.

The luggage was brought in, and was, indeed, in a condition to warrant the remark of Perkins, for it had been carelessly strapped together, and the soaking rain had free access to the contents within.

William, the waiter, was not the class of man to be put upon, if he could help it; but what is a man to do with a boy like Perkins? A verbal contest invariably gives such imps the victory, and as for a personal struggle with him, it could only end in a victory without honour, or possibly a defeat with utter ridicule and disgrace.

William was a man of mottoes, and he had one which was the guiding star of his existence—"If you can't get the upper hand, take the under;" and he took the under with Perkins.

When the luggage was all in William certainly thought Perkins would go; but nothing of the sort—he wanted the usual tip for his services, and asked to see Jolly Greene.

"He's engaged," said William.

"Oh! is he?" replied Perkins. "Then you just go and tell him I'm a-waiting. You public-house servants are getting too much cheek nowadays. One would think that you dewoted your lives to the service of a private gentleman."

"And aint our line of bis'ness as good as yours?" asked William, weakly entering into an argument.

"No!" said Perkins, emphatically. "One have a harystocratic flavour, and t'other's low and vulgar, if it aint mean. Now, are you going, or am I to run all over the house until I find 'em?"

"If you was a boy of mine——" began William.

"I a boy of yourn!" exclaimed the indignant Perkins. "Well, that beats all I ever heard. Have you gone mad? Have the wicissitudes of waiting on people in a low corfee-room turned your brain? Did you hever know a barn-door fowl the father of a helephant?"

William dared proceed no further, but hurriedly saying, "You will find the gents in that there room," retreated upstairs.

Perkins opened the door pointed out, and entered with his usual serenity.

Jolly was still asleep, but Billy was seated before the fire, reading a local paper. To him Perkins addressed himself.

"What cheer?" he said.

"Oh! it is you—is it, old chap?" replied Billy, thinking it best to be friendly. "What are you doing here?"

"Brought your luggage down," said Perkins.

"Much obliged, and now you are here will you stop to dinner?"

The words were out before he knew it, and ere he could recall them Perkins gave his reply. "Delighted, I'm shewure!" he said, with an aristocratic accent in his tone which he could either put on or cast off like a garment.

"Then," said Billy, "I think we had better have a private room," and rang the bell to give the order.

When William received the order he felt, as he afterwards said, "as if the top of his head was lifted up, and his tongue kind o' stuck to the roof of his mouth."

Reply to that boy he couldn't, and it was as much as he could do to get out of the room.

He spoke to the landlord, who said it was all right, and the private apartment was prepared. Thither Perkins, Billy, and Jolly presently repaired, to pass a pleasant evening.

CHAPTER XLVII.

MRS. COBBEM FOR ONCE IN A WAY MAKES A MISTAKE.

BEFORE giving an account of the dinner at the White Hart—a feast fraught with many little incidents—it is necessary to return to Warmington College and take a peep at the dinner there.

Mrs. Cobbem had prepared a feast, indeed—in mock turtle soup (from the tin—sold by Bross and Clackwell), veal cutlets, a curry, game, a joint, and sweets, with some really good wine, which the Reverend Copley inherited from his father.

"As there are only three of us," said Mrs. Cobbem to Jiggles, "you can wait without Perkins I hope. I have sent him out on an errand."

"Which I can, ma'am," replied Jiggles, "for to say that boy was of the least use to me would be for to tre pass on the trooth. I niver had a grey hair in my 'ed until I knowed him."

Mrs. Cobbem, ignoring the painful fact named, merely requested him to do his best, and retired to dress.

On the occasion of an entertainment of this sort Mrs. Cobbem was a sort of domestic whitened sepulchre. She was not a bad-looking woman, as I have said before, and when she was well dressed, and wore a sweet smile around her face, she was to the outer world a very pleasant woman.

No living being blessed with her casual acquaintance would have believed that she had ever clutched the Reverend Copley's whiskers, knocked the Reverend Copley's head against the wall, or shied dangerous missiles indiscriminately at the Reverend Copley's person; but, nevertheless, all these had she done from the day of her marriage up.

A bright fire, good light, and well laid-out table, are three things calculated to cheer the heart of man, and Uncle Ruddle, already warmed with the sherry, sat down in excellent humour. Mrs. Cobbem was amiable, the Reverend Copley more than cheerful, and all things promised a very pleasant evening.

Jiggles, too, was in a pleasant frame of mind. He could have his little perquisites out of the dishes and bottles in the hall without being harassed by Perkins, who, although a lover of black mail himself, saw fit to reprove the levying of it in others.

"Sherry, sir," said Jiggles, to Uncle Ruddle.

"Yes," he said, and raising his glass, held it up to the light. ' You drink good stuff here, Cobbem."

"Better drink none at all than bad wine," replied the Reverend Copley.

"True. By the way, do you give your boys wine?"

Jiggles, who was going round with the cruets, felt a rising sensation in his bosom which he found difficult to quell. He heard the question about the wine, and thought of the small beer which th Reverend Copley provided.

"We give them wine," replied the Reverend Copley, "when they require it medicinally."

"That's wrong," said Uncle Ruddle, emphatically. "Give them nothing of the sort. Bring children up on water. I wish I had never tasted a drop of this stuff in my life, but, having begun it, I suppose I must go on with it." Here he sighed, and emptied his glass. Jiggles, obeying a nod of his mistress, refilled it.

"I presume you are an advocate of temperance, Mr. Ruddle," said the Reverend Copley.

"Unswerving," replied Uncle Ruddle, as he went at his sherry again. "All stimulants are dangerous, if not absolutely poisonous."

"May I offer you a cutlet or curry?" asked Mrs. Cobbem.

"Curry," said Uncle Ruddle. "And here again you have the results of a pernicious early education. These hot dishes are the ruin of people; but once the system has become accustomed to them you must go on. By the way, we were talking of boys just now. Tell me the name of that young imp who went through the greenhouse."

"His name is Greene," said Mrs. Cobbem.

"Who is his father?"

"He has plenty of money," replied Mrs. Cobbem, hesitating a little. "But I fear he is hardly the sort of boy we ought to have taken."

"Why not?"

"Well, he is below our standard. At least, I think so."

She hardly knew what Uncle Ruddle was driving at, and for the present was extremely cautious. He was sipping his wine, and thinking.

"I knew a Greene once," he said, "a school chum of mine. His name was Greenly Greene."

"Why, that's the name of the father of this lad," said the Rev. Copley. "He was a drysalter or something of that sort, and made a heap of money."

"I'll warrant it's the same," said Uncle Ruddle. "Bring in that boy, and let me have a chat with him."

Mrs. Cobbem was aghast. Here was a most unexpected turn of events. The boy whom she had sent away as a relief to Uncle Ruddle, was the very boy that same uncle particularly wanted.

The Rev. Copley Cobbem, who knew nothing of the dismissal of his pupils, rose up to ring the bell for Perkins, but a look from his wife checked him. She, summoning Jiggles with a crooked finger to her side, asked him if Perkins had returned.

"Oh, no, mum," said Jiggles, "and it's raining 'eavens 'ard."

"Let me know the moment he comes in," she said. "I am afraid, uncle, that master Greene has retired. We always send the boys to bed early."

"Then let him get up again and come," said Uncle Ruddle.

"Champagne," asked Jiggles.

"Of course," said the old bachelor; "what brand is this, Cobbem?"

"Moet's best."

"I prefer Clicquot," said Uncle Ruddle. He was getting irritable again, and Mrs. Cobbem began to tremble.

"Jiggles," she whispered, "fill all the glasses, and go and look out for Perkins."

Jiggles went out, not once, but many times, and always returned with the same tale. Perkins was still away. As the dinner proceeded, Uncle Ruddle was continually inquiring after Jolly, and was each time assured he was getting up.

At last Mrs. Cobbem hit upon a desperate resource. The dinner was as good as over, and she determined upon sending Jiggles to the White Hart for the boys. The Rev. Copley was in an amazed state of mind; he could not understand it a bit, but he was a prudent man, and asked no questions.

Jiggles did not like the prospect of the expedition

The rain which he had been admiring, because he felt sure it was soaking Perkins, became suddenly distasteful to him, and he demurred.

"I haven't a dreadnought, nor nothing to keep the rain off," he said. "I should catch my death, mum."

"Get a coat of some sort," said Mrs. Cobbem, "and go."

He went when the wine and sweets were on the table, and being in a savagely reckless frame of mind, he put on a favourite coat belonging to Uncle Ruddle—a gorgeous fur thing, very popular with nobles in Russia, and men who are connected with a circus in our own country.

While he was gone Mrs. Cobbem had a trying time of it. It required all her tact to turn Uncle Ruddle's mind into channels apart from Jolly Greene. She gave him wine, she asked after his favourite ailments, got him to talk about foreign countries; but from each and all he always came back to young Greene.

"That boy must be a slow dresser," he said, at last.

"He is rather slow at most things," replied Mrs. Cobbem, "but he only requires time and the careful culture we give all here."

"I've no doubt you do wonders with the boys," growled Uncle Ruddle, "but you can't turn out the men they did in my time."

Jiggles came back in an evident hurry, entering the room with some explosive message in his mouth. Mrs. Cobbem rose, and promptly checked its utterance.

"I will go and see after that boy myself," she said. "Jiggles, get me a small lamp."

"Yes, ma-am. I've been to the——"

She got him out of the room into the hall, and then unable longer to hold himself, he told his sad tale.

"I've been to the White Hart, mum," he said, "and I've seen Perkins and t'other two, and a nice way they are going on, mum. That young Sharp said he shouldn't come back to-night, and young Greene said so too. As for that Perkins, he ordered me out of the house, and when I told him to come or take the consequence, he chucked a whole sauce-boat of parsley and butter over me."

He ought to have said the parsley and butter went over Uncle Ruddle's coat, but prudence forbade. Mrs. Cobbem wrung her hands in agony.

"What shall I do?" she said. "Oh! what shall I do? Go again, Jiggles."

"It's no use, mum, as they would only come it stronger. Now, if Mr. Cobbem——"

"He shall go," said Mrs. Cobbem. "Jiggles, go in and tell him he is wanted on urgent business."

The Rev. Copley, looking considerably flurried, came out, wondering who could want him at that hour. When he saw nobody but his spouse, his stout manly heart quailed.

"My love," he exclaimed, "what is it?"

"Uncle Ruddle! What is he doing?" asked Mrs. Cobbem.

"Snoring," replied her husband.

"Asleep!—that's good. Now put on your coat and go to the White Hart."

"Eh, my love, the White Hart?"

"Yes, the boys we want and Perkins are there, bring them all back."

"But how came they there? Boys of mine at a public-house! What monstrous breach of discipline is this?"

"Don't talk twaddle, but go," said Mrs. Cobbem. "You shall hear all when you return. Hasten, and you will be back with them before Uncle Ruddle awakens."

"But where is my coat?"

"Take any coat."

"Here's one, sir," said Jiggles, taking that down of Uncle Ruddle.

He helped him on with it, keeping the part with the parsley and butter upon it well out of sight, and with great dexterity put a pair of goloshe over his master's pumps, thrust an umbrella into his hand, and shot him out into the darkness of the night.

CHAPTER XLVIII.

THE WHITE HART DINNER PARTY ENDS IN SMOKE.

IT was wet indeed when the Reverend Copley Cobbem found himself outside his house. All the day the rain had fallen pretty smartly, but now the fury of the clouds appeared greater than ever. In every hollow there was a little pool, and the road was like a shallow stream.

As soon as he got fairly clear of his residence the reverend gentleman had a short but serious struggle with his umbrella. First it turned inside out, and he swung round to allow the wind to blow it back again.

This the wind did, but so roughly that it came off the top, and slid down the handle. He turned again to remedy this, and a violent gust took away the silk and bones altogether.

The Reverend Copley said something that was not a blessing, and in a fury strode on. Ere he was half over the playground he entered upon another battle with his hat.

There was a rush of air, and he, feeling it going, brought his hand violently down upon the crown, and wedged it over his ears. Unable to bear the pressure he raised it a little, and not holding with sufficient firmness away it went into the gloom before him.

His first impression was that it was gone for ever, but in a second or two he heard it bang against the schoolground wall, with such a noise as a muffled tin-kettle would have made, and, calculating the spot with admirable nicety, he bore down upon it.

He was right as to position, but not as to distance, and coming upon the hat all too soon, put his foot upon it, and barked his nose and knees against the wall. Again he said something that was not a blessing, and having secured his battered hat, put it on his head, and staggered forward at the mercy of the storm.

But he was full of good wine, and did not care. The rain beat upon him, but for the time he was as hard as a rock and hot as an oven, and he even sang fragments of songs quite cheerfully, as he opened the gate and went down the road.

He wilfully and deliberately chose the most soppy side of the road, and went on his way quite gaily, until he fell over the milestone. While lying for awhile on his back he saw luminous bubbles in the air, and made violent comments upon the parish authorities, who always will place milestones just where people are sure to fall over them.

But although harassed by these casualties there was life in him yet, and he got upon his feet again, and proceeding with more caution got to the four cross roads without any further accident. Then he ran against a human being, who went staggering back a dozen yards or so with an oath for every yard he travelled.

"I really beg your pardon," said the Reverend Copley, "but it is so very dark."

"Begging pardon aint much," replied the voice that had duly sworn. "Come and stand a drink. Who be you?"

"I am the Reverend Copley Cobbem."

"Then I'm jiggered if I don't have the life of you. I've sworn to have that of you and your missus too. I'm paid for it."

It was Goggles, returning from his favourite tap-room thoroughly soaked. He was on his way home, and was in a day-dream of what he would do to Mrs. Goggles if she talked to him about "wittles for the kids," when he ran up against the Reveren' Copley. On hearing who it was all his animosity turned upon that gentleman, and he included him in the awful promise he had made to Jolly Greene.

"Come here," he said, ferociously, "and let me git at your witalities. I'm ready for you. It's no use, you can't get away."

"My friend," said the Reverend Copley, cold with fear, "why this unseemly violence? How have I ever wronged you?"

"You've wronged them as loves me and pays me," replied Goggles, "and I'm bound for to have at your witalities."

"I have a knowledge of your voice," said the Reverend Cobbem, soothingly; "and, judging by the sound of it, I fear some friend has deluded you into imbibing horrible drinks.'

"I don't want no derluding," replied Goggles. "You come and see how I'll take it if you pays for it."

"If a shilling, now," said the Reverend Copley—"if a shilling would be of any use to you I think I have one about me, just one, and no more."

"I'm paid five times as much to have your witalities, and I must have 'em."

"What dreadful person is this?" thought the Reverend Copley, "and whose animosity can I have so raised? But I will flee from him."

And he ran.

Goggles heard him go, and, making a dashing but fruitless attempt to stop him, precipitated himself into a ditch, where the cold water, about a foot deep, gave his face what it needed—a washing—and sobered him.

Some guiding spirit hovered around the Reverend Copley as he fled, and bore him safely to the White Hart.

Pausing a moment to recover his breath, and to put his hat into a little shape, he entered.

William, the waiter, was in the passage, with four pewter pots in his hand, which he was regarding with an excited eye. He did not heed the new arrival, but, putting them down on a little ledge close to the bar, ruminated thus—

"That's Mr. Harris's pot—he wanted a pint of six ale. No, it's Mr. Jones, and he wants cooper. But didn't he say he'd have stout for a change? I fancy he did, and—no, it was Mr. Tomkins who said he wanted stout, and yet it wasn't, for he said he thought the beer was a little muddy, and would go on to cold gin. And yet, wasn't it Mr. Waddem who wanted cold gin? I'm bothered if I know what they want! Them boys have put me right off my 'ed."

"You have some of my pupils here, I believe," said the Reverend Copley.

William looked up with a vacant stare, but made no reply.

The reverend gentleman put the question again.

"Oh, yes," said William, waking up a little, and speaking in a sepulchral tone, "we has."

"Where are they?"

"Upstairs, a going of it," replied William, "fust floor, door right opposite. Mind how you go, sir, as the lamp's blowed out, and there's a hole in the mat, also holler out who you are afore you go in, as every time I've showed myself either that boy of yourn, or the haged boy, have throwed something at me."

The Rev. Copley took off his rough coat, and leaving it with William, went upstairs. He felt there might be a struggle before him, and it was not desirable for him to be hampered with more clothing than was necessary.

The caution given by William about the mat was very necessary, for even with it the Rev. Copley and that mat collided. He got his foot through it, and had a narrow escape of precipitating his head into a trayful of empty dishes, which William had considerately left upon the floor near he door. He got amongst them with his hands, nd made a terrible clatter, but fortunately broke othing.

"What a day, and what a night!" he exclaimed, as he got upon his feet. "Another such, and my earthly career must end. Now, which is the door?"

Doubt on this point was set at rest by the voice of Perkins, which came floating from a room close to him. Perkins was singing "Sally in our Alley," to a tune of his own with variations. He had also an imperfect knowledge of the words, and was filling up the gaps in his memory with little bits of his own.

"Of all the gals that are so smart,
There aint one up to the mark of our Sally;
She's werry nigh broke my young beating 'art,
And lives up our halley."

"Now, then, chorus—Ri tooral—tooral—tooral rum tum ti iddidy day!"

"I say," he said, "you chaps don't sing. Surely you aint done up with a bit of smoke. I've smoked scores of old Cobbem's cigars, and he never knowed it."

"Oh! that's where my cigars went to—is it?" muttered the rev. listener, "and I, in my heart, have suspected the simple, honest, truthful Jiggles. You little villain, I'll make you smoke and sing presently—I will. But for the present I must dissemble. I will listen, and hear more."

"The last box old Cobbem got wasn't so good," pursued Perkins. "They was rather green I fancy, wanted keeping, or else he's given a lower price, which is just like him. He grows meaner every day, and if he don't mind what he's up to I shall have to leave him, and then I wonder where that blesssed school will go to?"

"I see him now in his true light," muttered the Rev. Copley. "Oh! what a serpent I have taken and warmed at my hearth!"

"I don't think I could stand the place at all." Perkins went on, addressing somebody who, for some reason, offered him no reply, "if it wasn't for the fun I gets out of Cobbem. The way he gets warmed up by Mrs. Cobbem is the most amusing thing I know of."

"If Agatha could only hear this, surely she would repent," thought the Rev. Copley. "But I can bear no more. I must go in and check this infamous boy."

He pushed the door open a little, and peeped in. What a scene met his eyes! Never had he looked upon the like before.

Around a table, on which stood a decanter or two and a box of cigars, sat Perkins, Billy Sharp, and Jolly Greene. Perkins was in the full enjoyment of a blissful smoke, but both Billy and Jolly had had enough of it. Billy was asleep, and Jolly was in the throes of the sickness which often follows a first consumption of tobacco.

"Perkins," cried the Reverend Copley, in the usual voice of thunder, "what are you doing here?"

Perkins did not start, but turning in his chair he waved his hand and said "How de do?" and sent forth a creamy cloud from his cigar. Without the half-emptied glass of sherry by his side it would have been easy to see that Perkins had been stimulating himself.

Mr. Cobbem was staggered, as well he might be; but although a weak and yielding man in many things, he drew a line occasionally. He drew one now.

Springing forward like a tiger on his prey, he took Perkins by the collar and shook him until his teeth chattered like well played negro bones, and his eyes stood out like crocus bulbs. Then he boxed his ears half-a-dozen times, and sent him staggering over a footstool on his back upon the floor.

"Now you little villain," said the Reverend Copley, shaking his fist at him, "tell me what you mean by it."

"I didn't come here for to do it," pleaded Perkins. "Mrs. Cobbem sent me with the luggage, and they axed me up, sir, and that ain't no reason why you should knock me down."

GREEN AS GRASS.

A JOLLY SCHOOL STORY.

THE MOMENT IT WAS SEEN WHO WERE IN THE CAGE THE "WARMINTERS" SENT UP A GREAT SHOUT OF JOY.

"Don't talk to me," said his master, "for I won't have it. Popper! Popper!"

Billy opened his eyes and stared sleepily around him. At first he did not recognise the Reverend Copley, but when he did so he got upon his feet and did his best to make a bow.

"Popper, this is disgraceful."

"Mrs. Cobbem sent us here, sir," replied Billy, "and we've had some dinner"—(hic).

"Oh! no doubt you have. Greene, what has made you so ill?"

"Shmoke," replied Greene, feebly. "Ugh! I am so cold."

"This dreadful scene," said the Reverend Copley, "almost breaks my heart; but you must return at once. Perkins, ring the bell."

CHAPTER XLIX.

A NIGHT OF NIGHTS.

PERKINS slowly got up and obeyed the reverend gentleman's order. The rebellious spirit within him was in a measure subdued, but not utterly quelled. William, the waiter, answered with a promptness which left no doubt about his being outside listening.

"Can we have a conveyance?" asked Mr. Cobbem.

"It's a werry wet night, sir, and the ostler's ill in bed with a cold, replied William.

"But is there nobody who can drive us?"

"There's only old John in the tap-room, and if the landlord don't object he might drive you home in the shay."

"But is he used to driving? He is a very old man."

"He used to drive a team, sir."

"Well, let me see him, and ask if we can have the chaise."

William went out, and in a few minutes the oldest inhabitant came up. He had "had his whack" without a doubt, but he was able to keep upright.

"Well, John," said Mr. Cobbem, cheerfully, "do you think you could drive us home?"

"You gi' I the ribbons," said John, "and see what I'll do wi' um."

William, the waiter, came up with the information that they might have the old chaise and the grey mare, but it must be taken on the responsibility of Mr. Cobbem.

"I am agreeable," said that gentleman, "if you will assure me that John can drive."

"He used to drive," replied William.

"My grandfeyther druv a coach and four," said the oldest inhabitant; "it's in the blood of the family But it's a cold night, master, and a drop of that stuff won't be amiss."

He had some sherry, and went out to prepare himself for the drive.

The Reverend Copley took advantage of the waiting time to administer a lecture to all three culprits, and was especially down upon Perkins.

"I am not sure I shall not dismiss you when we return," he said, "but I must consult Mrs. Cobbem. Your conduct is almost past forgiveness. It was an evil day when I took you from the work—ahem! from your home."

Perkins had no desire to return thither, and wisely drew in his horns.

He was really brought down. The reaction of the evening's amusement was upon him.

The chaise was soon ready, and William came up to announce the welcome fact. He also brought Uncle Ruddle's coat, but it being very wet the Reverend Copley decided not to put it on.

The night, if possible, had grown darker, and the rain was as heavy as ever, but there were lamps to the chaise, and old John sat huddled up on the box wrapped in sacks and rugs, so that he looked more like a bale of linen goods than anything else.

"Get us home, John, as quickly as you can with safety."

This was the last warning the Reverend Copley gave, and in reply the oldest inhabitant assured him "he'd get he home, or know the reason why."

Then they started.

Old John cracked the whip, and with a very loose rein started the horse.

He also shut his eyes to keep out the rain—in short he left all to fate.

When people go trusting to chance fate generally proves unkind. On this occasion there was no exception made to the rule.

The horse went all right until he reached the four cross-roads, and being then divided in opinion as to which way to go, he ran into the guide-post, and took the off-side front wheel off and extinguished both the lamps.

The oldest inhabitant was shot off somewhere into the darkness, and roused from a sound sleep by coming down on his back, and the Reverend Copley, who was also dozing, was precipitated against the front window of the chaise with considerable violence.

"That wretched man," he exclaimed, "has he lost control of the horse?"

The old grey was skipping about like a mountain ram, and as the four occupants of the carriage bundled out, it shook the vehicle free of the post, and tried to make a run of it with three wheels.

This was a bit of a failure, and he gave it up at the end of fifty yards, where he and the chaise rolled over together, and lay perfectly still.

"A night of nights!" exclaimed the Reverend Copley. "What has become of the driver?"

"Where be ye all," cried the voice of the person alluded to, "and where be the horse? Stop he, and let me gi' he a taste o' the whip. Dang un, he ought to ha' seen the post."

"The driver has a duty also," said the Reverend Copley, "and but for your poverty I would hold you responsible for the mishap. Look after that horse and vehicle, and take it back to the White Hart. Now, boys, we must trudge home. Let me see, which is the way?"

The collision had confounded them all alike, and it was too dark to see any object upon the road. It was a very open question which was the way to the college.

"Can you tell us the way, John?" asked the Reverend Copley.

"I don't know and I don't care," muttered the oldest inhabitant, sulkily. "All I know is that where you go I go, and dang that horse and shay, I beant going to look arter they."

"This," said the Reverend Copley, "is gross impertinence."

"Be it what it may," said the old un, "I'm going to keep my word."

"The expense of this night," murmured the Reverend Copley "will be ruinous, and all because Agatha is rash enough to unwarrantably dismiss two of my best-paying pupils."

As there was no getting rid of the oldest inhabitant the Reverend Copley made him one of the party, and after a little deliberation selected a road he felt sure led to Warmington College.

"I think," he said, "we had better go hand-in-hand, and I will lead the way."

They went hand-in-hand, and old John brought up the rear. As he was constantly falling down, from old age, drink, and exhaustion, he not only retarded their progress, but often brought somebody down with him.

On each occasion he had to be helped up and allowed a minute's grace to rub his meagre legs, which he said had got the "rheumatiz."

"Judging by the distance we have travelled," said the Reverend Copley, after they had been feeling their way for an hour or so, "we ought to be near the college. But I see no lights."

"Is it the college ye be going to?" asked the old un.

"Yes, my friend."

"Then you would find it this way. This I reckon to be the Wittleton-road by the ruts in it."

"But Wittleton is just the opposite way."

"That's right, sir—so it be."

The oldest inhabitant was not much disturbed, but the Reverend Copley was very much so. Here was a nice predicament indeed — the rain each moment falling faster and the darkness becoming more appalling!

"Are you sure it is the Wittleton-road?" he asked.

"I'd take my hoath on it, sir," replied the oldest inhabitant.

"Then we must retrace our steps. Oh! what a night of nights! It is truly terrible."

The boys did not say anything, for they were too wretched to speak. All were wet through, and Jolly Greene's cold was worse than ever. Back they trudged, the oldest inhabitant leading until he announced they had reached the cross-roads again.

The Reverend Copley took his word for it, for he could not see, and they, under the able guidance of old John, bore away a little to the right, until a gate checked them.

"Stop a minute," said the old un, reflectively, "where have we got to? I think the t'other road must have been right arter all."

"How exasperating!" exclaimed the Reverend Copley. "Then let us go back."

"Don't be in a hurry, sir—don't be in a hurry; let us take the bearings."

"The bearings be ——!" the Reverend Copley paused, and got up a sneeze. "Now my good man, if you don't know the way, say so, and we will find it ourselves."

"If I don't know the way, you don't," said the old un. "But since you are so independent I'm off."

"Stay, my good friend, stay," exclaimed the reverend gentleman. "I did not mean to offend you." But the oldest inhabitant *was* offended, and when that was the case you could not expect to pacify him in a moment.

"Shall we follow him?" exclaimed the Reverend Copley.

"But he isn't going to Warmington College, sir," suggested Billy.

"Indeed, no. This is a sad fix. Oh! what a night of nights! But come, boys, we must go on until we find a house, and then, perhaps, we shall be favoured with a better guide."

Slowly and cautiously they crept along for awhile, dejected beyond measure by the weight of affliction upon them. It seemed as if they were like the old woman with the pig, not at all likely to get home that night, and all reflected upon the agreeable prospect of being out in the rain until the morning.

So, sadly and silently they wended their way, tripping over heaps of stones, stumbling against the grass growing at the road-side, and cannoning against each other. At last they were all startled by Perkins shouting out—

"A light, sir."

"Where?" asked the Reverend Copley.

"Over there—look, sir."

A dull red light it was, such as one sees through the red curtain of an inn, but broader.

"Right at last," exclaimed the Reverend Copley; "the end of the night of night's is at hand."

The next question was, how to get at that light. They went up the road until it was behind them, then they came back again until it was before them, and found no lane or opening leading to it.

"It must be some house in the fields, sir," suggested Perkins.

"Then let us cross the fields," returned his master, "we must get at it."

After a little blundering search they found a gate. It was locked, and garnished with thorns, but they pulled the latter away and climbed over.

"To the house," exclaimed the Reverend Copley, dramatically, and they all stepped out upon a miry newly-ploughed field.

CHAPTER L.

MRS. COBBEM IS ABSENT AND HER HUSBAND IS MISSING.

THERE is nothing like a good dinner for making a sound sleeper. Doctors will tell you that the repose following a very hearty meal is not one of real value, but positively injurious. Nevertheless, the hard and fast naps we sometimes get after food are very enjoyable.

Uncle Ruddle slept well, and enjoyed his little sleep; at all events he was in a very good humour until it suddenly occurred to him that he was alone.

There was coffee upon the table, but it was almost cold. He poured out some and tasted it, and pushed it aside with an angry exclamation. Next he rang the bell.

Mrs. Cobbem herself answered it, and came in with a flurried look, which she vainly endeavoured to conceal.

Uncle Ruddle perceived it, and charged it to her anxiety for his comfort.

"My dear uncle," she said, "we thought it best to leave you quietly by yourself. The day has been very fatiguing to you; let me ring for some hot coffee."

"Not at all," he said. "Where is Cobbem?"

"He will be here directly," replied Mrs. Cobbem, with the look upon her face of one who is listening to some sound outside.

"I thought he was too much of a gentleman to leave his guest."

"He was called away on important business," replied Mrs. Cobbem, "on what is business to him— the pupil you wish to see, young Greene, is rather unwell."

"Ah! yes, I had forgotten him, and was just going to bed."

"How stupid of me!" thought Mrs. Cobbem, and bit her lips with vexation.

But the thing was done, and could not be helped. In vain she threw out hints about retiring.

Uncle Ruddle, growing each moment more lively after his sleep, was bent upon seeing young Greene, and altering his mind, thought he would have some coffee and a cigar.

The hands of the ormolu clock upon the mantel-piece pointed to half-past eleven, and the fact was noted by the old gentleman, who compared it with his watch and found it was only a minute fast.

"Cobbem has been a long time fetching that boy, but if he is too ill to come, send for Cobbem, to have a cigar with me."

"Yes, yes," answered Mrs. Cobbem, and again there was that curious absent look upon her face, as if her mind was rather outside the house than in it.

She was listening for the sound of footsteps, but heard nothing but the pattering of the still falling rain, and the noise of the wind as it rushed by. What would she have given if she could have confessed the truth, and how thankful she would have been if she had that power no living creature possesses, of going back a few hours, so that she might have told another tale!

"What can have become of Cobbem?" she asked herself a score times; "can he have been mad enough to stop at the White Hart, drinking, or—" here she paused and put a hand upon her heart to still its palpitation, "can he have strolled into the bourn and drowned himself? It is sure to be high to-night."

Uncle Ruddle, keeping up his spirits somehow, told a tale of some of his adventures abroad. Mrs. Cobbem was more absent than ever, and put in all sorts of exclamations when a dim idea came upon her that they were needed. At last she put a "no" in the wrong place.

"You are not listening, Agatha," said Uncle Ruddle.

"I was—in a way—uncle dear, but I have a headache," she replied.

"You are rude, Agatha," said the old man, rising with a wrathful countenance, "and Cobbem is rude; in fact he is an ass. Can I have a chamber candle?"

"Of course you can, my dear uncle, but I beg of you to wait a few moments."

"Not another instant," he answered, savagely; "may I ring for the candle?"

He did not wait for permission, but jerked the rope with some violence, and Jiggles, who had been having a nap in the hall, came in with a frightened look.

"Candle," said Uncle Ruddle, glaring at him.

"Yes, sir—here, sir—in a moment, sir," answered Jiggles.

Uncle Ruddle got his candle, and with a short and sharp "good-night," bounced out of the room. Mrs. Cobbem sank upon the couch in tears, and Jiggles stood regarding her with well-timed commiseration.

"Jiggles," said Mrs. Cobbem, "do you think you could run over to the White Hart for your master?"

"The White Hart closes at eleven, and they don't keep open for nobody," replied Jiggles.

"But your master went there."

"And he must have left an hour ago, mum," returned Jiggles.

"What shall I do?" exclaimed Mrs. Cobbem, and again tears burst forth."

"It's my opinion, mum," said Jiggles, after a respectful pause, "that them boys are giving master a run over the country. Perkins is sure to indooce 'em to do wrong. And a nice thing it would be for master, seeing that the night is black as hink."

"I cannot bear this suspense," said Mrs. Cobbem, pacing up and down. "You must go at once. Take the odd man with you."

"He's gone home, mum."

"Then take a lantern and go alone."

Jiggles had the average pluck of his race, but he did not care to face the night alone, and said so. Mrs. Cobbem, too much distressed to be peremptory, offered him five shillings to go.

"I'll wenture, mum," said Jiggles, and went into the kitchen to see if he could induce the cook to go with him."

"We should never get there such a night as this," said the cook.

"Just my opinion," replied Jiggles, "and I shan't go."

So he made himself comfortable in the kitchen for an hour, and then went up and reported the White Hart closed, and all in bed.

"But what did they say?" asked Mrs. Cobbem.

"Nuffin," said Jiggles, staring at the fireplace. "I couldn't make them hear."

It was one o'clock, and no signs of abatement in the storm. Mrs. Cobbem made the fire up, and sat before it, hoping against hope that each moment would see her husband return.

A score of conjectures forced themselves upon her, and she weighed them one by one. He had remained at the White Hart on account of the storm—had never got there—had got there and left in the pursuit of the boys, who had fled before him—and then the terrible thought—"Perhaps he was dead."

She knew the bourn well. In dry weather it was a little rippling brook which a child could walk over, but in the winter, and after a heavy storm, it was very rapid, and deep enough to drown a man. She did not know whether her husband could swim or not—he had never exhibited the art before her, and to her knowledge had never heard him speak of his being acquainted with it, and if he could not and had got into the bourn, why, then—she was a widow!

From the time they were married she had never been particularly kind to him. A shrewish temper,

kept very lightly under control, had grown more imperious year by year, until it would have been unbearable to a man of strong temper; but the Rev. Copley was kind and generous—a very good sort of fellow, take him all round.

She could think of his good qualities as she sat by the fire that long autumn night, and she could think of them at their best. She also dwelt upon her own shortcomings and her violent temper, and was sorry she had not been a better wife to him.

If he had returned then, she would have caressed him and wept upon his shoulder, but the moments flew by without bringing him. When he did return she neither wept over him nor caressed him.

What a pity it was that some good spirit did not waft him home à la Mrs. Guppy! The Rev. Copley Cobbem being lowered through the ceiling to a sitting position on the table, and his wife with joy beholding the phenomenon, would have made a thrilling scene.

But it did not come off. A long long night passed, and Mrs. Cobbem was still alone.

Towards morning she fell into a fitful sleep, but after about forty false starts she at length fairly got away to the land of dreams. There she had a pleasant time of it with the corpse of her husband, who was drowned, shot, stabbed, crushed to death, and all sorts of other things in turn, and once he appeared with a placard on his breast, bearing the inscription, "Bullied out of my life!" She then recognised herself as a murderess, and wept in her sleep.

From this agreeable scene she was aroused by the opening of the door by Jiggles, who came in, breathlessly exclaiming—

"Oh! mum, they've come."

She started up and shivered as she looked about the room. The fire was out, and there was a cold grey light behind the window blinds. On the table was the skeleton of the last night's feast, which is never a very agreeable sight in the morning.

"Oh! mum, they've all come home in such a state!"

As the announcement fell from his lips the second time there entered four figures that would have served for ghosts by night, and millers by day. She thought she was still dreaming, until the Reverend Copley's voice came out of one of the white figures.

"Oh, my love," he said, "we have had a night of nights! We have passed the last six hours with the man who lives in the hut by the limekiln."

And what did she do? Fall upon his neck and weep? Oh, no! but went at him like a tigress.

"And how dare you," she said, "bring the boys into this room in that state? Send them into the stable to be brushed."

"My love," he said, "the boys are almost dead, and I have suffered——"

"Bother!" she replied. "A pretty thing to keep me out of bed all night. I shall be ill for a month. Send those boys away to change their clothes. Their appearance is disgraceful."

And sweeping proudly by she went upstairs. The Reverend Copley Cobbem, who with the boys was in a very exhausted condition, mournfully bade the boys go to bed and make up for lost time, then went aloft himself, and was talked into a dead sleep by his gentle Agatha.

CHAPTER LI.

UNCLE RUDDLE GOES FOR A WALK AND HAS TO RUN FOR IT.

THE Reverend Copley slept until ten o'clock, then awoke, and having heard of the furious state Uncle Ruddle had retired in, made up his mind to act for once alone and tell him the whole story.

Without consulting his wife he went to the old gentleman's room, and found him in bed, with a glass of brandy and soda by his side as an antidote to the performance of the previous evening.

He heard what the Reverend Copley had to say, and was immensely tickled with some parts of the narrative, especially where it related to falling into ditches, and running up against posts, trees, or gates. In the end it restored him to good humour, and he got up and went down to a late breakfast—smiling.

Mrs. Cobbem was overjoyed, although at first she knew nothing of the cause. But she soon heard all about it, as Uncle Ruddle told it in bits, and had little fits of laughter after each relation. He choked himself once with tea and twice with toast, and came out generally in the most agreeable manner.

It was Sunday, but those who had suffered the previous night did not go out in the morning. Mr. Cobbem was indulged with a lounge on the sofa, Perkins was taken off duty, and Jolly and Billy were entertained by Uncle Ruddle, who was entertained by them in return, as he asked over and over again all about their adventures, and laughed until his old face was as black as a nigger's. Surely there never was a more facetious old gentleman under the sun.

He took to Jolly, principally because he was always in a mess of some sort, and Uncle Ruddle spent a most delightful Sunday in listening to Jolly's piteous story of his own sufferings. He did not care much for Billy, and told him so.

"You are a cute un," he said, "and I fancy you make a good thing out of this young fool" (that was Jolly), "but that's no business of mine. Who was your father?"

"Professor Popper," replied Billy, compelled to fall back on the old lie.

"And who was Professor Popper?"

"Which I've told Mrs. Cobbem all about him," murmured Billy, who had forgotten what he had said, and was afraid to venture upon another tale.

As he had such a first-rate day's entertainment it was only fair that Uncle Ruddle should pay for it. He gave Jolly half a sovereign when he bade him "Good night!" and went into a fit of laughter as he left the room.

"I do like a downright born fool," he said to the Reverend Copley; "it is about the best fun out to talk to 'em. I'm rather fond of talking to you. Not that I think you a born fool, but you seem to have gone a little wrong, or how could you have passed a night in a limekiln? Ha—ha! it is very funny, but I would rather you had not married a niece of mine."

On retiring that night the Reverend Copley made a remark to his wife.

"Agatha," he said, "your uncle may be a very agreeable person, but I shall not be sorry when he is gone—ahem!"

"Whenever an opportunity to insult my relations offers itself you are ever ready to take it," replied his wife.

"I have not insulted your relation; he has insulted me."

And so they went on for an hour, and Mrs. Cobbem bedewed her pillow with tears.

Four or five days passed without Uncle Ruddle finding his new life pall upon them. He mixed with the boys, and made especial chums of those who were dull at learning or unfortunate generally, and a vast amount of amusement they afforded him.

"So you were licked this morning?" he said to Christopher Cobble.

"Yes, that I was; got it hot," replied Christopher.

"Why?"

"Didn't know my lessons."

"Why not?"

"Because I did not learn them last night. I was making a kite."

"Good fun," said Uncle Ruddle. "If I were you I would make a kite every night. Never mind the lickings."

"I don't," said Christopher.

"Boys ought not," replied Uncle Ruddle. "I

used to laugh at 'em, and I should now, only I don't know who would venture to thrash me."

These words were overheard by Dick Stager, and they set him thinking.

He had never cared over much for Uncle Ruddle, who was in his eyes, as I dare say he is in those of my readers, a spiteful old man, who could get more fun out of the pain than the pleasure of others. Dick thought he would very much like to give him something in return for his facetiousness.

That very day an opportunity presented itself.

Uncle Ruddle came into the playground towards evening, and after watching the boys at play some time, asked Dick Stager to point out a nice walk. Of all things this was what Dick would most have desired, and pointed out a road at once.

"I don't know much about this place myself," he said, "as we only occasionally go out, and I have not been long here, but if you go down the road, get over the first stile to the left, and go straight on, you will get a stroll through some very pretty fields."

"But are the grounds public?" asked Uncle Ruddle; "some people are very nasty about trespassers."

"All you have to say is," said Dick, "that you come from Warmington College, and that will put all right. It will settle everything."

This was very cruel of Dick, for Job Grumper was not at all likely to be found in an amiable temper. Matters between him and the Warminters had grown worse. In the early part of that very week the boys had encountered him unarmed, and fallen upon him in a body with tufts of grass and other comparatively harmless but very trying missile.

He fled, wisely, but chose, not too well, a path that led to the brook. In his haste he got into it, and tried to swing himself across with the aid of a branch of a tree. The branch miserably failed him, and he got a ducking.

The water was not deep, and, having satisfied themselves he would not drown, they chaffed him, and some of them indulged in a little bathing to give him an idea of the art of swimming. Beyond the wetting he did not suffer, but such things are not calculated to add to friendship or to heal old sores.

Uncle Ruddle was not exactly a dandy, but he was a bit of a buck in his way, and on this day he wore a bright blue coat and neat pepper-and-salt waistcoat and trousers. He also mounted a white hat, and carried a new silk umbrella under his arm.

On leaving he walked with jaunty step, and was evidently quite prepared to ogle any girls who might be thrown in his way. Uncle Ruddle had been almost fast once upon a time, and often made casual reference to a girl who was found in the Thames three weeks after he sailed for India. But that was many years ago, and the grief he felt had died away into a feeling of pride that any girl could break her heart for him.

Two hours afterwards he was seen from the schoolroom window by the boys, returning in hot haste without his hat, and his neat clothing covered with mire. He dashed into the playground, closed the gate and locked it in frantic haste. The next moment Job Grumper rushed up, and raged at the gate like a wild bull at the bars of a cage.

Uncle Ruddle only stayed to shake his fist once at his foe before rushing into the house. Dick, who had witnessed the scene with a score others, sprang down from the window, and opened the schoolroom door.

The voice of Uncle Ruddle was wafted up the stairs.

"Cobbem!—Cobbem!" he cried, "where are you?"

"Here I am, my dear sir," replied the Reverend Copley, emerging from some room in the hall, most probably the breakfast-room.

"And a pretty fellow you are when you are here. Why don't you put down the infamous outlaws who infest this place?"

"Outlaws, my dear sir?"

"Outlaws, yes, outlaws! Come, I speak plain enough, I hope. Outlaws—madmen—lunatics—highwaymen—and footpads!"

"All this," exclaimed the Reverend Copley, "is Greek to me!"

"All is not Greek to me!" roared Uncle Ruddle. "I have been grievously and atrociously assaulted. I have been bruised and beaten. My hat, which I have only worn twice, was knocked off my head and trodden upon by a beef-headed, red-faced fellow, in top-boots and cord breeches. You call yourself a gentleman, and permit this within a four-mile radius of your house!"

"My dear sir, I beseech you to be calm," said the Reverend Copley. "I am not the lord of the manor. I cannot control everybody around me. If you have been assaulted, as your appearance warrants me to——"

"My appearance!" cried Uncle Ruddle. "Yes, look at it! Here's an appearance for a gentleman of my position."

"The author of this outrage," said the Reverend Copley, "shall be punished by the law."

"Don't talk to me about the law!" cried Uncle Ruddle, "but go out and fight him. He is at the gate, braying with triumph like a jackass."

"I will see who the offender is. Jiggles, my hat."

The Reverend Copley departed, and Uncle Ruddle remained raving in the hall.

From what he said the boys gathered that he had been upon the farm leased by Job Grumper, and had met that individual, who, at first, had only asked him what he meant by walking over his land. Uncle Ruddle promptly answered that he came from Warmington College, and Job Grumper responded with equal promptitude with a blow between the eyes. Uncle Ruddle went down, and Job Grumper threw himself upon him, and tore him to bits.

This, as far as his clothing went, was literally true. Uncle Ruddle had as many rags fluttering about him as a ship has flags upon a gala day.

"It's a serious thing," he kept saying to Jiggles, into whose sympathetic soul he poured his woes during the absence of the Reverend Copley. Strange that he should find his own woes so serious when the sufferings of others were to him so intensely comical.

The Reverend Copley came back with the intelligence that he could find nobody, and on hearing this Uncle Ruddle went off again.

"You are in league with him, sir!" he cried. "You conspire with all the ruffians in the neighbourhood to annoy and insult me, but I'll have the law on them and you!"

In vain the Reverend Copley tried to pacify him; he raved on, and even roared at the unoffending Jiggles.

Mrs. Cobbem came, and went so far as to throw herself upon the bosom of her uncle, but he cast her off, and insisted upon his things being packed immediately.

The time for his departure had, however, not yet come.

The excitement proved a little too much for him, and on reaching his room he was obliged to sit down and ring for brandy and water.

Mrs. Cobbem lighted him a fire, brought up a little copper kettle and a bottle of good pale brandy, and mixed him a stiffish dose. He drank half of it, and asked for a cigar. Mrs. Cobbem fetched the box, and sat with him while he smoked and drank three glasses of grog.

A series of soft answers turned away his wrath, and he softened down, but not towards Job Grumper. The brandy and water made him feel valiant, and he declared he would go out to-morrow and "do

for him," but what he was going to do he did not say.

"And I'll have a talk with that youngster who told me to say I came from here," he said, "for I believe he was joking with me, and boys who joke with me will find I am not to be lightly trifled with."

CHAPTER LII.

UNCLE RUDDLE ENJOYS A JOKE THAT ENDS SERIOUSLY.

THERE is an event in the life of Mrs. Cobbem on which some reticence has been shown. A portion of it was described in a previous chapter, and a veil was drawn where her husband, who had good cause to be indignant, arrived upon the scene.

This was the time when she entertained Professor Popper, alias Sharpley Sharp, and it will be remembered that Mr. Cobbem arrived just at the moment when the professor, overcome by what he had eaten and drunk, combined with his feelings, was getting more tender than a man of honour should have been under the circumstances.

Not lacking ready wit he was wise enough not to show any confusion, but still holding the lady's hand cleverly ignored the presence of the Reverend Copley, and counted her pulse.

"One—two—seventeen—eleven—twenty-nine—eighteen! Ah! my dear madam," he said, "I should recommend a little soothing mixture. I will give you a prescription in a friendly way before I go."

"Permit me to ask if you are a qualified practitioner," said the Reverend Copley, advancing with an austere face.

"Dear me! the Reverend Copley Cobbem, I believe?" said Mr. Sharp. "Very glad to see you I came to have a look at my son, and rejoice to find he has progressed amazingly under your kindly care."

"I am proud of your approbation," said the Reverend Copley, stiffly. "But again let me ask—are you a duly qualified practitioner?"

"No, but I have some knowledge of medicine, and Mrs. Cobbem feeling unwell I—ahem!—gave her my services free."

"Freely you might have said," said the Reverend Copley, and then he glared at Mrs. Cobbem, as she afterwards said, "like a demon."

However there was really nothing which he could openly complain of, and Mr. Sharp was accommodated with a room for the night. In the morning he breakfasted and took his leave, rather glad to get away. The Reverend Copley said very little, but it was plain he was thinking muchly.

No further allusion was made to this affair until the day after Uncle Ruddle's adventure, when the Reverend Copley, his wife, and their guest sat at dinner. Perkins, who was bringing in the dishes, stumbled over a footstool, and emptied a sauce-bowl into Mrs. Cobbem's lap, and she, irritated at the moment, boxed his ears.

"Come now!" cried the precious youth, "you aint got a right to do that; it aint legal. I'll bring an action agin you. If I don't soot give me the proper notice."

"Get out of the room, you impudent boy," said Mrs. Cobbem.

"Oh! I can go; but I aint going to be banged about," replied Perkins.

"Mr. Cobbem, will you remove that boy from the room?"

"Come, Perkins," said the reverend gentleman, "go out of the room quietly. You have no right to be rude to your mistress."

"Well, and I don't want to, but don't let her bang me about."

"Now, Perkins, go at once," and Perkins left, murmuring as he went.

"You encourage that boy—you know you do," said Mrs. Cobbem.

"I, my love?" exclaimed the Reverend Copley.

"Yes, you do; and well I understand the reason," returned his wife. "That boy is a standing disgrace to you, but I never see the blush of shame on your cheeks."

"Mrs. Cobbem," thundered her husband, "I will endure this no longer. The infamous libel scattered broadcast about me must and shall be put down."

"Hey! what libel is that?" asked Uncle Ruddle, pricking up his ears.

"It is asserted," said the Reverend Copley, red-hot with indignation, "that I am the father of that boy."

"Ha—ha! ho—ho!" roared Uncle Ruddle, wriggling about his chair in an agony of laughter; "that's the best joke I've heard here. Oh! Agatha, this is indeed good."

"Excellent!" replied Mrs. Cobbem, and then she laughed in concert.

"Madam," said the Reverend Copley, with the quiet dignity of outraged, yet patiently-bearing virtue, "this is approaching the infamous."

"Ha—ha! ho—ho!" roared Uncle Ruddle.

"It is extremely funny," said Mrs. Cobbem.

"Only a depraved mind in a woman could see anything to laugh at in an insinuation so base," said the Reverend Copley; "but you are lost to all shame, as I unfortunately know."

It was now Mrs. Cobbem's turn to be indignant, and she became stiff and savage in a moment.

"Mr. Cobbem," she cried, "have the goodness to explain yourself."

"It is done in two words," he said—"Professor Popper!"

"Hey! ho! what's this?" asked Uncle Ruddle, his ears rising another inch. "Who is Professor Popper?"

Mrs. Cobbem said nothing. She was debating within herself whether it would be better to faint, or to enter upon a warlike movement. She settled upon the last as the most damaging, and taking a boiled fowl out of the dish she aimed it with a dexterity springing out of pure practice, and caught her husband fairly in the face with it.

He staggered back into the seat from whence he had risen, and she, rising majestically, stalked out of the room. The Reverend Copley, with his amazed countenance bespattered with gravy, was a still better joke to Uncle Ruddle than the parentage of Perkins.

"Oh! this is rare fun," he said, rubbing his hands. "I shall stop, and live with you regularly if this sort of thing goes on."

"With my permission," said the Reverend Copley.

"Which you won't refuse," said Uncle Ruddle, with confidence.

"Don't be too sure of that, sir."

"Do you mean to say you would object?"

"Yes, and I do object."

"Why, confound you!" said Uncle Ruddle, "I won't leave you a shilling."

"Confound you and your shillings too!" said the Reverend Copley, now fairly aroused. "You go about sponging on people on the strength of your money, but I don't think you have any to leave."

Uncle Ruddle rose with a purple face, and doubled his fist.

"Come on, you insulting scoundrel!" he cried.

"I'm ready," replied the Reverend Copley "Here's at you!"

Jiggles, who had been a spectator and listener at the doorway, thinking it high time for him to interfere, came forward with a rush, and laid hands on Uncle Ruddle.

"There's a law agin fighting," he said, "hold 'ard, sir."

"Hit hard, you mean," said Uncle Ruddle, and planting one in the chest of Jiggles, he laid him out upon the hearth-rug, gasping.

By this time the Reverend Copley had recovered a little of his temper and his dignity, and remembering he was a host, came forward like a gentleman.

"Mr. Ruddle," he said, "I am sorry I insulted you. Pray accept my apologies."

"I will accept nothing," roared the old man, "and do nothing; except leave your house to-night."

"I regret, sir—"

"Your regrets be bothered, sir!" yelled Uncle Ruddle, and bounced out of the room, fully determined to leave the house that night, and within one hour his boxes were packed and he was on the way to the White Hart.

CHAPTER LIII.

ON THE TERRACE—A DEPARTURE.

THE usual dinner-hour of the Reverend Copley Cobbem was half-past six, it being a rule of that gentleman never to go to bed if he could help it, as some people do, with an amount of food inside them sufficient to tax the gastronomical arrangements of an ostrich.

It was not yet dark when the meal began, although the blinds of the dining-room were drawn and the lamps lighted, to give the meal an air of comfort, and Perkins, after his dismissal by his mistress, went out upon the terrace to enjoy himself in any way that presented itself.

Perkins had a forgiving nature. When smitten, all the wrath of his youthful nature bubbled up to the surface, and what he had to say or do was said and done. After that, he personally washed his hands of the business.

He had no animosity against Mrs. Cobbem when he went upon the terrace; on the contrary he was much obliged to that lady for having with one blow knocked off his fetters of servitude for the evening. For the time being he considered himself free, and like a bird newly released from a cage, he was bent upon making the most of his liberty.

Having found Mrs. Cobbem's favourite watering-pot, he took a cork out of his pocket and stopped up the spout inside in a very artistic manner, and tossed the rake, which happened to be handy, into the middle of a thick shrubbery, where it was not likely to be found for the next ten years, and then took a short perambulation upon his hands, until somebody came, and with a friendly but rather painful smack, laid him at full length upon the gravel walk.

"Who the juice is that?" he asked.

"Me, your friend," replied Billy Sharp, who, with Jolly Greene, had come out surreptitiously for a little fresh air.

"Can't yer be friendly without knocking me over?" asked Perkins.

"Don't be angry," said Billy, who was in excellent humour, "it was a temptation as I never could resist when I see the little chaps in the street doing of it for coppers. I say, is old Copley at dinner?"

"All on 'em," replied Perkins, "and they are guzzling away at sich a rate that they are ashamed to have me looking on, and so sent me out for a walk."

"Let's have a lark then," said Billy; "what do you say, Jolly?"

"I don't mind," replied Jolly, mournfully; "do what you like with me; I don't care."

"Oh! you beauty," said Billy, savagely, "allus a growling and a grumbling."

"You would grumble," replied Jolly, "if somebody was always taking your money."

"They would soon get the lot," rejoined Billy, "and there would be an end of it."

"What do you do with it then?" asked Jolly.

"Do with what?" asked Billy.

"Your money—my money."

"Here, come on," said Billy, "let's have a lark. Here's a barrer; let's have a ride. Jump in, Jolly."

"What for?" asked Jolly.

"For a ride."

Jolly got in as if he was getting into a hearse to be taken straight to the cemetery. They gave him a run up and down; then Perkins had the same, and finally Billy had a bit of a treat.

"One isn't much to run about—is it?" said Perkins.

"Nothing," replied Billy.

"I think I can manage two; you and Greene get in."

Jolly neither objected nor assented, verbally. He got in when he was told, and Billy squatted by his side. The pair made a very tight fit of it.

"Steady, Perky," said Billy; "now—off."

Perkins took up the barrow and started. It was as much as he could manage, and the vehicle rolled from side to side most ominously.

"Don't go near the steps," cried Billy, suddenly.

The warning came too late; the barrow had got into a good pace and was bringing Perkins with it. He saw the danger and strove to turn, but that only made matters worse, and the next moment the whole three, mixed up with the conveyance, were blundering down the steps.

Jolly, of course, got the worst of it. He had the back of the barrow on his spine, and his nose deeply imbedded in the gravel walk. Billy and Perkins lay on their backs counting the stars, which had apparently come out early to dance a highland reel.

"I hollered to you," said Billy, glaring at Perkins viciously.

"What's the good o' hollerin'," demanded Perkins, "when you've got a barrer like that—just like mother Cobbem, uncontrollable?"

"Oh! indeed, you low boy," said that lady, who was just behind him. She had come out to have a cooler after her warm domestic skirmish; "take that—and that."

"Oh! you are at it again—are you?" said Perkins, staggering to his feet; "you will drive me to have the law on yer, will yer? Look out to-morrow for a letter from my siliciter."

"Get up, all of you," said Mrs. Cobbem, dealing out equal portions of chastisement to Billy and Jolly. If anything, Jolly had the best or worst of it; at any rate, he suffered most, and went revolving about until he came to a flower bed, and falling over the border of it he sat upon a choice collection of asters, and squashed them flat.

Mrs. Cobbem was now at boiling point, and failing to find any other way of wreaking her vengeance, she dragged out Jolly by the hair of his head, and shook him as a terrier does a rat. He was so worried and bothered by this proceeding, that he even lost the power of asking for his "mar." He opened his mouth to do so, but shut it again without a word.

"I've borne enough," gasped Mrs. Cobbem; "I'm racked and tortured and driven half wild by a race of imps. As for you," she added, turning to Perkins, "if you live long enough, you will be the Father of Evil."

"Then," said Perkins, readily, "you'll be my daughter."

Billy Sharp was so tickled by this that he shut his eyes and went into a fit of that most powerful of all forms of laughter—silent laughter. For a time he was quite blind, but his sight was restored with a box on the ears that sounded like the crack of a whip.

"I'll teach you to laugh at his impertinence," said Mrs. Cobbem, "and you, Perkins, come here."

"Don't you wish you may get it?" said Perkins, facetiously skipping about. "Oh! my, what a treat it would be for you!"

The infuriated woman, justly irritated, made a general charge, and the trio fled. A boy in his proper attire will beat a woman in petticoats any day, and she soon gave up the chase. Turning away she walked to the front door, and there saw the carriage standing with the odd man on the box ready to drive.

"Who is this for?" she asked, abruptly.

"Gen'leman of the name of Ruddle. Party wot's been staying here," replied the odd man.

It may be mentioned here that the odd man was always very independent. He was one of those men who considered himself "worth his money," and was possessed of a firm belief that he "could get it anywheres." As he had no affection or regard for anything but himself, he was just as happy with one master as with another, so long as the wages and beer were equally dealt out to him.

"This," said Mrs. Cobbem, to herself, "must never be."

She waited at the door until Uncle Ruddle was heard coming through the hall. He was fuming and fretting like a steam-engine at a railway station, and must have seen Mrs. Cobbem, although he went by without taking any notice of her.

"Uncle Ruddle, hear me!" she cried.

Uncle Ruddle jumped into the carriage and bawled out to the odd man—"To the inn; what's the name of it?"

"White Hart, sir," replied the odd man, touching his hat. He could be polite when there was a prospect of a tip, but with the poor and needy, and those known to be stingy, he kept up his dignity.

"Uncle Ruddle be ——,"

The carriage started, and Mrs. Cobbem was left alone upon the door-step with the mantle of misery around her.

"Cobbem shall suffer for this," she muttered. "If his hair is not white in a month, my name is not Agatha."

CHAPTER LIV.

THE VENGEANCE OF JIGGLES.

THERE was one man under the roof of Warmington College, whose heart was full that night, and his name was Jiggles. He had been knocked down by a man, whom, from the first time of meeting with him, he had despised.

"He came in a bullyin'," he said, "and he kep' a bullyin' all the time he's been here. If he'd stopped at that I wouldn't have minded; but he gave me a buster, and I'll have revenge. But let me act as a gentleman."

Then came the question—"How would a gentleman act under the circumstances?" and that Jiggles was not certain about. He never was "genteel," for the cook had told him so; but he did not set himself up as a creature of birth and blood.

"I wonder if any of the young gentlemen would put me right," he thought; "them young Stagers are true bred uns. I wonder if they will help me. At any rate, I'll try 'em."

After a little reflection he settled upon confiding in them at once, and went up to the schoolroom. Opening the door, he said—"Two master Stagers wanted," and Dick and Nick, wondering, came out.

"Excuse me, gentlemen," he said, closing the door when they got upon the landing, "but it was the only way I could get at you by yourselves. I want a little advice from real gentlemen, and I've come to you."

"Much obliged, I'm sure," replied Dick, politely, and Nick bowed in acknowledgment of the compliment.

"What I want to know is what a gentleman does when he's downright insulted and trampled on?" said Jiggles.

"Depends upon who does it. If a cad does such a thing he locks him up, and gets him either imprisoned or fined," said Dick.

"But in the case of ekals—people of the standing?" said Jiggles.

"Then," said Nick, "he challenges him to fight a duel."

"That's so," confirmed Dick.

A slight shudder passed through the frame of Jiggles. Of duelling he had read about in books, and considered it an awful thing.

"A duel," he said, "with swords or pistols, I suppose, gentlemen?"

"One or the other," replied Dick.

"And fight until somebody's killed," said Nick.

Again a cold sensation passed through Jiggles, but he was resolved to go on. A duel was a great thing; the victor was always a hero, and if Uncle Ruddle fell, proud the cook would be of him.

"I'll do it," he said; "I'll have it out with him."

"Who?"

"Old Ruddle," said Jiggles, disrespectfully; "he's knocked me down, and I'll have his life or collapse in the attempt. Tell me how to go about it."

"You challenge him."

"How?"

"Through a second or representative—a friend," said Dick.

"Ah! there you fix me, sir," said Jiggles, mournfully. "I don't know a party as I can trust."

"Will you leave it to my brother and me?" asked Nick.

"In course I will, and proud of the honour," answered Jiggles, in trembling tones; "but when do you think it can come orf?"

"To-morrow morning," said Dick; "if you let us out the back way, we will take the challenge to-night."

"Oh! thank you, gentlemen," said Jiggles, but he would have looked as much obliged to the keeper of a prison who had brought him the cheerful intelligence that he was to be hanged in the morning; "there's my door, which leads into the lane; you can go by that."

"We shall not be long," said Dick; "fetch our hats from the hall."

Jiggles fetched the articles required, and escorted the two boys to the door. They sped off quietly and swiftly, and Jiggles, overcome by his emotions, sank down upon the door-step.

"I'm in for it now," he gasped; "but, Jiggles, be a man; remember the eye of a woman is on you and be firm."

The eye of woman alluded to was in the head of the cook, and at that moment was on a sweetbread, which she was cooking for the supper of herself and Jiggles, "which," she said, to the housemaid, "you'll find few men can refoose at supper. If ever you rises to be cook, give em a sweetbread and a smile, and you'll get 'em."

She had both the smile and the sweetbread ready for Jiggles that night, but somehow he did not seem to appreciate them. When he came in a little after the usual time he took his seat at the table, facing the cook, and looked over her head as if there had been a ghost behind her.

"Lor' a mercy, Mr. Jiggles," she said, "What do ail ye to-night?"

He started and sought to put a smile around his lips. But a man sitting on the sharp end of a tenpenny nail, and his naked feet in a bed of nettles, would have made a better job of it.

"Good gracious, Mr. Jiggles, are you ill?" muttered the cook.

"I?" said Jiggles. "Oh, no! I never was better; but, cook, hear me as you would a man who is a putting out his last words."

"Don't talk in that way, Mr. Jiggles."

"I must—it's a dooty I owe to everybody. If I—in—in the course of nateral ewents should be a corpses to-morrer."

"Oh, oh! Mr. Jiggles, what horrid talk!"

"If I," said Jiggles, firmly, "become a corpses—no matter how—think kindly of me, and—and if you can, put a stone over me. Don't give me a long hepitaph; don't rush into the poets for a hextract,

but get a man as knows his work, and pay him to cut 'Jiggles' on that stone. No more."

"What is the matter?" asked the cook. "You look like a death's 'ed."

"If I am one to-morrer," said Jiggles, "don't be surprised. Ask if they've come back."

"They—who?"

"The messengers of—death," replied Jiggles, in a voice sepulchral enough to be cut up and divided between a dozen ghosts in Hamlet.

The cook was in as dreadful a state of mind as any member of the gentle sex might be expected to be, but she struggled with her feelings, and fought them down, as she had seen Jiggles in a similar state once before, when there was a large dinner party on, and he had drunk about a pint and a half of wine dregs, mixed, and eaten the best part of a dish of lobster salad.

Jiggles went to the door and let in Nick and Dick, who were as chirrupy and cheerful as if they brought him news of wealth unexpectedly left to him instead of something the other way.

"Well?" said Jiggles.

"He will meet you," replied Dick.

"Where?" asked Jiggles.

"On the common, in the gravel pit," said Nick.

"It is well," returned Jiggles; "the pit is a handy place. It will save the trouble of digging a grave. Ha, ha!"

"At sunrise you are to meet," said Dick; "we will, with your permission, both accompany you."

"I'm much obliged, gentlemen, I'm sure," said Jiggles, wiping the perspiration from his brow; "nothing could be more kinder."

"Perhaps you would not object to a few more being present."

"The 'ole school there would be taken as a faviour," said Jiggles, with a forced smile. "I might be able to bear—the—the—worst—with—as I may say—a mob around me."

"I will arrange for a strong meeting," said Dick. "Good-night, Jiggles."

"Good-night, sir," replied Jiggles, "the blessing of—of a departing man be on you! But I forgot. Which is it, swords or pistols?"

"Pistols," replied Dick; "we have a pair upstairs loaded."

"Loaded with powder?" asked Jiggles.

"Yes," said Dick.

"And shot?"

"Yes, Jiggles."

"Then," said Jiggles, "a—a blow from one of 'em would be fatal."

"If you get over a bullet out of one of them," said Dick, "you will live to be as old as Methusaleh."

"Which won't be my lot," moaned Jiggles. "I'm more like a worm in the bud. I mean the bud in the worm. No, not that, but it don't matter. Good-night, gentlemen, and as you must pass the kitchen, kindly look in and tell cook that I'm gone to bed with an attack of indigestion—will you?"

CHAPTER LV.

AT THE APPOINTED SPOT.

THE morning broke cold and grey as Jiggles suddenly started up from a troubled sleep. All night long he had been fighting duels with all sorts of people, and mangled some of them most frightfully. Uncle Ruddle he cut up with a broad sword, but each separate part of the body was still alive, and had the power of following him about, of which full advantage was taken.

"What a dreadful time I've had of it," thought Jiggles, as he sat up in his bed, "but it doesn't matter, for it was all a dream. The most dreadful thing of all—a reality is at hand. Shall I slay him, or will he slay me? Whichever way it is, horrors on horrible heads will accumulate."

A light knock at his door made him leap up several inches. Whose dread hand was it summon-ng him at that hour? Another knock extracted rom him a quavering—

"Who's there?"

"Are you getting up?" said Dick Stager, putting his head in at the door. "It is as much as we shall do to get there in time."

"We shall be there soon enough sir," replied Jiggles, mournfully. "I'll be ready in two minutes."

He got into his clothes somehow, but the buttons were all anyhow and nohow when he presented himself before Dick and his brother. The face of Jiggles was white indeed, his eye had lost its brightness, and his broad mouth quivered.

"It's a—a cold morning, gentlemen," he said.

"Autumnal—nothing more," replied Dick, calmly. "Come on, or would you like to look at the weapons? We have them here."

"Don't let me look at the gashly things," replied Jiggles, averting his face. "Time enough for that when the hour of my destruction have come. Have you come alone, gentlemen?"

"Some, all we dare trust, have gone on before," replied Dick. "There will be enough to bury whoever falls."

"Ah!" exclaimed Jiggles, as he smote his forehead.

Outside the chill mists of the night lay thick upon the ground. The long grass at the roadside, the hedge-row, and the trees, were saturated with dew. The aspect of the earth would have turned one cold, and the very bones of Jiggles were chilled.

He was silent and thinking as he trod behind the two boys. He had not many friends to leave behind him. He had a brother somewhere, of whom he had not heard for ten years. He was in Yorkshire then, in the service of a gentleman who was going abroad, but whether he went with that gentleman or not Jiggles never knew. Neither were very facile with the pen, and writing to each other ceased when they were quite young.

And then there was the cook. Jiggles, in his way, loved her, and had looked forward to the time when he could marry, leave service, and take a public-house or some snug business; but now—alas! what was before him? An encounter with a man who might prove to be a remorseless ruffian, and who would take his life as he would take a pinch of snuff—without hesitation.

"I'll not fire at him," muttered Jiggles. "I'll fire in the hair like a 'ero, and when I receive his bullet I'll stagger forward, cast a reproachful look on him that shall haunt him to his grave, and die."

Jiggles, as most men would have done, forgot for the moment that he was the challenger, and had he not been such a terrible fire-eater the meeting need not have taken place. Danger and sickness oft make great men maudlin.

"You look pale," said Dick, as they halted at the turn of the road; "you want something to warm you, Jiggles."

"I've brought something," replied Jiggles, producing a physic bottle. "It's some of the bottoms of the bottles from last night's dinner. There's port and sherry and claret mixed, and I filled up the bottle with beer. I've tried it afore, gentlemen; it's werry stimerlating."

"It is a wonder it doesn't knock you down," said Dick.

Jiggles took a drain, and they moved on. A little colour came into his cheeks, and he walked with a more determined air, until they came in sight of the gravel pit. Then he was obliged to go at the bottle again, and emptied it.

"Now, Jiggles," said Nick, "bear yourself like a man."

"I'm ready, gentlemen," replied Jiggles. His knees were terribly bent, but otherwise he had quite a martial air.

There was about a score boys already in the pit, walking up and down to keep themselves warm. When Jiggles appeared they saluted him gravely, and some turned away, as Jiggles thought, to hide their emotion. Jiggles was right.

CHAPTER LVI.
JIGGLES AND UNCLE RUDDLE MEET.

COBBLE, Larry, Whisker, Greene, and Sharp were among the crowd assembled. Jiggles saw them, and recognised them, but the things which most attracted his eyes were a pickaxe and a spade.

"We brought them from the tool-house," said Dick, "in case they should be wanted. To save time I fancy we ought to begin to dig the grave."

Jiggles did not answer, but his knees went down almost to the ground, and he had in his face the appearance of one endeavouring to repress sea-sickness.

"On second thoughts," said Dick, "I think we had better leave the grave; it may not be wanted."

"I hopes not," murmured Jiggles.

It was a sad scene, and for awhile the silence was broken only by short choking gasps from some of the boys who were most affected by the solemnity of the time. The gravest face of the whole of them was that of Jolly Greene. He was a great sufferer himself, and sympathised with Jiggles.

"Our man ought to be here," said Jiggles, looking at his watch.

"I said half-past five," replied Dick, "and it is five minutes over the time."

"Perhaps he has overslept hisself," said Jiggles. It was a great hope that, and brought back a lot more colour to his cheeks.

"Overslept himself!" said Nick—"nousense! If anything he funks you."

"Afraid to come, sir?"

"Yes, Jiggles."

"And it is my belief such is the case," said Dick. "I'll run to the level and have a look."

Dick bounded up to the top of the gravel-pit, and looked carefully around on every side.

"Not coming," he said. "The fellow's afraid of you."

"The coward!" said Jiggles, now quite himself again. "What ought to be done in that case?"

"What's the usual thing, Nick?" asked Dick.

"To lie in wait for the fellow in public and pull his nose. It exposes him, and raises the other fellow in the sight of the public."

"But he wouldn't like that, sir," said Jiggles.

"Of course not, and it isn't intended that he should. If you are afraid to do it why there's an end of the matter."

"Afraid, sir—afraid, gentlemen!" said Jiggles, boldly. "Do you think a coward would have been here this morning?"

"All depends upon how you act afterwards," said Larry, winking at Dick.

"But where can this—ahem!—coward be found?" asked Jiggles.

"He went to the White Hart," said Dick, "to pass the night. He must be there still."

"I'll go—I'll have at him," said Jiggles, rolling up his cuffs. "The odd man said he was going away by a hearly train. I'll be at him!"

"Bravo, Jiggles!" cried Dick. "Now, boys, give him three cheers."

This they did, and what is more, they carried him thrice round the gravel pit, singing "See the Conquering Hero Comes" in a variety of keys.

It was the proudest moment Jiggles had ever known.

When they put him on his feet again he marched off in the direction of the White Hart with the gait of a lion.

"He'll do it," said Dick. "Now, boys, home, and back to your rooms quietly before Cobbem gets up. I am going to the White Hart to report progress."

When the Reverend Cobbem awoke from a sleep

that morning he found his wife in a very sad but amiable mood. She was mourning over the loss of her uncle, and she wanted her husband to seek him again.

"Copley, dear," she said.

"Yes, my love."

"It is a pity Uncle Ruddle should slip through our fingers."

"Well, so it is, my dear. But he is terribly offended."

"Too much so to be pacified again?"

"I fear so, Agatha, my love."

"We can but try. He is at the White Hart. You could obtain an interview with him almost against his consent."

"Well, my love, after morning school I will go to him."

"After morning school, you booby!" said Mrs. Cobbem, tartly. "What's the good of that? Before breakfast, you mean."

"Before breakfast, Agatha?"

"Yes, at once—this minute. Get up, dress yourself, and go."

"If you think it would be any use," murmured the Reverend Copley, as he put one leg out of the bed, "why I——"

"Use!" exclaimed Mrs. Cobbem. "Get along with you," and, giving him a push, he slid out and took up a sitting position upon the floor.

"Agatha—Agatha," he said, "this violence is scarcely necessary."

"Are you going or not?"

"Yes, my love, I am."

The Reverend Copley dressed with great rapidity, and went forth a few seconds after the boys returned from the gravel pit. Had he been half a minute sooner he would have detected about half of them in loose attire returning from surreptitious morning exercise.

On the road the Reverend Copley dwelt, as men are apt to do, on the joys of matrimonial life, and occasionally he gave the walking-stick he carried a very vicious dig into the ground. He also cut off the tops of nettles and other weeds, and gave out several more signs of not being in the most amiable of moods.

Before breakfast very few of us are fit for much, especially for business of a diplomatic nature, and the Reverend Copley saw failure before him.

On arriving at the White Hart he found that famous inn open, and a pile of mats by the door. The bar was empty, and when he called nobody responded.

There were voices, however, in the coffee-room, apparently in loud altercation.

"Servants quarrelling," thought the Reverend Copley. "This is a very ill-disciplined establishment. Perhaps my appearance may help to subdue them."

He opened the door of the coffee-room, and entered boldly, but the next moment stood transfixed with amazement as he looked upon the scene being enacted there.

On the hearthrug lay Uncle Ruddle, and on the top of him was Jiggles. About the pair were William the waiter, the ostler, and two housemaids. Jiggles was hammering Uncle Ruddle, and the four White Hart assistants were endeavouring to drag him off.

He clung like a leech with one hand, and the other went up and down like an inverted pump-handle. Uncle Ruddle was concealing his face with one arm, and bellowing for mercy. The blows for the most part descended upon the baldest part of his head.

"Jiggles," thundered the Reverend Copley, "how came you here, and what is the meaning of all this?"

"Wengeance!" replied Jiggles, looking up with a face like a harvest moon. "I swore for to do it, and I've done it. He knocked me down on your hearthrug, and I've put him on this."

Uncle Ruddle was now released by Jiggles, and bounced up like a Jack released from the box. His lowering eye fell on the Reverend Copley.

"You blackguard," he said, "to send this dirty scoundrel to assault me!"

"I, my dear sir!" exclaimed the reverend gentleman. "I did not even know he was here."

"It is a lie!" roared Uncle Ruddle. "You sent him here, and you've come here to enjoy the spectacle of his ruffianism."

"Sir," said the Reverend Copley, with dignity, "I never lie."

"You lie now."

"I do not. I came here to offer you any apologies you might be pleased to accept for the little mishaps you have suffered in my house. I decline to do so now, and bid you good morning."

"I'll summon that scoundrel for assault!" roared Uncle Ruddle.

"And he, sir, shall summon you," returned the Reverend Copley. "I am a witness of you dealing him a severe blow in my house."

"And he struck me first here," put in Jiggles—"didn't he?"

"He did," said William, the waiter. "I see it with my own ... and I'll be sworn a hoath on it."

"You scoundrel," said Uncle Ruddle, "you threatened to pull my nose!"

"And I did it," cried Jiggles, triumphantly—"didn't I?"

"With my own eye," said William the waiter, "I see your thumb on one side of his nose and the finger on the t'other. You was likewise punching him in the wesket."

"Brawling," said the Reverend Copley, addressing Jiggles, "is unseemly, and can never have my countenance; but in this case I entirely exonerate you. The provocation you received was more than man can bear. But who is this—who is this under the table?" and making a plunge at him he drew Dick Stager like a badger."

"This," said the Reverend Cobbem, "is another thread in the skein of mystery."

Dick was a fair-sized thread, and one that played an important part in the woof. As he stood up before the Reverend Copley there was a quiet twinkle of amusement in his eye but no dismay.

"Explain yourself, sir," said the Reverend Copley.

"In private, sir," replied Dick, "I will tell you all."

"We will retire into the passage and relieve my mind at once. Jiggles, go outside and wait for me."

What Dick told him may easily be guessed, as he told the truth. No challenge had ever been delivered to Uncle Ruddle, as he would in all probability have communicated with the police. Duels, Dick knew, did not come off nowadays, but he meant to get some fun out of the affair, and had done so. He was very sorry, of course, but pleaded youthful spirits. The Reverend Copley heard all with a very grave face.

"All this, Stager," he said, "is very wrong. You will find something serious come out of these jokes one of these days unless you abandon them. In this case I hardly know what to say, as ——"

"You rather approve of the punishment the old gentleman has received," replied Dick, coolly.

"I do not say that I do, and I will not say that I do not. It is past eight o'clock, and we shall be late for breakfast. Let us hurry home, only no more absence without leave, or I shall be bound to punish you."

"I hope you will, sir," replied Dick. "Whatever is just I am content to endure."

CHAPTER LVII.

PUDDLE TAYLOR, ESQUIRE, GETS INTO A MUDDLE.

THERE were several private residences of great respectability around the college—that is within a mile of it—and the most pretentious was owned by the Puddle Taylors, very great people in a small way, and accustomed to give themselves airs.

The Puddle Taylors were new to the neighbourhood—so was their house, which was mostly composed of lath and plaster, and had a stucco front, almost but not quite as handsome as a Greek temple. The garden and grounds were also new, and the shrubs were young. People walking there had a dim idea they had somehow got into a place where people were playing at gardening with rather superior toys—everything was so very neat and trim and so very small.

The great glory of the Puddle Taylors was a fountain in the middle of their grounds, supplied by a cistern at the top of their house, or "hall," as they called it, which was filled every morning by the page with a force pump. This page, by the way, was the antipodes of Perkins, being mild, gentle, tractable, and long suffering from an everlasting cold in his head.

The name of this boy was Coddles, and of course he was at war with Perkins—or, to put it more correctly, Perkins was at war with him. Scarcely ever did the gentle Coddles go out for Mrs. Taylor without returning in hot haste, pursued by his remorseless foe into the very heart of the private grounds.

Mrs. Puddle Taylor had written letters to Mrs. Cobbem about these "repeated outrages," to which Mrs. Cobbem offered no reply, because Mrs. Puddle Taylor had set herself up above Mrs. Cobbem and declined to visit her.

The one good thing Perkins did in the eyes of Mrs. Cobbem was his pursuing Coddles with an undying hatred, which he did whenever an opportunity offered itself and he had nothing better to do.

To return to the fountain. It was a very pretty thing, with a great stone basin, where two fish went round in melancholy mood, and a pedestal, on which was a little boy, considerably naked, who blew the water through a trumpet several feet in the air. You would not have found a prettier thing anywhere thereabouts, and the Puddle Taylors—husband, wife, and son—were never tired of contemplating this noble work of modern art.

But one morning when Puddle Taylor, junior, got up and went for a walk abroad in the garden, he looked at the fountain and suddenly sat down plump upon the ground, for the trumpet was gone and the considerably-naked boy was sputtering the water out of his little innocent mouth like one who had tried to swallow solids and liquids together.

The sight was very dreadful, and Puddle Taylor, junior, sat long enough upon the ground to catch a severe cold.

But when he did get up he rushed in with the sad tidings, and all the servants were called up to see if they knew anything about it.

Coddles knew nothing, of course—he never did know anything, nor did the others; but the gardener surmised it must be a "Warminter," as they were given to "bemeaning themselves," so the gardener said, "with all sorts of low tricks."

"All schoolboys are low," said young Taylor. He had a private tutor, and, of course, fancied he must be a great swell.

Mrs. Puddle Taylor wrote yet another letter to Mrs. Cobbem, and this time she was favoured with a reply.

"Mrs. Cobbem presents her compliments to Mrs Taylor (the Puddle was left out purposely to insult Mrs. P. T.), and very much regrets the loss she has experienced, but must, in the absence of evidence, decline to acknowledge it is the act of any of the college pupils, who are without exception gentlemen of birth, family, and breeding. Should the trumpet not be recovered, Mrs. Cobbem would suggest to Mrs. Taylor the advisability of putting her own, which she is so fond of blowing, in its place, as such a course would be a relief to Mrs. T. and people generally."

Mrs. Puddle Taylor bottled this insult, although the effect nearly brought her to an untimely end, but young Puddle, who was a great lubberly lout, took to harrassing all the smaller pupils of the college whenever he could catch them about.

Many of the little fellows suffered grievously, but they made no complaint to Mrs. Cobbem, only talking of it among themselves. At last the two Stagers took the matter in hand, and arranged most artfully an ambush.

It was done in this way.

Dick and half a dozen others hid among some gorse outside the Puddle grounds, and Christopher Cobble was instructed to walk up and down until Puddle Taylor came out, then to retreat into the bushes where he would inevitably be followed by the big bully.

As arranged, so it fell out. Puddle Taylor, beholding Christopher walking by, reading a book, rushed out upon him. Christopher retreated. Puddle followed and was captured.

They gagged and bound him, and boldly carried him in a state of mortal terror to the school grounds, round to the fighting corner, which was commanded only by the windows of the Rev. Copley's private room.

Puddle was put upon his feet, unbound, and a ring formed round him. He stood up white and ghastly in their midst, and in quavering tones asked them what they were going to do with him.

"To give you fair play," said Dick; "you will have to fight, old fellow."

"I never fight," gasped Puddle.

"Indeed," said Dick, "but we will see to that. Keep an eye on him, my boys. If he tries to bolt, down with him, and skin him alive for a coward."

"What a race of young demons I have fallen amongst," thought Puddle Taylor, cold to his very marrow; "I'm as good as killed."

A slight argument meanwhile was going on between Dick and Nick Stager. Both wanted to fight the bully, although he was a head over both, and neither would give in to the other; at last Billy Sharp put forth a suggestion likely to lead them out of the difficulty.

"Toss for it," he said.

"The only thing to do," said Dick. "Have you any money, Nick?"

"Not a copper. The last went for sweets yesterday."

"No more have I. Who's got any money?"

Impecuniosity was a frequent resident at the college, and was there just then, but Jolly Greene after a little hesitation brought out a shilling, and with this they tossed. Nick threw up the coin, and Dick called head. Head it was.

Dick was overjoyed, and began to peel with alacrity. Billy Sharp contemplated the sight and marvelled within himself.

"Fond of fighting," he mused—"death or hard knocks. Well, I never, but I suppose it's in him. Give me a good feed afore a fight. A suet dumpling is worth a dozen black eyes."

In Jolly Greene's opinion the whole business was delightful. He had suffered much, and in common with most sufferers he was not at all sorry to see somebody else travelling the same road. He was not particular—it did not matter to him which got the blows and bruises so long as both did not escape scot-free.

Puddle Taylor was in a bad way—a bully and a coward, he could scarcely relish the prospect before him. He had not a friend there—not one to give

GREEN AS GRASS.

A JOLLY SCHOOL STORY.

THE REV. COPLEY CORNER CAUGHT JOLLY GREENE—BILLY SHARP CAME HEAVILY TO THE FLOOR—AND PERKINS BOLTED.

him a little encouragement and stimulate him with a hopeful whisper. He was alone in his misery.

"Now," said Dick, when he was ready, "are you going to peel?"

Puddle Taylor looked round for one pitying or sympathetic face, but saw none. There were many whom he had injured, and of course he could expect no pity from them—still they were not malevolent, only in a state of quiet enjoyment over the fix he was in.

"It isn't fair," he said.

"Not fair," said Dick, contemptuously. "You great lubber, off with your things and stand up, or we will give you a lesson you won't forget in a hurry."

There was no help for it, and Puddle Talyor with much deliberation took off his coat and waistcoat. He had, as all people have, hope. Somebody might come in and stop this dreadful outrage as he deemed it, but the only spectator at all likely to do so was the Reverend Copley, who saw the assemblage from the window, and took no measures to interfere. He had heard indirectly of the doings of Master Puddle Taylor, and left him to his fate.

"If even Agatha was here she would not interfere," he thought, and the mind of the Rev. Copley was at peace.

He even took an interest in the fight, which presently began—watching it from behind the shadow of the blind with the complacent countenance of a man who entirely approved of what was going on.

And this is what he saw.

Puddle Taylor, with more than doubt in his countenance, faced Dick Stager, who was as calm and confident as the champion of England would have been in the presence of a coal-heaver. The attitude of Puddle showed his want of skill, that of Dick his knowledge of the fistic art. Puddle received heavily on the left eye, and went down.

"Good," said the Rev. Copley. "skill there. I approve of the last delivery."

They got Puddle Taylor up, more for the pleasure of seeing him knocked down than anything else, and Dick, little and nimble, went at him again. Dick was rather spiteful, because Puddle had been heavy on little boys. He performed upon the right eye this time, and Puddle went down with "half-shutters up."

"Truly skilful," said the Rev. Copley, "highly creditable—ahem! from a pugilistic point of view. But this sort of thing is bad—very bad, and it is my duty to interfere."

He looked round the room for his cane. It was not in sight, and he did not leave the window to look for it. By this time Puddle had been put on his feet again, but he had had enough, and would have "cut it" if he dared. But he was told to go on, and went.

It was a sight to see how Dick polished him off. He went round him, and in a workmanlike manner settled him completely. In using the old phrase "his mother would not have known him," we do not diverge from the truth. If Mrs. Puddle Taylor had been passing by she would not have recognised the face of her offspring in that damaged countenance.

"Really," cried the Rev. Copley. "I fear the stranger is terribly knocked about. It is time I interfered."

He found his cane, and rushed out just as Puddle Taylor received the final blow, and went down with gasp and a groan.

"Settled," cried Dick, as he fell. "Nick, give me my coat."

"Boys," cried the Rev. Copley, "what am I to think as I look upon this scene? Is it possible you can have been fighting?"

[...] replied Dick. "This is a [...] who has been a pest to us—a bully and a coward."

"Still," said the Reverend Copley, "he has no right here."

"We were just thinking of turning him out," replied Dick.

"Do it at once," said the Reverend Copley, looking at the gasping and groaning Puddle Taylor; "and tell him from me that if he dares to come here again I will have him prosecuted for trespass. How dare you, sir," he added, suddenly addressing Puddle, "come into this place, which is—a—a—strictly private, and—a—a—devoted—to the cultivation of—of the mind of the young?"

"I didn't come," said Puddle, wiping his face.

"How came you here then?"

"I was brought."

"That is an excuse which will not weigh with the proper authorities appointed for the punishment of trespassers," said the Reverend Copley.

"You will hear more of this," said Puddle Taylor, as he pulled on his jacket. "My father is rich, and will prosecute the lot of you."

"Your father," said the Reverend Copley, "is an arrant snob. Now go. Understand me, boys," he went on, addressing his admiring pupils, "I do not—I cannot—I will not approve of such scenes as these. They are an outrage upon the decorum of my establishment, and at another time I shall seriously reprove you for it. Meanwhile I will deal with the trespasser. Now, sir, are you going?"

"Do you want me to run?" asked Puddle Taylor, as he began to move away.

"Yes!" thundered the Reverend Copley. "Now, quick!"

He raised the cane, and ere Puddle knew what he was going to do it fell. With a wild cry he leapt forward, and ran.

Blundering out of the gate he ran against Perkins, who was coming from the village with some new-laid eggs for Mrs. Cobbem's breakfast. Perkins let the eggs fall, and dealt Master Puddle Taylor a fair blow between the eyes, that finished what Dick Stager had so well begun, and sent him home feeling his way like blind man.

There was much blustering and fuming in Puddle Hall that day, but Puddle Taylor senior was a man of the world, and knew he had no legal hold upon the Warmington boys. An action was more likely to fail than not, and a criminal prosecution for a boyish fight ridiculous; so he contented himself with a round of curses and threats of future vengeance.

CHAPTER LVIII

JOLLY GETS PHOTOGRAPHED.

MRS. COBBEM was simply informed that Uncle Ruddle declined to heal the breach, and after another burst of tears she came to the conclusion that her relative was an old brute—mean and selfish beyond compare.

"And I don't want to see him again," she said

"If he presents himself at the door," said the Reverend Copley, firmly, "I will take him by the collar and lead him off the premises."

"I hope you will," said Mrs. Cobbem, and Uncle Ruddle was dropped—for the time at least.

Perkins and Jiggles settled into their old places, after Perkins had received a wigging for his general impudence, and for two whole days nothing transpired worthy of record. Jolly got into a few inevitable messes; but scarce a day or an hour of his life ever passed without his being in something of that sort.

A travelling photographer one morning put in his appearance in front of the school—not one of those men who travel about with a clothes-trunk on two wheels—who insult the human form divine with black-and-white indistinguishable productions—but a master of his art, with a house on wheels, drawn by two horses, and divided into three compartments—a "studio," a waiting-room, and an inner apartment, where he and his wife an two

.... rank, aud slept—in faot, passed a very merry time of it.

Having secured the good offices of Mr. and Mrs. Cobbem by taking them for nothing, he solicited the patronage of the boys, and the Reverend Copley asked those who desired to be taken to put down their names.

Billy Sharp had never been photographed in his life, and the notion was both new and fascinating to him. He asked Jolly to put both their names down.

"Money isn't wanted," he said; "the charges are to go down in the bill."

"I don't care much about it," replied Jolly.

"But it will be so lovely," suggested Billy. "You will come out beautiful. That nose o' yourn will show up like a mountain."

"You let my nose alone," snarled Jolly; "it's as good as yours."

"Better," said Billy, softly, and after a little more buttering Jolly consented. Their names were put down, and they were the first on the list.

"You two will be taken together," said the Rev. Copley.

"Sich is our views," replied Billy, softly.

"Then go—the others will take their turn. If you went in a party I fear you would be up to mischief."

It was a reasonable fear, and one which the reverend gentleman fancied he had fully provided against.

The photographer's van was outside, on a piece of green at the bend of the road, and as Billy and Jolly wended their way thither Perkins crept out of the shadow of the hedge, and presented himself before them.

"I say," he said, with a keen interest depicted upon his face, "are you going to be took?"

"We are," replied Billy, proudly.

"Don't I wish I was?" sighed Perkins; "but I ain't got no money. Cobbem allows me a little weekly, but that wife of his puts it into a box for a rainy day, she says. Blow it!" he added, with disgust, "who cares for rainy days?"

"Being took comes expensive," said Billy.

"Then let me come and see you done," cried Perkins; "he wont charge me for that."

"Do you mind?" asked Billy, addressing Jolly.

"Oh, no!" he said, "I ain't particular any way."

"Then come," said Billy, and they all three went together.

The photographer was a very handsome man. He had black curly hair, a moustache like a shoe-brush, and a nose as red as the rose. He was dressed in a suit of loud tweed, and wore a smoking-cap. His appearance was quite professional, and Jolly was quite awed when he spoke to them. Not so Perkins and Billy Sharp Popper—they knew all about him, and were quite familiar.

"From the college?" he said.

"Yes," replied Perkins. "Cobbem sent us fust, as we are the s'periors of the place."

The photographer, whose name was Simmons (nearly all travelling photographers bear that name—the whole family must have rushed into the portrait business, and bound over their children by solemn oath to follow the same calling), looked at Perkins as if he knew all about *him*, but refrained from speaking his mind just then.

"You two gentlemen have come to be taken?" he said, pointedly addressing himself to Billy and Jolly.

"Yes," said Perkins, "and mind you do it well, or I'll report yer, and none of the rest will come then."

"Are you the appointed judge of my work?" asked Mr. Simmons, glaring at Perkins with the hope of aweing him (of course he signally failed). "What knowledge have you of art?"

"A pile of knowledge," replied Perkins. "My father took the r'yal family siveral times, and he's now having a run among the docks. Lor' bless yer, he wouldn't look at a chap like you!"

"Walk in, gentlemen," said Mr. Simmons, falling back upon his dignity. "This is the portrait-room. Visitors and friends in the next, if you please, as their presence is apt to disturb the sitting. Who first?"

"You, Jolly," said Billy.

"But can't one stop here?" said Perkins.

"No, you cannot," replied the photographer, "it is never allowed."

"But I am to see 'im through it, and let Cobbem know it was properly done," urged Perkins.

"I cannot have any one here," said the photographer, and Perkins, yielding to the force of circumstances, retired to the second room with Billy.

There, however, his restless spirit kept him in motion, and after examining all that was in the room, which was not much, he knelt down by the key-hole and peeped into the operating room.

"Nothing doing yet," he said; "but he's got Jolly's head fixed in the instrument of torture, and he looks as if he was a-choking. That man is a brute. Who knows? He may be a travelling murderer in disguise. Perhaps he's getting some corpses for the doctor to hoperate upon."

"Don't talk in that way," said Billy, with a shudder.

"It is just as well to know the wust," replied Perkins. "Hallo! here's another room," and not being troubled with many compunctions about prying into other people's affairs, he peeped into the domestic part of the establishment.

Mrs. Simmons was away, being down in the village making a few needful purchases, and the children were with her. The apartment was empty as far as human beings were concerned, but every little arrangement was in apple-pie order. The bedsteads closed up so as to look like chiffoniers, the table was open and in the centre of the room, and a bright fire was burning in a small grate—a poker put in to assist the burning being still there.

"Not bad for low people," said Perkins, sauntering slowly round the apartment; "quite a little snuggery. What a crib it would be for the Cobbems to fight in! Cobbem would have to stand his ground like a man here."

"Gentlemen," said the photographer, suddenly appearing, "this part of my establishment is strictly private."

"Why didn't you say so then?" demanded the undismayed Perkins.

"It is not necessary with respectable people," said Mr. Simmons, and, a little more flushed than usual about the face, he returned to Jolly—

"That's cheek!" said Perkins.

"Downright insolence!" said Billy.

"Which," pursued Perkins, "a boy of my spirit ain't going to put up with."

"What'll you do?" asked Billy.

"Anything you like," answered Perkins, recklessly; "let's see what he is a-doing of now."

The photographer at that moment was getting the focus, and had his head under the piece of black velvet. In this position he presented his back to Perkins, into whose brain an evil thought flashed instantly.

To conceive with Perkins was to act, and in a moment he had armed himself with the poker, and was advancing upon the unconscious Mr. Simmons with stealthy tread.

That great artist was talking to Jolly from under his covering in the usual way. "Keep still, sir; a little to the left—a little more hupright—and a little more expression in the hye. Steady now. Oh!"

It was done. The poker was applied, and he gave a wild leap forward with the machine, and descended upon Jolly, who went over with the iron rack chair, ornamental table, and a few other things, in a heap upon the ground.

The first impression upon Mr. Simmons was that he had been bitten by some animal, a dog most likely, which somehow had got into the van for the sole purpose of mutilating him. But a second impression was not long in coming, and that was the true one.

"Them boys!" he said, and sprang upon his feet with vengeance in his artistic eye.

The poker was on the floor, and the floor was smelling of burning. What more did a man of his intelligence want? Heedless of the gasps and groans of Jolly, who somehow had got the steadying apparatus round his throat, he dashed into the second room. It was empty. He flew into the third, and found that empty too.

"They are gone!" he cried, realising a fact with an intelligence that many men in and out of the photographic line would be proud of.

But he was a man who liked evidence for all things, and ran to the door just in time to see four legs whisk through the gate of the playground.

"They've made it hot for me," he said, "and I'll make it hot for them."

"Oh, lor'!" cried Jolly, "do help me out."

He gave Jolly a lift, and put him on his feet. The unfortunate one was almost dead, and leant against the wall limp and heedless.

"Am I taken—is it all over?" he asked.

Jolly, you see, laboured under the idea that the involuntary conduct of Mr. Simmons was part of the process of portrait-taking, but the artist soon undeceived him.

"Hi," he said, with emphasis, "was only getting the focus when I was interrupted in a way that admits of no extenuation."

"Then I'm not taken?" groaned Jolly.

"No."

"Why did you knock me down then?"

"That," said Mr. Simmons, exchanging his smoking-cap for a hat, "I have already explained. Wait here, sir; I will return in a few moments."

The Rev. Copley and Mrs. Cobbem were sauntering up and down the school-ground in deep conversation over domestic expenses, and for once in a way they were discussing them amicably. Mrs. Cobbem had found a man who sold things at least ten per cent. cheaper than the individual they previously dealt with, and her loving spouse was complimenting her upon her sagacious economy.

Suddenly two forms hove in sight, and the Rev. Copley recognised Perkins and Billy Sharp, both making for the boys' entrance to the house with all speed.

"Stay, my lads!" he cried; "why this extreme haste?"

"Oh, sir!" replied Billy Sharp—"that photographary chap!"

It was all Billy could say, for he really had no sound explanation to offer. Perkins, however, took up the refrain most successfully.

"Gone mad, sir!" he said; "barked like a dog, and he's got Jolly—Master Greene—down in the corner of his workshop a-worrying him."

"Human hydrophobia," said Mrs. Cobbem.

"And here he comes," said the Rev. Copley; "both retire. I will see you safe in. Agatha, you had better retreat."

They all got inside the house without delay, and the Rev. Copley having barred the door, went with Mrs. Copley to the first-floor window to warn off the photographer. Poor Jolly was quite forgotten.

Mr. Simmons rang first, and Jiggles being stopped on the way, he got no answer. Then he knocked, and was favoured with no response. Then he both knocked and rang, and did what most people do under similar circumstances, retreated into the road, and looked up at the windows.

Beholding Mr. and Mrs. Cobbem at one of them, he took off his hat and bowed, but his face was so malevolent that the Rev. Copley might be pardoned for underrating that act of courtesy.

"He looks quite mad," said the reverend gentleman.

"To me," replied Mrs. Cobbem, "he seems simply to be angry. Open the window and hear what he has to say. He can't jump up."

The Rev. Copley threw up the window, and in quavering tones, said, "Sir?"

"Sir to you," replied Mr. Simmons, taking off his hat, and bowing again.

"What do you—a—want here?"

"I've come to lodge a complaint against that liveried boy of yours. He burnt me, sir, with a poker—a hot poker, sir."

"Burnt you!" said the Rev. Copley, "where?"

"That I can't tell you, sir, just at present—ahem!" said Mr. Simmons, looking at Mrs. Copley with an apologetic eye.

"Mere subterfuge," exclaimed the Rev. Copley.

"Indeed it isn't, sir," said Mr. Simmons, earnestly, "and if the lady will retire, I will show you—you—my—my hinjuries. I had my head under the machine when 'twas done."

"Another trick," said Mrs. Cobbem. "I understand all."

"I don't," said the Rev. Copley. "The man's tale is anything but clear."

"You always were a dunderhead," said Mrs. Cobbem, regarding him savagely, "but I will retire. Then, perhaps you will understand."

And the Rev. Copley did understand, fully, after the retirement of his wife; and if ever his honest English blood boiled in his veins it did so that morning.

He went down and shook hands, promising to punish the offenders, and undertook to come in person and see the portraits taken without interruption. Compensation for the damage to his garments was also to be given to Mr. Simmons. His other injuries "no money," he said, "would pay for."

Before going over to the photographer the Rev. Copley sent for Perkins and Billy, and both those young gentlemen came, very blue about the mouth and shaky at the knees.

Both at once fell upon their knees, but there was no pardon. The Rev. Copley seldom wielded a cane, but when he did, those who came under it learnt to dance. Billy and Perkins left that room with watering eyes and a limping gait.

"Where was you cut about the most?" asked Perkins, as he crept upstairs.

"'Bout the legs and huppards," replied Billy.

"Ah!" sighed Perkins, "just my case; we got it pretty much alike."

CHAPTER LIX.

CORRESPONDENCE AND OTHER MATTERS.

THE arrival of the letter-bag is always a matter of interest in a house, and especially so at school, when so much in the way of tips, admonitions, warnings, promises, and outpourings of genuine affection is brought by it.

Mrs. Greene wrote frequently to Jolly, and not being much of a "schollard," letters were directed by her husband. The inside was all out of her own head, and very wonderful things she occasionally turned out. Here is one that came a few days after the visit of Mr. Simmons, the photographer.

"MI DARE JOLLEE,—Yure likeness was wunderful, and has yu sai wood hev Beene hall the better if the mann cood hev tackin you without the black i, wich yu gott wen he was maid to jump on yer bi that wicket boy in buttins. Eye notised him wen i was doon, and thort he was uncomen imperent. Wen i slippt on a peace of horange peel he sed 'Old up, old gal!' as bold as bras. Mr. Cobbem ort to send im back to the workus. Yure farther ses yu carnt hev so much munney; but I sends yu a fippund note. Yure farther must not noe of it, as e hev the gowt, and hav bene throwin bottels of fissic out of the winder. Toe nusses hev left, and the therd wil not stai unless she hev a bottel of gin per dyem toe kepe up her nerfs. Yu must be gettin quite clevver; you rite so large, and sum of the wurds air toe long for me to rede. Yure farther hev jest throne a bole of bred and milk at the nuss, and she is a goin on drefful, soe noe moor from yure affichshunait mother, to conclood, as it leafs me at present."

There was no signature, but the dear old hand-writing was familiar to Jolly, and it needed not her name to convince him it came from her. He was very glad to get the letter, and uncommonly glad to have the five-pound note, which he carefully secreted in his jacket pocket, and said nothing to Billy about it.

Billy also had a letter, a very peremptory affair, which had the effect of tightening the curls on that young gentleman's head. It began without any opening form of address, and it concluded, like Mrs. Greene's, without any signature. But Billy was also well acquainted with the parental scrawl, and was perfectly satisfied it came from his father.

This was the letter:—

"Just you look sharp, and keep the family name up. There are complaints about you. Mr. Spoons says you walk off with his brads, and show too many hooks. If you lose this chance of starting in life you will have to fall back on the old profession—that's all I have to say. Mind this, if it comes about I have done with you."

"I'll warm him up," growled Billy, glaring across the breakfast-table at Jolly, "a-going and writing home as if I was a wulture preyin' on his witals. A nice thing for a respectable chap to have his father down on him in this way. It makes my life a curse."

In the playground he fell upon Jolly, and asked him bitterly if he had ever done anything to injure him, and if he had not always been his friend.

"I don't know," replied Jolly. "What's the matter?"

"Oh! nothing," said Billy, "except what you know. Only mind this, if you lose me you are as good as alone in the world."

Jolly did not say anything, but looked particularly wretched. He certainly was friendless enough as boys go, for those whom he ought to have trusted he would have nothing to do with—indeed, of late he had grown suspicious of everybody, and indulged in close and secret thoughts.

He said nothing to Billy about the five-pound note, but he felt it a burden to him. How was he to change it, and where was he to hide the change when he had obtained it?

Had he been on better terms with Mrs. Cobbem he might have trusted her, but it was out of the question; and of the Reverend Copley and the usher he stood in too much awe to trouble them with his private matters.

Casting about in his mind for some fitting person to help him out of his difficulty, he alighted on Goggles.

Goggles had promised much at their first interview, but had performed very little, nevertheless Jolly was inclined to think he was working in secret, and decided upon trusting him.

Goggles soon gave him the opportunity he wanted, for that very day he was in a dreadful state of impecuniosity, and thinking over people likely to help him he thought Jolly Greene the person to do so. Accordingly he hovered about the playground until the boys came out in the afternoon, and peering through the gate caught the eye of Jolly as he wandered about disconsolately alone.

"Hist, master!" he said, "come here. I've summat to say to thee."

"And I want to speak to you," said Jolly, drawing near. "Only don't speak so loud, or the others will hear you."

"Stand agin the gate, and scratch the calf of thy leg," suggested the cunning Goggles. "Now then, master, what is it?"

"You haven't done much to Mrs. Cobbem," said Jolly.

"Oh! aint I?" replied Goggles. "I'm working in the only way to soot her. But you can't expect me to tame a woman of that sort in a day."

"I suppose not," said Jolly. "But she's as bad as ever, you know."

"Not quite, surely," said Goggles. "Come now, master, her's improved a bit."

"Is she?" said Jolly, doubtfully.

"Yes," replied Goggles; "everybody is a-talking about it."

"Well, it isn't that I want to talk to you about," said Jolly. "I've got some money that I want taken care of, and I don't want anybody to know a word about it."

"Then," said Goggles, with the air of a man on whom the whole world might rely, "I be the party for thee."

"It's a five-pound-note," said Jolly, "and I want you to get it changed, and to give me a little at a time."

"Give me the fi'-pun note," said Goggles, "and I'll give you as little as you like o' he."

"Here it is," said Jolly, "I shan't want any to-day, as I've some by me. Come to-morrow, and bring a little with you."

"I'm the man to be trusted," said Goggles hoarsely. The musical crisp of the paper brought his heart into his throat. He had never held so much in his grasp for years. "This bean't a Brummagem, I suppose."

"A what?"

"A bad un."

"Oh, no—my mother sent it."

"She got a lot on 'em, I suppose," said Goggles.

"Heaps—thousands," replied Jolly.

"And she wouldn't miss one more or less," asked Goggles—a very eager question this time.

"No, of course not," replied Jolly, contemptuously. "Now mind you don't lose it, and be here to-morrow about this time."

"All right, master."

Jolly left him, and went into the centre of the playground, and Goggles, with his blood on fire, hurried away.

CHAPTER LX.

CHANGE FOR A FIVE-POUND NOTE.

CHOOSING a shady and secluded corner of the road, Goggles sat down to look at his trust. There it was, a real bran new crisp five-pound note, legally issued by the governor and company of the Bank of England, and as good as gold in any civilised country in the world.

A five-pound note!

"Five suvrins," said Goggles, "let's see how many shillings—there be twenty shillings in the pound; five times ought is a ought, and five times two are ten. How much is that lot together? A hundred—a hundred shillings, and beer fourpence a quart! How many quarts will that be?"

The limited education Goggles received in his childhood did not enable him to work this out, but he knew the quantity of beer that note would purchase was immense.

"Not that I'm a-going to spend the chap's money and not pay him back agen," he argued. "No, he only wants a little at a time, and when he does, I'll go out and get a job and airn a little. That's how I'll do it. It would be a shame and a pity to let all this money lay dead."

But there was a difficulty in the way of spending it. Few men of humble means could change a five-pound note without exciting comment, and Goggles, who was never seen with more than a sixpence or a shilling at a time, could not hope to show up as the possessor of one without exciting a little troublesome inquiry; but again his cunning stood him in good stead. He hit upon a plan, and forthwith proceeded to work it out.

First he sought the oldest inhabitant, on whom very hard times had descended. He had been out of work for some time, and the Warmington College subscription had not come off as anticipated. Occasionally he got a few pence, but it was not up to out-door relief, which is about fourpence halfpenny a day, out of which a man has to find houserent, coals, food, candle, firing, beer, tobacco, clothing, and the means of recreation. To him Goggles addressed himself.

"Fine morning, John."

"It be," said John, indifferently; "though it be the arternoon."

"I was coming the dodge of the gentry folks," replied Goggles, facetiously, "who make it morning up to night, and then begin again. I say, John, did you know my uncle Richard?"

"No, I didn't," replied John; and it was scarcely possible for him to know the said Richard, as he was a myth.

"Not Richard on my wife's side, a farmer worth a mint o' money."

"No, I didn't know him."

"Then he's dead," said Goggles; "and a good thing it be for some folks, I can tell 'ee."

"But not for thee, Goggles," said John.

"Oh! beant it?" replied Goggles, "I was allus his favourite nevvy; but he couldn't a-bear my wife, and that's why he never came nigh us."

"And has he left thee anything?" asked John, who, always of a sceptical turn of mind, was never so sceptical as when dealing with Goggles.

"He ha' left me summat, John, I tell 'ee," said Goggles.

"His old boots, maybe."

"Nay, John, don't thee sneer at the old man now he be dead and gone. He ha' left me 'ard cash, and I'm coming round to the White Hart to stand thee and all as knows me a lot o' drink. Go and get thy favourite seat by the fire, and I'll come by-and-bye."

Mark the cunning of Goggles. He knew that John wouldn't be in his seat two seconds without blurting out the news, and in ten minutes it would be all over the house, up to the landlord, and who would refuse to change him the note then?

The plot succeeded. The story, doubted at first, was as good as confirmed by the arrival of Goggles at the White Hart. He swaggered in, dashed down the crisp paper, and bawled out—"Gi' I the change for that, and send in two gallon o' beer." All doubts were dispelled—joy and gladness filled the tap-room, songs were sung, the merry quart pot went round, and even old John's hard head succumbed to the o'erflowing generosity of Goggles.

The evening was appropriately and pleasantly finished by a general fight, arising out of an expression used by one of the party, who declared he had not a fair chance of getting drunk with the rest. One man, undoubtedly drunk, undertook to reply to the complainant, but not being able to find speech for the occasion, he threw a handful of pipes at him. The ball being opened all joined in and knocked each other about splendidly, until the potman came in and ejected the lot, clinging to each other like a bunch of worms.

Goggles went home and sought his bed. Mrs. Goggles said something about the children being hungry, but he only cursed her and them roundly, and went to sleep.

CHAPTER LXI.

THE OLDEST INHABITANT SMELLS A RAT.

THE fictitious story of "Uncle Richard" gained ground, and Goggles became a great man. As usual in cases with men who come into money, a number of vulture-like acquaintances descended upon him.

Old friends reminded him of favours past and gone when they had money and Goggles had shared it with them, but Goggles either could not or would not remember those happy days, and new acquaintances promised all sorts of good things to him whenever fortune should smile upon them. Some wanted a pound or two to help with the rent, others wanted a little help towards buying a pig; most of them had something to sell, and all wanted him to stand drink.

After the first night Goggles drew in his horns. He was wise enough to know that five pounds—enormous sum as it was—would not last for ever; he was also covetous enough to feel it would be a sin to spend any more of it upon friends. On his wife and children he never bestowed a thought.

The better part of one sovereign being gone he began to think of measures for taking care of the rest, debating much within himself what course to pursue.

"If I have they about me when I be drunk," he resumed, turning the solid-looking coins over and over in his hand, "it be like enough that I be fool enough to spend they. No, I'll bury 'em and take 'em out one at a time."

But where should he bury them? After a little more thought he decided upon the back of the pigstye. He had no pig—no loafer ever has—but he occasionally made use of the stye himself when he was able to have an extra night in the tap-room. That humble structure was not, therefore, thrown away.

To dig most people require a spade. Goggles had not one just then. The last he was the happy possessor of went for a pint of beer to a tramp, who had a keen eye for a bargain and no compunction of conscience about taking a man in when he was drunk. Goggles was obliged to fall back upon a small piece of board which had hitherto escaped the keen eye of Mrs. Goggles when in search of something to burn, and with it he slowly and laboriously dug a hole in the very centre of a thriving bed of nettles.

The money was deposited, securely covered, the ground trodden down, and he was rising with a countenance suffused with satisfaction, when the sound of a retreating footstep fell upon his ear.

In a moment he was at the ragged hedge which bordered his garden, peering over with a countenance at least forty shades whiter than his ragged shirt. There was nobody in the road but the oldest inhabitant, who was walking quietly but leisurely away.

"Old addle-pate don't suspect nothin'," he muttered. "I thout it might be some canny chap from the village. I'm glad it be nothin' worse than our John."

The oldest inhabitant was at that moment wending his way to Warmington College, with the object of extracting a little pecuniary juice from some of its youthful grapes.

He was very hard up, had never been more so, and Jenny Hall had been particularly hard upon him.

"I'm a hard-working woman," she said, "and I can't keep a lot of loafin' old villains for nout. Get out of the house, and don't come back wi'out some money—d'ye hear?"

He chose a time when the boys were likely to come out on one of their weekly half-holidays—red-letter half days, well known to the country for miles around—and calculated his arrival to a nicety. As he reached the gate the boys came bounding out

"Mornin', gentlemen—mornin'," he said. "Here's your frind, ready for you—willin' for to do all the sarvice a man can."

He bowed and scraped, but none of the boys noticed him.

To do them justice they were all eager to get away to the woods, where there was plenty of nutting. The last to come out was Billy Sharp, who looked back through the gate, and bawled out—

"You aint coming then?"

"No," replied a distant voice, "I'm not."

And off went Billy, ignoring a very polite bow from the oldest inhabitant.

"Well, I'm danged!" muttered the aged one "Here's a low lot. Not worth putting your nose out of the door to look at. Blow 'em!"

The grapes were getting sour.

"But who be the chap as said he wasn't coming?' he continued, and looking through the gate he beheld Jolly Greene approaching with a most disconsolate air.

"Morning, sir," said the old un.

Jolly looked up with a face flushed with expectation, but the colour died away as soon as he saw who addressed him.

"I'm your friend," said the old un, in a thrilling whisper. "I stands by yer."

"So the other said," replied Jolly, mournfully, "and he said he would be here to-day."

"Who's t'other—not Goggles?"

Jolly did not reply verbally, but his face gave the answer.

The oldest inhabitant bent down to give strength to what he had to say, and tapped the palm of his left hand with the forefinger of his right at every word.

"If you trusts the likes o' he," he said, "you are sure to be tuk in."

"Isn't he honest?" asked Jolly.

The aged one gave a contemptuous snort—then laughed aloud.

"Honest!" he exclaimed — "Goggles honest! Where do you go for your downright thieves, then? Surely you aint trusted him with nothing?"

"Yes I have," replied Jolly.

"What be it?"

But this Jolly would not say. If his secret became possessed by many, it would soon reach the ears of Billy Sharp, and then he would, as schoolboys says, "have to fork out."

Little did he dream to what extent he had forked out already.

The aged one tried him for a shilling and failed, asked him for tenpence and failed, dropped his claim down to sixpence and was denied, and finally offered to stand by him for fourpence. As this was considered too much, he humbly asked for twopence, and got it.

"Enough for a pint," he said, and off he went to the White Hart.

Good wholesome beer has the credit of stimulating thought, and the beer of the White Hart being quite up to the average, materially helped the working of the brains of the oldest inhabitant.

In the corner opposite was Goggles fast asleep, with his head thrown back in a most uncomfortable position, mouth open, and eyes rolling horribly. The aged one kept his eye on him, for the loafer played an important part in his thoughts.

Early in the afternoon the oldest inhabitant left the tap-room, and later on Goggles awoke from a most wretched slumber, and finding he had spent all his change, decided upon going home for another sovereign.

On his way thither he borrowed a spade of a neighbour, to save himself the trouble of scratching up the earth. The spot where the money lay was easily found, and thrusting in the garden implement he turned up the first spadeful.

Nothing there.

"Werry hodd," he muttered; "I only just scratched a little hole and put it in, wrapped up in a bit of my handkercher."

He tried another spadeful, and examined the earth most carefully, with the same result. No money was there.

"I can't have mistaken the place," he thought, as the dewdrops of agony rose to his brow. "I can't have buried it somewhere else. It was among these nettles, I'll swear!"

He dug all those nettles up, dived down to their very roots, and found nothing.

In the middle of his job his wife came out, and asked him what he was doing. He swore at her. When the job was almost finished his little ones came out to view the novel spectacle of their father at work, and he threw the spade at them. At the end of his task he was like a tiger robbed of his prey.

"Whose got 'em?" he cried, hoarsely. "Who's tuk my money—that—uncle Richard left me? I'll have his life's blood for it, I'll warrant 'ee!"

Unable to get a settled idea upon the subject he went into his house, and without any preliminary word knocked his wife down. This scared his children out of the house, and still boiling with fury he went off to the White Hart.

Before he got there he was overtaken by a brother loafer, who came up breathless, and red with heat.

"Have ye heard the news, Goggles?" he asked.

"No," replied Goggles, surlily, "I aint. What be it?"

"You had a uncle Richard as left thee money," replied the other, "and now our John have had a like bit o' luck. He ha' got a uncle Thomas dead, who ha' left he money, and he's now standing treat to all comers."

It was not a cry, it was not a howl, neither was it a roar, that burst from the lips of Goggles, but a compound of all three. The misery, the helplessness of his position burst upon him in all its force. One tale was as good as another. If he had an uncle Richard, why should not the old un have an uncle Thomas? And, granted that they had such relatives, they would be no more than mortal, and their dying was quite natural.

He was in a fix.

He knew as well as the old un himself where that money came from. But how could he tax him with the theft?—how prove it was his own? It was a difficult thing to swear to a particular sovereign or sovereigns, and he was beaten—hoist with his own petard, like the duffing engineer he was.

"If I had knowed," he groaned, "I'd ha' marked 'em."

"Marked what?" asked his brother loafer, who had witnessed his emotion with surprise.

"Never mind what," replied Goggles, "but come wi' I to the White Hart, and see me mark our John."

CHAPTER LXII.

TRAVELLING WILD BEASTS AND UNTAMED SAVAGES.

"MY love," said the Reverend Copley, as he laid down his toast after giving it a most respectable circular bite, "I have received a circular this morning."

"Is there anything remarkable in that?" asked Mrs. Cobbem. "You are always receiving circulars of some sort. Schoolmasters are inundated with such things."

"Do not, my love, use that vulgar word 'schoolmaster.'"

"It is as good as any other—for you," said Mrs. Cobbem, shortly. She had, as the saying goes, got out at the wrong side of the bed that morning, and was ready for anything but domestic peace.

"To return to the original subject, my dear," said the Reverend Copley, producing a printed paper from his pocket; "I have here a circular sent me by the proprietors of Saunders' menagerie. It will halt outside the village, near our school, and be exhibited this afternoon and evening."

"Of course you are going to take the boys?" said Mrs. Cobbem.

"Such was my intention," replied the reverend gentleman.

"I wonder," rejoined his wife, "that you do not give up studying altogether, and entertain them with an endless round of amusement."

"With your permission, my love," said the Reverend Copley, rising and going to a desk, "I will read you an extract from my prospectus."

She did not answer him, and he, taking silence for consent, took out one of the prospectuses alluded to, and, running his eye down to the middle of the first page, read aloud—

"The Reverend Copley Cobbem feels it incumbent upon himself to admit that he is not of the so-called 'grinding' school. Education must, in his opinion, be imbibed with ease, and not thrust down the throats of the young. To gain this point amusement in due proportion is considered by the Reverend C. C. to be necessary, and parents who entrust their children to his charge will find recreation an item in his accounts. The experience of many years justifies him in this course, and those who fall in with his views will find it to the advantage of all."

"That's the paragraph, my dear," he said.

"Which I wrote out, and you copied," said Mrs. Cobbem.

"Just so; but it stands there, and we must act up to it."

"You may do what you please, Mr. Cobbem."

"The recreation items are not entirely without profit—please to remember that," he replied.

"Oh! take them."

"But you will go too, my dear?"

"Perhaps."

The "perhaps" was Mrs. Cobbem's usual expression of assent. As a woman of true dignity she could not be expected to bend any further.

The menagerie came in due course—a very respectable concern indeed—with five lions and lionesses, a litter of cubs, two elephants, giraffes, and all sorts of animals known and unknown; and last, but not least, a band that played selections, arranged by the leader, from the great masters. Feeding-time, it was announced, was five o'clock, and the charge to see the untameable beasts of the forest gorge themselves was sixpence extra.

"It will be as well for our boys to see the feeding," said the Reverend Copley, "as they may thereby learn a lesson on the folly of over-eating, and have an opportunity to contrast the hungry instincts of the wild brutes with the cultivated manners of a Christian table."

"And while you are about it," said Mrs. Cobbem, "you might take a lesson."

She was putting her bonnet on as she delivered this final stab, and neither noticed nor cared for the wincing of her husband. He felt it keenly, for he esteemed himself a most delicate feeder.

Going to the menagerie! What boy has not felt a thrill go through him at such a time, especially if it has never been his lot to go to such a place before!

Great was the joy in Warmington College. Even Jolly was quite elated, and neither sucked his thumbs nor complained of being "shoved about," all the afternoon.

There was one sad heart in the house that day, and it lay under the buttons Perkins wore. That morning he had broken a basin, and excited the deepest ire in Mrs. Cobbem's gentle breast. He, therefore, did not dare to ask her if he might go.

To make matters worse Jiggles had leave to have an hour in the evening to view the untameable, and was going to take the cook. Perkins was especially wroth at this, and eased his anguished mind by giving all sorts of insulting warnings.

"You keep away from the monkey cage," he said to Jiggles, "unless you want a lot of your relations to claim you; and stick tight to that old woman cookey, or they will collar her and show her as a hipperpotlemus."

"Mr. Jiggles," said the cook, "if I was you I would crush that boy for his imperence."

"He crush me!" said Perkins. "Let him come and try it, and I makes a corpser of him. Arter that you can go into mourning for a year, just to keep up decent aperiences, and then marry me."

"Give me my rolling-pin," said the cook, with a resolute air, and Perkins, knowing what she could do in a passion, beat a prudent retreat.

"But I'll go," he said, "in spite of the lot of 'em." How was it to be done?

He had neither money nor leave, and was in bad odour with his mistress, who generally regulated the movements of the servants. The prospect was not cheering, but his dauntless young heart was not by any means cowed.

He tried the Reverend Copley, and met with a mild refusal. He asked the ushers to lend him a shilling, offering to give them an I. O. U. bearing his invaluable signature, but was told they had no money to spare. As a last and desperate resource he attacked Mrs. Cobbem.

"Please mum," he said, "I feels wery unwell."

"What's the matter with you?" asked Mrs. Cobbem.

"Too much confinement," he replied. "If I don't get a little change at once I shall break down, and be unfit for dooty."

Mrs. Cobbem did not immediately answer him, but putting on a mild, almost benevolent expression, drew up to him. Perkins, in the innocence of youth, not dreaming of evil, allowed his mistress to come nigh. Immediately he was within reach she seized him by the collar and shook him, until all creation, as far as he was concerned, was reduced to a mass of fiery sparks and buzzing sounds.

When set free again his illness had disappeared, and he found himself upon the mat with Mrs. Cobbem, panting and breathless, standing over him.

"If it were not for the madness of Mr. Cobbem, who took you for a term of years," she gasped, "I would discharge you on the spot."

"Discharge me!" cried Perkins, loudly, "send me away! I'd rather be a sugar nigger than be what I am."

"I know what you will be," said Mrs. Cobbem—"a convict in chains on board the hulks."

"It couldn't be wuss than this," said Perkins; "nuffin couldn't."

Mrs. Cobbem made another dart at him, but he being on the alert this time, dodged, and got away to his own private apartment, where he barricaded himself in, and sat down to reflect.

"Go I will," he muttered, "if I'm taken straight orf to the Tower and battleaxed all over. If I don't go I shall bust right orf, and there'll be an end of me. The t'other coves are going; I'll have a peep at them."

CHAPTER LXIII.

CAGED BIRDS.

THE "other coves," as Perkins disrespectfully called the pupils, filed out of the college, with Mr. and Mrs. Cobbem in the rear. The tutors did not accompany them, as their charge for admission could not be put down in any bill, and their attendance to keep order was in the eyes of Mrs. Cobbem superfluous.

"Leave the boys to me," she said, with an expressive eye, "and I will see if they are to indulge in any tricks."

To do the Reverend Copley justice it must be admitted he would have taken the tutors, and paid for them, as he was not at all ungenerous, but in all such matters he was guided by his better half, who was in reality his three-quarters and a trifle over.

Perkins saw them leave with an aching heart, but he speedily recovered and sallied forth, bent upon seeing the show with the rest of them.

He had a dim idea he might creep in under or through some defective part of the exhibition, but the arrangements were too complete. A mouse would have had some difficulty in getting in without payment.

The band was playing fragments of Mozart, mingled with some popular airs a little upside down, and the tender strains made Perkins sad.

"I must and will get in," he said, and walked boldly up the steps, trusting to chance to aid him in his purpose.

A stout man, with a big head and bow legs, whose garments were quite equal to anything that the most renowned of advertising tailors ever turned out, met Perkins on the top step, and held out his hand.

"Kids half price," he said. "Sixpence, young un."

"But I aint come to go in reg'lar," replied Perkins. "Is the Reverend Copley Cobbem here?"

"Yes, he is," said the man.

"I'm his walley," said Perkins.

"Oh, indeed!" said the man, with a stony eye.

"And I've got a message for him," pursued Perkins.

"Who from?"

"His mother, who's just been took ill."

"Give me your message, youngster, and I'll deliver it."

"I can't," said Perkins, desperately; "I was to give it myself."

"All right," replied the man, "you can go to the bottom of the steps, and deliver it. Swiper!"

"Yes," answered a voice from below.

"Come up here. Stop a minute youngster."

Perkins was preparing to descend, but perforce he halted when desired so to do, and Swiper came up. Swiper was short and thick, and his dress was corduroy and a fur cap. He carried a large whip, and was undoubtedly one of the keepers.

"Take this kid to the bottom of the steps," said the man, "and holler for the reverend gent to come and speak to him. Place pretty full, aint it?"

"As good as and better than we could expect."

Swiper took Perkins down, and in a few minutes came back alone. His face was flushed, and he looked like a man who had run a race and lost it.

"I no sooner got down," he said, "than the kid dived under the camel's legs, and bolted into the thick of the people, running in and out like a heel."

"All right," said the other man, with an evil eye. "Let him be, and I'll collar him as he comes out."

Swiper returned to his duties, which were to go round periodically and in forcibly graphic language describe the contents of the cages. As the time was up, he bottled his indignation, mounted the little official stool, and began.

"This, ladies and gentlemen, is a wild untamed rhinoceros—one of the finest of the tribe, and the largest ever seen in captivity. You will observe that it has a powerful tusk upon its nose with which it repels the assaults of its enemies. Ladies and gentlemen, this rhinoceros with its tusk can rip up deal boards, and even tin—and you will please to observe its cage is lined with sheet-iron. In the wild wilderness it is monarch of all—even the lion shuns it and the sagacious elephant flies before it. A bullet will not pierce its 'ide, and notwithstanding the smallness of its hye, it can see to an immense distance, and observe the most minute hobject at its feet."

"Most interesting," said the Reverend Copley. "Boys, attend. This is a valuable lesson in natural history."

The Reverend Copley was well to the front, and his broad back shut out the view from several small boys, among others Billy Sharp and Jolly Greene,

who, in retreating a little way to get a better peep, stumbled upon Perkins, prudently hovering in the rear.

"So you've come," said Billy Sharp.

"I was 'arf in mind to stay away," replied Perkins, "but Cobbem implored of me to show up—almost went down on his bended knees, he did—and Mrs. Cobbem shed tears, and said she had been a mother to me, and I ought to come."

To all of which Billy Sharp put his finger against his nose, and simply said—

"Walker!"

"The fearocious leopard," continued Swiper—"a rapacious quadruped of the cat group. It lies in wait for its prey on branches of trees, the summit of rocks, and sich like places. It is untiring in pursuit of food, and morseless when anything comes in its clutches. Observe its coat, its lissome limbs, and its tail, which, in hopposition to the dog, waggles when it is angry."

"I can't see anything," said Jolly.

"No more can I," said Billy.

"It's all because old Cobbem sticks hisself in front," said Perkins. "I say, there's a empty cage opposite, let's get into that."

Not only was the cage empty, but the door open, and a most eligible position to see the opposite side of the exhibition was at their command.

Perkins gave Jolly and Billy a leg up, and they gave him a hand up, and then they were all three in decidedly the best position in the place.

"Aint this jolly?" said Perkins.

"Lovely!" exclaimed Billy.

"It smells frightfully," remarked Jolly.

"You," said Billy, "are never satisfied. We aint going to live here—are we?"

The eye of Swiper had marked their ascent, but he gave no outward sign of having perceived it. He recognised Perkins at once, and the thirst for vengeance came upon him.

Passing between the cages he came upon one of the keepers, who was raking out the giraffe cage. To him he whispered—

"Jim, there's some kids in a cage opposite. Go quietly round and let the spring bolt fly. Keep 'em there till I come."

"All serene," was Jim's reply, and not ill-pleased with a change of duty, walked quietly round the caravan, and unobserved by the occupiers of the cage, secured the door.

"I don't know that iver I enjoyed myself so much afore," said Perkins. "It's like having a stall at the hopera—quite a swell persition."

"They will be round this side in a minute," replied Billy, "and then we must clear out."

"I shall be glad to get away," said Jolly, "I never smelt anything like it."

"I say," said Perkins, suddenly, "he's coming round sharp. Here, let's get out of it. I say, who closed this door?"

"I didn't," replied Billy.

"Then it must have been you," said Perkins, to Jolly.

"No, it wasn't," replied Jolly. "But it's not locked, is it?"

"It's fast," moaned Perkins, "which is just the same thing. What shall we do?"

"Go to the back and lie down," suggested Billy.

"But won't they see us?"

"No, I should think not."

"I can't lie down in a place like this. It is no better than a pigstye," said Jolly.

"You must!" growled Perkins. "Here they come, with old Cobbem stuck in front, as if he wanted to see the hins and houts of everythink."

Lying down was the only chance of escape from observation, and Perkins and Billy, getting Jolly between them, lay down at the far end of the caravan. Swiper, pursuing his descriptions with an unmoved face, bore down upon them.

"The armadiller," he said, "a member of the pig tribe, found in South Ameriky. Please to notice the scales on its back. When persood it makes for a precipice, rolls itself up like a ball, and bounds over. A fall of two hundred feet is said not to damage it. We will now pass on to the next cage, where—hallo! what's this?"

Every eye was strained and every neck craned to get a view of the supposed strange animal at the back of the cage. The light being dim nobody could make out what was there.

"Jim!" cried Swiper.

"Yes, sir," replied Jim.

"Wot's in this cage?"

"Don't know, sir."

"Bring the pole."

Jim, entering into the spirit of the joke, although he scarcely understood the full depth of it, brought out a pole, shod at the end with a spike.

"Stir 'em up," said Swiper.

Perkins got the first and last dig. With an agonised "Oh!" he sprang up, and the others followed his example. The moment it was seen who was in the cage the Warminters sent up a great shout of joy.

The Reverend Copley had often doubted his eyes, but on this occasion he doubted them more than ever. It was such a startling thing for him to find three prominent members—perhaps the most prominent members—of his establishment in a cage usually appropriated to wild beasts.

"Agatha," he exclaimed, "can I believe my eyes?"

"Don't talk to me," she replied, "but have them got out. This thing will bring us into ridicule and disgrace. I wonder at your allowing it."

"My dear, I—"

"Get them out, I say."

"My good man," said the Reverend Copley, addressing Swiper, "will you have those lads taken out?"

"I want to know what they are doing, trespassing there," said Swiper, with a dogged air.

"I do not know; but they shall be punished, my good man."

"Will you lay it on thick with that chap in buttons."

"If you mean me to punish them severely you may rely upon my doing so."

"All right," said Swiper, and opened the door.

Perkins prudently allowed the others to get out first, to see what was coming; and nothing being done to them, he came out with a confidence that only made his after humiliation the greater. Mrs. Cobbem was waiting for him, and the moment he was free gave him a sounding box on the ear.

"Go home—this instant," she said.

Swiper smiled—he at least was avenged.

Perkins, who had more dread of Mrs. Cobbem than all other living things, made for the entrance and ran up the steps. The man who took the money saw him coming, and having a private account of his own to settle, left off counting his gains and spat upon his hands.

For impending trouble Perkins had an excellent eye. He read the evil intentions of the man he had deceived, and quailed—only for a moment, however. Close by was a sack of sawdust, used to keep the stairs sweet and clean. Perkins took a handful, cast it into his face, and under cover of the blindness which came upon his foe, fled in safety.

CHAPTER LXIV.

THE REVEREND COPLEY ENGAGES A PRIVATE CONJURER.

"THE subject for our next evening lecture will be 'Illusions,'" said the Reverend Copley Cobbem, after the studies of one Tuesday were over, "and on this occasion I propose to illustrate my address with the nimble fingers of a conjurer, or professor of legerdemain, who will attend with his apparatus, and prove to you how little the eye can be trusted."

The Reverend Copley often gave lectures, and they were very popular, especially when he gave them in the dark, and illustrated them with a magic lantern.

These entertainments were, of course, "extras," and were justly profitable, like everything else at Warmington College. Occasionally the servants were admitted to a back sitting, but of late Perkins, owing to a long course of misconduct, had been excluded, to his great grief and despair.

Fortunately for him, however, the conjurer wanted a boy with him on the stage, to hold things, to be shot at, to have watches found up his back, and so on; and the Reverend Copley, thinking it infra dig. for one of his pupils to figure in that way, Perkins was told off to fill the part.

"And mind you do exactly what the gentleman tells you," said Mrs. Copley, "or I will punish you severely."

Now the conjurer was a gentleman, who had, as he thought, a turn for conjuring, and was only too glad when he could get any one to put up with his mild attempts at the mysterious art. His proposal to exhibit before the boys of Warmington College was a welcome one, for it would cost nothing but a dinner, bed, and breakfast.

He came on Wednesday afternoon, with a large box containing his apparatus. He was a mild-looking man, with red hair, and, to the astonishment of the boys, wore a white neckcloth.

"What! a clergyman a conjurer!" exclaimed the boys, and so indeed it turned out. [A fact—the author of this story knew the gentleman intimately.]

His name was the Reverend Charles Ohler, and being in a living of which he himself was the patron, and where the whole duty was done by a curate for a tenth of the pay, he was quite independent of all public opinion. He was not at all fit for the church, and always admitted it, but he clung to his living even as the best of men will cling to worldly profit.

That he did so was more the fault of the system that permitted these things than anything else. He only acted as you and I, dear reader, might act if we were in a similar position.

"Where is the boy I am to have?" was the first question he asked, and the Reverend Copley rang for Perkins, who speedily appeared, his face flushed with excitement.

"This," said the Reverend Copley, "is the boy —a sharp boy," he added in a whisper; "but he wants looking after."

"Boy," said the Reverend Charles, "come here."

Perkins went over to him, and was asked if he was prepared to do as he was told, and if he would keep secret such portions of the tricks as it was necessary to entrust him with.

Of course he had but one answer to give: he would die a score of times, would Perkins, rather than hint, suggest, or in any way allude to the confidence reposed in him. Then he was dismissed for the time.

"I've got an eye for boys," said the Reverend Charles, "and I can see that he is afraid of me. We can trust him. Boys, I have generally found, have a great awe of them who deal in the mysterious art."

The Reverend Copley coughed a little, and ventured to hint that Perkins was not a very impressionable boy; but the Reverend Charles pooh-poohed that idea, and said he had Perkins "under his thumb."

As it was a half-holiday, the schoolroom was at once prepared, and the private performer entrusted with the key. Jiggles and Perkins took the box of things upstairs, and the Reverend Charles having locked the door, went in for a private rehearsal.

They were closeted for two hours, and Perkins

came out a man of some importance, for he had of necessity been admitted to a knowledge of some of the mysteries of the coming evening. On his way downstairs he met the boys coming in from a walk, and on their way to wash themselves for tea.

Questions were poured upon him, but he was inflexible.

"I've taken a hoath," he said, "not to reveal nothink, gentlemen—so it is no use questioning me."

Nevertheless, when the two Stagers asked for a private interview, he promised it them, and, what is more, gave it. Whether he revealed anything or not our readers must judge by the events of a later part of the day.

"I know that Reverend Charles Ohler," said Dick, in the dormitory, where some dozen boys were washing, "and a mighty conceited prig he is—fancies he can do everything—row, run, play cricket, shoot, and all that; and he is but a lame duck at them after all."

"Of course we know him," said Nick, "but he doesn't know us. I met him as he came in, and said 'how do you d ?' and what do you think he said, 'ah! boy, I hope you are well.' Ah, boy—confound him! Such a swaggering conceited ass!"

"But if he can do the tricks well," said Larry, "it will be good fun."

"Oh, I dare say we shall have some fun any way," said Dick, carelessly.

Meanwhile Perkins had descended to the kitchen, and, to his amazement, the cook had provided him with some buttered toast for tea. If the Lord Mayor and all the aldermen of London had called to take him for a walk he could not have been more astonished.

"What, cookey, have you gone mad?" he politely asked. "Toast for me! Have you given up Jiggles, or have you grown cold and faithless?"

"There, none of your imperence," replied the cook, "but sit down and eat what I've got ready for you. You want something to sustain you to-night."

"So I does," said Perkins, "for I tell you no common man can do these tricks. That carroty chap will do nothing but jaw. All the real work falls on me."

"And what are the tricks?" asked the cook, softly.

Perkins understood the mystery of the buttered toast now. It was a bribe for him to reveal the secrets of the art, but he smiled within himself at the notion. Had he not given his word, and was he to sacrifice his honour for buttered toast? Never."

"The tricks," he said, "are things you will see when you look at 'em, and all you find out you are welcome to keep."

"But, Perkins, surely you can trust me with some of 'em?"

"I'll tell you this much, that you won't have a blessed hair on your head to part after you've seen what he can do, and Jiggles will have to put up with a woman in a wig."

"And this is gratitood," said the cook, making a grab at the remnant of the toast; but Perkins was too quick for her, and seizing the plate he bolted out of the room, and finished his toast on the stairs.

"As if I," he thought, scornfully, "was to be deluded by a woman, like Jiggles."

The time for the entertainment to begin was seven, and at six o'clock Perkins was entrusted with the key to light the candles and arrange the seats. Prior to doing this the Reverend Charles arranged certain articles about the room which were to be afterwards discovered, as such things usually are at these performances.

At five minutes to seven the Reverend Copley and his wife and the tutors took up a position in front, the boys crowded behind them, and the servants—Perkins excepted—ranged themselves against the wall. At seven precisely the Reverend Charles and Perkins emerged from behind a red curtain, and were received with much applause.

Perkins, to Mrs. Cobbem's unmeasured indignation, continued bowing up to the finish of the feet stamping and hands clapping. Then he drew back a pace, and smiling affably upon the assembled company, as if to assure everybody that there was no need to be afraid of him, as he was not going to summon any evil spirit or perform anything beyond the ordinary feats of legerdemain.

"My friends," said the Reverend Charles, advancing and blushing until his hair was quite pale in comparison with his cheeks, "I—I—am as—you know—not—a—professor."

"Public professor," put in the Reverend Copley.

"Just so—not a public professor—but I—I—a—ahem!—will—now—in a way—do my best."

"The first trick," said Perkins, advancing to the front, "is the conversion of a pigeon into a—"

"I said you were not to speak," said the Reverend Charles, in an audible whisper; "you have to show the box round to let them see it is empty."

The trick on hand was to put a figure apparently into the box, and shake it into feathers. It is a very simple one—the pigeon is slipped through the bottom into another box, made to look like a table. At the back of the first box there is a concealed panel, which opens by the touch of a spring. Behind this panel there is a lot of feathers, closely compressed. These are released after the box is shown round and closed with the pigeon apparently in it. On opening it the feathers are found in great profusion.

This is a very good trick when well done, and the Reverend Charles would have done it well on that occasion if Perkins had not, when showing it to Mrs. Cobbem, touched the spring, and out flew about a pound of very small feathers all over that lady.

"I told you so," said Perkins, calmly turning to the Reverend Charles; "the spring isn't strong enough."

"Bobby!" growled the Reverend Charles, pushing him back; "Mrs. Cobbem, I must apologise for this mistake."

"It doesn't matter," replied that lady, "only I do object to feathers. I hope there are none in the next trick."

"None, I assure you," he replied; "the next trick is performed with a mouse, which I will place under this wine-glass, cover over with this paper cone, and change to a piece of toasted cheese. Now, Perkins, take that mouse out of the box and give it to me. Be careful."

Perkins thrust his hand into the box pointed out and immediately called out—"oh !" and jerking it out again revealed a small mouse holding on to his forefinger, as if it relied upon it for sustenance.

"Here, give it to me," said the Reverend Charles, "Quick!"

But it was too late. The mouse dropped, and scuttled off the platform. This was the signal for a scream from Mrs. Cobbem, and another from the cook. The former got upon her chair, and the latter sank into the arms of Jiggles.

"Catch that mouse !" cried the Reverend Copley, "or we shall be swarmed with them."

Down went every boy, and a grand hunt ensued.

"I've got him !" cried Billy Sharp, and produced poor mousey squashed flat.

"I am glad it is caught," said the Reverend Charles, faintly smiling. "I think I can perform the trick with it even now."

"Oh! take away the awful horrid thing," said Mrs. Cobbem, and the trick was not performed.

The confusion of the Reverend Charles Ohler became each moment more apparent. Naturally a nervous man, the two failures weighed heavily on his spirits, confused his mind, and turned him from half a conjurer into the tenth of one. It would really have taken ten men like him, as he was then, to have performed a trick decently.

It would fill a volume to enumerate all the disasters of that evening. Nothing went well. The pudding was made in the hat, but would not come out when it was made; the performing cards turned rebellious, and declined to perform ; the bowl of gold fish that was to have come out of a handkerchief was dropped, and broken before the trick had fairly begun ; and when the school clock was opened to show that a florin had been spirited there from the inside of a tumbler, the pet cat of Mrs. Cobbem—a big Tom—flew out in a fury, and cantered all over the room like a young tiger.

But the crowning mishap of all was when the Reverend Charles borrowed the Reverend Cobbem's watch, to smash to pieces, and to ram into a pistol, to fire it out whole again on a blackboard. A dummy watch was to be smashed of course, and Perkins had instructions to change the real for the false one.

He forgot to do so. The Reverend Charles took the real watch, and knew it not. Determined upon doing this trick well he pounded away, until that watch was dust and ashes, and he rammed it down the pistol, and prepared to fire.

Perkins was in front of him, making signs of agony, but he understood them not. He was blind to all but the watch trick.

"Ladies and gentlemen," he said, "this trick is one of the most remarkable illusions practised in necromancy. It has excited the admiration of—of millions, and defied the detection of the keenest eyes."

"I say," whispered Perkins behind him, "you've done it."

"This trick— What do you want?" he asked, turning savagely upon Perkins.

"You've done it," said Perkins.

"No, I have not," replied the Reverend Charles, "I am only doing it. Get away!"

"All right," said Perkins, retiring, "we'll have the trick t'other way," and playing the part of confederate, he put the dummy watch where the real one ought to have been, at the back of the board, ready to be jerked up when the pistol was fired.

"Spirits of departed watchmakers," said the Reverend Charles, "I call upon you to restore this watch. Hey, presto! One two, three—fire!"

He let off the pistol, and a watch appeared upon the board.

The applause was immense.

The Reverend Charles unhooked it from the board, and advanced, smiling.

"Your watch, I believe," he said.

"Well, no, not exactly," replied the Reverend Copley, smiling.

The Reverend Charles looked down, saw his mistake, and turned faint. Faintness, however, turned to fury, and, shaking his fist at Perkins, he exclaimed—

"Fiend, you have ruined everything to-night!"

"I aint done nothing of the sort," replied Perkins.

"You have."

"I haven't. Can I help your being such a duffer?' demanded Perkins.

"If you call me names I will pull your ears," said the Reverend Charles

"You!" exclaimed Perkins, with contempt. "It's as much as your life is worth to try it."

Infuriated beyond measure by his own failure and the impudence of his confederate, the Reverend Charles rushed upon Perkins, who stood his ground, and the two closed.

CHAPTER LXV.

A SERIES OF ENTERTAINMENTS.

"REALLY this is most unseemly!" exclaimed the Reverend Copley, springing upon the extemporised stage. It was a weak affair, and under the combined weight of himself and the others it gave way.

Down came all the apparatus. False bottoms came out of boxes—double extinguishers revealed their structures—hidden corn, feathers, and a live rabbit concealed in a tea caddy, all came to light, and the confusion, destruction, and uproar, were immense.

"Ohler, Ohler!" cried the Reverend Copley, "I call upon you to desist."

"A boy like that ought to be strangled," said the Reverend Charles, as he loosed his hold of Perkins, and gained his feet, heated with the fray.

"I'll have the law on yer for this," said Perkins, who did not seem to have suffered much, except in the buttons of his jacket, half of which had disappeared. "I'll have you up before the Lord Justices."

"Hurrah!" shouted a score of voices at the back of the room.

"Silence!" thundered the Rev. Copley. "I will not have this unseemly display. Boys, depart; Perkins remain here."

"I aint going to be knocked about again," said Perkins, backing out of the ruins of the stage; "it aint right to put it on me. Did I bust the watch up?"

"You will not be beaten again," said the Rev. Copley.

"Of course not," said Mrs. Cobbem, sarcastically; "whatever happens, and whoever is put about, he must not suffer, but it is only natural, I suppose."

"Madam!" said the Rev. Copley, his voice coming forth with a hissing sound, like steam from a safety valve, "I thank you for that—stab."

When the room was cleared, a mighty lot of wrangling ensued. The Rev. Charles laid everything upon Perkins, but in this he met with little or no support. Even Mrs. Cobbem was inclined to think that a conjurer ought to be responsible for the success or failure of his tricks. In the end Perkins was dismissed, and the Rev. Charles, with the tears of mortification in his eyes, went down to supper.

It was a sad meal. The Rev. Copley was thinking of his watch and the cruel sarcasm of Mrs. Cobbem, the Rev. Charles lamenting the failure of the evening, and Mrs. Cobbem busy calculating how it would be possible to charge enough for such a miserable affair to cover the loss sustained.

The failure of the Rev. Charles Ohler had not the effect of deterring others from attempting all sorts of things out of their ordinary course of life, as might have been expected. On the contrary, a mania for conjuring and acrobatic performances set in, and many failures and much disaster consequently ensued.

Perkins borrowed a shilling from the cook to conjure with. He put it into a tumbler, and covered it up with a napkin. When the napkin was taken off the shilling was gone, and could not be found until she boxed his ears and threatened him with the rolling-pin. Then he produced it from his pocket, and complained of having his trick cut short in the middle.

Jiggles also did a little. He tried to twirl a plate on the top of a walking-stick, and he broke that plate, did Jiggles, and as it happened to be a favourite china plate, a gift to Mrs. Cobbem from her mother, he heard of it extensively, and heated by a mountain of epithets piled upon him, gave a month's warning on the spot, and he would have gone if it had not been for cook. Her charms held him chained to the spot, and the warning was conveniently forgotten on all sides.

Among other acrobatic feats, Perkins, Billy Sharp, and Jolly Greene attempted to form a "pyramid"—that is, Perkins tried to carry Billy Sharp and Jolly Greene upon his shoulders.

How he ever induced them to risk their neck in attempting such a feat must ever more remain a mystery, but they certainly yielded to his gentle persuasions, and in the corridor, near the Rev. Copley's room, they tried the feat.

The Rev. Copley heard staggering feet and gasps

GREEN AS GRASS.

A JOLLY SCHOOL STORY.

A PARTY OF YOKELS—CARRYING AN EXTRAORDINARY SPECIMEN OF HUMANITY IN A BASKET—WERE ADVANCING.

and groans. He opened his door and rushed out just in time to save Jolly from breaking his neck right away. The Rev. Copley caught him in his arms, and staggered up against the wall holding him in tight embrace.

Billy Sharp came heavily to the floor, and Perkins bolted.

"I really," said the Rev. Copley, "can have no more of this. Loath as I am to use corporal punishment, I really must resort to it."

"It aint my fault," said Jolly; "I don't want to do it."

"Why then do you do it?" was the natural question of the reverend gentleman.

"Because they tell me to," replied Jolly.

"Now attend to me," said the Rev. Copley, bent upon giving an illustration that would make Jolly a wiser and better boy. "If I were to ask you to put your head into the fire, would you do it?"

"Yes, sir," replied Jolly, and the Rev. Copley stared at him in dismay.

"You really would," he said.

"Yes," said Jolly.

"And upon my life," thought the Rev. Copley, "I believe he would. He is as green as grass and greener. To you, sir," he added, turning to Billy Sharp, "I have nothing to say. You *know* better —come in here a moment."

Billy went in, and was there but a brief time, but yet too long, and when he came forth again he had one hand behind him, and was wailing bitterly.

"Order," said the Reverend Copley, as he resumed his book—"must and shall be preserved."

While these things were going on, Jolly went down day by day to the gate with the hope of meeting Goggles and hearing something of his five-pound note; but Goggles, as may readily be guessed, never came.

That uncle Thomas of the oldest inhabitant had proved a little too much for him, and the old un had a merry time with the money which Goggles considered to be his by the right of appropriation.

Goggles did not mark our John at the White Hart, but he asked him what he meant by spending *his* money, and to him the aged one replied—

"Thy money, man, when hadst thou any?"

"It was left me by my uncle Richard," replied Goggles, feebly.

"Thy uncle!—thee never had one," said the old un. "Prove it—will 'ee?"

"And where is thy uncle Thomas?" added Goggles, furiously.

"I ha' money to prove he," replied the aged one, slapping his pocket facetiously.

Goggles was goaded almost to madness, but he was an arrant coward, and was afraid of even old John. Having nobody else to take it out of, he went home and ran a-muck among his family.

But an avenger was at hand, who was to punish both evil doers. Jolly Greene, after a long and weary waiting, at length grew suspicious, and went down to the village in search of Goggles.

He found him outside the White Hart, lounging against the wall. His attitude was limp and his eye was evil, for he had had no liquor that day, and old John, the aged one, was getting drunk as fast as beer could make him so.

Dwelling upon his wrongs, Goggles had no eye or thought for the outer world, until Jolly came up and addressed him.

"I say," said Jolly, "I want a little of my money."

Goggles started, and looked for a moment like the guilty thing he was, but his native impudence shortly came to his aid, and in a voice of mingled surprise and indignation he asked—

"Wot money?"

Jolly was staggered, but he rallied quickly for him, and boldly said—

"The money I gave you."

"Thee never gave none to I," said Goggles.

Jolly was staggered yet the more, but his head did not quite give way under the shock, and so he turned to the attack.

"You know I gave you five pounds to take care of," he said; "so don't deny it."

"Well, thee needn't holler," said Goggles; "suppose so, what then?"

"I want some of it."

"Then," said Goggles, "thee can't have it. It's been stole."

"Who by?"

Goggles paused. Accusations of theft are very serious, and sometimes difficult to prove. If he accused old John, and failed to bring home the crime to him, he might be in a bit of a fix. Better hold off for awhile.

"Dunnow!" he said, "but I'm arter he. So go thou home and wait a bit."

"But I haven't *any* money," said Jolly. "Can't you let me have a few shillings?"

In reply to this, Goggles bitterly swore to a statement of his having spent his last twopence on the night previous, and being at that moment thirsty as a fish. Barely had he finished this declaration when the oldest inhabitant reeled out of the White Hart door, and threw his hat into the air.

"Three cheers for uncle Thomas!" he cried; "'oller boys, 'oller!"

Then he saw Goggles, and sarcastically asked, "Why don't thee cheer for thy uncle Richard? He left thee a little money, which thou spent freely."

"Has he been spending money?" asked Jolly, with a quickness that would have staggered even his parents.

"He ha' been a gettin' drunk, and a treatin' everybody," replied the oldest inhabitant, gravely, "and there be a whisper about that the money bean't fairly come by."

The audacity of that old sinner literally froze up Goggles, and Jolly Greene, awakening to his wrongs, hurried off to debate within his mind what he ought to do.

But while he debated, the question was settled by another—viz., William, the waiter, who had overheard every word of the foregoing.

Now William had marvelled much at the stories of uncle Richard and uncle Thomas, not entirely believing in those myths, as many men of weaker minds did.

The conversation between Jolly and Goggles, and the few words subsequently uttered by the oldest inhabitant, gave him every clue he wanted, and five minutes later he sought his employer and asked for an hour's leave of absence.

"There's only one commercial in the coffee-room," he said, "and it's the party as travels with Doctor Nundger's hinfants' food, and never takes anything arter dinner."

"You may go then," said his master, and William, the waiter, having brushed his hair and put on his best coat, hurried off to Warmington College, and rang the bell of the front-door boldly, like an ordinary visitor.

Perkins answered him, and no sooner saw who it was than all the bitter indignation buried in his young carcase came to the front.

"Wot next?" he asked; "ain't their such a thing as a kitching door?"

"I want to see your *master*," said William.

"And who may he be?" demanded Perkins, "come, out with it—who's he? Not you or ho' Jiggles. I'd take the two on yer with my left han behind my back. If you've got a message leave it on the door-step and go back to your beer-shop."

"Perkins, who is that?" cried out the Reverend Copley Cobbem, from the stair-head.

"A man from the public-house, sir," replied Perkins, "who wishes to know if you want any beer, sir."

"That, sir," said William, darting into the hall, "is not the truth."

"Ah! William, do you want me?"

"Yes, sir. I've something to tell you as will make your 'air curl."

The Reverend Copley did not want his hair to be curled, for he was not a vain man; but he desired Perkins to show William into the breakfast-room, and said he would be down directly.

"Show him into the breakfast-room," muttered Perkins; "here, bring a pint o' p'ison, and I'll swaller it first. Now old truckle-penny, that's the breakfast-room, and don't you go a perluting the chairs by sitting down in 'em."

"You are a boy," said William, breathing hard, "or I would make you answer for this."

Perkins laughed scornfully, and walked away. William ushered himself into the breakfast-room, and despite the warning he had received, sat down.

The moment he did so the door was opened, and Perkins thrust his head in.

"Oh! you will—will you?" he said; "perhaps you would like to order 'arf a piut of stout and a long clay pipe. Don't be bashful. The imperence of them pot-house waiters."

"The White Hart," said William, who ought to have been wise enough to keep silence "is not a pot-house, but a tavern."

"It's a disriperable house," said Perkins, "and I'm a-coming up at the next sessions to take away your licence. Now are you going to stand up or shall I come and let into you? I'm responsible for the furniture and the plate and glass, and the way old Jiggles ruins things is bad enough. Here's Copley Cobbem coming, and don't you let him catch you sitting down. The young man, sir," said Perkins, turning to his master, and speaking in a confidential tone, "is in the breakfast-room, and is, I think, a little the wuss for drink."

William was certainly excited, but he was sober. Nevertheless the Reverend Copley regarded him with a stern and suspicious eye as he entered. William stood up and told his tale.

"And is this true?" said the Reverend Copley, doubtfully.

"Ax the young gentleman if he didn't give Goggles the money," said William, "and lock me up if I've told a lie."

"I thank you very much for this communication," said the Reverend Copley, "and will see into the matter. Will you have anything to drink?—or perhaps you have had as much—as—as you care for to-day."

"Indeed, sir," said William, fervently, "I haven't touched a drop."

"Then I will tell Perkins to give you some beer. Good morning."

"He's a real gent," said William, when he was alone, "and I do like to deal with 'em. I suppose I had better go into the hall and wait for my beer."

Perkins kept him waiting a good ten minutes, and then brought him a mug full of a liquid half-and-half—half the boys' table-beer and the rest water, which he had put in on his own account.

"Now," he said, "don't drink that all orf at once, or it will get into your head."

"What do you call this?" asked William, having taken a sip.

"Warminter stingo," replied Perkins. "But of course you won't like it, as your taste have got witiated by the White Hart p'ison. Better not drink it, as you aint got the intellects to stand it."

William, however, drank it off, and found something at the bottom of the mug looking like a piece of gold-beater skin.

"There's something here," he said.

"It comes off the blackin'," said Perkins, easily. "We put it in for finings."

"I've got this to say to you," said William, in a warning tone; "you'll come to a bad hend. I thank 'iven that all my children is different. Now open the door."

"I had horders to take you out the back way," said Perkins.

This was not true, but William was of humble mind, not given to trespassing upon his superiors, and he followed Perkins to the back of the house, where that youth bolted and barred him into a small yard from whence there was no exit.

William was there five minutes wandering about, and knocking occasionally at the door by which he entered, until Jiggles came round accidentally, and asked him what he was doing there.

"Trying to get out," replied William.

"But how came you here?"

William explained.

"Oh! he's a beauty," said Jiggles, sympathising with a fellow-sufferer. "But it's no use. We must take him as we has him, and bear with his ways. I wish there was no law, I'd p'ison him."

"And I," replied William, "axes 'for nothing better than to be public hexecootiner when he's growed a man, and to have the pleasure of hanging him."

It may please some of our readers to learn that ere Jiggles and William parted they shared a jug of something better and stronger than the "brew" Perkins had produced, and William after all went back to the White Hart well satisfied with his visit.

CHAPTER LXVI.

ARREST OF CERTAIN MALEFACTORS.

THE Reverend Copley had a long interview with Jolly Greene, and having received strong confirmation of the truth of William, the waiter's story, resolved to have both Goggles and the oldest inhabitant arrested.

Accordingly Perkins was despatched for Mugs, the policeman of the district, but not being furnished with the particulars of the case, Perkins took upon himself to create a case of his own, and having found the said Mugs, bade him hurry up, for there was a bad business on at the college.

"And what may it be?" asked Mugs. He was a quiet sedate man, not fond of being hurried at any time.

"Old Copley have settled his wife at last," said Perkins, "and wants to give hisself into custody for murder."

"I thought it would come to that," said Mugs, whose stolid nature was seldom impressed by the trouble or misfortunes of others.

"I knew it," returned Perkins, "for you see I've watched the case all through, and I believe he would have done it before if I hadn't said to him orfen and orfen, 'Bottle yourself up, Cobbem, and hold on.' 'All right, Perky,' he used to say, 'you are a friend indeed.'"

Mugs was not astonished, being a firm believer in the parental story, and in his eyes it was natural and right that a father and a son should thus communicate. Having armed himself with a pair of handcuffs and a truncheon, in case the Reverend Copley should repent of his confession, and become refractory, he and Perkins turned their steps towards the college.

"Where's she lying?" asked Mugs on the way.

"In the bedroom, with her head in the fender, just where she fell," replied Perkins.

He had a mind for detail, and lost no opportunity for exercising it.

Mugs was let in by Jiggles by the front door, but Perkins prudently left him, and made his way round to the back of the house. The train was fired, and he did not want to be present at the explosion.

"This is a bad business," said Mugs to Jiggies.

"Werry," replied Jiggles, who knew nothing whatever about it, but did not like to appear ignorant.

"Where is he?" asked Mugs.

"Who?"

"The Reverend Mister Cobbem."

"He's in the study—a-sitting in his chair, think-ing."

"Then I dare say I shall be able to take him quietly," said Mugs.

"Take *him!*" exclaimed Jiggles—"take Mister Cobbem!"

"Why not?" asked Mugs. "Persition aint no-thing in the eye of the law—is it?"

"I don't know," said Jiggles. "Oh! good gracious—who would ever have thought that it would come to this? Shall I show you the way?"

"Ah! do; and stand by the door to give help in case I wants it."

Jiggles, with a dim idea of having a nightmare upon him, ushered Mr. Mugs to the study door, and allowed him to walk in unannounced. The Rev. Copley was seated at the table writing.

"Making a confession in pen and ink," thought Mugs.

"Ah, Mugs!" said the Reverend Copley. "I'm glad you've come; I want you very particularly."

"So I'm informed, sir," said Mugs. "It's a bad business."

"Well, so it is, Mugs; but I suppose the punish-ment will be light?"

"All depends on the werdick," said Mugs.

"What verdict?"

"On the body, sir."

"The body, Mugs! What are you talking of? You are altogether wrong."

"May be, sir," said Mugs, who was gifted with professional obstinacy to a remarkable degree; "but it's no use shirking out of it now. If you've hid the body we are sure to find it."

"*I* hid the body!" exclaimed the amazed gentle-man. "What body?"

"Mrs. Cobbem's," said Mugs, "which it was a-lying agin the fender this morning."

"What preposterous story is this? Who can have told it you?"

Mugs hesitated a moment, then came out with the truth.

"Your young un," he said.

"*My* young one! One of my pupils?"

"No—Perkins—your hoffspring," said Mugs. "He come and told me that you had murdered Mrs. Cobbem, and wanted to charge yourself with it."

"What evil spirit was at my elbow when I en-gaged that boy?" thought the Reverend Copley, smiting his forehead. "Mr. Mugs," he said aloud, "attend to me—the whole story is preposterous."

"Is it?" said the sceptical Mugs.

"Yes; Mrs. Copley is alive, and went out shop-ping half an hour ago. But I will soon prove it, as you seem to doubt me. Please ring that bell."

Mugs kept an eye upon the Reverend Copley as he did so. Jiggles answered the ring.

"Send Perkins here," was the command given. "If he won't come bring him by force."

Perkins came quietly, and presented himself before his master, serenely unconscious of having done anything wrong.

Mugs began—

"He come this morning and he said to me—he says ——"

"Oh! Mister Mugs," interrupted Perkins, "what are you going to say ag'in an orphan boy?"

But Mugs was firm, and pursued his story, despite half a score interpositions on the part of Perkins, such as "Oh! Mister Mugs, how can you?" "Mister Mugs, what have I done for you to come and take away my character?" and so on, all of which did not avail the culprit, who had to make a confession in the end.

Perkins was dismissed with a promise of future punishment, and Mugs was told what he was really wanted for. He was regaled with beer and bread and cheese as a bribe to keep the Perkins business a secret, and went in search of Goggles and the oldest inhabitant.

Late in the day he came to announce the success of his mission. The law had asserted itself, and both villains were in custody.

"And," said Mugs—"they will come up afore Justice Puddle Taylor to-morrow morning."

"Mr. Puddle Taylor!" said the Reverend Copley Cobbem—"is he a magistrate?"

"Made one last Toosday, sir," said Mugs.

"Then," exclaimed the Reverend Copley, "I fear there will be but scant justice in this dreadful case."

CHAPTER LXVII.
COUNTRY JUSTICE.

JOLLY GREENE, on being informed that the culprits were arrested, received the news most dismally.

"What's the use of that?" he asked; "I want my money."

"You must sink personal interest for the public good," replied the Reverend Copley Cobbem; "persons of this stamp must be punished. Be ready by nine o'clock, in your best, to accompany me to the seat of justice, Puddle Hall."

"Yes, sir," replied Jolly, and went back to the schoolroom with the news.

"What would I give to be there!" said Christopher Cobble. "I say, do you want any witnesses? I saw you against the gate that day."

"And I—and I—and I!" called out a dozen voices.

"Yes," said Dick Stager, "there were a lot of us who saw you, and you must have witnesses, or the case will fall through. I shall see Cobbem about it."

It was quite true that all had seen Jolly Greene against the gate on the day when he put his trust in Goggles, but they had seen nothing further. Their attendance was in a measure superfluous, but when Dick put the case to the Reverend Copley, he was pleased to acquiesce in their coming—so, to their amazement, did Mrs. Cobbem.

"With all the confirmatory evidence I shall bring to bear against the prisoners," said the Reverend Copley, "even Puddle Taylor must deal out justice."

"I hope the boys will walk straight through the trumpery flower beds," said Mrs. Cobbem.

"My love," said her husband, "why this malice?"

"Of course you will go against me," said Mrs. Cobbem, "and all because you are fond of that coarse creature, Mrs. Puddle Taylor."

This was the first time such a thing had ever been hinted. The Rev. Copley, if he had any feeling towards Mrs. Puddle Taylor, rather despised her as an upstart, but he said nothing. He was gradually giving up the notion of reasoning with his wife, which was a proof of growing wisdom.

At nine o'clock the following party started for Puddle Taylor Hall: Mr. and Mrs. Cobbem, Perkins (selected by Mrs. Cobbem with the hope that he might have the opportunity of heaping further com-motion and dismay upon Coddles), Jolly Greene, Billy Sharp, the Stagers, and Christopher Cobble. The grounds of the hall were reached by half-past nine, and the house five minutes later.

Mrs. Cobbem knocked and rang, taking this duty upon herself in case her husband should be too mild about the matter. A long delay ensued, and she rang again, this time keeping the bell going until Coddles, white and ghastly, opened the door.

"His wuship," he said, "don't sit till ten o'clock."

"Nevertheless," said Mrs. Cobbem, pushing her way in, "you can show us where the justice-room is."

"I havn't got no order," said the frightened Coddles.

"It's this room on the right, ma'am," said Perkins, whose keen eye had seen through a half-open door the signs of magisterial sittings in the form of a long table and sundry chairs, all new and neatly arranged, to give an official air to the place.

"You can't go in yet," said Coddles, making a feeble effort to bar the way.

Mrs. Cobbem gave him a push, and Perkins gave him another, depositing him in a sitting posture at the foot of the hat-stand. Then the party marched in, and all the front or upper seats were taken.

"There is nothing like reading these people a lesson," said Mrs. Cobbem.

"Just so, my dear," replied the Reverend Copley; but he felt very uncomfortable, and had a strong conviction upon him that the day would end in tumult.

Everything had been provided to give the room an awe-inspiring effect. At the upper end there was a raised platform, on which was a table and a chair for Mr. Puddle Taylor, and such brother magistrates as might occasionally favour him with their presence. The lower table was covered with green baize, and about it a number of inkstands, pens, and blotting-pads were scattered. To the right was an iron rail, behind which the prisoners were to be placed.

They were all silent—the boys for the most part occupied in covering the blotting-pads with libellous sketches of the Puddle Taylor family — the Reverend Copley reading, and Mrs. Cobbem calmly waiting. Perkins whiled away the time with shifting a score or so of marbles one by one from his right-hand pocket to the left, and back again.

Mr. Puddle Taylor was in no hurry, and those who were his assistants took their time also. Mugs brought in the prisoners about a quarter past ten, and put them behind the rail with a warning to be quiet, of which there was little need, as both were in a frame of mind which a few gifted persons might conceive within their brains but never find language to adequately describe.

At twenty minutes to eleven somebody at the door called out silence in the court, and Mr. Puddle Taylor, followed by his clerk, a ferret-faced half-bred lawyer, came bustling in. Behind them was a stout man in a red waistcoat, who, as the worthy magistrate took his seat, bawled out again—

"Silence."

Mr. Puddle Taylor was an iron-headed man of perhaps fifty years, with a short round body and features of insignificant type, small eyes, small nose, and shapeless mouth. He was clad in a gorgeous dressing-gown, and tried to look at his ease, but the business was new to him, and he was palpably nervous.

"Silence!" cried the man in the red waistcoat, for the third time.

Mr. Puddle Taylor took up a bundle of papers and affected to examine them, as if he had half the law of the country in his hands. But he really read nothing, and soon put them down again.

"Any charges this morning?" he asked, as if he didn't know all about it, and had not been talking an hour or so to Mrs. Puddle Taylor of the way he would settle that Cobbem lot.

"One, sir," replied Mugs—"breachy trust case, your wusship."

"Who are the prisoners?"

"Goggles and old John, your worship."

"Who charges?"

"The Riverand Copley Cobbem."

"What address?"

The question was a miserable piece of affectation, and Mrs. Cobbem was down upon it immediately.

"The old address," she said, "where you have sent so many impertinent letters to."

"My love," whispered the Reverend Copley, "you must control yourself. Remember he is——"

"Fiddlesticks!" said Mrs. Cobbem. "Look at him; he won't try that again."

Mr. Puddle Taylor was indeed slightly abashed, and called upon the first witness to stand up. This was Mugs.

The clerk gave him the book—he kissed it, and went ahead.

He arrested the prisoners in the White Hart tap-room, and when he told them the charge both said they were innocent, and could call their uncles to prove it.

"We will see if their uncles are needed," said Mr. Puddle Taylor. "I think this is rather a doubtful case. Is it not, Mugs?"

Mugs did not want to answer definitely one way or the other—so he smiled a gentle smile, and put on a look that might have meant anything.

"Answer me, sir!" thundered Mr. Puddle Taylor.

He felt he was safe with Mugs, and could bully him with impunity.

"It aint, sir," replied Mugs. "I thinks both of 'em are guilty."

"Stand down," said Mr. Puddle Taylor. "Next witness stand up."

The next witness was Jolly Greene, who gave a pretty clear narrative of what had taken place between Goggles and himself, so clear that the Rev. Copley was heard to murmur

"There is, indeed, light in the darkness of us all."

To which Mrs. Cobbem said—

"Don't be a fool, Mr. Cobbem!" and Mr. Puddle Taylor was seen to smile. He had a wife, and could fully appreciate such matrimonial courtesies. As a woman who went in for her rights Mrs. Puddle Taylor could have given Mrs. Cobbem two years' start, and beaten her into fits. It is doubtful if Mrs. Cobbem would have even turned Tattenham-corner with her.

If a man wishes to be truly happy, let him take unto himself a wife who knows her rights—who chalks a line of life from which nothing less than the entire disruption of creation will turn her. Let him do so, I say, and live happy ever afterwards—if he can.

Jolly having given his evidence, Mr. Puddle Taylor undertook to cross-examine him—in a way not entirely in accordance with the general idea of magisterial duty.

CHAPTER LVIII.
DEFEAT.

"YOUR name is Greene?" said Mr. Puddle Taylor to Jolly.

"Yes, sir."

"Don't say sir; say your worship," said Puddle Taylor.

"Don't say anything of the sort," advised Mrs. Cobbem; "say simply yes and no, and all the laws in the universe can't make you do more."

"My love, my Agatha!" whispered the Reverend Copley; "do not forget that it is to the position you pay respect—not the man."

"And your name is Polly, I think you said?"

As this was a joke, of course Mugs smiled, and the man in the red waistcoat smiled; but Jolly did not smile as he replied.

"My name isn't Polly, and you know it—it's a girl's name; you are old enough to know better."

This was a spontaneous outburst from Jolly, not intended by him to be a repartee or a joke, or any insult, but everybody laughed, Mrs. Cobbem especially, and Mr. Puddle Taylor became very red in the face.

"Perhaps," he said, "you will tell me what your name is?"

"Jolliffe Greene."

"Your name is Greene! It is not a low nickname—is it?"

The Reverend Copley rose up, stiff and indignant.

"He is a pupil of Warmington College, he said, "and we have no nicknames—ahem!—that I know of there."

"You say you gave this money to the prisoner Goggles?" pursued the worthy magistrate, ignoring his explanation.

"Yes."

" Was the other prisoner present ?"

" No."

"Then," said Mr. Puddle Taylor, "he is discharged."

"And this," said Mrs. Cobbem, "is justice. Cobbem, get up and say something."

"I must have silence in the court," said the magistrate. "Are there no ushers in attendance ?"

There was one, and no more—the man in the red waistcoat, who had fallen into a gentle doze. Mugs dug him in the ribs, and he woke up instantly, but unfortunately mistaking the justice-room for the interior of the White Hart, and the morning for the evening, he said—

"I think, William, I will have a drop of 'old Tom' cold."

The delight his order gave to all in court was very exasperating to Mr. Puddle Taylor, but being a little afraid of his usher he said nothing, and took refuge in making a few notes about nothing.

The man in the red waistcoat was unconscious of having committed himself in any way, until Mugs whispered a few words in his ear. Then his confusion swelled him out like a frog, and he seemed like to burst, and would have done so if something that sounded like the whole of the back of his waistcoat had not given way with a crash and relieved him.

"Witness," then proceeded Mr. Puddle Taylor, "attend to me. I must have more expedition in this case. My time is too valuable to be frittered away. Did you, at the time you gave the prisoner Goggles that money, forbid him to spend it ?"

"No," replied Jolly Greene.

"Then that prisoner is discharged, and the case is over."

"Dogberry," said Mrs. Cobbem, "still lives and breathes. Put his real name down if you please."

"Good," chuckled the Rev. Copley Cobbem —"good!"

But the ferret-faced man was upon his feet, and whispering in the ear of his superior something which seemed to be very interesting. Mugs, who had had considerable experience of county magistrates, did not release his prisoner as he was told to, but awaited further orders.

"Oh! Mugs," said Mr. Puddle Taylor, "before releasing the prisoner Goggles, I think there is a second charge of breach of trust."

"Yes, your wusshup."

"Does that refer to the same five-pound note?"

"Of course it does," said Mrs. Cobbem. "Mr. Cobbem put the case before that noodle."

"My love, my love, be dignified," whispered the Rev. Copley, as he got upon his feet.

"You may sit down," said Mr. Puddle Taylor. "I decline to hear you."

"I appear here to prosecute," said the Rev. Copley, "and I warn you at your peril against refusing to hear me. The prisoner Goggles is charged—"

"I decline to hear you, sir."

Again the ferret-faced man stood up and whispered words that were like oil on the troubled waters. Mr. Puddle Taylor sank back again, and said—

"Go on, sir."

But here the voice of Perkins was heard declaring that he (Perkins) had "niver come anigh such a old himage of a magistrate, and the sooner they put him in the Court of Queen's Benches the better."

"I will not have talking in the body of the court," said Mr. Puddle Taylor. "Usher, do your duty."

The said usher, however, having the effects of the previous night's potations upon him, had gone to sleep again, and Mugs gave him another friendly jog

His mind being on this occasion with the partner of his bosom, he was heard to say—

"Do let me sleep, Mary; it can't be six o'clock yet."

"It's Mr. Puddle as wants you," whispered Mugs.

"Oh, old Puddle aint up yet !" muttered the usher, as he closed his eyes again. "Don't bother."

Even the ferret-faced man smiled at this, but it was no joke to the sitting magistrate, who felt the dignity of his office, and had determined from the first to uphold it. But what could he do? The man inside the red waistcoat had gone to sleep again, and if awoke he might say something more inharmonious to the decorum of the court of justice; so, reserving reproof for a more fitting opportunity, Mr. Puddle Taylor proceeded with the case.

"You will swear you gave the prisoner Goggles five pounds ?"

"Yes," said Jolly.

"And have not received any of it back ?"

"No."

"Sit down."

Jolly was glad enough to sit down, and rejoined his fellows with all speed.

Then came another conference between the learned magistrate and the ferret-faced man. Out of this came a joyful opportunity to Mr. Puddle Taylor and confusion to the prosecution.

"Is there any confirmatory evidence ?" asked Mr. Puddle Taylor.

There was of a sort, but certainly not good enough for any court of law, and if the Reverend Copley Cobbem had been wiser, or had relied a little less upon the judgment of his wife, he would have left it out.

The ferret-faced man hailed the evidence of the two Stagers and the rest with ill-concealed joy, and Mr. Puddle Taylor treated it with open contempt.

"And am I supposed to commit the prisoner on such evidence as this ?" he asked.

"Certainly you can," replied the Reverend Copley.

"I should be committing a gross outrage upon—a—upon—a——"

"Justice," said the ferret-faced man.

"Yes, justice, if I did so," said Mr. Puddle Taylor. "But I have too much respect for the laws of the country, and a—a—the—the—ah! the——"

"Position I hold," said the ferret-faced one.

"Yes—ah!—position I hold to be led away by evidence that is—on the face of it—fa——"

"Unreliable," sharply put in the ferret-faced one.

"Unreliable, and I may say that in many cases of a less——"

"Undecided character," said his prompter.

"Undecided character have resulted in breaches for action—I mean actions for false breaches—action for——"

"False imprisonment."

"False imprisonment," wound up the wise and worthy magistrate. "The case is dismissed—the prisoner may go."

And, rising, Mr. Puddle Taylor, followed by the ferret-faced man, retreated with as much haste as was consistent with dignity, leaving Mr. and Mrs. Copley Cobbem in a state of mind bordering on insanity.

Mugs hustled out his prisoner, and retreated too, and the only object left on whom vengeance could be wreaked was the man in the red waistcoat, who had gone to sleep again, and was apparently smoking a long pipe in his dreams.

"And this," said the Rev. Copley, "is justice !"

"And where were you," asked Mrs. Cobbem, "to permit it ?"

"I, my love ?"

"Yes, you to let a low fellow like that ride over me, and trample me in the dust; but you are in league with him, or rather with that base creature—his—"

"Boys," exclaimed the Reverend Copley, "our business here has ceased. Let us retire."

"Shall I wake this gentleman up afore we go?" asked Perkins, pointing to the individual in the red waistcoat.

"You may—do what you like with him," said the

Reverend Copley, striding out of the room, followed by his wife.

"Now, gentlemen," said Perkins, addressing the boys, "have you all got a pin?"

All but Jolly Greene had one of those small but useful articles, and Perkins, from quite a little store, fitted him up.

"But what are we to do?" asked Jolly.

"Stick 'em in all together," replied Perkins, "and run for it. Now then, gentlemen, all ready, give it to him."

The pins did their work as one, with a power and pain equal to a well-applied Spanish stiletto, and he of the red waistcoat gave a mad leap into the air, at the same time exclaiming—

"Wot now, Mary?"

Short as this sentence was it revealed to several acute young listeners that the object they had so ably operated upon was in the habit of being treated to little experiments by his wife occasionally; but without pausing to reflect upon it they ran for their lives.

In the hall they came upon Coddles, gazing through the window at something outside which gave him unqualified delight. Perkins only waited to smite him heavily with a handy boot-jack, and was followed by the others, on whose ears the voice of the Reverend Copley in angry accents fell.

In the garden they found that gentleman in tribulation—the gardener having accidentally, while watering the garden, pumped about two pailfuls of water over him.

"Quite a haccident, sir," the man said.

"It is false," said the Reverend Copley; "you only obey the instructions of your low master. Boys, wreck that infern— that machine!"

In a twinkling the gardener was in the middle of a freshly-watered bed of flowers, and that watering machine a thing of the past. Dick Stager saved the brass nozzle from the wreck, and bore it triumphantly away. At the gate they came upon Mrs. Copley, who had retreated thither in case she should share the fate of her husband.

"Boys," she said, "you have done well; but it was the work for a *man* to do—but there are some who never care to risk their own precious bodies if they can get women or children to do it for them. Mr. Cobbem, are we to wait all day for you?"

"Coming, my dear," said the Reverend Copley, bottling up the wrath of ages; "the sooner we get away from this polluted atmosphere the better."

At the first bend of the road they came upon the oldest inhabitant and Goggles, who were for the time united in the bonds of brotherhood for the purpose of assailing the common enemy, and as the Reverend Copley advanced, with the fixed purpose of not heeding either, they stood out in the middle of the road and shook their fists threateningly at him.

"I'll have the law on ye, measter schoolmaster," said the old un.

"What remarkable fine poplars, my love," said the Reverend Copley, addressing his wife, "and they harmonise so well with the middle distance of the landscape."

"Perhaps you will cease to talk nonsense and get along a little quicker," said Mrs. Cobbem; "get out of the way, you low fellows."

She raised her umbrella, and the pair prudently got out of the way, but they hovered in the rear, and harassed the party up to the very gates of Warmington College with threats of—

"We'll ha' the law on ye for this, we will."

CHAPTER LIX.

UP IN A BALLOON, BOYS!

TWO days after the events recorded in our last, the Rev. Copley Cobbem received a notice, Elisha Goggles and John Straddle v. Yourself, wherein it was set forth that they, the said John Straddle and Elisha Goggles, had instructed a certain Mr. Meddle, of an adjacent town, of the profession of the law, to bring an action against him for false imprisonment, and damages were laid at five hundred pounds.

"Preposterous!" said the Rev. Copley; "two drunken loafers bringing an action against me!"

"It all comes of a fool in the place," replied Mrs. Cobbem.

"Well," said the Rev. Copley, "I do not deny that the boy is to a certain extent dull, but—"

"Mr. Copley," whispered his wife, "I did not mean to refer to any boy. No, my words bore reference to something in the form of a man."

"Oh!" said the Rev. Copley, and retired to cogitate upon the letter in private.

It disturbed him without a doubt, for he knew that a sharp attorney sometimes makes a great deal of such cases. The radical papers of the adjacent towns would of course put it down as "another attack upon the people," and call upon the public to aid the poor and oppressed to obtain justice. And it was just on the cards that these two loafers might get damages out of him. So he had cause for uneasiness.

"It won't do to let them have it all their own way," he thought. "I'll go and see Stingem, and get his advice."

Stingem was his lawyer, and lived in the town of Grippenham, from whence the notice had been issued, and in addition to seeing the lawyer himself he wished that Jolly would also go to tell his own tale, and give the lawyer an idea of the sort of witness he would make for the defence.

Before doing this he asked Mrs. Cobbem for her advice, and was told to go his own way as he always did, and he took it. The odd man put the pony in, and the Rev. Copley, with Jolly Greene, started for Grippenham. Perkins was in the little seat behind.

Nothing happened on the way except that Perkins' hat fell off just as they got to a muddy part of the road, and being bowled along by a stiff breeze, was made, as the Rev. Copley said, "unsightly and loathsome to the eye." But Perkins brushed it up and made it almost pretty again.

They put up at the Castle Inn, and walked towards the office of Mr. Stingem—the Rev. Copley remarking on the way that there seemed to be an unusual number of people about the town that day— a fact presently explained when they came upon a flaring poster announcing that a balloon ascent would take place that day at the Royal Sea Shell Gardens of that town.

"A balloon ascent?" said the Rev. Copley; "dear me, how interesting! See, Greene, how aspiring— nay, audacious—man is. He strives to master all the elements, and to o'ertop the clouds."

"I have never seen a balloon ascent," remarked Greene.

"There is only one objection to it here," returned the Rev. Copley, and that is, it takes place at a public tea-gardens—a class of place which helps to demoralise and deprave the humbler classes. He said no more just then, but hurried on to the lawyer's office, where he inquired if Mr. Stingem was in; the reply was in the affirmative, and he was ushered into an inner room.

After being closeted for a few minutes, he emerged again, in company with the lawyer—a stout man, with rather a jovial expression of face—who cast a keen glance at Jolly, and turning to the Rev. Copley, slightly shook his head.

"Then you won't hear his story?" said the Rev. Copley, in a low tone.

"Not a bit of use," was the reply, "a junior counsel would make rags of him in less than five minutes."

"You think so?"

"Sure of it," was the answer.

"Then I think we had better go and see other friend," said the Rev. Copley.

"Just so," said the other.

"Remain here, boys," said the Reverend Copley, "until we return. We may be an hour or perhaps more."

Now the prospect of waiting at that office was not a very agreeable one, especially as there was a balloon ascent, and as soon as the backs of the gentlemen were turned, Perkins suggested to Jolly that there would be no harm in going outside just to see if the balloon was up.

Now we all know that as soon as the first step towards a sin or indiscretion is committed, the tempter has succeeded—the second and third and others follow, until the thing is done.

Within a quarter of an hour of leaving the lawyer's office, Perkins, who knew the place well, led his companion to the exterior of the outside of the Sea Shell Gardens, where a motley mob were waiting the advertised ascent.

"Don't you think we had better go in?" said Perkins. "We shall see nothing here."

"But Mr. Cobbem said it's a bad place," returned Jolly.

"That was his fun," said Perkins. "I was looking at him, and he never deceives me. It's only sixpence each. Come on."

Jolly was terribly anxious to see the ascent, and as it was announced to take place immediately, he produced the shilling, and paid for himself and Perkins.

The Sea Shell Gardens were of the ordinary type, and therefore need no explaining here. The gravel walks were almost empty, but upon a lawn usually devoted to bowls there was a crowd of people, and high in the centre rose the great balloon.

There are few things made by man more majestic and awe-inspiring than the silken bag with its net and car, by the aid of which the aëronaut ascends above the clouds.

Jolly involuntarily clapped his hands, and uttered a shout of joy, and Perkins, all excitement, pressed forward into the crowd.

I do not say that boys love to sit in high places, but I do assert that when there is anything to be seen in public they dearly love to be in front.

Nay, more, they insist upon it, and manage somehow to work their way through such dense masses of humanity as would be impregnable to the majority of adults.

Perkins, towing Jolly in his wake, soon succeeded in getting near the car, so close that he could handle it and look over and see what was inside of it, two advantages he fully availed himself of.

This was the scene. Some dozen men holding the balloon down by ropes, awaiting the word "Let go!" on one side of the car, Perkins and Jolly on the other, and the aëronaut taking leave of a few friends. Around, and pressing close up, was the crowd before alluded to.

"What a jolly thing to sit in!" said Perkins. "Get in, and see how you like it."

"I dare not," said Jolly.

"Oh, go on," urged Perkins; "that fellow isn't looking. Now, then, in you go."

As Jolly still hesitated, Perkins gave him a little physical help, and fairly tilted his companion into the car. The moment he had done so he became aware of two eyes fixed upon him from the opposite side, and in an instant he recognised them as being in the head of his master, the Reverend Copley Cobbem.

Without pausing to reflect upon the position in which he had placed his companion, he turned and worked his way into the crowd again, leaving Jolly lying upon the bottom of the car, a little confused by his sudden introduction into it.

It was to be a sensational ascent; the aëronaut was to go up under the car with his foot in a stirrup, and to climb up when at a certain height.

Just as Perkins retreated the eventful moment had arrived, the aëronaut cried "Let go!" put his foot in the stirrup, and ere Jolly Greene knew what

had really befallen him he was half way up towards the clouds.

CHAPTER LX

JOLLY GREENE GOES IN STRONG FOR THE AERIAL BUSINESS.

THE finding of any person in a place where no person is expected to be has always a startling effect, but in the case of the aëronaut, who ascended to the car and came upon Jolly, it must have been doubly so.

In the first rush of astonishment the aëronaut nearly let go his hold of the ropes, and had he done so he would have gone straight down to Mother Earth, and Jolly, alone in his glory, would have gone up to the clouds; but the strong-minded man held on, and getting into the car, asked—

"Who the devil are you?"

"I was shoved in," replied Jolly; "I am always being shoved about."

"Shoved in—was you? What do you mean by that?"

"I think it was Perkins," returned Jolly; "he is always up to some trick. But I'll get out, if you please."

"You can't get out," said the aëronaut, "unless you want to dash out your brains. We've started."

"Started, sir?"

"Yes we are going up."

"Not into the sky?" shrieked Jolly.

"Yes, we are. What are you doing? Keep quiet."

But Jolly, with a cry of "I can't stop! I daren't go!" gave a wild leap over the side, and if his companion had not seized him by the collar he would have gone down some half-mile or so and put his father and mother into mourning.

"Bless the fool!" gasped the aëronaut, "Come in again—can't you? Put your hand on the side of the car. Oh! what a fool!"

Jolly, terrified out of his senses at finding himself like a cherub, very much aloft, only kicked and wriggled about in a wild purposeless manner.

"If I drop him," thought the aëronaut, cold with fear, "I shall be tried for murder perhaps, and I can't hold on for ever. Here, you ass, put your hand here—will you? I can't haul you up alone."

He might as well have appealed to the clouds to turn and work against the wind.

Jolly went his own wriggling way, and the balloon shot into a great white cloud.

The chill dense mist alarmed Jolly the more, and his wild attempts to get free increased in force. He kicked, he even scratched, and the aëronaut felt he must soon drop him whether he would or no.

On they drifted for another minute or so, not much when looked at upon the roll of time, but a great deal to a man in that aëronaut's position; and they were free of the cloud, and wet to the skin, shooting higher and higher into space.

"I say, you fellow, can't you listen to reason? If you get in here again you will be quite safe, but I can't get you in alone. Put your hands here—higher—no, not there—don't scratch me—here, on the side of the car."

To all of which Jolly only answered—

"Where's my mar?"

"Your mar be hanged!" muttered the aëronaut. "Come, I'll give you another chance. Good heavens, I must drop him!"

*　　*　　*　　*　　*　　*

Meanwhile the Reverend Copley Cobbem, unconscious of the fate of Jolly Greene, gave chase to Perkins, and captured him as he sought to make his exit from the gate.

"You bad boy," he said, cuffing him, "what do you mean by coming to such a place as this?"

"Aint it as good for me as you?" demanded the defiant Perkins. "If you hadn't come don't you think I should have stopped away?"

"Where is Master Greene?" asked the Reverend Copley, declining to pursue the subject of his being there any further.

For the first time Perkins began to suspect what had become of his companion, and a feeling akin to remorse sprang into his gentle breast. He looked, and saw the balloon high in the air, with the aëronaut climbing into the car, and then a cloud shut out the balloon and all from view.

In his eyes Jolly was as good as done for, but even this, so evil were his ways, did not prevent Perkins from prevaricating.

"How should I know?" he asked. "He wasn't stuck to me with gum—was he?"

"You are a dreadful boy—an awful boy," replied the Reverend Copley, "and I would give fifty pounds if your time with me was out."

"Then pay my passage to the West Injies," said Perkins; "I don't want to stop with you. I would rather live in a hut on an island, instead of being pushed about and wolloped from morning till night."

"I would do it if I thought I should get rid of you," said his master.

"You try it," returned Perkins; "that's all I want."

They were now joined by the lawyer, Mr. Stingem, and, signalling to Perkins to follow, the Reverend Copley took his friend's arm, and they went back to the office.

Perkins followed them, and was very quiet on the whole. He had only two skirmishes with boys of his own type upon the way, and was not more than five minutes behind his master.

They waited an hour for Jolly Greene, but as he did not turn up two of the clerks were despatched to find him.

Perkins saw them go with a sad smile, for he knew their search would be fruitless.

"What can have become of that wicked lad?" said the Reverend Copley. "Something always seems to be wrong with him."

"Where was he seen last?" asked Mr. Stingem.

"I left him here with Perkins," was the reply.

"Have Perkins in."

"I have already examined him."

"My dear Cobbem, you examine him! A very tame piece of business, I'll warrant. Let him come to me."

So Perkins was sent for, and found in the lawyer a very different man from his master. Facts were drawn from him, like teeth by an experienced dentist, and the truth was soon known.

"I didn't go for to put him in," said Perkins, wofully. "I just ketched hold of his leg, and with a kind o' skip in he went."

"Don't you lie!" said Mr. Stingem, calmly, "or one of these days you will find yourself on trial at the Old Bailey for perjury."

"Don't go and take a poor boy's character away," pleaded Perkins.

"It would be a very good thing if your character was taken away," said the lawyer. "It is not such a good one that you need cry over its loss. Go into the clerks' office and wait."

Perkins, considerably worsted, and feeling very uncomfortable, returned to his seat in the outer office, and for full five minutes was as quiet as a mouse and did not once get up to stare at the clerks through the rails of their desks as if they had been wild beasts on show.

"This is a sad affair," said the Reverend Copley, when he and the lawyer were alone.

"Aye!" replied the lawyer, "especially as a boy of that stamp may give a great deal of trouble to the aëronaut, and bring destruction on them both. However, if we send a message to the gardens we may in the course of the evening hear what has become of the balloon."

"Mrs. Cobbem expects me home to dinner," said the Reverend Copley, nervously. "She objects very much to dine alone."

"Go home, then, and I will send you a message."

"But about the boy——"

"Say nothing to her at present; and if he returns safely get him quietly off to bed. If he comes here I will send one of my clerks on with him."

CHAPTER LXI.

PERKINS COMMENCES AND JIGGLES FINISHES IT.

"BEFORE I go," said the Reverend Copley, drawing on his gloves, "tell me what you think of the case."

"The false imprisonment business?"

"Yes."

"Well, it is in good hands, and I fancy they will pull through."

"Do you mean that I shall have to pay?"

"Very likely, for really there was no case against the men, especially the old man. It was rash of you—very rash."

"Before paying such a pair of villains one farthing," cried the Reverend Copley, firmly, "I will suffer imprisonment—I will starve and rot in a dungeon!"

"About three days of much milder form of imprisonment would make you sing another tune," replied the lawyer, calmly. "I am speaking to you as a friend, and I should advise you to square it. A few shillings will be enough if you pay Meddle's costs."

"I won't."

"They must be paid eventually."

"Not by me. I'll die first."

"We shall see; but perhaps a split may take place between the men. In that case we may be able to defeat Meddle."

"You mean Goggles and the other?"

"No I don't. It is Meddle's business—got up by Meddle for his own benefit. Suppose you have to pay damages, the better part of it will go into Meddle's pocket."

"What direful villainy!"

"He is a representative of the law, and he acts legally," replied Mr. Stingem, "and while the law stands you must not abuse the man."

They parted, and the Reverend Copley, as near red-hot as a man can be, went home, giving Perkins on the way strict injunctions not to say a word about the adventures of the day.

"If you do," he said, "I will take measures to secure your dismissal from my house."

Perkins fervently promised, and on his return home said nothing until he got into the kitchen, where he found cook and Jiggles finishing their tea.

"Oh! here's Mister Himp again," said the cook.

Perkins, instead of replying in his usual impudent strain, smote his forehead and sat down in the attitude of one overwhelmed by despair.

"What is the matter with you?" asked the cook, who was always suspicious of some new trick.

"This place," replied Perkins, "is as good as broke."

"Broke!" exclaimed the cook and Jiggles together.

"Yes. Master's been and sent young Greene up in a balloon, hoping as how he'll break his neck," replied Perkins.

"Oh! come," said Jiggles, "that won't do. It's too strong. Me and cook saw the balloon go by this afternoon; but there was only one head in it as I could see."

"He was sent up by master, I tell you," returned Perkins; "and it's all on account of that filthy loocre."

"What do you mean?" asked the cook.

"I suppose you will say as you didn't know master and young Greene was related," said Perkins, scornfully.

"Never heard of it afore," said his listeners.

"Everybody in the house but you knows it," said

Perkins; "and closely related too. If young Greene's father dies without leaving a male issoo alive, all the property goes to the next of kid. Master's the next of kid, and now don't tell me that you don't see no reason for sending that poor boy up in a balloon. But don't you say a word. It'll all come out to-morrer, when they brings the body home."

Both the cook and Jiggles were very much upset, and the latter, who waited at dinner, behaved so strangely that his conduct could not fail to be marked. Standing behind his master he was seen to shake his fist surreptitiously at the reverend gentleman by Mrs. Cobbem, who cried out in a voice like the closing of a steel trap—

"Jiggles, what are you doing?"

"Me, mum? nothing, mum," replied Jiggles—"a kind o' twitching."

"Then don't twitch here, please, but attend to the table."

"Sherry, Jiggles, please," said the Reverend Copley.

Jiggles, with a trembling hand, poured out a glass, and retreating to his waiting position, murmured—

"And he can drink while that poor boy is a-lying in his gore perhaps."

"What are you saying, Jiggles?" asked the Reverend Copley.

"Nothing, sir, I assure you, sir."

"It is my opinion," said Mrs. Cobbem, "that you have been drinking."

"I had nothing but the husual beer, mum," replied Jiggles, emphatically, "and he must be a wery weak man to get drunk on *that*."

"Don't be impertinent."

"I am not, mum; I only speaks the trooth."

"Really, Jiggles," said the Reverend Copley, turning round in his chair, "this is very unusual conduct on your part. I trust you have not been taking a lesson from Perkins."

"Oh! no, sir," said Jiggles, "it's not that; but why was he sent up?"

The Reverend Copley flushed. He saw that Perkins had been revealing something, but knew not the whole dreadful truth.

"Bread, Jiggles," he said, hastily, but Mrs. Cobbem, who saw something was wrong, quickly struck in.

"Why was he sent up? Who and where was he sent to?"

"Oh! nothing, mum," said Jiggles, looking at his master with a fixed eye, "but I hear as *somebody* havo gone—been sent hup in a balloon."

CHAPTER LXII.

THE REVEREND COPLEY MAKES A CLEAN BREAST OF IT.

"THERE was a balloon ascent at Grippenham to-day, my love," said the Reverend Copley, with the face of a lily.

"I saw it go over," returned Mrs. Cobbem; "but why it should so affect Jiggles, and turn you so awfully white I cannot comprehend. There is some mystery here which requires explanation."

"Better speak the trooth, sir," said Jiggles, "and hease your mind."

"My mind is easy enough," replied the Rev. Copley, turning from white to red; "the fact is, Agatha, young Greene is somehow missing, but how it came about is a mystery."

"Aye!" groaned Jiggles, "that is the mystery."

"Jiggles," said his master, "go out of the room."

"Jiggles," said Mrs. Cobbem, "have the goodness to remain, and perhaps you will be able to supply some of the missing links of your master's story."

"There is no story, Agatha," said the Rev. Copley. "I left Greene and Perkins together, and they got into the grounds to see the balloon ascent, and by some means young Greene was lost."

"Were you there?" asked Mrs. Cobbem, turning on him a piercing eye.

"I—there?"

"Yes, you, Mr. Cobbem."

"In a measure, my dear, I was."

"In a measure!" repeated Mrs. Cobbem, scornfully. "What do you mean by that?"

"Well, you see, Agatha," replied the Rev. Copley, "when a man has the mind of the young to cultivate, it is necessary to—a—a—know a little of—everything—to study in short—to know, in fact—ah—"

"Oh! I have no patience with you. Now come to the point, and tell me what has happened to-day. Something is wrong I know."

The reverend gentlemen was driven into a corner, and there was only one way out of it, to tell the truth.

"My love," he said, "by some mishap young Greene got into the car, and he has gone up in the balloon."

For a moment Mrs. Cobbem was unable to speak. Many strange things had happened to that unfortunate boy, but never aught like this. For once, at least, in her lifetime, she was fairly taken aback, and could only repeat—

"Up in a balloon!"

"Oh! yes, mum," proceeded Jiggles. "It's all true, although it's given to lying he is, which is the froots of a bad bringings up."

"What new impertinence is this?" asked the Rev. Copley, "how dare you, you scoundrel, charge me with being untruthful at any time!"

"Which it was Perkins I referred to, sir," replied Jiggles; "but although a liar, there's worse crimes."

"He *has* been drinking," said Mrs. Cobbem; "put him out of the room."

Jiggles left without much persuasion, for he was glad to get out of what he told the cook was a "chamber of 'orrors," where a man hitherto supposed to be meek and mild, and was a trained clergyman, could eat roast mutton and red currant jelly after compassing the death of an unfortunate boy, who stood between him and a considerable amount of property.

Left with his wife the Reverend Copley told all he had to tell, and Mrs. Cobbem listened with a quiet sarcastic expression of countenance, which showed she considered her husband the author of it all.

"And now the only question is," said he in conclusion, "what has become of the boy?"

"I think," replied Mrs. Cobbem, "that you ought to go out and see."

"Go where and see what, Agatha?"

"Oh! of course I am to guide you in this as I do in everything else," replied his wife. "Oh! you men, what addle-headed fools you are! Go to Grippenham of course, where you will hear some account of the balloon."

"I have left word with my friend Stingem to send me news as soon as he hears anything," replied the Reverend Copley, "and I fancy the messenger has arrived."

There was a ring at the bell, and it proved to be the messenger—one of the clerks of the office, who had driven over. The intelligence he brought was not at all satisfactory, being to the effect that the balloon and aëronaut were all right, but young Greene had jumped out of the car, and nothing was known of his fate.

The clerk delivered this message in the dining-room. Jiggles, standing unnoticed against the door, heard it, and uttered a loud groan.

His master turned upon him, but he rushed away into the kitchen, where he made the following announcement to the cook and Perkins—

"Young Greene's been thrown out of the car and bashed to bits, and master will rob him of his property."

It was now the turn of Perkins to be troubled, and with a face like a turnip he asked Jiggles if he was joking.

"Not I," replied Jiggles. "There is a young

man from the lawyer's office in the dining-room. He brought the news, and he says they were going to print off some fifty bills, offering a reward of a hundred pounds for the murderer."

"Oh!" cried Perkins, and beat a retreat to his own apartment, where he sat down upon an empty claret case, and shivered with fear.

He had never expected any harm would have come of the balloon business, beyond a scare for young Greene, and now, here was news telling of the poor boy's death, and one hundred pounds offered for the arrest of his murderer.

Who was that murderer?

Perkins if anybody, and he knew it.

There was precious little jocularity in him as he sat in his private scullery dwelling upon the probable consequence of his little practical joke. Grim visions of the scaffold and the hangman uprose before him, and wail after wail escaped his lips.

Then came the thought, should he run away? If so, where to?

Dim ideas of getting on board some ship, and going far away to some lone isle, floated across his mind. But he did not know where to find the vessel, and besides, the police were everywhere, and would most infallibly apprehend him.

It was a dreadful fix to be in, and Perkins groaned and groaned again.

Nor was his the only breast perturbed. The news getting into the schoolroom, Billy Sharp was much discomposed. With the death of Jolly his occupation would be gone, for it was not likely the Greenes would keep him there, unless—oh! happy thought—they adopted him.

"Not werry likely," thought Billy; "but if they does, I shall bless that balloon as long as I live."

He was a young brute by nature, as he came of a bad stock, and no doubt his life upon the streets had hardened him, but yet he felt a *little* unselfish sorrow over the recorded fate of young Jolly.

Many of the boys spoke regretfully and even tearfully of their missing comrade. He was never very chummy, but he was at the same time very harmless. Greene never injured anybody wilfully, although he was constantly doing something to bring trouble upon himself and others. There was very little of the usual skylarking going on in the house that night.

The clerk who came from Grippenham having been regaled, was sent back again, and the Rev. Copley, with the aid of his wife, concocted a tale to be told to the Greenes. Meanwhile, the clerk bore away a telegram to Grippenham, from whence it was to be despatched to London, asking the afflicted parents to come immediately.

It reached town by nine o'clock, and the afflicted parents left at once by the night mail, and arrived at the station in the middle of the night. As no conveyance could be had, they walked to the White Hart and knocked up the landlord, who let them in and roused a housemaid to light a fire.

"I must have a cup of tea," said Mrs. Greene, "for I'm in a dead faint. Then we will go on, my love."

"Let us read that ere telegram again," said Mr. Greene, taking it's from his pocket. "Come at once,—your son is missing. Has, we fear, injured himself seriously by a fall."

"Is that the young gentleman named Greene?" asked the housemaid, who was blowing up the fire.

"Yes," said Mrs. Greene.

"Then he had a big fall—he had," said the girl.

"You seem to know all about it."

"Yes, ma'am," replied the housemaid, "we had Mister Jiggles from the college over here last night, and he told us all about it. Mister Copley put him in the car, and he fell out of the balloon; but if he gets his rights, it won't be the property."

"My Jolly sent up in a balloon," screamed Mrs. Greene.

"Yes 'um, and fell through the clouds, and come down bang, and was bashed into bits."

What could Mrs. Greene do now but go off? And accordingly she went into hysterics, and got the whole house up in no time. Gin and peppermint brought her through, but she could not walk to the college, and the chaise, repaired after that night with the Rev. Copley, was brought round to the door.

At half-past six the Rev. Copley was roused from a troubled sleep to go downstairs and face those afflicted parents. They were in the breakfast-room, where Jiggles was dusting about in the most unconcerned manner, and not the least inclined to listen to anything that did not concern him—certainly not.

CHAPTER LXIII.
HOLLOA, BOYS!

"GOOD morning, Mrs. Greene, I hope you are well." It was a mere customary form of speech, but it enraged Mrs. Greene more than scoffing openly at her would have done. And we do not wonder at it.

"You villain!" she said, shaking [ ] umbrella at him, "how dare you send him up in a balloon? Give me back my murdered boy."

"Mariar," said Mr. Greene, "hendeavour to be calm while I talk to this party afore I hands him over to the police. Mister Cobbem!"

"Sir," said that astonished gentleman.

"We have hevidence that you put our child into the car of that balloon, and—"

"Stay," said the Rev. Copley, "before you proceed let me ask what evidence."

"The 'ousemaid of the White Hart, who had it from your man Jiggles."

"Who had the hinformation straight from Perkins," said Jiggles, stopping suddenly in his work, and facing about to defend himself, "which he see you do it, and is ready to swear to it."

"Fetch that boy here," said the Reverend Copley; "but do not tell him what he is wanted for, or he will concoct another string of abominable lies."

Perkins was cleaning boots, or trying to do so, but with his mind in such a troubled state a polish was out of the question. Jiggles found him pale, hollow-eyed, and with every appearance of having passed a sleepless night.

"Perkins," said Jiggles, "you are wanted."

"Wanted?" said Perkins.

"Yes, a strange gentleman in the breakfast-room. Come on."

"Oh! don't take me!" cried Perkins, falling on his knees, to the infinite amazement of Jiggles; "I didn't go for to do it, and I never knowed the balloon chap was ready, or I wouldn't have shoved him in."

"Perkins," cried Jiggles, seizing him by the collar, "what is this?"

"I—I—shoved young Greene into the car," replied Perkins.

Jiggles let go his hold and staggered up against the wall, where he remained for full half a minute, glaring at Perkins as if he had just discovered some hideous reptile fresh from a cavern in the bowels of the earth.

"Oh, villain!" he said, at last; "but I've a dooty to perform. Come away to the justices."

Sobbing bitterly, Perkins was led into the breakfast room, where he made a full confession, and was then and there publicly thrashed. Jiggles was admonished not to listen to his idle tales again, and the Reverend Copley gave to the Greenes his version of the day's disaster.

"In a few hours," he said, "we shall have all the sad history. Messages have been despatched all over the country, and I am hourly expecting to have a full account of the terrible mishap."

"My poor—poor—Jolly!" sobbed Mrs. Greene, "Oh! what an awful thing!"

Such consolation as could be offered was tendered her. Mrs. Cobbem came down, and in the presence of such deep grief was a changed woman. There was, indeed, a silence and a sadness over the whole house which nothing but the visage of death could have planted there. Jolly was believed to be dead, and the whole house mourned.

At eight o'clock breakfast was served, and the boys came in to partake of it. They ate much less than usual, and talked in undertones as they looked at a vacant chair.

"Poor Jolly!" was whispered round a dozen times, and all that could be thought of in a kindly way was said.

The party in the breakfast-room was the saddest of all, for there a parent's grief was to be seen. Absurd as Mr. and Mrs. Greene might have been in their everyday life, only a brute would have thought of smiling at them now. Hand in hand they sat, shedding tears and exchanging reminiscences of their lost child.

A shout outside drew the attention of all assembled there, and the Reverend Copley through the window beheld a party of yokels advancing with a strange fantastic figure in a basket. A noisy party it was, and even at that early hour must have been making merry.

Goggles and the oldest inhabitant, dressed in roughly-made garlands, came in front, next the guy for such indeed it was, and in the rear a worthy assemblage of general followers.

"Good gracious," exclaimed the Reverend Copley, "this is the fifth of November. I had forgotten it. Much as I love old institutions such as these, this is no time for revelry, and these men must depart."

"Go out then and set them going," said Mrs. Copley, and her husband hurried out hatless.

She saw him check the procession a few yards from the house, and heard their shouts of derision as he bade them go away. The guy, too, a spare living figure with blackened face and hideous sack-cloth attire, appeared to speak to him and tossed it's arms seemingly in derision.

"The cold, brutal, heartless monsters," said Mrs. Cobbem; "they ought to be hanged."

Mrs. Greene's eyes were turned upon the scene, and the words of Mrs. Cobbem passed unheeded. Suddenly Mr. Greene felt himself clutched by the hair at the side of his head, and the voice of his spouse shrieked in his ear—

"That's our Jolly!"

CHAPTER LXIV.

EXPLANATIONS AND REJOICINGS.

IN the early part of life—in my infant days in fact—I have many and many a time cried over the story of a little boy who was stolen and recognised after a lapse of years by his mother, whose maternal instincts enabled her to recognise her child through the garb of a sweep. Soot could not disguise him from one who had held him to her heart and examined each feature a thousand times.

It must, in my opinion, have been maternal instinct, and maternal instinct alone, that enabled Mrs. Greene to recognise Jolly through the disguises which some hand or hands had put upon him. He was clothed in sackcloth, his face was as black as the nigger's on whose countenance it is recorded a piece of charcoal made a *white* mark; there was a wreath of corn and poppies about his brow, and in his hand he carried an enormous carrot, supposed to do duty for a sceptre.

Yet through all his mother knew him.

As soon as the words "That's our Jolly!" escaped her lips, both she and her husband, acting upon a common impulse, made for the door, and darted out into the thick of the Guy Fawkes group.

"You villains!" cried Mr. Greene, and with the family umbrella, which he had instinctively grasped as he left the room, he gave Goggles and the oldest inhabitant each a blow upon the head that took the fun out of them for at least five minutes, and while

Mrs. Greene seized her child and dragged him with sobs and tears from his perch, her husband made a general onslaught upon the crowd, and did much execution, even to striking the Reverend Copley in his blind rage, and treating him to a cheap public daylight illumination.

Mrs. Greene bore Jolly indoors, and, all accoutred as he was, laid him down upon the sofa in the drawing-room, and hugged him and cried over him until the black ran off his face and left indelible traces upon Mrs. Cobbem's chintz covering.

"Oh! my poor boy—my Jolly—how came they to serve you in this way?"

"Harvesh home, mar," murmured Jolly, and there was a mildness in his general look which seemed to indicate that he had been joining in the festivity alluded to.

"Harvest home!" exclaimed the mother; "I thought all such rubbish was over months ago."

"They are kept late here," said Mrs. Cobbem; "but I cannot see how your son can have been to one. Let him explain."

"He is overcome with fatigue," cried his mother; "he is almost speechless. Oh, my Jolly!"

"Harvesh home," said Jolly, again; "great fun. Old Mister Grumpy say we have larsh with old Cobby."

"He is ill—he his dying!" cried Mrs. Greene.

"No, he only wants sleep," said Mrs. Cobbem, calmly; "let us leave him here."

"But he must be washed."

"Let him be washed by-and-bye. For the present a little sleep will do him good. When he awakes he can tell us how he came in this plight."

Meanwhile the Reverend Copley Cobbem and Mr. Greene assailed the mob, and their arms being nerved by truth and justice, they very much prevailed. The whole party was driven out, leaving their fifth of November, from their guy downwards, behind them. Goggles and the old un took away more than they brought, in the shape of a pair of broken heads; otherwise there was no sport.

While Jolly slept his mother watched over him with a fondness above soot, sacking, and corn wreaths, and when he awoke he told his story. The substance of it here follows—

We left him, it will be remembered in a very perilous position, hanging outside the car, with the aëronaut holding on to the collar of his coat with the tenacity of despair.

The man's coolness, however, did not entirely fail him, and a means of redeeming himself from his present predicament came to his mind. Holding Jolly with one hand, he groped about with the other for the rope of the safety-valve, got hold of it, and tugged away furiously.

The gas rushed out with big sobs, and in a second they were in the cloud again, shooting down through it like a falling rocket-stick. Down, down at a terrific pace—Jolly, with staring eyes, seeing the earth apparently rushing up towards him, and all objects beneath growing and expanding at an alarming rate. Down, down, to within a couple of hundred feet of the earth, when the safety valve was closed, and the pace of the downward rush considerably lessened.

If ever the skill of man was fully taxed, it was just then; but the aëronaut was equal to the occasion. Just as the car was about to touch the earth he let go of Jolly Greene, and the machine, lightened of the boy's weight, sprang into the air again, and drifted far away out of sight.

And Jolly lay upon his back in a state of amazement, such as in the whole course of his eventful life he had never known before, and he was still lying dazed, when some half-dozen yokels, who had followed the balloon over two fields, came up to see if he was injured.

"Be ye hurt, measter?" asked the foremost, but Jolly, with his eyes fixed in the direction the balloon had gone, neither heeded nor answered him-

GREEN AS GRASS.

A JOLLY SCHOOL STORY.

A GHOSTLY HEAD APPEARED OVER THE TOP OF THE DOOR GLARING DOWN ON MR. AND MRS. GREENE.

"He ha' got a mortial hurt," said another, and among themselves they debated how to get him to a place where his supposed injuries would be attended to.

The yokels were four in number, and they were all a little flushed in the face, partly on account of their having followed the balloon at country racing pace, and partly in consequence of that being a festal day.

"Ha' ye got any bones broke?" asked one.

Still no answer. Jolly's eyes remained fixed aloft, and his lips moved, but nothing more.

"Let us get 'im to the farm," said another. "Here be a potatoe-basket and a pole. Let us carry 'im whoam that way."

So they got the pole and the basket and put him into it, and moved on. Ere they had travelled a hundred yards, Jolly awoke from his trance, and asked for his everlasting "mar." That lady, not being forthcoming, he wanted to get out of the basket and go and find her, but this the yokels would not permit.

"Noa, noa!" said one, who appeared to be a wag among them, "it ain't orten as we get a wisiter from the clouds, and we mean to ha' ye at our harvest whoam that's comin' off to night. You sit still and we'll carry ye there."

And in rude triumphant percession they bore him off to their rustic feast.

That feast turned out to be at Job Grumper's, where, as we know, he could hardly expect to meet with a friendly reception if he was recognised as a "Warminter."

Recognised he was at once; but Job was in a humorous mood, and he resolved to entertain his guest courteously. He pressed him to eat and drink, particularly to drink, and Jolly, who had received no real injury, soon became merry with his new-found friends.

They kept him there all night, and just about dawn somebody said it was "Guy day," the fifth of November, and Job Grumper then and there hit off an idea that was for long after considered the most brilliant one of the age.

"This chap must go back," he said, pointing to Jolly, who was asleep in a corner; "and he be too tired to walk, so let us take un back as a guy."

That idea was acted upon, and on the way to the college they picked up Goggles, the oldest inhabitant, and sundry other people, who helped to make an imposing procession, which, however, was entirely routed and destroyed by the vigorous onslaught made by the Reverend Copley Cobbem and Mr. Greene.

It took a long time to get the black off Jolly, for he unnatural monster had painted him with grease and soot, and his ears and eyes were almost stopped up with it; but the maternal hand and arm, combined with hot water and soap, got him pretty clean at last, and great was the general rejoicing.

Mr. and Mrs. Greene, in the fulness of their heart at getting their son again, "shelled out" amazingly, and all the fireworks in the village were bought right away, also a load of faggots for a bonfire, and the skilful hands of Dick Stager and his brother built up a capital resemblance of Job Grumper for the burning.

Mr. Greene also undertook to defend the action brought by Goggles and the old un, and to send down a detective to fathom the five-pound note business, "Which can easily be done," he said, "as I can get the number from my banker and thus trace it."

The evening was a jolly one. Fine weather, a heap of fireworks, and a glorious bonfire kept up the spirits of the boys, and Jiggles looking on, said it made him feel quite young again.

Perkins, however, only caught a glimpse of the proceedings through the grated window of the scullery, where Mrs. Cobbem locked him up to pass the night as a punishment for his deliberate false-hoods. But Dick Stager passing by heard a piteous voice, "Chuck us a cracker, do," and gave him a few fireworks to let off in his prison-house, and with these he singed his hair and set fire to a heap of dusters, which, smouldering, nearly choked him before he found out they were ignited.

"It is a pleasing sight," said the Reverend Copley, as he drank his wine at dinner; "a very pleasing sight, Mr. Greene, to see how Protestant the country is, and how it still looks with abhorrence upon the dastardly attempt upon our dear old monarch, James."

"I suppose they did try it on?" said Mr. Greene.

"No doubt of it, my dear sir. It is in history; but what were you saying just now about a house?"

"I think I shall take one near this school if I can, and come and live down here."

"My dear sir!" said the Reverend Copley, warmly, "I shall be delighted to hail you as a neighbour."

"And it will be nice for you and me," said Mrs. Greene, addressing Mrs. Cobbem, "to drop in on one another and have a cup of tea together."

"Oh! yes—no doubt," replied Mrs. Cobbem, a little stiffly, "although I think four o'clock tea a pernicious meal."

"Then," said Mrs. Greene, amiably, "we will have it at five, and if the two gentlemen don't like tea they can have a pipe together. It will be quite jolly, I am sure."

*   *   *   *   *   *

It was a great idea which Mr. Greene had of coming to live near the school, and it gave much satisfaction to both his wife and son.

"It will be so nice to be able to see Jolly every day," thought Mrs. Greene.

"I shall always be able to get money out of my mar now," thought Jolly.

Houses in the country are not easily got, but it so happened there was one to let close to the Puddle Taylors, of the dimensions suitable for the Greene family. Mr. Greene took it at once, and employed a local jobbing builder to clean and paint and repair it. Then he and Mrs. Greene went to London, promising to come down and take up their abode in a month.

One day Jolly and Billy Sharp Popper took advantage of a half-holiday to have a look at the new house, and on the way they met Perkins, who had been on a journey to the village, and was slowly and painfully returning home, burdened with half a dozen stay-laces for his mistress, and half a quire of notepaper for the cook.

"Hallo!" he said affably, "going out?"

"I am going to look at my new house," replied Jolly.

"Then I'll go too," said Perkins, readily, "and give you my opinion of it."

"Oh! but won't you be wanted at home?" asked Jolly, who would rather have been without him.

"No doubt I shall," replied Perkins, "but it's nothing new. They must wait. I aint a born slave to be run off my legs for everybody. Besides, if I did, it would be all the same. Do whatever I does, I am sure to catch it from Mrs. Cobbem."

There was a little truth in this declaration. Mrs. Cobbem showed him little mercy, and it will be generally admitted he did not deserve it. Perhaps he would have been a better boy if he had been more considerately treated, and there was his workhouse training in the background, which was not a good foundation to build a life upon.

They went to Jolly's house, where a number of workmen were busy cleaning and painting and repairing, and Perkins surveyed the house from top to bottom, and criticised the labours of those engaged there.

The grounds—which were very extensive—were next the object of attention, and Perkins pointed out to Jolly where to erect a "marky" when he gave a dinner party, and where to put the band for them "as chooses to have a kick-up;" and, having run through the greenhouses, they started for home. Now, there are [some people born to ill-luck, on whom misfortune waits as an untiring attendant. Jolly Greene was one of them, and Coddles, the Puddle Taylor page, was another—as we shall show.

CHAPTER LXV.

A FIGHT INDEED!

CODDLES did not often get out for a walk, but when he did he always met his mortal foe, Perkins, who never failed to harass him most terribly.

Even now, when starting forth on an errand, he fell in with his old foe. Always a good boy in the execution of errands, Coddles felt the harassing attacks of his enemy, as they made him longer on the road than he otherwise would have been; and, catching sight of Perkins advancing, he put up his arm instinctively, and cried—

"Come now—you let me alone. I am in a hurry."

"Let you alone! Oh, yes! that's a good un," said Perkins, "Put down that basket and fight. I niver did see a feller like you—all paste; and it comes about because you won't take exercise."

"Master says he will have you locked up if you don't leave me alone," said Coddles, backing into the road.

"I'll have your master taken off the bench," returned Perkins, sternly. "Let you alone, indeed! I like that! Am I to be robbed of my hordinary amusement by that bloated tyrant? Niver!"

Coddles had backed up against a heap of mud-scrapings from the road, and Perkins making a feint as if he would hit him, he started back and sat into it. Even Jolly Greene was amused at this, and went into a roar of laughter. Perkins and Billy performed a dance of ecstacy.

It was bad enough to be laughed at by those he was afraid of; but Coddles was decidedly averse to being grinned at by one whom he was not at all in fear of, and, scrambling to his feet, he put down his basket and stepped up to Jolly Greene.

"What are you laughing at, you fool?" he asked.

"I'm laughing at you," replied Jolly, with spirit; "and don't you call me a fool or I'll knock you down."

"Good again!" said Perkins, and clapped his hands rapturously.

"He's a-coming out," said Billy. "Go at him, Jolly. We'll back you up."

"I can't fight everybody," said Coddles, with a shiver.

"Nobody axed you to," returned Perkins, "but you'll have to fight Master Greene. Now go at him."

Coddles was a little startled at finding himself defied, but having a knowledge of Jolly Greene he did not hesitate about pitching into him, and putting down his basket he went for him.

Jolly stood his ground.

"Good again," said Perkins.

"Prime," remarked Billy.

It was a fight indeed. In after years it was talked of by those who witnessed it and those who heard the story of it afterwards.

Coddles, exasperated by long suffering, and imbued with the notion of having an easy victim to deal with, fought his best, and Jolly, excited with the novelty of a contest, brought all the pugilism of his nature to bear upon the hour.

Neither of the combatants could be considered pugilists by those who understood the art of boxing. They had no defence, no regular mode of attack, but gave and took in a wild blindfold fashion, which was more amusing than the most scientific display possibly could have been.

Coddles wore a tall hat a little too big for him, and this was the principal point attacked by Jolly, who, distrusting the ordinary mode of hitting out straight, made circles in the air with his hands, and whenever Coddles got in the way his fist came down upon the crown of that hat with a noise like the beating of a drum.

The result of this mode of assault was that Coddles' hat was gradually beaten down over his eyes, and shut out all objects from his view. He was as helpless as the principal figure in the game of blind man's buff, but still he fought on, and dealt stinging blows whenever Jolly kindly and considerately put himself in the right place to receive them.

It ought to be said that as far as seeing went the pair were pretty equal, for Jolly for the most part kept his eyes shut, and placed himself in the hands of fate.

Fate was kind to him, and although he came into the possession of some pugilistic property in the form of two black eyes and a nose like an Orleans plum, he came off victorious.

That hat of Coddles was perhaps the main cause of his downfall, for it got past his eyes, over his nose, and finally, in a smashed condition, covered his mouth. On the verge of stifling he fell upon his back in the road and uttered smothered howls of mercy.

Jolly, too much absorbed in working his arms, was unconscious of what had befallen his foe, until he fell over him, but Billy had him up and in his arms in a moment, and there he remained working his arms, until Perkins pinioned them to his side, and compelled him to desist.

"It's all over," he said, "you've won. Rool Britanniar!"

Jolly opened his eyes, and looked upon his fallen foe, who was still engaged in getting off his hat—a process which appeared to be a slow one, for his nose and eyes were still beneath it. He could breathe, and his life was safe, and that was all.

"Did I knock him down there?" asked Jolly.

"You did," replied Billy Sharpe. "Tom Crib couldn't have done it better. He's done for!"

"But I haven't killed him, I hope," said Jolly, anxiously.

"Oh, no! he'll come round by-and-bye. Come on, you Champion of England. Let us get home and put something on your eyes. They are swelling up tremenjously."

"I can hardly see out of the right one," said Jolly.

"And you won't see out of either long if you ain't sharp."

They left Coddles in the road, and Perkins took one arm and Billy the other, but ere they reached the college-gate, Jolly was as blind as a bat.

"Here's a go!" said Perkins, "but I can't show in it. Where's my little parcel?"

"You put it down in the road," replied Billy. "Didn't you take it up again?"

"You know I didn't," said Perkins, savagely; "here's a go! I must run back. You had better take this noble 'ero into my pantry, and pu this head under the tap. Cold water is as good as anything now."

CHAPTER LXVI.

WHAT HAS BECOME OF GREENE?

BILLY SHARP lost no time in getting Jolly into the house by the back way, and having a good knowledge of the place, he reached the pantry, or boothole, as it ought to have been called by Perkins, without being observed.

"You put your head here," said Billy, "under the tap, and I'll set it a-running. Now keep it there, and I'll look for a towel."

He looked all over the place, but not a vestige of one could be seen, and bidding Jolly keep his head in the position he had placed it in, he ran upstairs to get one from his bedroom. On the top of the stairs he met the Rev. Copley Cobbem.

"Ha! Popper," he said, "just the very boy I

want. I have been looking for you. Where have you been?"

"With Greene, sir, to look over his house," replied Billy.

"It was my intention to have kept you in for an hour to have examined you in geography," said the Reverend Copley. "Yes, I perceive you are lamentably deficient in that branch of learning. Come into my room and I will instruct you a little. I have globes there which are of immense assistance to young beginners."

Billy dared not disobey, nor say anything about where he had left Jolly Greene.

It was a very trying lesson that. Billy, with thoughts far away, answered the questions put to him in the wildest manner. He said that Austria was the capital of Australia, and declared the United States to be in the Bosphorus, and nearly lengthened his studies to double the duration they would otherwise have been.

At last he was released and hurried downstairs, where he saw Perkins with tears of agony in his eyes. He and Mrs. Cobbem had been settling accounts over his long absence.

"Hallo! Perky, seen young Greene?"

"No."

"Aint he in your pantry?"

"No—haven't seen him."

"Must have gone up to his room," thought Billy, and hurried upstairs. He was not there, nor was there any sign of his late presence. Down to the schoolroom—no Jolly there; into the play-ground, and every place he was likely to have been, but no sign of his lost friend could he find.

"Where's he got to now?" asked Billy; "he must be as good as blind, and can't have run away in that state."

The bell rang for tea, and Billy of necessity went. Jolly's vacant chair was soon noticed, and the usher, who presided at the meal, asked where he was.

"He went out with me, sir," replied Billy, "and we came in together."

"And where have you been since?"

"Having a lesson on jography with Mr. Cobbem, sir."

"And you did not see Greene afterwards?"

"No, sir."

The report of his absence was sent in to the Reverend Copley at once, and was delivered just in time to spoil his dinner.

"That boy again," said Mrs. Cobbem; "what has become of him?"

"I don't know, my dear," replied her husband; "but I will see after dinner."

"No, Mr. Cobbem, that will not do. The boy ought to be found at once."

"But he is perpetually being lost and found again, Agatha."

"He may be lost for good now, for all we know. Go and find him."

Accustomed to obey, the Reverend Copley departed, and had the whole school brought before him. Billy confessed to their having been out and coming in together, but he said nothing about where he left him, nor of his manful encounter with Coddles. Perkins was not questioned as he was not even suspected of having been in his company.

"Has the house been searched?"

"Yes, the house has been searched," replied the tutor, "in all likely places."

"Then he must have gone out again," said the Reverend Copley.

A number of the most active boys were told off to scour the neighbourhood, and, delighted with their mission, they started off, and the reverend gentleman went back to his dinner, which had grown cold in the meantime.

"I fear, Agatha," he said, "that boy is lost."

"He will be the ruin of the college in the end," replied Mrs. Copley. "He seems born to get into trouble and to give trouble."

"His lot, like that of many others," said her husband, with a sigh, "is cast in stony places."

Mrs. Cobbem cast a quick glance at him, and, smiling sarcastically, went on with her dinner.

The scouts returned, bringing no tidings of the lost one, and the night grew on apace. A messenger was sent to the police, but the Reverend Copley decided upon not communicating with his parents until the morning.

"I wonder where he is?" was the Reverend Copley's constant comment. "He must be outside, for why should the boy skulk or hide about the house?"

"What has become of young Greene?" was asked all that eve, and when the hour for retiring came it was still in every mouth.

CHAPTER LXVII.

PERKINS HEARS A GHOST.

"PLEASE, ma'am, it is ten o'clock," said Perkins, as he brought in the usual candlestick.

"Have you cleaned your knives and forks?" asked Mrs. Cobbem.

Perkins hesitated a moment, and then said—

"Yes, ma'am."

"Bring them here, and let me see them."

The face of Perkins turned white and red, and there was a faltering on his tongue as he asked—

"Do you mean the reg'lar knives and forks?"

"Of course I do," said his mistress, tartly.

"Then," said Perkins, as if enlightened on an important point, "I haven't cleaned them."

"Go and do them at once," said Mrs. Cobbem, rising, "and when done bring them here for me to look over."

Perkins guessed she was coming at him, and fled away to his pantry.

There he turned out about a bushel of knives and forks, got out his board and Bath-brick, and, with bitterness in his heart, began his distasteful labour.

"I wish I was dead—I do," he muttered. "I may die if I don't. There niver was a nigger treated as I am. I wish that old woman was dead too."

He began his work, rubbing a knife upon the board with a violence that threatened to clean it all away, and rubbed and rubbed until he was obliged to pause for breath.

"That's one on 'em," he said, and threw it savagely at the basket.

It missed the usual receptacle, and stuck into the floor, where it stood upright quivering. At the same moment, and apparently from the very spot, there arose a deep groan.

"Oh! who is that?" asked Perkins, feeling his flesh creeping. "Come, no larks—don't go to frighten a chap. Come out, whoever you are."

The pantry was large and gloomy, and Mrs. Cobbem only allowed the smallest and cheapest cotton candle for pantry use, and the one by which Perkins was now working failed to light up a third of it. It was an odd-shaped place, and there were at least half a dozen dark corners suitable for any sort of ghost.

"Come now," said Perkins again, "no larks, or you'll get it. I wonder if it's Jiggles. Anyhow, I aint going to let him get a rise out of me."

And Perkins, to show how little he was afraid, began to sing—

"Ri fol, de riddle lol, so early in the mo-orning, so early in the mo-o-orning, afore the break of——"

"Oh-h-h!"

It was a groan indeed that came to his ears, and it appeared to come from the floor just where the knife was still sticking. And the floor itself rose up and creaked, as if some spirit imprisoned beneath it was seeking to get free.

Perkins waited ro longer, but, with every hair of his head stiffened, he dashed out of the place into the kitchen, where he came upon Jiggles bidding the cook good-night in an attitude that left no doubt as to the amiable relations between them.

"I'll knock your head off!" began Jiggles, wrathfully. "What do you mean by coming into the kitchen like a lunatic?"

"A ghost—a ghost!" replied Perkins, with staring eyes.

"Where?" asked Jiggles.

"Under the floor of my pantry. Come and hear it groan."

"I think master ought to know about it," said Jiggles.

"But surely, Mister Jiggles, you are not afraid," said the cook.

"Oh, no!" replied Jiggles; "it is only some trick of this boy's. Let us all go."

Perkins put them in front, and they all went to the pantry, where the aforesaid cotton candle was burning, with a wick shaped like a mushroom. It was as much as they could see half-way across the place.

"Now where is that ghost?" asked Jiggles; "here, come out you, sir, and show yourself!"

"Oh-h-h!"

"Good 'ivens!" exclaimed the cook, and throwing her arms around Jiggles, checked him in a precipitate retreat.

"I told you so," said Perkins, "but you wouldn't believe me. There it is again."

The groan that now burst on their ears was really something awful, and stouter hearts than any of the three could boast of would have quailed at the sound. Jiggles simply lost all use of his legs, and sank upon his knees, with the cook, a mighty incumbrance, round his neck.

Perkins stood up against the wall, stiff with horror.

"It's real!" gasped Jiggles. "Oh! Perkins, why did you bring us here? This will be the death of cook. I'll go for master."

"No, I'll go," said Perkins.

"Let us all go," suggested the cook, and they all went.

The Rev. Copley was sitting up with his wife, debating the absence of young Greene, and was speaking mournfully of his probably untimely end when the door opened, and Perkins, Jiggles, and the cook came in together. It was a tight fit in the doorway, and Perkins being between the other two, had half the breath squeezed out of his body.

"A ghost, sir," they said together, "in the pantry."

"A ghost—nonsense!" replied the Reverend Copley. "Go away; I am busily engaged with Mrs. Cobbem."

"It's true, sir," said Jiggles, whose face bore testimony of his sufferings. "Do come and hear it, sir. It's awful!"

"Really——"

"Why don't you go?" said Mrs. Cobbem.

He went then, and heard two groans which made his hair as stiff as the others, and he also saw the floor lift up a little, as if the ghost was trying to get out. It was a horrible sight, and he trembled visibly.

"Stay here," he said, "and I will fetch Mrs. Cobbem."

But this would not do. They dare not be left, and the whole party went back to Mrs. Cobbem. Swollen to the number of five they came to the pantry again.

Mrs. Cobbem, with a sarcastic smile upon her face, said—

"Where is it?"

"Be quiet, Agatha, a moment, and you will hear."

"Oh-h-h!"

"You hear that, Agatha?"

"Oh, yes," she said, calmly, "I hear it. What of that?"

"But, my love, have you no fears? Do you not tremble in the presence of the invisible?"

"Invisible, but not unknown," she said. "It's that booby, Greene."

"Now, my dear, how can that possibly be he?"

"Go in one of those cupboards. Look for him."

The pantry, like the rest of the college, was very old, and in it there were the innumerable cupboards which our forefathers were wont to make, and no doubt fondly loved.

The solution of the mystery as regards the sound appeared to be at hand.

The cupboards in question, it may be said, were never used, and seldom if ever opened. Perkins looked into them occasionally in the daytime, and that was all. They were roomy affairs, some of them half the size of a drawing-room in a Camberwell "villa."

"Show a light here," said the Reverend Copley, opening a door. "Now this appears to be a large cupboard, but he is not here—oh!" and suddenly, to the amazement of all but Perkins, he disappeared.

"That's the cupboard," he said, "where there's no floor to it."

"Give a light here," said Mrs. Cobbem, snatching the candle impatiently from Jiggles. Advancing she looked down and saw her beloved husband about three feet down, blinking and sneezing on a bed of dust which must have taken a score years to accumulate.

"Good gracious!" she exclaimed, "I had no idea of this."

"Have I fallen, or is the house down?" asked the Reverend Copley, with a bewildered stare around him.

"Don't ask foolish questions," replied Mrs. Copley, "but get up and help that boy out. He is groping among the foundations of the house."

It was indeed Jolly who lay beneath the flooring, and hearing voices he came groaning towards them on his hands and knees, and turning up dust enough to smother one.

The Reverend Copley got him out, blind and covered with dust and cobwebs—a strange, pitiful object, that would have melted a heart of stone.

"Why didn't you come before, Billy?" he asked; "I fell through the floor. Oh! what would my mar say?"

"It is fortunate for both of us," said the Reverend Copley, trying to look cheerful, "that we only fell into the foundation of the house, instead of into a cellar. We might have broken our necks."

"I don't know that it would have mattered much," said his spouse; "but what is the matter with this boy's eyes?"

"That's not Billy speaking," said Jolly; "who is it?"

"How came you in this state?" asked Mrs. Cobbem.

"I opened the door to go into the passage, and the floor fell in," replied Jolly. "I've been feeling about ever so long. Oh, dear!—oh, dear!"

"But your fall didn't blind you. I am Mrs Cobbem—speak."

"I was hit about the eyes in a fight," replied Jolly, trembling before that awful presence. "Perkins and Billy know all about it."

"That's right," said Perkins, from the rear, "shove it all on me."

"I knew you were at the bottom of it," said Mrs. Cobbem, shaking an angry hand at him. "Mr. Cobbem, why don't you get rid of this low boy?"

"I will call upon the authorities to-morrow," said Mr. Cobbem; "meanwhile, don't you think Greene would be better for a wash?"

"Of course he would. Jiggles, get the bath-room ready, and when he is washed put him to bed, and let him have a cold poultice over his eyes."

These orders were faithfully obeyed, and Billy Sharp had once more the gratification of his friend's society by half-past twelve o'clock. By one all the house, except Perkins, was in repose, and he was lying awake wondering whether Mr. Cobbem would really call upon the parish authorites, and have him taken to the dreadful home of his infancy again.

CHAPTER LXVIII.

GOGGLES BROUGHT TO BAY.

THE last adventure of Jolly Greene secured him from the toils of the schoolroom during the next day. He could see just a little on the following morning, and would have been better out and about, but Mrs. Cobbem, who loved to make the boys feel the sinfulness of being sick, insisted upon his lying in bed.

Early in the morning the Reverend Copley Cobbem, having, as everybody will admit, given Perkins a fair trial, had his horse put into the trap, and drove over to the workhouse to know on what terms they would take their precious boy again. The guardians were sitting, and the reverend gentleman being much respected, was granted an audience at once.

He told his story in a few words—not being too heavy on the sins of his page, but declaring that he could do nothing with him. In the end he offered to pay sufficient to apprentice him to a business if they would take him back, and the guardians after a little debating, accepted the offer.

It was a bad day for Perkins. He awoke in the morning with the conviction of his days at Warmington College being numbered. Repentance was upon him, for in spite of the drawback of Mrs. Cobbem's discipline it had been a comfortable home for him, and he ought to have behaved better. He saw the Reverend Copley depart with a heavy heart, and saw him return two hours afterwards with one of the officials of the workhouse.

"I'm done for," said Perkins.

Many boys in his place would have shed a tear—but he did not. Perkins drove back the briny drops and put on a smiling face. He was a stoic in his way, and went into the kitchen as bold and impudent as ever.

"How de do, Jiggles?" he said; "morning, cook. I've just come to say that this place don't soot me, and I'm going back to rest in the family mansion, till I can find a better place. I sent Cobbem for my walley this morning, and I see they've just returned. It won't be long afore I leave yer, so get out your pocket-handkerchers, and if you've got such a thing as a parting present shell it out, will yer? but let it be something 'andsome or I shan't take it."

"I wish you were going, young imperence," said the cook, shaking her head; "but I knows you. All lies, from the crown of your wicked head to the soles of your boots."

"The likes of him are a sort of crumpets, which sticks to the rocks from the moment they comes to life until they dies, or somebody picks 'em off," said Jiggles.

Jiggles meant "limpets;" but his knowledge of natural history was limited, and it was near enough for him.

"Any how," said Perkins, "I've had enough of this low crib, and I'm going. When next you see me I shall be behind the Lord Mayor's carriage, with silk tights and gold lace hanging all the way down my back. If you feel low, Jiggles, you can call on me while I'm resting."

"There's master's bell," said Jiggles; "I suppose I had better answer it?"

"If you don't nobody will," said Perkins, "for I've done with *him*."

Jiggles was not long away, and came back with a face beaming with joy. "You are to pack up your things," he said, "leave your livery behind you, and go."

"And do you think I'd take the fetters of servitood away with me?" asked Perkins, scornfully; "do you think I'm a-going to let everybody know as I've been a slave at a kids' 'ot-house? I fancied

you thought better of me. Well! good-bye cookey, shake hands, for I bear you no malice."

"I never met the like o' you," returned the cook, as she shook hands good-naturedly with him; "and I fears you will come to a bad end."

"Ta, ta! Jiggles," said Perkins, and to the great rage of Jiggles gave him *two fingers* to shake. He took them, however, and Perkins left the room with a step too jaunty to be natural.

He took off his livery and put on an old suit of clothes. Then he gathered together his worldly possessions. There were many odds and ends such as boys of his stamp get together—broken mousetraps, small bottles, bits of indiarubber, stumps of pencils, brass rings, buttons, pieces of string, and so on—these he stowed away in his bundle and in his pockets, and presented himself before his master.

The official from the workhouse was standing by the window, slowly and respectfully sipping a glass of beer. Perkins took no notice of him, but addressed himself to the Reverend Copley.

"So," he said, "it seems I don't soot."

"You do not," was the reply; "I have done my best with you, and I'm sorry to say you have turned out a very bad boy."

"He gave us a deal of trouble in the house, sir," put in the official with a bow; "he was worse than all the rest put together."

"I have done my wery best," said Perkins, loftily ignoring the workhouse party; "and I should have been better if I'd been more understood. I've too much talent for this 'ere place. If I'd been put with the Lord Chief Justice or somebody with a hopening, I should have got on; but I've been worried here. Now, if you are ready, young man," addressing the workhouse official, "I am."

"Oh! he's a bad un," said the man, "but all that will be taken out of him in the house. We know how to stop that while they are with us."

"The thing you stops most down there," said Perkins, "is the wittles. But the country aint benefited. What we lose, you gets. The regulation allowance aint enough for all that fat——"

"Take him away," said the Rev. Copley.

Perkins and the official left the room, and Perkins closed the door with a bang behind him. In the playground the boys were disporting themselves, and a little lump rose in the throat of Perkins, but he kept his eyes ahead, and passed out of the playground without showing any signs of emotion.

He had left Warmington College as a servant for ever, but he had not done with Warmington College, as we shall see anon.

Within ten minutes of his departure, a quiet-looking man of fifty years or so came lounging into the ground. As he strolled across it the boys stopped their game to look at him, for he was a stranger. Merely glancing at them as he went by, he kept on until he came near Billy Sharp, on whom he bestowed a gaze as keen as the look of a hawk.

Billy tried to look unconscious, but those eyes were too much for him, and he turned away.

"Curious," muttered the stranger, "I have seen that face in town, and yet it can't be, for how comes it here?"

He passed on, however, and rang the bell. When Jiggles appeared he gave him a card, on which was inscribed Mr. Bowlem, Scotland-yard. Jiggles was all deference in a moment.

"Walk in, sir," he said, "master's just finished luncheon, and will be werry glad to see you."

Mr. Bowlem simply said "all right," and walked into the reception-room, where he put his hat down upon the table and took a survey of the room.

"Usual pattern," he said. "I could have sworn it belonged to a school if I had seen it floating in the middle of the Atlantic. Good morning, sir."

"Good morning," returned the Rev. Copley, as he entered. "Mr. Bowlem, I believe."

"That's my name, and the business is about a five-pound note."

"It is," replied the Rev Copley, adding to himself, " a very sharp man, and comes to the point."

" Got the number, sir ?" was the next question.

" Yes, I have it in a letter here."

The reverend gentleman found the letter—one he had received from Mr. Greene. The detective made a note of the number—four hundred and twenty seven thousand two hundred and ten.

" Whose was it ?"

That was explained, and the detective next inquired—

" Who had it ?"

That was also put before him, and then he desired to see the party who had parted so freely.

Jolly was sent for, and the moment he entered Mr. Bowlem read him through and through. The detective smiled more in sorrow than in anger, and evidently considered Jolly a party not quite accountable for his actions.

Jolly told his simple tale, and Mr. Bowlem reflected upon it for a minute before pursuing his questioning. At length he said,—

" Why did you part ?"

" Part, sir ?" said Jolly.

" Yes, why give it up ? What was your reason? Were you afraid you should lose it ?"

" No."

" Were you against trusting this gentleman, Mr. Cobbem, with it ?"

" No."

" What then ?"

" Billy Popper was always borrowing my money, and saying he hadn't got it."

" Who is Popper ?" asked Mr. Bowlem, looking up at the Reverend Copley.

" I'll send for him instantly," said that obliging gentleman.

" No, don't, and do not say that I have asked about him. Point him out to me—that's all. This window looks out upon the ground. Which is he?"

" That boy leaning against the wall with his hands in his pockets," replied the Reverend Copley.

" Oh! that's the party, is it ?" said the detective. " I thought he was a fly cove."

" A fly—ahem !—what ?" asked the Reverend Copley.

" Beg pardon, sir. A fly cove is one up to snuff, down to anything, and has all his eye teeth in his head. Was, in short, rocked on the sharp side of his mother !"

The Reverend Copley shook his head slowly to intimate that all this was Dutch to him, but the detective saw that he understood, and favoured him with no further explanation.

" All that has to be done now is to keep quiet," he said. " I hope that young man with the black eyes knows how to hold his tongue."

" I hope so," said the Reverend Copley. " You hear, Greene ?"

" Yes, sir," replied Jolly.

" If you go tattling," said the detective, " your five-pound note will take fright, run away, and never be seen no more! That's all I can tell you."

" I won't speak, sir," said Jolly.

" Don't. Keep mum, even among your own pals."

" I will, sir."

Jolly was dismissed, and the detective and the Reverend Copley entered into a conversation which received material assistance from a luncheon and bottles of sherry, served up for the former's benefit.

" I'll settle this matter in two days—perhaps one," said Mr. Bowlem, as he rose to take his leave. " Meanwhile, I shall put up at the White Hart."

Passing through the grounds on his way out, he purposely made a little detour so as to come up to Billy, who, for certain reasons of his own, had a wish to avoid him. But Mr. Bowlem, who would not be avoided on particular occasions, brought him to bay near the gate.

" How do you do, young gentleman ?" he said.

" How do you do, sir ?" said Billy, with a scared look.

Mr. Bowlem contemplated him with an interest somewhat mournful for twenty seconds or so, and finished with a shake of his head.

" The likeness," he said, " is very remarkable—very remarkable! What is your name, young gentleman ?"

" Popper, sir," replied Billy, in a low tone.

" Not the name," murmured Mr. Bowlem, " but the relationship may be upon the mother's side. Father alive, young gentleman ?"

" Yes, sir."

" Lives in Canonbury, I think ?"

" No, sir."

" Oh! I thought he did—Highgate, perhaps ?"

" No, sir; he's secretary to Mr. Greene," replied Billy, getting more and more alarmed in his looks.

" Ah! that's it—is it ?" said Mr. Bowlem, apparently much relieved. " Then I see I am mistaken. I thought you were a son of a second nevvy of mine, and really the likeness is most remarkable ! Good-day, young gentleman."

" Good-day, sir," replied Billy, in a tone of voice scarcely audible.

Mr. Bowlem, with his hat at a knowing angle, strolled off in a casual way and never once looked back Billy gave a little sigh of relief when he was gone, but all the afternoon he was very pale and silent. That night he wrote as follows to his father:

" A bird from Scotland roosting here. He's been flapping his wings about, and wants to have a peck at somebody. Mind your eye, and keep at home for visitors.—BILLY."

Mr. Bowlem, on returning to the White Hart, asked where the post-office was ; and William the waiter, whose instinct never erred, politely told him where to find one, and offered to post his letters.

" Give me a telegraph form," said Mr. Bowlem, " and I'll take it myself, as I write very badly, and they may want it explained."

His telegram was very short, being only the number of the note. " Four hundred and twenty seven thousand two hundred and ten ;" and it was sent to his chief in Scotland-yard.

Late that night came the reply.

" Pass—from your quarter—bank there."

" All right," thought Mr. Bowlem, and asked William if the landlord of the White Hart was disengaged. William made inquiries, and ascertained he was at the guest's disposal.

The landlord was one of the usual types of men found in such places, heavy in look, slow of speech, but not by any means a fool at business. He kept his accounts pretty straight for one thing, and this now proved to be of great service.

" I am sorry to trouble you," said Mr. Bowlem, " but I may as well tell you who I am. My name is Bowlem, and I am a detective. A five-pound note has been lost. Have you changed one lately ?"

" Several," was the reply, after a little thought.

" Do you know the numbers ?"

" I've kept 'em, with the names of the parties I took 'em from."

" You ought to have been in the force," said Mr. Bowlem; " you've got a head, you have. Let me see your cash-book."

" In welcome, sir," replied the gratified landlord.

The book was produced, and Mr. Bowlem ran his eyes rapidly over its pages. Presently he came to what he wanted, with the name of Goggles attached to it.

" One down in the name of Goggles, I see," he said.

" Yes," replied the landlord.

" Curious name, Goggles."

" Yes, sir, and he came into that money all of a sudden. His uncle Richard left it to him."

" Thank you," said Mr. Bowlem, rising, " that's all I want. Much obliged to you."

CHAPTER LXIX.

A PARTICULAR MESSAGE.

THERE was joy in the tap-room of the White Hart. There were also melancholy and despair. The joy lay in the breast of the oldest inhabitant and the companions who drank with him, and the melancholy and despair were the property of Goggles and two or three loafers who were at low water-mark and were cast aside by their old companions.

Old John was standing drink to them he loved, and them he had ceased to love were out in the cold.

The old un was pretty well soaked as Mr. Bowlem opened the door and strolled in with the most careless air you ever saw. He walked to the fireplace, and standing with his back to it, surveyed the room easily.

"Is there a gentleman of the name of Goggles here?" he said.

The surprise was general, but Goggles could not deny himself, and replied—

"Here I be."

"I've a message for you," said Mr. Bowlem, "from your uncle Richard, lately deceased."

The face of Goggles was a splendid study. Faithfully depicted, it would have made the fortune of any artist, even if it had been painted on a tea-paper.

"Un—uncle Richard?" he gasped.

"Yes, he who left you that money," replied Mr. Bowlem. "I am a doctor, and attended him in his last illness. He sent a particular message by me to you, and it's so important that I can't deliver it in company. Come into the passage and I will deliver it to you."

It was plain that Goggles thought he was dreaming. He rose with a dazed look, and tried to get out of the room through a cupboard. A friend put him right, and he got into the passage. Mr. Bowlem followed and closed the door.

"Hold out your hands," he said, "I've something for you."

Goggles innocently held out his hands.

"Put them together."

Goggles obeyed, and in a moment the "cuffs" were on.

"There we are," said Mr. Bowlem, "all right and comfortable."

"But—but what be they here for?" asked Goggles.

"By the desire of your uncle Richard," replied Mr. Bowlem. "He says you stole that five-pound note."

Goggles said no more. The position was clear to him and he gave in. But ere he left the beloved spot, perhaps for ever, he had a last request to make.

"I'll go quiet," he said, "but give I half a pint o' beer afore I go. I be as dry as a fish."

Bowlem would have arrested his grandfather as a matter of business, and show no quivering muscle in his face, but he was not all stone.

"It's a neat job," he said, "and I'll stand two penn'orth."

Goggles had a pint of half-and-half, and Mr. Bowlem had a small quantity of gin cold. Then they sallied forth, and Mr. Goggles was duly assigned to the lock-up.

In the morning he was brought before Mr. Puddle Taylor again, much to that gentleman's amazement, and this time the worthy magistrate did not have it all his own way. Mugs and Bowlem were two different men. Mr. Taylor sang uncommonly small before the London detective.

The evidence was clear. Goggles had been entrusted with the bank note, and spent it on himself. He pleaded guilty, and the case was worked up and treated as one of petty theft. Goggles was sent to prison for four months, and he was taken away limp with the prospect of going all that time without beer.

A fairish crowd was in attendance, and as Jolly left the court somebody put a small parcel into his hand. On opening it outside he found it contained one pound, one shilling, and a penny, and the following words—

"Hall that is lef' of the banc noat! Forgiv' yure hennymes!"

Jolly put the money into his pocket, and as his mother had sent him another in its place, he was a pound and more in pocket by the business. He forgave his enemies, and said nothing to his friends about that money.

"I'll not trust any one," he thought; "I'll find a place and hide it away."

A hole in the floor of his bedroom seemed to offer the place desired, and not thinking how he was to get his money out again, he dropped it down—fresh bank note and all!

"There, that is safe," he said. "Nobody will be able to get at it."

The detective, Mr. Bowlem, after being liberally refreshed (his dinner was put down in Jolly's bill), took train for London; and having changed his somewhat official-looking apparel for a suit of complete black and a white choker, in which he rather flattered himself he bore a strong resemblance to the Reverend Copley Cobbem, he sought Mr. Greene's residence, and rang the bell.

But Billy's letter had arrived before him. Mr. Sharpe was ready to receive the visitor, and answered the door himself, with a pen in his mouth, and a white wig over his not too abundant locks.

"Mr. Greene at home?" asked the detective, looking hard at him.

"No, sir," replied Sharpe. "He's gone to Margate for a week. Will be back by next Tuesday—ten o'clock train."

"Thank you," said Mr. Bowlem, and went away, apparently satisfied.

Mr. Sharpe closed the door, cut a caper in the passage, stuffed his white wig and spectacles into his pocket, and went back to his own room to enjoy a cigar!

"What an ass that fellow is!" he thought. "Call him a knowing bird—gad! he is a goose!"

But the goose just then was hanging round the corner, and thinking something in this way—

"That was the man I wanted who opened the door; he has disguised himself to deceive me. Must have had the straight tip from his precious son. I know that young— who is the beggar? I must run through my list of photographs at home."

So you see Mr. Bowlem was not quite such an ass as Mr. Sharpe took him to be, and there were clouds of a threatening nature gathering around the uncommonly cute father and son. While the storm gathers let us look to others who figure in our story.

*   *   *   *   *   *

It was not until Jolly wanted some tarts that he realised the sort of bank into which he had put his money, and when the nature of the receptacle burst upon him, despair for awhile held him for its own.

In the daytime the boys of Warmington College were supposed to keep out of the dormitories, but for all that they often went there when they wanted anything from their boxes, and Jolly was now a frequent visitor to his.

The money was wrapped up in the note, and it lay in a bunch about nine inches from the hole, upon the ceiling of the room below. It was safe enough in a certain sense—too safe in fact, and all Jolly's inventive faculties were in active service to find out how it could be got out again.

Twenty times a day he stole up to his room and poked his finger through that hole, in the vain hope of being able to touch his property lying many inches lower down. He could touch it and feel it with a stick, and hear it shift about as he stirred it up, but that was all; it never left its resting-place.

"There never was such a boy as I am," thought Jolly, "always being shoved about, and losing my money, or being robbed of it. How shall I get it out again?"

He was sitting on the floor, mournfully cogitating, when Billy entered the room. Billy had marked his frequent absences, and now came up to ascertain, if possible, the cause.

He had suspicions in the right direction, but they went no further than concealed tarts or hidden gingerbread.

"Hallo, Jolly," he said, "you look down."

"I'm not very well," replied Jolly.

"Been a-gorging of yourself most likely."

"Gorging myself with what?" asked Jolly.

"That depends on wot you've been a-buying," replied Billy, cheerfully. "Wotever you've invested in must be the cause of it. Aint you been eatin' nuffin?"

"No, I haven't," replied Jolly, and his tone carried conviction with it.

"It's a rum go," thought Billy. "He comes up here for something, but if it aint wittles what is it?"

Billy's ideas seldom rose above things to eat and drink, and would not even now be turned aside from their ordinary course. "It's tarts or sweets," he said, "and I won't leave him till I gets my share."

He watched Jolly, and Jolly, conscious of being watched, did not go up to the room again that day. Persons with a small amount of real ability may be endowed with a vast amount of cunning, and Jolly was so favoured.

CHAPTER LXX.

JOLLY AND HIS MONEY.

JOLLY GREENE was not brilliant, he had no head for learning, but he could be as wily as a fox when aroused to preserve himself or something he dearly loved.

And Jolly loved money for what it brought him.

He meditated all that afternoon upon a variety of plans, which presented themselves for his acceptance, for the recovery of his money. The one which found most favour in his eyes was to sharpen the end of his walking stick, thrust it through the bank note, and slowly and cautiously haul it up.

It was really a good notion if it could only be carried out, and Jolly, with his pocket-knife, sharpened his walking stick until it was like a new-made skewer. He put it into his bed to keep it from the sharp eyes of Sharp Billy, and when they retired for the night lay upon it until Billy was fast asleep.

Determined not to give a chance of being detected, Jolly lay awake a good two hours before he got out of bed and commenced operations. Then putting on his lower garments he crept to the spot where his money lay, felt out the hole, and thrust in the stick.

The first dig, though a mild one, stirred up the money, and the second, a little more vicious, brought no better result. In desperation Jolly began to dig more viciously, very much like a man who is trying to get the last onion out of a pickle bottle, and the money, like the onion, slid here and slid there, and did anything and everything but come out.

At last Jolly gave a tremendous dig, and the stick went down at least a couple of feet. A less sagacious mind than his ought to have known that the stick had gone through the ceiling, but he kept pegging away until the absolute lack of all resistance forced the truth upon him.

"I've pushed a hole quite through," he said, "and my money's gone!"

Despair was no stranger to our green young friend, but on this occasion its visit was trebly painful. If this money had been dropped overboard in mid-ocean he could not have felt it keener.

"All gone!" he said, and sat up on the floor, staring about him in the darkness until he was chilled to the bone. Sobs burst from his heart, and these expressions of bitterness and sorrow woke Billy Sharp.

"Here, what's the game?" he asked, sitting up in a fright.

"Never you mind," replied Jolly. "It's no business of yours."

"What are you snivelling about?" asked Billy. "Thinking of your mar?"

"No—I'm not," returned Jolly.

"Then what is it?"

"Never you mind."

Billy had matches—as most schoolboys have—in case of need, and while he was striking a light Jolly retreated to his bed and got into it, in company with his walking stick, on which he lay to hide it from the keen eyes of his friend.

Having lighted a small piece of private candle, Billy came over to Jolly's bedside to have a look at him. He was in a very grimy state with dust and tears, but under the whole lay a large amount of obstinate resolve not to reveal his secret.

"I see how it is," said Billy; "you have been spending your money and having a private feed. Now, did you never hear the story of greedy Tommy?"

"No," returned Jolly, "and you need not tell it. I don't want to hear it."

"There's a smell of stale tarts about the room," said Billy, sniffing; "raspberry jammers I should think by the odour. Have you got any left? If so, shell out, for I could eat a tenpenny nail!"

"I haven't been eating tarts," said Jolly, surlily.

"Then it's gooseberry puffs, or sponge roll, or gingerbread. Come, don't say you've eaten the lot."

"It don't matter to you what I've eaten; I've got none now."

"Greediness," said Billy, sadly, "is a vice that brings its own punishment. If you had acted friendly with me you wouldn't be ill now. I would have eaten half if you had offered it, or the lot rather than you should suffer."

"Much you care about vice," said Jolly, "but I haven't had a tart these three days."

"Haven't you got them in bed with you?"

"No, I haven't—let me alone," snarled Jolly.

But Billy would not let him alone, and he rummaged in the bed until he fished out the walking stick. Its pointed end puzzled him more and more.

"Wot's this?" he asked.

Jolly turned his back upon him and refused to reply.

"It's a curious move—this," said Billy, sadly. "What were you going to do with this? Not going to stab yourself, I hope—and, I say, don't you say that you were going to murder ME!"

"I wouldn't mind doing so," replied Jolly.

"What!" exclaimed Billy, appalled—"you wouldn't mind doing so. You little skinflint-stuffing beggar take that." Here he gave him a prod with the stick. "You murderous young villain, to think of taking the life of your best friend; there's another for you." Jolly jumped up several inches, but refused to howl. "I'll have you charged to-morrow before the justices—I will, and when your mar reads the case in the papers it will be a oner for her, I guess—she who have loved you so and thought you so young and innocent!"

"You let me alone," said Jolly.

"Yes, I will," replied Billy, "but it's only to hand you over to the proper authorities to-morrow. The likes o' this I never see. Only think of my being so a-nigh my end, and sleeping so peacefully too!"

Billy gave him another prod with the stick and retired to his couch, bearing that terrible weapon with him; but however alarmed he might have been at the murderous intention of his friend, he could not ward off sleep, and was speedily in sound repose again.

CHAPTER LXXI.

BLACK AND WHITE.

WHEN a man marries a white woman he does not expect or desire her to change her colour. This observation may have a slight flavour of the absurd about it; but the Reverend Copley Cobbem, awaking from his sleep on the following morning, experienced such a change, for on looking at his gentle Agatha he beheld the usual lily-white countenance almost as dark as a black-a-moor's.

The daylight came strongly through the blinds, for the sun was shining outside, and it was no dark shadow that lay upon the face of the woman he had espoused. Sitting up in his bed he pinched himself to make sure he was awake.

Wide awake as a man could be, and his wife was blacker than any respectable woman ought to be.

And not only the face of Agatha was black, but all around her was a smutty sort of halo—on the pillow, on the sheets, on the blanket, and on the counterpane.

Agatha, who was a good sleeper, did not appear to have turned on her couch in the night, and there was still an aspect of gentle repose upon her which would have been exceedingly charming to see but for the black with which her face was garnished.

"Where on earth can it have come from?" the Reverend Copley asked himself.

An indefinite thought about sprites coming in and playfully peppering her entered his head; but dismissing it, he looked about him to see how this marvellous transformation came about.

Gazing around, his eye fell upon a packet, likewise smudgy, upon the bed. Taking it up in his hand he heard the rustle which once heard is never forgotten—the rustle of a crisp bank note. It also gave out that most unmistakeable of all jingles, the jingle of gold against silver.

He opened the packet and found one pound, one shilling, and a penny—a mysterious and talismanic sum, which only gave the reverend gentleman additional wonderment.

"I have lived in a shroud of mystery for weeks," he murmured, "ever since that unfortunate young Greene came—why! what in the name of all that is marvellous is this?"

His eyes were fixed upon the ceiling, where a hole about the size of the crown of a man's hat was visible; and above that was a small hole in the floor, through which the daylight could be seen.

"This is some boyish prank," he thought, "but then—why the bank note—the gold? Ah! it is a mystery upon mysteries. Agatha, my love, awake."

Agatha would not be aroused without a shaking, and she was shaken accordingly.

When she opened her eyes she was inclined to be cross, as usual.

"Could you not let me rest five minutes?" she asked. "I have scarcely closed my eyes all night."

This was a mistake upon the face of it, but her husband did not tell her so.

"My love," he said, "a most mysterious affair has happened in the night. Look at the ceiling."

Mrs. Cobbem looked, and looked long. Not that she doubted the existence of the hole, but she was working her way mentally over the house to find out who occupied the room above. She was a woman of great mental power, and speedily came to it.

"It is the room that fool occupies," she said; "go up and ask him what he means by his audacity."

The Reverend Copley Cobbem went upstairs, and found Jolly with only his night garments on, kneeling down with his eye at the hole in the floor, staring down at his work with amazement. If he had opened the cavern of the forty thieves he could not have been more amazed.

But he was speedily aroused by the Reverend Copley, who, enraged at what he considered to be sheer impudence on the part of his promising pupil, gave him an open-handed smack that was heard half over the house.

"You little villain," he said. "What next will you be up to?"

"Oh! sir," cried Jolly, "I was only looking for my money."

"Your money—is this it?"

"Yes, sir."

"And how dare you make a hole and drop it into my room?"

An explanation followed, and it seemed that Jolly in the morning had revealed his disaster to Billy, who at that moment was roaming about downstairs with a rug round him endeavouring to find the room into which the money had fallen.

The Reverend Copley, who was much enraged, because he knew that the whole brunt of this business would fall upon him, went out and hid on the landing, determined upon venting some of his wrath upon Billy.

Presently he came up, with his rug around him, so that he looked like a young savage chief. Unconscious of an ambuscade he ascended the stairs, and on reaching the landing bawled out—

"I say, Jolly, you've done it; the tin have gone into old Cobbem's room."

"How dare you go about the house in this disgraceful condition?" asked the Reverend Copley, darting out upon him; "you low-bred boy—how dare you?"

Billy received a couple of staggering blows before he could make good his retreat, and the Reverend Copley, appeased, went downstairs to his wife, who, with the consistency of women, asked to have the ceiling repaired before she got up.

"My love, it is impossible," said the reverend gentleman, "but I will take care it is done to-day."

"What had the donkey to say for himself?" asked Mrs. Cobbem.

The Reverend Copley explained all; his wife grimly smiled.

"Where is that money?" she replied.

"Here," replied her husband; "shall we spoil the Egyptian?" he asked, with an insinuating smile. "I think we might also look upon this as treasure-trove."

"Give it to me," said Mrs. Cobbem, "and I will put it into my box for the mission to the benighted savages of the coast of Patagonia. Mr. Chump Chawler says we are doing wonderful work there."

"Ahem!" said the Reverend Copley, "let us hope so. The last man sent has not been heard of since, and his wife is writing to the papers questioning the conduct of the society."

"Let her write," said Mrs. Cobbem. "I dare say she was very glad to get rid of him. If you wish to go, do so by all means."

"I," said the Reverend Copley, sweetly, "have my mission here. The youth of the British Empire have need of me."

"Have need of a drumstick!" returned his wife. "But it is like you, selfish in all things. You will never do anything to give me peace."

"Do you mean to say," exclaimed her husband, aghast, "that my being roasted by savages would give you rest?"

"Of course it would," she said, shortly, "and you know it."

After this the Reverend Copley dressed himself in silence, and went sadly down to breakfast, murmuring—

"'Oh! woman, in our hours of ease,
Uncertain, coy, and hard to please.'

Oh! dear me, if I had only remained a bachelor! I was happy then, but now— But no matter, I must bear it, even as Job did, to the end."

CHAPTER LXXII.

MR. GREENE GIVES A PARTY.

THE house was soon ready for the Greenes, and they came down to take possession of it. Mr. Sharp did not accompany them, being left behind to arrange the sale of the town house—a very congenial piece of business for him, especially as it was left entirely in his own hands.

A house-warming was the first thing thought of, and Mrs. Greene determined it should be a good one.

"We will ask the Cobbems," she said, "and all the young friends of Jolly, and we will give them a reg'lar flare up. I do so like to have children about me."

"What shall we do to amoose them, Mariar?" asked Mr. Greene.

"If there was a gals' school nigh," said Mrs. Greene, musing, "we might have some dancing."

"So we might," replied Mr. Greene, "but I don't think there's such a thing about. Anyhow we can give 'em fireworks. I can write up to London and get a rare load down."

"Fireworks are pretty, but who's to manage 'em?"

"We'll have a man down with 'em."

A letter was written to the firework-maker, telling him to send down a good assortment, and a man to fix them. The Rev. Copley and his wife were asked, with the school and ushers, and there was every promise of a happy day and evening.

"A hospitable neighbour is a most desirable acquisition to the neighbourhood," said the Rev. Copley.

"Any place where rioting and drinking go on is pleasing to you," returned his wife.

He did not argue the point. Why should he? A wise man does not waste his breath in reasoning with the unreasonable, but went out for a walk and called upon the Greenes, where he had the last part of a capital bottle of sherry, and came home as mellow as a ripened pear.

Jolly was a great star in the school pending this day of festivity. He never was disliked, for he was not vicious in any way, and he would have commanded the sympathies of his fellows had his disasters not been of the ludicrous order. He might, indeed, as it was, have made many friends, but his connection with Billy Sharp made him suspicious of all boy kind, and he held aloof.

But now, for once, his heart was warmed, and he promised all sorts of good things to his school associates, and was continually writing home to his "mar," to press her to have everything in profusion. To which he received compliant answers, combined with further promises.

Mr. and Mrs. Greene were in their element. They were vulgar if you like, but they were a kindly old couple, possessed of a considerable amount of this world's goods, and willing to dispense the same among their friends and neighbours. "Let the boys have all they like to eat and drink," said Mr. Greene, "and let everything be first-rate."

The morning of the eventful day arrived, and the man with the fireworks came. An entire van was taken up with the combustibles. There were catherine-wheels, rockets, squibs, jack-in-the-boxes, set pieces, and a large variety of other pyrotechnic articles, all ready for almost immediate use.

The man in charge was a true Britisher. He knew his right, and stood upon his dignity. Those who attempted to trifle with him found themselves in the wrong box, I can tell you.

At the station he made the porters tremble.

"You mind what you are up to with that lot," he said, "or your heads will be blowed orf, and look here, if you don't want to send a rocket through the station-master don't go a-banging 'em about that way. Only t'other day I was at a station with just sich a lot, and there was two chaps just sich as you;

and they began a-banging the things about, and all of a sudden the lot went orf, and each o' the chaps was taken up on the top of a big rocket, and was seen no more. Both was married, and both left a large family behind them."

Railway porters have quite a mania for knocking things about, and the more fragile the articles are the greater their violence generally is; but on this occasion they showed a gentleness that was quite touching. Both of bucolic breed, they had wild ideas about the power of rockets and such things, and they worked silently and carefully with bated breath until the whole of the dangerous manufactures were safely stowed upon a waggon, and were being moved away. Then they breathed freely, and exchanged a grasp of the hand in token of their grateful recognition of danger passed.

That man in charge must have been intended by nature to have cut a fine figure in the army. He would have been just the party to storm a breach or to walk up coolly to the cannon's mouth and put his head into it—he was so daring and reckless.

Prior to leaving London he had indulged in a little rum and milk, a quart of beer, and about half a pint of gin cold, and on the way down he had taken sundry sips out of a flat bottle containing some rare old Jamaica from his favourite public, but no impartially-minded man would have insinuated that he had been drinking.

Nevertheless those who loved him best had they been there would have warned him against stopping at every roadside inn for a drink; but alas! they were far away, and he took in liquor freely.

He was not a man of fanciful mind or taste. It was all fish that came to his net. At one house he had whiskey, at another four-ale, at another brandy and water hot, and at the White Hart he tried nearly all the taps before leaving.

The man in charge of the waggon shared his cups, and by the time they left the White Hart both were in an extremely independent and defiant state of mind.

"My name's Bungey," said the firework man, "and I'm afeard of no man and nothing. I've lighted the mine o' golden jewels with my pipe, and the biggest rockets with a common lucifer. I've been among fireworks all my life."

"Have you?" said the admiring waggoner.

"Yes, I have," replied Bungey, "and so was my father. When I was ten year old he and I was blowed out of the workshop together, and the old man went head fust into the mud of the canal, and there he stuck like a post, with his feet up in the hair, until the jury came to sit upon the body. I was throwed right across, and wasn't hurt. Since then I've been blowed up seven times—five times out of the shop and twice out of my own house, when I've been doing piece-work at home. I've been knocked down twice by rockets, have been nigh burnt to death in consequence of going to sleep under the fiery cascade at the Crystal Palace, and seen no end of other sort of fun. Ah! it's a jolly sort o' life, I can tell you."

"So I should say," returned the waggoner, with just a shade of hesitation in his manner.

"Now, where can we have a last drink?" asked Bungey. "I'm as dry as a fish."

"There beant no more houses bout here," replied the waggoner; "but Measter Greene beant a bad sort. He'll gi' ee plenty enough, and more than ye can drink."

"You think so," replied Bungey; "but I'll bet you a pint he give in afore I do. Is this the place?"

"That be the place."

"Then draw up just by the lane, while I go and see Mister Greene, and taste his liquor."

CHAPTER LXXIII.

THE ENTERTAINMENT BEGUN.

MR. BUNGEY presented himself before Mr. Greene with all the independence of a noble son of toil. He entered the room with his hat on, and with a simple "Here I am!" sat down in a chair.

In addition to Mr. Greene, there was the Reverend Copley in the room, and this gentleman undertook to reprove Mr. Bungey for his uncourteous behaviour.

"My friend," he said; "it is not customary for man to enter the house of another with his hat on."

Mr. Bungey waved his arm, implying that he was not going to argue the point, and turning to Mr. Greene, said—

"I suppose you've got the drink handy? I'll take a drop of old Tom."

Mr. Greene flushed with indignation, and was about to say something that would have ruffled the tender feelings of Bungey, if the Reverend Copley had not interposed.

"Leave him to me," he whispered; "the working men of large cities are terribly independent. They require a little management and smoothing down. My friend," he said, aloud, "come with me outside. Your drink shall be brought to you. I want to show you the site for the fireworks."

"I don't stir a peg till I gets something to drink," replied Mr. Bungey; "a nice way to treat a man who got out of his bed at a quarter arter four this morning, and come away without a bit of wittles. But it don't matter; I'm off, and you may manage the fireworks yourself."

"Hasty conduct," said the Rev. Copley, "is often the father of repentance."

"And I'm a father too," said Mr. Bungey, "and has my feelings. Is this drink a-coming, or is it not?"

"Coming? Certainly," said the Rev. Copley, "and in a few minutes the feelings of Bungey were soothed with a stiff tumbler of gin and water. As he consumed it he grew quite amiable and chatty, but he did not take off his hat.

"There's nuffin' like fireworks," he said; "they are fun to them as makes 'em, to them as lets 'em off, and them as sees 'em. I've been among 'em all my life, and I looks upon 'em as my best friends."

"I have some knowledge of the pyrotechnic art myself," said the Rev. Copley. "I used to make my own."

"Did you?" returned Bungey, gruffly; "and werry pretty things they must ha' been."

"I do not suppose they were at all like your work," said the reverend gentleman, soothingly. "I am but a child in those things. It is my purpose, with your permission, to assist you to-night."

"I'll see if there's anything in yer," returned Bungey, "and if there is, I'll give yer some lighting to do. I've brought some shells—regular busters—quite a new invention. We've only tried one on 'em as yet, and it killed the party as put the port fire to it."

"Indeed!" said the Rev. Copley, turning slightly pale. "Perhaps he was not a careful man."

"The most careful as we had at the works. And no mortial man could have got away from that shell. If these don't go orf right, we are going to give up the idea. I'll hand 'em over to you."

"Wouldn't you like something to eat?" asked Mr. Greene.

"Not at present," replied Bungey.

"When would you wish to have anything?"

"I don't want to put you out of your reglar meals," said Bungey, amiably; "give me my drink, which don't give no trouble to get, and I'll take the wittles as it comes."

He would have had some more drink then, but it was not forthcoming, and the Reverend Copley and Mr. Greene rising, Bungey was obliged to follow their example.

They took him to the grounds, and showed him where the platform for the fireworks was erected, and he at once declared it must all come down, and be put up in another place. As this would take all the day to do he, after a stubborn resistance, yielded the point.

"Only don't blame me for what happens," he said. "If you has a hinquest after it don't have me up afore the coroner, or I shall speak out pretty plain."

"About these shells, my friend?" said the Rev. Copley.

"I have 'em here," said Bungey, opening a box, and exposing to view some packages about two feet long, and as thick as a man's leg. "There they are, reg'lar beauties!"

"And what is inside them?" asked the Reverend Copley.

"Sulphur and brimstone, gunpowder, and little bits of iron," replied Bungey. "There was also a few nails clenched in, and the lot's rammed home as tight as a mining blast. The touch-paper is on the top, you see. It aint the werry best, for we was out of it, but if you blows on it, it will soon go orf."

"Those shells and I," said the Reverend Copley, mentally, "will ever be strangers."

Bungey's stock of combustibles was looked over, and he was left to fix them up, tie the rockets to the sticks, and so on.

The Reverend Copley, as he was retiring to the house with Mr. Greene, remarked—

"Our friend seems to understand his business, but don't you think he is—a—little—as I may say—excited?"

"Perhaps it is only his manner," said Mr. Greene.

"Aye, aye!—just so, his manner. I hope it is nothing more," rejoined the Reverend Copley, but he had not a perfect faith in Bungey.

When a man of his sagacity has doubts you may rely upon there being grounds for it.

The reverend gentleman stayed to luncheon, and then went home for his wife. Meanwhile the boys arrived.

Mr. Greene received the first intimation of their presence as he sat with Mrs. Greene enjoying his afternoon glass of something nice and sweet. The door opened and a most ghastly head appeared over the top of it, with a long demoniacal-looking arm thrust out at the side.

"Good heavens!" exclaimed the worthy old gentleman, "who is this? He must be eight feet high."

But it was only Dick and Nick Stager, with Jolly Greene and that faithful follower, Billy Sharp. Jolly during the past day or two had been getting rather intimate with the Stagers, and as this did not suit Billy's book he was even more attentive to his friend than usual.

"How do you do?" asked Mr. Greene. "Ah! you young dogs, to come and scare a poor old man in this way."

"It was only a mask and a false arm in sticks," replied Dick; "but we thought you would be surprised."

"It gave me that turn," said Mrs. Greene, "that I saw everything as red as a piony. Well, Jolly, my dear—dear boy, how are you?"

"Quite well, mar—at least nearly so," replied Jolly. "I fell downstairs just before we started."

CHAPTER LXXIV.

THE ENTERTAINMENT PROCEEDS.

"MASTER GREENE got into a tin pail which the girl left on the staircase," explained Dick, "and nearly broke his neck."

"Well—well," said Mrs. Greene, cheerfully, "as long as it is not broken we will say no more about it. Where are the rest?"

GREEN AS GRASS.

A JOLLY SCHOOL STORY.

—LIKE A CANNON-BALL PERKINS' HEAD "WENT FOR" WILLIAMS' STOMACH AND A WILD RALLY ENSUED.

"Below," replied Jolly; "we came up to say they were all here."

"Fust have a bit of cake and a glass of wine," said Mr. Greene, "then out into the garden to play; but don't touch the fireworks."

"Certainly not," they said in chorus.

They went below, where all the school had assembled, and Mr. Greene addressed them in the following manner—

"My lads, I'm glad to see you. I like boys. I've got one, and wish I had more of 'em; it would be better for me and them. Make yourselves at home, enjoy yourselves, and you will please me. There are cake and wine in the dining-room—that door to the right. Go in and help yourselves. I shall see you by-and-bye."

They lost no time in complying with this request, and a very hearty turn-out it was. Dick Stager took the chair, and made a neat speech, proposing the health of their host.

"He's a jolly old cock," he said. "Long life to him! Now, Chris Cobble, don't you drink any more of that sherry, or you will be drunk. Take his glass away. Larry."

"You let my glass alone," said Chris.

A struggle ensued, and between them the glass was broken.

Dick Stager got upon his feet.

"Look here, boys," he said, "I've something to say to you. Order, there!"

"Silence!" cried half a dozen voices, and there was a lull, so that Dick could be heard.

"I'm taking a lot upon myself, Jolly," he said, addressing our friend.

"A mighty lot!" growled Billy.

"What did you say?"

"Nothing."

"Then don't say nothing again, or I will pull your ears. Have I your permission, Jolly, to speak?"

"Do what you like, say what you like," replied Jolly.

"Thanks. Now, boys, you are here under the roof of a very hospitable gentleman, and all I want you to do is to be merry and wise. No pranks with the fireworks, and so on—no dancing. That's all. By the way, I think we have all had enough now, and may as well adjourn to the grounds."

By this time Mrs. Cobbem had arrived, and her husband was wandering about the grounds in search of Bungey, who was nowhere to be seen.

"There is nothing done," said the Rev. Copley, in despair. "Where is he?"

After considerable searching Bungey was found in the tool-house, down behind the wheelbarrow, fast asleep. The Reverend Copley took upon himself the task of awakening him.

"Get up, my friend," he said, shaking him by the shoulder. "The night will soon be here, and all the fixed pieces ought to be in their places."

It took some time to wake Bungey, but at last he suddenly sat up, and began striking out right and left like a maddened pugilist. Having dealt the Reverend Copley a staggering blow, and knocked the skin off his own knuckles against the wheelbarrow, he got up, and gave vent to speech.

"Now then," he said, "get on with your work. Fill them rockets, and give me a candle to go into the cellar for more powder. Hallo! Why, what the jeuce is this?"

"You have been dreaming," said the Reverend Copley, gently.

"If I have wot's that to you?" growled Bungey. "Wot are you doing here?"

"The day," said the Reverend Copley, "is almost done, and the fixed pieces ought to be up."

"You leave 'em to me," said Bungey, "and I'll have 'em up in time. I knows my business, and you knows yours. Who are them kids?"

"Those boys," said the Reverend Copley, with emphasis, "are the pupils of Warmington College."

"Your pupils?"

"Yes, my friend."

"I thought so—blowed if I didn't," said Bungey, "'cos you are so fat and they are so lean. You don't give 'em drink enough; that's the stuff to fatten 'em."

Bungey himself was a member of the lean kine fraternity, but nobody ventured to tell him so. Taking his pipe out of his pocket, he lit it, and began to smoke with a defiant air.

"I knows my work," he said, "no man better—so we'll begin. Now here," he said, diving down, and bringing up a small tube, "is a few pounds o' dry powder, and we'll begin to mix at once if——"

But the Reverend Copley and the boys had already departed in amazement and horror, and put a good hundred yards between them and the tool-house before they stopped for breath.

"That man will blow himself and the house to pieces," said the Reverend Copley. "Hi! my friend, come out there."

"Wot do you want?" asked Bungey, coming to the door.

"That pipe of yours is dangerous."

"Pooh! I allus smokes at home when I'm mixin'," said Bungey. "It's all right if you keeps the bowl straight. But I'll put it out if you'll get me some drink."

"He has had more than he ought now," murmured the Reverend Copley, "but anything is better than that perilous pipe."

Bungey, being very thirsty, elected to have ale, and insisted upon having a full quart. This he drank off at a draught, and declared himself ready for work.

"I'm a-goin' to make this powder into a spit-devil," said Bungey, "and we'll have some water to begin with. Now, my man, make yourself handy, and damp it."

The Reverend Copley was only too glad to destroy the explosive powers of the powder, and pocketing the familiarity of Bungey, he emptied a watering-can into the tube, and began his work.

All that afternoon he was engaged with Bungey, and all went well until just before dusk, when a terrific report was heard, and the Reverend Copley, with a blackened face and without his hat, was seen hurrying across the lawn towards the house.

CHAPTER LXXV.

A PIPE PUT OUT.

THE boys of Warmington College, who had been engaged in various games at the bottom of the lawn, came running over in a body to know what had happened to their chief. At the same time the inmates of the house, alarmed by the explosion, came running out to know what was the matter.

"I told him not to smoke," said the Reverend Copley, waving his arms about, "but he would do it; and then he kept putting the odd bit of touch-paper and crackers, and all sorts of fiery things into his pocket, and at last he put his pipe there, and then came an explosion."

"Is he dead?" said a dozen voices.

"I don't know," replied the reverend gentleman. "Great bundles of fireworks went off. I was hit in the back with a rocket, and had a dozen crackers about my head at the same time. All is confusion and ruin in the toolhouse."

"But is the man dead?" asked Mrs. Cobbem, impatiently.

"I don't know."

"Then go and see."

"Well, my dear——"

"Let us all go," said Mrs. Cobbem, and the whole party advanced to the toolhouse."

There the ruin was found not to be so great as might have been expected. Bungey lay under a heap of tools and a great deal board, and there were a few smouldering bits of paper lying about, but nothing more.

Bungey was using strong language, and he was using it for some time after they got him up and put out his smouldering coat, and he came out still stronger when he asked for his pipe and nobody could tell him where it was.

"I had it the minute afore that white-chokered chap blowed hisself up," he said, "and I'd like to know where it is."

"Hear that!" said the Reverend Copley, "*I* blew myself up!"

"I dare say you did it," replied his wife, "and tried to cast the blame upon this poor, simple, unoffending, honest man."

"It is enough!" exclaimed the Reverend Copley ; "*I* did it, of course, Agatha!"

"Mr. Cobbem," said Agatha, "don't be a fool."

Mr. Bungey, having had his pipe put out, and having been put out himself, went in for more drink, and only people with hearts of stone would have refused him then.

"Never mind whether I'm hurt or not," he said. "I'm used to it. If you was to see me without any clothes," here Mrs. Cobbem gave a little scream, and made preparations for a retreat, "you would find me as black as a nigger. I've got at least ten coatings of powder over me."

His face bore testimony of the many accidents he had been in, and Mrs. Cobbem finding he was going no further in explaining the state of his frame, called him a manly sufferer, and asked to be allowed to bring him drink with her own fair hands."

"It don't matter to me who brings it," replied Bungey, gallantly, "so as I gets it."

Shortly after a repast was announced, the boys to have their feed in one room, and their elders in another. The youngsters smuggled Bungey into their apartment, and put him at the head of the table, where he gave them excellent food for mirth, while they ate and drank the good things provided.

He discoursed a little upon the merits of the Reverend Copley, who he said " was not a bad chap, but without the genius to be a fireworker."

"He wants to be blowed up oftener," he said.

"Oh! no he doesn't," said Dick Stager.

"I know he does," insisted Bungey ; "look at me. I've been blowed up a dozen times."

"And he is blown up every day by Mrs. Cobbem," said Dick, and a roar of laughter followed. It was a small joke, but it was founded on truth, and took immensely.

They put Bungey into a sort of witness-box, and examined him somewhat after this style. He answered every question readily.

"What is your name?"

"Noddy Bungey."

"Your age?"

"Somewheres about forty."

"Married or single?"

"Been married twice. The first was blowed out of a hattic as we was mixing powder. I went with her, but stuck to the tiles. She went into the street, and there was a hinquest."

"Any children?"

"Four living, and three dead."

"Blown up too?"

"One went up with his mother, and 'tother two put a candle into the powder-barrel, and was never seed arterwards."

Here Bungey was much affected, and stopped to drink. Having refreshed himself, the examination was resumed.

"What made you take to the firework business?"

"Was born on the fifth of November," replied Bungey.

"A regular guy," said Dick Stager.

"Thanky, young gentleman," said Bungey—"no more guy than you."

"Beg pardon. Yours is a dangerous business, isn't it?"

"Uncommon."

"Your neighbours object to it?"

"They hate us like pison," replied Bungey, "and if we wasn't blowed up occasionally accidental, I'd get up a job o' that sort to spite 'em. You'd larf fit to split if you was to see some places as I've cleared out. Not even a sarspan left in the house. All cleared out into the street—slap bang."

While Bungey was giving the account of his life and things, the elders in the other room were talking of him in a way he would probably have resented had he been present. An addition had been made by the Rev. Charles Ohler, who had come to assist. He, of course, understood fireworks, as he did conjuring and everything else—at least, so he said.

"The man," said the Reverend Copley, "cannot be relied on. He has been drinking all day, and may do some mischief unless he is carefully watched."

"I should be sorry for any accident to happen," said Mr. Greene; "but fireworks are dangerous in the hands of ignorant people."

"Or drunken persons," put in the Reverend Charles Ohler.

"I did not think the man was under the influence of drink," said Mrs. Cobbem.

"I was inclined to think he was," said Mrs. Greene.

"Let me suggest something," said the Reverend Charles Ohler, with a soft smile. "After dinner let us have the man in, and examine him ; then put the matter to the vote. If you reject the man you can have the fireworks still, as Cobbem and myself both understand them."

"Are you sure you do?" asked Mr. Greene, dubiously.

"I assure you that I am quite an experienced hand," replied the Reverend Charles.

So it was settled that Bungey should be summoned before the council, and judged according to his state. If considered sober he was to have the working of the fireworks; if not he was to be induced, if possible, to keep himself out of the way until all was over.

Had they sent for him at once he would have come in what some people of charitable minds would have called tolerably sober, but having the run of the good things in the other room, and nobody to check him, he managed to get into a state which the most inveterate toper must have admitted as diabolically drunk.

He did manage to stagger into the room, but as soon as he got there he pitched upon his head at the feet of Mr. Greene, and lay like a warrior taking his rest. And wonderfully well he slept, considering the suddenness of his going off, as his snoring bore witness to.

They picked him up and put him on the sofa, thinking he had got a fit. The Reverend Copley beat the palms of his hands, and the Reverend Charles emptied half the contents of a water-bottle over his manly brow.

Bungey was almost a stranger within and without to the pure liquor, and the effect upon him was electrical: He gave a great bound in the air, kicked the Reverend Copley in the watch-pocket, knocked the water-bottle out of the hand of the Reverend Charles, and coming down with a bang upon the floor, shook the house to its foundation.

He was awake, but he would not get up. Wiping his forehead with a red cotton pocket-handkerchief, which was as much a stranger to water as he himself was, he heaped all sorts of anathemas upon the assembled company, sparing neither age nor sex.

One great desire appeared to be upon him, and that was to have what medical men call the abdominal organ lying under the fifth rib of somebody, and finding nobody willing to make him a present of it he bounced up and ran to the table, where he secured the carving-knife, and made grand preparations for a little rough-and-ready dissection.

Now was the day and now the time for the Rev. Copley to distinguish himself, and he came out nobly. Dodging Bungey's first thrust, he dealt that party a blow delivered from the shoulder, and sent him into a distant corner of the room, where he lay huddled up like a hedgehog.

Still he did not appear to be much hurt, for when they cautiously advanced and bent over him, he was sleeping like a child, and snoring like two full-grown men.

"He will be quiet for hours now," said the Rev. Copley; "let us put out the lights, lock the door, and leave him here until the fireworks are over.

"Couldn't possibly do better," said the Reverend Charles, and the ladies having retired to put their bonnets and shawls on, this very wise suggestion was acted upon, and Bungey was left in the dark dining-room to sleep in peace.

CHAPTER LXXVI.

SOME STARTLING PYROTECHNIC DISPLAYS.

IN addition to the platform erected for the display of fireworks, there were comfortable garden seats arranged about fifty yards away for the spectators. The boys had already taken up their positions when their elders came out. The arrival of Mr. and Mrs. Greene was hailed with a hearty cheer.

"I likes to hear 'em," said Mr. Greene; "it does my heart good. I'd sooner hear a boy give a good honest shout than listen to a song from the finest singer in the world."

"Your sentiments, my dear sir," returned the Rev. Copley, "do credit to your head and heart."

"Don't stand here talking nonsense," interposed his wife, "but go and begin the fireworks. The dew is enough to chill one to the bone."

"Have another shawl, mum," said Mr. Greene; "stop a moment and I'll get it," and away went the good-natured old man on his errand of kindness, Mrs. Cobbem bestowing a compliment upon him as he retreated.

"There is a true gentleman," she said, "one of Nature's gems. There are some men all politeness before their marrage, but after it bears are nothing to them."

"Now then, Ohler," said the Rev. Copley, "I think we ought to get ready."

The two efficients accordingly retreated to the platform, on which were fixed sundry posts, but none of the fireworks were up yet.

"There," said the Reverend Copley, turning the light of a bull's-eye lantern he had provided himself with upon a lot of curious-looking things, like gigantic hieroglyphics, lying upon the ground, "are the set pieces. They are various in design. Here, I believe, is one which when diplayed will represent the word 'Welcome,' and there is another to finish with, which says 'Good night!'"

"Which is that?" asked his friend.

"It is rather difficult to tell," said the Reverend Copley. "In this light one can hardly see, and the forms themselves are imperfect until displayed. That is 'Good night.' Yes, I am sure of it."

"What are in these big boxes?" asked the Rev. Charles.

"The smaller things—roman candles, squibs, crackers, and so on."

"And where are the rockets?"

"Just behind you; and the board for letting them off is close by."

"We are then, as we may say, ready to begin."

"Quite ready."

"First let us hoist up 'Welcome.' This is it, you say?"

"Yes."

The piece was hoisted and tied to the post. Then came the question—how was it to be lighted? The Reverend Charles discovered the touch-paper at last, and lighting it the pair retreated behind.

A minute elapsed, and nothing took place. All was darkness and suspense.

"You can't have lighted the touch, Ohler," said the Reverend Copley.

"Oh! yes, I have."

"I am sure you have not. I'll go and see."

The Reverend Copley accordingly went to the post, and the moment he arrived there a great rush of flame sent him staggering back. He went over the edge of the platform, and fell heavily, with his bull's-eye lantern under him.

Lying on his back, in a painfully reflective mood, he saw to his amazement the words "Good night!" blazing away in their full glory, while his ears were saluted by cries of astonishment from the spectators. In a few brief moments all was over, and darkness was upon the land again.

"Cobbem," whispered the Reverend Charles, "where are you?"

"Down in front here," replied the other. "I have fallen."

"Are you injured?"

"Not much; but the lantern is put out, and quite flat. I am trying to put it straight."

"Was it good?—the fireworks I mean."

"We had 'Good night' up, instead of 'Welcome.'"

"Oh!" said the Reverend Charles Ohler, and there was a moment's silence.

The Reverend Copley returned to the platform with the battered lantern in his hand. It was hopelessly ruined, and could be of no more service that night.

"How you smell of oil!" said the Reverend Charles.

"It's that confounded lantern," replied the other, gloomily. "The reservoir burst, and I have lain in oil."

"Like a sardine," said the Reverend Charles, with a chuckle; "but you always were an odd fish."

The Reverend Copley said nothing, but at that moment he felt daggers towards his friend.

"Let us go on," he said, "or they will grow impatient. But we have no light."

"I have brought a dozen boxes of vesuvians with me," returned the Reverend Charles. "I always think of emergencies of this sort, and provide for them. What shall we have next?"

"A few rockets, I think."

"Here they are. I'll fix 'em. Now, which end do you light?"

"Ah! that is it," replied the Reverend Copley. "Some go one way, and some the other, I think. That drunken old scoundrel told me so!"

"He must have been jesting."

"I don't know. Light that one underneath," said the Reverend Copley.

"There is no touch-paper there; it is at the top."

"Light it at the top, then."

The Rev. Charles, after groping about for a stick for some time, eventually found one, and, fixing a vesuvian to the end, applied it to the top of the rocket.

The only defect in this article was that it was tied on to the stick upside down. The consequence was it rushed down with terrific force, struck the Reverend Charles on the crown of his hat, smashed it over his eyes, and covered him with blue and red blazing stars.

He was not much hurt, but he was terribly frightened, and danced about until he, too, fell off the platform, and the light went out.

"That seems to me to be a new sort of firework," said Mrs. Cobbem.

"I aint seen anything prettier for years," remarked Mr. Greene.

Nobody understood it, but everybody was pleased, and the boys cheered until the woods around rang again.

"They mock me," groaned the Reverend Charles from the darkness below.

"Oh, no! they do not think it was an accident,"

whispered his companion above. "Come up; all is well for the present. We are getting on famously!"

The Reverend Charles returned to his post, and his companion immediately remarked—

"How you smell of sulphur!"

"It is those confounded coloured lights," was the reply. "My coat is full of holes, I think. What shall we have on next?"

"Another set piece. Here is one—the fountain of fire."

This was an article that required very strong fixing, but they knew it not, and tied it on but feebly. The Reverend Copley lighted it, and off it went with a terrific spirt of fire, then leapt from its moorings, and went straight into the box of crackers and other things.

"Stop it!" cried the Reverend Copley, "or we shall be blown to atoms."

"Have you got a pail of water here, Cobbem?"

"No."

"You ought to have had. Always in these cases make provision for accidents."

"Fizz! fizz!" went the fountain, spirting about the box. The reverend gentlemen started dancing about outside like a couple of maniacs. Bang! bang! went the crakers, Roman candles shot stars in every direction, and coloured fires illumined the sky with shafts of varied light.

"This," said the Reverend Copley, "is destruction and ruin."

But it was very pretty, and pleased the spectators immensely.

Everybody thought it was a novel display, skilfully arranged and designed. It was almost equal to Mount Vesuvius, and almost as dangerous.

The exhibitors were behind the box, and in consequence unable to retreat from the platform, the front of which was one mass of flaming fire and shooting lights, so they lay down, and threw their coats over their ears, awaiting the end of this accidental display.

But the box was a large one, and the contents numerous and various. Rows of crackers, packets of Roman candles, squibs, Chinese fire, and many other things, and under all about fourteen pounds of blue and red fire in packets.

These caught at last, and only those who have sniffed the odour of blue and red fire at a short distance can understand its power. The fumes are of the most deadly description, and as the horrid mass sent forth its flames and smoke the two reverend performers gasped for breath.

"Death is approaching," groaned the Reverend Copley. "Ohler, push the box over."

"It is red hot, Cobbem."

"Kick it then."

The Reverend Charles gave it a kick with his foot, and the box went over, throwing its burning contents among the rockets and remaining set pieces. "Welcome!" upside down, burst into a blaze, huge Catherine wheels spun about like humming tops, rockets darted about in every direction, and the great shells, spoken of by Bungey, went off with a force that shook the earth.

Aghast, and terrified half out of their senses, the two exhibitors rushed towards the spectators, and were received, to their further amazement, with an overwhelming round of applause. Nobody was hurt, and all things were looked upon as the result of pre-arranged display.

"Brayvo! brayvo!" cried Mr. Greene, clapping his hands. "Splendid—magnificent—couldn't have been better!"

The Reverend Copley, with instinctive genius, grasped the position, and seized his companion's arm.

"Ohler!" he hissed in his ear, "not a word. They know nothing. We are safe."

"All right," was the reply.

The last lights were out, and only scattered masses of burning material lay about to bear witness to the glory that had come and gone. The applause had subsided into quiet congratulations, which the two humbugs received with much complacency.

"Marvellous!" said Mrs. Greene. "Wonderful!"

"It was really very pretty," said Mrs. Cobbem, condescendingly.

"I liked it amazingly," said Mr. Greene, "but," he added, taking the Reverend Copley by the button-hole and drawing him aside, "don't you think these things are rather dangerous? A rocket as big as my leg went just over our heads."

"If directed with care," replied the Reverend Copley, calmly, "there is no danger whatever."

There was only one dissentient voice as to the success of the display, and that was Dick Stager.

"The whole thing was a myth," he said, "and it was a wonder nobody was killed. But it was rare un in its way."

The fireworks over, the party adjourned to the house. The servants, who had all been out, hurried in first, but in a few moments they came out again in a mighty hurry, and rushed in a body up against their master and mistress.

"What is the matter?" cried Mr. Greene.

"Oh! sir—please sir!" gasped half-a-dozen voices, "There is such a noise in the dining-room. Everything seems to be being smashed."

"It's that ruffian, Bungey," said the Reverend Copley.

They all went into the house—the ladies and boys were warned to stand back, and the men boldly unlocked and threw open the dining-room door.

As soon as it was thrown back, Bungey, mad and furious, burst forth. In one hand he had the leg of a chair, and in the other all the fire-irons.

"Who's been letting off my fireworks?" he cried. "I heerd 'em a going. Who's been a doing of it? Pint him out, and let me have his——"

The Rev. Copley skilfully got behind him and pinioned his arms, or he would have done a lot of mischief. His weapons were taken away, and he was put into a chair, and held there until he became calmer.

"But I'll have somebody's life for it," he kept muttering, and that was his last utterance prior to going to sleep again, which he did in a few minutes from sheer exhaustion.

His work in the dining-room was complete. Not a whole article was left; even the table was split in two, and the hearthrug torn.

"A sad spectacle," said the Rev. Copley; "showing what man in wild ungovernable and unreasonable fury is capable of."

"But it's not like broken bones—is it?" said Mr. Greene, cheerfully. "Nobody's hurt, and it isn't a bit o' use grieving—is it, Mariar?"

"It is not, my dear," replied Mrs. Greene.

"And there's lots of the house left to have some fun in," continued Mr. Greene, "and so we will make the best of a bad job."

Which they did. The boys had a splendid supper, and their elders a glorious feed. On the way home the Rev. Copley told his wife that he still adored her, and the gentle Agatha was for a brief time subdued. The Rev. Charles Ohler never got home at all until the morning, for he took the wrong road, and wandered about the fields all night, and at early dawn he was found by a shepherd, seated on a stile, shedding tears.

"I grieve over those fireworks like lost children," he said to the man; "lost—lost for ever. I say, my good friend, which is the way to Dumplington Rectory?"

"I'll show ye the way, measter," replied the man.

"Do, and I'll give you half-a-crown."

"Done, measter."

And shepherd and pastor went amiably over the fields side by side to the rectory aforesaid.

"Whatever you do, my friend," said the Rev. Charles, as he shook the shepherd's hand tenderly at parting, "shun fireworks. They are the sources of most evils, and in combination with drink lead to *ruin*. You hear me—RUIN. Good night. Call me early. Farewell!"

"He was allus a rum 'un," muttered the shepherd, as he moved away, "but every day he seems to I to grow more rummier."

CHAPTER LXXVII.
THE CLOUDS THICKEN.

JOLLY and a few select friends stayed in the house all night, and had breakfast on the following morning with Mr. and Mrs. Greene.

Billy Sharp, the two Stagers, and Christopher Cobble were thus honoured. Billy for old acquaintance-sake, and the others on account of a growing intimacy between them and Jolly Greene.

The Greenes altogether were getting tired of the Sharps, as their rascality was growing each day more apparent. In all the world it would have been difficult to find a family more confiding and innocent than the Greenes; but the eyes of even the most innocent and confiding are generally opened in the end.

Billy could see the growing coolness, for he was almost left out in the cold at the breakfast-table. His wants were attended to as a matter of hospitality; but nobody talked to him, and more than one observation he made remained without an answer.

In the middle of the meal the letter bag came in, and Mr. Greene having apologised, proceeded to read his letters, some five or six in number.

The first made him stare and then flush indignantly. Throwing the letter down on the table he asked if anybody knew who Puddle Taylor was. This was explained to him, and he read aloud a letter he had received from that gentleman.

"Mr. Puddle Taylor presents his compliments to Mr. Blue, and will thank him not to disturb the peace and imperil the property of his neighbours by foolish and childish exhibitions of fireworks. If the scene of last night is repeated, Mr. Taylor will take cognisance of the same, in his capacity as magistrate of the county."

"Confound the fellow!" said Mr. Greene, "who is he?"

"A jumped-up nobody," replied Dick Stager—"a mushroom judge, a Dogberry, a judicial jackass."

"What does he take me for?" cried Mr. Greene; "does he think I have lived all my life in the world for nothing? Here, Mariar, give me pen and ink. I'll answer him. Mr. Blue, indeed, as if he did not know my name."

"Don't be too violent," said Mrs. Greene; "or he may come here and fight."

"I should like him to," replied Mr. Greene; "I would put down two poun' ten and fourpence to have a round with him to-day."

"Hear, hear—bravo!" cried the delighted boys.

"I'll give him a letter that will make him swear," continued Mr. Greene, "and then he will have an opportunity to fine himself for using bad language. Now for pen and ink. Let me dash it off while I'm hot."

They brought him writing materials, and, inspired by the insult he had received, he wrote as follows :—

"Mr. Greene presents his compliments to Mr. *Fuddle* Taylor and begs to say that he will have fireworks as often as he pleases, and shoot 'em when he likes. If Mr. *Fuddle* T. don't like it he had better move.

"N.B.—All future letters from Mr. F. T. will be put into the fire without being read, and my name is Greene, not Blue—confound you!"

"There," said Mr. Greene, "I think that is a cork for his bottle, and if you will ring, Mariar, I'll send the boy off with it at once."

Nick Stager sprang up and rang the bell, and the page was sent off with the letter.

CHAPTER LXXVIII.
A BATTLE ROYAL.

MR. GREENE, having relieved his mind, went on with his correspondence. The next letter he read was from Bowlem, the detective. Thus it ran :—

"DEAR SIR,—I am sorry to trouble you with a matter which you will say does not in any way concern me; but I am a public man holding a public post and have a public duty to perform. That party of the name of Sharp, who lives with you, is no good—in fact he is an old associate of criminals, *and I can prove it.* If you like to take this hint, and act upon it, you can write to me or my chief, at Scotland-yard.—Your obedient servant,
"J. BOWLEM."

"Humph!" said Mr. Greene, this must be looked to.

"What's the matter, my dear?" asked his wife.

"Nothing, Mariar," he said, looking at Billy, who caught the glance and muttered to himself "something about the governor. I reckon the game is nearly up."

He turned very cold at the thought, but he went on with his breakfast, and laid in a stock of food, as if preparing for the dearth to come.

Breakfast over the boys went back to college, and Mr. Greene wrote an answer to the detective, thanking him for the information, and asking for particulars. After that he went for a walk, and as invariably happens in such cases, the first person he ran against was Mr. Puddle Taylor.

Now, the magistrate was well aware that in such a locality as that he had no power to stop fireworks or any other display Mr. Greene chose to indulge in, but he thought he would try it on, and having failed, he was doubly annoyed. In a rash moment he read the reply to his wife, and she immediately said—

"You must thrash that man."

"I, my dear," said Puddle Taylor. "Ahem! as a magistrate—"

"You stand first as a man of honour," said Mrs. Taylor, "and you must thrash that man, I say."

"How can I, my love? If I go to his house—"

"Lie in wait for him. He is sure to walk out soon. He goes out every morning, I fancy."

"I don't think he will walk this morning," replied her husband.

"Pooh! don't be afraid of him," said Mrs. Puddle Taylor. "You are nearly a head taller, and twice as fat. If you can't fight him, fall on him."

"My dear, if there is any difference, Mr. Greene has the advantage, and as he is not quite so fat he will be more nimble."

"You *must* fight him," insisted his wife. "Go outside and walk up and down until he comes out."

There was no help for it. Puddle Taylor could not escape, and with many inward groans he went forth and wandered up and down until Mr. Greene came out. Mrs. Puddle Taylor, to keep him up to the mark, walked about the ground, occasionally coming to the gate and taking a look at her husband, to let him know that she had her eye on him.

When the two men met there was a moment's silence. Mr. Puddle Taylor was white with fear, and Mr. Greenly Greene very red with rage.

"Well," said Mr. Greene at last, "who the devil are you?"

"Sir," stuttered the other, "did you—a—write this letter?"

"I did," replied Mr. Greene, boldly; "and pray what then?"

"Sir, it's an—an—insult."

"Is it? I am glad you think so," said Mr. Greene. "I intended it for nothing else."

"Sir."

"Sir to you."

"Are you aware of the—the penalty of insulting a gentleman?"

Mr. Greene laughed scornfully.

"Oh, yes," he said. "I know all about it; but I never do such a thing."

"But you have insulted me," said Mr. Puddle Taylor.

"That," replied Mr. Greene, "is quite another matter."

After this there was nothing but fighting to be done. Mr. Puddle Taylor rolled up one cuff and advanced one step, Mr. Greene advanced two, and thus both struck an attitude. Mrs. Taylor was now glued to the gate by the prospect of the encounter.

Had she any womanly fears?

None at all. She was a modern Spartan, and loved to see those she loved engaged in manly warfare. Hitherto opportunities for witnessing the prowess of her husband had been rather scarce; now, however, as he had an opportunity of covering himself with glory, she was bent upon seeing the whole business.

Mr. Puddle Taylor was, however, speedily covered with mud in the place of glory. One feeble blow he dealt, and then, receiving heavily on his nose, went down upon his back.

"Now, sir," said Mr. Greene, dancing about him like a sprite, "do you want any more? I'm on for a month of it."

"A man indeed!" murmured Mrs. Puddle Taylor —"quite a gladiator."

Her husband, who had now had enough of fighting for the present, lay on the ground, holding his nose and exclaiming, "Oh, dear! this is very painful; I don't know when I felt anything like it. You have killed me, sir."

"I ask you," said Mr. Greene, "if you want any more? If so, get up and come on."

The reply was in the negative, and Mr. Greene, swollen to the size of a small balloon in the pride of victory, passed on. He saw Mrs. Puddle Taylor, and received a most unexpected and very polite bow from her.

He raised his hat in response, and went on his way. Mrs. Taylor opened the gate and went out to her husband.

"Get up," she said, short and sharp.

"Is—he—gone?" asked Mr. Puddle Taylor.

"Oh, yes! he's gone," replied his wife; "and Coddles is coming up the lane. Perhaps you would be more at home fighting him."

Mr. Puddle Taylor made no reply, but, rising, dusted his clothes in a way intended to let Coddles know that he had just slipped down and nothing more.

Coddles was a dull boy, and really bestowed no thought on how his master became in that condition. Touching his hat, he passed on to the house.

"Coddles is a good boy," said Mr. Puddle Taylor; "no impudence about him."

"Oh! Coddles will do," said his wife. "I think of calling on the Greenes this afternoon."

"Calling on who!" exclaimed Mr. Puddle Taylor, staggering back, and narrowly escaping, in his amazement, another tumble.

"The Greenes—our next-door neighbours. I like Mr. Greene—there's something valiant and noble about him. The way he knocked you down was one of the prettiest sights I ever saw."

"Oh! was it?" said her husband. "The feeling wasn't very pretty. But do as you like. I quarrelled with them first to please you, and now I make friends with them just to keep peace in the house."

Mrs. Puddle Taylor did not, however, call that afternoon, but first wrote a note apologising for her husband's *rudeness*, and expressing, on his and her behalf, sorrow that he should have been led away by the excitement of the moment.

To this Mrs. Greene replied "that she would rather at any time be on good than ill terms with her neighbours, and that Mr. Greene shared her feelings, but neither of them cared to be reproved and threatened with legal proceedings for having simply given a quiet entertainment to a number of innocent children."

An opening thus made, general good-humour rushed in. The Puddle Taylors called on the Greenes, and the Greenes called on the Puddle Taylors. The gentlemen shook hands, while the ladies kissed.

Mr. Greene hoped he had not hurt Mr. Puddle Taylor, and Mr. Puddle Taylor assured Mr. Greene that he only fell to stop the fight, as he was sure both would be sorry if it developed into a serious encounter.

So far all is well, but how this friendship ended will in due course be revealed.

CHAPTER LXXIX.
A NEW BOY AT THE WHITE HART.

THERE are few servants in the world who do not consider themselves overworked, and those who generally make the most complaint have the least to do.

Among the multitude of grumblers was William, the waiter, at the White Hart. William had as little to do as any waiter need desire for a good old sleepy country inn, where everything is done in a jog-trot easy style. What could there be to overtax a man who had simply the coffee-room and casual visitors to attend to ?

But William was overworked.

He insisted such was the case, and was constantly laying before the landlord of the inn the necessity of having a boy. "If," said William, "I am looking after spittoons and sich like, it stands to reason that some gent in the coffee-room must be kept a-waiting. Only 'tother day Mr. Stringer said it was a wonder I did it at all."

"All right," said the landlord at last; "you shall have a boy."

Boys, however, in that part of the country were rather scarce. The agricultural interest swallowed up all juvenile help, and the landlord was driven to the workhouse to seek for the required aid.

Even there youthful labour was scarce, or at least the authorities said so, and Perkins was the only available assistant to be had.

"I'll take him," said the landlord.

"If you do," stipulated the guardians, "you must have him for a twelvemonth."

The landlord, who was not well up in the antecedents of Perkins, agreed, and had that promising young gentleman handed over to him. When William the waiter saw who was to be under him he felt like a novice in the magician's art who had thoughtlessly breathed a spell, and raised up an attendant spirit of whom he was afraid.

"This boy, sir," he said, respectfully, "won't do."

"I have taken him for a year," replied the landlord, sharply, "and you must make the best of him."

William saw that a twelvemonth's unceasing battle lay before him, and like a true warrior girded up his loins to meet the foe.

"I must put him down from the first," he said. "Give him a hinch and he'll take an ell."

It was a great come down for Perkins, especially after the way he had sneered at those who serve in public-houses, but do not for a moment imagine he was at all cowed by this reverse in his life. Not he. Brisk and bright he turned up at the White Hart, with his small bundle of necessaries, and walked into the place as if it belonged to him.

Entering the coffee-room he came upon William, who was engaged in preparing for the evening company. William breathed hard, for he felt that the battle was about to begin.

"Ha! young man," said Perkins, affably, "how d'ye do?"

"Look here," said William, shaking a two-tined fork at him, "don't you come a-young-manning me for I won't stand it. I'm head here, and you've come to be under me—so sing smaller—will you?"

"Me under you!" said Perkins, in surprise, "when I'm a sort of harticled clerk to the business, and you a common waiter. Oh! I say, you mustn't talk in that way—it's taking liberties. Perhaps you'll tell me which is my room?"

"Your room is the hattic on the left side of the hupper part of the house," replied William; "you'll know it by the door being yaller, bordered with green."

"All right," said Perkins; "and as you are so busy I'll take my traps up myself. Mind you clean that fork properly—will you? At present you are only digging holes in the duster with it."

William breathed harder, but he said no more, and Perkins softly whistling, went upstairs to seek out his apartment.

He found it, and proceeded to look about him to see what arrangements had been made for his comfort.

"H'm!" he said, "bit o' carpet close to the bed, washstand, and lookin'-glass, to start with—box and nails for clothes. About on a level with Cobbem's crib. The bed's a mattress one of course. They have no mercy on a boy's bones. I'll try it."

He threw himself down, and immediately a bright smile overspread his intelligent countenance."

"Dashed if it aint a feather un," he said. "What a treat!"

The enjoyment he derived from it was very great, and he continued to revel in it until he fell asleep.

The excitement of the change and the long walk from the workhouse, combined with the soothing influence of a soft bed, entirely overcame him.

William finished his knives and forks, breathing harder and harder as the minutes flew by without the return of Perkins, and the conviction that the struggle would be a severe one grew upon him.

"He must be crushed," he thought, "and if he don't come down soon I'll go up for him."

Darkness was close at hand before he carried this fearful threat into execution. With a weight upon him as if he had undertaken a mission of awful importance, he went upstairs to Perkins's room, opened the door, and walked in.

Perkins was still asleep, and dreaming hard of the place he had so lately left—the workhouse. Now his visions were of encounters he had had with his juvenile friends within its sheltering walls.

"Are you going to get up or not?" asked William.

"Touch me—touch me not," said Perkins.

"But I will touch you," said William, shaking him. "Get up."

Perkins, still in his dreams, struck out, and dealt William a blow that sent him staggering against the washstand. The earthenware upon it rattled violently, and Perkins awoke.

"Hallo!" he said, "wot's the row? Is it time to get up, Jiggles?"

"You will not be hable to assault me, and then get off by a subtyfuge," replied William. "What do you mean by a-hitting of me, you young wiper?"

"Oh! I forgot," said Perkins, sitting up; "I've been harticled to a new shop. Wot's that about hitting you?"

"I came to wake you up, and you struck me."

"Then if you hadn't come you wouldn't have been hit. The next time you want me, young man, knock at the door until I tell you to come in."

"I tell you," said William, emphatically, "that I won't be 'young-manned' by you. Get yourself ready for waiting, and come down instanter."

Perkins smiled pityingly, but he got up, as he was good enough to recognise that he had really enjoyed an excellent rest. William retired, leaving the door open—an insult Perkins resented.

"Come and close this door, will you, you—himage?" he said.

William did not reply, but walked deliberately downstairs, and sought out his master.

"Sir," he said, "I axed you for a boy, and you have got me a demon, sir."

"You will not get perfection in any boy," replied the landlord, "and must make the best of what you have."

"Sir," said William, "if I might be so bold, I think I would rather be without him."

"I have engaged him for a year," replied the landlord, testily, "and I must keep him. Surely you are man enough to manage a boy."

"A boy," said William, "I can subdoo, but he ain't a boy.'

"What is he?"

"A fy-end," replied William.

"A what?"

"A fy-end, sir, a sort of devil as is too much for anybody."

"Oh! a fiend. Now I understand you. Be he what he may, he is here for a year, and you must look after him."

"A year," thought William, as he returned to the coffee-room—"twelve months—three hundred and fifty-six—no, ninety-six—sixty-nine—how many days are there in a year? Don't know. Oh! misery! William, thou wert born to suffer."

The coffee-room company had assembled by this time, and Perkins was there also—not going round deferentially for orders, but standing with his back to the fire and his arms behind his back, regarding the customers with a patronising air.

They, for the most part, were taken aback with the phenomenon, and only one of the customers had ventured to ask for anything. This was Mr. Stringer—a grocer—who asked for a pint of old ale.

"William," replied Perkins, "will be here in a minute."

"Are you not the under waiter?" asked Mr. Stringer in surprise.

"Oh! no," said Perkins; "that was a mistake of sweet William's. I'm dooly harticled to learn the ins and outs of the business—nothing more."

When William returned Perkins neatly transferred the order to him.

"Young man," he said, "that gentleman in the corner wants a pint of old ale. Look sharp, as he have been a long time a-waiting."

"How orfen am I tell you not to young man me?" asked William.

"As orfen as you find convenience," replied Perkins. "Now, get the ale."

"Was the order given to you?" asked William.

"Yes, it was."

"Then go and get it."

"This," said Perkins, appealing to the room generally, "is downright imperence. But he don't know no better. He was badly brought up."

"I see," said William, rolling up his sleeves, "I must bend this. Go and get the hale, you cantankerous, im—possible young himp!"

Perkins neither moved nor spoke, but remained calm and confident in the strength of a superior position. William now did a very rash thing—he smote Perkins on the ear.

The next instant he was kicked on both shins, and a head came like a cannon ball into his stomach—a wild rally for life and liberty followed, and then he went down.

"You come a-hitting me!" said Perkins. "What next, I wonder!"

The noise created brought the landlord to the room. He arrived just in time to see William rise to his feet, and make a frantic rush at Perkins.

"William," he said, "what are you doing?"

"Doing!" replied William, with a wild stare—"I don't know. This boy will drive me mad."

"What have I done?" asked Perkins. "Can you expect me to know the whole business in a minute?

I want to know the ways of the house before I takes orders. I asked you to get the ale for the gent, and why didn't you do it?"

"You axed me!" said William. "You hordered me!"

"Really, William," said the landlord, "I am surprised at you. The boy is right. You cannot expect him to learn the business at once—it's as much as he knows his way to the bar."

"Oh, he's uncommon hinnocent!" muttered William, as he hastened out; "but I'll get the better of him somehow."

Whether he did or not we shall hereafter see. Meanwhile the victory most decidedly remained with Perkins.

CHAPTER LXXX.

MR. BOWLEM AT WORK.

THE friendship between Jolly Greene and the Stagers quickly ripened, and this opened out to Jolly a better life among the boys at the school.

They saw he was not quite so keen as he might have been, that he had many narrow qualities, but under all they perceived he had a spark of generosity which few boys are without.

Hitherto, Jolly had been systematically plundered by Billy Sharp, whom he looked upon as his only friend, but with the Stagers and others things were vastly different. They were willing to share in the good things his money provided, but they did not sponge upon him, and often invited him to a little school feast of their own providing. The gulf then was gradually dividing between Jolly and Billy. The latter was keen enough to see that his reign was over, but he was also bold enough not to give up his rule without a struggle.

"A nice lot you've got mixed up with," he said, sneeringly, as he and his companion were dressing one morning.

"Very nice," replied Jolly, who took the observation literally. "But I thought you didn't like them."

"Oh! yes," said Billy, sarcastically, "I am very fond of them. So would you be of a lot of fellows who came sneaking about and took me—your only friend—away from you."

"I dont know that I should mind it much," returned Jolly.

"Of course you won't," said Billy, "because they butter you and say all sorts of nasty things of me—I, who've always stood your friend when you've been in trouble."

"They neither butter me nor say anything against you," replied Jolly; "they never mention your name; and as for getting me out of trouble you were always getting me into it."

"All right!" said Billy, with a mock air of resignation; "go it! What are you doing now?"

"Packing up my things," said Jolly.

"What for?"

"I am going to sleep to-night in Stagers' dormitory."

Billy turned upon him with a savage growl.

"Who told you to do that?" he asked.

"Mrs. Cobbem," replied Jolly.

"And am I to sleep here alone?"

"Don't know, and don't care," replied Jolly, and, taking up his box, he marched out of the room.

"I see," muttered Billy, when he was alone, "they are bringing him on. I've not done with you yet, Jolly Greene. It will be hard to go back to the old life, but I don't think I have made the best of this. I haven't run quite so straight as I might have done; still I don't care much, school life's rather tiring. I'll go and fasten on the governor, and make him keep me."

There was every prospect of his governor, Mr. Sharp, having as much as he could do to keep himself, for Mr. Bowlem was at work. He had got the clue he wanted, and was going back step by step to that dingy house in Drury-lane, to all its criminal and miserable surroundings.

About this time he obtained sufficient information to put a tolerably clear report before Mr. Greene, and for the purpose of doing so he came down to that gentleman's country house.

Mr. Greene received him kindly, and invited him to have some luncheon before reading his report. The detective, in no wise loth, fell to, and while making a hearty meal he asked many questions about young Billy.

The answer he received amused him mightily. Many times he laughed heartily, apologising for doing so. "But you see," he said, "it was such a downright clever game. Of course, they were not father and son. Oh, dear, no!"

"Father and son!" exclaimed Mr. Greene. "Who do you mean?"

"Why, this young Popper and old Sharpe. Not at all related. Ah! certainly not!"

"Do you mean to say," said Mr. Greene, "that they are father and son?"

"I do," replied Mr. Bowlem, "and I can prove it."

"Well, I never," exclaimed Mrs. Greene. "Did you ever hear of such deceit as that?"

"Bless you, mum," said the detective, "the world is full of it; society is made up of sharps and flats. This Sharp is sharp indeed, and you are, pray excuse me, a little the other way."

"Yes," said Mrs. Greene, simply, "we never pretended to be very clever people, but we knew how to manage our business respectably and honestly, and we made money."

"I suppose you have a lot to tell me about these two," said Mr. Greene, who looked indignant.

"I don't want to be very hard on the boy," replied Mr. Bowlem, "for he's only a young un, and has always been under the guidance of his father. Old Sharp is a downright regular bad un, and will die as he has lived. He's grown so precious old and tough in sin that nothing can change him."

"If all you tell me is correct," said Mr. Greene, "he must be bad indeed. Of course the boy has been educated by him?"

"Entirely."

"I shall not blame the boy," said Mr. Greene, thoughtfully.

"Certainly not," said Mrs. Greene.

"Nor should I like to send him back to his old life—eh, Mariar?"

"Not to be thought of for a moment."

"If there were a few more like you in the world," said the detective, admiringly, "there would not be half the vagabonds, who now infest society, in existence."

Luncheon over, the two men retired to Mr. Greene's study, where further revelations of Mr. Sharp's career were made. With him Mr. Greene was resolved to have nothing more to do, and the only question remained was how to deal with the son.

"Send for him," said the detective, "and let us hear what he has to say for himself."

A note was despatched to the Reverend Copley Cobbem, asking him to send William Sharp Popper on at once, and in due time Billy arrived, wondering on the way what on earth he was wanted for.

When he entered the room, and saw the detective, he changed colour, and shrank back. "The game's blown," he thought, "and it is a sure lagging."

"William," said Mr. Greene, kindly, "I have been talking to this gentleman, and he has told me many things—painful things—of your past life."

"It's like him, meddling with other people's business," replied Billy.

"Stay a minute and hear me further," said Mr. Greene. "I have heard, as I have told you, these things with pain. Now, tell me, are you really sorry for your past life?"

"Werry sorry," replied Billy, and indeed he really felt so.

"And if I endeavour to bring you up respectably you won't ever return to it?"

"I'd die first!" said Billy, and meant it as much as ever he meant anything in his life.

"What do you think?" whispered Mr. Greene to the detective.

"Worth a trial, sir," was the reply.

"So I think," said Mr. Greene. "Now, Sharp—you see I know your name—as you have begun with Popper, you had better go on with it—keep to Popper. You will remain at school, and I trust your future conduct will be of such a nature as to give me satisfaction."

"I'll try my best—indeed I will," said Billy.

He was quite overcome with this unexpected kindness, and his eyes were full of tears.

"You shall have an advance of pocket money," pursued Mr. Greene, "and if I find you deserving I shall take steps to put you out comfortably into the world. You can go now, and you need not say anything about this to any one. Go on as usual, and be as kind to my son as you have hitherto been."

"I never was kind to him," said Billy, remorsefully; "but I'll be so now. I didn't know how kind you were—indeed I didn't; but I feels it here now a-stabbing me."

"His remorse is genuine, I fancy," said the detective, approvingly.

CHAPTER LXXXI.

MR. SHARP IS SETTLED WITH.

BILLY SHARP'S remorse was genuine. He made a fervent promise to do his best and took his leave. From that day a new and better life was open to him.

Mr. Sharp passed an anxious time in town after the departure of his patron, feeling none the better as day after day passed without receiving a letter from him.

The communication he received from Billy upset him too, and in a general way Mr. Sharp was very much troubled in his mind.

"I'll get up an excuse to run down," he thought, "just to see which way the wind blows. The gutters on the roof want looking to, and I can plead that as an excuse for going down for advice on the subject."

It was on the very next morning that he took train and went down to the country residence of the Greenes, arriving there a few minutes before the luncheon hour.

"Just in time to peck," he thought. "Travelling does make one hungry, to be sure."

He rang the bell, and a servant strange to him appeared at the door.

"Your master in?" he asked.

"Yes, sir," was the reply. "What name?"

"His private secretary—Mr. Sharp."

The name was taken in, while Mr. Sharp was left in the hall.

"Snug place," he thought—"better than the crib in town. I think I must come down here for a month or two."

The servant returned, and asked him to walk into the study. Thither he went, and was again left alone.

The study also pleased him. He admired it exceedingly. It was so snug, so well furnished, and looked out upon such a pretty piece of garden.

"This chair," he murmured, turning round the one generally used by Mr. Greene, "is a good one—seems the best of the lot. I think I will have that, and I'll sit here. There's more light, and I can look out. Ha! my dear friend and benefactor, I hope you are well. But I need not ask. You have the flush of youth and strength upon you."

Mr. Greene, who had just entered, bowed coldly, and asked Mr. Sharp what his business was. Mr.

Sharp, a little taken aback, but not entirely floored, sat down in Mr. Greene's chair—to explain.

"Don't sit there," said Mr. Greene, "that's my seat. Don't sit at all; you can hear the little I have to say standing."

"My friend," murmured Mr. Sharp, "I fear there have been whispers of evil abroad."

"You unmitigated scoundrel!" cried Mr. Greene, suddenly firing up, and shaking his fist at him.

"Eh?" exclaimed Mr. Sharp.

"You—you impostor! you liar! you thief!" cried the old man, white-hot with fury.

"This language to a gentleman, sir," said Sharp, with well-assumed indignation, "is actionable."

"To a gentleman," cried Mr. Greene. "You low beggar, how dare you come here?"

"How dare I, sir?" said Sharp.

"Yes, how dare you? Stay! don't put on that look. I have a friend of yours here," he added, as he struck the bell upon the table.

At the word "friend" Mr. Sharp turned all sorts of colours. He was a shrewd man, and knew well what sort of friend he was about to meet. The entrance of Mr. Bowlem confirmed his worst fears.

"Now, sir," said Mr. Greene. "Do you deny what I have said?"

"No," replied Sharp, in a low tone.

"Are you not an impostor?"

"Indeed I am."

"And a liar?"

"I have occasionally diverged from the truth."

"And a thief?"

"I have, like other men, fallen into temptation, and sinned grievously."

"Don't be a hypocrite," said Mr. Greene, "for that is the worst character of all. Now I want you to tell me how much you have robbed me of. Out with it, for I will know the truth."

Mr. Sharp, now that he was well in the toils and without hope, put on the calmness of a man resolved to die game.

"May I sit down at the table and work it out?" he asked.

"You may," replied Mr. Greene.

As unmoved as he would have been in performing any of the ordinary duties of a secretary, he sat down at the table, took a pen and paper, and began to work out a calculation. It occupied about ten minutes, and at the end of that time he handed the paper to Mr. Greene.

"I think everything is there," he said; "and you will perceive the principal items are connected with repairs never executed by tradesmen who do not exist. I have cheated you to the amount of between six and seven hundred pounds, and appropriated the money to my own use."

"And what have you done with it? asked Mr. Greene.

"Spent it," was the brief reply.

Mr. Greene looked at the detective, who nodded and said—

"Take your oath it's true, sir. He couldn't keep a penny if he knew he was going to starve to-morrow."

"For past robberies," said Mr. Greene, "I forgive you, but do not look for mercy in the future. Go away, and keep clear of me and those who belong to me."

Mr. Sharp rose and bowed.

"Being dismissed without notice," he said; "and as a secretary usually engages by the half year, I trust—"

Mr. Bowlem uttered a short laugh and turned to the window. Mr. Greene flushed scarlet.

"You will get nothing from me," he said; "I think you ought to thank me for not prosecuting you."

"At this present moment," said Mr. Sharp, "I am the possessor of sixpence and a return railway ticket."

"I will give you nothing—go at once," replied

his late patron. "Your conduct has been shameful. Go back to London, and do not go near my house, as Mr. Bowlem has telegraphed to a brother officer to arrest you if you show your nose there."

"Mr. Bowlem is very attentive," said Sharp—"too attentive, I might say. Perhaps his turn will come one day. At least, Mr. Greene, let me fetch away my clothes."

"You came with nothing, and you can leave as you came," was the reply.

"I think, sir," said the detective, "his boxes had better be examined."

"Ah!" sighed Sharp, "I see I shall get no mercy; but, Mr. Greene, before you go I have to ask you one question. Young Popper—how is he getting on?"

"*Your son*," replied Mr. Greene, with considerable emphasis, "will have another trial. I blame you for his being what he is."

"Sir," said Mr. Sharp, "I thank you for your clemency, and wish you good morning. Ta-ta, Bowlem. When you come down to the old quarter look me up—will you?"

"I shall look you up one day when you least expect me," replied the detective.

"Glad to see you at any time," was the impudent reply—"only don't think you will find me napping."

He went out jauntily, humming an air; but as soon as he got the other side of the door he turned and shook his fist, grinding his teeth with rage.

"I'll square accounts one day with you both!" he hissed. "And you, Bowlem, look to it—better men than you have disappeared and never been heard of again!"

As he passed through the hall there was a desire upon him to appropriate something—if only an umbrella—but he checked it, and went out of the house as poor as he entered it, and much hungrier.

"Dine I must," he muttered, "but where can I dine about here for sixpence? In London I could fill myself out for half the money, but here— Stay—the White Hart. I do not think they will know me; I was disguised when I went there before; I will dine sumptuously, if I never dine again. Ah, me, what a falling off is here!"

But even at the White Hart they seemed to be prepared for him. As he entered, William, the waiter, who was in the passage, blocked the way, and asked him what he wanted.

"To dine," replied Sharp.

"Are you Mr. Greene's secretary?"

"I am," incautiously replied Mr. Sharp.

"Then you can't have nothing here," said William, "and if you don't go at once I'll fetch a perliceman."

"You insolent varlet I will——"

"Oh, fiddlesticks!" said William, ringing a bell. "Now are you going, or am I to send for the stable chaps to throw you out?"

"I'll go," replied the other, "but I'll bring an action against the proprietor of this place, and ruin him. As for you, I'll——"

"Tom," said William to a boy, who now appeared in answer to the bell, "ax a couple of men to come here with a pail of water."

Mr. Sharp saw all was up. He could have knocked William down for satisfaction, but that might have brought trouble upon himself so he went away with a bitter heart, and footed it to the railway station, a-hungered and a-thirst.

At the station he had to wait an hour for the train, and, to escape the keen eyes of the porters, whom he had once deluded, he was obliged to spend the time in a small stifling waiting-room, with only a time-table and the advertising frames upon the walls to read.

Hungry and miserable, he felt he had been there a week when the train came in.

The next morning Billy received a letter from his affectionate parent, characteristic of the man and the fatherly affection within him:—

"DEAR BILLY,—I'm blown on, and have come back to the old shop. I was glad to find that you had managed to soap them over, so that we can still work together. Meanwhile, if you get any tin send it to me, for I'm good for outdoor relief. When you catch the Greenes in a melting mood lead them on to talk about me, and then draw a picture of me repentant and starving, lying on my dying bed in an attic. If they talk of coming to see me give me the straight tip, and I will get up for the occasion. I can get some lovely starving paint quite equal to the most delicate shades of nature. I hardly know what lay to be up to, but I think of making a collection to give two hundred ragged children, stifling in these wretched courts, a day in the green fields. A little late in the year, but I can talk of taking them south. Don't forget to send me something at once, if only a bob.—Your affectionate dad,
"S. SHARP."

In reply Billy sent a little money and a letter, informing his father of his intending to live a new life, and that his "lay" was to be respectable and have nothing more to do with swindling in any shape or form. He concluded by advising his father to get a situation as light porter, and live honestly by the sweat of his brow.

To this his amiable parent rejoined:—

"BILLY,—I'm disgusted with you to go and try and humbug your poor old father, who never deceived you. *You* on the respectable lay—*you* wasting your talents among the flats! No, William—I never can and I never will believe that your education has been thrown away upon you. Turn again, Billy, and be Lord Dodger of London. Do what you like with other people, but don't try to impose upon your only surviving parent—that is coming it a little too strong.—Your pained but still affectionate father,
"S. S."

"But I don't care," said Billy, as he tore this precious epistle into shreds. "I am going to be respectable. He may say and think what he likes of me, and it don't matter: He may do what he likes, and I won't go back to the old life. A feller might just as well be a rat, hunted, and chivied, and sneaking about. No, I'll have no more of it. Dad may do and say what he pleases."

CHAPTER LXXXII.
BREAKING UP.

THE changes wrought by the revelations made by Mr. Bowlem were many, but not of a nature to be dwelt upon at any length here. Billy retained his gastronomical powers, but certain qualities of a more objectionable nature were put aside for the time, if not for ever.

The Stagers, who knew enough of Billy's past life to understand his true position, were too generous to say anything to their schoolfellows. What they knew they kept to themselves, and although they could never look upon him as a friend they were as civil as ordinary acquaintances are after the time Billy set about reforming himself.

And Jolly Greene changed also. Not that he became remarkably bright or distinguished himself in any way. Get into messes he would, and was likely to go on in the same way until he was called away from this vale of tears; but his troubles lessened, and he sometimes learnt something from his books, and kept it in his head for nearly a week.

He went home from Saturday to Monday now and then, and would astonish his mother with his knowledge of things. He told her the north pole was at one end of the world, and the south pole the other, and that Australia was under our feet, and that there the people walked upside down without falling off; and he also did sums, multiplying and dividing and adding in a way that would have driven the great Cocker mad, and killed the mighty Babbage right away. And wasn't his mother pleased, for the sums were a complete maze to her, and she could not but think they must be very clever?

Mr. Greene might not have thought quite so much of his son's performances as his wife did, but he had nevertheless a father's prejudices, and firmly believed his son Jolly was getting on.

"I don't mind what I spend," he said, "so that I can make a man of him."

Mr. Cobbem, to whom these words were addressed, said that Jolly would undoubtedly make a man of the world if he lived long enough.

"It is a remarkable and well-known fact," he said, "that the brightest boys often make the dullest men. They have mushroom intellects, in fact, which come up in the night, and will not bear the noonday light upon them. Your son's intellect now is like the oak, or let me say it is but the acorn at present; but by-and-bye it will grow into a big tree, and spread branches sturdy and strong, defying the winds of the world around it."

"That's uncommon good—aint it, Mariar?"

"It is," replied Mrs. Greene, "and Mr. Cobbem ought to know what our Jolly is, having had so much to do with boys."

"Madam," replied that learned gentleman, "boys' brains are the rough materials out of which I mould great intellects. I've told you what your son is like, but I warn you not to be astonished at the slow development of his mind, although it is under my anxious care."

Mr. and Mrs. Greene both expressed themselves perfectly satisfied, and told the Rev. Mr. Copley not to spare any expense in the education of their offspring. He promised he would not, and faithfully kept his word.

Perhaps the most remarkable change in the little community figuring in our story was that observable in the ladies.

The Greenes and the Puddle Taylors became intimate in due course of time, the Cobbems met their old enemies, and in place of warfare reigned a most loving and promising peace.

Mr. Puddle Taylor could not quite forgive his reverend friend for having thrashed his son, but as a matter of policy he conveniently forgot the event; nor could Mrs. Puddle Taylor entirely obliterate from her mind the pungent letters she had received from Mrs. Cobbem. She was nevertheless all honey and sweetness.

Visiting backwards and forwards and dining together was established, and for the time being a very pleasant little circle was formed.

While all this was going on, Christmas was approaching, and the breaking-up of the school was at hand. The boys began to talk of what they would do in that pleasant time of rest from study, and to write to their friends, saying how they would like to have so and so home with them, or to ask if they might go here or there for a time with some boy friend, and at least quite a fortnight before the day for leaving half the boys had packed their things ready for a start.

In Warmington College there were—as there are in every school—boys who looked gladly on the coming holidays, and others who regarded them with aversion.

It was not every boy who had a comfortable home to go to, or parents to hail their coming with pleasure, or brothers and sisters to greet them; and Christopher Cobble was one of these unfortunates. He had neither father nor mother alive, and his guardian, being a grumpy old sinner, arranged for his stopping at the college during the vacation.

"And a precious game that will be," growled Cris, "with Cobbem and his wife away five days a week, and I left at home, thinking how jolly you fellows must be with your friends. Don't be surprised, when you come back, to hear that I have hung myself in my garters."

Dick Stager, who was going to spend the first part of the holiday with the Greenes, and then take Jolly up to the admiral's for the rest of the time, suggested that Nick should take Cris up with him.

"The admiral won't mind," said Dick, "and he will be company for you before I come up with Jolly."

"Had I not better write first?"

"If you do that," replied Dick, "he's just likely to say 'no.' Take Cris with you, and it will be all right. You know his ways."

"All right," said Nick, "and you square it with the guardian—will you?"

The guardian of Cris Cobble was written to, asking his leave, and in reply he amiably said the boy might go anywhere he pleased so long as he didn't trouble him.

This was accepted as a favourable reply, and great was the joy of the orphan Cris.

Time sped on, and the breaking up drew nigh.

Great was the general joy, except in the heart of one poor lad, who received a letter informing him that his mother had suddenly died. He was to go home with the rest, but all the anticipated joys of the Christmas holiday were lost to him.

CHAPTER LXXXIII.
EXCHANGING CONFIDENCES.

AMONG others Larry was leaving for good. He was a great hero with the boys, for he was going over the sea to India, where he had an uncle who had grown rich as a merchant there—a childless man. If Larry behaved well he was to inherit the said uncle's property.

"And when I come into it," he said, "I'll have all you fellows over, and we will ride about on elephants, and have black slaves to fan us and fill our hookahs. You shall stop as long as you like. We will have a rare time of it."

It was a boy's promise, but he meant it at the time. But Larry went his way, and in the new life over the sea speedily forgot the old. Not even a letter came to one of his old friends. But it's only the way of the world, and we need neither blame him nor repine over it. Who among us have not either made or received similar promises, and do we not know too well how soon they have been forgotten?

To return. The day at last arrived for the breaking up, and early in the morning the prizes were distributed by the fair hands of Mrs. Cobbem, who was all smiles and graciousness on the occasion. Jolly Greene got one for "general good behaviour," and the Reverend Copley made a neat speech on the occasion, declaring that, although he could not help admiring talent, he had the greatest love for perseverance, even if it were unaccompanied by success.

After the prizes were given out the boys were told to go and play until eleven o'clock, when they were to have cake and wine, and be sent about their business.

It had been snowing all night, and was snowing still. But what of that? All the more fun. Snowballing is a capital exercise if you can give all and take but a few, and at it the youngsters went. Jolly got it heavily as a matter of course, for he came in the way of all sorts of white missiles not intended for him, and speedily bore strong resemblance to a figure belonging to twelfth cake.

Others got into a similar state, but everything was taken in good part, as it ought to be, and when the bell rang for cake and wine they all trooped in, ignoring the blows they had received, and disregarding the wet without, and in some cases within, their clothing.

The cake was not bad, and the wine was very fair for school wine, as it was a policy with the Rev. Copley Cobbem not to upset the stomachs of his pupils just as they were going home. Then came the shaking hands all round and general adieus.

Jolly, Dick Stager, and Billy Sharp walked off to

the residence of Mr Greene. Vehicles came up to take the boys to the station, or if they lived within a dozen miles straight to their homes. Nick Stager and Cris Cobbles took train for home, and the Reverend Copley and his wife took up a position before the fire, and thanked their stars they were at peace for five weeks.

"And pray, Copley, dear," said Mrs. Cobbem, "how do you mean to spend the time?"

She was always particularly sweet when she wanted anything of her husband, but unfortunately she generally put a little acid in the honey of her disposition, and spoilt it.

"Christmas here," said the Rev. Copley, "and the rest of the time in London, to see the pantomimes and other amusements. I do not care for such things, but one must be kept posted in what the world is doing. We have an invitation for Christmas-day, my dear."

"Indeed! And pray who has asked us? This is the first time I have heard about it."

"It is from the Greenes, and came as the boys were going. In the confusion I forgot it for the moment."

"So like you, so addle-headed!" she said. "What will you do?"

"What will you do, Agatha, dear?"

"Go, of course. It might save a turkey. We can give the servants a piece of beef and a pudding."

"Yes, my dear. Will you answer it at once? The letter was addressed to you, but I opened it by mistake."

"So like you," said Mrs. Cobbem, again, as she sat down to write a reply. I say, Copley, dear."

"Yes, Agatha, my love."

"I think we shall be able to do very well with the Greenes."

"We shall make fruit of them," replied the Rev. Copley. "I hope to gather many a plum from that flourishing tree."

CHAPTER LXXXIV.
ICE SCENES.

"I WANT you boys to make yourselves at home," said Mr. Greene, to his two guests; "do as you like and be as merry as you can, but don't forget to be in punctual to meals."

"I'll never be a minute behind," replied Billy, and if ever a boy meant to keep a promise he did.

Dick Stager also said he would attend to Mr. Greene's desires, and they were then shown their rooms, each one with a separate apartment, furnished with every comfort.

"Think of giving up all this to mouch about the streets again," thought Billy, as he lay curled up in bed that night. "No, it wouldn't do; honesty is best—the best—what is it?—never mind, it's right. Bless old Greene for his kindness; he's a regular trump!"

He was soon asleep, and slept until he was aroused in the morning by a knock at the door.

"Who's that?" he said. "Come in."

"It's me," said Dick Stager, putting his head in. "It's been freezing awfully hard all night. As this is the third day of it I fancy the pond in the garden will bear. Jolly and I are going to try it; will you come?"

"Thanks," replied Billy, "I will."

"Mighty civil of him," thought Billy, as the door closed. "Not a bad fellow after all, although he knows more about me than is quite pleasant."

On going down into the hall he found Jolly and Dick with skates in their hands, and another pair ready for him.

Billy looked at them with doubt, and Jolly passed them over to him, with a gimlet to put them on.

"But I never had such things on," he said. "I don't know how to skate a bit."

"Nor I," replied Jolly, "but it is so easy. I've seen people on the ice, and it's no trouble at all."

"I warn you not to fancy it is so easy," said Dick, with a smile, "but I dare say you will soon get on. The stable boy is already there brushing away the snow. The ice is as firm as a high road. Can you swim, Sharp?"

"To the bottom," was the reply.

"And you, Jolly? Oh! I remember—you tried once."

"Yes, with bladders," replied Jolly, woefully. "I tied them to my feet, if you remember, and went down head under. It was so painful. I tried to call out for my mar and couldn't—the water stopped me."

"It was a close shave," replied Dick. "Come on and let us get an appetite for breakfast."

"I've got one already," replied Billy, "but a little of an edge on it won't matter."

The pond in the garden was a very fair-sized one, being quite a hundred and fifty yards across, and about two hundred long. It had fish in it, and a pair of swans upon it. The latter had kept a clear space for themselves at one end, by swimming round almost constantly, and here, as the young fish came up for air, they made a meal of them, and put the little things out of their misery.

The rest of the pond was apparently sound. The boy with the broom went all over it sweeping, and it did not even crack. Dick Stager put on his skates in a few seconds, and went off, skimming to and fro like a swallow.

"It's lovely—isn't it?" said Jolly; "help me on with my skates, please," he said to the boy, who threw down his broom and went to work.

"It goes through the 'eel, I think, sir," he said.

"Yes, in the middle," replied Jolly.

The boy, a strong country lad, went to work vigorously, and bored away, when Jolly suddenly shrieked out—

"Oh!"

"What's the matter, sir?"

"You've got it into my foot."

"Beg pardon, sir," said the boy, and reversing the gimlet he put on the first skate and strapped it tight.

The other was put on without any mishap, and Jolly, with a confidence beyond his years, ran upon the ice to make a start.

The next moment all creation seemed to him to turn upside down, and somebody or something hit him violently on the back of the head. Then he saw a dozen boys bending over him, which presently dwindled down to his two friends and the stable boy.

"Are you hurt?" asked Dick.

"What's the matter?" said Jolly, feebly.

"You have had a fall—that's all," replied Dick.

"Was that a fall?" asked Jolly.

"Yes."

"Then I think I'll have the skates taken off."

"Don't give them up," said Dick, "you will get on by-and-bye. Let me take one hand and Popper can take the other. Now, up you get and off we go."

"I don't think I ever felt anything so dreadfully slippery," said Jolly, as he started afresh, with his legs well in front, and his dead weight on those who supported him; "don't let me fall."

"Can't help it," replied Dick, and down all three went together.

The tumble this time hurt nobody, and only made Jolly laugh. They got up again and started afresh. Little by little he progressed, until he could stand alone several seconds without falling down, and he began to feel quite proud of himself.

Billy next put on the skates, and with the aid of Dick and the stable-boy made a fairish start. It was not long before he said he thought he could manage by himself, and asked them to let him go. They did so, and he went up at once and came down like a stone upon the ice. He lay there with what he had not before—a fellow-feeling for Jolly, who had preceded him in the tumbling feat.

All round, however, they got on pretty well, and

went into breakfast full of health, and as rosy as ripe apples—"perfect picters" Mrs. Greene called them—and didn't they punish the food upon the table, Billy in particular utterly destroying and demolishing so much bacon, toast, and eggs that Mrs. Greene was doubtful if he would ever get up from that table alive.

But he was not at all hurt, and seemed as light as ever when the meal was over.

After a short rest the boys got out their skates again, and while arranging them the Reverend Copley Cobbem arrived. He, too, had skates with him, and evidently intended to disport himself upon the pond.

Mr. Greene came out on hearing his voice, and they shook hands.

"I thought your lake would be frozen," said the Reverend Copley, "so I came over. Mrs. Cobbem intends coming a little later to watch us at the exhilarating exercise. Do you skate?"

"Never had such a thing on a foot of mine in my life," replied Mr. Greene. "Now you are here you will stop to luncheon?"

"With pleasure," replied the Reverend Copley.

"Well, go on to the pond," said Mr. Greene, "and I'll get the missus to come down. Why, here's Mr. Taylor and his son!"

"Morning, gentlemen," said Mr. Puddle Taylor. "I've come to have a bit of skating. Hope I don't intrude, you know. We have no water to speak of except the fountain in our grounds, and that's not big enough, you know."

"Glad to see you, sir," said Mr. Greene. "And so you skate?"

"A little," replied Mr. Taylor, "or I used to. My son is anxious to learn, and I am going to teach him."

So they all went down and put on their skates, and the Reverend Copley started first, going off like a wild duck upon the wing, and cutting all sorts of figures on the ice, to the intense admiration of the boy with the broom, whose services were retained to sweep the ice occasionally.

After the Reverend Copley went Dick Stager, and he joined the tutor in making a figure of eight, and they kept at it until Mr. Puddle Taylor came in between them under the entire government of his skates.

They all went down together, and everybody laughed, even the boy with the broom, who dropped down upon the ice quite limp, and got his ears boxed by Mr. Greene for his impudence. But on they went again, Jolly and Billy among the rest.

Jolly was down a great deal, but he made considerable progress and got about famously, sometimes going quite three yards without pitching upon his nose or falling upon the back of his head. Billy was down often, and the stable-boy put him down in his mind as being one "mash of bruises."

Mr. Puddle Taylor teaching his son was an exhilarating sight. In years gone by he might possibly have skated, or tried to skate, somewhere, but on this occasion he did not come out very strong. He spent most of his time as a "sitting" magistrate upon the ice, and whenever he took his seat his son, overcome with filial affection, immediately fell over him.

Anon came the ladies, and the Reverend Copley Cobbem, having obtained a chair, gave his wife, the gentle Agatha, a push round the pond, which pleased her much.

Next he took Mrs. Puddle Taylor for a ride, but in this Mrs. Cobbem saw no fun, and muttered something about a brazen face pleasing men more than anything.

Nor did Mr. Puddle Taylor quite approve of it, for he was jealous of his wife in a way, and wondered what she could see in the parson schoolmaster to look up into his face and smile as she had not smiled upon her loving husband for very many years.

CHAPTER LXXXV.

A CATASTROPHE.

IT was a festive scene, and at the very height of the festivity everybody suddenly became aware of an intruder upon their privacy, and that intruder was—Perkins.

No longer clad in gorgeous livery, but simple corduroy and a green baize apron, he was not recognised at first. It was not until he spoke that he was known.

Perkins had a basket with four partitions in it, and in each partition there was a bottle of spirits for some customer, who, of course, had to wait the convenience of Perkins for the goods he had ordered.

There was not the least malice in the heart of Perkins. He had forgiven all his enemies there assembled, and smiled upon them sweetly. He was as much like a full-grown cherub as a boy in corduroy can be.

"Ah!" he said, "I thought so. I jest heerd the skates a-screaming, and I come in to see how you was a-getting on."

The Reverend Copley Cobbem, recognising his old pest, wisely forbore to attack him, but Mrs. Cobbem charged at him like an Amazon.

"Go away, you low boy," she said. "These are private grounds."

"Why aint there a notice put up, then?" he asked. "The gate was open, and besides, there aint no such things as private grounds when there's hice about."

"This," said Mrs. Cobbem, "is monstrous impudence!"

The Reverend Cobbem came skimming over to the side of his wife.

"Agatha," he whispered, "it is no use being violent with a boy of this description. He will only annoy you. Deal gently with him."

"Like a parent?" said Mrs. Cobbem, sarcastically.

The Reverend Copley made an angry gesture, and seemed as if he were about to clutch his hair, but the action threw him off his balance, and he went down for the first time that day, and went down heavily.

"Never mind," said Perkins, cheeringly: "Hup again, and go at it like a man."

Mr. Greene saw it was time for him to interfere, and in an authoritative tone he bade Perkins begone.

"Wot's the harm of a boy looking on?" asked Perkins. "I aint a-going to eat any body—am I? I aint so werry hungry as all that."

Mr. Greene was wise enough to know that struggling or fighting with a boy is a mistake—so he told his stable boy to remove Perkins from the grounds.

The stable boy was quite half a head over Perkins, and, no ways loth, went at the bold intruder. Perkins received him like a valiant knight, and the pair closed.

"That boy," said the Reverend Copley, "is a demon. Wait until I have removed my skates and I will stop this disgraceful scene."

But while he was taking his skates off Perkins tripped up the stable boy, who fell upon the basket and broke two of the bottles.

This stopped the fight; Perkins, dismayed at the disaster, gave in.

"Here, come," he said, "you pay for this damage some of yer."

"Pay for it, you wicked boy," said Mrs. Cobbem. "How dare you ask such a thing?"

"Did I break 'em?" asked Perkins.

"You threw that boy down," said Mr. Cobbem.

"He fell a purpose; you told him to do it," said Perkins. "It's werry hard that a poor boy can't come and see a bit o' skating without getting his bottles smashed. Wot harm had I done?"

"You were intruding."

"Come—come my lad," said Mr. Puddle Taylor, "take your basket and go away. Perhaps you don't know that I'm a magistrate?"

"Oh! yes, I know you," replied Perkins. "I was present at the case when you made a mess of it and Mrs. Cobbem chawed you up."

This was rather awkward, all the parties being present, and the Reverend Copley felt he must do something. That something he did promptly and well. Taking Perkins in one hand and the basket in the other, he carried them bodily off, put them outside, and locked the gate.

"Now go back," he said, "and don't you ever intrude here again."

He turned away and the next moment received a lump of frozen snow in the nape of his neck.

Infuriated, he made a dash at the gate, but Perkins—the offender—seized his basket and fled.

"I heard that boy was at the White Hart," muttered the Reverend Copley, as he went back to the pond, "but I thought I was safe from him. Is he to haunt me for ever? I wish he would repent of his sins and—die. What a relief it would be!"

Boys of the Perkins stamp—as the Reverend Copley knew—do not so readily depart this life. They are scourges upon mankind.

Having resumed his skates he joined the festive throng again, and with a view to conciliating his wife asked her to have another ride in the chair.

She graciously consented.

"And take me round quick," she said—"as quick as you did that impudent Mrs. Puddle Taylor."

"Hush, my dear, not so loud. She will overhear you."

"I don't care if she does," replied Mrs. Cobbem. "Women of that stamp want a lesson. Are you ready?"

"Quite, my love."

Off they went, the Reverend Copley driving the chair at a furious rate, desiring to please his Agatha. But in his hot haste he forgot the swan hole before alluded to, and made straight for it.

"Copley, where are you going to?"

Her scream was loud, but it came too late. In she went with the chair, and her loving husband plunged in head first after her.

CHAPTER LXXXVI.
BILLY GOES AWAY.

THE disappearance of Mr. and Mrs. Cobbem was so sudden and unexpected that at first nobody moved forward to the rescue, but stood staring at the swan hole as if they rather expected something to come up, instead of having just seen a man and wife go down.

The stable boy with the broom was the first to move, and he, with a wisdom and discretion passing that possessed by ordinary mortals, ran towards the house calling out "Murder!" at the top of his voice.

The next to come round was Dick Stager. He rapidly whipped off his skates and ran forward to the rescue just as the two feet of the Reverend Copley emerged from their temporary hiding place. His body and head came next, and in the midst of spluttering his voice was heard.

"A hand—a line—a stick—anything!" he said. "I have—hic—"

Dick gave him a hand, and the others, now well on the way to the restoration of their ordinary faculties, formed a chain, and pulled the reverend gentleman out.

In his left hand he held his walking stick, and in his right his wife—his gentle Agatha—who was snorting like a grampus and sending forth from her nose two jets of water, whale fashion.

An umbrella she had with her she still held, and when the Reverend Copley, forgetful of his own misery, offered her sweet consolation on being saved, she raised that umbrella and hit him with a force seldom exhibited by, or to be found in, gentle woman.

"I do not feel the blow here," he said, as he put his hand to his head, "but here," laying his hand upon his heart.

"Come in at once, both of you," said Mr. Greene; "change your clothes, and have a warm bath, or you will catch your death of cold."

It was a wise and good suggestion, and the sufferers were hurried into the house. Their friends and servants relieved them of their wet clothing, and after a warm bath they went to bed—in separate rooms—for Mrs. Cobbem said—

"I will never look upon his face again. It was a glaring attempt to drown me."

When the Rev. Copley heard this he tore his hair, but shortly after he and Mr. Greene were playing cribbage on the bed and drinking brandy and water, to their mutual enjoyment.

The rest of the guests kept to the ice until luncheon time, the boy with the broom being appointed to stand near the swan-hole to prevent further accidents.

Mrs. Cobbem got up after luncheon, and her husband too, but she would not relent towards him.

She glared at him whenever he spoke to her, and in a hollow tone said nothing else but "murderer!"

She even said she would not go home with him unless she was protected by another man; but as neither Mr. Greene nor Mr. Puddle Taylor offered themselves for the post, she eventually went back with the Rev. Copley.

When they got home she gave him two days' real domestic bliss and then forgave him.

The frost continued for two or three days, and then broke up for a time. It snowed all Christmas-day, but that only made the comforts of Mr. Greene's house more appreciable. Good cheer warmed the hearts of all, and the day passed happily and merrily.

In due time Jolly and Dick Stager went to London, and had rare fun at the old Admiral's, where they did pretty much as they liked.

Jolly got into a good many scrapes, but none of them so serious as in the days of yore. He was becoming wiser, and in the society of boys more clever than himself was getting a vast amount of good.

"He will never be Lord Chancellor," said the Admiral, "but I don't think he will make a bad sort of fellow in his way."

"The little nonsense he has in him," replied Dick, "will soon be taken out," and so said Nick.

While staying in London Jolly received a letter from his mother, informing him that Billy Sharp had expressed a wish to go right away to a school in Yorkshire, among people who knew nothing whatever about him. It was a wise desire, and it was to be complied with.

The fact is, Billy was afraid of his father. He knew what that amiable gentleman was capable of in the way of sponging upon him, and making use of his son's position to obtain money in some way; so he had asked to be sent away.

With a lingering affection, which surely everybody must feel, however bad their parents in some cases may be, Billy did not state the real cause of his wishing to be sent away, but Mr. Greene suspected it, and thought none the less of the boy.

"He will make a sharp man of the world," thought the benevolent old gentleman, "and a good one, I hope."

When Jolly returned home he found his old companion gone, but a letter had been left for him, in which Billy boldly and candidly set forth all the petty wrongs he had inflicted upon Jolly, and asked his forgiveness.

Jolly forgave him. "What's the use of bothering about it?" he wrote in reply—"it's all over and will soon be forgotten."

So it was by Jolly, but Billy remembered it still, and he is not an atom the worse for it, seeing that he remembers that forgiveness with gratitude.

CHAPTER LXXXVII.

FINALE.

THE career of Jolly Greene need not be further pursued just now, for he is no longer as "Green as Grass." Contact with the world has considerably changed his colour, and although he will never make much impression on the public mind by his abilities, he will, if he lives, become a sober and fairly sensible man of the world, which is as good as being a genius.

Great geniuses are occasionally neither sober nor sensible.

Mr. and Mrs. Greene continue to live in the country, and to dispense their hospitality as heretofore, to the great comfort and satisfaction of their neighbours, and Jolly, in his slow but sure progress with his books, is a great joy and comfort to them.

The Puddle Taylors remain fast friends with the Greenes, and tolerable friends with the Cobbems; but Mrs. Cobbem and Mrs. Taylor have not quite forgiven each other, and never will. Women of that stamp have fixed and abiding principles of the vinegar-cruet order. Young Puddle Taylor is at Oxford, and is one of the best known puppies there. As a preparatory step towards bringing his father's grey hairs with sorrow to the grave, he is running into debt and taking great pains to avoid receiving honours. Next term his rooms at college will in all probability be taken by another.

The boys of Warmington College are, as a body, progressing satisfactorily. They have the usual fun, cares, sorrows, and joys of school life, as of old. Many well-known faces have disappeared and new ones come, and so the mill goes round, grinding the grist of childhood into educational flour. What sort of bread the boys will make by-and-bye is their look out. The Rev. Copley Cobbem having given them the raw material has nothing more to do with the business.

The reverend gentleman goes on with his wife as heretofore, trotting over almost daily the same old wrangling ground on which grow the weeds of a woman's inconsistency. The Rev. Copley cannot complain of want of change, as there is ever something new cropping up in Mrs. Cobbem's breast. He lives a life of ever-varying light and shade—smiles one moment, a frown the next, and occasionally a few scratches to follow. But it is all part of the matrimonial pie, and the Rev. Copley takes it accordingly.

I now come to a very painful part of my winding-up—the present career of Perkins. I would have preferred giving a good account of that boy if I could, but truth permits and insists upon being here set down.

Perkins is not a good boy. William, the waiter, looks twenty years older since that young torment went to the White Hart. Long ago William gave up the struggle for supremacy, and he is now the slave of Perkins, who has somehow picked up the art of waiting, and being about twice as brisk as William is in executing orders, is rather popular in the coffee-room.

He has often talked of going to London as a waiter, and will probably go one of these days, and then he will be in his element. It is within the bounds of possibility that he may get on, but it is not kind of him to chaff William before customers, or to call him a "hannimated tortoise," or to ask him why he don't learn the use of his legs, or to sarcastically allude to his having been unfortunately born without a head.

William bears all, but breathes hard and longs for the day when Perkins will depart for the metropolis.

Goggles loafs about still, but keeps honest, as the confinement of a prison does not suit his constitution. But the old one—our John—the oldest inhabitant—is in the workhouse, where he has established himself as an oracle, and heads the deputations that wait upon the guardians once a week to complain about the quantity and quality of the food and drink provided for the consumption of the inmates.

Among other marriages of the period is that of Jiggles and the cook, who are now realising the joys of matrimony in a newsvendor's and sweetstuff shop in the town of Grippenham. Mrs. Jiggles is the guiding spirit of that establishment, and in the evening Jiggles is often very glad to get away and have a smoke and a little drink at the Angel hotel. He has taken to politics as a balancing power to his overwhelming bliss.

A few days ago news of Uncle Ruddle came to Warmington College. He was dead, and had left nothing but a long string of unpaid debts. The old humbug never had much money, but had put all sorts of falsehoods abroad, and lived on the cupidity of his relatives.

And lastly, Mr. Sharp. He is still in the flesh, and exists, as he did before, by little arts which bear very poor fruit, although they are so very clever. He tried to find out where Billy was, but failed. Mr. Green threatened to prosecute him if he did not keep away—so he took to writing begging letters to his son, who writes back without any address, occasionally, enclosing a few stamps out of his pocket money. It is to be feared Mr. Sharp will never wholly abandon his evil ways.

And so the world wags—the wise and foolish, the knavish and honest, running their courses to the end, some to weal and others to woe. And so I fancy it will be until the story of this great world is ended.

THE END

www.ingramcontent.com/pod-product-compliance
Lightning Source LLC
Chambersburg PA
CBHW080828250626
47160CB00008B/2878